INDIA
SHASTRA

ALSO BY SHASHI THAROOR

NON-FICTION

Pax Indica: India and the World of the 21st Century (2012)
Shadows Across the Playing Field: 60 Years of India-Pakistan Cricket (2009)
The Elephant, the Tiger, and the Cell Phone: Reflections on India in the 21st Century (2007)
Bookless in Baghdad (2005)
Nehru: The Invention of India (2003)
Kerala: God's Own Country (2002)
India: From Midnight to the Millennium and Beyond (1997)
Reasons of State (1982)

FICTION

Riot (2001)
The Five Dollar Smile and Other Stories (1993)
Show Business (1991)
The Great Indian Novel (1989)

INDIA
SHASTRA

REFLECTIONS ON THE NATION
IN OUR TIME

SHASHI
THAROOR

ALEPH

ALEPH BOOK COMPANY
An independent publishing firm
promoted by *Rupa Publications India*

Published in India in 2015 by
Aleph Book Company
7/16 Ansari Road, Daryaganj
New Delhi 110 002

ISBN: 978-93-84067-28-1

1 3 5 7 9 10 8 6 4 2

For sale in the Indian subcontinent only.

Printed and bound in India by Replika Press Pvt. Ltd.

As the Republic of India turns 65
This book is for my grandmother
Mundarath Jayasankini Amma
As she turns 98
And for my mother
Lily Tharoor
On her 78th birthday

CONTENTS

INTRODUCTION

India Shastra is a collection of 100 articles and essays, some longish, some rather short, that seek to convey a portrait of contemporary India from the perspective of late 2014. Many of the pieces began life as columns in the media, but have been updated and expanded for this volume; some are adapted from speeches. Few have been left as they were originally written and delivered, since they are meant to be read at the dawn of 2015. The judgements in the book should stand as contemporary reflections of the India in which they are now being published.

With *India Shastra* I have concluded a de facto trilogy of works attempting to explore what makes my country what it is. *India: From Midnight to the Millennium* (1997), slightly revised and republished at the turn of the century as *India: From Midnight to the Millennium and Beyond* (2000), took in the broad sweep of India's politics, economics, society and culture in its first fifty years of Independence. *The Elephant, the Tiger and the Cellphone* (2007) was a collection of various writings on the same themes, bringing the narrative of India's transformation up to the sixtieth anniversary of India's Independence. *India Shastra* (2015) updates the story with more recent writings, and takes into account the dramatic change in Indian politics today with the ascent to power of Prime Minister Narendra Modi and his Bharatiya Janata Party. In a sense, the three books have evolved as my personal works of Smriti (memory), Shruti (hearing), and Shastra (thinking).

Section I, 'India Modi-fied', looks critically at a number of initiatives and actions of the new government in its first six months of existence. Section II, 'Modi's India and the World', discusses the foreign policy actions of the current government. Section III, 'The Legacy', groups together a number of essays relating to the political inheritance received by the new government from its forerunners. Section IV, 'Ideas of India', goes beyond reaffirming my long-held (and often expressed) faith in India's democratic pluralism to discuss a number of ideas relating to different aspects of Indian political life and the national ethos. Section V, 'The Pursuit of Excellence', covers a variety of areas in which India is striving, with varying degrees of success, to achieve quality outcomes. Section VI 'Issues of Contention', picks up a number of issues on which political opinion in contemporary India is sharply divided. Section VII, 'A Society in Flux', casts an eye on recent developments that point to changes in aspects of Indian life and society. And finally, Section VIII, 'India Beyond India', takes up a number of globally-relevant issues of interest and concern to India, but are not principally about India alone, except as part of the worldwide themes in which India is also implicated.

Taken together, the eight sections in this volume do not pretend to amount to a comprehensive portrait of India. Rather, they reflect my preoccupations relating to India over the past seven years, which happen to coincide with my return to my homeland after more than three decades abroad, first as a student and then as a career official of the United Nations. Though there is little by way of memoir or autobiographical reflection in it, except for a look back, in the final section, on my years at the United Nations, the book embodies many of the concerns that dominated my political life during this time. If there are glaring omissions—caste, for instance, hardly features, except in one essay—it is not because these issues are not important, but because, for one reason or another, I did not write about them very much during this period (caste is, however, extensively discussed in *India: From Midnight to the Millennium*).

My basic thesis about India has remained consistent in these three books. It is a land of extraordinary pluralism and diversity, where political democracy is indispensable to national survival; a country of great economic potential held back by some of its own policies and practices, many of which are in the process of being re-examined and reinvented; and a lively, contentious and exciting society which is far removed from the timeless and unchanging land of well-worn cliché. A Rip Kumar Winkle who had fallen asleep at the end of the Second World War seventy years ago would be unable to recognize the India of 2015. Everything has either changed dramatically or is in the process of changing: the nation's politics, its economic preferences, its social assumptions, the relations amongst castes, the material and professional choices available in the country, the patterns and habits of daily life, and the intangible attitudes of Indians towards everything from religion to profit-making.

I am, I suppose, an old-fashioned liberal, one who believes in political liberty, social freedoms, minimal restrictions on economic activity, and a concern for social justice. This has tended to put me in a very small minority in India, where political opinion is divided between a 'left' pledged to upholding socialism and state command of the economy, and a 'right' defined principally by its adherence to religious and cultural nationalism rather than economic or political convictions. The one liberal political party that largely embodied my views, C. Rajagopalachari's Swatantra Party, disappeared in 1974, and it was only after the liberalization policies undertaken by the Congress in 1991 that I was able to find a congenial home there, albeit, on some issues, on its fringes. My political isolation in many respects has been compounded by the robustness of my views on foreign policy and national security, laid out in greatest detail in *Pax Indica: India and the World of the 21st Century* (2012). A liberal hawk is a rare bird anywhere, but particularly in an India whose social and economic pieties and peace-loving credentials were sanctified by the hallowed freedom movement led by Mahatma Gandhi.

And yet, as this book suggests, India may be coming increasingly around to the point where my beliefs might one day even appear mainstream. Prime Minister Modi's speeches and sound bytes since his election could certainly have been scripted by a liberal, though the gap between articulation and implementation, in his case, remains currently wide enough to drive a rath through. What can one make of a man who speaks of tolerance and accommodation while condoning hate speech by party members he has appointed as ministers? How does one interpret a PM who speaks of 'minimal government, maximum governance' but is in the process of running the most centralized, top-down, bureaucracy-driven, personality-cult dominated central government since Indira Gandhi's Emergency rule? What conclusion can one reasonably derive about a leader who says 'the government has no business to be in business' but has never said a word to question the anomaly of his government owning and running airlines and hotels? How can one interpret the intentions of a prime minister elected on a promise of delivering results, whose very fine speeches and liberal pronouncements appear completely disconnected from any tangible action plan, adequate funding or execution capacity?

So the jury is still out on how much we can celebrate the 'Modi-fication' of India. What are the prospects for the expansion of the liberal space in India over the next two decades? This desirable objective requires both growth and equity. Progress is being made on both, but there's still a lot that needs to be done before we get there.

We cannot think of economic growth in India without also thinking of bringing its benefits to all our countrymen and women. (As I have written elsewhere, whether we grow at 9 per cent or at 5 per cent, we have to ensure the benefits reach the bottom 25 per cent of our population.) The most significant facts about the Indian people today are that the majority of them are young, and the majority of them are poor. I have discussed the promises and opportunities of our current demography in this volume. But the availability of human resources of such magnitude only means anything if we can feed, house, clothe, educate and train these young people so they can actually contribute to achieving socio-economic change in their own lives and in the country's fortunes. If we can't do that—if we fail to provide them the opportunities to make something of their lives in the new India—the same youthful and aspirational population could be not only a burden but even a threat, since so much of terrorism and extremist violence in our country is carried out by embittered, under-educated and unemployed young men.

How are we going to give them these opportunities? Plainly it cannot be through agriculture alone, because rural India already cannot sustain the 700 million people who are currently trying to live off the land. That is why India is suffering the painful tragedy of farmer suicides every time the monsoon disappoints and the harvests fail to sustain a debt-ridden farmer's family. I have no doubt that one of the phenomena we will witness in India over the next two decades is a significant and massive migration from the rural areas to the urban, both to existing cities and towns and through the transformation of rural centres into urban townships. In turn this will have an impact on other vital aspects of Indian life. First, on our education system, which will have to cope with hundreds of millions of young people who no longer intend to be farmers and peasants, but who will actively seek the educational tools that will equip them to lead viable urban lives. Second, on our infrastructure—not just roads and railways, but sanitation systems, health care facilities, educational institutions. And third, on our demand for and consumption of energy, which will multiply exponentially as new infrastructure is built and as urban dwellers seek electricity, water, drainage, roads, telephone connections and mass transit. Today, 600 million Indians, overwhelmingly in rural areas, are not even connected to the electricity grid. Tomorrow they will be.

If, say, 300 million Indians were to move from the villages to the towns in the next two decades or less, can we absorb all of them, educate all of them, employ all of them? Can we even contain all of them within India, or will there be a natural magnetic pull from those countries with ageing populations who need fresh young blood to man their factories, till their fields, drive their taxis? Can our cities and our national infrastructure cope with the challenges that these new demographic changes impose on us?

The stresses of economic development have created disparities which risk becoming centrifugal forces, dividing our society between rich and poor, urban and rural, high-caste and lower-caste, Hindu and Muslim. To counteract this, we need to devise creative, ambitious responses to deal with the challenges faced by our people—to connect them to the opportunities the 21st century offers, while uniting them in the perception that what divides them is irrelevant to fulfilling their core aspirations for themselves and their families.

I have not addressed all these issues in detail in *India Shastra*, but I have, I hope, raised the essential questions. As a political representative in India today, I certainly do not take the prospects of success for granted. The process of doing what I have described is not just huge in itself; it also involves something no society, not even China, has yet attempted. And that is to connect millions of citizens in a functioning democracy to their own government: not just to announce entitlements that they are expected to grasp for themselves, but to create delivery mechanisms that ensure that these entitlements are not just theoretical, but real and accessible.

Prime Minister Modi seems to understand this, if his speeches are anything to go by. But in India the right diagnosis does not always result in the right prescription, and even when it does, there is no guarantee that it will cure the condition—implementation of good ideas has long been our national weakness. If Modi can change this familiar narrative, he will have earned his place in history. So far, we in the Opposition have not seen enough to dispel our scepticism, though it is reasonable to argue that six months is far too short a time to draw emphatic conclusions either way.

There is a paradox at the heart of Modi's ascent to the prime ministership. His speeches and rhetoric appear to recognize, and harness, a vital shift in our national politics from a politics of identity to a politics of performance. Yet, he has ridden to power at the helm of a party, the Bharatiya Janata Party (BJP), which is ill-suited to the challenge of delinking India's polity from the incendiary issue of religious identity that it had built its base on. And his rise to office has empowered the khaki-shorts-wearing 'cultural organization', the Rashtriya Swayamsevak Sangh (RSS), whose views on every subject—economics, politics, history, culture, morality, gender relations, even matters of appropriate dress or conduct—are totally illiberal. Mr Modi has built his appeal by putting the focus on what the Indian people manifestly need—more development, better governance, wider socio-economic opportunities. But having won an election by attracting voters to these themes, he has given free rein to the most retrograde elements in Indian society, who are busy rewriting textbooks, extolling the virtues of ancient science over modern technology, advocating protectionism and self-reliance against free trade and foreign investment, and asserting that India's identity must be purely Hindu. Mr Modi cannot be oblivious to this fundamental contradiction, but he can only resolve it by jettisoning the very forces that have helped ensure his electoral victory. I am not sure whether such a fundamental contradiction can even be resolved, and in that may lie the seeds of Modi's future failure.

Beyond politics, *India Shastra* casts its eye on a wide variety of socio-cultural phenomena, from the controversy over the wearing of traditional Indian dhotis at posh clubs to the excitement aroused by India's Mars mission, and from the successes and failures of our educational policies to the relevance of non-alignment to today's India. Readers familiar with my passionate pieces on cricket during the same period should be advised that I have not included them in this book, to retain the interest of the general reader seeking a volume on the main currents of today's India. Perhaps in due course my cricket pieces might find space in a separate volume devoted to that most enthralling of sports!

Many of the essays included in this volume have been extensively rewritten, merged, and updated, though the more recent ones have required minimal editing. All have appeared, in somewhat different form, in the following publications, which are gratefully acknowledged: the *Asian Age/Deccan Chronicle*, *Financial Times*, *Hindu*, *Hindustan Times*, *Huffington Post/World Post*, *India Today*, *Indian Express*, *Mail Today*, NDTV.com, *Outlook*, *Sahara Samay*, *Times of India*,

Week, and in a number of international publications worldwide through my syndicated column for Project Syndicate.

Though I alone am responsible for the contents of this volume, some of the individual pieces in it benefited in their gestation from close collaborators, for whose intellectual inputs and wordsmithing I am most grateful. I would like to thank, in particular, Abhinav Kumar, who worked with me on some of the speeches that find themselves transmuted in this volume, Keerthik Sasidharan, with whom I co-authored earlier versions of two of the essays in this book, Sandeep Chakravorty, Samir Saran, Ria Vesta (for invaluable research assistance, and for this volume's title) and Dinesh Kapur. My trusted assistants during this period, Manu Pillai, Ameya Naik and Yashshri Soman (in order of appearance), helped me in innumerable indispensable ways, and though their inputs are not specifically visible in any of the text, without their support I could not have written it as I have. My diligent, conscientious and hard-working editor at Aleph, Simar Puneet, worked closely with me to bring the book to its final shape against very tight deadlines. Her deft touch is invisibly present throughout and I am most grateful for her excellent collaboration.

India Shastra is in many ways the brainchild of my close friend and publisher for over thirty years, David Davidar, who conceived the book, persuaded me to undertake it at a difficult time in my personal and political life, and took the personal trouble to wade through seven years of my articles to suggest the outline and contents of the present volume. If the finished product differs in important respects from his original conception of it, it is only because I embraced his idea with such enthusiasm that I found much more to include and to redo. To David, for his almost lifelong faith in me and my work, this book is a personal tribute.

Shashi Tharoor
New Delhi, December 2014

I

INDIA MODI-FIED

INDIA'S ELECTIONS: A PROCESS, NOT AN EVENT

India's 2014 general elections—which took place over a staggering thirty-seven days in nine 'phases', some a week apart from each other, from 7 April to 12 May—constituted, once again, the largest single exercise of democratic franchise in the world. Some 814 million eligible voters elected, for the sixteenth time, a new Parliament and government for India (casting their ballots this time at over 930,000 polling stations) from an estimated 15,000 candidates belonging to over 500 political parties in a process that was universally considered free, fair, honest, and by and large peaceful.

Democracy, of course, is a process, not an event. But the event of India's elections—with their amazing logistical and security challenges, their myriad languages, their candidates identified not just by name but by electoral symbols to aid the illiterate voter—is an astonishing spectacle, one that never ceases to evoke admiration each time it occurs. They are conducted with scrupulous impartiality by India's independent Election Commission, protected by its security forces and watched over by a hyperactive citizenry and a robustly free media. It takes the felling of a sizeable forest to furnish enough paper for posters, electoral rolls and voting slips; thousands of electronic voting machines are manufactured that can survive heat, dust and power failures and retain their results safely until they are ready to be counted, sometimes weeks after they are used (since no votes are counted till the last ones are cast); and every election has at least one story of returning officers battling through snow or jungle to ensure that the democratic wishes of remote constituents are duly recorded.

And yet there are larger issues behind the electoral spectacle that must not be overlooked. India's elections have, over the years, deepened and broadened the composition of the political establishment: sociologists have analysed the class-composition of India's legislatures and traced an important change from a post-Independence Parliament dominated by highly-educated professionals to today's motley crew of MPs, who are more truly representative of the rural heartland of India.

However, the fact that, particularly in the northern states, our voters elect people referred to openly in the press as 'mafia dons', 'dacoit leaders' and 'anti-social elements' is a troubling reflection on the way the electoral process has served Indian democracy. A hundred members of each of the last four Parliaments have had criminal cases pending against them. The resultant alienation of the educated middle-class means that fewer and fewer of them go to the polls on Election Day.

On the other hand, the poor do. Whereas psephological studies in the United States have demonstrated that the poor do not vote in significant numbers during elections (the turnout in the largely poor and black district of Harlem during the pre-Obama US presidential elections was 23 per cent), the opposite is true in India. Here it is the poor who take the time to queue up in the hot sun, believing their votes will make a difference, whereas the more privileged members of society, knowing their views and numbers will do little to influence the outcome, have been staying away from the hustings. Voter studies of Indian elections have consistently demonstrated that the lowest stratum of Indian society vote in numbers well above the national average, while graduates turn out in numbers well below.

The significant changes in the social composition of India's ruling class, both in politics and in the bureaucracy, since Independence are indeed proof of democracy at work. But many lament that the poor quality of the country's political class in general offers less cause for celebration. Our parliamentarians increasingly reflect the qualities required to acquire power rather than the skills to wield it for the common good. Many cynics see democracy in India as a process that has given free rein to criminals and corrupt cops, opportunists and fixers, murderous musclemen and grasping middlemen, kickback-making politicos and bribe-taking bureaucrats, mafia dons and private armies, caste groups and religious extremists.

And yet it is democracy that has given Indians of every imaginable caste, creed, culture and cause the chance to break free of their lot. Where there is social oppression and caste tyranny, particularly in rural India, democracy offers the victims a means of salvation. Amongst the victors in recent elections have been people from traditionally underprivileged backgrounds who have risen through the power of the ballot to positions their forefathers could never have dreamed of. There could be no more startling tribute to the Indian system.

Yes, elections also allow many to vent extreme views: there are those who wish India to become a Hindu Rashtra, a land of and for the Hindu majority; those who seek to raise even higher the protectionist barriers against foreign investment that had begun to come down; those who believe that a firm hand at the national helm would be preferable to the failures of democracy. As the victors in May, the Bharatiya Janata Party whose leaders and supporters include all these elements, established their government, the challenge remains to sustain a pluralist India, open to the contention of ideas and interests within it, unafraid of the power or the products of the outside world, and determined to liberate and fulfil the creative energies of her people.

Reassuringly, India's democratic process has historically served to ensure inclusiveness rather than fragmentation. The only possible idea of India is that of a nation greater than the sum of its parts. And yet the tactic of promoting communal polarization in a state like Uttar Pradesh, with a view to consolidating a good proportion of the Hindu majority vote, appears to have paid off, with the BJP and its ally winning an unprecedented 75 out of 80 seats in the state.

This is undoubtedly a warning sign. Yet, on the whole, India has reasons to celebrate its electoral process. Across the globe, there will always be a choice between a world of edicts and crusades, where orthodoxies rule and foreign heresies are ruthlessly suppressed behind exclusionist walls, and a world in which the virtues of tolerance, dissent and co-operation are recognized and practised. Every time it goes to the polls, India, which in the second decade of the 21st century has a sixth of the world's population, offers the world an instructive paradigm of the latter.

IS THERE A MODI 2.0?

When Narendra Modi swept to a dramatic victory in India's general elections, becoming the first prime minister in three decades to command an absolute majority in the lower house of India's fractious Parliament, many in India worried about what his victory would portend. To political opponents and members of India's liberal intelligentsia, Modi was a divisive, sectarian, authoritarian figure who had presided over the massacre of some 1,200 innocents, mainly Muslim, as chief minister of Gujarat in 2002. The thought of such a figure leading a diverse and multi-religious polity that had long been built on the 'Nehruvian consensus' developed by the Congress party, was anathema to many.

In the event, Modi overcame this negative perception, re-branding himself as an apostle of development and pointing to his successful record in Gujarat, a state of high growth rates that under his leadership has been a magnet for investors. His brilliantly-organized, lavishly-funded election campaign saw 'Hindutva', the ideology of Hindu chauvinism with which he and his BJP have long been identified, relegated to the back burner, while Modi promised voters he would remake India in the model of prosperous Gujarat. The electorate rewarded the BJP—which had never previously won more than 186 seats in India's 543-member Lower House—with 282 seats, as the National Democratic Alliance led by the BJP claimed 333. The ruling Congress party, of which I am a member, was relegated to its worst showing in history, winning a mere 44 seats.

To almost everyone's surprise, however, in his first six months in office, Modi and the BJP eschewed the hubris and triumphalism they might have been assumed to have earned with their sweeping victory, except during electoral campaigns for by-elections and for State Assemblies. Immediately after his election, Modi was conciliatory and inclusive in both his pronouncements and his actions. I was a beneficiary of this unexpected generosity on the very day of his victory, when I received a startling tweet of congratulations from him on my own victory in my constituency. 'Let us work together to move India forward,' he declared in his message to me.

This tweet to a prominent adversary, with whom he had crossed swords in the past, was one of many signals to the nation that he was putting old enmities behind him. 'I will be prime minister of all Indians, including those who did not vote for me,' he announced in one of his first speeches. Cynics might point out that this was only prudent, since his party won its resounding majority with just 31 per cent of the national vote, benefitting from the Westminster-style 'first-past-the-post' system in constituencies with multiple contesting parties. But coming as it did from a man with a reputation for brooking no dissent and riding roughshod over opposition during his twelve years at the helm in Gujarat, it was a welcome surprise.

In a series of speeches, Prime Minister Modi has gone out of his way to avoid confrontational language, to omit issues and imagery that India's religious minorities would find offensive, and to extend a hand of friendship to his critics. After having attacked the large number of government projects and schemes named for members of the Congress party's Nehru-Gandhi dynasty during the election, he stopped his ministers from renaming these programmes, saying it was more important to get them to work more effectively. (There are signs, however, that this restraint may not last.) His early Cabinet appointments rewarded the party's brighter and younger professionals, omitting many of the Hindu nationalist veterans and rabid ideologues who epitomized many Indians' anxieties about the BJP.

In a striking departure from precedent, Modi also quelled concerns in India's neighbourhood about his rise by inviting the heads of government of India's seven South Asian neighbours, as well as that of Mauritius (the Indian Ocean republic whose population is 63 per cent Indian), to his swearing-in. India's prime ministers have never enjoyed lavish inaugurations like American presidents, traditionally assuming office after sparsely-attended and low-key oath-takings behind closed doors. Modi converted this routine into a grand, opulent 4,000-guest ceremony on the forecourt of Rashtrapati Bhavan and invited his foreign guests to attend the televised coronation. The gesture instantly disarmed many across the borders who had been alarmed by his combative rhetoric during the campaign, in which he had promised robust action on the borders, assailed Pakistani sponsorship of terrorism, criticized Sri Lanka's treatment of its Tamil minority and warned some 30 million Bangladeshi illegal immigrants in India that they should be prepared to pack their bags on the day of his victory. His cordial welcome to, and subsequent bilateral meetings with, the leaders of these and other neighbouring countries reassured them that the Modi government would not feel obliged to live up to the belligerence of the Modi campaign. Indeed, on my own visits to Nepal and Bangladesh, I was struck by the highly positive comments about the new Indian prime minister that I heard from many prominent leaders who would have been happy to describe themselves as friends of my Congress party.

So does this all add up to a Modi 2.0, a very different figure in government from the ogre some of us had feared and demonized for years? It is still too early to tell; despite the breathless pronouncements of the media, two hundred days is far too soon to judge a new prime minister or his government. But the initial signs are encouraging. Prime Minister Modi would hardly be the first opposition leader to temper his views and conduct once in office, but there seems to be something more fundamental involved here. An ambitious man, Modi appears to realize that if he wants to make a success of his government, he will have to lead the nation from the centre and not from the extreme right where he had built his base in the BJP. His overwhelming majority, won on the back of a highly personalized campaign which led many to vote for Modi rather than for the BJP, has also liberated him from the party's and his own past positions. Just as he remade himself from a hate-figure into an avatar of modernity and progress, he is seeking to remake the BJP from a vehicle of Hindu chauvinism to a natural party of governance. This will require a change in both language and tone, as he has demonstrated from Day One. Whether he will succeed in pulling it off beyond the honeymoon period, or whether he will lapse back to Modi 1.0 at the first sign of public disenchantment or mounting criticism, remains to be seen.

For an Opposition Member of Parliament like myself, it would be churlish not to acknowledge Modi 2.0's inclusive outreach and to welcome his more conciliatory statements and actions. The moment he says or does something divisive or sectarian in the Modi 1.0 mould, however, we will resist him robustly. India's people, and its pluralist democracy, deserve no less.

MODI: PLUS CA CHANGE, PLUS C'EST LA MEME CHOSE

According to Prime Minister Narendra Modi's supporters, his overwhelming victory in the general elections was a sweeping repudiation of everything for which the previous United Progressive Alliance (UPA) government, led by the Indian National Congress, stood. Will Modi live up to voters' expectations?

There has certainly been a lot of hype. Modi, it was claimed during the election campaign, would reverse the UPA's 'poor governance' and 'policy paralysis', introducing a radically new approach, based on his corporatist 'Gujarat development model'. In doing so, he would transform India, liberating it from the UPA's exhausted and ineffective policies, thus improving the lives of millions. 'Achhe din aane wale hain'—'the good days are coming'—his supporters declared upon his victory.

In particular, the Modi public relations machine proclaimed an end to the sops and compromises that supposedly characterized the UPA coalition. Modi pledged to make the tough decisions that the UPA could not, weaning Indians from the statist culture of 'doles' and subsidies, while pursuing bold policies aimed at spurring economic growth and job creation. Indians today, he averred, want jobs, not handouts.

It took just a few weeks for the hollowness of these claims to become apparent. A commonly cited example of the outgoing government's alleged economic mismanagement was its sugar-price policy. Powerful sugarcane cooperatives, led by major UPA supporters, supposedly drove the government to fix extravagant prices and write off sugar farmers' bad debts, leading to over-production.

Instead of eliminating this system, as expected, Modi's government has augmented subsidies for sugar exports to support higher output, raised import duties on sugar to discourage foreign competition, and increased the percentage of sugar-based ethanol that must be blended with petrol. His motivation is not difficult to discern: his party hoped that such concessions would help it to wrest control of Maharashtra, India's main sugar-producing state, from the UPA in the state assembly election, which indeed it duly did.

This goal explains another policy reversal as well. The UPA's critics long claimed that unsustainably low, state-dictated passenger fares and freight charges for rail services—which could not cover the cost of maintenance to ensure the safety of trains and tracks, much less enable expansion and improvement of service—reflected the government's inability to make tough decisions.

It is true that coalition politics prevented decisive action, with a railway minister being summarily dismissed by his own party leader—whom the UPA was politically unable to confront—after attempting to raise fares. But, in the pre-election interim budget, the UPA government finally bit the bullet, proposing a 14.2 per cent increase in rail fares and a 6.5 per cent hike in freight rates. Per India's code of political conduct, the budget changes were deferred until after the election.

Soon after taking office, the Modi government announced its intention to implement the price increases, though officials made sure to emphasize that they were merely following through on an existing mandate. Then, faced with public resistance, they moderated the planned hikes, particularly of the significantly discounted monthly pass currently available to suburban commuters—an important segment of the electorate in Mumbai, Maharashtra's capital.

Modi had previously derided the UPA's populist railway ministers for distorted policies that punished businesses, declaring during his election campaign that India's railways should be run more like China's, with increased government investment, including for bullet trains. Yet, no sooner had he been sworn in than he acquiesced in precisely the kind of political compromise to which he and the BJP—which won a parliamentary majority, and thus does not depend on coalition partners for its government's survival—was supposed to be immune.

Modi's government has adopted an even weaker stance on another unpopular but necessary decision: fuel-price increases. In order to align Indian fuel prices more closely with world market prices, thereby enabling domestic oil and gas producers to finance exploration and extraction, the UPA government had announced that natural gas prices would be doubled from 1 April. But, as with railway fares, the final decision was left up to Modi. And, instead of doing what was needed—even while blaming his predecessors—Modi postponed the decision until September. As it happens, luck came to Mr Modi's rescue; international oil prices plummeted from $128 a barrel to $78 by late November, making it easy for Mr Modi to deregulate prices at the pump. The true test of his government will come only if and when international prices rise again.

This hypocrisy about rhetoric and action has characterized virtually every policy decision that the BJP government has taken so far. Despite the BJP's strident criticism of the United States–India Civil Nuclear Cooperation deal—the UPA administration's signature foreign-policy triumph—Modi's government quietly ratified an India-specific 'additional protocol', granting the International Atomic Energy Agency access to India's civilian nuclear sites.

Moreover, the BJP had opposed interaction with Pakistani Prime Minister Nawaz Sharif, pending satisfactory progress on the prosecution and punishment of the perpetrators of the 2008 Mumbai attacks, which killed 164 people and injured more than 300. Yet Sharif was an honoured guest at Modi's inauguration, exchanging gifts with India's newly affable leader.

The Modi government has also adopted the UPA-proposed Goods and Services Tax, which had been stalled by opposition from BJP-ruled states (including Modi's Gujarat), and is advocating its adoption by Parliament after opposing it tooth-and-nail for five years. And it will strengthen the national anti-terrorism effort, which Modi previously denounced as an assault on Indian federalism.

Many Modi supporters in the media have already begun to decry the series of policy abdications Modi has conducted since his campaign. Indian citizens who thought that they voted for change are beginning to wonder if the BJP has simply reprised the UPA government's policies. As a member of the previous government, I must say that that may not be such a bad thing.

THE MODI BUDGET

The finance minister, Arun Jaitley, delivered himself of the longest Budget speech in living memory in July 2014—16,473 words lasting nearly two hours and a half, versus just 6,581 words in less than an hour that his predecessor P. Chidamabram took to deliver the 2013 Budget. We know this was literally back-breaking work for the minister, since he had to sit down mid-way to rest his aching back, but it was one more confirmation that length is no substitute for substance.

After hearing my good friend Arun Jaitley's views on the UPA's Budgets over the last five years, I have to confess I was disappointed in his own Budget's lack of 'big, bold ideas', to cite a phrase he has often used against the UPA. For the last decade the BJP has been critical of the UPA's Budgets and could have been assumed to have a pretty good idea of what they would offer in our place. I had expected some path-breaking reforms, some radical departures from UPA policies, and of course a few of Prime Minister Modi's 'bitter pills'. We got none.

No fewer than twenty-nine projects have been allocated Rs 100 crore each. (Indeed, the repeated announcements of 100-crore sums reminded listeners of a statement of Bollywood hits' box-office collections, without the entertainment value.) A Budget cannot be a laundry list of assorted 100-crore sops to various constituencies—though of course we understand that for the most part these are meant to be initial allocations for this year alone and not complete numbers for the total duration of the project. Still, a Budget has to have a vision and a clear policy direction. Where are those?

These 100-odd crore allocations merely confirm a worrying lack of coherence in the government's mindset. What is the desired overall outcome, and how does each 100 crore serve that objective? For instance, when there is no overall approach on women's issues, a mere 100 crore for gender security is meaningless, especially when there is not enough outlay for core sovereign functions like law and order.

But in keeping with Mr Jaitley's own preferences when he was in Opposition, let us focus mainly on the big picture. There are four questions we all need to ask when we evaluate the 2014 Budget.

First, as this is a new government, does it have an overall vision and is it clear how it is going to be implemented? Second, have the economy's problems been diagnosed correctly and is the prescription appropriate? Third, who gains and who loses from the budget proposals? Fourth, does it live up to the expectations generated by the ruling party's statements when it was in opposition?

I am sorry to say there are grounds for disappointment as we analyse the Budget with each of these four questions in mind.

What does the aam aadmi look for in the Budget? At a personal level, more income and a lower cost of living; at the macro level, policies that will create growth and job opportunities, reduce prices, widen his life prospects. India needs an economy which is efficient, competitive and, in an era of growing inequality, also humane.

In his Rajya Sabha speech on the UPA's Budget in 2012, Mr Jaitley declared that the Budget should help 'increase the width and volume of economic activity'. That is a good yardstick, but his own Budget fails to meet it. Where is the road map for national recovery?

Any Budget in today's India must address five issues: (i) fiscal consolidation, that is, a policy aimed at reducing government deficits and debt accumulation; (ii) job creation through boosting manufacturing; (iii) increasing savings in order to boost investments; (iv) inflation control; and (v) improving investor sentiment—both domestic and foreign—for growth revival. One can throw into this list a few subsidiary points: sound tax policies, energy policies, human resource development incentives, issues of banking and pensions. We don't have the time to address each one in detail—but the finance minister did. He chose not to.

Take one item, manufacturing. To be internationally competitive, India requires policies that will reduce the cost of manufacturing: affordable interest rates, improved infrastructure, better trade facilitation, lower cost of power and so on. One of the key reasons for the fall in the GDP growth rate is the slowing Index of Industrial Production. But this government's Budget has failed to give us such a coherent set of policies to improve manufacturing.

For a government that had long deprecated the UPA's alleged 'indecisiveness', there were no concrete decisions on offer on any of these or our country's other fiscal priorities. For instance, after decrying the UPA's tax policies for years, Mr Jaitley announced no decision on introducing the pending Direct Tax Code. Instead he gave us a series of committees—an expenditure management commission, a high-level committee of the CBDT on retrospective taxation, another to interact with industry on taxation, a fourth one to examine micro, small and medium enterprises (MSMEs). This from a party that routinely accused the UPA of delegating decision-making to groups of ministers!

Now on the Expenditure Management Commission proposed by the Modi government: we have seen this movie before, four times in fact. The Atal Bihari Vajpayee government too had an Expenditure Reforms Commission, led by Mr K. P. Geethakrishnan. The report, which covered thirty-six subject areas, was consigned to the archives. As usual, a commission becomes an excuse for inaction. How many times must the wheel be re-invented for the NDA engine to start cranking?

No specific measures were announced to reduce inflation. Price rise is the worst kind of tax on the poor and the lower middle-class, the issue that most hurts the aam aadmi, but the party that rode to power on public resentment of high prices had no inflation-busting solutions to offer. The cuts in fuel subsidies by about Rs 22,000 crore mean that the prices of petrol and diesel will increase, leading to a cascading impact on other essential commodities. (In the event, crashing global oil prices have prevented that from happening.) We would at least have hoped the FM would say that he encourages and supports the Reserve Bank of India to manage interest rate policies that complement the fiscal efforts to reduce inflation. But he has not even addressed this concern.

People below the poverty line get short shrift in the focus on the so-called 'neo middle-class'. But for aspirational young Indians, there is no indication of where new jobs will come from for the 12 million young people entering the employment market each year.

We all know that containing the fiscal deficit to 4.6 per cent of GDP is important to manage and contain public debt at sustainable levels in the long term, and to curb inflation in the short term. After accusing the UPA of fudging the numbers in claiming a fiscal deficit of 4.6 per cent, the NDA budget now accepts those numbers. But it gives no specifics on how it will bring that down to 4.1 per cent, a target it endorsed without cavil.

From a macro-economic perspective, there are some real worries about how the finance minister will achieve any fiscal consolidation with his budget. The finance minister based his deficit calculations on a nearly 20 per cent increase in revenue, which most analysts say is overly ambitious. The global ratings agency Moody's criticized the Budget for its lack of detail on specific revenue and expenditure measures to shrink the deficit. Are global investors more likely to heed Moody's views or Modi's?

The government is betting on a sharp increase in revenues in a slow growth year, which is implausible. Some of the budget numbers strain credulity. Tax revenues are projected to grow by nearly 20 per cent. That defies credibility, given that nominal GDP growth is unlikely to exceed 13 to 14 per cent (9 per cent for inflation plus 5 per cent for real GDP growth). It also defies credibility because in the first quarter of this fiscal year, 45 per cent of the annual deficit number has already been reached.

The fine print in the Budget documents shows that the government expects Rs 99,000 crore from non-tax revenues, a 24 per cent increase from last year's revised estimates. Where's that coming from, if not from selling national assets? Yet, Mr Jaitley didn't even mention the word 'disinvestment' in his speech. Still, disinvestment proceeds are projected to rise from Rs 25,000 crore in 2013-14 to Rs 63,000 crore in 2014-15, much higher than the interim

Budget's target. The finance minister needs to spell out exactly what he will do on disinvestment. Which bits of the family silver is he planning to sell off?

In addition to disinvestment, he hopes for a bunch of other non-tax items to further plug the deficit—telecom spectrum auctions (Rs 45,000 crore), and dividends and profits transferred to the government from public sector undertakings (PSUs) and other bodies (Rs 90,000 crore). How realistic are these numbers? Widespread scepticism has been expressed, which I share.

To turn to taxes: As leader of the Opposition, Arun Jaitley had demanded that the IT exemption limit be raised to Rs 5 lakh, which he has not been able to fulfil as finance minister. The very fact that the BJP's promise of increasing the exemption limit to Rs 5 lakh has resulted in only a 25 per cent increase in the exemption limit from Rs 2 lakh to Rs 2.50 lakh has disappointed people across the country. The average taxpayer will save Rs 416 a month—which won't even cover the increased price of tomatoes, onions and milk for a family of four.

The Budget implies a tax buoyancy* of 1.3, which is higher than the last ten years' average of 1.0 and is too optimistic given muted GDP growth expectations (5.4–5.9 per cent), no increase in tax rates and cuts in excise and customs duties. Mr Jaitley has projected tax revenue growth well above GDP growth for 2014-15. And despite only a 6 per cent growth in customs duty revenues in 2013-2014, the government budgeted a 15 per cent jump in customs duties for 2014-15 as well. All this is, at the risk of euphemism, unduly optimistic.

There is no comprehensive roadmap to step up the country's tax to GDP ratio, which is at a low level of 17 per cent. And no measures to address the lack of progressivity in the country's tax structure, which depends on indirect taxes to the extent of almost two-thirds of total tax revenue.

Mr Jaitley had long attacked the UPA's service taxes, joking that he couldn't use the 'sulabh shauchalaya' at Lodhi Garden on his morning walks because toilet use is not on the negative list of service tax exemptions. Now, he has in fact increased the number of items attracting service tax. He has flushed his own objections down the toilet.

In the absence of clear measures to increase revenues or tax collection efficiency, how will the NDA manage the fiscal deficit? Won't there inevitably be cuts in development expenditure?

Persistent inflation is due in large part to rising government borrowings and is the cause of high interest rates that have hurt investment, consumption and job creation. Clearly, debt must be reduced, even retired altogether, if interest rates are to be lowered. Mr Jaitley rightly said in his speech: 'We

---

*Tax buoyancy is the percentage increase in tax revenue for every 1 per cent increase in GDP.

cannot leave behind a legacy of debt for our future generations.' Yet, this year, the Government of India will spend more than it did last year, borrow more than it did last year—approximately Rs 69 crore an hour—and spend more on subsidies than it did last year.

Strikingly, resource mobilization for infrastructure is meagre. In 2013, then Chief Minister Narendra Modi had called for Rs 55 lakh crore to be devoted to infrastructure improvements: his finance minister hasn't come close, his numbers clocking in at around 2 per cent of Mr Modi's preferred figure.

The Budget did not spell out clear plans for rationalizing subsidies, recapitalizing PSU banks, and did not repeal the retrospective tax amendment as was widely expected by the investing community. The Economic Survey envisaged reducing direct taxes to the ASEAN level, a Fiscal Responsibility and Budget Management Act with teeth, and food stamps and cash transfers instead of subsidized goods. Mr Jaitley has avoided all these reforms.

No wonder that, in the wake of the Budget announcements, the BSE Sensex extended its losing streak to a fifth straight day during which the blue chip index shed over 1,000 points. So while the 100-crore giveaways make it look like a 'something for everybody' Budget, the stock market reaction proves it is really a 'not enough for anybody' Budget.

Agriculture—one area in which the country has been growing relatively well—has been woefully neglected by the NDA Budget, in a year where farmers are particularly vulnerable to the consequences of a bad monsoon. Yes, the Rural Youth Entrepreneurship Scheme is an innovative idea, but can Rs 100 crore be a serious figure for a scheme for the rural young, in a country where 67 per cent of the population is rural and 65 per cent is young (under 35 years)? The Budget does nothing to cater to agricultural labourers. It directly hits funds for rural housing, provision of drinking water and sanitation—sectors which require a big increase in allocation.

Mr Jaitley has made no budgetary allocation under the Integrated Scheme for Farmers' Income Security. In the run up to the country's 2014 general elections the BJP manifesto promised that it would 'increase public investment in agriculture...enhance profitability in agriculture by ensuring a minimum of 50 per cent profits over the cost of production, cheaper agriculture inputs and strengthen and expand rural credit...welfare measures for farmers above 60 years in age, small and marginal farmers and farm labours...implement farm insurance scheme to take care of crop loss', etc. Keeping in view the stunted growth of the agriculture sector over the years, the promises made in the election manifesto as well as the deficient rainfall that has already been experienced (which seems certain to hit agriculture production), one would expect the Union Budget 2014-15 to give top priority to this sector, particularly a boost to rural employment under the Mahatma Gandhi National

Rural Employment Scheme (MGNREGA) and for agricultural activities in 'the dryland'. The development and sustainability of agriculture in India critically depends on public investment in the sector. There is practically none. Yes, there is provision for farm credit, and increasing the targets each year might not be beneficial for the large proportion of small and marginal farmers as they do not have access to such formal sources of credit.

Even more painful is the issue of pensions for retired government servants, teachers and the like. The Modi Budget fails to raise minimum pension to living wage levels: I have met people in my constituency with forty years' service behind them who are getting Rs 500 a month. Current Employees' Provident Fund Organisation participants and members should be given the option to migrate to the New Pension Scheme. Like the provident fund, employee-employer contributions to life and health insurance should be mandatory. But these easy wins have been spurned.

Some of the Budget allocations raise eyebrows, and some others might raise hackles. The Rs 500 crore offered to Kashmiri Pandits pales in comparison with the Rs 1,600 crore allotted by the UPA in its 2008 Budget for the Kashmiri Pandits' relief and rehabilitation. Rs 100 crore has been set aside for the training of sports persons for the (then) upcoming Commonwealth Games in Glasgow and the Asian Games in Incheon, but it's not clear how much training they will get, since it cost Rs 678 crore just to train our medal-winning athletes in the 2010 Commonwealth Games.

In other areas, the lack of specifics is maddening. There was no indication of where new jobs will come from for the 12 million young people entering the employment market each year. You can talk all you want about affordable housing and smart cities, but where is the land available to build them?

In some areas, however, the BJP has adopted the very UPA policies it had criticized, opposed and blocked. I am glad to see the BJP embracing the Goods and Services Tax (GST), which had been opposed tooth and nail by BJP-ruled state governments even though business groups had said that it could add 2 per cent a year to India's GDP. But again, no specific deadline has been announced for its adoption. GST rollout is critically dependent on the states and the roadmap must be set in stone. (The key is assuring states as to how you will compensate for their loss of fiscal flexibility.)

Some of the UPA's social sector schemes have remained intact, including MGNREGA, which—in an unscripted statement not found in his published text—Mr Jaitley assured the Lok Sabha would be maintained at its current levels. But there is no increased expenditure for the MGNREGA programme, which means the Budget has reduced the funds available in real terms. With a drought being predicted, a huge expansion of the programme to provide drought relief to the 60 per cent agriculture-dependent working population of our country was essential.

NREGA is not the only UPA scheme that continues. 'Skill India' is merely a new name for the UPA's National Skill Development Mission and the proposals already approved by the UPA for funding under the Nirbhaya Fund have been announced again by the BJP. The AIBP Scheme (Accelerated Irrigation Benefit Programme) initiated by the UPA has been now named the Pradhan Mantri Krishi Sinchai Yojana for which Rs 1,000 crore has been given. Jawaharlal Nehru National Urban Renewal Mission along with Bharat Nirman, which had almost about $8 billion allocated to it, has been turned into the Shyama Prasad Mukherjee Rurban Mission. So instead of a game-changing Budget, Mr Jaitley has given us a name-changing Budget. As Mr Chidambaram memorably put it, the BJP campaigned for a 'Congress-mukt Bharat', but they couldn't even deliver a Congress-mukt Budget!

I can't imagine the prime minister is too happy with this, judging by his critique of the UPA's 2013 Budget: 'This budget is…piecemeal. UPA wants to play safe', Mr Modi had written in the *Economic Times*. His 2013 commentary had mocked the UPA repeatedly for not thinking big. How ironic that his own government's first Budget is guilty of exactly the same defect.

Even in one of the PM's favourite areas during the last decade, federalism, there is nothing new on offer. The campaign rhetoric waxed eloquent on the need to empower states. The reality of the Budget doesn't reflect this. Authority for clearances could have been reverted to the states with caveats, but investors—whether in mining, gas, smart towns or power projects—will still have to visit Delhi for clearances. It is clearly a case of 'where you stand depends on where you sit': when Mr Modi was sitting in Gujarat he wanted to empower the states; now that he sits in Delhi he prefers centralized top-down rule.

Finally, the Budget fails to address some of the deep-rooted problems in the country, like that of growing inequality. The findings from the NSSO's survey on the level and pattern of consumption expenditure during July 2011 to June 2012 show that the spending gap between the rich and the poor in India has almost doubled in the last five years. The monthly per capita consumption expenditure of the top 5 per cent of the rural population is nearly nine times that of the bottom 5 per cent. This is even worse in the urban areas, where the average consumption by the top 5 per cent of the population was about 14.7 times that of the bottom 5 per cent. In 2013, India ranked 136th in the Human Development Index (HDI) among 186 countries in the world in the Human Development Report released by United Nations Development Programme (UNDP). Currently, the education and health indicators in India fare poorly in comparison to other developing countries.

Women's issues have suffered woeful neglect. It is an indication of the NDA's skewed priorities when it allocates only Rs 100 crore for a 'beti bachao/beti padhao' scheme, while finding Rs 200 crore for a 'Unity' statue in Gujarat. I suppose for the BJP, the 'beti''s voice counts for even less than that of the 'murti'. To rub further salt into the gender wound, the Budget allocation for the statue, at Rs 200 crore, is equal to the allocations for the home ministry's scheme for women's safety in cities (150 crore) and the project for the safety of women on public transport (50 crore) put together!

Though, according to the National Crime Records Bureau, there has been a drastic increase of 26 per cent in crimes against women, we see no comparable reflection of this in the Budget. The BJP manifesto sought to dispense funds for the rehabilitation of rape victims on a priority basis. Yet, how much does the Budget allocate for medical help, shelter and counselling of rape victims? A measly Rs 91 lakh for the whole country, in a scheme called 'SAAHAS'. Even 100 crore would not have been enough for this purpose. 'One stop crisis centres' are to be set up for women victims of crime—but only in cities that have a population of more than 2.5 million. So even a city like Thiruvananthapuram would not benefit from this scheme.

Let me, however, applaud some of the interesting new schemes the FM has proposed. The National Mission on Pilgrimage Rejuvenation and Spiritual Augmentation Drive (PRASAD), which I am glad to see has not been named for any individual (it would be a stretch to suggest the BJP were thinking of President Rajendra Prasad!), is praiseworthy. I have however requested that three major pilgrimage centres in Kerala not be omitted from the minister's rather short list of places to be favoured, namely Sabarimala, the Sree Padmanabhaswamy temple and Kurishumala, the latter two in my constituency.

As Indians, we all want India to succeed, and Indians to prosper and lead decent, productive lives. If the government can ensure that, it would be uncharitable of us in the Opposition to dissent. But they will have to do better than this Budget if they are to persuade sceptics here and around the world that they can take us there.

BJP apologists have argued that their government had forty-five days to present a Budget and this is only a beginning. Fair enough, except they have been broadcasting their trenchant opinions for ten years and should not have needed even forty-five days to act on views they have expressed for so long. Former prime minister Manmohan Singh had just a month after his surprise appointment as finance minister in 1991 to come up with the most revolutionary Budget India has ever had. Mr Modi campaigned on the promise of showing voters the light at the end of the tunnel. In this Budget, though, his finance minister hasn't even built the tunnel.

Since the finance minister did not favour us with the usual couplets we have become used to in Budget speeches, I thought I should offer him a couple that are appropriate to this story. The first:

कहाँ तो तय था उजाला हर घर के लिए
कहाँ चिराग़ मयस्सर नहीं शहर के लिए

(The promise was to illuminate every home
Not even a lamp lights up the city today.)

But we on the other side of the House are not surprised. After all, as the immortal Ghalib put it:

तेरे वादे पर जिये हम, तो ये जान झूठ जाना
कि ख़ुशी से मर न जाते, अगर एतबार होता

(I lived by your promise, as I knew that it was false
Wouldn't I have died of happiness, if I had believed it to be true?)

It would be better for the Modi government to fulfil its promises than to disappoint the young voters whose hopes and aspirations voted them to power. This Budget is not one to make anyone die of happiness.

THE HYPOCRISY OF MODI'S 19 COMMANDMENTS

The news that the Government of India has amended the All India Services (Conduct) Rules, 1968, by inserting assorted sub-rules, is rather piquant. First of all, what do these amendments require civil servants to do?

Under sub-rule (1A), every member of the Service shall maintain:

(i)   High ethical standards, integrity and honesty;
(ii) Political neutrality;
(iii) Promoting of the principles of merit, fairness and impartiality in the discharge of duties;
(iv) Accountability and transparency;
(v)   Responsiveness to the public, particularly to the weaker section;
(vi) Courtesy and good behaviour with the public.

Under sub-rule (2B), every member of the Service shall:

(i)   Commit himself [yes, good old linguistic sexism continues in the Government of India] to uphold the supremacy of the Constitution and democratic values;
(ii)   Defend and uphold the sovereignty and integrity of India, the security of State, public order, decency and morality;
(iii) Maintain integrity in public service;
(iv)   Take decisions solely in public interest and use or cause to use public resources efficiently, effectively and economically;
(v)   Declare any private interests relating to his public duties and take steps to resolve any conflicts in a way that protects the public interest;
(vi)   Not place himself under any financial or other obligations to any individual or organisation which may influence him in the performance of his official duties;
(vii) Not misuse his position as civil servant and not take decisions in order to derive financial or material benefits for himself, his family or his friends;
(viii) Make choices, take decisions and make recommendations on merit alone;
(ix)   Act with fairness and impartiality and not discriminate against anyone, particularly the poor and the under-privileged sections of society;
(x)   Refrain from doing anything which is or may be contrary to any law, rules, regulations and established practices;
(xi)   Maintain discipline in the discharge of his duties and be liable to

implement the lawful orders duly communicated to him;

(xii) Be liable to maintain confidentiality in the performance of his official duties as required by any laws for the time being in force, particularly with regard to information, disclosure of which may prejudicially affect the sovereignty and integrity of India, the security of State, strategic, scientific or economic interests of the State, friendly relations with foreign countries or lead to incitement of an offence or illegal or unlawful gains to any person; and

(xiii) Perform and discharge his duties with the highest degree of professionalism and dedication to the best of his abilities.

Phew! Quite a list. But is there, in fact, anything new in there? Wasn't the civil service always supposed to behave this way? After all, were our civil servants ever meant to be discourteous, partial, corrupt or anti-national? There was a time when the colonial-era Indian Civil Service was neither Indian, nor civil, nor imbued with any spirit of service; but that was all supposed to have changed with the advent of Independence and the creation by Sardar Vallabhbhai Patel of an indigenous 'steel frame' for the Government of India. Very clearly, all that these amendments do is to make explicit what has always been implicit.

Perhaps it is a reflection of our times that the government feels the need to spell out the obvious in such excruciating detail.

But that's hardly a crime, and the list of prescriptions and proscriptions is in itself quite unexceptionable—what the Americans call 'motherhood and apple pie', things that no one can oppose. All Indians would want their civil servants to adhere to the code spelled out in Mr Modi's 19 commandments. (Though nineteen does seem a bit much: as Clemenceau remarked in a different context, 'even the good Lord only needed ten!')

But there's more than a bit of irony to the fact that it's a BJP government that, under sub-rule (1A), point (ii), urges 'political neutrality' in the civil service. After all, it is this very government that—in an action unprecedented in the history of Indian democracy—issued a circular decreeing that any civil servant who had served on the personal staff of a UPA minister was ineligible to serve in the NDA government. While the UPA had earlier issued rules saying that no officer could serve more than ten years on any minister's personal staff, the NDA circular made length of service, or indeed competence, irrelevant in its instruction: any personal staff who had served the UPA government in such a capacity for any length of time had to be removed from the offices of NDA ministers.

As a result, many officers of unimpeachable integrity and impressive service records were rusticated from the personal staffs of NDA ministers. Their only sin was not a negative performance report, or excessive length of service on personal staffs—no, their only deficiency was that they had been tainted by association with the preceding government.

This decision by Mr Modi's government represents the worst politicization of the civil service in living memory, and a betrayal of the fundamental principles of our civil service. After all, governments may come and go, but the civil service is meant to be permanent, and immune to the vagaries of changing political fortunes. Some senior civil servants in the mid-1990s ended up serving four prime ministers in five years, without ever changing their own jobs!

As for myself, I had no hesitation in blessing my former aide's wish to serve an NDA minister: his duty was, after all, to the government, not to me or my party, and I did not begrudge him the recognition of his administrative talents by a different party. This was as it should be. In any government, ministers will naturally exercise their powers in a politically partisan manner, because that is what they have been elected to do—they arrive in their jobs on a platform that requires them to cater to their political constituency and voter preferences. But our system of democratic government, as the founder of the IAS, Sardar Patel, made clear, requires that laws and rules be administered without prejudice. Politicians make policies, but the actual application of laws or rules underpinning those policies is meant to be done by civil servants without any political bias.

That is the logic of our bureaucracy: a new government can announce a new benefit it has advocated politically, but once that benefit is established and funded by the Government of India, it must be given fairly to all eligible beneficiaries, whatever their political persuasion. That's why we are supposed to have politically neutral civil services which are only accountable to the Constitution and the laws for their execution of policies - and to their political masters, the ministers, for their conduct and their impartial functioning.

The NDA's decision to make service to UPA ministers the sole grounds for transferring officials is a disgraceful violation of that principle. It establishes a new principle, that bureaucratic service will henceforth be seen as evidence of political allegiance. When the NDA loses power, as it surely will in five years, the bureaucrats who served them will, by the same logic, be seen as having been politically committed to the Modi government—because the NDA chose them on that basis.

How hypocritical of the very same government to mouth pious homilies about civil service neutrality!

These new rules appear to be a fresh example of the politicians' PR disease, 'watch what I say, not what I do'. What the NDA says is civil servants must be politically neutral; what it has 'done', in fact, is to move no fewer than seven senior civil servants from Gujarat to the prime minister's office in New Delhi, presumably for having shown their political commitment to

Mr Modi while serving under him there.

We are learning to get used to more and more examples of the gulf between proclamation and actual implementation in the Modi era. For a prime minister who professedly admires Sardar Patel, it is a pity that Mr Modi has trashed one of the doughty Sardar's most invaluable legacies while issuing rules codifying his adherence to it. One can only hope that the bureaucracy will live up to the new amendments and not to the hypocrisy of those who have issued them.

YES, MR JAVADEKAR, LET'S LOSE THIS JOB

The dangers of trying to say something profound and political on Twitter is that 140 characters restricts you to a pithiness that can give rise to ambiguity. I tweeted the other day, 'Javadekar says he wants to abolish the Information & Broadcasting Ministry. We heard the same thing from his predecessor LK Advani—in 1977!' Some read that tweet as implying dismissiveness of the idea. Far from it: I was just pointing out that we'd heard this a long time before, but for good or bad reasons, it had never been done.

This is not to doubt Mr Javadekar's sincerity in wanting to do himself out of a job. (Or rather one of his jobs—he's also the Minister of State for Environment and Forests, and while some of his party's backers might well want to see that ministry abolished too, Mr Javadekar isn't suggesting it yet.) Speaking on television recently, he said that both 'philosophically and ideologically' he believed his ministry ought not to exist, adding for good measure that I&B 'has no place in a democracy'. But he needs to give us reason to believe that the outcome of his philosophical and ideological views will be a little more conclusive than those of Mr Advani turned out to be nearly four decades ago.

Mr Javadekar added, in the same interview, that he would consider appointing a professional editor-in-chief for Doordarshan and AIR with full freedom to cover the news as he or she thinks fit. He promised not to interfere in appointments, transfers and promotions in Prasar Bharati, which he said for good measure he wanted to make accountable to Parliament and not 'only' to himself. If he follows through on those intentions, he could certainly take a meaningful step towards the withering away of his own ministry.

So what does I&B do that would no longer be done if it ceased to exist?

It would no longer run the government's PR arm, the Directorate of Audio-Visual Publicity (DAVP); presumably the government would have to decide whether it needed a PR arm at all, or whether it would simply hand out contracts to private sector PR agencies when it needed paid publicity. (This could be done through the e-tendering route trumpeted by the Modi government in the President's Address.)

It would also stop running Doordarshan and AIR (once dubbed All-Indira Radio by the critics of that formidable prime minister in the early 1970s), leaving that task to an autonomous public-sector Prasar Bharati; even Mr Modi's most passionate acolytes have not taken his faith in minimal government to imply that our venerable public service broadcasters would be privatized. Some BJP ideologues want the Modi government to deregulate news and public affairs on radio, which would give us the same cacophony on FM that we currently get on TV. But the public-service duties of a government-funded broadcaster—notably relaying information in the border states and getting out authoritative and authentic official messages in times of national emergency—would be lost if Prasar Bharati were privatized.

There's a case, therefore, for keeping Doordarshan and AIR in the public sector, but not necessarily for preserving I&B to oversee them. If I&B were abolished, an autonomous Prasar Bharati would no longer have a political boss to be accountable to—but as long as it is even partly funded by taxpayers, it needs political oversight. The solution is to make it answerable to a committee of Parliament, which is also the body that votes its funding.

The I&B Ministry also plays a key role in the world of Indian cinema. It appoints and runs the Central Board of Film Certification (and its regional affiliates), conducts national and international film festivals, and funds and runs such worthy institutions as the National Film Development Corporation, the Film Finance Corporation, the Film and Television Institute of India and the National Film Archives. These are all things that need to be done, but there is absolutely no reason why, in the 21st century, they must be done by the government.

Why not oblige the film industry to do the job itself, by creating a Cinema Corporation of India or a National Motion Picture Association as in the US, with regional versions for each language in which films are made in our country? The government could transfer its assets to these bodies in return for equity, and ask the industry to finance itself thereafter. Can the film industry be trusted to censor itself responsibly? Other democracies have proved that it can, because the market is often a more sensitive barometer of public tastes and of what society will tolerate than a bureaucrat or politician might be. One area where the industry might be less willing to do what the government has been doing is to finance and encourage the making of experimental or innovative films with limited commercial appeal. It could either be obliged to do so by law, or these functions—and these alone—could be retained by the government under the rubric of the Ministry of Culture.

One task we haven't discussed is that of the I&B Minister himself, as the principal spokesperson of the government and boss of the Press Information Bureau (PIB), which diligently puts out press releases daily about whatever the government is up to (or says it is up to). The government obviously needs a spokesperson, but this role could be performed by a minister in the PMO instead, with the PIB assigned to his or her supervision. Or if that makes the PMO too heavy, park the task in the Cabinet Secretariat, which after all has the responsibility for co-ordinating the work of all ministries, and which could easily house the government spokesperson too.

In other words, I&B could indeed be abolished, with other ways of ensuring that its essential functions are still performed inside or outside the government.

So dear Mr Javadekar, I wasn't trying to dismiss your intent—merely trying to say that we've seen this movie before. It's your job to ensure that this time the tangled and long drawn-out tale of your own ministry's demise has a different ending.

MR MODI MISSES A TRICK: ENLARGED COUNCIL OF MINISTERS IS NOT ABOUT 'MINIMUM GOVERNMENT'

I must confess, as an unabashedly old-fashioned liberal, to being rather attracted to Prime Minister Narendra Modi's oft-repeated maxim, 'minimum government, maximum governance'. I have no illusions about the fact that the prime minister's talent for sound-bytes is not often accompanied by matching action. But the recent Cabinet expansion has confirmed that his definition of 'minimum government' is rather stretchable.

When Mr Modi began his innings in government with a Council of Ministers of just 44, including the allocation of several related portfolios to select ministers, it seemed he might actually be serious about reducing the size of our central government. According to our Constitution, 'there shall be a Council of Ministers with the Prime Minister at its head, to aid and advise the President who shall, in the exercise of his functions, act in accordance with such advice'. But the Constitution is silent on the size of such a council. Ministers are appointed by the president on the advice of the prime minister (Article 75.1) and the PM decides not only how many ministers he or she wishes to have, but what portfolios they will be allocated. There is nothing immutable about the specific ministries of government, which can be created, merged or dissolved by a PM at will.

While this has made for varying sizes of Councils of Ministers over the years, the Administrative Reforms Commission has regarded 10 per cent of the total membership of the Lok Sabha (that is, 54 ministers, including cabinet ministers, ministers of state, and deputy ministers, the three recognized categories of ministerial office) to be the ideal size. But this has been exceeded in practice by every Government of India since Indira Gandhi's day.

Still, the question of the optimum size has never been properly addressed in Delhi. A law passed during the tenure of Atal Bihari Vajpayee limits the size of the Council of Ministers in state governments to 15 per cent of the strength of the lower house of the State Assembly. An informal convention has sprung up that such a percentage should also be adhered to in the central government, so that the Council of Ministers is not too large in relation to the lower house of Parliament. Since the Lok Sabha has 543 members, that suggests an upper limit of 81 ministers. The last government of Prime Minister Manmohan Singh came closest to that number, with 78 ministers, but did not breach it.

The reasons for the ballooning size of ministerial councils have nothing to do with administrative logic; the calculations involved are unabashedly political. In a large and diverse democracy like India's, ministerial appointments need to reflect the range and diversity of the country: all regions of India must be represented, whether or not the ruling party or coalition has worthy candidates from all regions, and this being India, the same logic applies to all religions and castes. Appointments are also made to reward long political service, to quell brewing dissidence, to test mettle, to grant rewards and to send a signal to the appointee's state in advance of assembly elections. Whether or not the recipient of such ministerial honour is actually capable of doing the work allotted, is often beside the point. It is accepted that the country is really run by the bureaucracy and by a key handful of top ministers handpicked for powerful positions by the prime minister.

Over the years, the tendency to use the Council of Ministers to offer political rewards to MPs meant that other practices developed which moved the government away from administrative efficiency in the interests of distributing ministerial rank. The position of parliamentary secretary, used to reward young MPs, usually first-termers, who worked as understudies to their ministers, was discontinued. More surprisingly, the slots of deputy ministers, commonly filled in the Nehru governments, fell into disuse as well. The intermediate level of Ministers of State (MoS) became the de facto deputy ministers, devaluing the rank. Over successive governments, many MoSs complained of having no work allotted to them, and no authority over the work that did come their way. While, as MoS for External Affairs, I benefited from a genuine division of responsibility and served as de facto minister for Africa, the Middle East and Latin America, as well as for passport and consular matters, policy planning and for the Haj, as MoS in the Ministry of Human Resource Development (MHRD), no files stopped their journey at my desk except on their way to the cabinet minister, with whom ultimate decision-making on all issues resided. This meant my role was limited to influencing and articulating policy, but not to making it. (I could not resist tweeting, as the Modi government was being sworn in, that 'being MoS is like standing in a cemetery: there are a lot of people under you, but no one is listening'.)

Mr Modi's first Council of Ministers, which was the smallest one for decades, seemed a refreshing change from this usual practice. It seemed he was determined not to worry about giving ministerial office to his own party's experienced seniors, many of whom were sidelined, or to touching all political bases or even to stocking his Council with the right number of minorities, lower castes and so on. Many of us grudgingly acknowledged that streamlined government might well mark a major departure for a political class overly fond of the perks of ministerial office—the cars with red beacons, the offices and extra staff—rather than their ministerial duties. We looked forward to seeing what fewer ministers could accomplish, apart from reducing traffic congestion in Lutyens' Delhi.

But in his first cabinet reshuffle, Mr Modi has increased his Council of Ministers by 50 per cent, from 44 to 66. If his initial cabinet gave him bragging rights over his predecessors in speaking of 'minimum government', especially thanks to his placing some related ministries (coal and power, for example) under the same minister, now his government looks little different in size from the last several governments, all of which had between 70 and 80 ministers. And given that the South is still under-represented in his ministry, as are minority groups (other than in the Minority Affairs Ministry), further expansion seems inevitable, and Mr Modi's minimum government may soon reach the maximum permissible size.

So has Mr Modi missed a trick here? I'd argue that he has, and offer an alternative vision that really could deliver the 'minimum government' he speaks of.

What are the existing ministries that simply cannot be done without and so should remain intact? The four 'big ones'—Home, Finance, Defence and External Affairs—brook no argument. Since agriculture still engages ('employs' would be a disingenuous word) 67 per cent of our population, an Agriculture Ministry is indispensable. The core needs of our people—health, education, transport, law and justice, and environment follow; so do some of the core responsibilities of government, to provide our nation with energy, and to steward our domestic commerce and industry.

That gives us twelve indispensable ministries. But the list can't stop here: in a developing country, the government has to undertake to help the nation grow and develop its urban infrastructure as well as meet the range of its rural development challenges, as well as promote tourism and build tourist infrastructure. Then we need a strong PMO to help keep the whole lot in line.

That's sixteen ministries we absolutely can't avoid retaining. Give each a cabinet minister and one or two MoS (or deputy ministers), and you could have a Council of Ministers totalling no more than 40-45, with the PM and a 15-strong Cabinet at the helm.

So why do we have so many more today, and in earlier governments of the last few decades? Simple—the more ministries you create, the more political interests you placate. So functions that really belong together were divided up amongst different political heavyweights, not because they warranted a separate governmental machinery but because the individual in question had to be given a chance to exercise authority over something tangible, however undemanding that share of the pie might be.

So though we have a Ministry of Industry, we have managed, over the years, to create separate ministries for heavy industries, micro, small and medium enterprises, steel, mines, textiles, chemicals and fertilizers, and food processing, all of which, properly speaking, are merely different kinds of industries. The heavy hand of regulatory and licensing authority in each of these industries was then exercised by a different minister in each case, spreading the clout (that comes from having the authority to grant permissions) to many hands. That's anything but 'minimum government', and if Mr Modi meant it, he could have put a stop to it.

He seemed to have recognized this principle when he clubbed together the separate ministries for coal, power, and new (or 'alternative') and renewable energy under one minister (but still as different ministries located in different buildings). But he still retained atomic energy in the PMO, and excluded the largest source of India's energy, petroleum and natural gas, which stands as a ministry by itself. Wouldn't it have been more logical to have one all-inclusive Ministry of Energy to ensure that the nation has a comprehensive and co-ordinated energy policy—one that sees multiple sources of energy as elements in one national energy mix, needing policy direction from one minister? Instead of a single minister deciding, for instance, to alter the proportions of that mix, increasing the national output of solar, for instance, in preference to petroleum imports or incentives for coal production, we have different government policies on coal, alternative energy (wind and solar), and of course on the pricing of gas, petrol and diesel. Mr Modi has foregone an obvious win here.

Similarly, shouldn't the agriculture minister subsume Food and Public Distribution, while Consumer Affairs goes to Commerce and Industry? Yet, currently these are three ministries (and Food Processing is a fourth). Forty years ago all of them came under one food and agriculture minister.

One good step by the PM was to club our highways and shipping into one Ministry of Surface Transport, but why should Water Resources and River Development be taken out, as it now has been? After all, shouldn't the minister be developing national waterways for transport alongside national highways? For that matter, should railways and civil aviation be exempt? After all, aren't they all forms of transport of India's goods and people, and wouldn't costs and rates (e.g. for freight) charged in one sector impact the demand on the others? There just might be a case for a separate ministry to deal with the complicated challenges of international and domestic civil aviation, but I'm not convinced that couldn't be left in the hands of competent specialists in the Airports Regulatory Authority, rather than justifying a separate ministry.

(Similarly do we need a communications and information technology minister, rather than just a competent regulatory authority in these areas? And a minister for statistics and programme implementation, seriously? Why not appoint competent technocrats instead, Mr Modi?)

Mr Modi's decision to place the Ministry of Overseas Indian Affairs under the MEA was wise, especially since the former relies almost entirely on the latter to get its work done overseas, where its 'clients' are. He has also parked drinking water and sanitation under the rural development minister. The same logic does not seem to have been applied, however, in keeping the Ministry of Law and Justice separate from those of Social Justice and Empowerment, Minority Affairs, Women and Child Development, and Tribal Affairs. Surely a Justice Minister's job is to ensure justice for all? Some functions of the present ministries could then be placed in more logical departments—for instance, maternal health issues could go from the Women's Ministry to the Health Ministry, minority education to MHRD, and so on. Similarly, housing and urban poverty alleviation should be part of the Urban Development Ministry (just as rural housing and poverty alleviation in the countryside should be under the Rural Development Ministry). Where an issue is of sufficient importance, the PM could always declare a national mission that subsumes two or more ministries, and take the co-ordinating lead himself, as he has done with the Swachh Bharat Abhiyan. That could be the case with Ganga Rejuvenation, for instance, which could be an Abhiyan rather than a Ministry.

I have already argued that the I&B Ministry can be abolished, and that Prasar Bharati could be given genuine autonomy. The same for Corporate Affairs, which surely belongs to either Finance or Industry, depending on the issues involved. We also have a plethora of small ministries exercising functions that belong outside government, or in specialized institutions not requiring ministerial intervention. These include Science and Technology (for which few ministers are qualified anyway) and Earth Sciences (which usually ends up in the PMO, where it is understandably neglected). Couldn't the latter just go to the Geological Survey of India and the former to MHRD?

Indeed, the Ministry of Human Resource Development was conceived by Rajiv Gandhi as an omnibus ministry, but over the years it has been whittled down to just managing education. Why does Mr Modi need separate ministries of Skill Development, Labour, Culture, Youth Affairs and Sports, all of which were once under a single MHRD minister?

I am not seeking to diminish the importance of the tasks being undertaken, at least in some cases, by the separate ministries. But the answer lies not in creating more silos that make for inefficiencies in policy co-ordination and convey an impression of policy incoherence. The answer lies in giving real work to the Ministers of State to handle these portfolios under the overall direction of powerful co-ordinating ministers. Give real departmental power to Ministers of State, and you solve two problems in one; but also revive the post of deputy minister, and use it for the younger and less experienced MPs to work under cabinet ministers and MoSs.

There, Mr Modi, you would have 'minimum government, maximum

governance'. Interested? Or might it be, as many fear, that the phrase is not an agenda for action, but little more than a slogan for the sound-byte era?

'DIS'APPOINTING GOVERNORS

The decision of the NDA government, in its first months in office, to elicit the resignations of several UPA-appointed governors prompts a number of interesting questions. Predictably, UPA supporters have raised the issue of constitutional propriety (and a non–UPA critic, CPI(M) leader Sitaram Yechury, has called it 'politically unethical and constitutionally incorrect') while NDA supporters have cited precedent, not least pointing to a similar action by the UPA in removing four NDA-appointed governors in 2004. The Samajwadi party's Naresh Aggarwal, meanwhile, has alleged the replacement of governors is the first step in an RSS agenda to 'saffronize' the country's institutions. The battle lines are being drawn over an issue that ought to be, ideally, beyond the realm of contention.

First, let's get the blame game out of the way. If we go back far enough, the practice of turfing out governors appointed by the defeated government started in 1977, when the victorious Janata Party defenestrated a number of Indira Gandhi appointees. Changes of government have often seen a recurrence of the practice by all sides, though it is also true that many governments have left governors appointed by their predecessors in place. But what is happening today has happened before.

However, what is different this time is that since the last round of gubernatorial musical chairs in 2004 (when Haryana's Babu Parmanand, Uttar Pradesh's Vishnu Kant Shastri, Goa's Kidar Nath Sahani and Gujarat's Kailashpati Mishra were replaced by the UPA government), the Supreme Court has weighed in. Earlier decisions had been justified (though justifications had not earlier been deemed necessary) by a principle advanced in October 1980, when Tamil Nadu Governor Prabhudas Patwari was dismissed on the basis of the argument that governors serve at the President's 'pleasure' under Article 156 (1). At the time, given the precedent of 1977, it was generally accepted that the prime minister of the day could dismiss any governor for political reasons, and without giving any explanation, since the PM alone decided when the president would grant or withdraw his 'pleasure'. But in 2010 the Supreme Court differed, concluding, on a petition moved by one of the governors dismissed in 2004, that the government cannot arbitrarily transfer appointed governors without 'compelling' reasons. It declared: 'Nor can he be removed on the ground that the Union government has lost confidence in him. It follows, therefore, that a change in government at the Centre is not a ground for removal of governors holding office to make way for others favoured by the new government.'

What reasons could the government advance that would be so compelling as to pass the Supreme Court's test? The BJP today is making the same argument that the UPA did before the Supreme Court in 2004—that a governor appointed by a defeated government would have a different view of national policy than the new government, giving rise to conflict between the governor's views and the government's. It is on this basis that UP Governor B.L. Joshi and Kerala Governor Sheila Dikshit have already resigned; Rajasthan Governor Margaret Alva, Kerala Governor Sheila Dikshit, Governor of Nagaland Ashwani Kumar, West Bengal Governor M.K. Narayanan, Maharashtra Governor K. Sankaranarayanan, Assam Governor J.B. Patnaik, Goa Governor B.N. Wanchoo and Karnataka Governor H.R. Bharadwaj are said to be in the firing line.

But this argument had explicitly been rejected by the Supreme Court, which wanted evidence of such conflict to be cited before a governor was dismissed or even transferred. It is safe to assume that the Modi government would consider such a requirement to provide evidence an inadmissible interference in its executive prerogatives. Yet one could also make the counter-argument that the very same principle could, by the same logic, be extended to a president of India elected under the previous dispensation, yet no government has dared suggest the president should leave office when 'his' government loses an election. Any conflict between the president's views and the government's simply has to be resolved in favour of the latter; that is what our democracy requires. Why can't governors be told that, whoever appointed them, they must now follow the directives of the new government? Surely that would end the issue of any potential conflict?

But the truth is that this really isn't about a conflict of principles or policies at all; it's really all about jobs—jobs for 'our' people rather than 'theirs'. Various defeated or superannuated BJP leaders need to be accommodated in comfortable sinecures, and it galls them to see the Congress party's favourites enjoying the perks of palatial Raj Bhavans around the country while they languish in semi-retirement, itching to be appointed. So when Congress leader Ghulam Nabi Azad calls the NDA's decision 'arbitrary and capricious', using the Supreme Court's words, the fact is he's right. It's about emptying chairs for BJP people to occupy—nothing more and nothing less.

Azad found the removal of governors to be 'against the very grain of democratic traditions and constitutional propriety'. If taken forward, he warned, the move would be 'fraught with serious repercussions and have a debilitating impact on our constitutional democracy'. So what can we do to ensure we don't go through the same problems after every election?

There are two alternatives. The first is to insulate the office of governor from politicization altogether, by various measures that I suggest below. The second alternative is the more radical one: to abolish the post of governor altogether, as a colonial relic that democratic India can dispense with. Except in the increasingly rare resort to president's rule, the governor has little of substance to do, and his few substantive and mainly ceremonial tasks could easily be divided between the chief minister and the chief justice of the state. But that would mean depriving the ruling party of twenty-nine comfortably-provisioned freebie positions to hand out to its loyal supporters. And what are the odds of that happening?

I considered the first option in depth when Sheila Dikshit's resignation as governor of Kerala brought to eight the number of UPA-era gubernatorial appointees who had been coerced by the BJP government into demitting office prematurely.

As the MP for Thiruvananthapuram, I didn't conceal my disappointment at seeing her go. Sheilaji brought to her office a wealth of political experience and administrative ability, as well as the indefinable qualities of style and grace. Her tenure as governor lasted barely six months, but it was marked by swift and impressive decision-making in the few areas under her direct authority, as well as a genuine interest in Kerala and its cultural heritage.

Her decision to demand the resignation of the vice chancellor of Mahatma Gandhi University, against whom charges had been pending on her predecessor's desk for nearly a year, was one of several examples of the former. Her active involvement in the promotion of the arts, and her regular attendance at performances of Kerala dance and music, including at the Raj Bhavan, confirmed the latter. She adorned her office, and will be missed.

But 'The Sad Case of Sheila Dikshit' need not be the title of a tragic opera if we use the situation her case epitomizes to review the entire problem of governors, their appointment and what one may, not entirely jocularly, call their dis-appointment.

Isn't it time we developed an all-party consensus on a code of conduct regarding Governors, so that we can put an end to the unseemly and unedifying spectacle we have all been forced to witness in recent weeks—the slow-motion assassinations of some of the highest constitutional authorities of our land?

Though the suggestion that the very post of governor be done away with is tempting, it is going to be far more difficult to evolve a political consensus on amending the Constitution to achieve that, than to reform the process and criteria by which governors are appointed.

The governor represents in each of our States what the President of India does in the country as a whole. The president is universally considered to be above politics; even when a government changes, a president elected under the previous dispensation remains above controversy, and no government has dared suggest that a president should leave office when 'his' government loses an election. It doesn't need to; the president clearly understands, both as matter of constitutional principle and political reality, that he may be the nation's First

Citizen for protocol purposes, but it's the popularly-elected government that calls the shots. Indeed, what is known as the President's Address to Parliament is merely the performance of a figurehead reading out a script given to him or her by the elected government of the day. And that, in our parliamentary democracy, is exactly how it should be.

It is true that the president is elected by MPs and MLAs, whereas governors are appointed. But what the governor, as the president's representative in the State, must be is a carbon copy—just as apolitical as the president, equally subordinate to the elected government (in his case that of the state as well as that of the centre), owing primary allegiance only to the Constitution of India.

Such an institution of governorship should ideally, like the presidency it mirrors, be beyond the realm of contention. But we all know it's not: the practice of the last several decades has sometimes, though not always, dragged the institution into disrepute. Amongst the reasons for the plummeting stature of the office have been: the appointment of political time-servers who conducted themselves in office as agents of their parties; the profusion of decrepit sinecure-seekers long past their use-by-dates, who brought neither energy not distinction to their posts; the elevation of a number of active politicians who used Raj Bhavans as a rest-stop on their way to resuming their political careers; and the occasional misuse of governors by a party at the centre at loggerheads with one in the state to dismiss elected governments on spurious (or at least contestable) grounds. If all these practices span the range of evident transgressions of the intent of the framers of the Constitution, there have also been men and women of integrity and class who served their states, and the country, ably as governors.

How do we ensure that we get more such men and women to be governors in the future? There is a crying need for an all-party consensus, to be embodied in law, to achieve this.

The consensus would require agreement on insulating the office of governor from politicization by adopting these principles, or something very like them:

1. Anyone appointed governor must:
   - renounce primary membership of any political party;
   - be ineligible for future appointment as office-bearer of any political party;
   - be disqualified from election or appointment to any post, bar that of president or vice-president of India, or Lokpal.
2. In turn, a governor shall be immune from
   - being removed from office till the completion of his or her term;
   - being transferred to another state, except by mutual consent;

- receiving instructions from any functionary of the government other than the president of India.

3. A governor may, of course, be impeached for gross misconduct or dereliction of duty, but only through a procedure akin to that currently governing the impeachment of members of the country's senior judiciary.

If such a code were to be adopted, it would elevate the office of governor to the status intended by the founding fathers, which it no longer enjoys. It would ensure the position attracts men and women of integrity and ability, while simultaneously ending the spectacle of politicians taking a breather in some Raj Bhavan before returning to the electoral fray for their parties, and so conducting themselves in office with an eye on their own political future.

There should be no bar on former politicians becoming governors, as some are advocating: it would be a pity to lose their political experience in such an office. But these rules would ensure that upon appointment, they cease to be politicians. Their lifelong allegiances would not disappear overnight, but they would be empowered, and expected, to transcend them.

If our new government is serious about reform, and about working with the Opposition, fixing the institution of governor would be a good place to start. But something tells me that the timeless and irresistible appeal of 'jobs for the boys' will ensure that the BJP too, will continue to use Raj Bhavans as retirement homes for their apparatchiks. And therefore, five years from now, we will see the same disgraceful mess all over again, as a new government exacts the resignations of the very governors being appointed with such shameless glee in 2014.

MODI'S SILENCE AND THE SINISTER
REVIVAL OF COMMUNALISM

'Eid Mubarak!' is one of the most routine of all wishes a non-Muslim extends to a practising Muslim celebrating one of his faith's major festivals. So it was not surprising that Prime Minister Narendra Modi routinely wished all his Muslim brothers and sisters on the auspicious occasion of the first Eid of his prime ministership. It is the kind of thing he rarely forgets to do. But there is a lot more that Modiji has forgotten—or omitted—to say to his Muslim fellow-citizens that we should be concerned about.

Much has been written and spoken in recent days about the prime minister's surprising public silence. He has neither been communicative nor accessible to the press; he has broken with prime ministerial practice in not taking journalists on board his official plane on his international travels; he has held no press conference nor granted any interviews. Our media is feeling spurned. The man they had hailed as the talking, tweeting, orating alternative to 'Maun'mohan Singh's taciturnity has turned out to be far less friendly to them institutionally and personally than they had taken for granted he would be.

It is yet another example of how much Modi-in-power differs from Modi-on-the-campaign-trail and the expectations raised by his electoral insurgency. But there's something more important that Eid reminds us and our new government of: that they rode to power despite the fears of large sections of our society—shared by 69 per cent of the electorate—that the Sangh Parivar is too divisive a force to govern a pluralist society like India. In particular, given the horrors of 2002 perpetrated on his watch, and his subsequent rhetorical excesses, there were real doubts as to whether Narendra Modi would reach out to Muslims, and indeed whether their needs even figured in his idea of India.

It is in this context that the prime minister's silence bothers me. It's not just that he's ignoring the media, which, given the quality of much of our media, may well be what they deserve. My bigger concern is that I believe the prime minister is missing an opportunity to send a signal of reassurance to a vulnerable minority that needs it. This sin of omission is all the more glaring because of the litany of recent incidents involving Muslims that his government's silence has slighted.

'There is no communal violence problem in India,' insisted Parliamentary Affairs Minister Venkaiah Naidu, admonishing Congress party MPs in the Lok Sabha for demanding a debate on the subject. 'Please don't raise unnecessary issues.'

'You can't speak about communal violence in general,' added Speaker Sumitra Mahajan, rejecting a Congress party adjournment motion on the same issue. 'You must have specific instances to discuss.'

No problem, Mr Naidu? Specific instances, Madam Speaker? Among the spate of tragic episodes of communal violence that occurred in the first three months since the BJP government came to power were over 600 incidences of violence against religious minorities all over Uttar Pradesh, especially in Western UP, 60 per cent of them in areas near constituencies where by-elections were occurring. Police records of communal incidents during this period scrutinized by the *Indian Express* show some 120 of them were triggered by the use of loudspeakers at places of worship—the largest contributor to tensions, alongside construction activities involving masjids, madrasas and kabristans.

The death of a man in an accident triggered communal riots in Tauru, a town 32 km from Gurgaon, leaving at least fifteen people injured. Tensions in the Northeast have escalated since BJP MPs from Assam started spouting communal rhetoric targeting 'Bangladeshi immigrants' and intimidating all Bengali Muslims, whether Bangladeshi or not. They were warned that if they did not leave the state within a fortnight, the activists of the BJP's youth wing would embark on a door-to-door search for Bangladeshis. Armed attacks in the Bodoland Territorial Area killed over forty people, almost all of whom were Bengali Muslims.

Then there was the horrific killing of the 24-year-old Pune techie Mohsin Shaikh, who was beaten to death with hockey sticks by the goons of the Hindu Rashtra Sena in retaliation for the uploading of 'derogatory' pictures of Maratha icon Shivaji and the late Shiv Sena supremo Bal Thackeray on a social networking site. Young Mohsin had nothing to do with the uploading, but the Hindu Rashtra Sena activists were looking for a Muslim to exact revenge upon, and he was visibly Muslim, emerging from namaz at a mosque in a beard and skull cap. This was a classic 'hate crime' that was universally condemned across the country—by everyone but the prime minister himself.

Modi did eventually mention the tragedy in Parliament, where he included Mohsin Shaikh's murder, without mentioning his name, in a list of recent incidents he deplored: 'whether it is the Pune killing, or the killings in UP, the drowning of students in Manali, the rapes of our sisters…all these incidents must provoke us to look inwards and seek answers.' But those words were too little, too late—too little for the gravity of the crime, and too late to avoid the damage done by his initial silence, which allowed a fringe right-wing group like the Hindu Rashtra Sena to assume quiet acceptance of their misbehaviour at the highest level. (It's an old truism, after all, that silence means acquiescence.) And if Modiji is 'looking inwards and seeking answers' he hasn't shared any of those answers with the Indian public, which is entitled to know what they are.

In early July 2014, the BJP called for a 'Hindu Mahapanchayat' in Moradabad following a communal clash over the removal of a loudspeaker from a temple in Kanth. Clashes between party leaders and local police, and the BJP leadership betraying a deal that had been brokered to defuse the situation, led to communal tensions over the issue simmering for days.

A few weeks later, footage emerged of a Shiv Sena MP, Rajan Vichale, trying to force a chapatti into the mouth of a Muslim caterer at Maharashtra Sadan during the Ramadan period of fasting. Vichale's excuse—that he didn't know the man was Muslim and he was protesting the quality of the food—was just as outrageous, since it implied that it was acceptable for MPs to go around showing their displeasure in this manner, by shoving food down unwilling throats. Muslims were not the only ones disgusted by this BJP ally's conduct. Modi again had nothing to say.

Around the same time, communal riots between Muslims and Sikhs erupted over a land dispute in Saharanpur, left nineteen people injured, killed three and led to the deployment of additional security forces. Police arrested thirty-eight people for rioting and arson. The district administration imposed curfew and shoot-at-sight orders in the area. Responding to this serious situation, BJP MLA and party National Executive Member, C.T. Ravi, issued a tweet advocating the 'Gujarat Model' to stem the Saharanpur riots. He said 'Only the Gujarat model, that worked from 2002 in containing their [i.e. Muslims'] rioting elements, can work. Apply across Bharat.' Alarm bells sounded in every liberal Indian's brain at these words.

Separately, a BJP politician in Telengana, K. Laxman, questioned the national credentials of India's greatest woman tennis star ever, Sania Mirza, because she had married a Pakistani and was now a 'daughter-in-law of Pakistan'. (The BJP hadn't earlier showed such touching faith in daughters-in-law's allegiance to their husband's land when they attacked Sonia Gandhi as irremediably Italian.) Sania broke down during a television interview, saying it was unfair that she had to keep asserting her Indianness. 'I am an Indian who will remain an Indian until the end of my life', she said on Twitter. Would a non-Muslim Indian, even one married to a Pakistani, have had to face such an inquisition on her identity?

Each of these incidents is deplorable in itself, but cumulatively they add up to a disturbing vindication of all the fears the BJP's ascendancy had created since 1989, and which had been sharpened by the events of 2002 that Modi had sought to live down. The prime minister's silence on these actions and utterances by his followers leaves the worrying impression that he condones them.

According to National Crime Records Bureau data concerning incidents of rioting, the years under Dr Manmohan Singh's rule were the most peaceful in Independent India's history. That record appears in danger of being rapidly overturned.

The Bharatiya Shiksha Niti Aayog has been constituted by the RSS-affiliated

Shiksha Sanskrit Uthan Nyas, under the leadership of the notorious Dinanath Batra, with a mandate to 'suggest corrective steps' to 'Indianize' the education system. In Gujarat under Chief Minister Anandiben Patel, an intense wave of 'saffronization' has already begun. And the Gujarat government has reinstated a police officer, G.L. Singhal, who was accused of being complicit in the Ishrat Jahan fake encounter case.

Intangible factors have also contributed to the sense of communal polarization across our country. The election campaign afforded the first egregious instances of such rhetorical transgressions. Bihar BJP MP Giriraj Singh declared that 'those who want to stop' BJP prime ministerial candidate Narendra Modi would soon have 'no place in India...because their place will be in Pakistan'. Amit Shah, the current president of the BJP, reportedly claimed in a speech that the election was a chance to seek 'revenge' for the 'insult' inflicted on the Hindu community during the riots in Muzaffarnagar in 2013, in which nearly sixty were killed, hundreds raped and thousands displaced. (Most of the victims were Muslim.) Shah also condoned the violence: 'Nobody wants riots. But when there is one-sided action, people are forced to come out on the streets.'

Electoral victory has emboldened Hindutvawadi voices across the country. Goa State Cooperation Minister Deepak Dhavalikar told his state assembly that 'If we all support it and we stand by Narendra Modi systematically, then I feel a Hindu Rashtra will be established.' Goa's Catholic deputy chief minister, Francis D'Souza, rushed to support him, declaring, in a perverse fulfilment of Savarkar's and Golwalkar's views, that he considers himself a 'Christian Hindu'. 'India is already a Hindu nation' and 'all Indians in Hindustan are Hindus', he added.

It is easy to discount such verbal violence—and there have been worse from the likes of Pravin Togadia and Ashok Singhal, whom the BJP prefers to dismiss as fringe figures—but the words in fact reflect a harsher reality. For the first time in the history of India, the ruling party has no Muslim representation in the Lok Sabha.

Indeed, the state that has historically sent Muslims to Parliament after every single General Election, Uttar Pradesh, failed to do so in 2014, when the BJP and its Apna Dal ally swept 75 seats out of 80 there. There is no starker evidence of polarization imaginable.

Prime Minister Modi has been either ambivalent or utterly silent on all these incidents. He has missed several opportunities to reach out and reassure the Muslim community. Indeed, the Prime Minister's statements on the communal issue have not been reassuring. Before the election, he had notoriously compared Muslim victims of the 2002 Gujarat pogrom to a puppy, when he told an interviewer in July 2013: 'If one is driving a car or someone else is driving a car and you're sitting behind, and a puppy comes under the wheel, will it be painful or not?' But even after becoming prime minister, Mr Modi's language has betrayed a Hindu nationalist mindset: '1,200 saal ki ghulami ki mansikta Hindustaniyon ko pareshan karti rahi hai' (Colonial slavery of 1,200 years has weakened/troubled Indians), he said as recently as June 2014. The reference is not to British colonialism, which only lasted less than 200 years. It is to the advent of Muslim rule 1,200 years ago. If 'Muslims' are a foreign element that enslaved 'Indians', isn't it time the tables were turned on them?

Since the PM refuses to speak, can we find any reassurance in his earlier statements? In a video conference addressing NRIs in the US, Modi had said, 'My definition of secularism is simple: 'India First'. Whatever you do, wherever you work, India should be the top priority for all its citizens. [The] country is above all religions and ideologies.'

That's unexceptionable: but do any of the examples I've cited conform to such a vision? In an interview to ABP News, he was asked specifically whether his desire to reach out to every Indian citizen would include Muslims. Mr Modi replied, 'I will never go by this terminology of yours. Even if you drag me, I will not. I will meet my countrymen. I understand only one language that they are my countrymen, they are my brothers.'

It doesn't seem that Messrs Dhavalikar, Vichale and Laxman, not to mention the thugs of the Hindu Rashtra Sena, have got the message.

As Monobina Gupta pointed out in *Caravan*: 'the prime minister is powerless to speak on communal violence because his landslide victory in the Hindi heartland and elsewhere, to a large extent, was propelled by communal polarization and the consolidation of the majority Hindu vote bank... By speaking on these issues—which he is not entirely free from—he might implicate himself in a past he tries constantly to escape. Therefore, the fact that he chooses to remain silent says a lot.'

Modiji must know that there is a great deal of concern throughout the country, and particularly among our Muslim fellow-citizens, about whether the Bharatiya Janata Party and its fellow-travellers have the desire or the willingness to work for all of India's communities, or whether they seek to profit from dividing the nation on sectarian lines. A few words of reassurance from the master orator could have gone a long way towards calming our disquiet. Instead, the prime minister has chosen to stay silent. He has not even made the simple gesture of attending an Iftar during Ramadan, let alone hosting one as his predecessors did.

This will not do. I believe the prime minister is missing an opportunity to send a signal to a vulnerable minority that their fears are unjustified, and that there is no divisive communal agenda in the ruling party. It is time for Mr Modi to live up to his professed intention to be a prime minister for all Indians.

WHY THE HINDI-FIRST ORDER
THREATENS EFFICIENCY

The unnecessary controversy over the use of Hindi by the government in official communications and social media revealed two essential truths about our country. The first is that, whatever the Hindi chauvinists might say, we don't have one 'national language' in India, but several. The second is that zealots have an unfortunate tendency to provoke a battle they will lose—at a time when they were quietly winning the war.

Hindi is the mother tongue of some 50 per cent of our population; the percentage has been growing thanks to the spectacular failure of population control in much of North India. It is not, however, the mother tongue of the rest of us.

When Hindi speakers emotionally decry the use of an alien language imposed on the country by British colonialists and demand that Hindi be used because it speaks for 'the soul of India', or when they declare that 'Hindi is our mother, English is a stranger', they are missing the point twice over.

First, because no Tamil or Bengali will accept that Hindi is the language of his soul, and second because injecting anti-English xenophobia into the argument is utterly irrelevant to the issue at stake.

The issue is quite simple: all Indians need to deal with the government. We need government services, government information and government support; we need to understand easily what our government is saying to us or demanding of us. When the government does so in our mother tongue, it is easier for us. But when it does so in someone else's mother tongue with which we are less familiar than our neighbour, our incomprehension is intensified by resentment. Why should Shukla be spoken to by the Government of India in the language that comes easiest to him, but not Subramaniam?

The de facto solution to this question has been a practical one: use Hindi where it is understood, but use English everywhere, since it places all Indians from all parts of our country at an equal disadvantage or advantage. English does not express Subramaniam's soul any more than it does Shukla's, but it serves a functional purpose for both, and what's more, it helps Subramaniam to understand the same thing as Shukla.

Ideally, of course, every central government document, tax form or tweet should be in every one of India's languages. Since that is not possible in practice—because we would have to do everything in twenty-three versions—we have chosen to have two official languages, English and Hindi. State governments complement these by producing official material in the language of their states. That leaves everyone more or less happy.

The new government's requirement that Hindi be privileged actually works against the interests of efficiency. Obliging a Keralite bureaucrat in Delhi to read and write file notations in Hindi to be submitted to a superior officer from Odisha makes no sense, since neither man would be using a language with which he is at ease. Obliging both to digest a complex argument by a UPite subordinate writing in his mother tongue is unfair to both. Both may write atrocious English, for that matter, but it's the language in which they are equal, and it serves to get the work done.

Language is a vehicle, not a destination. In government, it is a means, not an end. The Hindi-wallahs fail to appreciate that, since promoting Hindi, for them, is an end in itself.

The result is episodes like the time that Mr Mulayam Singh Yadav, who punctuates English speeches in Parliament with cries of 'Hindi bolo' from time to time, became defence minister of India and wrote to the chief minister of West Bengal, Jyoti Basu, in Hindi. In due course he received a reply—in Bengali. One is only grateful that no urgent issue of national security was involved in either communication.

The irony is, as I observed earlier, that the Hindi chauvinists should realize they were winning the war. The prevalence of Hindi is far greater across India today than it was half a century ago. This is not because of Mulayam Singh Yadav's imprecations or the assiduous efforts of the Parliamentary Committee on the Promotion of Hindi. It is, quite simply, because of Bollywood, which has brought a demotic conversational Hindi into every Indian home. South Indians and Northeasterners alike are developing an ease and familiarity with Hindi because it is a language in which they are entertained. In time, this alone could have made Hindi truly the national language.

But it would become so only because Indians freely and voluntarily adopt it, not because some Hindi chauvinist in Delhi thrusts his language down the throats of the unwilling. The fact is, its vocabulary, gender rules and locutions do not come instinctively to everyone: native speakers of languages like Malayalam that do not use gender can understand why a woman must be feminine ('woh aurat aayi hai') but are genuinely mystified as to why a table should be feminine too. If you've grown up with Hindi at home, it's a matter of instinct for you that it should be 'desh ki haalat achhi hai' rather than 'desh ka haalat bura hai', but for the rest of us, there's no logical reason to see anything feminine about the national condition.

Still, if we watch enough Bollywood movies, we'll pick it up one day. Just don't tell us that we must, or else. Language should be an instrument of opportunity, not of oppression.

It is time to let sleeping dogmas lie.

MADAME SPEAKER, JUST SAY YES: WHY PARLIAMENT NEEDS A LEADER OF THE OPPOSITION

The controversy over whether the Congress party should be awarded the formal position of Leader of the Opposition in the Lok Sabha hinges on both legal and political principle. Every parliamentary democracy has a Leader of the Opposition, a title accorded to the head of the largest single political formation not in the government—whatever its size. It is only in India that we have chosen to require a party to hold 10 per cent of the seats in the House before its chief can qualify for the honour. Those wedded to the letter of that rule (a directive, Rule 121, issued by Lok Sabha Speaker Mavlankar in the 1950s) argue that the Congress, with 44 seats in a House of 543, falls short of the 10 per cent number and so cannot put forward the Leader of the Opposition.

It's a peculiar argument, all the more so since the ten per cent rule comes from a Speaker's directive, whereas the only law on the books that mentions the position is a law enacted a quarter of a century later, the Salary and Allowances of Leaders of Opposition in Parliament Act, 1977. This law never mentions 10 per cent or any other figure; it simply states that the status of Leader of the Opposition shall attach to the leader in the Lok Sabha of that party 'having the greatest number' amongst parties not in government. Common sense would suggest that this law supersedes a mere rule; legal theory confirms that laws passed in Parliament trump directives issued by any individual authority, even a Speaker.

Ah, but there's a catch, say those who want to deny Congress the position. The 1977 law speaks of the party 'having the greatest number', but adds, 'and recognized by the Speaker as such'. There's the rub: the Speaker, in granting that recognition, is bound, they argue, by the 1950s directive that obliges her to do the 10 per cent math. Ergo, no Leader of the Opposition for the 9 per cent Congress.

Those who make that argument are wrong. The law doesn't require the Speaker to be bound by the earlier directive; in fact, it doesn't even mention that, or any other, directive. In any case, a rule issued by a Speaker in the 1950s can always be changed by another directive issued by a Speaker half a century later. The only way a Speaker is bound by that rule is if she chooses to be bound by that rule. And such a choice, you can be certain, would be an implicitly political one.

But there's a further complication: various other laws passed since 1977 not only assume the existence of a Leader of the Opposition, but require the holder of such a post to participate in the implementation of key acts—the Human Rights Act of 1993, the Central Vigilance Commission Act of 2003, the Right to Information Act of 2005 and the Lokpal and Lokayuktas Acts of 2013. The selection of a Lokpal or a CVC, for instance, is made by a committee that includes the Leader of the Opposition. A Speaker's directive from the 1950s can't be allowed to dilute the intent of legislation written decades later—the intent being to ensure that, in our democracy, such key constitutional positions are only filled with the involvement of the democratically-elected Opposition.

That's the heart of the matter. Reducing the issue to an argument amongst lawyers about the relative precedence of rules, directives and laws completely misses the spirit of the question at stake. We need a Leader of the Opposition because our democracy recognizes that an elected government, even one with an overwhelming majority like the BJP enjoys today, cannot fully reflect the wishes and feelings of all the people of our diverse nation.

The BJP came to power with 31 per cent of the vote; it needs to pay heed to the views of the 69 per cent that did not wish to see it in power. Those views are best reflected institutionally in the position of a formal Leader of the Opposition. The trappings that come with that position—Cabinet rank, a car, an office, staff—are not important, except inasmuch as they reflect the value attached to such a function in Indian democracy. The formal status of Leader of the Opposition honours our country's pluralist system far more than it honours the occupant of the post.

A final clincher: even insistence on the 10 per cent cut-off won't matter if you recognize that the UPA fought the election as a pre-poll alliance and won 60 seats on a common platform. All 60 UPA Lok Sabha MPs have signed a letter to the Speaker asking her to recognize their leader, Mallikarjun Kharge, as Leader of the Opposition. As the Delhi University students who deal with their own cut-offs might put it, it's really a no-brainer. All you need to do, Madame Speaker, is to just say yes.

She didn't. This Lok Sabha no longer has an official Leader of the Opposition.

MODIFYING SANITATION:
THE 'CLEAN INDIA' CAMPAIGN

I landed in Romania on Gandhi Jayanti—Mahatma Gandhi's birthday, 2 October 2014—to attend and address the Bucharest Forum, only to be greeted by a flurry of messages. The Prime Minister's Office had been trying to reach me while I was airborne. While I was travelling and uncontactable, the PM had gone ahead and announced his invitation to me to join a panel of nine prominent Indians to promote his new Clean India campaign (Swachh Bharat Abhiyan). Some in the media, inevitably, were trying to stir up a controversy: I was the only politician, and worse, the only Congressman, on his list. What did this portend? Was I defecting to the BJP? Would my party be furious if I accepted?

I was honoured, of course, by the invitation. Which Indian worthy of the name would not be humbled to be tapped by his prime minister for a national cause? At the same time, I was a bit mystified by the fuss. This was not the first time the PM had reached out to me for a non-political purpose: less than a year ago, then Chief Minister Modi had asked me on Twitter to join him in exhorting young Indians to register to vote. I had already been doing just that in my constituency, and I had no difficulty in adding my voice to his on social media to make an appeal to young voters. I saw the Clean India campaign in much the same light.

A clean India would benefit all of us, and I was delighted, in principle, to support the prime minister's initiative. At the same time, as I also said in accepting his invitation, I am not a fan of tokenism, and I was worried the campaign would descend to symbolic photo opportunities for grandees who would never touch a broom again after 2 October. Clean India is a great campaign idea, but the real challenge will be to sustain it beyond a week of photo ops. The prime minister asked those who joined him at the campaign launch at Rajpath to take a pledge to 'remain committed towards cleanliness and devote time for this' and to 'neither litter nor let others litter.' That pledge will have to be honoured not just for a week, but every day for the rest of our lives.

As for the Congress party, it initially reacted maturely to the announcement, with former minister Rajiv Shukla rightly decrying the silly speculation about 'Tharoor inching towards the BJP'. 'Why should we be surprised about it?' he asked. 'There are a lot many things which every government has to do and the Opposition has to cooperate'. Shuklaji was right: indeed, as he said, the Congress would have welcomed it if the prime minister had invited many other Congressmen and women to join his effort. After all, it had been launched on the birthday of the greatest Congressman of us all, Mahatma Gandhi, who once said, 'Sanitation is more important than Independence'. Later, however, the party decided that the prime minister, given his somewhat confrontational campaigning style, was the wrong person to espouse a Gandhian cause: the Mahatma had always insisted on means and ends being pursued in the same spirit. As I, too, reminded the prime minister on Twitter, the Mahatma's idea of cleanliness was not only literal: he also spoke of cleanliness of the heart, soul and spirit, and so a campaign on his birthday would have done well to pursue an India cleansed also of bigotry, sectarian hatred and communal violence, as well as clean streets.

At the same time, I was aware of Mr Modi's pronounced interest in sanitation issues. Every once in a while a story slips through the media net that might have received more attention at a different time. With all the media in mid-July focused on the Budget (and the Railway Budget before it), very little attention was paid to an intriguing item that emerged from the prime minister's meeting schedule.

A week before Finance Minister Arun Jaitley presented the 2014 Budget to the Lok Sabha, Prime Minister Modi met Facebook chief operating officer Sheryl Sandberg in Delhi. The fact that he thus became probably the first prime minister anywhere to devote time to a social media executive should not surprise us—he has, for some time now, shown his considerable penchant for 21st century methods of mass communication. That he asked her, in his own words, 'about ways through which a platform such as Facebook can be used for governance and better interaction between the people and governments' is fascinating too, and I can't wait to see what new methods of government-citizen interaction emerge from their conversation. But what I found most striking— and deserving of much more attention than the media gave it—was the news that the key issue Modi asked Sandberg to help India with was sanitation.

Public hygiene was, of course, one of the topics that candidate Narendra Modi had raised in his election speeches, and it featured among the issues mentioned by the prime minister-elect in his first public address in Varanasi after his victory. Many will recall the backlash he received from his usual supporters on the Hindu right when he declared some months before his victory, echoing Congress minister Jairam Ramesh, that toilets were more important to him than temples. Still, it seemed an odd topic to raise with a Facebook executive. The *Economic Times* reported that when asked by Sandberg how her company could help the prime minister achieve his objectives, he mentioned sanitation. 'India has vast tourism potential but poor cleanliness standards hold it back', the paper reported Modi as telling the Facebook COO.

On the face of it, it's an odd request. But the prime minister confirmed it was raised, in his own Facebook post: India intends, he declared, 'to commemorate

Mahatma Gandhi's 150th birth anniversary year [2019] with a special focus on cleanliness and I spoke to Ms Sandberg on how Facebook can assist us in this endeavour'.

How exactly will Facebook do that? It is quite common these days for techno-enthusiasts to turn to social media for pretty much everything, but cleaner streets? Better waste disposal? More and cleaner public toilets? Surely matters like open defecation are far too tangibly physical to lend themselves to 'virtual' solutions? The call of nature, after all, doesn't occur in cyberspace, but in the real and limited public space we all live in, and for too many of our fellow Indians, in open fields, against walls, and on our roadsides.

There isn't much detail on offer from Sandberg herself. Sure enough, she publicized the meeting on Facebook. The Indian prime minister 'believes that direct communication with people all over the world is critical to effective governance and he plans to continue using Facebook and other social media to communicate with the people of India and the world', Sandberg revealed. No surprises there. But sanitation didn't feature big in her post. 'The prime minister asked us to develop local content and reach out to more languages', Sandberg declared (Facebook is currently available in nine Indian languages). So can we look forward to multilingual versions of that quaint wall-sign, 'Make No Nuisance'?

Jokes apart, how exactly would Facebook 'assist the government in all its endeavours', as Sandberg is believed to have assured Modi? More precisely, how would Facebook help India address its vexed, visible and smelly problems of public hygiene?

No clue. Apparently when Communications and IT minister Ravi Shankar Prasad asked Sandberg about the areas in which Facebook could assist the Indian government, she replied by proposing 'cooperation in the fields of health and education, referring to her experience as a World Bank research assistant in Madhya Pradesh in 1991', according to the *Economic Times* again, the only publication that seems to have taken an interest in the content of the meeting.

What little we know officially about the entire episode, in other words, raises more questions than it answers. One obvious use of social media outlets like Facebook is in putting out information about what the government is doing and seeking public participation, suggestions and feedback as inputs into the process. Doing this for a campaign on sanitation would not only raise public awareness—the usual 'agenda setting' function of any media, including social media—but also promote civic engagement. Since Facebook has 100 million users in India, a number that keeps growing, it could serve as the catalyst for a major national effort to engage the Indian public in the cause of improving public hygiene. (And, since Modi is nothing if not a shrewd politician, add to his support base of followers and fans, and expand his multi-million strong list of potential backers in the next election.)

But—there is a 'but'. The sanitation problem is neither caused by, nor affects the basic existence of, the 100 million Indians who are educated enough to use Facebook. It's a nuisance and an inconvenience to have around us, but India's internet users are unlikely to live in homes without toilets, or have to take a lota to the fields in the morning, or seek to perform our ablutions when it's too dark to be observed. The challenge of addressing public sanitation in our country is to reach those who suffer those privations.

So Facebook can serve as a springboard, but not as an exclusive platform. It can at best help kick-start the process of constructing a virtual community to mount a campaign on cleanliness. But to reach and help the people most affected, the government will need grassroots engagement, and Facebook can't provide that by itself. It will take a concerted effort by central and state governments, political workers, the best brains in the advertising community, the most committed activists in the non-profit sector, and sanitation specialists like Sulabh International, to come together in a massive public education effort that actually mobilizes people to transform our culture of public hygiene.

And even that won't be enough. Awareness is half the battle, but only half. Then the government will actually have to go out and build the toilets, install the dustbins, improve the drainage facilities, create waste management systems and improve public sanitation. You can't do that on Facebook, Modiji. But getting the denizens of social media to spend more time on toilets than trolling would be a good place to start.

There is no doubt that Mr Modi has been effective in using his prime ministerial position—what Americans, in Theodore Roosevelt's phrase, like to call the 'bully pulpit' that comes with high office—to drive change from the top. Like so many others, I myself have written articles about our appalling lack of public hygiene (one of which, long before I entered politics, was made a required text in Kerala high schools by the state's communist government), but no individual Indian can match the reach of a Prime Ministerial initiative. When a PM picks up a broom, it is news; the country pays attention. By launching his Swachh Bharat (Clean India) campaign on the occasion of Gandhi Jayanti—which over the years has been reduced to a casual holiday in which the last thing on anyone's mind is the Mahatma or his beliefs—the prime minister has grabbed the nation's attention. His invitation to nine people who are not part of his government helped portray it as a people's movement rather than a government drive. Who would be churlish enough, I reasoned, to refuse an offer to participate in a people's movement, inspired by Mahatma Gandhi, that would improve the lives of all Indians?

Let's also remember that the Swachh Bharat campaign is an attempt by PM Modi to give a new fillip to a national effort of successive governments—one that has failed to achieve its objectives for years. It was the Congress party that gave the nation a Rural Sanitation Programme, which in 1999 was changed by the first NDA government to a Total Sanitation Campaign, with equally modest results. The UPA government in 2012 subsumed that into a Nirmal Bharat Abhiyan, with the objective of making the nation Open Defecation Free by 2022. Modiji, who acknowledged the work of previous governments, has advanced the UPA's deadline by three years and given the effort a national visibility that sanitation has not enjoyed before. But there is no guarantee that it will succeed any more than its predecessor programmes. The fundamental problem lies in our people's ingrained behaviour patterns—and mindsets are the hardest things to change.

The government has announced that it would spend about Rs 2 lakh crore on building more than 111 million toilets, and invited contributions to a new 'Swachch Bharat Kosh' (Clean India Fund) from corporates and well-heeled individuals. The UPA named swachhata preraks or sanitation coordinators who were working in the rural districts. The Clean India effort would make swachhata preraks of us all.

The PM's personal involvement, his websites and Twitter feeds, his Walkathon and the reach-out to nine Indians (who are each supposed to reach out to nine more, and so on) are intended to enhance national awareness of the campaign. It reminds me of the mass movement that brought Kerala to full literacy, as volunteers fanned out to remote hamlets, leper colonies and tribal hutments to reach the unreached. That's the kind of sustained effort that will be needed to make Indian clean.

As then health minister Harshvardhan pointed out, poor sanitation breeds infections and leads to major public health problems; studies have proved a correlation between poor public hygiene and the stunted growth of many poor Indian children, while better sanitation leads to lower infant-mortality rates. A study by scholars Dean Spears and Sneha Lamba proves that children using toilets have better cognitive skills than those who don't. 'Our results suggest,' they conclude, 'that open defecation is an important threat to the human capital of the Indian labour force.'

But our government has discovered that even when toilets are built, people continue to defecate in the open, most out of sheer habit. An estimated 53 per cent of Indians still do so: one survey across several north Indian states learned that 47 per cent found open defecation 'pleasurable, comfortable or convenient'. Litter is everywhere because we are used to discarding things in public places—roads, pavements, beaches—and because there are few public garbage bins anywhere. An attempt to install wastebaskets at every street corner in Delhi and Mumbai found they were being stolen; when they were replaced by iron or concrete bins that could not be removed, those became tempting targets for terrorists to drop lethal explosives into, or so the security wallahs claimed. Thus ended our very brief attempt at abolishing littering. As one who habitually carries everything from used chewing-gum to discarded wrappings in his pocket till I can throw them into a bin, I can testify from personal experience how difficult it is to find a public dustbin on the streets of India.

We also have a cultural problem: we are a nation full of people who live in immaculate homes where we bathe twice a day, but think nothing of littering public spaces, spitting on walls, dumping garbage in the open and urinating and defecating in public, because those spaces are not 'ours'. It is this individualistic mindset and lack of civic consciousness that makes our country a land of private cleanliness and public squalor. Educating Indians about public hygiene must start in schools and be drummed into the minds of adults through information campaigns, exhortations and warnings—as well as fines and punishments for wilful disobedience. If we can fine people for exceeding the speed limit or not wearing a helmet—on the grounds that such behaviour is a menace to others and a cost to society—we should fine litterers and despoilers of public spaces on the same grounds.

It's a long hard road ahead. All over the country, thousands of government employees attended office on Gandhi Jayanti to put in a few hours of manual labour to clean the premises and the surrounds. As one who has long argued that the best way to commemorate the birthday of the man who declared 'Work is Worship' is to work rather than take a holiday, I find that gratifying. But the challenge is sustainability. Once the initial enthusiasm has waned, how do we keep it up? And what about the structural problems—where do we get rid of the waste we sweep up? Do we have enough landfills, waste disposal plants, incinerators, recycling plants, compost heaps? Building toilets is not enough—we have to create entire systems, while changing mindsets all the way.

Since I was in Bucharest, I asked the ambassador if the embassy needed cleaning, but she and her staff had already just done that. When I came back to India, I was enveloped in a political storm over my politically unwise commitment to the prime minister—and the nation—and taken to task by my party. But my involvement is marginal to the larger issue: will Indians, whether mobilized by the prime minister or not, change their habits and help clean up the country—and even more, keep it clean? Given all the factors I have described, a high degree of scepticism is understandable. Let's see whether by next Gandhi Jayanthi we have all succeeded in making a visible difference, or whether 'Clean India' too will go down as one more Modi public-relations gimmick, more visible in the headlines than in the streets.

MR MODI, AREN'T YOU FORGETTING
SOMETHING? AN OPEN LETTER TO
THE PRIME MINISTER

Respected Pradhan Mantri, dear Modiji:

I have not yet had the pleasure of writing to you, except on Twitter. I hope you will forgive me for sending my first direct communication to you in public, because I believe it is on a matter that should also engage the entire public of India.

Ever since assuming the highest executive office in our land, Modiji, you have so far, not even once, mentioned the illustrious name of our first prime minister. I am sure you recall his name, since in the past you have said it has been used too often: it is Jawaharlal Nehru. (Like me, you are not overly fond of titles, but for the record, he was generally known as Pandit Jawaharlal Nehru, hence 'Panditji' for short.)

I mention Jawaharlal Nehru because this year, on 14 November 2014 to be exact, we will be reaching the 125th anniversary of his birth. As you know, we are a country that is very fond of marking anniversaries. We commemorate births, deaths, events of various kinds. Normally, the 125th birth anniversary of a nationalist leader who fought for our independence, graced the high office that you now hold, and guided the destiny of our country till he passed away on 27 May 1964, would be the occasion for a major national commemoration. I am sorry to say that I see absolutely no sign of any such intention on the part of your government.*

Prime Minister Jawaharlal Nehru was, I am sure you will concede, unrivalled as an architect of modern India. I have not forgotten the other great icon you have been lauding of late. Again like you, I am a great admirer of Sardar Vallabhbhai Patel, and his role in merging the princely states into the Indian Union—and his setting up of the administrative structure of independent India—is unquestionably of great value. But the great Sardar passed away in 1950, and his impact on our country was therefore limited by comparison with that of Nehruji, who helped shape our nation's foundations for another fourteen years.

---

*In the end, Mr Modi appointed himself chairman of a commemorative committee, which public sources suggest met only once. A perfunctory commemoration was held, with none of the fanfare that might have been expected from a government of a less anti-Nehru coloration. Mr Modi's own contribution was a one-sentence tweet stating that he was 'remembering' Nehru on his birthday.

Jawaharlal Nehru was no ordinary political leader. An exceptionally gifted writer and speaker, he authored some of the most remarkable books on Indian history and politics. He was a thinker, a humanist, a passionate democratic socialist and internationalist, and a statesman respected around the world even by those who may have disagreed with him. With his rationalist and liberal worldview, his scientific temperament and his faith in modern industry, he was very much a man of the 20th century, whose vision laid the foundations for a progressive India. His abiding faith in Indian pluralism helped keep the nation united; his commitment to democracy and democratic institution-building meant that we never strayed down the path of dictatorship that afflicted so many other newly-independent nations.

At the risk of immodesty, I would like to draw your attention to my short biography, *Nehru: The Invention of India*, which describes all this with a brevity that might commend itself even to a busy prime minister. Jawaharlal Nehru's life is a fascinating story in its own right, and I tried to tell it whole, because the privileged child, the unremarkable youth, the posturing young nationalist and the heroic fighter for independence were all inextricable from the unchallengeable prime minister and peerless global statesman. At the same time I sought to analyse critically the principal pillars of Nehru's legacy to India—democratic institution-building, staunch pan-Indian secularism, socialist economics at home and a foreign policy of non-alignment—all of which were integral to a vision of Indianness that you and your party fundamentally challenge today.

Today, Modiji, you lead the India Nehruji made possible. You say you will be the prime minister of every Indian. The very term 'Indian' was imbued with such meaning by Nehru that it is impossible to use it without acknowledging a debt. Our passports incarnate his ideals. Where those ideals came from, whether they were brought to fulfilment by their own progenitor, and to what degree they remain viable today were the themes of my book, and are legitimate subjects for discussion on his 125th birthday. I started delving into his life as divided between admiration and criticism as I was when I finished my work; but the more I delved into the life, it was the admiration which deepened.

Jawaharlal Nehru's impact on India is too great not to be re-examined periodically. His legacy is ours, whether we agree with everything he stood for or not. What we are today, both for good and for ill, we owe in great measure to one man. That is why his story is not simply history. A history, it would seem, that you, your party, and your government prefer to ignore.

Panditji never claimed he was infallible. He once said that only the dead don't make mistakes. You and your party spokesmen have relished dwelling on his mistakes. Jawaharlal Nehru's achievements in ensuring the stability, unity, development and progress of our country find no acknowledgement in your own speeches or those of your party leaders, but anything and everything that has gone wrong in India is routinely ascribed to him. As the historian Ramachandra Guha has observed, 'No man has been so greatly revered in his lifetime and so viciously vilified since his death'.

There is one exception in the BJP's constant reviling of Jawaharlal Nehru, and it came from none other than your only predecessor as a BJP prime minister of India, Atal Bihari Vajpayee. Speaking in Parliament on Nehruji's death, Vajpayee declared emotionally—and poetically—that with his passing 'a dream has remained half-fulfilled, a song has become silent, and a flame has vanished into the Unknown. The dream was of a world free of fear and hunger; the song a great epic resonant with the spirit of the Gita and as fragrant as a rose, the flame a candle which burnt all night long, showing us the way'. The loss, Vajpayee averred, was not merely that of a family or even of a party. Mother India, he said, was in mourning because 'her beloved Prince has gone to sleep'; even humanity was sad because its servant and worshipper had left it forever. Vajpayee went on to describe the departed prime minister as a 'benefactor of the downtrodden' and the 'chief actor of the world stage' whom he compared to none less than Lord Ram, for like Valmiki's (and the Hindutvawadis') hero, Nehru was 'the orchestrator of the impossible and inconceivable'. He too (I'm still quoting Vajpayeeji) 'was not afraid of compromise but would never compromise under duress'.

You might say that these words were only to be expected from a gracious adversary in tribute to a deceased prime minister. But Vajpayeeji's statements went far beyond the claims of ritual. He called on the nation to rededicate itself to Nehruji's ideals. 'With unity, discipline and self-confidence', Vajpayeeji said, in words that could have been yours, 'we must make this republic of ours flourish. The leader has gone, but the followers remain. The sun has set, yet by the shadow of stars we must find our way. These are testing times, but we must dedicate ourselves to his great aim, so that India can become strong, capable and prosperous...'

Modiji, these are the very objectives you say you share. You may disagree with Nehruji's policies, but like Vajpayeeji, you can have no quarrel with his ideals. You have often expressed respect for your illustrious predecessor and party founder—but none for your very first predecessor, the nation's founder. Is it not time you heeded the former's advice and used the 125th anniversary of our founding prime minister's birth to re-examine the latter's great contributions to our country? And should your government not be preparing to use the occasion to rededicate our nation to his ideals?

As pointed out in an earlier footnote, no such rededication or even affirmation occurred, and Mr Modi's government continues on the path of seeking to bury Mr Nehru and his contributions deep into the recesses of a now unlamented past.

II

MODI'S INDIA AND THE WORLD

MODI AND THE FOREIGN SERVICE

On 12 June 2014, the new prime minister, Narendra Modi, met with the young diplomats of the 2012 batch of the Indian Foreign Service. According to press reports, he told them four things which point to his international priorities in the years ahead. One is right, one is partly right, one is wrong and one is disastrously wrong.

According to PMO sources, the prime minister told the group of twenty-nine young Indian would-be envoys that their focus should be on expansion of trade and commerce and technology transfer; they should become 'catalytic agents to convey the strengths of India to the world, so that mutually beneficial exchanges can take place'. This is right. The days when diplomacy consisted largely of attending receptions and meetings (and faithfully reporting every marginally-useful snippet of political speculation to an indifferent headquarters) have given way to the era of diplomacy as business. Every Indian diplomat must understand that his or her brief includes the facilitation of trade, the promotion of India as an investment destination and the smoothing of barriers for Indian businessmen abroad and foreign ones wishing to come to India. This is no longer something to be sneered at as beneath the dignity of a diplomatic grandee; it is the very warp and woof of modern diplomacy. In this, the prime minister—the first Indian leader who seems capable of echoing US President Calvin Coolidge in claiming that 'the business of India is business'—is indisputably right.

But then he seems to have gone too far. Asking them to focus on 'zero-defect manufacturing' and 'packaging and presentation' to boost exports, the PM apparently illustrated his argument by stating that Indian herbal medicines were among the best in the world but are lagging behind Chinese products in international markets because of poor packaging. Similarly, he told the young diplomats, they needed to ensure that the huge diversity and range of Indian handicrafts is presented better to the world; they have not been made or showcased properly. Fair enough, but this is not for diplomats to remedy: the PM's diagnosis is right but his prescription is wrong. The problem embodied in the PM's accurate observation is one that needs to be fixed at home, by manufacturers and a vigilant regulatory system, not by diplomats. As the BJP itself has observed in a different context, if the product has flaws, no amount of marketing will sell it. The same applies to diplomats: they can only represent Indian products as they are. Making them better, and packaging them better, is the job of manufacturers and the government at home, not of diplomats.

Understandably, the PM seems to have affected the fashionable disdain for the fripperies associated with diplomacy—the 'alcohol, protocol and Geritol'

aspects lampooned by many in the past. 'Chammach kahan rakhna hain…
in sab baton se hatke kaam karo,' he is reported to have said. ('Where your
spoon has to be laid…ignore that kind of issue and do your work'). Sorry
Modiji, aise desh ka kaam nahin chalega. If you don't know where to place
your spoons when hosting a diplomatic dinner, you come across as gauche or
uncultured, and are regarded by foreigners—the others you are trying to win
over with your hospitality—accordingly. There is a reason why the procedures
of protocol, forms of address, laying of tables and so on were devised and
followed by diplomats around the world. They provide the common basis or
platform for dialogue and civilized discourse without which the more substantive
discussions and understandings would not be possible. No, you can't afford to
get your spoons wrong.

Finally, Prime Minister Modi also seems to have reverted to his nativist
populism of old by telling the young IFS trainees not to be swayed by the
cultures of the developed countries they would be posted in, but to take pride
in projecting the strengths of Mother India. 'Apni ma phate purane kapdon
mein bhi toh bhi ma hoti hain,' he told them in Hindi according to press
accounts; 'aur mausi agar ache kapdon mein ho toh bhi mausi hi rehti hain.'
('Your mother's still your mother even in old and torn clothes, whereas your
aunt, even in her best finery, is still an aunt.') Aside from an unsuspected, and
almost Wodehousean, distaste for aunts, what Modiji's statement implies is the
very antithesis of what an effective diplomat should do. Diplomats should be
curious about, and receptive to, the outside world; they should seek to engage
with and understand the cultures of the countries to which they are accredited.
If you want to represent India effectively to a Ruritanian, you will do by
taking an interest in Ruritania and its way of doing things, learning its language
and customs, and listening to its concerns. The Modi notion of diplomacy
as stoutly resisting the siren call of foreign countries while haranguing others
about the strengths of your own is wrong-headed and downright dangerous.
No one will listen to you if you behave like that; and why should they? The
very thought is disastrously wrong.

So here's my advice to the young IFS trainees who have just emerged
wide-eyed from their audience with the prime minister: listen to him attentively,
as you must. Heed his exhortations and feel inspired, if you are. But go back
and listen to what your seniors taught you in basic diplomatic training. Unlike
the prime minister, they've been there. They know what it takes to tell the
India story to foreigners. And here's wishing you all success in doing so.

EXTERNAL APTITUDES: TIME TO REFORM THE IFS

When my book, *Pax Indica*, a study of Indian foreign policy, was launched in New Delhi in 2012, a good portion of the discussion on it focused on my recommendation that the Foreign Service be strengthened, enlarged with the addition of new personnel, and reformed in significant ways. Since my brief stint in the ministry I have been arguing the case for increasing the numbers in the service. India is served by the smallest diplomatic corps of any major country, not just far smaller than the big powers but by comparison with most of the larger emerging countries.

At just about 900 IFS officers to staff India's 120 missions and 49 consulates abroad, India has the fewest foreign service officers among the BRICS countries. This compares poorly not just to the over 20,000 deployed by the United States, and the large diplomatic corps of the European powers—UK (6,000), Germany (6,550) and France (6,250)—but also to Asia's largest foreign services, Japan (5,500) and China (4,200). The picture looks even more modest when compared to the 1200 diplomats in Brazil's foreign ministry. It is ironic that India—not just the world's most populous democracy but one of the world's largest bureaucracies—has a diplomatic corps roughly equal to tiny Singapore's 867.

The size and human capacity of the Indian Foreign Service suffers by comparison with every one of its peers and key interlocutors. While this may partially be a tribute to the quality and the appetite for work of the 900 who staff the foreign service, it lays bare some obvious limitations. I remember the frustrations of the nineteen Latin American ambassadors in New Delhi at the near-impossibility of getting an appointment with the sole joint secretary (assisted by one mid-ranking professional) who was responsible for all their countries. At a time when India is seen as stretching its global sinews, the frugal staffing patterns of its diplomatic service reveals a country punching well below its weight on the global stage.

A few examples will suffice. The joint secretary in charge of East Asia has to handle India's policies regarding China, Japan, the two Koreas, Mongolia, Taiwan, Tibetan refugees, and the disputed frontier with China, in addition to unexpected crises like those relating to India's response to the Japanese earthquake, tsunami and nuclear disaster. Inevitably China consumes most of his attention and relations with the other crucial countries within his bailiwick are neglected or assigned to one of the five junior officials working under him. Another joint secretary is responsible for India's relations with Pakistan, Afghanistan and Iran, while a colleague of equivalent rank handles Bangladesh, Sri Lanka, Myanmar and the Maldives, all countries of significant diplomatic sensitivity and security implications. One more joint secretary has been assigned the dozen countries of Southeast Asia, with Australia, New Zealand and the Pacific thrown in! It is instructive that the US embassy in New Delhi, with a twenty-person political section, has more people following the MEA than the MEA has to deal with the US embassy—in its own country.

As an acute observer, Canada's former High Commissioner to India, David Malone, wrote, the MEA's 'headquarters staff work punishing hours, not least preparing the visits of the many foreign dignitaries laying siege to Delhi in ever growing numbers as India's importance has expanded.... India's overburdened Foreign Service is, on average, of very high quality, but because it is stretched so thin, its staff spends too much of its time conducting India's international relations through narrow diplomatic channels, managing ministerial and other visits, negotiating memoranda of understanding of no great significance, and by other means that reflect only a fraction of the rich reality of international relations today and of official Delhi's actual international interests.'

The problem has not escaped the attention of the professionals. In 2008, Foreign Secretary Shivshankar Menon moved a Cabinet Note proposing a doubling of his effective diplomatic strength. The government agreed to increase the cadre by 520 personnel (320 in the IFS category and 200 additional support staff), but the hierarchy-minded bureaucracy immediately stepped in to forestall any dramatic expansion—which would have required, for instance, the infusion of external professional talent at all levels of the MEA by mid-career recruitment from the other services or even (perish the thought!) from the private sector.

Instead of reaching beyond the government to people who could fill the gaps in the service—more French and Spanish speakers, for instance, or more professional journalists for public diplomacy positions—the implementation of the Cabinet decision was stretched out over ten years by simply increasing the annual intake into the IFS (including promotions from the clerical grades of the IFS 'B') by thirty-two a year. Even this has not materialized, since the MEA has not found thirty-two additional worthy candidates in each of the three years since the Cabinet approved Menon's proposal. Lateral entrants have not been encouraged; a circular to the other government departments soliciting candidacies have turned up few whom the MEA is excited about. The chronic understaffing is therefore likely to continue for more than a decade.

The irony is that as far back as 1966, the Pillai committee that studied the IFS had recommended a broader-based recruitment process that would seek out professionals in various fields, between the ages of 28 and 35, for mid-career employment in the foreign service. The idea was to compensate for the lack of experience (and the consequently more restricted vision) of the standard process which recruited only 21-to-24-year-olds, who 'grew' in the MEA within the norms and confines of the foreign office bureaucracy. The Pillai report suggested that 15 to 20 per cent of the annual recruitment be set aside for older recruits 'to permit entry of persons with specialized knowledge of international relations and area studies, experience in management and administration and public relations'.

The recommendation was never implemented and the thinking behind it continues to be strongly resisted by the entrenched bureaucracy. Ironically the need is even greater today than when Pillai did his work nearly half a century ago. In today's multilateral diplomacy, for instance, the MEA needs expertise that it cannot provide from its own ranks. For instance, climate change has become a hot-button diplomatic issue that needs to be discussed and negotiated in multilateral forums where other delegations rely on technical and scientific expertise that they find indispensable, but which the MEA eschews because it is unwilling to look beyond its own ranks (or those of its retired grandees). In an era when a certain level of specialization is considered essential by many foreign ministries, Indian diplomacy still abounds in talented generalists.

This is why the Parliament's Standing Committee on External Affairs has recommended that the MEA adopt a practice of augmenting its ranks with mid-career recruits from outside, including the private sector. I'm not holding my breath for their response: the IFS is totally resistant to the idea.

Which raises a related question: what kind of diplomats do we need?

The Indian diplomatic corps has long enjoyed a justified reputation as among the world's best in individual talent and ability. It includes men and women of exceptional intellectual and personal distinction who have acquired formidable reputations in a variety of capitals. Indian diplomats over the years have won in print the admiration of Henry Kissinger, Strobe Talbott and other distinguished memoirists who have dealt with them professionally; several have distinguished themselves not only in India's service but in international organizations and conferences. Nonetheless there are institutional failings which are evident despite the quality of the individuals who operate within them.

The Indian Foreign Service is recruited by competitive examinations held by the Union Public Service Commission (UPSC) across the country, followed by a personality test. The diplomatic corps is selected from the same examinations from which emerge the domestic services, like the Indian Administrative Service, the Indian Police Service, the Indian Revenue Service, and so on. The examinations have always been firmly grounded in the generalist tradition; it's overall talent that is sought, not specialization.

For decades, the cream of the examination crop opted for the Indian Foreign Service: in the years after independence, when resources and foreign exchange scarcities made travel abroad a rare privilege, a job that took you frequently abroad was prized by the middle-class families whose sons (and sometimes daughters) took the civil service examinations. From the 1950s to the 1970s, it was customary for the foreign service to draw its entrants almost exclusively from the top ten finishers in the annual examinations.

This has now changed dramatically. Not only has the far more powerful Indian Administrative Service supplanted the IFS as the service of choice, but even the more lucrative Indian Revenue Service—which places officers in the customs and tax administrations, where financial incentives are considerable—is preferred over the IFS by many applicants. As a result it is now common for the IFS to find itself selecting officers ranked below 250 in the examinations, something that had been unthinkable to the officers currently heading the MEA.

The decline in prestige of the foreign service has also been enabled by the relative ease of foreign travel, which has negated what used to be seen as the IFS's principal perquisite, and the widespread perception that diplomats neither wield as much clout nor have as many opportunities to salt away a retirement nest-egg as their domestic counterparts. The further complication of this problem is that several civil service aspirants are thrust unwillingly into the MEA while their real ambition is to serve elsewhere—a far cry from the glory days but one that does not produce a dedicated and proud foreign service.

The mandarin-style approach to recruitment—which requires all entrants to come through a one-size-fits-all civil services examination, the same one that produces generalist administrators, tax officials and police officers—has evident limitations. Since working abroad for the government has lost some of its allure, this is no longer the best way to find the most suitable diplomats; indeed, for many applicants the IFS is a third or even fourth preference among the career options available to those who do well in the exams. I feel strongly that a diplomat should not be someone who fell short of his or her 'real' goal of becoming an administrator, a customs official or a crime-busting sleuth.

We need internationalist-minded young Indians who see the chance of serving the country abroad not only as a privilege, but as something indispensable to India's growth and prosperity. A separate foreign service exam, with a greater emphasis on international relations and languages, is one possibility. Such an exam would test different skills from today's UPSC, because we need diplomats, not bureaucrats, in the Foreign Service: young people with an interest in world affairs, an aptitude for languages and an engaging personality, who know how to talk to foreigners. It's by no means clear that a majority of our recent recruits would fill the bill. An IFS exam should be offered not only within India but in places like Dubai, Singapore, New York and London, which abound with bright young Indian citizens who have grown up abroad, are at ease with foreign cultures, speak foreign languages, know how to communicate with foreigners—and who would never make it past the current UPSC exams.

Not every diplomat emerges from the current training process well-enough equipped in the 'soft skills' required in international diplomacy to function effectively, though their mastery of their assigned foreign language is now usually impressive. But then language training, too, is not always reflected in assignments: I have frequently come across Indian diplomats in non-Anglophone European capitals whose foreign language was Chinese; a number of ambassadors in Paris who could not speak French; and (as I pointed out in a Parliament question in 2011) not one of India's nine ambassadors stationed in the countries of the Gulf at that time spoke or had learned Arabic. Surely we can aim at a time when every national language is spoken by at least one Indian officer and an eventual time when every one of our missions is headed by an ambassador who knows the language, be it Khmer or Korean, Spanish or Swahili?

When I presented my book to then External Affairs Minister S.M. Krishna, he seemed receptive to my thoughts on staffing and language skills. I hope the new foreign minister, Sushma Swaraj, will grasp the nettle. If it is left to the bureaucracy, reform will never happen. Whatever is decided, the time for reform is desperately overdue—though little of the urgency required is visible in the corridors of South Block, once known, in the early 1960s, as the 'Ministry of Eternal Affairs'.

Surely the eternal must now make way for the urgent. The time for reform is now.

AB KI BAR, CONFUSED SARKAAR:
THE FOREIGN POLICY U-TURNS

If there were ever to be an object lesson in the fundamental political wisdom that opposing is different from governing, Narendra Modi and the BJP epitomize it.

We have already seen the Modi government reverse half a dozen domestic positions of the Modi campaign. Our new BJP rulers now support GST (the proposed Goods and Services Tax), sugar subsidies, railway and diesel price hikes, FDI in insurance and other key UPA Budget measures, all of which they had ferociously denounced, obstructed and prevented progress on when they were in Opposition.

Nowhere is the U-turn more apparent, though, than in foreign policy. As we know, one of the first acts of the newly-elected prime minister was to invite Pakistan's Prime Minister Nawaz Sharif to his inauguration, after attacking the Congress party and his predecessor Manmohan Singh for being too soft on our neighbour. Modi, who had excoriated the Congress for 'serving chicken biryani' to a Pakistani visitor, now exchanges shawls and saris with his Islamabad counterpart. (I mischievously tweeted my hope that chicken biryani would be on Modi's dinner menu for his Pakistani guest: it wasn't.)

In the election campaign, Modi had breathed fire and brimstone about Bangladesh, accusing it of sending millions of illegal immigrants into India and promising that the moment he won the election, they would all have to 'pack their bags' and leave India for home. Bangladeshi officials had publicly and privately expressed their disquiet that any attempt to do this could be deeply destabilizing for their politically fragile state. Within weeks of his victory, however, Modi's Foreign Minister Sushma Swaraj was all smiles on her first official visit abroad—to Bangladesh. Illegal immigration wasn't even mentioned in Dhaka.

The Land Boundary Agreement with Bangladesh concluded by Prime Minister Manmohan Singh, which Indian diplomats had considered vital to removing bilateral irritants, had never been implemented because UPA couldn't win the BJP's support in Parliament to ratify the territorial swaps required. Now the Modi government is the biggest votary of the Land Boundary Agreement, with the BJP leadership calling for it to be ratified.

The BJP had been virulently critical of the Indo-US nuclear deal, Manmohan Singh's signature foreign policy triumph. They had even supported a no-confidence motion against the UPA government on the issue of the deal. Yet, in a quiet and under-reported move, the Modi government wisely ratified the India-specific Additional Protocol, a UPA undertaking to grant greater access to India's civilian nuclear sites to the UN's International Atomic Energy Agency.

In the lead-up to and during his election campaign, Modi and the BJP had constantly berated the Government of India for being unable to do anything about frequent Chinese incursions across the disputed frontier. Today, the same Modi has not only had effusive meetings with both the Chinese President and Foreign Minister, but is inviting China to help modernize the Indian railways. As to the border incursions, the BJP government echoes the very line it had denounced when the Congress government uttered it—that since the two countries have differing perceptions of where the border lies, each patrols in areas the other considers to be theirs. What was excoriated by Modi as pusillanimity and appeasement in the Congress has become wisdom and statesmanship in the BJP.

The most poignant issue relates, of course, to the most sensitive: the killings of Indian jawans in shooting incidents on our Line of Control with Pakistan. Every time any such tragedy occurred, Modi and the BJP used to savage the Congress. Their campaigners frequently said that if Modi won, the killings would stop because Islamabad knew that a Modi government would retaliate ruthlessly in taking ten Pakistani heads for every Indian one that fell.

The first killings occurred immediately after the BJP victory, but before Modi had been sworn in: the victors' silence was understandably not held against them. But shortly afterwards, when news again came in of a jawan being killed on the LoC, the silence of the Modi government was deafening. In a tweet on 11 August 2013, Narendra Modi had declared with typical bravado: 'India is going through a troubled situation. China intrudes our borders, Pakistan kills our soldiers time and again but Centre doesn't act!' The implication was clear to his fans: this won't happen on my watch.

Well, it just has, repeatedly. As one critic sarcastically reposted Modi's tweet from August 2013: Completely Agree with Narendra Modi. China Intrudes border, Pakistan Kills Soldiers. Centre doesn't act.

Prime Minister Modi has wisely chosen not to rise to the bait. Where you stand on foreign policy, in other words, depends on where you sit. Your stand is different when you're sitting in South Block and not in Gandhinagar.

Just a few days after Foreign Minister Sushma Swaraj had attempted to prevent discussion of the Gaza crisis in Parliament, and barely forty-eight hours after she had responded to the Rajya Sabha by stressing that India would not take any position on the tragedy there that might vitiate our relations with Israel, the government did its latest about-face. It voted for a United Nations Human Rights Council resolution on Gaza that 'strongly condemned' Israel's 'prolonged occupation' of Palestinian Territory, and condemned 'in the strongest terms' the 'widespread, systematic and gross violations of international human rights and fundamental freedoms arising from the Isareli military operations' in Gaza.

Such language, endorsed by twenty-nine countries and opposed by only one—the United States (as usual), though seventeen nations preferred to abstain—was entirely consistent with India's traditional positions on the Palestinian issue, which have remained more or less the same for the last three decades. Our position can be summarized thus: strong support for the Palestinian cause, opposition to Israeli occupation and illegal Jewish settlements, but acknowledgement of Israel's right to exist, and support for a peace process that would conclude with two states living side by side in peaceful co-existence. Voting for UN resolutions that condemned Israeli excesses was in keeping with this policy, and long-time followers of Indian diplomacy would have felt no surprise in seeing how New Delhi voted in Geneva.

But after listening to the foreign minister in recent days signalling a new even-handedness between the two sides ('both are our friends,' she declared, equating the 700 innocent civilian victims, including 170 little children, with those who had killed them) the vote did come as a surprise. The resolution not only avoided all pretence of equal blame, it explicitly suggested that 'the Isareli military operations carried out in the Occupied Palestinian Territory since 13 June 2014…may amount to international war crimes'. War crimes are not something you expect 'friends' to be happy to be accused of.

Israelis and their sympathizers, who had expected—indeed, been led to expect—something different from the BJP, will be told that in fact the Modi government's position was carefully calibrated: after all, it didn't co-sponsor the Pakistani resolution, merely voted for it, and it took care to ensure that reference was included to Israeli civilian victims (of whom there have been precisely two). Indeed, the resolution 'condemns all violence against civilians wherever it occurs'. Israel would clearly have preferred that a government professing even-handedness abstain, as most Europeans, some African countries and the Republic of Korea did. India rightly thought that would be too much of a departure from its traditional position and its normal pattern of voting, and went with its usual vote.

So India was consistent, but the BJP was not. The Government of India behaved as all Indian governments for the last thirty years have done. The BJP, with its words and actions in Delhi, its joining the Fortalezza consensus of BRICS countries and now its vote at the UNHRC, has signalled complete incoherence on its Israel policy.

Israeli apologists are justified in pointing out, of course, that their military action was in response to an incessant fusillade of Hamas-fired rockets raining down upon their citizenry. But these rockets, thwarted by the impressive solidity of the anti-missile defence system called the 'Israeli Dome', caused very little damage and no loss of life in 2014. Israel has every right to defend itself, but its right to do so cannot trample on the basic human rights of others. An air assault and military invasion that has killed 700 people and injured or maimed over 4,000 more is grossly disproportionate to the wrong it is claiming to set right. The BJP, however, has refused to see this so far. Its diplomatic representatives have. This is the incoherence.

The resolution India voted for says three other things the Israelis will resent. It sets up an international commission of inquiry, but it is a foregone conclusion that the Government of Israel will not co-operate with such a commission or facilitate its work. It asks Switzerland, as custodian of the Geneva Conventions, to call a conference of all contracting parties—that would be a prelude to finding Israel guilty of war crimes, and the Israelis will leave the world in no doubt that making this demand is an unfriendly act. Finally, it calls for an end to Israel's blockade (the resolution terms it an 'illegal closure') of the Gaza Strip. This, of course, is a long-standing Hamas demand, and it is also Hamas's only precondition to accepting a ceasefire.

So Israel will portray the UN resolution as giving aid and comfort to its enemies, and those who voted for it as dupes of Hamas terrorism. It is a strange place to be for a BJP leadership that just a few days ago didn't even want Indian parliamentarians to express their concern at the unfolding humanitarian tragedy, lest it offend Israel.

As it struggles to come to terms with the unfamiliar demands of being in power and acting for India on the world stage, it's clear the BJP will find itself in a lot more strange places in the months to come.

The cerebral American politician, New York Governor Mario Cuomo, once memorably observed that you campaign in poetry, but govern in prose. Hard reality, he suggested, replaces the fights of policy fantasy that afflict those without power.

With power comes responsibility. And with responsibility, Modiji, comes realism. Welcome to Indraprastha.

INDIA AND AFGHANISTAN: WELL DONE, SUSHMAJI

The news that Indian Foreign Minister Sushma Swaraj made a successful visit to Afghanistan early in her tenure should gladden the hearts of all of us in the Opposition who believe that our political differences stop at the water's edge and the border line. When it comes to India's national interests, there is no Congress foreign policy or BJP foreign policy—there is, or should be, only India's foreign policy.

This was already amply demonstrated at the time of the very first non-Congress government in 1977, when the Janata Party's foreign minister, Atal Bihari Vajpayee, conducted a Nehruvian foreign policy with style and grace. Sushma Swaraj shows every sign—in Nepal, in Bangladesh and now in Afghanistan—of doing the same.

India and Afghanistan share a strategic and development partnership based on historical, cultural and economic ties. We have an abiding interest in the stability of Afghanistan, in ensuring social and economic progress for its people, getting them on the track of self-sustained growth and thus enabling them to take their own decisions without outside interference.

The binding factor in our relationship is that the interests of Afghanistan and India converge.

In our efforts towards the stabilization of Afghanistan, the focus has been on development. Our $2 billion assistance programme, modest from the standpoint of Afghan needs, is large for a non-traditional donor like India, and is in fact our largest aid programme in any country. Our assistance programmes are being implemented in close coordination with the Afghan government, and are spread all over Afghanistan. They straddle all the socio-economic sectors of development: humanitarian; infrastructure; small and quick gestation social projects; and skills and capacity development. India is the fifth largest bilateral donor in Afghanistan.

The principal objective of this effort is to build indigenous Afghan capacities and institutions for an effective governance system that is able to deliver goods and services required by the Afghan people, who have suffered years of unremitting violence.

India has helped build the infrastructure of the new Afghanistan. The 218 km (130 mile) Zaranj-Delaram highway, in southwest Afghanistan near the Iranian border, was an Indian triumph and has opened an alternative route for Afghan goods and services which were otherwise totally dependent on Pakistan. The Pul-e-Khumri to Kabul power transmission line and the sub-station at Chimtala—constructed by brilliant Indian engineers at a height of 3,000 metres—has lit up Kabul, which, thanks to India, has round-the-clock electricity supply for the first time since 1992. We have constructed the Salma Dam on the Hari Rud River in Herat and the Afghan Parliament building, a visible and evocative symbol of India's commitment to Afghan democracy.

We have simultaneously commissioned around 100 small development projects, which are typically quick gestation, smaller-scale social sector projects in outlying and frontier provinces, conceived and executed by local authorities.

India has five medical missions providing treatment and free medicines to over 1,000 patients every day, most of whom are poor women and children. We continue to support the Indira Gandhi Centre for Child Health in Kabul and have connected it through a telemedicine link with two super-speciality medical centres in India. We provide 100 grams of high-protein biscuits to 2 million of the 6 million Afghan schoolgoing children, a third of whom are girls.

We are digging tube wells in six provinces, running sanitation projects and medical missions, and working on lighting up 100 villages using solar energy. India has also given at least three Airbus planes to Afghanistan's ailing national airline, Ariana. Several thousand Indians are engaged in development work.

Funds have been committed for education, health, power and telecommunications. There has also been money in the form of food aid and help to strengthen governance. For capacity development, we are providing 675 scholarships each, annually, for undergraduate and graduate students in India, and for Afghan public servants to train in Indian public training institutions for up to 180 days in areas of their choice. These are the largest such programmes that India has for any country and the largest among the skills and capacity development programmes offered to Afghanistan by its development partners.

Bilateral trade has grown rapidly, but could grow much more if transit through Pakistan was made less cumbersome. It is a shame that the Pakistani military still sees Afghanistan as a zero-sum game—that anything that is good for India must be opposed and obstructed, even if doing so is bad for Afghanistan. In fact both Pakistan and India stand to benefit from enhanced and smooth trade and transit to and from Afghanistan.

Given its geographic location, Afghanistan has immense potential to develop as a hub of trade, energy and transport corridors, which would help the long-term sustainability of development efforts in Afghanistan. There is a need for greater regional cooperation and economic integration of the Afghan economy with South and Central Asia. The historical and cultural relationship of Afghanistan with the other South Asian countries makes it a natural member of SAARC, which it joined only after some delay. As its westernmost country, Afghanistan is the key link for SAARC member States with Iran and Central Asia. This economic interdependence could catalyse peace and prosperity in the region at large and in Afghanistan in particular. But it needs Pakistani co-operation for Afghanistan to be able to fulfil its great potential as a transit hub for the region.

We have ensured that our projects are dictated by the needs and priorities of the local population. As a long-standing friend of the Afghan people, and one with deep civilizational and historical ties, India is gratified at the progress that has been made in Afghanistan in recent years.

We believe it is important for the international community to maintain its commitment to the people of Afghanistan even after the planned American withdrawal. India remains fully committed to assisting our Afghan partners in the process of reconstruction, and economic and human resource development, as they build a prosperous, democratic and pluralistic Afghanistan.

The 2014 presidential elections conducted by the Afghan Election Commission are a landmark event in Afghanistan's evolution as a democracy, marking a transition from the first post-Taliban Presidency of Hamid Karzai, a friend of India. As a fellow developing democratic country, India appreciates the resoluteness and determination of the Afghan people who participated in the election process, notwithstanding threats and intimidation by the Taliban. It is heartening that the campaigns were conducted in a democratic spirit, that there were no incidents of violence resulting from any clashes between supporters of the candidates, that participation in the elections was broad-based, and that voting was across ethnic lines.

The elections were hotly contested and ended in a bitter standoff, with the results in favour of Ashraf Ghani being passionately challenged by the apparent loser, his former Cabinet colleague Abdullah Abdullah. Still, in a land so ravaged by civil war and terrorism, neither of the contestants is reaching for his gun.

As in India, free and fair elections have permitted a complex and divided society to manage an important political transition. Following a protracted electoral imbroglio, Ghani was declared the president-elect after he signed a deal to share power with his rival Abdullah Abdulla. The new Afghan government and the international community will need to come together to configure the contours of their partnership for the next five years. This is why Sushma Swaraj's visit is particularly timely.

The threat of terrorism is never absent in Afghanistan and India has faced it unrelentingly. Local Taliban are blamed for attacking and kidnapping Indians in the country. There have been explosions and grenade attacks on the Indian consulates in Herat and Jalalabad, and two major attacks on the Indian Embassy in Kabul, one of which killed two senior Indian diplomats. Both took a heavy toll of the lives of Afghan passers-by. In January 2008, two Indian and eleven Afghan security personnel were killed and several injured in an attack on the Zaranj-Delaram road. In 2006, an Indian telecommunications engineer was abducted and killed in the southern province of Zabul. In November 2005, a driver with India's state-run Border Roads Organization was abducted and killed by the Taliban while working on the road. In 2003, an Indian national working for a construction company was killed by unknown attackers in Kabul's Taimani district. There have been other attacks on Indians too.

Given the turbulence of the recent past and the dramatic decline in security, there is need for an intensified focus on security, governance and development by the Afghan government. Here, India and the rest of the international community should do what it can to assist. Failure in Afghanistan's stabilization will entail a heavy cost for both the Afghan people and the world at large. India cannot send troops, but it is doing its best to train Afghan military and police personnel in India, and these efforts should continue.

The international community has tended to place the responsibility for institution building and governance mainly on the shoulders of the Afghan people and government, without adequately resourcing that effort and eliminating the growing threat from terrorist groups destabilizing the country. This transition is the last opportunity for the country to extricate itself from its endemic entanglement with violence and under-development and settle on a track of stability and sustainable progress.

All stakeholders now agree on the need for greater Afghanization of the development process. The Afghan National Security Forces (ANSF) should be enlarged and developed in a professional manner, at a much faster pace. ANSF should be provided appropriate resources, combat equipment, and training.

As for the process of reconciliation, India supports the Afghan government's determination to integrate those willing to abjure violence and live and work within the parameters of the Afghan Constitution, which provides the framework for a pluralistic and democratic society. This should, of course, go hand-in-hand with the shutting down of support and sanctuaries provided to terrorist groups across the border.

There is a growing understanding that the increase in terrorist actions in Afghanistan is linked to the support and sanctuaries available in the contiguous areas of Pakistan. That explains the particularly high level of violence in the border areas of Afghanistan.

The international community should put effective pressure on Pakistan to implement its stated commitment to deal with terrorist groups within its territory, including the members of Al Qaeda, Taliban's Quetta Shura, Hezb-e-Islami, Lashkar-e-Taiba and other like-minded terrorist groups.

The world has come to realize, at considerable cost, that terrorism cannot be compartmentalized, and any facile attempts to strike Faustian bargains with terrorists often result in such forces turning on the very powers that sustained them in the past. The Indian foreign minister's visit occurred days after Al-Qaeda chief Ayman al-Zawahiri announced the establishment of an Indian branch of his terrorist movement in a 54-minute video in which he said that

Al-Qaeda would recognize the overarching leadership of the Afghan Taliban leader Mullah Muhammad Omar. Her visit at this time underscored the shared interests of Kabul and New Delhi in resisting Al-Qaeda terror.

As American withdrawal looms, a sense of defeatism pervades certain sections of international opinion. This needs to be guarded against, because it runs the risk of encouraging insurgent groups, besides weakening the authority of the central government and its institutions.

What we believe Afghanistan needs is a long-term commitment, even while remaining mindful of the challenges. The Afghan people have displayed resilience and a survival instinct even against the greatest odds. We must do our utmost to support them. There are really only two choices confronting the international community—invest and endure or give up and exit. India has already made up its mind—invest and endure—because we believe in the cause of peace, democracy and development in Afghanistan. Sushma Swaraj's visit was a signal to the rest of the world that India was not giving up.

PRESIDENT XI OR PRESIDENT XXX?

From the heady days of 'Chindia', when China and India were twinned together in the global imagination, comparisons between the two countries have taken on a more modest hue. Once united by their shared status of being giant Asian countries with booming demographies and unlimited economic potential, the two are perceived to be very different today. India's incomplete domestic transformation, recently slowing economy and its flourishing and contentious democracy mark it as starkly different from China, which has shot ahead economically, with a GDP four times India's size, while remaining resolutely authoritarian, under one-party Communist rule.

Despite these stark differences—and the bitter legacy of the 1962 war between the two nations, which culminated in a decisive Chinese victory and bequeathed to both nations the world's longest unresolved border dispute—the two nations are moving towards each other in a wary embrace. China's new leader, President Xi Jinping, who has impressively consolidated his power in Beijing, arrived in India in early September 2014, at a time when India's new prime minister, Narendra Modi, was still basking in the glow of a decisive electoral victory. The two even met in Mr Modi's home state of Gujarat on his sixty-fourth birthday.

Though there have been no clashes on the frontier in decades, both countries' media tend to bristle at each other's alleged provocations. A series of irritants has continued to plague the political relationship. Delhi is miffed by China's claim to the northeastern Indian state of Arunachal Pradesh, which Beijing calls 'South Tibet', its support for Pakistan in the acrimonious geopolitics of the subcontinent, and its insistence on issuing stapled visas to Indians living in Kashmir rather than directly on their Indian passports, to underscore Beijing's view that Kashmir is disputed territory. In turn, China looks askance at India having given refuge to the Dalai Lama and his followers since 1959, and his maintaining a Tibetan government in exile on Indian soil, though New Delhi fully recognizes Beijing's sovereignty over Tibet and does not allow Tibetan protestors to disrupt Chinese leaders' visits. At the same time, Mr Modi has tended to align his government with those critical of China's territorial claims in the South China and East China seas, and signalled his determination to prioritize India's relations with Japan and Australia as well as countries in India's immediate neighbourhood.

But economic relations tell a different story. Of course, China is way ahead. China started its liberalization a good decade and a half before India, shot up faster, hit double-digit growth when India was still hovering around 5 per cent, and with compound growth, has put itself in a totally different league from India, continuing to grow faster from a larger base. Indian visitors to China, including then Chief Minister Narendra Modi, emerge with acute cases of infrastructure envy, contrasting China's gleaming skyscrapers and six-lane expressways to India's own ramshackle facilities and congested roadways.

Yet bilateral trade volume has multiplied several hundredfold in the last three decades, crossing $70 billion by the end of 2013 from a level of only $30 million in 1992. (The trade balance is, however, skewed 2 to 1 in China's favour.) China has now overtaken the US as India's largest single trading partner, and the two countries seem well on course to reach their proclaimed target of $100 billion in annual trade by 2015. Indian information technology firms have opened offices in Shanghai and Hangzhou, and Infosys recruits Chinese staff for their headquarters in Bangalore. There are dozens of Chinese engineers working in (and learning from) Indian computer firms and engineering companies from Gurgaon to Bangalore, while Indian software engineers in Chennai and Bangalore support the Chinese telecoms equipment manufacturer Huawei.

By and large, India is good at things that China needs to improve at, notably software, where it has been unable to rival India's IT dominance; China excels at hardware and manufacturing, which India sorely lacks. So India's Mahindra and Mahindra manufactures tractors in Nanchang for export to the United States. The key operating components of Apple's iPod were invented by the Hyderabad company PortalPlayer, while the iPods themselves are manufactured in China. Philips employs nearly 3,000 Indians at its Innovation Campus in Bangalore who write more than 20 per cent of Philips' global software, which in turn goes to Philips's 50,000 strong workforce in China to turn into brand-name goods. China's manufacturing muscle is on display in India, with telecoms equipment maker Huawei clocking $800 million in Indian sales, amounting to about 2 per cent of its global revenues.

Politically too, the temperature has begun warming. India and China both see themselves as having outgrown a world order dominated by the West. They are moving beyond traditional bromides like their joint advocacy of the 'Five Principles for Peaceful Coexistence', to pragmatic co-operation in the framework of the BRICS grouping: they recently came together to announce the creation of the BRICS Bank, which will be located in Shanghai and headed by an Indian. China has supported Indian participation in the Shanghai Co-operation Organisation and India has extended China observer status in SAARC. Strikingly, in 2013, China's new Premier Li Keqiang chose India, rather than America or any European country, as the destination for his first-ever official foreign visit. The Chinese Foreign Minister was also the newly-elected Modi's first official visitor, and President Xi had already met the new Indian prime minister at the BRICS summit in Brazil in July. Neither leader appeared at the UN climate change summit, a reflection of their shared rejection of Western attempts to place the onus for global warming on developing countries rather than where it rightly belongs.

Prime Minister Narendra Modi has taken to the international responsibilities of his office with gusto, and has generally earned high marks for his energy and style. But it's fair to say that the visit of Chinese President Xi Jinping to India must rank among the first major disappointments of his fledgling forays into foreign policy.

The visit was hyped enormously by the PM's hyperactive PR machinery and an overzealous media. Nothing wrong with that: here was the leader of Asia's biggest economy, who has in a short while impressively asserted his control over a nation gearing up to be the next global superpower, coming to pay court to a renascent India.

Not just that: President Xi had actually rearranged his schedule to accommodate President Pranab Mukherjee's absence in Vietnam; he had cancelled the Pakistani leg of his trip, eliminating the usual hyphenation that so often irritates New Delhi; and he agreed to arrive in Ahmedabad on Mr Modi's sixty-fourth birthday. Even a stray remark by Mr Modi in Japan about some countries' expansionist inclinations, widely read as implied criticism of China, did not provoke the Chinese, whose assistant foreign minister declared, 'China has never, and will not, used so called military or other means to try and hem in India.' It all seemed to add up to an extraordinary effort by the Chinese leader to warm up to India. The Modi government's PR build-up at first appeared totally justified.

Headlines and breathless articles in the days leading up to Xi's visit announced that the Chinese would be announcing $100 billion worth of investments into India, almost three times the amount pledged by Tokyo during Mr Modi's recent visit to Japan. The visiting Chinese president, who travelled with a delegation of over 100 senior business executives, including the heads of China Harbour, China Railway Construction Group and Huawei, as well as of the four biggest Chinese banks, was expected to announce some $20 billion of Chinese investment commitments a year over the next five years, much of it in the new Indian industrial parks, a pet project of Mr Modi's. In advance of the visit, it was reported that China would initially invest $7 billion in industrial parks in Pune (for automobile manufacturing) and Gandhinagar in Gujarat (for power equipment), as well as set up an industrial park in Tamil Nadu for the textile sector. Other areas of likely investment, according to Chinese diplomats in India, include the modernization of railways, with $50 billion worth of investments contemplated in improving rolling stock and running bullet and hi-speed trains in India; upgrading highways and ports; power generation, distribution and transmission; and food processing. The billions of dollars that will be needed in loans to finance Indian infrastructure projects (which will mostly take place as joint ventures with Chinese firms) will be funded by Chinese banks. Such loans, often tied to purchases from Chinese equipment manufacturers, have already relieved pressure on heavily indebted Indian companies.

In all fairness to our prime minister, the promises came not only from his spin-masters but from the Chinese themselves. Liu Youfa, China's consul-general in Mumbai, told the *Times of India* (13 September 2014) that 'on a conservative estimate, I can say that we will commit investments of over $100 billion or thrice the investments committed by Japan during our President Xi Jinping's visit next week. These will be made in setting up of industrial parks, modernization of railways, highways, ports, power generation, distribution and transmission, automobiles, manufacturing, food processing and textile industries'.

Unfortunately, the mountain laboured, and produced a mouse.

India and China signed sixteen bilateral agreements, but all they added up to was the promise of some $30 billion, not only not three times Japan's offer, but less than the $35 billion already pledged by Tokyo.

The centrepiece of the visit was a five-year trade and economic development plan signed by the two countries' commerce ministers, under which China committed to investing $20 billion in India over the next five years. (The pre-visit spin was $20 billion a year over each of the next five years.) In addition, China committed to an investment of $6.8 billion in two industrial parks in Gujarat and Maharashtra, and some twenty-four Chinese companies entered into agreements with Indian companies that, if and when delivered, would add up to investments of another $3.6 billion.

Do the math: 20+6.8+3.6 = $30.4 billion. Not $100 billion. And even the $30.4 billion is still a set of promises, not actual cheques in the bank.

The Doordarshan newsreader who charmingly referred to President Xi as President Eleven could as well have named him President Xxx, the man who promised a hundred and offered thirty.

If this wasn't disappointment enough, the visit's deflating economic news was overshadowed by fresh reports of Chinese incursions into Indian territory along the two nations' long-disputed frontier. The movement of Chinese troops and civilians into Chumar in Jammu and Kashmir's Ladakh region was now the third such incursion by the PLA in recent weeks. It was hard to believe that President Xi, with his formidable control over the governmental and military machinery in a one-party authoritarian state, was unaware of what was happening, or could not have prevented it from casting a shadow on his hosts' over-the-top bonhomie.

It is true that the two countries have differing perceptions of where the Line of Actual Control lies between them, and that each patrols in territory claimed by the other side. But when so much effort was being expended on the atmospherics of the Xi visit, surely it was not beyond Beijing to tell the PLA not to run their patrols at least for the duration of their president's presence on Indian soil?

It is hard to escape the conclusion that the Chinese were sending a deliberate signal: you Indians want our money and investments, but remember we still claim land you think is yours, and we will assert our claims even while we pursue business with you. Our president may be all smiles and warm rhetoric, but underneath the cuddly exterior, we're reminding you who's boss.

Beijing has for years used the border dispute to its tactical advantage, permitting border incidents to flare up from time to time to throw India off balance. In this case the incursion may have constituted a Chinese riposte to President Mukherjee's Vietnam visit, which concluded with India agreeing to increase its role in exploring offshore oilfields in Vietnamese waters that China disputes. The PLA's strolls onto sensitive ground may well have been to send the message: don't think we haven't noticed what you were doing in Vietnam, and don't think you can get away with it quite so easily.

Whatever may have been the reasons, there is no doubt that a visit that was built up by the Modi government as a major foreign policy triumph in the making instead turned out to be a damp squib. Xi's India visit will now be remembered less for the photo-ops of the Chinese First Couple on a swing at Sabarmati than for the disappointment of the $100-billion-that-wasn't and the Chinese incursions that shouldn't have been.

Nor were any breakthroughs announced in the significant areas where progress is needed. India's complaints about the trade balance are augmented by worries about Chinese dumping and non-trade barriers to Indian investment in China. People-to-people contact is limited: though tourism, particularly of Indian pilgrims to the major Hindu holy sites in Tibet, Mount Kailash and Lake Mansarovar, can be said to be thriving, nearly 600,000 Indians visited China for business, tourism and study in 2012, while only 140,000 Chinese returned the compliment. No practical solution to any of these problems was on offer.

Clearly, there's a long way to go before Sino-Indian relations can be described as truly close. But they're improving. It's just that President Xi's visit fell short of being the capstone of this rising edifice.

For Mr Modi, the Xi let-down has taken some of the shine off his burgeoning foreign policy credentials. Of course, it's never too late to learn that in international relations, it's always better to promise less and deliver more. Mr Modi really should give his PR machine a rest before the next foreign visitor comes calling.

MR MODI GOES TO WASHINGTON

Mr Smith Goes to Washington was a heartwarming 1936 film about a small-town guy, decent and straightforward, who finds himself in the senate where he leads a courageous battle against corruption and abuse of power. 'Mr Modi Goes to Washington' is a somewhat less inspiring tale.

Fresh from his triumphant visit to New York, the new Indian prime minister appears to have cut something less of a swathe through the American capital. Far from the hysterical cheers of his fans in Madison Square Garden, and even from the company of actor Hugh Jackman before 60,000 concert-goers in Central Park, Mr Modi found himself in the decidedly more prosaic environments of the Beltway, drinking warm water at a Presidential dinner and exchanging talking points with US officialdom. If New York was all flash and celebration, Washington was, as always, about the dull but necessary practices of formal diplomacy.

New York first: Mr Modi is undoubtedly already a considerable presence on the world stage. We should take with a fistful of salt the over-the-top pronouncements of his being a 'rock star of diplomacy', but it is undeniable that with his style, commanding presence and overwhelming confidence, our prime minister has made an impact wherever he goes. (I was in Nepal the previous week and heard similar enthusiasm for his words and deeds there.)

This does not necessarily deliver results for India, but it does mean that the Indian leader's presence is noticed, in a very different manner from his understated predecessor. Dr Manmohan Singh was greatly respected for his intellect and his unrivalled expertise and wisdom on global economic issues; no one would seek Mr Modi's views on fiscal markets or quantitative easing. But as Mr Modi arrived at the UN with a thousand supporters cheering him on, or as he alighted from his vehicle to glad-hand curious onlookers, it was evident that India's leadership had emerged from the conference chambers and meeting rooms of international diplomacy to make a mark on the imaginations of people who have no place behind those closed doors.

The prime minister's speech to the UN General Assembly was a strong one. It was marked by a soaring internationalism that one could unembarrassedly call Nehruvian, effective messaging on environmentalism and terrorism, and a good response to Pakistan's needling on Kashmir. I did not hesitate, when asked by Barkha Dutt on NDTV, to award Mr Modi's performance at the podium an 'A', a high rating indeed in the long and largely uninspiring annals of prime ministerial speeches at the UN.

By speaking in Hindi at the UN, Mr Modi reasserted his now-familiar brand of nativism and reached out to his principal audience back home. There was nothing intrinsically wrong with doing so; though Hindi is not one of the six official languages of the United Nations, leaders may speak in another one, provided they bear the costs of interpretation. Mr Modi is very much more comfortable in Hindi than in his somewhat wooden and stilted English, so he was right to play to his own strengths. The price he paid for that was that everyone in attendance at the General Assembly hall heard him through the filter of a translation—and his audience was not as attentive as he deserved.

The dangers of extempore speaking in international affairs also became apparent when the PM referred carelessly to Pakistan-Occupied Kashmir as 'Pakistan'—unwise for an Indian prime minister, given that New Delhi still claims the territory to be ours. The official written transcript put out by the Indian delegation hastily corrected the error, but there must have been some gleeful chortling in Islamabad over the apparent relinquishing of a perennial Indian claim.

The visit to Ground Zero, site of the 9/11 terrorist attacks, was an excellent idea and situated India firmly on the right side on the issue of international terrorism. Pushing at the UN for a Comprehensive Convention on Terrorism was also well taken, though we still have a lot of work to do to overcome the reservations of many Islamic countries about the idea of such a convention and the specifics of the draft text we have been promoting.

Dropping in at a rock concert for charity at Central Park and saying a few words to the crowd there was a neat trick. One cannot imagine any other Indian prime minister doing it. Mr Modi is well on his way to creating a distinctively different prime ministership that is singularly his. Whether that can be leveraged to India's benefit, and not just for the PM's PR, remains to be seen.

The Madison Square Garden extravaganza went exactly as planned, even if it left some observers bemused. Mr Modi wanted to doff his cap to his enthusiastic supporters in the US, who had stood by him during the dark days of the visa denial and contributed heavily to his electioneering campaign efforts. His remarks were clearly addressed to them and to his broader circle of supporters across the US and of course in India: it was, in effect, a political campaign speech conducted on foreign soil. It inspired the audience, which was overwhelmingly BJP in orientation, and showcased the kind of crowds an Indian leader can command in the US. But though it was an Indian-American celebration of India in America, it received very little traction in the mainstream American media.

For all the razzmatazz, its relevance to Mr Modi's overall trip, however, was debateable. Perhaps it might have served to remind his critics in the US government how popular he is and that he should not be trifled with, but they knew that already. Perhaps, by having forty-one US Congressmen waiting on stage for his arrival, he was signalling to Indian-Americans that he embodied their own increased political clout in the US, which they should not shy away from using in defence of the motherland. But at bottom it was a self-indulgent love-fest for a leader who never seems to tire of reaffirming his larger-than-life heroic status in the public eye.

The subtext of his New York peregrinations is amply clear, and he wants us all to know it: Prime Minister Modi has arrived, and the rest of the world had better pay attention.

✍

In Washington, though, Mr Modi had very much less to show for himself. If his encounter with Chinese president Xi Jinping was marked by breathless PR about an imminent $100 billion investment, whose reduction to $30 billion amid reports of Chinese military incursions left a sour taste in Indian mouths, expectations of his meetings with President Obama were decidedly pitched at a lower key. This was as it should be: just months ago, Mr Modi featured on the USA's visa-ban list for failing to prevent the Gujarat killings of 2002, and this was more of an opportunity to restore normalcy than to be serenaded by his hosts. And it turned out to be just as well that there were no great expectations from the visit, since there were no great breakthroughs either.

The US is not a country from which one returns clutching big-ticket promises of investment: American capitalists are, in any case, much less amenable to government direction than their Chinese counterparts. Nor is Washington, a notoriously worldly-wise city, susceptible to Mr Modi's brand of alliterative rhetoric. The 3 Ds and 5 Ts that are so rapturously received by Mr Modi's Indian audiences leave Washington cold. The Americans have heard great sound-bytes before. What they are looking for is action, not words; results, not hype.

Here, Mr Modi's government still has a long way to go. Mr Modi's promises of translating India's demographics into a manufacturing engine for the world are precisely what the UPA government had promised, but progress in implementing such a vision has been slow, given the enormity of the challenge facing the country. Meanwhile, on concrete issues where Americans want deliverables from India—backing off its obstructiveness on the WTO talks, removing barriers to trade and investment, easing the entry of US nuclear businesses and pharmaceutical companies—Mr Modi had little to offer but words. On WTO, his pieties about India's food security masked a cynical devotion to the profits of the middlemen who are a reliable vote-bank for the BJP; on nuclear liability, the onerous clauses in the current law had been introduced by his own party in Parliament. On pharma, Mr Modi's surrender to American dictates had already been announced before he got there, much to the dismay of Indian patients who will now have to pay much more for patented American medicines that they have been getting in generic form at a hundredth the price.

In turn, India too had hoped for some good news from the US, notably in willingness to aid Indian defence production by offering state-of-the-art equipment to Indian manufacturers, and the transfer of environmentally-friendly green technologies at an affordable price. On neither issue was any concrete announcement forthcoming.

Instead, the Indian leader was fobbed off with a poetically-titled Joint Vision Statement, 'Chalein Saath Saath: Forward Together We Go', a joint op-ed in the names of the US president and Indian prime minister, and a greeting in Gujarati at the White House. These are the sort of optics that Washington has long specialized in offering visiting Indian PMs: remember the hype about Prime Minister Manmohan Singh getting the first-ever state banquet of the Obama Administration in 2009? Once again, though, there was little beyond the blather: bromides abounded about democracy, common values, peace, and partnership, weasel words that have long since been sucked of any meaning by overuse. An American writer in the *Wall Street Journal*, Michael Kugelman, summarized the visit as 'long on pageantry and short on substance'. It is hard for the most die-hard Indian chauvinist to disagree.

After the near-hysteria that greeted Mr Modi in New York, Washington was a sobering reminder that the really hard work of building a strategic partnership requires a lot more than skilful public relations.

But it would be wrong to see the Washington leg of Mr Modi's US tour purely as an anti-climax. By going to the US capital, Mr Modi administered a necessary corrective to the negative image many American opinion-makers had of him. He achieved the basic objective of introducing himself to those who had not been his friends, and to showing American politicians and business leaders that he is a man they can do business with. How much business they will do depends largely on how well he is able to translate his words into tangible outcomes, and the vision of his speeches into actual solutions.

Mr Modi starts off from a solid platform of sound relations. Democrats and Republicans in the White House have both been responsible for this development. President Obama's successful visit to India in 2010 and his historic speech to a joint session of Parliament capped the most significant recent milestone in India–US relations. This was one of many encounters Obama has had with then Prime Minister Manmohan Singh in various forums since his assumption of office, often in multilateral summits like the G-20, and it set the seal on the consolidation of a relationship that has changed dramatically over the last decade. Then, when Narendra Modi was elected prime minister of India in May 2014, there were worries that the US's earlier visa ban on him, for his complicity in the pogroms that took more than a thousand lives in Gujarat in 2002, would bedevil the relationship. That didn't happen: he was received with great warmth and hospitality in Washington. But if the trip achieved Mr Modi's own rehabilitation as a worthy and befitting Indian interlocutor for the US president, it is hard to see what else was accomplished for India.

Throughout 2014, we saw Modi the campaigner. Soon, we will have to start seeing Modi the implementer, delivering the results his rhetoric has promised. Once he does so—if he does so—Washington won't be the only world capital that will give him a much better reception when he goes back.

HAVE WE FORGOTTEN KHOBRAGADE?

Reports of the prime minister's visit to the US were conspicuously silent on whether he raised the issue of the still-pending charges against Indian diplomat Devyani Khobragade in the United States, but all indications are that it did not feature in his talking points. It would be a disgrace if New Delhi developed amnesia on the entire affair.

Months after US authorities arrested India's Deputy Consul-General in New York, Devyani Khobragade, outside her children's school, and charged her with paying her Indian domestic worker a salary below the US minimum wage, relations between the two countries, which for some years had featured great amity, remained tense. The UPA government reacted with fury to the mistreatment of an official enjoying diplomatic immunity, and public indignation over the strip-search and 'cavity search' of Khobragade, who was detained with common criminals before being released on bail, was widespread and near-unanimous. Even our mild-mannered then Prime Minister Manmohan Singh declared the US' conduct 'deplorable', National Security Advisor Shivshankar Menon called the US action 'despicable' and 'barbaric', and Foreign Minister Salman Khurshid refused to take a conciliatory phone call from Secretary of State John Kerry.

Emotions ran high in India's Parliament and television talk shows. In writing to her diplomatic colleagues after her arrest, Khobragade, who denied all of the charges, mentioned that she 'broke down many times as the indignities of repeated handcuffing, stripping and cavity searches, swabbing, holdup with common criminals and drug addicts were all being imposed upon me'. A former Indian foreign minister, Yashwant Sinha, publicly called for retaliation against gay American diplomats in India, whose sexual orientation and domestic arrangements are now illegal after a recent Supreme Court ruling. The government did not take him seriously, but that such a suggestion could be made is a measure of how inflamed passions have become.

Some retaliation occurred. The initial American excuse (that foreign consuls in the US enjoy a lower level of immunity than other diplomats) led New Delhi to wake up to the very different situation that prevails in India, where US consular officials enjoy a number of privileges unavailable to their Indian counterparts in the US. These privileges—including full-fledged diplomatic ID cards, access to the restricted customs areas of airports, tax-free shipments of items for personal consumption and no questions asked about the terms of their employment of local domestic staff—were swiftly withdrawn. The cardinal principal of diplomatic relations is reciprocity, and India realized it had been naïve in extending courtesies to the US that it was not receiving in return.

In addition, bollards and barriers that had unilaterally been placed by the US embassy on the street in front of its complex in New Delhi, and which blocked free circulation on a public road, were removed by the Delhi Police. India had tolerated the barriers in a spirit of friendship, but when it realized the same spirit was not being extended to it, it reviewed its approach. The government, however, reiterated its commitment to the security of US embassy premises, outside which Indian police pickets were reinforced.

Tempers remained inflamed, with then US Ambassador to India Nancy Powell, in a New Year's message to Indians, ruefully acknowledging that ties have been 'jolted by very different reactions to issues involving one of your consular officers and her domestic worker'. Secretary of State John Kerry also expressed 'regret' over the incident. But Indians were bewildered that the US State Department would so willfully jeopardize a relationship that Washington had been describing as 'strategic', over a practice routinely followed by foreign diplomats for decades. Most developing country diplomats take domestic staff with them on overseas assignments, paying them a good salary by their national standards, plus a cost differential for working aboard, and perquisites including (in Khobragade's case) a fully furnished room in a pricey Manhattan apartment, a free television set, mobile phone, medical insurance and tickets home. The cash part of the salary might have been low by US standards—Khobragade herself, as a mid-ranking Indian diplomat, earns less than what the US considers a fair wage for her maid—but with the other benefits, was attractive for a domestic helper. More to the point, Khobragade did not find her maid in the American labour market and 'exploit' her—she brought her from India to help her in her representational duties, on an official passport, with a US visa given for the purpose. In almost no other country are the local labour laws of the host country applied in such a manner to a foreign diplomat's personal staff.

Privately, American diplomats expressed frustration at their helplessness in the face of theatrical grandstanding by the ambitious New York prosecutor Preet Bharara, an Indian-American who has been seeking political legitimacy with a series of high-profile prosecutions of Indians in America. For once, however, the zealous American law-enforcer seemed to have slipped up on his homework, since Khobragade was arrested at a time when she enjoyed full diplomatic (and not just consular) immunity as an adviser to India's UN mission during the General Assembly. The state department's handling of the matter—which included giving a green light for Khobragade's arrest—was, to say the least, inept.

It was only when a court ruled that Khobragade enjoyed full diplomatic immunity at the time of her arrest that she was released and flown out of the country. The authorities promptly slapped fresh charges on her, which now make it impossible for her to visit the US without facing arrest on landing. Surprisingly, despite all the bonhomie attendant upon new Prime Minister Narendra Modi's visit to Washington in September 2014, the US has shown no signs of moving to drop the charges to defuse the crisis. (Ironically, Khobragade's husband and children are American citizens; she is in effect barred from visiting them in their own country.)

To make matters worse, an air of conspiracy surrounded the spiriting out of India, just before the arrest, of the maid's family on US 'trafficking' visas. The suggestion that an Indian diplomat in a wage dispute with her maid is by implication guilty of human trafficking understandably riles Indian diplomats, as does Khobragade being treated in detention like a drug-runner. The American habit of imposing its worldview self-righteously on others is deeply unwelcome. To most Indians, you can't try to dress up common discourtesy as moral virtue.

Indian–American relations had been riding high as a celebration of shared democracy, common concerns about China, increasing trade and investment, and an absence of geopolitical conflict. The Khobragade affair suggests, however, that all this is not enough: to sustain a strategic partnership, what you need above all is mutual respect.

India had handled American diplomats with a generosity of spirit that it felt the bilateral relationship deserved. Now, with the same spirit shown to be lacking from the other side, the friendship has suffered. Can we afford to just drop the whole matter, leaving an Indian diplomat with criminal charges pending against her in a foreign court?

Until the US develops and displays a regard for the sensitivities, pride and honour of other peoples and cultures, it will continue to be resented around the world. And until the Indian government insists on standing up for those who serve it around the world, we should drop all talk of a robust foreign policy, let alone of aspiring to become a superpower. Superpowers don't allow other countries to put their diplomats in the dock, and they certainly don't leave their faithful servants in the lurch.

THE GLOBAL INDIAN

No other country has anything like it—an annual jamboree of its diaspora, conducted with great fanfare by its government. India has been doing it, with great success, for a decade, timed to recall the return to India of the most famous Indian expatriate of them all, Mahatma Gandhi, who alighted from his South African ship in Bombay on 9 January 1915. Each January, a selected Indian city overflows with expatriate Indians celebrating their connection to their motherland. The centenary of Gandhiji's return will be marked by the grandest Pravasi Bharatiya Divas (Expatriate Indians' Day) of them all so far, slated for the Mahatma's—and by no coincidence, Prime Minister Modi's— home state, Ahmedabad.

India is the only country that has an official acronym for its expatriates— NRIs, or Non-Resident Indians. In my book *India: From Midnight to the Millennium*, I suggested, only half-jokingly, that the question is whether NRI should stand for 'Not Really Indian' or 'Never Relinquished India'. Of course, the nearly 25 million people of Indian descent who live abroad fall into both categories. But the nearly 2,000 delegates who flock to India from over sixty countries for each Pravasi Bharatiya Divas (or PBD, as our bureaucracy has inevitably abbreviated it) are firmly in the latter camp. They come to India to affirm their claim to it.

It is curiously appropriate that the event, organized by the Ministry for Overseas Indian Affairs (another unique Indian creation) in cooperation with the Federation of Indian Chambers of Commerce and Industry, take place in Gujarat in 2015. After all, though the state of Gujarat contains just 3 per cent of the country's population, it accounts, together with comparably modestly-sized Kerala, for the largest number of Indians living and working abroad.

And what a collection the delegates make: the president of Mauritius, the former governor-general of New Zealand, former prime ministers of Fiji and Guyana, Malaysian politicians, Gulf-based entrepreneurs, tycoons from Hong Kong, and corporate titans from the United States, all united by the simple fact of shared heritage—the undeniable reality that even exiles cannot escape in the mirror. As former Prime Minister Manmohan Singh put it in one of his inaugural addresses to the gathering, they were united, too, by an 'idea of Indianness'.

Indianness embodies the diversity and pluralism of both the country and its diaspora. India was again using the Pravasi Bharatiya Divas celebrations to provide Indians—including former Indians—from all corners of the world the assurance that they were indeed at home.

There have been four waves of Indian emigration. The first, in pre-colonial

times, included those who left as travellers, teachers, and traders; the second
involved the forced migration of Indian labour as indentured servants of the
British Empire; the third was the tragic displacement of millions by the horrors
of Partition; and now we have the contemporary phenomenon of skilled Indians
seeking new challenges and opportunities in our globalized world.

I would probably divide the fourth wave further into two distinct categories:
highly educated Indians, often staying on after studies abroad in places like the
US; and more modestly qualified (but often harder-working) migrants, from
taxi drivers to shop assistants, who generally see their migration as temporary
and who remit a larger share of their income to India than their higher-
earning counterparts do. But both sets of fourth-wave migrants remain closely
connected to their motherland.

The ease of communications and travel today enables expatriates to be
engaged with India in a way that was simply not available to the plantation
worker in Mauritius or Guyana a century ago. To tap into this sense of
allegiance and loyalty through an organized public gathering was an inspired
idea, which India continues to build upon each year.

India regards its successful expatriates as a source of pride, support, and
investment. According to a recent US survey, Indian-American households'
median annual income is nearly $88,000, more than $12,000 higher than
Japanese-American households and more than $20,000 higher than the national
average. That kind of success is not merely at the elite end of the scale: in
England today, Indian restaurants employ more people than the steel, coal, and
shipbuilding industries combined. (Many are the ways in which the Empire
can strike back.)

The presence of successful and influential Indians in so many countries
is also a source of direct support for India, as they influence not just popular
attitudes, but also government policies, to the benefit of India. There is also a
political benefit for the politicians who can tap into their base: Kerala politicians
have often travelled to the Gulf in quest of support, and the rapturous reception
our new prime minister received from 18,000 raucous NRIs at what is being
dubbed 'Modison Square Garden' in New York shows the effectiveness of his
outreach to Indian-Americans. India also received more than $70 billion in
remittances in 2013—more than double the level of inward foreign direct
investment—and most of it came from blue-collar workers in the Gulf sending
money home to support their families.

There is undoubtedly a utilitarian aspect to the Pravasi Bharatiya Divas
celebrations, as suggested by the many parallel seminars run each time by
state governments to attract expatriate investment. The importance of diaspora
financing—from the remittances of working-class Indians that have transformed
Kerala's countryside to the millions poured into high-tech businesses in

Bangalore or Gurgaon by Silicon Valley investors—simply cannot be minimized, especially during a global financial crisis.

But we should not get carried away: overseas Indians still invest a lower proportion of their resources in India than overseas Chinese do in China. Encouraging them to do more, and giving them emotional reasons to do more, is certainly a worthwhile task for the Indian government—and an overt goal of the annual conclave.

Sometimes the real value of a conference, however, lies in the conferring. Indians have learned to appreciate how much it means to allow NRIs from all over the world the chance to share their experiences, celebrate their commonalities, exchange ideas, and swap business cards. Because when India allows its pravasis to feel at home, India itself is strengthened. I can think of one more meaning of NRI: the National Reserve of India.

INDIA: THE UNLOVED GIANT?

One temptation every sensible analyst must resist is, of course, the urge to generalize from the particular—especially when the particular is anecdotal and trivial. And yet sitting in the stands in Colombo in September 2012, watching India being thrashed by Australia in the world cricket T-20 tournament, was sobering not only to the cricket fan in me. The student of foreign policy was shaken as well, because the Sri Lankan crowd, almost to a man, shouted and cheered and applauded every four and six by the rampaging Australian batsmen. When the game ended, the abject Indian failure was greeted with gleeful joy by the throngs, who sang and danced and blew triumphant horns outside the stadium as if their own team had triumphed.

My wife was upset enough to take on the Sri Lankans sitting near her. 'Whenever we see Sri Lanka playing anyone, we always cheer for your team,' she expostulated. 'Why are you so anti-us?' She was greeted with an embarrassed silence, for no answer was possible.

What does this undoubtedly trivial experience tell us about ourselves, and the ways others see us? I won't draw sweeping conclusions about Indo-Sri Lankan relations or specific details of Indian foreign policy in the island state, because this was a cricket match, not an international relations seminar. But there's no doubt that being a giant neighbour is not exactly an asset in the 'how to make friends and influence people' sweepstakes. The Mexicans used to lament that they were 'so far from God and so close to the United States'. The Sri Lankans probably feel the same way about us.

OK, so we can't help being as big as we are—we account for some 70 per cent of the subcontinent's population and some 80 per cent of its GDP. We do take up a lot of room and we can't be ignored by our neighbours. If we're resented merely because of our size, there's nothing we can do about it: we are not going to apologize for being ourselves. But if basically friendly neighbours like the Sri Lankans relish seeing India put down, even on the cricket field, it suggests we haven't done a good enough job of earning their affection.

A rising India has an obvious interest in the success of its neighbours, since a stable neighbourhood contributes to an enabling environment for India's own domestic objectives, while disturbances on India's borders can act as a constraint on India's continued rise. As Prime Minister Manmohan Singh remarked during his October 2011 visit to Bangladesh, 'India will not be able to realize its own destiny without the partnership of its South Asian neighbours.'

India's geopolitical strategists, both inside and outside government, have tended to see India's interests globally (witness the attention paid to relations with

the United States, or India's role at the UN and the Non-Aligned Movement).
In our own neighbourhood, they have focused mainly on the threats to the
nation's rise from the Pakistani military and its terrorist proxies, and to a
somewhat lesser degree from the emergence of China and its impact on India's
stature in the region. The result has been that the rest of the neighbourhood has
sometimes been treated with neglect rather than close attention, and occasionally
with a condescension that some have seen as arrogance.

In Nepal, India's not-always-positive reputation for interference in that
country's domestic affairs has generally not been undeserved. The border with
Bangladesh has witnessed more shooting incidents in recent years than is
explicable or reasonable. Relations with Sri Lanka remain complicated both by
the history of India's prior involvement—support for the Tamil militancy, then
a disastrous military intervention that engaged Indian troops in battles with
the Liberation Tigers of Tamil Eelam (LTTE) and resulted in our ignominious
withdrawal—as well as by India's legitimate desire, made more urgent by our
own domestic political imperatives, to see a political accommodation on the
island that respects the aspirations of the Tamils. In all cases, India's prioritization
of relations with global powers like the United States and China and our
disproportionate focus in the neighbourhood on Pakistan have come at the
cost of due attention to our other neighbours.

Of course it would be wrong to cite these examples as a reason to place
the entire onus for any subcontinental dysfunctionalities on India alone. The
fact is that there are a number of challenges that continue to beset the region
and that hold back the true potential of our countries, individually as well
as collectively. These include terrorism and extremism, and the use of these
as instruments of state policy; and the daily terror of hunger, unemployment,
illiteracy, disease and the effects of climate change. And less obvious but equally
potent, restrictions on regional trade and transit that belong to an older, more
mercantilist century.

That many Indian states, in India's federal polity, have serious issues with
their neighbours (concerns in Bengal and Bihar about movement of goods and
people from Bangladesh and Nepal, for instance, or the treatment of Tamils in
Sri Lanka, and at one time Pakistani support for separatist Khalistani militancy
in Punjab) injects domestic political compulsions into New Delhi's thinking,
particularly in an era of coalition governance, where the views of political
allies must be imperatively taken into account.

A political tendency in some of the neighbouring countries to adopt 'blame
India' as a default internal political strategy has in turn bedevilled perceptions.
These are among the factors that drag the people of the subcontinent back
from the path of sustained peace, development and prosperity.

For the Indian foreign policy-maker, there is no getting away from the fundamental verities underpinning our relationships on the subcontinent. A subcontinent at peace benefits all who live in it; one troubled by hostility, destructive rivalry, conflict and terror pulls us all down. To achieve it, the Modi government needs to show our neighbours that apart from being large, we also mean well.

III

THE LEGACY

THE RAVAGES OF COLONIALISM

In September 2014, on the very day that Scotland was deciding its future, six of us gathered in London to debate the past.

To commemorate the 400th anniversary of the British presence in India—King James I's envoy, Sir Thomas Roe, arrived at the court of Emperor Jahangir in 1614—the Indo-British Heritage Trust held a debate, in the chamber of the UK Supreme Court, on the motion 'This House believes that the Indian subcontinent benefited more than it lost from the experience of British colonialism.' Needless to say, I spoke against, alongside two Indophile Brits, authors William Dalrymple and Nick Robins. The proposers were Pakistan's Nilofar Bakhtiar, an editor, Martin Bell, former BBC war correspondent, and Kwasi Kwarteng, a Conservative Party MP of African descent.

It was a lively affair. As the debate began, its Chair, Labour MP Keith Vaz, called for an initial vote, which went 35 to 28 for the motion. When it was over, voting took place again, and the needle had moved dramatically: 26 to 42 against. The anti-colonialists had carried the day.

Why was our case so compelling? At the beginning of the 18th century India's share of the world economy was 23 per cent, as large as all of Europe put together. By the time we won independence, it had dropped to less than 4 per cent. The reason was simple: India was governed for the benefit of Britain. Britain's rise for 200 years was financed by its depredations in India.

Britain's Industrial Revolution was built on the de-industrialization of India—the destruction of Indian textiles and their replacement by manufacturing in England, using Indian raw material and exporting the finished products back to India and the rest of the world. The handloom weavers of Bengal had produced and exported some of the world's most desirable fabrics, especially cheap but fine muslins, some light as 'woven air'. Britain's response was to cut off the thumbs of Bengali weavers, break their looms and impose duties and tariffs on Indian cloth, while flooding India and the world with cheaper fabric from the new satanic steam mills of Britain. Weavers became beggars, manufacturing collapsed; the population of Dhaka, which was once the great centre of muslin production, fell by 90 per cent. So instead of a great exporter of finished products, India became an importer of British ones, while its share of world exports fell from 27 per cent to 2 per cent.

Colonialists like Robert Clive bought their 'rotten boroughs' in England with the proceeds of their loot in India (loot, by the way, was a word they took into their dictionaries as well as their habits), while publicly marvelling at their own self-restraint in not stealing even more than they did. And the British had the gall to call him 'Clive of India', as if he belonged to the country, when all he really did was to ensure that much of the country belonged to him.

By the end of the 19th century, India was Britain's biggest cash cow, the world's biggest purchaser of British exports and the source of highly paid employment for British civil servants—all at India's own expense. We literally paid for our own oppression.

As Britain ruthlessly exploited India, between fifteen and twenty-nine million Indians died tragically unnecessary deaths from starvation. The last large-scale famine to take place in India was under British rule; none has taken place since, since free democracies don't let their people starve to death. Some 4 million Bengalis died in the Great Bengal Famine of 1943 after Winston Churchill deliberately ordered the diversion of food from starving Indian civilians to well-supplied British soldiers and European stockpiles. 'The starvation of anyway underfed Bengalis is less serious' than that of 'sturdy Greeks', he argued. In any case, the famine was their fault, for 'breeding like rabbits'. When officers of conscience pointed out in a telegram to the prime minister the scale of the tragedy caused by his decisions, Churchill's only response was to ask peevishly 'why hasn't Gandhi died yet?'

British imperialism had long justified itself with the pretence that it was enlightened despotism, conducted for the benefit of the governed. Churchill's inhumane conduct in 1943 gave the lie to this myth. But it had been battered for two centuries already: British imperialism had triumphed not just by conquest and deception on a grand scale but by blowing rebels to bits from the mouths of cannons, massacring unarmed protestors at Jallianwallah Bagh and upholding iniquity through institutionalized racism. Whereas as late as the 1940s it was possible for a black African to say with pride, 'moi, je suis Francais', no Indian in the colonial era was ever allowed to feel British; he was always a subject, never a citizen.

(No wonder the sun never set on the British Empire: even God couldn't trust the Englishman in the dark.)

What are the arguments for British colonialism benefiting the subcontinent? It is often claimed that the British bequeathed India its political unity. But India had enjoyed cultural and geographical unity throughout the ages, going back to Emperor Ashoka in the 3rd century BC and Adi Shankara travelling from Kerala to Kashmir and from Dwarka to Puri in the 7th century AD, establishing his temples everywhere. As a result, the yearning for political unity existed throughout; warriors and kings tried to dominate the entire subcontinent, usually unsuccessfully. But with modern transport and communications, national unity would have been fulfilled without colonial rule, just as in equally fragmented 19th century Italy. And what political unity can we celebrate when the horrors of Partition (1 million dead, 13 million displaced, billions of rupees of property destroyed) were the direct result of deliberate British policies of 'divide and rule' that fomented religious antagonisms?

The construction of the Indian Railways is often pointed to as benefit of British rule, ignoring the obvious fact that many countries have built railways without having to be colonized to do so. Nor were the railways laid to serve the Indian public. They were intended to help the British get around, and above all to carry Indian raw materials to the ports to be shipped to Britain. The movement of people was incidental except when it served colonial interests; no effort was made to ensure that supply matched demand for mass transport.

In fact the Indian Railways were a big British colonial scam. British shareholders made absurd amounts of money by investing in the railways, where the government guaranteed extravagant returns on capital, double that of British government stock, because the difference was paid for by Indian taxes. Thanks to British rapacity, a mile of Indian railways cost double that of a mile in Canada and Australia.

It was a splendid racket for the British, who made all the profits, controlled the technology and supplied all the equipment, which meant once again that the benefits went out of India. It was a scheme described at the time as 'private enterprise at public risk'. Private British enterprise, public Indian risk.

Despite such flagrant exploitation, apologists for the British have sought to claim credit for giving India the rule of law. Of course we are glad to have it, but Britain has saddled us with an adversarial system, excessively bogged down in procedural formalities—a legacy of interminable trials and long-pending cases, far removed from India's traditional systems of justice. And laws are enforced by a colonial-era police system based on the Irish constabulary, not the London bobby—under colonialism, policing was an instrument of oppression rather than empowerment, and we are still living with the consequences of that.

Still, it is argued that Britain left us with self-governing institutions and the trappings of democracy. To anyone who knows how hard it was to win a smidgen of self-government after many broken British promises, this is preposterous. Let me cite one who actually lived through the colonial experience, Jawaharlal Nehru. British rule, Nehru wrote in 1936 in a letter to a liberal Englishman, Lord Lothian, is 'based on an extreme form of widespread violence and the only sanction is fear. It suppresses the usual liberties which are supposed to be essential to the growth of a people; it crushes the adventurous, the brave, the sensitive, and encourages the timid, the opportunist and time-serving, the sneak and the bully. It surrounds itself with a vast army of spies and informers and agents provocateurs. Is this the atmosphere in which the more desirable virtues grow or democratic institutions flourish?' Nehru went on to speak of 'the crushing of human dignity and decency, the injuries to the soul as well as the body' which 'degrades those who use it as well as those who suffer from it'.

This injury to India's soul—the very basis of a nation's self-respect—is what is always overlooked by apologists for colonialism.

The English language comes next on the claimed credit list. It too was not a deliberate gift but an instrument of colonialism. As Macaulay explained the purpose of English education: 'We must do our best to form a class who may be interpreters between us and the millions whom we govern; a class of persons, Indians in blood and colour, but English in taste, in opinions, in morals and in intellect.' The language was taught to a few to serve as intermediaries between the rulers and the ruled. That we seized the English language and turned it into an instrument for our own liberation was to our credit, not by British design.

(I cheerfully conceded that we couldn't have enjoyed Shakespeare and P.G. Wodehouse without the English language. But a non-colonial Britain could have sent us a whole bunch of toothsome VSOs instead of sturdy Welsh master sergeants and a free India would have learned the language better!)

The day we defeated the motion, Scottish voters rejected the proposal to leave the United Kingdom. But it's often forgotten what cemented the Union in the first place: the loaves and fishes available to Scots from participation in the exploits of the East India Company. Before 1707 the Scots had tried to colonize various parts of the world, but all had failed. After Union with England, a disproportionate number of Scots were employed in the Indian colonial enterprise, as soldiers, sailors, merchants, agents and employees. Though the Scots made up barely 9 per cent of Britain's people, they accounted for 25 per cent of those employed by the British in India. Earnings from colonialism in India pulled Scotland out of poverty and helped make it prosperous. With India gone, no wonder the bonds are loosening...

FORGOTTEN HEROES: INDIA IN WORLD WAR I

Exactly one hundred years after the 'guns of August' boomed across the European continent in 1914, the world wallowed in commemorations of that seminal event. The Great War, as it was called then, was described at the time as 'the war to end all wars'. Ironically, the eruption of an even more destructive conflict twenty years after the end of this one meant that it is now known as the First World War. Those who fought and died in the First World War would have had little idea that there would so soon be a Second.

But while the war took the flower of Europe's youth to their premature graves, snuffing out the lives of a generation of talented poets, artists, cricketers and others whose genius bled into the trenches, it also involved soldiers from faraway lands that had little to do with Europe's bitter traditional hatreds.

The role and sacrifices of Australians, New Zealanders, Canadians and South Africans have been celebrated for some time in books and novels, and even rendered immortal on celluloid in award-winning films like *Gallipoli* and *Breaker Morant*. Of the 1.3 million Indian troops who served in the conflict, however, you hear very little. As many as 74,187 Indian soldiers died during the war and another 67,000 were wounded. Their stories, and their heroism, have long been omitted from popular histories of the war, or relegated to the footnotes.

India contributed a number of divisions and brigades to the European, Mediterranean, West Asian, North African and East African theatres of war. In Europe, Indian soldiers were among the first victims who suffered the horrors of the trenches. They were killed in droves before the war was into its second year and bore the brunt of many a German offensive.

It was Indian jawans who stopped the German advance at Ypres in the autumn of 1914, soon after the war broke out, while the British were still recruiting and training their own forces. More than a thousand of them died at Gallipoli, thanks to Churchill's folly. Nearly 700,000 Indian sepoys fought in Mesopotamia against the Ottoman Empire, Germany's ally.

Letters sent by Indian soldiers in Europe to their family members in their villages back home speak an evocative language of cultural dislocation and tragedy. 'The shells are pouring like rain in the monsoon,' declared one. 'The corpses cover the country like sheaves of harvested corn,' wrote another.

These men were undoubtedly heroes: pitchforked into battle in unfamiliar lands, in climatic conditions they were neither used to nor prepared for, fighting an enemy of whom they had no knowledge, risking their lives every day for little more than pride. Yet they were destined to remain largely unknown once the war was over: neglected by the British, for whom they fought, and ignored by their own country, from which they came.

Part of the reason is that they were not fighting for their own country. The soldiers were all volunteers: soldiering was their profession. They served the very British Empire that was oppressing their own people back home.

The British raised men and money from India, as well as large supplies of food, cash and ammunition, collected both by British taxation of Indians and from the nominally autonomous princely states. It was estimated at the time that the value of India's contribution in cash and kind amounted to 88,000,000 pounds sterling, worth some 30 billion pounds in today's money.

While raising men and money from India, the British had insincerely promised to deliver self-rule to India at the end of the war. Perhaps, had they kept that pledge, the sacrifices of India's First World War soldiers might have been seen in their homeland as a contribution to India's freedom.

But the British broke their word, despite strong support for the war effort from Indian leaders. Mahatma Gandhi, who returned to his homeland for good from South Africa in January 1915, supported the war, as he had supported the British in the Boer War. India was wracked by high taxation—and the high inflation accompanying it—to support the war, while the disruption of trade caused by the conflict led to widespread economic losses. All this while the country was reeling from a raging influenza epidemic that took many lives. Yet Indian nationalists did not seek to take advantage of Britain's vulnerability by inciting rebellions, or even disturbances, against the Empire. Instead, Indians rallied to the British cause: there were no mutinies against the British, though political unrest did continue in Punjab and Bengal.

By 1917, as the Allies—newly reinforced by the United States—began assuming the upper hand in the war, Indian nationalists began demanding recognition of their compatriots' sacrifices. Sir Edwin Montagu, the Secretary of State for India, responded with the historic 'August announcement' in Parliament, declaring that Britain's policy for India was 'increasing association of Indians in every branch of the administration and the gradual development of self-governing institutions with a view to the progressive realization of responsible government in India as an integral part of the British Empire'. This was widely understood to mean that at the end of the war India would receive the Dominion status hitherto reserved for the 'White Commonwealth'.

It was not to be. When the war ended in triumph for Britain, India was denied its promised reward. Instead of self-government, the British imposed the repressive Rowlatt Act, which vested the viceroy's government with extraordinary powers to quell 'sedition' against the Empire by silencing and censoring the press, detaining political activists without trial, and arresting without a warrant any individuals suspected of treason against the Empire. Public protests against this draconian legislation were ruthlessly quelled. The worst incident was the Jallianwallah Bagh massacre of April 1919, when Brigadier-General Reginald Dyer ordered his troops to fire, without warning, on 15,000 unarmed and non-violent men, women, and children demonstrating peacefully in an enclosed garden in Amritsar, killing 1,499 and wounding 1,137.

The fact that the British hailed Dyer as a hero, raising a handsome purse to reward him for his deed, marked the final rupture between British imperialism and its Indian subjects. The wartime hopes of Dominion status and 'progressive self-government' were dashed forever; Gandhi and the nationalists concluded that nothing short of independence would end the immoral injustice of British rule in India.

With British perfidy providing such a sour ending to the narrative of a war in which India had given its all and been spurned in return, Indian nationalists felt that the country had nothing for which to thank its soldiers. They had merely gone abroad to serve their foreign masters. Losing your life in a foreign war fought at the behest of your colonial rulers was an occupational hazard; it did not qualify to be hailed as a form of national service. Or so most Indian nationalists thought, and they allowed the heroism of their compatriots to be forgotten. When the world commemorated the Fiftieth Anniversary of the First World War in 1964, there was scarcely a mention of India's soldiers anywhere, least of all in India.

India's absence from the commemorations, and its failure to honour the dead, were not a major surprise. Nor was the lack of First World War memorials in the country: the general feeling was that India, freshly freed from the imperial yoke, was ashamed of its soldiers' participation in a colonial war and saw nothing to celebrate. The India Gate in New Delhi, built in 1931, is a popular monument, visited by hundreds daily who have no idea that it commemorates the Indian soldiers who lost their lives fighting in World War I. Historical amnesia about the First World War is pervasive across India.

In the absence of a national war memorial, though, many Indians see it as the only venue to pay homage to those who have lost their lives in more recent conflicts. I have stood there many times, on the anniversaries of wars with China and Pakistan, and bowed my head without a thought for the men who died in foreign fields a century ago.

As a Member of Parliament, I had twice raised the demand for a national war memorial (after a visit to the hugely impressive Australian one in Canberra) and been told there were no plans to construct one here. It was therefore personally satisfying to me, and to many of my compatriots, when the Government of India announced in its budget for 2014-15 its intention finally to create a national war memorial. We are not a terribly militaristic society, but for a nation that has fought many wars and shed the blood of many heroes, and whose resolve may yet be tested in conflicts to come, it seems odd that there is no memorial to commemorate, honour and preserve the memories of those who have fought for India.

It appears that the centenary is finally forcing a rethink. The British have been flocking to an exhibition showcasing the role of the Indian troops; the French are making a film about the brown-skinned and turbaned men who fought to save their land from the Germans. Remarkable photographs have been unearthed of Indian soldiers in Europe and the Middle East, and these are enjoying a new lease of life online. Looking at them, it is impossible not to be moved by these young men, so visibly alien to their surroundings; some about to head off for battle, others nursing terrible wounds. For many Indians, curiosity has overcome the fading colonial-era resentments of British exploitation. Indians are beginning to see the soldiers of World War I as human beings, who took the spirit of their country to battlefields abroad. The Centre for Armed Forces Historical Research in Delhi is painstakingly working to retrieve memorabilia of that era and reconstruct the forgotten story of the 1.3 million Indian soldiers who had fought in the First World War.

The Commonwealth War Graves Commission maintains war cemeteries in India, mostly commemorating the Second World War rather than the First. The most famous epitaph of them all is inscribed at the Kohima War Cemetery in Nagaland. It reads: 'When you go home, tell them of us and say/ For your tomorrow, we gave our today.'

The Indian soldiers who died in the First World War could make no such claim. They gave their 'todays' for someone else's 'yesterdays'. They left behind orphans, but history has orphaned them as well.

It is a matter of quiet satisfaction that their overdue rehabilitation has now begun.

THE 1940s: WHERE IT ALL BEGAN

The 1940s were, to use a cliché, a decade of triumph and tragedy. They witnessed two instances of nationalist assertion—the Quit India Movement and the Indian National Army—that ended in failure; both inspired the nation, but the first resulted in Congress leaders being jailed and their movement driven underground, and the second had no discernible impact on British military might. The same decade saw the country win independence—a moment of birth that was also an abortion, since freedom came with the horrors of Partition, when East and West Pakistan were hacked off the stooped shoulders of India by the departing British. Before the 1940s were over, India and Pakistan were embroiled in war over Kashmir, whose consequences still affect us today. But they also saw the extraordinary work of the Constituent Assembly, which in January 1950 gave us the Constitution that laid the foundations for more than six decades of Indian democracy.

When the British government announced in early 1947 that they would withdraw from India, and that the transfer of power would be executed by the blue-blooded Lord Mountbatten, it was already apparent that Pakistan, in some form, would have to be created. The experience of the interim government had proved that the League was simply not going to work with the Congress in a united government of India. Jawaharlal Nehru nonetheless tried to prod leaders of the League into discussions on the new arrangements, which he still hoped would fall short of an absolute Partition. By early March, as communal rioting continued across northern India, even this hope had faded. Both Sardar Patel and Nehru agreed that, despite the Mahatma's refusal to contemplate such a prospect, the Congress had no alternative but to agree to partitioning Punjab and Bengal; the alternative (of a loose Indian union including a quasi-sovereign Pakistan) would neither be acceptable to the League nor result in a viable government for the rest of India.

Some critics see in all this an exhausted Jawaharlal's anxiety to end the tension once and for all; others suggest that he allowed his regard for the Mountbattens to trump his own principles. Such arguments do a great disservice to Jawaharlal Nehru. His correspondence at the time shows a statesman in great anguish trying to do the best for his country when all other options had failed. Communal violence and killings were a daily feature; so was Jinnah's complete unwillingness to co-operate with the Congress on any basis other than that it represented the Hindus and he the Muslims of India. As long as the British gave Jinnah a veto over every proposal he found uncongenial, there was little else Nehru could do. Nor is there evidence in the writings and reflections of the other leading Indian nationalists of the time that any of them had any better ideas. The only exception was Gandhi: the Mahatma went to Mountbatten and suggested that India could be kept united if Jinnah were offered the leadership of the whole country. Jawaharlal and Patel both gave that idea short shrift, and Mountbatten did not seem to take it seriously.

There is no doubt that Mountbatten seemed to proceed with unseemly haste, and that in so doing he swept the Indian leaders along. Nehru was convinced that Jinnah was capable of setting the country ablaze and destroying all that the nationalist movement had worked for: a division of India was preferable to its destruction. 'It is with no joy in my heart that I commend these proposals,' Nehru told his party, 'though I have no doubt in my mind that it is the right course.' The distinction between heart and head was poignant, and telling. On 3 June, Jawaharlal, Jinnah, and the Sikh leader Baldev Singh broadcast news of their acceptance of Partition to the country. 'We are little men serving a great cause,' Nehru declared. 'The India of geography, of history and tradition, the India of our minds and hearts, cannot change.'

But of course it could change: geography was to be hacked, history misread, tradition denied, minds and hearts torn apart. Jawaharlal imagined that the rioting and violence that had racked the country over the League's demand for Pakistan would die down once that demand had been granted, but he was wrong. The killing and mass displacement worsened as people sought frantically to be on the 'right' side of the lines the British were to draw across their homeland. Over a million people died in the savagery that accompanied the freedom of India and Pakistan; some 17 million were displaced, and countless properties destroyed and looted. Lines meant lives.

Reading the debates in the Constituent Assembly, as the founding fathers (and mothers) of India grappled with fundamental questions of the kind of political system they would bequeath to the new nation—and discussed threadbare vital issues of human rights, affirmative action, social uplift and economic development—would be awe-inspiring at the best of times. But to think that these debates happened in the wake of the savagery of Partition, when rioting and murder scarred the land, millions were uprooted from their homes and billions of rupees worth of property were damaged and destroyed, is little short of astonishing. A nation exploited for two centuries by the British, which had effectively a 0 per cent rate of growth throughout the first half of the 20th century, a land riven by religious, regional and caste conflict, and full of poor, malnourished and diseased people, faced with the enormous political challenge of integrating several hundred 'princely states', came together through its elected representatives to produce, in the soaring majesty of its Constitution, a compelling vision for the future.

Four men, alongside dozens of remarkable statesmen, embodied this vision in the 1940s—Gandhi, Nehru, Patel and Ambedkar. Mahatma Gandhi took the issue of freedom to the masses as one of simple right and wrong and gave them a technique to which the British had no response. By abstaining from violence, Gandhi wrested the moral advantage. By breaking the law nonviolently, he demonstrated the injustice of the law. By accepting the punishments imposed on him, he confronted his captors with their own brutalization. By voluntarily imposing suffering upon himself in his hunger strikes, he demonstrated the lengths to which he was prepared to go in defence of what he considered right. He was not alone. Gandhi's moral rectitude, allied to Jawaharlal Nehru's political passion, made the perpetuation of British rule an impossibility. Sardar Patel's firm hand on the administration integrated the nation and established peace and stability. Ambedkar's erudition and legal acumen helped translate the dreams of a generation into a working legal document that laid the foundations for an enduring democracy.

Upon the Mahatma's assassination in 1948, a year after Independence, Nehru, the country's first prime minister, became the keeper of the national flame, the most visible embodiment of India's struggle for freedom. Gandhi's death could have led Nehru to assume untrammeled power. Instead, he spent a lifetime immersed in the democratic values Ambedkar had codified, trying to instil the habits of democracy in his people—a disdain for dictators, a respect for parliamentary procedures, an abiding faith in the constitutional system. Till the end of the decade, his staunch ally, Patel, provided the firm hand on the tiller without which India might yet have split asunder.

While the world was disintegrating into fascism, violence and war, Gandhi taught the virtues of truth, non-violence and peace. While the nation reeled from bloodshed and communal carnage, Ambedkar preached the values of constitutionalism and the rule of law. While parochial ambitions threatened national unity, Patel led the nation to a vision of unity and common purpose. While mobs marched the streets baying for revenge, Nehru's humane and non-sectarian vision inspired India to yearn again for the glory that had once been hers.

The principal pillars of Nehru's legacy—democratic institution-building, staunch pan-Indian secularism, socialist economics at home and a foreign policy of nonalignment—were all integral to a vision of Indianness that sustained the nation for decades. Today, both legacies are fundamentally contested, and many Indians have strayed from the ideals bequeathed to them by Gandhi and Nehru, Ambedkar and Patel. Yet they, in their very different ways, each represented that rare kind of leader who is not diminished by the inadequacies of his followers.

The American editor Norman Cousins once asked Nehru what he hoped his legacy to India would be. 'Four hundred million people capable of governing themselves', Nehru replied. The numbers have grown, but the very fact that each day over a billion Indians govern themselves in a pluralist democracy is testimony to the deeds and words of these four men and the giants who accompanied them in the 1940s march to freedom.

The man who, as Congress president in Lahore in 1929, had first demanded 'purna swaraj' (complete independence), now stood ready to claim it, even if the city in which he had moved his famous resolution was no longer to be part of the newly-free country. Amidst the rioting and carnage that consumed large sections of northern India, Jawaharlal Nehru found the time to ensure that no pettiness marred the moment: he dropped the formal lowering of the Union Jack from the independence ceremony in order not to hurt British sensibilities. The Indian tricolour was raised just before sunset, and as it fluttered up the flagpole a late-monsoon rainbow emerged behind it, a glittering tribute from the heavens. Just before midnight, Jawaharlal Nehru rose in the Constituent Assembly to deliver the most famous speech ever made by an Indian:

> Long years ago we made a tryst with destiny, and now the time comes when we shall redeem our pledge, not wholly or in full measure, but very substantialy. At the stroke of the midnight hour, when the world sleeps, India will awake to life and freedom. A moment comes, which comes but rarely in history, when we step out from the old to the new, when an age ends, and when the soul of a nation long suppressed finds utterance.

One man did not join the celebrations that midnight. Mahatma Gandhi stayed in Calcutta, fasting, striving to keep the peace in a city that just a year earlier had been ravaged by killings. He saw no cause for celebration. Instead of the cheers of rejoicing, he heard the cries of the women ripped open in the internecine frenzy; instead of the slogans of freedom, he heard the shouts of the crazed assaulters firing their weapons at helpless refugees, and the silence of trains arriving full of corpses massacred on their journey; instead of the dawn of Jawaharlal's promise, he saw only the long dark night of horror that was breaking his country in two.

In his own Independence Day message to the nation, Jawaharlal Nehru could not help thinking of the Mahatma:

> On this day, our first thoughts go to the architect of freedom, the Father of our Nation who, embodying the old spirit of India, held aloft the torch.... We have often been unworthy followers of his, and we have strayed from his message, but not only we, but the succeeding generations, will remember his message and bear the imprint in their hearts....

It was a repudiation as well as a tribute: the Mahatma was now gently relegated to the 'old spirit of India' from whom the custodians of the new had 'strayed'. We have strayed much farther in the decades that have followed.

THE LEGACY OF MAHATMA GANDHI

Every year the Nobel Peace Prize attracts great attention and celebration of the laureate, but (unless an acolyte wins it, as four have done) little is heard of arguably the most remarkable man who never won the Nobel: Mahatma Gandhi. Despite that omission, there is no doubting Gandhiji's huge worldwide significance. The Mahatma's image dominates the globe, featuring in advertising campaigns for everything from Apple computers to Montblanc pens. When Richard Attenborough's film *Gandhi* swept the Oscars in 1983, posters for the film proclaimed that 'Gandhi's triumph changed the world forever'. But did it?

Gandhi's life was, of course, his lesson. He was unique among the statesmen of the 20th century in his determination not just to live his beliefs but to reject any separation between beliefs and action. In his life, religion flowed into politics; his public persona meshed seamlessly with his private conduct. The claim emblazoned on those publicity posters for the film suggested that the lessons of his life had been learned and widely followed. But even for the man who swept aside the British Raj, Paul Newman and Tootsie in his triumphal progress towards a shelf-full of golden statuary, this was a difficult claim to sustain.

Mahatma ('Great Soul', a term he detested) Gandhi was the kind of person it is more convenient to forget. The principles he stood for and the way in which he asserted them are easier to admire than to follow. While he was alive he was impossible to ignore. Once he had gone he was impossible to imitate.

Shortly before he was killed, Gandhi had just announced his intention to spurn the country he had failed to keep united and to spend the rest of his years in Pakistan, a prospect that had made the Government of Pakistan collectively choke. But that was Gandhi: idealistic, quirky, quixotic and determined, a man who answered to the beat of no other drummer but got everyone else to march to his tune. Someone once called him a cross between a saint and a Tammany Hall politician; like the best cross-breeds, he managed to distil all the qualities of both and yet transcend their contradictions.

Gandhi was the extraordinary leader of the world's first successful non-violent movement for independence from colonial rule. At the same time he was a philosopher who was constantly seeking to live out his own ideas, whether they applied to individual self-improvement or social change: his autobiography was typically subtitled 'The Story of My Experiments with Truth'. No dictionary imbues truth with the depth of meaning Gandhi gave it. His truth emerged from his convictions: it meant not only what was accurate, but what was just and therefore right. Truth could not be obtained by 'untruthful' or unjust means, which included inflicting violence upon one's opponent.

To describe his method, Gandhi coined the expression satyagraha—literally, 'holding on to truth' or, as he variously described it, truth-force, love-force or soul-force. He disliked the English term 'passive resistance' because satyagraha required activism, not passivity. If you believed in Truth and cared enough to obtain it, Gandhi felt, you could not afford to be passive: you had to be prepared actively to suffer for Truth.

So non-violence, like many later concepts labelled with a negation, from non-cooperation to non-alignment, meant much more than the denial of an opposite; it did not merely imply the absence of violence. Non-violence was the way to vindicate the truth not by the infliction of suffering on the opponent, but on one's self. It was essential to willingly accept punishment in order to demonstrate the strength of one's convictions.

This was the approach Gandhi brought to the movement for India's independence—and it worked. Where sporadic terrorism and moderate constitutionalism had both proved ineffective, Gandhi took the issue of freedom to the masses as one of simple right and wrong and gave them a technique to which the British had no response. By abstaining from violence Gandhi wrested the moral advantage. By breaking the law non-violently he showed up the injustice of the law. By accepting the punishments imposed on him he confronted his captors with their own brutalization. By voluntarily imposing suffering upon himself in his hunger-strikes he demonstrated the lengths to which he was prepared to go in defence of what he considered to be right. In the end he made the perpetuation of British rule an impossibility.

Of course, there was much more to Gandhism—physical self-denial and discipline, spiritual faith, a belief in humanity and in the human capacity for selfless love, the self-reliance symbolized by the spinning-wheel, religious ecumenism, idealistic internationalism, and a passionate commitment to human equality and social justice (no mean conviction in a caste-ridden society). The improvement of his fellow human beings was arguably more important to him than the political goal of ridding India of the British. But it is his central tenet of non-violence in the pursuit of these ends which represents his most significant original contribution to the world.

The case for Gandhi's worldwide relevance rests principally on the example of Martin Luther King Jr, who attended a lecture on Gandhi, bought half a dozen books on the Mahatma and adopted satyagraha as both precept and method. King, more than anyone else, used non-violence most effectively outside India in breaking down segregation in the southern states of the USA. 'Hate begets hate. Violence begets violence', he memorably declared, echoing Gandhi who has said: 'We must meet the forces of hate with soul force.' King later avowed that 'the Gandhian method of non-violent resistance…became the guiding light of our movement. Christ furnished the spirit and motivation and Gandhi furnished the method'. In November 2010, President Barack Obama told India's Parliament that were it not for Gandhi, he would not be standing there as president.

So Gandhism arguably helped to change America forever. But it is difficult to find many other instances of its success. India's independence marked the dawn of the era of decolonization, but many nations still came to freedom only after bloody and violent struggles. Other peoples have fallen under the boots of invading armies, been dispossessed of their lands or forced to flee in terror from their homes. Non-violence has offered no solutions to them. It could only work against opponents vulnerable to a loss of moral authority—governments responsive to domestic and international public opinion, capable of being shamed into conceding defeat. In Gandhi's own day, non-violence could have done nothing for the Jews of Hitler's Germany, who disappeared unprotestingly into gas-chambers far from the flashbulbs of a war-obsessed press.

The power of non-violence rests in being able to say, 'to show you that you are wrong, I punish myself'. But that has little effect on those who are not interested in whether they are wrong and are already seeking to punish you whether you disagree with them or not. For them your willingness to undergo punishment is the most convenient means of victory. No wonder Nelson Mandela, who told me that Gandhi had 'always' been 'a great source of inspiration', explicitly disavowed non-violence as ineffective in his struggle against apartheid.

On this subject Gandhi sounds frighteningly unrealistic: 'The willing sacrifice of the innocent is the most powerful answer to insolent tyranny that has yet been conceived by God or man. Disobedience to be "civil" must be sincere, respectful, restrained, never defiant, and it must have no ill-will or hatred behind it. Neither should there be excitement in civil disobedience, which is a preparation for mute suffering.'

For many smarting under injustice across the world, that would sound like a prescription for sainthood—or for impotence. Mute suffering is all very well as a moral principle, but it has rarely brought about meaningful change. The sad truth is that the staying power of organized violence is almost always greater than that of non-violence. And when right and wrong are less clear-cut, Gandhism flounders. The Mahatma, at the peak of his influence, was unable to prevent the partition of India even though, in his terms, he considered it 'wrong'. Gandhi believed in 'weaning an opponent from error by patience, sympathy and self-suffering'—but if the opponent believes equally in the justice of his cause, he is hardly going to accept that he is in 'error'. Gandhism is viable at its simplest and most profound in the service of a transcendent principle like independence from foreign rule. But in more complex situations it cannot—and, more to the point, does not—work as well.

Gandhi's ideals had a tremendous intellectual impact on the founding fathers of the new India, who incorporated many of his convictions into the directive principles of state policy. Yet Gandhian solutions have not been found for many of the ills over which he agonized, from persistent sectarian (or 'communal') conflict to the ill-treatment of Untouchables (whom he renamed 'Harijans', or Children of God, a designation its beneficiaries found patronizing, for were we not all Children of God? Today, they prefer to be known as Dalits, 'the oppressed'). Instead his methods (particularly the fast, the hartal, and the deliberate courting of arrest) have been abused and debased by lesser men in the pursuit of petty sectarian ends. Outside India, too, Gandhian techniques have been perverted by such people as terrorists and bomb-throwers declaring hunger-strikes when punished for their crimes. Gandhism without moral authority is like Marxism without a proletariat. Yet few who wish to use his methods have his personal integrity or moral stature.

In his internationalism, the Mahatma expressed ideals few can reject. But the decades after his death have confirmed that there is no escape from the conflicting sovereignties of states. Some 20 million more lives have been lost in wars and insurrections since his passing. In a dismaying number of countries including his own, governments spend more for military purposes than for education and health care combined. The current stockpile of nuclear weapons represents over a million times the explosive power of the atom bomb whose destruction of Hiroshima so grieved him. As the Mumbai terror attacks of 26/11 demonstrated, India faces the threat of cross-border terrorism to which the Mahatma's only answer—a fast in protest—would have left its perpetrators unmoved. Universal peace, which Gandhi considered so central to Truth, seems as illusionary as ever.

As governments compete, so religions contend. The ecumenist Gandhi who declared, 'I am a Hindu, a Muslim, a Christian, a Zoroastrian, a Jew' would find it difficult to stomach the exclusivist revivalism of so many religions and cults the world over. But perhaps his approach was always inappropriate for the rest of the world. As his Muslim rival Mohammed Ali Jinnah retorted to his claim of eclectic belief—'only a Hindu could say that'.

And finally, the world of the charkha, the spinning-wheel, of self-reliant families in contented village republics, is even more remote today than when Gandhi first espoused it. Despite the brief popularity of intermediate technology and 'small is beautiful', there does not appear to be much room for such ideas in an inter-dependent world. Self-reliance is too often a cover for protectionism and a shelter for inefficiency in the Third World. The successful and prosperous countries are those who are able to look beyond spinning charkhas to silicon chips—and who give their people the benefits of technological developments which free them from menial and repetitive chores and broaden the horizons of their lives.

But if Gandhism has had its limitations exposed in the years after 1947, there is no denying Gandhi's greatness or the extraordinary resonance of his life and his message. While the world was disintegrating into fascism, violence and war, the Mahatma taught the virtues of truth, non-violence and peace. He destroyed the credibility of colonialism by opposing principle to force. And he set and attained personal standards of conviction and courage which few will ever match. He was that rare kind of leader who was not confined by the inadequacies of his followers.

Yet Gandhi's Truth was essentially his own. He formulated its unique content and determined its application in a specific historical context. Inevitably, few in today's world can measure up to his greatness or aspire to his credo. The originality of his thought and the example of his life inspires people around the world today, but Gandhi's triumph did not 'change the world forever'. I wonder if the Mahatma, looking at today's world, would feel he had triumphed at all.

SARDAR PATEL AND THE HIJACKING OF
INDIA'S HISTORY

As the political temperature heated up in India, in the lead-up to the 2014 general elections, one would have expected Indian leaders to be duelling over visions of the future. Instead, they were engaged for weeks in an unseemly brawl about the past.

The main Opposition leader, now prime minister, Narendra Modi moved aggressively to lay claim to the legacy of one of India's most respected founders, Sardar Vallabhbhai Patel. Like Modi, Patel was from Gujarat, where Modi served twelve years as chief minister. Patel was a determined nationalist, a key leader of the independence struggle, and a lieutenant of Mahatma Gandhi.

As independent India's first deputy prime minister and home minister, Patel is credited with the integration of roughly 600 princely states, sometimes by persuasion and sometimes by force. A firm, tough, and effective administrator, Patel, who died in 1950 at the age of 75, is revered as the 'Iron Man' of India.

In the normal course of events, Patel's illustrious life might have been left to the history books. But Modi, seeking to wrap himself in a more distinguished lineage than the BJP can claim, has called on farmers across India to donate iron from their ploughs to construct a giant 550-foot statue of the Iron Man in Gujarat. When finished, it will be by far the world's largest statue, dwarfing New York City's Statue of Liberty and Rio de Janeiro's Christ the Redeemer. But it will be a monument less to the modest Gandhian it ostensibly honours than to its builder's overweening ambitions.

Modi's identification with Patel is an effort at character-building by association. As we know, Modi's own image has been tarnished by his inaction (or worse) during the massacre of more than a thousand Gujarati Muslims in a pogrom on his watch in 2002. Modi would rather be perceived as embodying Patel's decisiveness than as the destructive bigot his enemies decry.

To hear Modi tell it, India would have been better off with Patel—who forged national unity, defended the country's Hindus during the horrors of Partition, and stood firm on issues like Kashmir—instead of the allegedly pussyfooting Jawaharlal Nehru, as its first prime minister. During the campaign, the implication was clear—a vote for Modi is a vote for a latter-day Patel.

That message resonated with many Gujaratis, who were proud to be reminded of a nationally admired native son, and with much of India's urban middle class, whose members yearn for a strong leader to cut through the confusion and indecision of a sprawling country's messy democracy.

But the ruling Congress party was not about to relinquish one of its greatest leaders. Congress politicians reacted with robust indignation to Modi's attempt

to appropriate Patel's legacy. Both men were faced with a serious breakdown
of law and order in their respective domains, involving violence and rioting
against Muslims. But Patel's conduct during the violence that accompanied
Partition stands in stark contrast to Modi's behaviour in office.

In Delhi in 1947, Patel immediately and effectively moved to protect
Muslims, moving 10,000 in the most vulnerable areas to the security of Delhi's
historic Red Fort. Because he feared that communal passions might have
infected the local security forces, he moved army troops from Madras and
Pune to Delhi to ensure calm. He attended prayers at the famous Nizamuddin
Dargah to convey to Muslims that they and their faith were unquestionably
part of India. He even went to the border town of Amritsar and pleaded with
Hindu and Sikh mobs to stop victimizing Muslim refugees fleeing to the new
Islamic state of Pakistan.

In each case, Patel succeeded. Tens of thousands of people are alive today
because of his interventions.

The contrast with what happened in Gujarat in 2002 is painful. Whether
or not Modi bears direct responsibility for the pogrom, he certainly cannot
claim to have acted as Patel did. He took no direct and immediate action, as
the state's chief executive, to protect Muslims. Nor did he publicly condemn
the attacks, let alone visit a masjid or a Muslim neighbourhood as a sign of
reassurance. On the contrary, many believe that he provided protection and
comfort to the rioters.

There is a particular irony to a self-proclaimed 'Hindu nationalist' like
Modi, whose speeches reveal a thinly veiled contempt for Muslims, laying
claim to the legacy of a Gandhian leader who would never have qualified
his Indian nationalism with a religious label. Patel would have been outraged
not only by Modi's conduct in his chief ministerial office, but by the kind of
remarks that Modi has repeatedly made against minorities during his twelve-
year tenure and in his vitriolic election campaigns.

History has often been contested terrain in India. The Gujarat riots in
2002 were, after all, directly linked to the destruction in 1992 of the 16th-
century Babri Mosque, which was allegedly built on the site of an ancient
Hindu temple.

Modi is of course well aware that the past retains a powerful hold over
India's present. How Indian voters judged his attempt to reinvent himself as a
latter-day Patel could have a major impact on the country's future. But one
thing is certain: though they have placed Modi in the prime minister's office,
the voters have not placed him on Patel's pedestal.

WHAT SWAMI VIVEKANANDA STOOD FOR

I had the great honour, in August 2013, on the occasion of his 150th birthday, to unveil a stone sculpture of Swami Vivekananda in Kanyakumari. What was particularly unusual about the occasion was that it was a monument to Brother Narendranath Dutta, as was fondly called by the organizers of the event, the Masonic Brotherhood, of which he was a member. The fact that Swami Vivekananda, a man who has been a source of inspiration for many, was a Mason, is hardly known in India, and rarely features in the many accounts of his life.

Swami Vivekananda was an inspiration to me right from my formative years, and one of the few accomplishments I remember from a hyper-active extra-curricular life at college was being the youngest person asked to deliver, in 1974, the annual Vivekananda Memorial Oration at Delhi University. Men like him, who spend a lifetime—in his case a tragically short lifetime since he passed away at 39—performing selfless service, come along rarely in history. The term 'Renaissance Man' or 'Yugapurush' is coined for precisely such exceptional souls. His teachings, and the timeless truths he spoke, transcend generations, and borders, making him one of the most revered men in modern Indian history.

Of the many roles the Swami played during his life, as a teacher, a patriot, a spiritual leader, an intellectual and philosopher, what is perhaps least known is his life as a Freemason. This can be attributed to the fact that the membership in Freemasonry has always been shrouded in mystery, despite its members having been some of the finest minds from all walks of life, and all corners of the world. From Benjamin Franklin and George Washington, to Pandit Motilal Nehru and Wyomesh Chander Bonnerjee, they have all been a part of this fraternal organization. Therefore, it gave me great pride to be present and to address the first ever public event of the Masons in India on such a splendid occasion.

Despite the organization's esoteric nature, there is no doubt in anyone's mind about the importance and continued relevance of the central tenets of Freemasonry—charitable work, moral uprightness, as well as the development and maintenance of fraternal friendship. The Society of Freemasons started as a congregation of stone masons in Europe and from these humble beginnings went on to become a complete perspective on the place and role of humanity in this world. Akin to the way a mason shapes and polishes a stone, members of the fraternity are supposed to shape character and make the world a better place to live.

The philanthropic work done by the fraternity, from hospitals to social service centres, is particularly commendable, given the fact that the money for all charitable purposes is collected entirely from the members. The Masonic Service Association, the Masonic Medical Research Laboratory, and the Shriners Hospitals for Children are just a few of the community service initiatives that the fraternity in India have founded and supported in recent times, both intellectually and monetarily.

The 150th birth anniversary of Swami Vivekananda was the occasion for India's Masons to reclaim him as one of theirs, in a fitting tribute to a man whose teachings remain relevant even in this day and age, and who continues to live on in our hearts, defying the transient nature of human existence. A few days later, the vice president of India unveiled an even grander statue in the city I represent in Parliament, Thiruvananthapuram. In both cases, the eyes of Vivekananda are the most striking feature—eyes that shone with a luminous light to take India forward.

As we honour the Swami's great life and achievements, we look back at the rich legacy he has left behind. He was far ahead of his time, as respect for all other paths and religions was an integral part of what he preached. He combined ancient wisdom with modern insights in spreading his profound message of interfaith harmony. In his writings, he explains how religion and science are not contradictory to each other, but are in fact, complementary. He is widely credited for being a major force in the revival of Hinduism and bringing it to the status of a major world religion.

The Swami felt that Hinduism, with its openness, its respect for variety, its acceptance of all other faiths, is one religion which should be able to spread its influence without threatening others. At Chicago's Parliament of the World's Religions, exactly 120 years ago, he articulated the liberal humanism that lies at the heart of his (and my) creed: 'I am proud to belong to a religion which has taught the world both tolerance and universal acceptance. We believe not only in universal toleration, but we accept all religions as true. I am proud to belong to a country which has sheltered the persecuted and the refugees of all religions and all countries of the earth. I am proud to tell you that we have gathered in our bosom the purest remnant of the Israelites, who came to southern India and took refuge with us in the very year in which their holy temple was shattered to pieces by Roman tyranny. I am proud to belong to the religion which has sheltered and is still fostering the remnant of the grand Zoroastrian nation.' He went on to quote a hymn, which he remembered from his formative years at school: 'As the different streams having their sources in different places all mingle their water in the sea, so, O Lord, the different paths which men take through different tendencies, various though they appear, crooked or straight, all lead to Thee.' The wonderful doctrine preached in the Gita echoes the same idea, saying: 'Whosoever comes to Me, through whatsoever form, I reach him; all men are struggling through paths which in the end lead to me.'

Vivekananda went on to denounce the fact that 'sectarianism, bigotry, and its horrible descendant, fanaticism, have long possessed this beautiful earth'. His confident belief that their death-knell had sounded was sadly not to be borne out. But his vision—summarized in the Sanskrit credo Sarva Dharma Sambhava, 'all religions are equally worthy of respect'—is, in fact, the kind of Hinduism practised by the vast majority of India's Hindus, whose instinctive acceptance of other faiths and forms of worship has long been the distinctive hallmark of Indianness, not merely in a narrow religious sense, but in a broader cultural and spiritual sense too.

The Swami made no distinction between the actions of Hindus as a people (embodied by their grant of asylum, for instance) and their actions as a religious community (visible in their tolerance of other faiths): for him, the distinction was irrelevant because Hinduism was as much a civilization as a set of religious beliefs.

In a different speech to the same Chicago convention, Swami Vivekananda set out his philosophy in simple terms: 'Unity in variety is the plan of nature, and the Hindu has recognized it. Every other religion lays down certain fixed dogmas and tries to compel society to adopt them. It places before society only one coat which must fit Jack and John and Henry, all alike. If it does not fit John or Henry, he must go without a coat to cover his body. The Hindus have discovered that the Absolute can only be realized, or thought of, or stated through the relative, and the images, crosses, and crescents are simply so many symbols—so many pegs to hang spiritual ideas on. It is not that this help is necessary for everyone, but those that do not need it have no right to say that it is wrong. Nor is it compulsory in Hinduism. The Hindus have their faults, but mark this, they are always for punishing their own bodies, and never for cutting the throats of their neighbours. If the Hindu fanatic burns himself on the pyre, he never lights the fire of Inquisition.'

During the Swami's time in Chicago, it was the Freemasons who supported his travel and stay. It is no wonder then that he began those inspiring speeches to the Parliament of the World's religions with the words, 'Sisters and brothers of America...'

Each of these qualities, in my view, make him the first globalized Indian thinker. The doctrines and ideas he preached are taught all around the world. For instance, he was a key figure in the introduction of the Indian philosophies of Vedanta and yoga to the Western world. He later founded the Ramakrishna Math, a religious monastic order, to carry on the good work. Based on the twin ideals of self-realization and service to the world, and eponymous with his Guru Sri Ramakrishna Paramahansa, the work done by the Ramakrishna Math and Mission have made Swami Vivekananda a modern day apostle of tolerance and humanism, two ideas that underpin the modern conception of the world and our place in it.

One of the major contributions with which the Swami is widely credited is for having leveraged his position as a spiritual leader effectively, to revolutionize the traditional image of sannyasis in India. He made social service an integral part of their lives. Although a formal shape to his ideas was given by him in 1897, all his activities from 1886 onwards helped prepare the ground for introducing so radical a change. When he came to the south of India, it is said that he travelled by foot from Ernakulam to Kanyakumari, during the time around Christmas of 1892. At Kanyakumari, he meditated on the 'last bit of Indian rock', which we now know as the Vivekananda Rock Memorial. It was at this juncture in his life that the Swami pondered over his experiences of observing the miseries of the poor in the various parts of the country, which culminated in his 'Vision of One India'. This has now come to be called 'The Kanyakumari Resolve of 1892', about which he famously wrote in a letter from America:

> At Cape Comorin, sitting in Mother Kumari's temple, I hit upon a plan: we are so many sannyasins wandering about, and teaching the people metaphysics? It is all madness. Did not our Gurudeva once say, 'An empty stomach is no good for religion?' That these poor people are leading a life of brutes is simply due to ignorance. Suppose some sannyasins, bent on doing good to others, go from village to village, disseminating education and seeking in various ways to better the condition of all down to the caāla—can't that bring forth good in time? We, as a nation, have lost our individuality, and that is the cause of all mischief in India. We have to give back to the nation its lost individuality and raise the masses...

These ideas galvanized his followers, in a country which had long grown indifferent to the tyranny and oppression faced by a majority of the people. And thus began a new epoch in his life.

I feel our modern systems of governance have a lot to learn from the teachings of this sage. His assessment of the social problems of India was realistic, rather than academic, largely owing to the fact that he wandered all over the country for years, with a few followers behind him and a begging bowl in his hand. He connected with the common man to a degree that would be the envy of most modern politicians. Initially, after the passing away of his guru, Sri Ramakrishna, he had thought of going on a pilgrimage to the holy places like Varanasi, Ayodhya, Vrindavan, and the ashramas of yogis in the Himalayas. However, after a couple of years spent on such visits, he turned his gaze to the common people for whom the only reality in life was their struggle for survival.

What bothered the Swami, even more than poverty itself, was the gulf between the rich and the poor, between the high-placed and the low-born, and further, the ugly sight of the strong regularly dealing a death-blow to the weak. 'This is our native land', he often bemoaned, 'where huts and palaces exist side-by-side'. Such was the dichotomy of the times that it seemed inconceivable to him that India could have the unity and brotherhood which are preconditions for national greatness. Born, as it were, a 'disunited mob', we could not combine.

Along with such oppression of the masses, he also voiced his opposition against the manner in which women were kept, in conditions of servile dependence on men, which made them 'good only to weep at the slightest approach of mishap or danger'. These dissensions pained Swami Vivekananda all the more, because they were being adhered to in the name of religion. 'A girl of eight is married to a man of thirty and the parents are jubilant over it. And if anyone protests against it, the plea put forward is that our religion is being overturned', he lamented.

Of the many angles from which the social problems of India could be analysed, he placed the greatest emphasis on the religious and spiritual perspectives. Therefore, the Swami laid the foundation of the Ramakrishna Mission, a philanthropic, volunteer organization to work alongside the Ramakrishna Math. The Mission bases its work on the principle of 'karma yoga', the path of selfless, altruistic service propounded by him. Ever since its inception, they have stayed true to their motto of 'Atmano mokshartham jagad hitaya cha', which translated from Sanskrit means 'For one's own salvation, and for the good of the world'.

We all speak of the Swami's contributions to Indian spiritual traditions, his importance in intellectual circles, as well as the contemporary relevance of his teachings, but it would be an incomplete tribute to the man not to mention his deep nationalist sentiment during the colonial era in India. In fact, he has often been given the title of a 'patriotic saint'. It is no wonder then, that his list of admirers include the likes of Gandhiji and Tagore. The extraordinary story of his life, his charismatic personality, and his benevolent nature shall continue to serve as an inspiration to people from all corners of India. He shall live on in our hearts, and his undying message of peace and oneness shall be recounted for generations to come.

It is unfortunate that there has been some unnecessary contestation over laying claim to the legacy of Swami Vivekananda. The truth is that he belongs to all of us. After all, his was a message of inclusion, not of exclusivity. His was a message where he celebrated Hinduism as an ancient faith which has taught the world not only the language of tolerance but of acceptance, the acceptance of all ways of belief as equally true. And that non-judgmental spirit that underlay his spirituality is what gave Swami Vivekananda the capacity to deliver the secular message that remains profoundly relevant today.

It is important to remember that Swami Vivekananda—despite being a spiritual figure, despite being a disciple of the immortal Ramakrishna Paramahansa, despite being a sannyasi who travelled the length and breadth of India and taught the message of Vedanta and the Gita, the message of religion and spirituality as he understood it—that Swami Vivekananda was also very much anchored in the real needs of today, of his people at that time and in the future. He argued that instead of wandering from village to village preaching, sannyasis should go from village to village and teach, offering people modern education to bring them out of wretched ignorance. He wanted an educated India, an objective we have not yet fulfilled a century and a half later.

Swami Vivekananda was an extraordinary figure, an advocate of social justice, of national unity and of material and spiritual progress. Even though he died at 39, the ideas and thoughts can animate another 39 decades of discourses and discussions. But the remarkable thing about his legacy to us is that all of us can lay claim to it with the openness of heart that was his, with the brightness in his eyes that shone the path for all of us. He was a giant of his time; he was also a human being capable of human behavior. But the fact is that he never considered himself detached from the world; his spirituality was anchored in the world. And that, to my mind, is the great lesson he leaves to those of us in public life: that we must have values, that we must join the quest for attainment of some knowledge of the divine, for that is ultimately what all spirituality is about, but that spirituality is meaningless if it is not anchored in a genuine concern for the well-being of ordinary people in our country.

Swami Vivekananda taught us a nationalism that was anchored in a spiritual yearning. He taught us values that actually mandated change in the arrangements of our society. He refused to accept it when religion was cited in favour of iniquitous social practices like child marriage: he was a religious reformer as well as a social reformer. And of course he was a great visionary.

Long may we all bask in the light cast by those amazing eyes and walk in the shadow of that amazing figure. That son of India belongs to us as much as he belongs to the Belur Math. A lifetime would not suffice to understand and appreciate the profound philosophies of this towering intellectual. At a lecture on Raja Yoga he said, 'Take up one idea. Make that one idea your life—think of it, dream of it, live on that idea. Let the brain, muscles, nerves, every part of your body, be full of that idea, and just leave every other idea alone. This is the way to success, this is the way great spiritual giants are produced.'

As an Indian, I am proud to lay claim to the tradition of thought that has Swami Vivekananda as one of its fountainheads.

THE MYSTIQUE OF GURUDEV

One of the striking things about Rabindranath Tagore that never fails to bewilder educated Indians is the extent to which his reputation has plummeted in the West even as it has grown into immortality in India. When the Nobel Prize-winning polymath Amartya Sen published his brilliant book, *The Argumentative Indian*, few, if any, Western reviewers paid attention to his essay in it about Tagore. And yet, while the book was rightly lauded for Sen's superb marshalling of arguments for the existence of the liberal tradition in India, this masterly essay was a much-needed effort to reclaim Tagore's international reputation. The reason it was necessary is, of course, that whereas Tagore's greatness seems self-evident to most Indians (and all Bengalis), Tagore is now unjustly misjudged in the West as a mediocre mystic poet, rather than as the remarkable rationalist and humanist genius Sen convincingly depicts.

The fact is, though, that it is genuinely difficult to explain to foreigners the scale of Rabindranath Tagore's accomplishments. Some have made glib comparisons to Shakespeare and Goethe, but neither man, despite his undoubted greatness, excelled in as many fields as the Bengali Gurudev, nor dominated his culture to the extent that Tagore did his. Think of it: he was not merely an extraordinary poet, the only Indian to win the Nobel Prize for Literature (in 1913, for his *Gitanjali,* profoundly moving verses written in Bengali in 1910, after he had lost his father, wife, second daughter and youngest son). He was also a prose-writer and essayist of the first rank, whose articles, books and monographs commanded a wide readership around the world. As a philosopher and mystic, he was perhaps the first to develop a synthesis of Eastern and Western approaches, and he developed political ideas of great depth and humanity (of which more later). He was a great, if uneven, novelist and short-story writer who produced several masterpieces that continue to be read a century and a half after his birth; his 'Kabuliwallah' is among the few short stories most Indians remember from their childhood. He was also a playwright of rare distinction: 'The Post Office', for instance, was one of the most popular plays in the world before the Second World War.

But, added to all that, were the extraordinary other talents. He was a painter of high quality and perceptiveness, an artist with a poet's eye. He was a composer of over 2,000 immortal songs, of which he authored both the lyrics and the tunes, and through which he essentially founded his own discipline of Indian music, known as 'Rabindra Sangeet'. He is the only person to have created the national anthems of two different countries (India's 'Jana Gana Mana' and Bangladesh's 'Amar Sonar Bangla'), though both nations were born after his own death; and he inspired the composer of Sri Lanka's anthem as

well, who translated Tagore's lyrics and set them to Tagore's music in a tribute
to his mentor.

As if this were not enough, he was an educator of great vision and courage,
founding Vishwa Bharati University at Santiniketan to offer an authentically
Indian experience of higher education, following systems and approaches of
his own devising. It educated the likes of Satyajit Ray and Indira Gandhi
(not to mention offering a cradle to Amartya Sen, whose first name, with its
evocations of immortality, was given by Tagore—probably the only instance
of a Nobel laureate baptizing another!)

If all this were not more than extraordinary—representing a level of
achievement so towering that it is difficult to imagine an individual in any
other culture who comes close—there is also the remarkable fact of Tagore's
huge worldwide impact in his own time, which even today's Indians may have
difficulty imagining. Tagore was a global giant before the era of globalization.
When he was to speak at New York's 4,000-seat Carnegie Hall in 1930
(itself a rare enough honour, since the hall is usually reserved for concerts,
not orations), more than 20,000 people were turned away from the sold-out
event, creating a mass of humanity on the streets outside that blocked traffic
for miles. No living writer on the planet had ever had something comparable
happen, and what's more, Tagore was handsomely paid for his speeches. One
American critic, not without a tinge of jealousy, wrote acerbically that the
Indian 'scolds Americans at $700 per scold'. (By today's standards that would
be more like $700,000.)

Tagore himself was modestly dismissive of his fame and the attention it
got him. 'The perfect whirlwind of public excitement it [the Nobel prize] has
given rise to is frightful', he wrote to his friend, the artist William Rothenstein
in 1913. 'It is almost as bad as tying a tin can to a dog's tail, making it
impossible for him to move without creating noise and collecting crowds all
along.' Eight years later he confided to Edward Thompson: 'What an immense
amount of unreality there is in literary reputation, and I am longing—even
while appreciating it like a buffalo the luxury of a mud bath—to come out
of it as a sannyasi, naked and aloof.'

Like all fine writers, he had a rare gift of phrase. His description of the
Taj Mahal as 'a teardrop on the cheek of time' can scarcely be bettered, and
which poet would not want to have authored his line, 'Who can strain the
blue from the sky?' His descriptions of nature are startlingly original, and
thought-provoking in their imagery. 'The rose', he wrote, 'is a great deal more
than a blushing apology for the thorn'. Dawn is 'the departing night's kiss
on the closed eyes of morning'. A picture is 'a memory of light treasured by
the shadow'.

Sometimes the metaphor is explicitly metaphysical: 'In the mountain, stillness surges up to explore its own height; in the lake, movement stands still to contemplate its own death.' He lent to spirituality a literary succinctness few others could master: 'Life is given to us, we earn it by giving it.' Or the poignant 'And because I love this life, I know I shall love death as well.' His stories and letters overflow with literary gems, each bearing an insight thoroughly steeped in Indian tradition. 'While God waits for his temple to be built of love, man brings stones.' Or 'He who does good comes to the temple gate, he who loves reaches the shrine.' And 'Darkness travels towards light, but blindness towards depth.'

This was also true of his more social reflections. 'Nowadays men have acquired what God did not choose to give them', he wrote in a short story. Or, as he turned 50: 'Elders have become cheap to modern children, too readily accessible; and so have all objects of desire.' And throughout, his awareness of the divinely-created cosmos: 'The world is an ever-changing foam that floats on the surface of a sea of silence.' Or 'Man has in him the silence of the sea, the noise of the earth, and the music of the air.'

W. B. Yeats, in his famous introduction to *Gitanjali*, quoted an anonymous Bengali doctor as saying that 'We have other poets, but none that are his equal; we call this the epoch of Rabindranath. No poet seems to me as famous in Europe as he is among us. He is as great in music as in poetry, and his songs are sung from the west of India into Burma wherever Bengali is spoken. He was already famous at nineteen when he wrote his first novel; and plays when he was but little older, are still played in Calcutta. I so much admire the completeness of his life; when he was very young he wrote much of natural objects, he would sit all day in his garden; from his twenty-fifth year or so to his thirty-fifth perhaps, when he had a great sorrow, he wrote the most beautiful love poetry in our language…. After that his art grew deeper, it became religious and philosophical; all the inspiration of mankind are in his hymns. He is the first among our saints who has not refused to live, but has spoken out of Life itself, and that is why we give him our love.'

(Tagore returned the compliment in elegant terms, writing of Yeats: 'Like a cut diamond that needs the light of the sky to show itself, the human soul on its own cannot express its essence, and remains dark. Only when it reflects the light from something greater than itself, does it come into its own.')

Yeats himself went on to observe: 'These lyrics—which are in the original, my Indians tell me, full of subtlety of rhythm, of untranslatable delicacies of colour, of metrical invention—display in their thought a world I have dreamed of all my life long. The work of a supreme culture, they yet appear as much the growth of the common soil as the grass and the rushes. A tradition, where poetry and religion are the same thing, has passed through the centuries, gathering from learned and unlearned metaphor and emotion, and carried back again to the multitude the thought of the scholar and of the noble.' For Yeats, their Indian spiritual content was their principal value: 'we fight and make money and fill our heads with politics—all dull things in the doing—while Mr Tagore, like the Indian civilization itself, has been content to discover the soul and surrender himself to its spontaneity.' Again, Tagore himself would have disowned such grand claims: 'Since it is impracticable to be uncivilized, I had better try to be thoroughly civil,' he wrote in 1892 to his niece Indira.

But enough of mutual literary adoration: let us consider the content of his writing as well. I mentioned his two national anthems, but perhaps greater than either is his poem from *Gitanjali*, which gives nationalism a meaning few anthems can:

> Where the mind is without fear and the head is held high;
> Where knowledge is free;
> Where the world has not been broken up into fragments
> By narrow domestic walls;
> Where words come out from the depth of truth;
> Where tireless striving stretches its arms towards perfection;
> Where the clear stream of reason has not lost its way
> Into the dreary desert sand of dead habit;
> Where the mind is led forward by thee
> Into ever-widening thought and action;
> Into that heaven of freedom, my Father, let my country awake.

Typically, Tagore's is an inspirational poem that could serve as the anthem for any nation seeking freedom—while giving no indulgence whatsoever to jingoism or chauvinism. For the chauvinist glee with which I, as an Indian writer, am celebrating Rabindranath Tagore, would not particularly have appealed to him. Though his decision to return his British knighthood after the Jallianwallah Bagh massacre led Indians to regard him as a great hero of the nationalist struggle, Tagore did not really believe in nationalism but in the values of the human spirit, transcending all national boundaries. 'My religion,' he told Albert Einstein, 'is in the reconciliation of the superpersonal man, the universal human spirit, in my own individual being.' He had little patience for parochial forms of thinking: 'Our mind has faculties which are universal,' he declared, 'but its habits are insular.' In his magisterial essay on nationalism, written as the First World War was raging, he expressed the view that 'There is only one history—the history of man. All national histories are merely chapters in the larger one.' National pride does not feature in his thought, only the immutable goals of knowledge, learning, and the pursuit of truth.

He dreamt of freedom for India, but it was not merely freedom from foreign rule that he sought for his countrymen. It was in a place 'where the mind is without fear and the head is held high; where knowledge is free' and 'where the mind is led forward…into ever-widening thought and action' that Tagore hoped his India would awake to freedom.

Indeed his idea of freedom was far more profoundly individual than national. 'Freedom of movement is not the only vital liberty,' he said in 1916, 'freedom of work is still more important. Nor is subjugation the greatest bondage, narrowness of opportunity is the worst cage of all.' One of his poems perfectly captures the paradox of the nature of personal freedom in an enslaved land:

> The tame bird was in a cage, the free bird was in the forest;
> They met when the time came; it was a decree of fate.
> The free bird cries, 'O my love, let us fly to the wood.'
> The caged bird whispers, 'Come hither, let us both live in the cage.'
> Says the free bird, 'Among bars, where is the room to spread one's wings?'
> 'Alas,' cries the caged bird, 'I should not know where to sit perched in the sky.'

His was a voice of freedom; but it was more important to him that every individual be free to pursue his destiny. 'Give me the strength never to…bend my knees before insolent might,' he prayed in *Gitanjali*. As a result he was an iconoclast, dissenting not only from Empire but even from the political orthodoxies of his own country's struggle for Independence.

Perhaps, in this context, his disagreements with Mahatma Gandhi are not so surprising. He objected to the Mahatma's non-cooperation movement on what one might term philosophical grounds. He considered it 'political asceticism', and asceticism was not something of which he approved. '"No" in its passive moral form is asceticism and in its active moral form is violence,' he argued in a letter to the Mahatma's British associate C.F. Andrews. Nor did he have much patience for the Mahatma's method of fasting unto death. 'Fasting, which has no direct action upon the conduct of misdoers,' he wrote to Gandhiji in 1933, 'and which may abruptly terminate one's power further to serve those who need help…is all the more unacceptable for any individual who has the responsibility to represent humanity.' Gandhi was not convinced, but their exchanges are amongst the most stimulating intellectual pleasures of the freedom movement.

At the same time, Tagore was not exactly an internationalist in the classic sense beloved of UN aficionados like myself. He died before the UN was created, but he did not think highly of its forerunner organization, the League of Nations. Tagore wrote of the League that it was well conceived in theory but not in practice, because it was an institution in which the world was represented by national governments and nationalist political leaders. 'It is,' he wrote, 'like organising a band of robbers into a police department.' There is no reason to believe he would have felt any differently about today's UN, which is also an organization of States rather than peoples.

When he won the Nobel Prize for Literature in 1913, his acceptance speech, read out at the grand official banquet by the British Charge d'Affaires in Norway, consisted of one sentence: 'I beg to convey to the Swedish Academy my grateful appreciation of the breadth of understanding which has brought the distant near, and has made a stranger a brother.'

If Tagore, the man of sophisticated political, educational and spiritual ideas, has dominated this appreciation, it would be wrong to omit the other Tagore, the author of some of the finest love poems and songs ever written in Bengali. My personal favourite is one I read to my wife upon our engagement, and I will repeat it here, for it is too good to omit:

I seem to have loved you in numberless forms, numberless times,
In life after life, in age after age forever.
My spell-bound heart has made and re-made the necklace of songs
That you take as a gift, wear round your neck in your many forms
In life after life, in age after age forever.

Whenever I hear old chronicles of love, its age-old pain,
Its ancient tale of being apart or together,
As I stare on and on into the past, in the end you emerge
Clad in the light of a star piercing the darkness of time:
You become an image of what is remembered forever.

You and I have floated here on the stream that brings from the fount
At the heart of time, love of one for another.
We have played alongside millions of lovers, shared in the same
Shy sweetness of meeting, the same distressful tears of farewell—
Old love, but in shapes that renew and renew forever.

Today it is heaped at your feet, it has found its end in you,
The love of all man's days both past and forever:
Universal joy, universal sorrow, universal life,
The memories of all loves merging with this one love of ours—
And the songs of every poet past and forever.

With his long beard and his flowing white robe, Rabindranath Tagore epitomized for many the archetype of the Indian sage, the precursor of so many godmen and gurus who have followed his footsteps to the West. There is little doubt that his magisterial mind and his authoritative presence did a great deal to inspire admiration across the world, and to spark a revival of interest in Hinduism and in the teachings of Hindu spirituality. Tagore's Hinduism had little to do with the Hindu-ness sought to be promoted by today's Hindutva brigades; it was a faith free of the restrictive dogma of holy writ, untrammelled in its yearning for the divine, and universalist in its conception and its appeal. This is what made his ideas so attractive to non-Indians. He had a great respect for Christianity, which he saw as emerging in many ways from Asia: 'I think it has been the good fortune of the West,' he wrote, 'to have the opportunity of absorbing the spirit of the East through the medium of the Bible.'

When the great British poet Wilfred Owen (author of the greatest anti-war poem in the English language, 'Dulce et Decorum Est') was to return to the front to give his life in the futile First World War, he recited Tagore's 'Parting Words' to his mother as his last goodbye. When he was so tragically and pointlessly killed, Owen's mother found Tagore's poem copied out in her son's hand in his diary:

> When I go from hence
> let this be my parting word,
> that what I have seen is unsurpassable.

> I have tasted of the hidden honey of this lotus
> that expands on the ocean of light,
> and thus am I blessed
> —let this be my parting word.

> In this playhouse of infinite forms
> I have had my play
> and here have I caught sight of him that is formless.

> My whole body and my limbs
> have thrilled with his touch who is beyond touch;
> and if the end comes here, let it come
> —let this be my parting word.

And yet this magnificent wielder of words spoke modestly of the value of poetry. 'Words are barren, dismal and uninspiring by themselves,' he said in a 1922 lecture, 'but when they are bound together by some bond of rhythm they attain their significance as a reality which can be described as creative.'

With his typical generosity, Tagore said of the artist William Rothenstein, 'He had the vision to see truth and the heart to love it.' The same was true of himself. Rabindranath Tagore would have won immortality in any of his chosen fields; instead he remains immortal in all.

THE ORIGINAL ANNA: THE LIFE AND TIMES OF
C.N. ANNADURAI

I have long argued that in a vital sense we are all minorities within the immensity and diversity of India. Nowhere does this seem more apparent than in Tamil Nadu, a state where consciousness of difference from the rest of India has been elevated to an existential principle. The man who both embodied this sentiment at its most extreme and tamed it most effectively was Conjeevaram Natarajan (C.N.) Annadurai, universally known simply as Anna.

Anna, or 'elder brother', as he was affectionately known even as a young man, made the journey from separatism and the contemplation of secession to cultural nationalism and finally political integration with the rest of India. His mission evolved from awakening Dravidian consciousness to winning Tamils their rightful place within a quasi-federal Indian polity in a peaceful manner. His impact still resonates in contemporary Indian politics, with Tamil Nadu being ruled alternately for nearly half a century now by two rival parties, each seeking to claim his mantle and portray themselves as the true inheritors of his legacy.

Anna belongs amongst the very few Indian leaders who were not drawn to the Independence Movement and consequently to the Congress party. Anna's college years—the formative period of his life—had drawn him to the Non-Brahmin Movement led by the charismatic Periyar Ramaswamy Naicker, founder of the Self-Respect Movement and leader of the Justice Party. Anna was swept up in his mentor Periyar's almost magnetic attraction to the youth of the Madras Presidency. But he was no slavish follower: there evolved a complex relationship between the two leaders, some thirty years apart in age and in many ways fundamentally different.

The star disciple's novel contribution to Periyar's movement was his harnessing of the theatre to draw new recruits to the Dravidian Self-Respect Movement. The use of the new medium of cinema followed, bringing ordinary Tamils flocking to be both entertained and not so subtly educated in Annadurai's political beliefs. Together, the two leaders were a formidable force, as was evident from the 1938 agitation against the introduction of Hindi and the conversion of the fading Justice Party to the popular Dravidar Kazhagam in 1944. But the relationship was strained at times because of the divergent personalities and visions of the two leaders.

Anna was known for his mesmerizing speaking and writing abilities. He edited the party publications and founded *Dravida Nadu*, the flagship journal. The accounts of Anna's associates testify both to Anna's towering oratory and his humility. To operate in an age where communication was not as swift or wide as now and to enlist support and garner recruits for a cause distinct from the Gandhian struggle for independence must have been a herculean task. Today, thanks to the media and the internet, people are recognized instantly. But in Anna's time the opposite was the problem. So much so that a lorry driver from whom Annadurai once attempted to hitch a lift told Anna to his face, 'Don't kid me! As if you are the great Annadurai and the meeting would be cancelled because of your absence!' The man had obviously heard of Anna but had not seen him. Once Anna reassured him that he was in fact 'that Annadurai', he was promptly given a ride to the event where his expectant audience was waiting.

In Anna's early years with Periyar, he was still under the intellectual thrall of his mentor. He initially echoed Periyar in calling for setting Hindu religious texts on fire for having 'enslaved' the Tamil psyche. But in time, his more pragmatic nature asserted itself, for Anna realized how deep-rooted religious yearnings are in the Indian soil. He began to speak against superstition but not against faith. His view of religion was 'One Race, One God' (Onre Kulam Oruvanae Thevan) and his secularism took on Gandhian echoes when he described himself as a Hindu without the sacred ash, a Christian minus the holy cross, and a Muslim sans the prayer cap. Rather than echoing Periyar in disavowing religion altogether, he advocated that religion should serve the poor. His movies advanced this view, much to Periyar's displeasure.

The two also differed on tactics. Anna worked to develop a mass movement, but Periyar, who did not suffer fools gladly, preferred to eschew populism for hardcore reform; in 1944 he announced that his party would not contest elections, a tactic with which Anna disagreed. Slights, real and imagined, irked Anna. In August 1947 the first open split occurred over a fundamental issue: Anna, always conscious of public opinion, rightfully differed with his mentor on India's independence, which Periyar denounced as a fraud on the Dravidian people, calling for a day of mourning in southern India. To Anna such a view would bring 'indelible blame' to the movement, and he disagreed openly, preferring to hail a national achievement that was being celebrated by the masses. At that stage, though, he did not disavow his mentor's advocacy of a Dravida Nadu, separate from the Indian Union.

But Hindi brought them together again and the two resumed their joint struggle for Dravidian self-respect in independent India. Attempts to impose Hindi on non-Hindi-speaking people as India's official language were resisted as inevitably reducing the latter to second-class citizenship; majoritarianism, Anna feared, would result in the tyranny of the Hindi-speaking North. As he put it: 'It is claimed that Hindi should be the common language because it is spoken by the majority. Why should we then claim the tiger as our national animal instead of the rat which is so much more numerous? Or the peacock

as our national bird when the crow is ubiquitous?' In this he went beyond
Periyar in seeing the potential of the issue to mobilize the Tamil masses.

For fourteen years together the two had spoken against caste, superstition
and a host of other ills that plagued Indian, and specifically, Tamil society.
When the break came in 1949, it was over Periyar's marriage to a much
younger woman and consequent doubts about Periyar's intentions regarding
the leadership of the movement, which many had assumed would eventually
be handed over to Anna or to Periyar's nephew E.V.K. Sampath. Anna left
Periyar and started his own organization dedicated to the same ideals—the
Dravida Munnetra Kazhagam. Sampath joined him (they later parted over
Sampath's distaste for the influence of cinema personalities in the party). The
DMK soon developed a much wider mass base than the parent party, fighting
for social justice, the advancement of the poor and the rights of the Tamil
people, and fiercely opposing the imposition of Hindi.

Strikingly, Anna never spoke ill of his mentor, nor indeed of any of his
adversaries, a standard of conduct not all his followers have been able to maintain.
He brought to public life a level of political decorum and decency that is rare
today, proclaiming that Periyar was his only leader and would remain so, even
while they went their separate ways. Periyar was not quite so gracious: he
made it his mission to fight Anna and the DMK and supported the Congress
leader Kamaraj as a 'true Tamil'. When Anna vanquished the Congress in the
elections of 1967 and became chief minister, he was advised against paying a
visit to Periyar to seek his blessings, given the old man's political hostility to
him. Anna bristled with rage and, declaring that he was what he was because
of Periyar, made the journey to seek the benediction of his former mentor.

Anna's political evolution and vision after his split with Periyar continued
on the issue of separatism. By 1962, as the nation braced for war with China,
his party's growth triggered the 16th Amendment to the Indian Constitution,
banning secession. Anna, after arguing unsuccessfully against the amendment
in Parliament, recognized that it had invalidated a central plank of his party;
pursuing secession now would drive his movement underground and destroy
its effectiveness as an instrument of much broader goals. Anna therefore deftly
used the Chinese intervention to give up the movement's advocacy of a
Dravida Nadu, rallying the Tamil people to the national cause in the face of
the foreign peril. It was to prove a turning point in the DMK's achieving
acceptability as a plausible claimant to power in the state.

The difficulties of founding and heading a party for eighteen years against
the formidable Congress and the communist movements in Tamil Nadu should
not be underestimated. It was he who wielded the DMK into a formidable
political movement, using his own and his aides' creative talents to fashion highly
effective propaganda for the fledgling party's beliefs. Theatrical plays, blockbuster

cinema and agitprop methods against price rise or against the imposition of Hindi as a national language fuelled the DMK's steady political rise. Anna, his star disciples, the brilliant screenwriter Kalaignar Muthuvel Karunanidhi and the star M.G. Ramachandran, known throughout the south as 'MGR', used the tinsel world to the advantage of the movement and the party.

The Congress party in Tamil Nadu was led by a giant, K. Kamaraj Nadar. Kamaraj was a hugely popular leader, credited for the success of the 1956 Avadi Congress which had made him a national figure. Uniquely, Kamaraj had visited each of the more than 16,000 villages in Tamil Nadu twice, an incredible feat for anyone in those days of bad roads and atrocious transportation. The developmental projects he initiated and his initiatives in education, rural electrification, mid-day meals and the relative prosperity that was ushered by the Kamaraj dispensation meant that Anna was challenging not a leaderless ruling party or a party in decline but a towering figure. But Kamaraj's success led to a revolution of rising expectations and as Anna himself declared, he was able to tap into these greater expectations from the masses.

As an agitationist, Anna had been fiery, effective and popular, courting arrest with his defiance and being jailed multiple times. In power, Anna was a very different leader. He could not fall asleep the night before his swearing in, not because of the impending new and exalted status he would receive, but because of the huge responsibilities before him. The teeming millions of poor and the depressed came to his mind and kept him awake.

It was Anna who, as chief minister, introduced rice subsidies, legalized 'self-respect marriages' that did not require a Brahmin priest, ordered the removal of pictures of Hindu gods and goddesses from government offices and schools, dropped Hindi from government schools and renamed the state of Madras as Tamil Nadu. He conducted the Second World Tamil Conference in Madras in January 1968 and travelled to the US as a recipient of a Chubb Fellowship from Yale University. Sadly he was not to be able to serve his people long. Anna's failing health in office limited his governmental role and the falling standards in public life dismayed him greatly. As cancer ate into Anna's health, he was acutely conscious that the cancer of corruption was eating into the state's political ethos.

During his brief tenure, though, Anna made an inestimable contribution to India's political unity through his enlightened advocacy of federalism and co-operative Centre-State relations. The DMK had been seen by many as on a par with the other sub-nationalist movements of that time—the Naga struggle in the northeast, the Akali agitation for a Punjabi Suba and the Kashmiri nationalist movement led by Sheikh Abdullah. Anna's victory had led many in New Delhi to fear that his former separatism would reappear. But Anna proved a wise and moderate statesman, using his position to advocate a greater devolution of power to the states, arguing that more self-reliant states would actually strengthen the centre. Anna began the process, still evolving, that has taken India to a more genuine federalism in recent years.

At a meeting with the media, Anna was asked why the Congress had lost. 'Because they were in power for long,' Anna responded. 'No party should be in power for more than ten years... As you get used to power you become intoxicated by it. That is what I pray to the Almighty every day; that I should not be intoxicated by power.' 'Do you welcome a Congress government in Delhi and an opposition government in Madras?' To this Anna replied, 'Indira Gandhi is ruling ably. Only in the issue of language, she had taken a hasty decision. Other opposition parties have not grown to a stage where they could take up the responsibility of government in Delhi. Therefore, as far as the nation's future goes I would like the Congress returning to power in Delhi.' Almost every word in this exchange echoes with relevance in the political environment of India half a century later.

Anna was a multi-faceted personality, modest, creative, compassionate and humane. He was unique in the annals of Indian leadership in being an accomplished playwright, screenplay writer, and journalist as well as a highly effective party leader, organizer and administrator. A mesmerizing orator in Tamil, Anna rivalled Pandit Nehru in his ability to draw crowds, and like Narendra Modi today, tickets were sometimes sold for his speeches. Yet his humility, probity and discretion were unquestionable. His conquest of the hearts and minds of his people was earnest and well deserved.

Anna, though known to the Tamil diaspora as the apostle of Tamil nationalism, surprised many by his mature speeches and interviews as an Indian federalist on his trips to Malaysia and Singapore as well as to the US and Japan. On foreign policy, he quelled any thoughts abroad of India being a divided house by declaring, 'That is Delhi's issue. There is no authority for the state government [to conduct its own diplomacy]. Yet, we generally concur with the Indian government's foreign policy.'

He was also a world citizen. In New York, Anna met the United Nations secretary-general, U. Thant. The UN head's Chef de Cabinet, C. V. Narasimhan of Madras, a crusty Tamil Brahmin and a formidable figure whom I had the privilege of knowing in his last years, accompanied Anna to U. Thant. Narasimhan might have been expected to look askance at the Dravidian firebrand, but the 59-year-old Anna disarmed them both. He told the secretary-general that more than 2,000 years ago the Tamil poet Kaniyan Poongunranar had espoused the UN idea of universalism in his lines 'Yaadhum oore, yaavarum kelir' meaning 'to us all places are one, all men our kin'.

His flair for the theatrical built his party, but it was his substantive vision that helped the movement he began retain power in Tamil Nadu for five decades, despite splitting, not over beliefs but personalities. Cinema had become such a success that it would bring divisions into the party, but even that preserved Anna's legacy, for it gave impatient voters a choice of Dravidian parties to opt for, rather than obliging them to turn to a non-Dravidian party if they wanted change.

He was also perhaps unique in contemporary Indian politics as the only leader of any party who encouraged the emergence of a second line of leadership in his own lifetime. Anna made it a point to groom promising leaders like Karunanidhi and MGR, identifying their talent and encouraging them to develop their leadership aspirations under his tutelage. When he passed away at the tragically young age of 59 from throat cancer—said to have been brought on by his lifelong habit of chewing tobacco—no one needed to ask, 'After Anna who?' The movement continued in government, and in its variants as the DMK and the Anna DMK (founded by MGR), has remained in power since.

Leaders such as Anna are rare. He was a giant of our age who deserves to be far better known outside his native Tamil Nadu. The impact of Anna's life and message still endures. Every thinking Indian should be aware of it. Sadly, most outside Tamil Nadu are not.

THE MANMOHAN LEGACY

Twenty years ago, India's mild-mannered finance minister delivered a startlingly bold Budget to the nation with the memorable words, 'No power on earth can stop an idea whose time has come.' The idea he was advancing was that of the liberalization of the Indian economy, and the reforms he ushered in proved almost revolutionary, lifting many of the controls of the 'licence-permit-quota Raj' and transforming India's derisory 'Hindu rate of growth' from below 3 per cent to a galloping, even tigerish, 8 per cent plus in the decade and a half that followed.

Twenty-odd years later, that finance minister, and later prime minister is being pilloried by every pundit with a soapbox, for indecision, pusillanimity and presiding over 'policy paralysis' while corrupt colleagues allegedly made off with the nation's silver. His mildness dismissed as timidity, his calm and unflappable manner excoriated as complacency and ineffectiveness, he is being blamed for the bloom coming off the Indian rose. He was even damned as an 'underachiever' by a prominent international newsmagazine.

So as Manmohan Singh turned octogenarian, had he lost the plot? Or are his critics being grossly unfair? This is the same man who did more than anyone to earn his country a worldwide reputation as the world's next big economic success story. Manmohan Singh deserves better.

Yes, there was bad news: some investor flight (mainly because of the passing of a retrospective tax law designed to net taxes from foreign transactions involving Indian companies), mounting inflation as food and fuel prices rose, and political troubles for his ruling coalition which had, for example, delayed the introduction of a new policy to permit Foreign Direct Investment in India's retail trade—a policy that was announced and then suspended for a year because of domestic political opposition. But all this was a minor blip in a graph of long-term success. The pessimism infecting most of the criticism was as exaggerated as the earlier boosterism about India was overblown.

Manmohan Singh's accomplishments were extraordinary. The India he took by the scruff of the neck in 1991 was an inefficient and under-performing centrally-planned economy which for forty-five years had placed bureaucrats rather than businessmen on its 'commanding heights', stifled enterprise under a straitjacket of regulations and licenses, thrown up protectionist barriers and denied itself trade and foreign investment in the name of self-reliance, subsidized an unproductive public sector and struggled to redistribute its poverty. Today's India boasts a thriving, entrepreneurial and globalized economy, with a dynamic and creative business culture, treating with the world on its own terms and pulling over 10 million people a year above the poverty line. The contrast is extraordinary—and no one deserves a greater share of the credit for this transformation than Manmohan Singh.

Even as the planet faced an unprecedented global economic crisis and recession, India weathered the worldwide trend and remained the second fastest growing major economy in the world after China—at a time when most countries suffered negative growth rates in at least one quarter in the last four years. Manmohan Singh's stewardship had a lot to do with this. His was the voice heard with greatest respect when the G-20 gathered to discuss the world's macro-economic situation. President Obama has mentioned him first amongst the top three world leaders he admires.

The Indian economy grew nearly 7 per cent in 2011-12; the services sector grew at 9 per cent, and accounts for 58 per cent of India's GDP growth—a stabilizing factor when a world in recession can't afford to buy more manufactured goods. According to the 2011 census, the country's 247 million households, two-thirds of them rural, saw literacy rates rise to 74 per cent (from 65 per cent in 2001); 51,000 schools were opened and 680,000 teachers appointed in just two years (2010-2012). An impressive 69 per cent of Indians had phones, up from just 9 per cent a decade before that; 100 million new phone connections were established each year during UPA's second term, including 40 million in rural areas, and India had 943.5 million telephone connections. Thanks to the ethos brought in by Manmohan Singh, nearly 60 per cent of Indians have a bank account (indeed, more than 50 million new bank accounts had opened in three years (2009-2012), mainly in rural India). Some 20,000 megawatts (MW) in additional power generation capacity was added in 2011, with 3.5 million new electricity connections in rural India; also in 2011, 8,000 new villages got power for the first time, and 93 per cent of Indians in towns and cities had at least some access to electricity.

The real picture of the UPA's and India's clear progress in the face of myriad challenges is far removed from the biased portrayal of a government beset by inaction and failure. Take education, the subject of the ministry I was a minister in. Literacy rates rose to 74 per cent; more than 75,000 schools were opened and nearly a million teachers appointed in just three years (2009-2012). The number of central universities increased from seventeen to forty-four during 2004 to 2013; nine IITs (Indian Institute of Technology) were added to the seven existing IITs; the number of IIMs (Indian Institute of Management) more than doubled from six to thirteen; and five IISERs (Indian Institute of Science Education and Research) and two IIITs (International Institute of Information Technology) were also established by the UPA. Despite a tragedy in Bihar (described separately in this volume), more than ten crore schoolchildren received nutritious hot meals every day under the Mid-Day Meal Scheme, which kept children in school, nourished them and reduced dropout levels.

Yes, corruption did exist, but it's an Indian problem, not a problem to be blamed on Manmohan Singh alone. Corruption has been endemic despite, before and beyond his Prime Ministership. Though many of the lurid newspaper headlines about corruption may yet prove to have been exaggerated, the revelations that have fuelled them are at least proof of Indian democracy at work—institutions like the Comptroller and Auditor-General, the judiciary, the media and civil society functioning with fierce independence and passion. And the irresponsibly destructive behaviour of the Opposition did more to foment the worst perceptions about India's performance as a nation unready for the opportunities of the 21st century than any of the government's alleged failures.

The UPA never argued that everything was perfect in India. Of course we had problems and challenges: the point is, were we on course to overcome them? The UPA was not guilty of either complacency or inaction. It had taken the measure of India's major problems and devised far-seeing, practical and effective remedies to overcome them. From the Right to Information Act, which empowered the citizenry and made public officials more accountable, to the Right to Education Act, which brought a record number of children to school and pumped resources into moribund classrooms, UPA governance changed the face of our society. The average Indian is better off now than he or she was ten years ago. In that simple reality lies the UPA's real vindication, even if the electorate rejected its claims to return to power on that basis

A more accurate and balanced portrayal of the Manmohan legacy would look before the beyond the current 'received wisdom' of a government beset by inaction and policy paralysis. As the former prime minister himself modestly put it: 'I will be the first to say we need to do better. But let no one doubt that we have achieved much.'

FOOD SECURITY AND LAND ACQUISITION

In the last few months of its existence, India's 15th Parliament, often justifiably derided for the frequent disruptions that marred its work, surprised its detractors by passing two crucial pieces of legislation that could transform the lives of hundreds of millions of people.

The first, a Food Security Act, grants 67 per cent of India's population a right to 35 kg of rice or wheat at the price of Rs 3 a kilo. Together with related provisions that would provide nourishing meals to infants and expectant mothers, and subsidized pulses to supplement the cheaply available foodgrains, the law would add some $6 billion a year to the Indian government's fiscal deficit, but abolish the risk of starvation and malnutrition in a land where too many have gone to bed hungry for too long.

The second Act assures fair, indeed generous, compensation to people, often small landowning farmers, whose land is acquired by the State for developmental purposes. In a country where two-thirds of the population is still dependent on agriculture and the pressure of population on land means that small holdings are all that a majority of Indians live on, the new law confers rights to fair compensation on people who have often felt exploited and deprived of their livelihoods by the State's power of eminent domain. The new law requires the consent of 80 per cent of landowners before the state can acquire a major tract of land, and adds exacting provisions for the rehabilitation and resettlement of those affected, as well as compensating even tenant farmers for their loss of livelihoods and requiring that those displaced by land acquisition find employment in the institutions that displace them. The BJP, then in Opposition, voted unanimously for the law, unwilling to risk the electoral costs of thwarting such legislation. Once in power, however, they are arguing that its provisions are unreasonable, have made land acquisition virtually impossible, and require amendment. As of this writing, however, no specific change has been proposed; there is little doubt that any far-reaching amendment will be resisted by the Congress, the other parties of the UPA and the socialist 'Janata Parivar' grouping.

Taken together, the new food security and land acquisition laws are the capstone of the Indian government's gradual but firm move towards making the world's largest democracy a welfare society based on rights and entitlements rather than ephemeral charity. Critics from the right have alleged that they are unaffordable schemes that will break the budget and retard development. But critics from the left say they do not go far enough in covering all the poor and vulnerable in India. The government feels that this two-pronged attack suggests that they have got it about right.

At a time when democracies are struggling with various models of welfarism, seeking to balance the imperatives of restraining budgets with the insecurities of vulnerable populations, India has unhesitatingly moved in a direction that few thought a developing country would be able to. From the RTI Act, which has empowered the citizenry and made public officials more accountable and governance more transparent, to the RTE Act, which has brought a record number of children to school and pumped resources into moribund classrooms, the Congress government which preceded the current NDA one brought in a number of far-reaching changes.

Every fifth rural household in India benefits from MGNREGA, which provides employment mostly to the SCs, STs and women in villages (in my own state, Kerala, 92 per cent of the beneficiaries are women, whose lives have been transformed by their new income). The employment scheme has successfully raised the bargaining power of agricultural labour, resulting in higher agricultural wages, improved economic outcomes, greater purchasing power for the rural poor and reduction in distress migration. Consistent governmental investments in public health are showing better results as our country's infant mortality rate, maternal mortality rate and life expectancy levels have improved steadily.

These measures cost money, but they also empower the poor and help them break free of their poverty. When governmental policies keep India's telecom rates among the lowest in the world, it is to ensure the poor can have access to a technology that gives them autonomy and freedom. When the government promotes food security, it is emboldened by its own efforts to strengthen agriculture, which have led to record production of foodgrains.

At the same time, the Manmohan Singh government did not abandon economic reform. It pursued the decision to permit FDI in multi-brand retail and civil aviation even at the cost of losing a recalcitrant coalition ally; subsidies on diesel and cooking gas were reduced in the face of vociferous opposition in Parliament and on the streets; pension reforms were passed.

India has suffered, like most developing countries, from declining foreign investment, poor export performance and a depreciating currency. But for the common man—the 'aam aadmi' of Indian political parlance, in whose name every party claims to speak—these debates pale in significance beside the major steps taken to build a social safety net in a country where everyone had been expected to fend for themselves.

Cynics say the new measures were motivated by electoral compulsions. One wit joked that the Food Security Bill offered 'food for the poor, security for the ruling party and the bill to the taxpayer'. But it is hardly surprising in a democracy that the government should pursue policies that are popular with a majority of the voters. The fiscal costs of such measures are high, but the average Indian is better off now than he or she was nine years ago. In that lies the Manmohan Singh government's vindication.

CONGRESS—THE WAY FORWARD

When I was first asked, in the wake of the Congress party's historic election defeat in 2014, to write on the way forward for the Congress, my initial reaction was one of hesitation. After all, as a freshly-elected second-term MP, I am something of a newcomer to the party. I am not a member of the Congress Working Committee, nor of any of its decision-making bodies. But I decided to rise to the challenge as an elected representative of the Congress, who is dismayed to be reading so many premature obituaries for my party. Though I am an AICC spokesman, however, I wish to stress that these are purely my personal views.

Let it be said up front: Reports of our demise are greatly exaggerated. The Congress is very much alive and well and retains a significant hold on the affections of the public. That we obtained just under 20 per cent of the national vote hardly makes us an irrelevance in a divided and competitive polity. We are in power in thirteen states and retain a pan-national presence second to none. Yet to be reduced to 44 seats in the Lok Sabha is sobering and points to the need for a course correction. What might that consist of? Here are eight suggestions embracing both policy and practice:

• Decide what we stand for and communicate it effectively and repeatedly. The Congress' core message has been the values it has embodied since the freedom struggle—in particular inclusive growth, social justice, abolition of poverty and the protection of the marginalized, including minorities, women, Dalits and Adivasis. These have been distorted and portrayed as pandering to vote-banks rather than as the sincere, indeed visceral, convictions they are. We are the political embodiment of India's pluralism and have been a strong and committed voice for the preservation of secularism as its fundamental reflection. We need to reaffirm our belief in these values and keep reiterating them at every opportunity. This means that our top leaders need to eschew their habitual reticence and speak out more often and more loudly. Doing so would set an example of accessibility and transparency about our values, our actions, our motives and concerns. If we share our thinking with the people, we will find it easier to bring them to our side. The media-driven mass politics of the 21st century requires open communication which the Congress in recent years has shied away from.

• Articulate a vision for the future that embraces the aspirations of India's majority—the young. A startling 40 per cent of voters in 2014 were under thirty-five. They need to hear what we have done and can do for them.

Our party has done a great deal of work in the areas of education and skill development, but not enough in job creation strategies. We need to evolve policies in this area to be implemented in the states we rule and to be advocated at the Centre. Young Indians must believe we understand their aspirations and can be trusted to promote them in government.

- Do not allow the BJP to monopolize the nationalist narrative. As the party with the most experience in safeguarding India's national interests, the Congress must proudly articulate its own nationalism and remain vigilant on security and foreign policy issues that could be mishandled by the BJP government. Though our tradition is that political differences stop at the water's edge and that foreign policy is India's, not any one party's, we must not allow the BJP to use its governmental position to be identified as the sole protector of Indian national pride, which we may define very differently.

- Be a constructive Opposition inside and outside Parliament. This does not imply meek surrender to the BJP majority. But knee-jerk opposition for the sake of opposing (the style adopted by the BJP during UPA rule) will put us out of sync with the mandate given by the people of India to Narendra Modi and invite public rejection. There is a broad sentiment in the country saying 'they have ruled for so long, why won't they give him a chance?' It is in our interest to co-operate whenever the BJP lives up to Mr Modi's conciliatory pronouncements and truly governs for the benefit of all Indians, but to oppose him robustly whenever he pursues a sectarian or divisive agenda.

- Devote most of the party's attention to the grass roots. The Congress is rightly accused of having lost touch with the grass roots in many states. We must focus more on panchayat and local government elections, and pay more attention to the petty problems of governance and corruption that beleaguer most Indians and which voters blamed us for when they occurred under our rule. We have to return to the ethos of politics as social work for those who cannot help themselves.

- Promote inner-party democracy and rein in internal dissent. Rahul Gandhi has been consistently right on this. Open up the party to internal elections for its key positions, including membership of the CWC. Allow, indeed encourage, the emergence of local, state and regional leaders, ratified by periodic votes of party members. At the same time, crack down severely on the disloyalty and dissidence stoked by those who put their personal ambitions above the party's interests, a habit visible in many places during the recent elections. When such behaviour occurs against elected leaders, it is easier to discredit than when it is conducted against those who can be portrayed as unelected courtiers.

- Explore pragmatic coalitions so as not to cede the anti-government space to regional parties. It would damage us if a coalition of regional parties were to take over the visible and audible role of the main opposition to the BJP government. We are the largest national opposition party and must reach out to embrace them in our common efforts to resist unacceptable BJP policies. Political arrangements and adjustments will also permit us to put up a stronger fight both in Parliament and in state assembly elections. But we have to be careful not to let our own local party structures atrophy as a result of such understandings. In the long term we must revive the Congress as a credible alternative in those states where we have not been in power for a quarter century or more—especially UP, Bihar, West Bengal and Tamil Nadu—and which account for 205 seats in the Lok Sabha that we can't just write off.

- Wield leverage on the central government through the issue of centre-state relations. This is an issue on which we can make common cause with regional parties. When the Congress lost power at the Centre, it still controlled thirteen state governments. Two fell by the wayside when elections ended Congress rule in Maharashtra and Haryana; prospects in forthcoming State Assembly elections do not appear very promising. Still, the Congress remains the only party with a national footprint larger than the BJP's. At the same time, we must use our performance in state governments to demonstrate that we are the natural party of governance— the very status that BJP is seeking to usurp. This will mean sending some of our national stalwarts back to their states to strengthen the party there, rather than congregating in Delhi where they are less needed in the new dispensation.

These suggestions are by no means an exhaustive list. But in my view they offer some pointers to the way forward for India's oldest, most inclusive and most experienced party to restore its past glory.

INDIA'S ECONOMIC MIRACLE

Surviving the 2008-09 global financial crisis

As the world begins to breathe a little easier, Indians are looking back with particular satisfaction at how we have coped with the recent global economic crisis. Even as the planet has faced an unprecedented worldwide recession, India still happens to be the second fastest growing economy in the world. During the global financial crisis, when most countries in the world suffered negative growth rates in at least one quarter in the last two years, India's gross domestic product (GDP) grew over 6 per cent in every quarter and reached 7.9 per cent in the last quarter of 2009.

India's achievement is all the more striking because the Pakistani terrorist attacks on Mumbai—India's financial nerve-centre and commercial capital—in late November 2008 had come in the midst of the financial crisis. The terrorists dented the worldwide image of India as an emerging economic giant, a success story of the era of globalization and an increasing magnet for investors and tourists. In late 2008, foreign investors withdrew $12 billion from the stock markets. And yet, India's resilience in the face of adversity, and its mature restraint in the face of violent provocation, encouraged investors to return. Foreign direct investment reached $27.3 billion in 2008-09 in spite of the global financial crisis, and hit a rate of $1 billion per week in May 2009.

It helped that India is a country much less dependent than most on global flows of trade and capital. India relies on external trade for about 20 per cent of its GDP; its large and robust internal market accounts for the rest. Indians continued producing goods and services for other Indians, and that kept the economy humming. Though India's merchandise exports did register declines of about 30 per cent, our services exports continued to do well. Indians abroad stayed loyal to India: remittances from our overseas Indian community remained robust, reaching $46.4 billion in 2008-09, the bulk of which came from the mainly blue-collar Indian expatriate community in the Gulf.

India's generally conservative financial system played a vital hand too. Our banks and financial institutions were not tempted to buy mortgage-supported securities and credit default swaps whose toxicity ruined several Western financial institutions. Among the domestic growth drivers, domestic capital formation retained much of its momentum from the preceding years. The Government of India adopted a proactive fiscal policy, rolling out two rounds of fiscal stimulus packages. India's financial authorities have pursued policies providing for lower interest rates, expanded credit and lower excise duties, all of which have served to boost economic growth.

There are still challenges. Reform is pursued with the hesitancy of a coalition government constantly looking over its electoral shoulders. Privatization of India's bloated public sector (from massive coal and steel enterprises to the loss-making national carrier Air India) has been slow to get off the ground. The ever-persistent complaints of corruption and bureaucratic red tape have not faded with liberalization. The infrastructure remains woeful, as any visitor to India notices. Power shortages are frequent. Forty per cent of the population still remains below a poverty line drawn just this side of the funeral pyre. Yet, during the rule of the Congress-led coalition, reform continued to be pursued. And, although there were still many problems when it was voted out of power, it made a real difference to the lives of people. In the fifteen years till 2008, India pulled more people out of poverty than in the previous forty-five years—averaging some 10 million people a year in the last decade. The country visibly prospered, and despite population growth, per capita income grew faster and higher in each of these years than ever before.

The global financial crisis, far from prompting India to retreat, was treated as an opportunity to safeguard those gains and to build on them. Indeed, one of the more interesting (and largely unremarked) developments in recent Indian politics was the startling shift in the nature of the country's discourse about capitalist economics.

In a pattern common to (or emulated by) many developing countries, 'self-reliance' and economic self-sufficiency were India's national mantra for more than four decades after independence. Whereas in most of the West most people axiomatically associated capitalism with freedom, India's nationalists associated capitalism with slavery—for, after all, the British East India Company had come to trade and stayed on to rule. (One of the lessons history teaches us is that history often teaches us the wrong lessons.) So India's nationalist leaders were suspicious of every foreigner with a briefcase, seeing him as the thin edge of a neo-imperial wedge.

This had implications for India's role in the world economy as well. Instead of integrating India into the global capitalist system, as only a handful of post-colonial countries like Singapore chose to do, India's leaders (and those of most former colonies) were convinced that the political independence they had fought for so hard and long could only be guaranteed through economic independence. So self-reliance became the slogan, the protectionist barriers went up and India spent forty-five years increasingly divorced from global trade and investment.

Domestically, bureaucrats rather than businessmen were placed on the 'commanding heights' of the Indian economy, and India shackled itself to statist controls that emphasized distributive justice above economic growth, stifled free enterprise, and discouraged foreign investment. As the nation sputtered along at

2 to 3 per cent GDP growth while the 'Asian tigers' roared ahead, economists derisively spoke of the 'Hindu rate of growth'. 'Self-reliance' guaranteed both political freedom and freedom from economic exploitation. The result was that for most of the first five decades since independence, India, despite the best of intentions, pursued an economic policy of subsidizing unproductivity, regulating stagnation, and distributing poverty. We called this socialism.

Socialism, Indian style, was a compound of nationalism and idealism. It was the conviction that items vital for the economic well-being of Indians must remain in Indian hands—not the hands of Indians seeking to profit from such activity, but the disinterested hands of the state, the father and mother to all Indians. In this kind of thinking, performance was not a relevant criterion for judging the utility of the public sector: its inefficiencies were masked by generous subsidies from the national exchequer, and a combination of vested interests—socialist ideologues, bureaucratic management, self-protective trade unions, and captive markets—kept it beyond political criticism.

The 'permit-license-quota' culture of statist socialism allowed the ruling politicians and bureaucrats to use politics as a vehicle for self-gratification, giving birth to a culture of corruption that still persists. India's misfortune, in Jagdish Bhagwati's famous aphorism, was to be afflicted with brilliant economists. And clamorous politicians: for every group claimed a larger share of a national economic pie that decades of protectionist economic policies prevented from growing. It is sadly impossible to quantify the economic losses inflicted on India over four decades of entrepreneurs frittering away their energies in queuing for licenses rather than manufacturing products, paying bribes instead of hiring workers, wooing politicians instead of understanding consumers, and 'getting things done' through bureaucrats rather than doing things for themselves.

It was only after a world-class balance of payments crisis in 1991, when India's government had to physically ship its reserves of gold to London to stand collateral for an International Monetary Fund (IMF) loan, failing which the country might have defaulted on its debt, that India liberalized its economy under then finance minister Manmohan Singh. The amount of gold possessed by the women of the household has often been seen, in Indian culture, as a guarantee of the family's honour; surrendering the nation's gold to foreigners betokened a national humiliation that the old protectionism could not survive.

Since then, India has become a poster child for globalization. A country whose share of global trade had fallen from some 2 per cent in 1947 to 0.2 per cent by 1987, decided it should open itself further to the world economy. A country whose nationalists were deeply suspicious of foreign investment became convinced it could not survive without it. The Information Revolution connected India's bright young white-collar workers to Western employers and clients; IT and IT-enabled services, call centres and business process outsourcing operations, became the hallmarks of the new Indian economy. The rate of growth more than tripled, averaging 9 per cent in the decade from 1998 to 2008. It is now widely accepted across the political spectrum that India's growth and prosperity would be impossible without the rest of the world.

The young generation has grown up with liberalization and will not accept it being rolled back. Young Indians today are likely to spend a lot of their adult lives interacting with people who don't look, sound, dress or eat like them. Unlike their parents, they might well work for an internationally oriented company with clients, colleagues or investors from around the globe; and increasingly, they are likely to take their holidays in far-flung destinations. It is a far cry from the assumptions their parents grew up with.

The change has now been deeply internalized. Three different coalitions have led India's government from 1991 to 2014, including one (from 1996 to 1998) that included the Communist Party of India, and none of them departed from the new New Delhi consensus. The liberalization of the Indian economy, and of the Indian political mind, has proved irreversible.

The renewed crisis of 2012-13

And yet, to hear some people tell it, the bloom is off the Indian rose. Bad news again assailed the economy in 2012-13 as growth rates plummeted and inflation soared. Investors fled in the wake of stringent tax action against some major ones, notably following a retrospective tax passed in 2011 and sought to be applied against Vodafone. These developments even prompted some to declare that 'the India story' was over. But the pessimism was as exaggerated as the earlier optimism had been.

India, home of the oldest stock market in Asia and a thriving democracy, has the basic systems it needs to operate a twenty-first century economy in an open and globalizing world. One can say with some confidence that India will continue to prosper and pull more millions out of poverty than it has ever done; that Indian companies will compete effectively with Western corporations for business, purchase foreign companies and assets, expand their trade and overseas investments, invent and develop new technologies, and displace more economic weight around the world.

There are other reasons for being confident that India will weather the storm. One is domestic capital generation: ours is a society which has considerable resources of its own to put towards investment. And then, as the global recession shows every sign of persisting, investors looking for a place to put their money are not going to find any worthwhile returns in the West. They will look anew at India, and I believe we will start attracting significant foreign direct investment again.

If one is inclined to compare India unfavourably with China, as many are, there are a few financial numbers worth considering first. Half of India's growth has come from private consumption, less than 10 per cent from external demand; this compares with 65 per cent of China's real GDP growth coming from exports, and only 25 per cent from private consumption. (In other words, China is far more vulnerable to the vicissitudes of other countries' economic troubles). India has the highest household savings rate in Asia, at 32 per cent of disposable income. In fact, 65 per cent of our national annual savings come from households (it's under 40 per cent in China). Indian banks have only 2 per cent bad loans, versus 20 per cent in China. And our workforce has been growing at nearly 2 per cent a year in the last decade, while China's grew at less than 1 per cent.

Putting China aside, India has some plus points of its own. The economy grew nearly 7 per cent in 2011-12; the services sector grew at 9 per cent, and accounts for 58 per cent of India's GDP growth—a stabilizing factor when a world in recession can't afford to buy more manufactured goods. McKinsey estimates that the Indian middle-class will grow to 525 million by 2025, one and a half times as large as the United States' will be. Some 20,000 MW in additional power generation capacity was added in 2012, with 3.5 million new electricity connections in rural India; also that year, 8,000 new villages got power for the first time, and 93 per cent of Indians in towns and cities had at least some access to electricity.

These trends and others have mentioned earlier in this section augur well for India's macroeconomic future. And they aren't slowing: India is looking for $1 trillion in infrastructure development over the next five years, most of it under public-private partnerships. This offers hugely exciting opportunities to investors. The prospects are bright, whether a Modi government profits from it or not. India is poised to win.

THE END OF THE NEHRUVIAN CONSENSUS?

The sweeping election victory 2014 of the Bharatiya Janata Party's Narendra Modi, on a platform of aggressive nationalism and business-friendly corporatism, has raised a larger question in the minds of long-time observers of India: are we witnessing the end of the Nehruvian socio-economic consensus?

The Nehruvian consensus, named for India's first prime minister, the socialist democrat Jawaharlal Nehru, was what at one time brought India together, facilitating our maturing as a democracy and accommodating the country's many diverse interests without letting any one group or section dominate the nascent nation state. It is fashionable today to decry Nehruvian socialism as a corrupt and inefficient system that condemned India to many years of modest growth levels. But at its core was the conviction that in a land of extreme poverty and inequality, the objective of government policy must be the welfare of the poorest, most deprived and most marginalized of our people. In Nehru's day, the best way to accomplish that was by building up structures of public ownership and state control of national resources, as well as enhancing the nation's economic capacity through government intervention.

The economic aspects of Nehru's vision did, one could argue, develop certain flaws, notably those of the so-called 'licence-permit-quota Raj', under which government control stifled entrepreneurial activity, reducing growth rates below that of India's Southeast Asian neighbours. India saw a slow repeal of much of this in the 1980s under Nehru's grandson Rajiv Gandhi, until, under the reforms initiated by his Congress party successors Narasimha Rao and Manmohan Singh, India marched into a confident new era of flourishing growth and socio-economic dynamism. The astonishing victory of the BJP under Prime Minister Modi, however, is attributed by many to his success in tapping into the restless (and rightful) aspirations of India's young. This is where the Congress party is deemed by its critics to have failed, focusing as it did on the needs of India's poorest.

Congress can justifiably argue that it helped build on the economic structures of Nehru's day while liberating them from excessive restrictions. But it remains committed to an inclusive idea of development, social justice and opportunities for the deprived and marginalized in our society—which, of course, are sometimes not easily marketable to a youthful electorate that wants change here and now. Admittedly, Congress could have communicated its values and objectives better to voters, but Modi's ability to convince our fellow citizens that he is their messiah of change, aided by a general anti-incumbency after ten years of Congress rule, led to the BJP's historic victory and prompted some to argue that the Nehruvian consensus has unravelled. In my view, reports of its demise are exaggerated.

It is alleged that the Congress failed to read the mood of the country—that growth rather than doles is what it wants. This is unfair: painting social legislation as a mere handing out of doles by the state is a caricature. Leaving aside the last two years, India witnessed record levels of growth under Congress governance. Our objective, which was supported by eminent economists, lawyers, and social activists with tremendous first-hand experience, was to distribute the fruits of this growth more equitably. And it is a fact, even if a superficial assessment of electoral results might suggest otherwise, that the lives and standards of living of most Indians have changed for the better in the last ten years.

This was not because of 'doles' but because of more generous and effective government. In fact it is exactly these doles, as critics term them, that put more children in school, got more people jobs and ensured that their basic needs were taken care of, so as to enable them to demand more from their government, which is their right, and which wave of aspirations the BJP rode so successfully. In a way, Modi owes some credit to the Congress for helping create this new aspirational India that has voted him to power. The alleged 'doles' were in fact not mere handouts but empowerment—enabling those who have little, to meet their basic needs so they can stand on their own feet and aspire to better their lives.

Some see the Congress moving further left economically to distinguish itself from the BJP, and pre-emptively argue that this would be counterproductive considering that voters have seemingly rejected socialist policies. In a country where the majority in every electoral constituency lives on less than $2 a day, writing off 'pro-poor' policies would be unwise. Congressmen can argue that it is their policies that have enabled most Indians to come out of a more basic existence into a position where they are better informed and more empowered to demand new and different things from their government.

The Nehruvian emphasis on socially inclusive growth is not simple 'leftism'; the Congress party supports growth and led the liberalization that made growth possible, but we wish to see the benefits of that growth reaching the weakest and poorest sections of our society. In the long run, I am certain that the Congress' Nehruvians will be remembered for not abandoning vast sections of society to hanker after a notion of growth that only favours a select few, at the cost of everybody else, who remain where they were.

India must shine, but it must shine for everybody. Until that is ensured, Mr Modi's triumph will prove short-lived. The Nehruvians will return.

THE FALL OF AN OLD RETAINER

I have long had enormous respect for Kunwar Natwar Singh. Intellectual, diplomat, man of letters, a raconteur par excellence and extraordinarily well-networked, Natwar Singh enjoyed the kind of career people like me grew up to admire: Stephanian, IFS officer, writer, politician, foreign minister, all at progressive levels of responsibility and accomplishment. I had met Natwar, read him, reviewed his books (always appreciatively), heard his stories, enjoyed his company and looked up to him in many ways.

That Natwar Singh would write a memoir was hardly a surprise: he has been doing so for years, mining his life, career and acquaintances for several books and multiple newspaper columns. His last two, *My China Diary* and *Walking With Lions*, were memoirs of his diplomatic and political experiences. The Natwar formula in these books and many others was fixed: anecdotal, engaging, episodic in its narrative form, often marvellously-written, with an indiscreet revelation or two, but nothing to rock any boats in the world in which he lived or offend the people he still met socially. Most of us would have expected his autobiography, *One Life is Not Enough*, to be in a similar vein.

But of course it is not: the wounds of his defenestration by the Congress party, and more particularly by the Nehru–Gandhi family he had loyally served for four generations, are still too raw. I have not yet read the book, and as a writer myself, I feel one cannot review a book one has not read, but Natwar's own revelations, in well-publicized television interviews, have indicated that at least parts of this volume are intended to settle scores.

From what one has heard, though, the most explosive of the reported revelations—that Sonia Gandhi was apparently persuaded by her son Rahul to sacrifice the prime ministership in 2004 because he feared she would be assassinated—turns out to be a damp squib. Critics of the Congress party have been spinning this story for all they are worth, to suggest that this somehow diminishes Mrs Gandhi's sacrifice. Nobody else who was allegedly present at this conversation has confirmed the story, but even if it turns out to be true, my own reaction is: so what? Mrs Gandhi would undoubtedly have sought the views and inputs of her family and close advisers before coming to a decision as to whether to accept the position the UPA coalition had just offered her. Each would have had their own reasons and motivations for advocating whichever course of action they did. Ultimately the decision was hers, and whatever be the clinching factor, many considerations, both political and personal, would have gone into making up her mind. That one of those considerations was the ever-present risk to her security should hardly surprise anyone, given that she had lost a husband and a mother-in-law to assassins. After turning down the prime ministership, she still did not shirk the risks and responsibilities that came with leading the country's largest party and ruling coalition.

So I don't make too much of this headline-grabbing story, nor of the other supposedly damning nuggets—from Rajiv Gandhi not consulting the Cabinet before offering Sri Lanka the IPKF, to government files being carried to Sonia Gandhi (again without a shred of proof). What saddens me, though, is that Natwar Singh should have descended to this level.

The aristocratic Natwar has always prided himself on being a gentleman: well-bred, well-educated, not the sort to tell stories out of school. One incident is revelatory. As a distinguished Stephanian he addressed the college's annual Games Dinner of 1974-75, which I, never proficient at games of any sort, was invited to attend as the elected President of the College Students' Union. He surveyed us, 17-to 22-year-olds with bright eyes and scrubbed faces, and chose to express a candour none of us was accustomed to from Indian officialdom. 'I look at you all,' he said bluntly, 'the best and the brightest of our fair land, smart, honest and able, and my heart sinks. Because I know that most of you will do what I did and take the civil service examinations, little realizing that if you succeed, your fate will be to take orders from the dregs of our society— the politicians.' He could see the shock on the faces of his audience as he went on: 'Don't make the mistake I did. Do something else with your lives.'

I have never forgotten the speech, thinking about which kept me awake most of that night—and helped change my own career plans. If someone as successful and important in the bureaucracy as Natwar Singh could feel this way, I wondered, what satisfaction could ordinary people without his rank or connections derive from government service? Of course, Natwar went on to put his money where his mouth was: he resigned from the government before he could attain the post of foreign secretary that most of his peers considered inevitable, and entered politics instead. This gave him a stint as Minister of State and then Minister for External Affairs, where he could give orders to the foreign secretary of the day. I am sure he relished the opportunity to set standards of which the 'dregs of society' were incapable.

Today, he has, it seems, descended to the dregs. Natwar has said he wrote *One Life Is Not Enough* because he did not want to 'take his bitterness to the funeral pyre' but the adjectives he has reportedly used to describe Sonia Gandhi, from 'authoritarian' and 'capricious' to 'Machiavellian' and 'secretive', do him little credit. If you see such traits in a person only after they dispense with your services, does it discredit them, or you?

Sadly, he has let himself down. As former Prime Minister Manmohan Singh cuttingly remarked when asked about Natwar's memoir: 'Private conversation should not be made public for capital gains.' There was a time when Natwar would have disdained a politician or a bureaucrat for doing what he did: he would have seen it as the sort of grubby and self-serving action that was beneath him. But it seems there is no level to which an embittered former confidant will not stoop: he has even described a visit to his home by Priyanka and Sonia Gandhi to urge him to respect their past confidences. That ought to make him feel ashamed.

In one of the many anti-Natwar stories he relishes telling, Mani Shankar Aiyar recounts how, at St. Stephen's College, he came across a visitors' book in which Natwar had grandly written: 'All that I am, I owe to the College.' Aiyar says he promptly scrawled beneath this notation, 'Why blame the College?'

It is a story that can be turned around to fit today's less amusing circumstances. Natwar could truthfully have written: 'All that I am, I owe to the Gandhis.' And one of us, reading his book, could truthfully have asked: 'Why blame the Gandhis?'

SAINT ANTONY AND SECULARISM

So what did A.K. Antony mean? The reticent veteran Congress leader, known nationally for his reticence and his rectitude (which have resulted in his being dubbed 'Saint Antony' by both admirers and critics), raised a few eyebrows, and some hackles, when he declared at a meeting in Thiruvananthapuram that 'there is a doubt created by the party's proximity towards minority communities. 'Some sections of society,' he said, 'have an impression that the party is inclined to certain communities or organizations. Congress policy is equal justice to everyone. But people have doubt whether that policy is being implemented or not.'

'People have lost faith in the secular credentials of the party,' he went on. 'They have a feeling that the Congress works for a few communities, especially minorities... Such a situation would open the door for the entry of communal forces into Kerala.'

The national punditocracy was quick to react to these comments, suggesting that Mr Antony was blaming the Congress party's commitment to secularism for its recent electoral setback. BJP leader L.K. Advani was quick to applaud his Congress rival for 'acknowledging' that the politics of 'minority appeasement' no longer worked.

In vain did Mr Antony's colleague, Kerala Pradesh Congress Committee president, V.M. Sudheeran, point out that his leader's statement, delivered in Malayalam to an audience of young Keralite Congress party political workers, was Kerala-centric. 'Antony has made this comment with the Congress and the UDF it leads in Kerala in mind. These were well-intentioned and meant to guide the party and coalition in proper direction,' Sudheeran told reporters. But despite his clarifications, commentators and political observers have chosen to read a national message into Mr Antony's remarks, and issued reams of exegesis questioning the relevance and effectiveness of our party's secular policies across India.

Mr Antony is probably mortified. He was making a point he had made before: in 2003, as chief minister of Kerala, he was reported to have criticized the Muslim community, calling them powerfully organized, and saying that they had secured excessive privileges by their collective clout. This, some reports claimed he said, 'could not be allowed'. The resultant backlash from Muslim voters may, in some accounts, have played a part in ensuring that Congress lost every seat it contested in Kerala in the 2004 Lok Sabha polls.

So why would he repeat that ill-fated comment? Perhaps because, in Kerala, it's true. The Congress rules at the head of a United Democratic Front (UDF) coalition whose two prominent constituents are the Indian Union Muslim

League, with 20 MLAs to the Congress' 39, and the regional Christian party, the Kerala Congress-Mani (KC-M), which has 11 MLAs. With the addition of four single-member coalition partners, each of whom has a ministry, the Congress presides over a government with a distinctly minority hue. The League provides five ministers to the Cabinet, having won the fifth two years ago after threatening to leave the government if it was denied; the KC-M and other allies furnish several Christian ministers, and the Congress itself includes Christian and Muslim leaders, leaving the 'majority community' in a minority in the UDF government. Its opponents, including both the Left and the BJP, have not hesitated to exploit the perception that the UDF government in Kerala is run by and for the minority communities. As a result, the Congress undoubtedly failed to garner a plurality of the Hindu vote in Kerala in the recent elections, even though, thanks to minority support, the UDF won 12 of the state's 20 Lok Sabha seats.

This is what Mr Antony was alluding to in his speech. He emphasized that the perception that the Congress was more inclined to minority interests needed to be addressed. 'A situation should not be created in which anyone feels that the party or the government is for someone else,' Mr Antony said. In Kerala (and particularly in my own constituency of Thiruvananthapuram, where he was speaking), this has meant that the Congress has made itself vulnerable to a consolidation of Hindu votes behind the BJP (what Mr Antony referred to as 'the entry of communal forces'). The veteran leader was reminding Congress workers that the party needed to allay this perception and win back Hindu voters.

It is easy to see why so many have extrapolated his analysis from the specific circumstances of Kerala to the national scenario. Though it is unfair to Mr Antony to suggest this, his thoughts seemed to echo those of some at the 20 May 2014 CWC meeting who blamed the election outcome on the party's 'anti-Hindu' image. Outspoken general secretary, Digvijay Singh self-critically stated in an interview on 22 May that 'the word secularism is, unfortunately, being identified with Muslim appeasement'. Though Mr Antony never used the word 'Muslim', his allusion was understood by all to be to that community.

There is a major problem with carrying this analysis too far. Many Muslims feel the Congress hasn't done enough for them; some feel their socio-economic situation reflects anything but 'Muslim appeasement'. A few even voted for the BJP, swayed by the argument that a Modi model of high economic growth would improve their fortunes more than Congress' more statist approach. If Congress seems to be abandoning them now in competing for Hindu votes, it risks falling between two stools. A 'soft Hindutva' appeal will never win hard-line Hindu voters, while minorities, deprived of a committed patron, might start voting in what they perceive to be their parochial economic interests, rather than to 'protect' their community. This could be disastrous for the Congress.

Mr Antony, an atheist and lapsed Christian, who insists on taking his oath of office as a solemn affirmation rather than in the name of God, is an unlikely proponent of Hindu majoritarianism, however. He was simply enunciating a local truth in Kerala. Nationally, he is the last person to advocate a dilution of the Congress party's historic commitment to India's pluralism and the protection of its most vulnerable citizens.

I know Mr Antony truly embodies the secular spirit in his personal as well as political life. He is right, therefore, to suggest that the perception he mentioned must be managed better, not least by the Congress' own minority partners in Kerala, who should rein in their assertiveness. But secularism itself is too fundamental a part of what the Congress is all about—and what Mr Antony has devoted himself to—to be weakened, let alone abandoned. The Congress will remain secular to the core.

IV

IDEAS OF INDIA

DEMOCRACY AND DEVELOPMENT: THE EXPERIENCE OF INDIA

During the brief period of Indira Gandhi's Emergency rule in 1975-77, when democracy was suspended, the country became a poster child of the 'bread versus freedom' debate: the question of whether democracy can literally 'deliver the goods' in a country of poverty and scarcity, or whether its inbuilt inefficiencies only impede rapid growth. The Emergency was sought to be justified in the name of development; democracy in India, it was argued, had detracted from the focus on development that was the nation's duty.

That debate was resolved in India by the elections of 1977, which defenestrated the Emergency regime and restored democracy. But the question has not gone away, and the dysfunctional politics of democratic India in recent years has made it seem even more relevant. Is the instability of political contention, and of makeshift coalitions, a luxury that a developing country cannot afford? When, for a quarter of a century, India was ruled by governments in Delhi made up of over twenty political parties, political decision-making was determined by the lowest common denominator: the weakest link in the governmental chain determined its strength. The threat of withdrawal from a coalition was enough to persuade a government to abandon a policy it otherwise thought wise. Is that an efficient way of ensuring the well-being of the Indian people? Is political freedom less valuable to the masses than bread? Or to put it bluntly, is the Chinese answer to this question more appropriate than the Indian one?

Today development and democracy as concepts are being redefined. Development as a concept is increasingly seen as one where there is a general improvement in the lives of the people—not just impressive infrastructure or Gross Domestic Product (GDP) numbers, but a qualitative improvement in the daily lives of a large part of the population. This is usually measured in the growth of per capita income as well as the fulfilment of the political, social and economic rights of the majority. Democracy is being seen as a foundation for development, one which goes beyond mere economic growth and a tool which delivers better governance, which in turn leads to a better quality of life for ordinary people.

As a person who has spent the better part of his life in the United Nations before serving in the Parliament of India and as a minister in the government, I see democracy and development as intertwined concepts. As good governance has found a place in the Millennium Development Goals and a democratic system has become an increasingly important criterion to receive international approbation (and aid), it is important that we explore the link between democracy and development in both theory and practice.

It is a commonplace saying that good governance promotes growth and that growth further improves governance. But what *is* good governance? Good governance brings into its realm a variety of factors such as accountability, transparency, equitable treatment, inclusiveness and the rule of law. These values are not always in harmony with each other, but then managing them is the primary task of politics in a democracy. While it may also seem a glaring generalization, these are qualities that, more often than not, are amply found in democracies around the world. Research has shown that democracy can successfully create institutions which promote good governance and development across several indices.

My good friend, the distinguished Nobel Laureate Amartya Sen, has persuasively argued over the years that democracy as a system of government is in fact a form of public reasoning, the outcome of which emerges through elections. Democracy gives all citizens effective political and civil rights while having the ability to deliver welfare to the poor. For Sen, a nation is not 'fit for democracy', rather it becomes fit through democracy. Democracy's special strength is its responsiveness to the needs of the people, rather than merely the wishes of the rulers. One of Sen's most enduring insights is that a substantial famine has never occurred in a nation which has a democratic government and a relatively free press. Democracies don't starve their people; they respond to the public clamour for attention to the suffering.

This concern for public welfare is a characteristic of democracy. An analysis of forty-four African states in the year 2005 revealed that under democracies they saw their expenditure on education shoot up. Research has shown that there is a healthy connection between democracy and higher spending on public health, education and social services. In the long run, democracies tend to respect property rights, individual liberties and collective freedom, all of which promote human development. These freedoms recognize the importance of human dignity and allow citizens to be able to defend their interests in appropriate forums, develop their strengths and potential, and give themselves opportunities to grow while taking their families and communities on the path of progress.

Though India's challenges are enormous, as a democracy we have always known where our priorities lay: with the poorest of the poor. Our growth was never only about per capita income figures. It was always a means to an end. And the ends we cared about were the uplift of the weakest sections of our society, the expansion of employment possibilities for them, the provision of decent health care and clean drinking water. Those ends remain. Whether we grow by 9 per cent, as we once did, or by 6 per cent, as we are doing now, our fundamental commitment as a democracy must be to the bottom

25 per cent of our society.

Democracies are also far more responsive to the people, for they go to them over a period of time in the form of elections to renew their mandate and appeal for their mandate to remain in power. Democratic governments can never dispense with the consent of the people to maintain their legitimacy. This is a defining characteristic of political power in democratic societies. This periodic exercise of reaffirming public confidence in political authority in turn helps speed up the developmental process for the people.

This is essentially why the country has visibly prospered, and despite population growth, per capita income has grown faster and higher in the past decade and a half than ever before. For more than four decades India suffered from the economics of nationalism, which equated political independence with economic self-sufficiency and so relegated us to chronic poverty and mediocrity. Now its economics are the economics of democracy: giving the people the systems they want to fulfil their material aspirations.

Democracies are also conducive to internal and external peace, without which development becomes difficult to pursue. Democracy is the best system for managing diversity. In a multi-religious, multi-ethnic nation like India, democracy permits its citizens to determine their own way of life under a state which accommodates divergent religious practices without privileging any. This gives citizens the right to grow in an environment which fosters harmony and stability.

Of course not all is sweetness and light. Democracies allow disagreements to be openly expressed. But the process of free and fair public discussion and contestation gives people the power to be stakeholders in combating social issues of a local nature without the state of suppressing them or coercing an outcome. Such constructive processes, which play a crucial role in developing the character of a democratic people, are unlikely to occur in an undemocratic state.

There are some who dismiss these arguments for democracy, especially in the Asian continent. The former prime minister of Singapore, Lee Kuan Yew once said 'I believe what a country needs to develop is discipline more than democracy. The exuberance of democracy leads to indiscipline and disorderly conduct which are inimical to development.' Nations in East Asia have largely been led by this thought process and have not seen substantially democratic governments during what was termed as their miracle years of growth. Yet a lot of the methods employed by these nations to bring in development, which include economic competition, use of international markets, spread of education and land reforms, have in fact been consistent with democratic principles. And even as these East Asian economies have grown richer, the desire of their people to experience more democratic freedoms has also deepened. As a result, many formerly authoritarian states in East Asia have become democracies at no cost to their development success stories.

While rapid industrialization leading to development has also been seen in other authoritarian regimes, it has often come at great cost in human suffering. China may have grown at breakneck speed—but it has broken necks in the process. While not all democracies have been able to deliver substantial development, they have respected the rights and freedoms of their people. And it must also be noted that this difference can be sourced to the investment each society made towards institution building and development within the country. This is also the reason that countries in East Asia have done better with few democratic processes in play.

It is also fashionable to put up the example of China against this argument. This begs the question—is China's extraordinary growth story due to its authoritarian government or its skilled and hard-working population, which attracted considerable foreign investment in an export centred model of development? China leads one to conclude that non-democracies can indeed develop, but not merely because they are not democratic. Other factors have helped China that have nothing to do with the lack of freedoms in its politics.

In any case, though it is still far away from democracy, its free economic system has made China a more open country today, and greater popular participation and economic and gradually political decision-making is already beginning to happen.

The East Asian examples have led some to suggest that poor countries cannot afford democracy and that once they have developed under autocratic rule, democratization can follow. In other words, democracy has been seen as a hallmark of developed countries with a certain level of per capita income: achieve, say, $3,000 a year per person, and you can think of democracy; stay poor and you are better off with a firm hand at the tiller. But the Indian experience has given the lie to this theory, as have many African democracies. It has been found that in Latin America, democracies recovering from communist rule and military dictatorships in the 1980's were the ones which introduced the most inclusive economic reforms, leading their population towards greater development, economic and otherwise.

India, of course, is a prime example of democracy. At a time when most developing countries opted for authoritarian models of government to promote nation-building and to direct development, India chose to be a multi-party democracy. And despite many stresses and strains, including twenty-two months of Emergency rule in the mid-1970s, India has remained a multi-party democracy–one that is corrupt and inefficient perhaps, but nonetheless flourishing. One result of this is that India strikes many as maddening, chaotic, inefficient and seemingly lacking direction as it apparently muddles its way through the second decade of the twenty-first century. Yet it works because it brings all its citizens along in the great adventure of development.

Its economic liberalization in 1991 and subsequent years of record growth occurred despite fractious democracy, coalition governments and a decade in which different political parties each had a turn at power. Our institutions, both formal and informal, allowed economic reforms to reach the lowest rung of the population, helping us to pull millions above the poverty line and allowing them to climb the social and economic ladders to a life of better quality.

The legitimacy of democracy in India comes from the faith of the vast numbers of underprivileged rather than the minuscule elite. It is the poor who turn out in large numbers to vote, because the poor know that their votes matter. They also believe that exerting their franchise is the most effective means of demonstrating what they really demand from the government. Frustration with government manifests itself in voting against the rulers rather than in revolts or insurrections. When violent movements arise, they are often defused through accommodation in the democratic process, so that in state after state, yesterday's militants become today's chief ministers—and thanks to the vagaries of democracy, tomorrow's leaders of the Opposition.

The Indian example proves that democracy can manage the most complex societal systems with dexterity to create and execute policies which have far reaching effects, without disrupting either society or state. Research has also shown that second generation reforms, like banking and financial sector reforms and anti-corruption measures amongst others, requires competencies and political attributes which only democracy can offer.

Indeed, the absence of democracy can stifle development. The political scientist Larry Diamond once aptly wrote that 'predatory, corrupt, wasteful, abusive, tyrannical, incompetent governance is the bane of development'. Young nations need democratic institutions to respond to their populations, weed out corruption, have access to the lowest sections of society to understand their problems and formulate policies which can counter them. While these measures actively lay the foundation of human development, these will come to nothing if a nation does not makes its institutions accountable to the people through a free press and judiciary.

In democratic systems, development and prosperity fuel further growth through a virtuous circle; historical experience tells us that development in a democratic society creates an educated and enlightened middle class which creates for itself additional opportunities to explore and expand the political arena. Empowered people articulate themselves better while they press for social and political freedoms with the need to create an open line of discourse between the government and the public so that their voices are heard and priorities noted.

Democracy is also a necessity to allow people to become creative in pursuing their goals. Democracy fosters an environment of openness, giving opportunities to people to take risks, permits citizens access to information, and assures them the right to express themselves freely without fear of repercussions. The ability to think and debate freely without censorship frees the imagination, leading to innovative practices which are the cornerstone of development. We live in a time where the challenges we face can be tackled only with creative and innovative practices. Democracies have historically been better at innovation than authoritarian systems which stifle original thought.

Some experts have argued that democracy does not lend itself to rapid development—that compromises which are in fact an essential element of democratic governance, and the need for decision makers in a democratic society to take the wants of their constituents into account, are distractions that less developed states could ill afford if they are to make the hard decisions necessary to improve their futures.

Of course, this argument rests on a set of assumptions that countries like India have never accepted. The most significant of these assumptions is that development is solely about generating wealth. The Christian Bible (in three different places) offers the undoubted wisdom that 'man does not live by bread alone'—and neither, I might add, does a woman. After all, why does man need bread? Of course to survive! But why bother to survive, if it is only to eat more bread? Democracy recognizes that life is about more than survival. But we in India are also—perhaps uniquely among the large democracies—very well aware that neither man nor woman, nor country nor State, will live well or long unless adequate attention is given to both the baking and distribution of bread, the boiling of rice, the rolling of a chapatti.

The question of whether democracy and development can go together has been answered convincingly by India. And just as we are aware—and proud—of the strong democratic traditions in today's world, we are also aware of our responsibility to develop—to seek to bring all our people into the twenty-first century with comfortably full bellies and comfortably fulfilling occupations. Democracy and human rights are fundamental to who we are; but human rights begin with breakfast.

So countries like modern India have struggled to come to terms with what has sometimes been seen as the competing demands of freedom and development, just as it has struggled with the need to fully respect diversity and at the same time strengthen and pay homage to our sense of identity. Democracy, as precept and practice, will never wear the mantle of perfection. I have written extensively of the many problems that India faces, the poor quality of much of its political leadership, the rampant corruption, the criminalization of politics. And yet—corruption is being tackled by an activist judiciary and by energetic investigative agencies that have not hesitated to indict the most powerful Indian politicians. (If only the rate of convictions matched the rate of indictments, it would be even better...) The rule of law remains a vital Indian strength. Non-governmental organizations actively defend human rights, promoting environmentalism, fighting injustice. The press is free, lively, irreverent, and disdainful of sacred cows. All this is possible only in a democracy.

Indian democracy is a strength, not a weakness. India's strength is that it has preserved an idea of itself as one land embracing many—a country that endures differences of caste, creed, colour, culture, cuisine, conviction, costume, and custom, yet still rallies around a democratic consensus. And that consensus is on the simple idea that in a diverse democracy, you don't really need to agree all the time—so long as you agree, on the ground rules of how you will disagree. The reason India has survived and flourished despite all the stresses and strains since it became independent is that it has maintained consensus on how to manage without consensus.

While the world moves towards free markets, countries around the world, especially new democracies, have a major task on their hands. They have to manage the demands of political and social integration, economic growth, and good governance, while ensuring that development spreads across the population evenly. If the institutions of the nation are built well, these challenges can be met effectively. Today, the onus lies on us, actors of this theatre called democracy, to see to it that the link between democracy and development creates actionable policies which can make a tangible difference to the lives of the people of our respective countries. Social scientists have shown that democracies, especially ones which are new and have unified political party systems, strong governmental bodies and protected economies and central banking systems, are in a better position to execute policies which will create inclusive growth for their people. It is necessary that young democracies understand that sustained development will be a result of good governance allows political and civil rights to flourish.

Even the established yardsticks support the case for democracy. Examining the various human development indices that the UNDP came out with, one will find that the top ten nations are all different forms of democracies. It comes as no surprise that nine of the top ten economies of the world are also democracies. In the UNDP's Gross National Happiness Index, based on the concept Bhutan devised in the early 1970's, the countries which comprised the top ten are again democracies.

Understanding how Norway created the best human development index for its citizenry will be important for nascent Asian democracies like Bhutan. It has been seen that New Zealand's social cohesion, Switzerland's education and negligible corruption and the pursuance of one's personal freedom in the Netherlands, have proved beneficial for their populations, allowing these nations to top the Happiness Index. At the same time, access to quick, effective and inexpensive start-ups have given the Swedish people trust in their government.

India and other developing countries also made mistakes that their neighbours can learn from. For decades, the theory of development economics had suffered from two intertwined historical circumstances—the experience of the Great Depression in the 1930s, when only robust government intervention saved a number of economies, and the fight for freedom from colonial rule, which involved the overthrow of both foreign rulers and foreign capitalists (though few nationalists could tell the difference). The development gurus firmly believed in the wisdom of top-down rule and government planning by all-knowing, all-seeing economists, of whom India suffered from an abundance. Our rulers, in turn, mistrusted what ordinary people could achieve for themselves when they were freed to pursue their own prosperity within a framework of government-supported structures that ensured a level playing field, fair regulation and social justice (the model that came to be adopted in the Western democracies, though increasingly dismantled in Republican-ruled America). Instead they created a licence-permit-quota raj that denied Indian businesses the opportunity to prosper and grow. The disastrous inefficiencies of the old system were masked by subsidies from the national exchequer, and a combination of vested interests—socialist ideologues, political opportunists, bureaucratic managers, self-protective trade unions and captive markets—shielded it fiercely from economic reality, as millions of Indians languished in poverty. Is this really what we want to return to?

We must move on, to ensure that we do enough to keep our people healthy, well-fed, and secure—secure not just from jihadi terrorism, a real threat, but from the daily terror of poverty, hunger and ill-health. Progress is being made: we can take satisfaction from India's success in carrying out three kinds of revolutions in feeding our people—the 'green revolution' in food grains, the 'white revolution' in milk production and, at least to some degree, a 'blue revolution' in the development of our fisheries. But the benefits of these revolutions have not yet reached the third of our population still living below the poverty line.

And just as we are aware, and proud, of modern India's strong democratic traditions, we are also aware of our responsibility to develop—to seek to bring all our people into the twenty-first century with comfortably full bellies and comfortably fulfilling occupations. Democracy and human rights are fundamental to who we are; but human rights begin with breakfast.

That is why democracy and development go together, and why the India that develops into a strong, prosperous and just society can only be a democratic India.

PARADOXES OF INDIA

It has become a cliché to speak of India as a land of paradoxes. The old joke about our country, one I have used in speeches for three decades, is that anything you say about India, the opposite is also true. We like to think of ourselves as an ancient civilization but we are also a young republic; our IT experts stride confidently into the 21st century but much of our population seems to live in each of the other twenty centuries. Quite often the opposites co-exist quite cheerfully. One of my favourite images of India is from the last Kumbha Mela, of a naked sadhu, with matted hair, ash-smeared forehead, rudraksha mala and scraggly beard, for all the world a picture of timeless other-worldliness, chatting away on a cell phone. I even suggested it to the publishers of my previous book of essays on India as a perfect cover image, but they assured me it was so well known that it had become a cliché in itself.

And yet clichés are clichés because they are true, and the paradoxes of India say something painfully real about our society. How does one come to terms with a country whose population is still nearly 30 per cent illiterate but which has educated the world's second-largest pool of trained scientists and engineers, many of whom are making a flourishing living in Silicon Valley and have founded one of every three start-ups there in the last decade? How does one explain a land which successfully shoots an orbiter to Mars but can't provide enough toilets to prevent mass open defecation? A creative economy that makes eight times more movies than any other country but a third of whose population can't afford three square meals a day, let alone the price of movie tickets for a family of five? A place where whose software programming is amongst the most advanced on earth, but whose major industries suffer from crippling power cuts, and where no city is guaranteed uninterrupted electric power 24 hours a day?

The paradoxes go well beyond the nature of our entry into the 21st century. Our teeming cities overflow while two out of three Indians still scratch a living from the soil. We have been recognized, for all practical purposes, as a leading nuclear power, but 600 million Indians still have no access to electricity and there are daily power cuts even in the nation's capital. Ours is a culture which elevated non-violence to an effective moral principle, but whose freedom was born in blood and whose independence still soaks in it. We are the world's leading manufacturers of generic medication for illnesses such as AIDS, but we have three million of our own citizens without access to AIDS medication, another two million with TB, and tens of millions with no health centre or clinic within 10 km of their places of residence. Bollywood makes four times as many movies as Hollywood, but fifteen million Indians cannot see them, because they are blind, for the most part as the result of preventable conditions. India holds the world record for the number of cell phones sold each month, but also for the number of farmer suicides (4,000 in the Vidarbha district of Maharashtra alone in 2011).

The month that I published my optimistic book about India's transformation, *The Elephant, the Tiger and the Cellphone*, in mid-November 2007, the prestigious *Forbes* magazine list of the world's top billionaires made room for ten new Indian names. The four richest Indians in the world then were collectively worth a staggering $180 billion, greater than the GDP of a majority of member states of the United Nations. Indian papers reported with undisguised glee that these four (Lakshmi Mittal, the two Ambani brothers, and DLF chief K.P. Singh) were worth more than the forty richest Chinese combined. We seem to find less space in our papers to note that though we have more dollar billionaires than in any country in Asia—even more than Japan, which has been richer longer—we also have 260 million people living below the poverty line. And it's not the World Bank's poverty line of one dollar a day, but the Indian poverty line of Rs 900 a month, or fifty cents a day.

When I addressed the Fortune Global Conference in Delhi soon thereafter, it was the day the Sensex (the Bombay Stock Exchange Index) crossed 20,000, just twenty months after it had first hit 10,000; but on the same day, some 25,000 landless people marched on Parliament, clamouring for land reform and justice. We have trained world-class scientists and engineers, but 400 million of our compatriots are illiterate, and we also have more children who have not seen the inside of a school than any other country in the world does. We have a great demographic advantage in 540 million young people under 25 (which means we should have a dynamic, youthful and productive work force for the next forty years when the rest of the world, including China, is ageing) but we also have 60 million child labourers, and 72 per cent of the children in our government schools drop out by the eighth standard. We celebrate India's IT triumphs, but information technology has employed a grand total of 1 million people in the last five years, while 10 million are entering the work force each year and we don't have jobs for them. Many of our urban youth rightly say with confidence that their future will be better than their parents' past, but there are Maoist insurgencies violently disturbing the peace in 165 of India's 602 districts, and these are largely made up of unemployed young men.

So yes, we are a land of paradoxes, and amongst those paradoxes is that so many of us speak about India as a great power of the 21st century when we are not yet able to feed, educate and employ our people. I courted some controversy in 2009 when, in response to a question, I said that India could not hope to be a superpower when we were still super-poor. Both the challenge and the aspiration remain.

And yet, India is more than the sum of its contradictions. It may be a country rife with despair and disrepair, but it nonetheless moved a Mughal Emperor to declaim, 'if on earth there be paradise of bliss, it is this, it is this, it is this...' We just have a lot more to do before it can be anything like paradise for the vast majority of our fellow citizens.

THE ROLE OF CIVIL SOCIETY IN LAW-MAKING
(Remarks to the MLAs of the Kerala State Assembly, 3 September 2011)

India became conscious of the phenomenon of 'civil society', and its impact on national law-making, with two major developments in 2011 and 2012. The first was the national debate on the Lokpal Bill dominated by the agitation of Mr Anna Hazare and his followers, grouped together under the collective label of 'civil society', and their determination to affect the course of the legislation passed in Parliament on this subject. The second was the violent rape and murder of a 23-year-old physiotherapy student on a bus in Delhi, which spoke to the deepest anxieties of urban middle-class India. The public outcry over the young woman, dubbed 'Nirbhaya' or 'the Fearless One', out of deference to restrictions on naming her in the media, led to popular pressure on the authorities for more stringent anti-rape laws, prompting the government to name a retired Supreme Court Chief Justice, J.S. Verma, to propose changes, and then to rush legislation through passing most of his recommendations. With these two developments, civil society had arrived as a force for legislating change in today's India.

India is no stranger to protest movements, fasts-unto-death and the mass mobilization of citizens for a popular cause. But the 2011 fast by Annaji, culminating in an extraordinary Saturday session of Parliament to pass a resolution conceding his main demands, marked a dramatic departure in the country's politics.

The Anna phenomenon reflected a 'perfect storm' of converging factors— widespread disgust with the corruption revealed in two recent exposes of wrongdoing (in the allocation of telecoms spectrum and the awarding of contracts for the Commonwealth Games), the organizational skill of a small group of social activists committed to transforming India's governance practices, the mass media's perennial search for a compelling story to drive up the ratings, and the availability of a saintly figure to embody the cause. The result has raised important new questions about the role of civil society in Indian democracy.

This entire phenomenon brought to the fore issues of far-reaching importance which touch upon the very core of the functioning of our parliamentary democracy. It has unfortunately been converted into a debate where one side has been portrayed as putting up impediments in the way of 'national will' while the other was portrayed as being the custodians of 'national conscience'. The country's Executive, the elected Government of India, and even Parliament were accused of acting in a manner which is incompatible with or even diametrically opposed to the desires of 'civil society', a term which only serves to further add to the confusion.

What is 'civil society'? Civil society is broadly understood to be composed of the totality of civic and social organizations, voluntary social relationships and institutions, whether formal or informal, that form the basis of a functioning society—as distinct from the organized structures of the state. To some scholars, civil society does not embrace the commercial institutions of the market, nor the 'uncivil 'and criminal organizations of the underworld, but does take in the NGO community and the media. Other analysts have a broader understanding of the term. Browsing the literature, one finds references to any and all of these as examples of civil society: universities and schools, families and clans, companies and markets, trade unions and political parties, hospitals and clinics, temples and mosques, community and religious associations, cricket clubs and debating clubs, newspapers and media organizations, recognized non-governmental organizations and unrecognized 'neighbourhood watch' groups. Together, an entire society is made up of all these elements, and the relations between these components are often considered to be determinant in shaping the structure and character of a society.

So if that is civil society, what does it have to do with law-making? There is a fair amount of literature on relations between civil society and democracy, and the influence of one upon the other. The great 17th century political philosopher John Locke described civil society as comprising people who have 'a common established law and judicature to appeal to, with authority to decide controversies between them'. Locke and Hobbes, however, were more concerned with the construction of the state out of social disorder than with civil society per se. Indeed, as political philosophers grappled with theories of the state, they saw it increasingly as distinct from society: in the 18th century, German philosopher Georg Wilhelm Friedrich Hegel even saw the 'state' as diametrically opposed to 'civil society'.

Things have changed in more recent times. One of the earliest modern observers of civil society was the Frenchman Alexis de Tocqueville, who observed it in action in the new US republic in the early 19th century and wrote about the vigour and strength of American civil society institutions in his classic Democracy in America. In the 20th century, American political theorists like Gabriel Almond and Sidney Verba, using the tools of functionalism and largely motivated to study the evolution of political models toward a American democratic ideal, laid emphasis on the role of political culture in democracies. The concept of 'political development', largely credited to Almond, relied in part on his analysis of the contribution of voluntary community activities and non-governmental organizations to the development of democratic politics. Almond, building on Tocqueville, saw such organs of civil society as serving to increase social awareness of political issues, and by involving in their members in the processes of discussion, co-operation and collective decision-making, enhancing the practice (and therefore the evolution) of democracy.

The logic is clear. A thriving civil society creates a more informed citizenry, who make wiser voting choices, participate more effectively in democratic political life, and thus do a better job of promoting the accountability of democratic governments. Half a century after Almond, the American sociologist Robert D. Putnam, in his seminal study of contemporary US society and politics, *Bowling Alone,* has argued that social activities—like community sporting events—serve to strengthen political discourse and build democracy. This is because, through shared social activities, relationships of trust and shared values are built amongst members of a community, resulting in the creation of what is called 'social capital'. In turn, such relationships are transferred into the political arena, underscore the interconnectedness of society and help to bind a nation by holding society's various elements together. Equally, the decline or disintegration of such civil society institutions creates a more fractured politics and greater intolerance, with the adoption of extreme positions by people who are insufficiently connected to each other through civil society.

If this is how civil society works in a democracy, should it have a role in law-making? It can certainly be argued that laws are made by a society to regulate itself, and that therefore civil society is obviously a source of law. The associations of people for various civic purposes inevitably lead to opinion-making on various subjects, including those that are determined by legislation. The Australian lawyer and UN official Geoffrey Robertson QC, while writing of international law, claimed that 'one of its primary modern sources is found in the responses of ordinary men and women, and of the non-governmental organizations which many of them support, to the human rights abuses they see on the television screen in their living rooms'. Many would argue that in today's world the same impetus does and should play a role in making domestic laws in a democracy. Those of us who watched the incessant television coverage on our multiple all-news channels of the Anna Hazare movement can have no illusions whatsoever that the responses of much of the Indian public to the Lokpal issue have been driven and even shaped by what they saw and heard on TV. The Lokpal law that eventually emerged from Parliament undoubtedly had amongst its key sources 'the responses of ordinary men and women' to the mass media on this issue.

In a democracy, there are specific rights accorded to citizens by the state to help them exercise their political freedoms: freedom of speech and political association and related rights allow citizens—in other words, members of civil society—to get together, argue and discuss, debate and criticize, protest and strike, and even go on fasts and hunger-strikes, in order to support or challenge their governments. This is an essential part of promoting governmental accountability between elections: no one can seriously argue that a citizen's democratic rights begin and end with the right to choose his government through voting alone. Indeed, as Amartya Sen so brilliantly pointed out with reference to India in his *The Argumentative Indian*, it through such discussions and engagement that a deliberative democracy is created. There is often a useful distinction between law and legitimacy: the greater the extent to which ordinary people are engaged with, concerned by and empowered to determine their own political destiny, the more they accept the decisions of the state institutions and the more legitimate the law becomes to the people.

So to that extent, civil society does and should have an influence on law-making. But that is not the same thing as saying it should have a direct role. In Switzerland, for example, ordinary citizens can actually bypass the elected legislature and write laws by voting for them in referenda that are organized by the state and whose outcomes are recognized by the government as having the full binding force of law. That is not the case, however, in most other democracies, where civil society's impact is confined to the influence it is able to bring to bear on the elected law-makers, through the shaping of public opinion, effective lobbying, media campaigns and mass movements.

The recent debate in India on the role of civil society should be seen against this broader context. To some degree, however, it appears to be based on a misunderstanding about the workings of our democratic system. The Indian system of parliamentary democracy has stood the test of time and is highly respected by many nations and peoples across the world. This system was put in place by the founding fathers of our Constitution at the time of Independence from foreign rule. The learned founding fathers of our Republic had been clear in their minds that the Parliamentary form of democracy of the Westminster model was what they wished to establish in Independent India. (India's nationalists had been determined to enjoy the democracy their colonial rulers had long denied them, and had convinced themselves the British system was the best.)

This was understandable, not merely because we were demanding exactly the democracy that our colonial masters had enjoyed for themselves but denied us, but also because it could be said to suit the democratic temper of our people. Our ancient civilization had the history of having Sabhas and Samitis where kingdoms and even empires were ruled on the principle of democratic functioning, extending right from the grass-roots level in the form of panchayats and councils which represented the broad as well as specific segments of the populace, to the royal courts where maharajahs took advice from learned and wise elders. This tradition is very important to recall, since it confirms that both majority as well as minority opinion were given due importance in the formulation of public policy. This was no mean achievement in a nation and society as diverse and heterogeneous as India, with its innumerable groups and socio-religious identities. But it helps that the very idea of India is of one land embracing many. As I have long argued, pluralism is India's defining characteristic.

The working instrument of our democracy is the Constitution of India. It is the basic framework of our democracy. Under the scheme of our Constitution, the three main organs of the State are the Legislature, the Executive and the Judiciary. The Constitution defines their powers, delimits their jurisdictions, demarcates their responsibilities and regulates their relationships with one another and with the people. The adaptability of the Constitution to the ever-changing realities of national life has effectively made it a vehicle of social change.

Equally important, the above process has been substantially facilitated by our Parliament, the institution conceived for that very purpose by the Constitution. The Constitution created itself as a self-generating and self-correcting entity, a living document that allowed for its own amendment to meet the changes of the times. In a way, it reflected the confidence in the people of this land to make adjustments and rise to meet every new challenge to society. During the past six decades of Independence the Constitution, which came into force on 26 January 1950, has been amended more than a hundred times by Parliament, itself a creature created inter-alia for that very purpose by the Constitution. The small-minded may consider this as one of its weaknesses, but those with a broader vision would understand that it was actually a sign of its inherent strength—a strength that derives from its ability to be flexible without the risk of self-destruction. It has the exemplary in-built ability to adjust to the needs of the times and the fact that this is enabled through a thoroughly democratic and representative process has been the key to its effectiveness in moving our society forward in a democratic and reasonably efficient manner.

Under the Constitution of India, Parliament is the supreme legislative body at the national level. Only Parliament makes laws that affect the entire country and therefore help shape its society. The most important aspect of legislation lies in its vital social or sociological ramifications—think, for example, of the reservations policy for certain castes, decided by Parliament, which has proved a remarkable tool of social mobility and political transformation. Parliament has also not been found wanting in creating through legislation many institutions and mechanisms which today addresses issues crucial to the well-being of our society, for example national level bodies like the National Human Rights Commission, the National Commission for Scheduled Castes and Tribes, the National Commission for Women, the National Commission for Minorities, or the National Commission for Backward Classes, which are all creations of Parliament through appropriate legislation in response to specific policy initiatives for various sections of society.

The process of democratic elections in India, involving a multiplicity of political parties organized to reflect any conceivable interest and ideology in society, ensures the representative character of Parliament—and this in turn is reflected in the manner in which its members perform their legislative functions. This is why laws must be made by law-makers who are truly representative of the society they are seeking to regulate, and who are bound by oath to act for the fair and equal welfare of all sections of the people they are constitutionally elected to represent.

One defining feature of the parliamentary system, as opposed to the presidential, is that the Executive emerges from the Legislature and is sustained by its ability to maintain a legislative majority. In our system, therefore, the Executive—the government—introduces the laws and uses its legislative majority to pass them. Of course, it is usually open to the views of other members, including those belonging to the opposition parties, in making necessary modifications to its draft bills before passage, in order to command as wide a consensus as possible. But it is not obliged to do so as long as it enjoys a secure majority. And unlike, say, the US Congress, where any representative or senator can initiate and steer legislation, in the Indian Parliament it is almost always the government which does so.

Law-making anywhere is a complex process and this is all the more true in a multi-faceted, multi-ethnic, multi-lingual, multi-religious federal state like India. The formulation and enactment of a law which has all-India ramifications cannot be considered in isolation from other factors. Apart from the obvious political factors, there is also a host of administrative, legal, financial and technical factors that have to be considered. People often lose sight of the important fact that it is the duty of the government of the day to ensure that all these factors are considered in the process of law-making. The government has an onerous constitutional responsibility to ensure proper governance and it cannot overlook or ignore this responsibility. For example, a law may have financial implications which the government has to take cognizance of. Therefore, in a parliamentary system such as India's, law-making has necessarily to be a function devolving on the Executive and ratified through Parliament.

There are two important features of the constitutional legislative process which are relevant in this context. First, our parliamentary rules and procedures provide for the initiation of legislation by private members also. A member of Parliament, other than a minister, is known as a private member. A bill initiated by any such member is called a private member's bill. It could be argued that only a handful of private members' Bills have been passed in the history of the Indian Parliament. There is a general perception that the chances of a private member's bill being enacted are very bleak. But there have been many instances in our Parliament where the introduction of private members' bills—even where those bills did not themselves pass—expedited the process of government legislation on those very subjects. For example, The Companies (Amendment) Bill, 1963, seeking to amend certain provisions of the Companies Act, 1956, was introduced in the Rajya Sabha by Mr K.V. Raghunath Reddy in August 1963. However, after some time, the government brought forward a bill incorporating the amendments suggested by Mr Reddy, who, stating that the objective had been achieved, withdrew his bill in September 1963.

Many a time, private members' bills are not comprehensive in nature and require a broader perspective. But they do cause ripples and it is often the case that private members' bills, which are discussed in the House, are withdrawn after obtaining assurance from the government that it will bring forward a comprehensive legislation on the subject. Mr Atal Bihari Vajpayee during his term in the Rajya Sabha introduced a private members' bill, namely, the Companies (Amendment) Bill, 1962, seeking to ban donations by companies to political parties. The bill was, however, negatived by the House on 27 November 1964. Another member, Mr Chitta Basu, also introduced a similar Bill in 1967. Later on, the government accepted the suggestion in principle and in 1969 enacted legislation, inter alia, putting restrictions on contributions to political parties. Similarly, very few people know that Mr Bhupesh Gupta introduced a Constitution (Amendment) Bill on 10 March 1961 to change the name of Madras State to Tamil Nadu. Even though Mr Gupta's Bill was not passed, later on the government brought forward an official bill on the subject and it was enacted. In 2011, Congress MP Manish Tewari introduced a private member's bill to regulate India's national intelligence agencies, which, though it hasn't yet been passed, has had the undeniable effect of placing the issue of intelligence reform on the agenda, and the media coverage of his initiative alone has given prominence to the issue involved.

Since May 1952, more than 3,000 private members' bills have been introduced in the Lok Sabha alone. A total of 14 Private Members' Bills have found their way into the statute book. Out of these 9 were those that had been introduced in the Lok Sabha. These are The Muslim Wakfs Bill, 1952; The Indian Registration (Amendment) The Proceedings of Parliament (Protection of Publication) Bill, 1956; The Code of Criminal Procedure (Amendment) Bill, 1953; The Women's and Children's Institutions (Licensing) Bill, 1953; The Code of Criminal Procedure (Amendment) Bill, 1957; The Salaries and Allowances of Members of Parliament (Amendment) Bill, 1964; The Hindu Marriage (Amendment) Bill, 1964; and The Supreme Court (Enlargement of Criminal Appellate Jurisdiction) Bill, 1968 Bill. All of these are significant pieces of legislation that have had a serious impact on our country.

The second feature worth mentioning is the system of referring bills to the Standing Committees of Parliament for detailed examination after their introduction. This provides an opportunity for the expression of wide-ranging and diverse opinions on its contents, including by Opposition members, which may not be possible on the floor of the House due to lack of time or other reasons. The Standing Committees are enabled to go in depth into the provisions of the bills. At that stage they also invite the opinion of the general public and other persons and organizations who may like to provide suggestions and detailed inputs on the various provisions contained or omitted therein. Thus Anna Hazare and his representatives were invited to depose before the Standing Committee on Law and Justice. It can therefore, be nobody's case that the public has no say in the process of law-making and that it is left purely in the hands of representatives whom they may have once voted into power but with whose views they are no longer in sympathy.

Parliament is a microcosm of the nation. The question that has been posed by the civil society agittions was that the Executive Government was 'not listening to the voice of the people'. It may be argued that the mass mobilization witnessed in the streets, or in the Ram Lila Maidan in Delhi, behind Anna Hazare's demands point to a disconnect between the Government and popular sentiment on the Lokpal issue, just as the mass protests near Parliament Square and Rashtrapati Bhavan over the Nirbhaya killing pointed to estrangement between the mobilized public and the guardians of law and order But that does not mean, in a functioning democracy, that laws can be dictated by crowds in the street or the fast of a respected figure. Parliamentary debate is necessary and legitimate, for in a parliamentary democracy, only elected MPs can make laws. To allow any unelected group, however virtuous and idealistic they may be, to substitute its will, through demonstrations and fasts, for that of Parliament would be an assault on the very foundations of our republic and fundamentally violative of our Constitution.

In our democracy, there is an efficient, well-tried and constitutional law-making system in place in this country. It is hardly perfect, but then we can remember the famous remark attributed to the 19th-century German Chancellor Otto Von Bismarck, 'If you like laws and sausages, you should never watch either one being made'. Nonetheless, the important point is that nobody is excluded from having an influence, or bringing their point of view to bear, on this process. The members of Parliament are those very people who have been elected as representatives by the people. The Executive is derived from among the members of Parliament. The law-making process is transparent, as well as constitutionally, administratively and technically sound and the parliamentary procedures provide sufficient scope for further considering and incorporating all shades of public opinion. One is entitled to start doubting the real intentions and motives of those who go around insisting that some legislation drafted outside this process should be adopted in toto and made into law by Parliament without giving scope for the process of executive formulation and examination of the administrative, financial, legal and procedural requirements implicit in the constitutional, parliamentary and other statutory processes I have already mentioned.

And yet, it is true that in a dynamic and responsive polity like ours, extra-constitutional pressures often cannot simply be ignored. The most famous example of moral pressure outside Parliament causing an executive to bend was in 1952, when Prime Minister Jawaharlal Nehru's government reversed its position and constituted a States Reorganization Commission in response to a fast-unto-death by the Gandhian leader Potti Sriramulu who fasted to demand the creation of linguistic states and died in the process. That Commission's report led to the redrawing of India's administrative and federal map in 1956.

But exceptions often prove the rule, as the cliché goes, and the rule remains that law-making in this country is connected to civil society through the process of consultation and debate by people's representatives elected through democratic elections. The demand that 'civil society' ought to allowed to write certain laws goes far beyond a mere challenge of the constitutional provisions or of the supremacy of Parliament. That is objectionable enough. But in my considered opinion it goes further by attempting to obfuscate the core issue of representation. Elections are not easy; each Parliaamentarian knows this from his or her personal experience. Their claim to represent the people, whose votes they have campaigned for and won, cannot be lightly disregarded in favour of those who are not willing or capable of surmounting the essential first step of achieving a representative position through victory in an election. The notion that the ability to mobilize a crowd on the streets, or attract the television cameras to a cause, is enough to supplant the results of democratic elections, only reveals an attitude of contempt for the democratic rights of the people of this country. Those who do so are in effect advocating a dictatorship of the minority, an oligarchy which was never agreed to by the learned and visionary founding fathers of this nation, who had unhesitatingly reposed total faith in the electoral wisdom of the ordinary masses of this land.

I might add, on a personal note, that I myself had previously engaged with public issues as a member of 'civil society'—making statements and speeches to middle-class and elite forums, appearing on television, publishing articles and books. But when the opportunity presented itself for me to enter politics, I had no doubt that the right thing for me to do was to contest elections to Parliament, in my case the Lok Sabha. It was only by doing this that I felt I could truly claim to have earned the right to represent the people. If members of 'civil society' want to have a determinant voice in law-making, what they need to do is to organize themselves politically and not merely agitationally, contest elections and come into Parliament—where they can write and pass the laws they were trying to dictate from the street. This is precisely what a section of Anna Hazare's supporters did in forming the Aam Aadmi Party (AAP) and sweeping to power in the assembly elections in Delhi in 2013. But the challenge of converting their burning passion to rid the nation of corruption to effective legislative and governmental action became apparent when the AAP Chief Minister, Arvind Kejriwal, found himself fleeing his own mass meetings as they got out of hand, agitating in the streets against his own police, and resigning impetuously after a mere forty-nine days in power. Civil society agitation is not the same as the responsible use of governmental machinery and legislative authority to pursue the same aims.

Laws emerge from a political process that is itself reflective of our society. Parliamentarians are in that sense themselves products of civil society. Our democracy, our thriving free media, our contentious civil society forums, our energetic human rights groups, and the repeated spectacle of our remarkable general elections, have all made of India a rare example of the successful management of diversity in the developing world. It adds to India's 'soft power' and influence in the world when its non-governmental organizations actively defend human rights, promote environmentalism, fight injustice. It is a vital asset that the Indian press is free, lively, irreverent, disdainful of sacred cows. But to confuse the respective roles of Parliament and these civil society institutions will do our democracy no good.

I have no doubt that India's law-makers, as consumers of mass media and targets of agitational protest, will find themselves influenced in the future by the passions visible in the street and on their television screens. But it is still up to them to devise, amend and vote the laws that ultimately govern the nation. And legislation, like salad, is best served cold, not overcooked in the heat of the political kitchen. Civil society can provide the impetus of the moment, but only elected legislators can determine the laws that shape the future.

POLITICS AND THE INDIAN MIDDLE-CLASS

As I reflect on my writings on post-Independence India, I am conscious that, before I entered politics myself, one of my more frequent laments had been about the abdication by the Indian educated classes of our political responsibility for our own destiny.

My generation grew up in an India where a vast gulf separated those who went into the professions or the civil services, and those who entered politics. The latter, at the risk of simplifying things a bit, were either at the very top or the very bottom: either maharajahs or big zamindars with a feudal hold on the allegiances of the voters in their districts, or semi-literate 'lumpens' with little to lose who got into politics as their only means of self-advancement. If you belonged to neither category, you studied hard, took your exams, and made a success of your life on merit—and you steered clear of politics as an activity for those 'other people'.

But the problem with that approach—while completely understandable in a highly-competitive society where the salaried middle-class rarely enjoyed the luxury of being able to take the kind of risks that a political life implied—was that it left out of Indian politics the very group of people that are the mainstay of politics in other democracies. Around the world, the educated taxpaying middle-classes are normally the ones who bring values and convictions to a country's politics, and who have the most direct stake in questions of what government can and cannot do. Across Europe, for instance, it's people from the middle-class who set the political agenda: they make up the bulk of the activists, voters and candidates for political office. In most Western democracies, politics is essentially a middle-class pursuit.

But in India, our middle-class has neither the time for activism (they're too busy doing professional jobs to make ends meet) nor the money or the votes to count in politics. The money flows at the top, and the votes, in our stratified society, lie at the bottom, where the numbers are. So members of the educated middle-class abstain from the process, and all too often look at it with disdain. They don't show up to vote in large numbers; whereas in India the poor turn out en masse to vote, spending hours in the hot sun to cast their ballots. They believe, rightly, that their votes make a difference, whereas the middle-class disempowers itself by its disdain. No wonder there is so much disenchantment amongst ordinary middle-class people with the processes of our democracy, such cynicism about the lack of principle amongst our politicians, and such surprise in learning of an honest politician (because we routinely expect the opposite).

This is easily apparent in the public attitudes of middle-class Indians to politics and politicians. Growing up in India, I was used to a double standard:

most Indians accept, indeed assume, conduct on the part of politicians that we would never condone in our neighbours. Traditional middle-class morality required arranged marriages, marital fidelity, scrupulous honesty and adherence to the law at all times, whereas politicians were expected to be different from the rest of us, and therefore exempt from these norms. As larger-than-life figures, they enjoyed a societal carte blanche to lie, cheat, dissemble, and commit large-scale duplicity, adultery and tax fraud; only murder was a little more difficult, though even there a handful of major politicians have been released from jail in India after allegations of offenses that might have earned lesser mortals fates worse than death.

So it was with some astonishment that I first went to America and discovered the opposite double-standard in operation: Americans expected, indeed required, conduct on the part of their politicians that they would never have presumed to demand of their neighbours. Middle-class Americans, for the most part, lived in an environment of pre- and extra-marital sex, divorce and adultery, and lapped up soap operas and television talk-shows where these were the staple fare. But they expected their politicians to be models of moral rectitude, their CVs punctuated by the standard long-lasting faithful marriage and 2.5 clean-cut children. At least it meant that they idealized their political leaders; in India, we routinely disparage them.

The result is that whereas ten of the last twelve American presidential nominees of the two major US political parties were graduates of either Harvard or Yale, the products of our best educational institutions rarely venture into politics. In America, the commentator Michael Medved wrote that the skills and determination required to get into a Harvard or Yale are in themselves indicators of suitability for high office—'the driven, ferociously focused kids willing to expend the energy and make the sacrifices to conquer our most exclusive universities are among those most likely to enjoy similar success in the even more fiercely fought free-for-all of presidential politics'. In India, the kids who 'conquer our most exclusive universities' would for the most part consider it beneath themselves to step into the muck and mire of our country's politics. The attitude of most Indians is that if you're smart enough to get into a good university, you can make something better of your life in a 'real' profession. Politics, it is generally muttered amongst the middle-class, is for those who aren't able to do anything else. And the skills required to thrive in the world of Indian politics have nothing to do with the talents honed by a first-class education.

That statistic (ten out of twelve hailing from Harvard or Yale), remarkable in itself, strikes one as all the more astonishing when you realize that in these last twenty years the two parties between them have in fact only had twelve nominees altogether. In other words, only two major candidates in all this time did not attend one of America's top two universities—and this in a country whose higher education system, with over a thousand top-class universities and colleges to choose from, is second to none. It is extraordinary indeed that, as the columnist Michael Medved recently pointed out, Yale and Harvard degree-holders make up 'less than two-tenths of 1 per cent of the national population, but (have won) more than 83 per cent of recent presidential nominations'. The closest Indian comparators would probably be St. Stephen's and the IITs, neither of which has ever produced a prime minister. (As a Stephanian myself, I remember the ethos of the institution being one of diligent preparation for the IAS and IFS examinations as the summum bonum of career aspiration for anyone with the brains to pass those gruelling civil service examinations. Stephanians succeed disproportionately in getting into the civil services; very few venture into politics.)

Can this state of affairs continue indefinitely? No—and it probably won't. My vision for India in 2020 is of a country growing economically, whose economic transformation brings more and more people into the middle-class— and by 2020, this process may have begun to reach the point where the numbers of the middle-class will indeed begin to matter in elections.

We already have, in the current and previous Parliament, several educated and bright young professionals of the kind of background that for many years previously would not have been found in politics—people with good degrees, a national vision, international experience, intelligent ideas and the capacity to articulate them. It doesn't matter that a significant proportion of them are the sons of politicians: the fact that they are in Parliament brings a different standard to bear on the quality of our politics. As they change the public's expectations of what a politician should be like, they should be joined by 2020 by many others of similar qualifications but with no political background. In that, eventually, will lie our democracy's salvation.

So my message to young middle-class Indians who actually have principles and ideals is this: when you think about the future of India, think also of getting involved in politics. The nation needs you.

The Nobel laureate Archbishop Desmond Tutu, speaking of South Africa, once said he hoped his country would get leaders the people could look up to, 'not people we have to keep finding excuses for'. If well-educated, middle-class Indians—the kind of people who are the mainstay of our professions—want a return to era when our country's political leadership was full of people whom the nation admired, they will have to enter the fray themselves. Otherwise, all too often, we will have to pay allegiance to people we need to find excuses for. My hope is that, by 2020, there will be many more educated, professional middle-class Indians in politics—and that they will do better than I have managed to do so far!

THE NEW VOTER: FROM KHAP TO AAP?

In 2009 I became a new voter. I had left India for graduate studies at the age of 19 in 1975, at a time when you had to be 21 to vote. Serving the United Nations around the world meant I could not vote in any Indian election until, at the age of 53, I was able to vote for myself in as a candidate for the Fifteenth Lok Sabha.

According to the most recent figures available, another 149.36 million first-time voters became eligible to, and over a 100 million did, emulate my experience in 2014—a little over 22 per cent of the estimated electorate in the general elections. Aged 18 to 23, they appear to embody the urgent concern with India's compelling problems that animates young Indians across the country's political divides. An India seemingly outgrowing many traditional political allegiances is taking shape, as a better-educated, more aspirational, more urbanized and more vocal young population enters the hustings. Are we witnessing a decisive move from old-style politics to new—from khap to AAP?

India is a remarkably young country. The nation's average age is 28; half our people are under 25 and 66 per cent under 35, which means that the young are already a majority in India. But they are not the ruling majority; according to the *Economist*, India holds the world record for the largest gap between the average age of the population and that of the Cabinet (which is 65). The young are entering the political world, but still with diffidence—and they continue to be outnumbered by their seniors in political authority, though not on the electoral rolls.

This predominance of youth in the population is expected to last until 2050—which is both good news and bad news. The good news is that we will have a productive, dynamic, even youthful working age population for decades, while most of the planet, including China, is ageing. (China's current average age is 38; in ten years, it will be 50, while ours rises to 29). In the next twenty years, the labour force in China will shrink by 5 per cent, and in the industrialized 'northern' world, by 4 per cent; in the same time frame, India's labour force will increase by 32 per cent.

But then there's the bad news. The availability of a human resource of such magnitude only means anything if we can feed, house, clothe, educate and train these young people to take advantage of the opportunities the 21st century offers. If we fail to provide them the chance to make something of their lives in the new India, the same demography could be not only a burden but a threat, since so much of terrorism and extremist violence in our country is carried out by embittered and unemployable young men.

The government is conscious of the new voters' demands for rapid change. As a freshly-elected Member of Parliament myself in 2009, I recall then Prime Minister Manmohan Singh, himself a sprightly 78, urging us to respect 'the impatience of the young'. India's under-35 are a generation that holds our nation to new, higher standards befitting the globalized era, standards that they understand prevail in the developed world. They are a generation born in the era of liberalization, growing up with greater freedoms, more choices and opportunities than their forebears, impatient with the heavy hand of government and tired of shopworn rhetoric about socialism and upliftment of the masses. They want action, not slogans; results, not bromides.

And yet there is a significant gap between the political process and the participation in it of India's brightest young sons and daughters. It was not so at the time of the freedom struggle, when the best and most energetic minds, cutting across all professional classes, actively participated in the nationalist movement. After the first flush of independence, though, cynicism and indifference set in. The middle-class, educated young turn to the professions, to civil service exams and to multinational corporations, but few amongst them spare a thought for politics.

Today it seems that change is in the air. More educated young people are beginning to think the previously unthinkable and contemplate a political career, or at least active participation in the political process. More and more young persons are convinced that they cannot afford to be 'apolitical' anymore. There is too much at stake.

I welcome this. Three years ago I wrote a letter to young professionals in my constituency, urging them to get involved in politics. I argued: 'politics is not merely about elections every few years. It is about determining the choices your country makes, which intimately affect your daily lives wherever you live and work. Our government is doing a great deal that young people can't afford to be indifferent to. Decisions are being taken on life and death issues about yourself and of your families—and if you are not involved in the process that arrives at those decisions, it simply means that you do not care. Vital decisions that will affect your professional opportunities, the investment climate in our country, the way in which revenues are raised and spent, and the policies that will affect your own advancement, are being formulated and taken in various forums—by local bodies, the state legislature and at the national level through our Parliament. It's the political process that establishes these institutions and determines their composition. Please join it.'

The response I got was modest, but the young have begun to stir. Many have turned out in the streets to voice their concerns, whether about corruption or other urgent social wrongs, more recently and tragically the brutal gang-rape and murder of a 23-year-old Delhi woman dubbed 'Nirbhaya', in December

2012. The challenge is to channel their energy into constructive political action.

The previous ruling party had already understood the need to involve the young generation by actively encouraging the participation of the citizenry in grass-roots governance. Path-breaking legislation, creating and strengthening the Panchayati Raj institutions, establishing the Mahatma Gandhi National Rural Employment Guarantee Scheme and promulgating the Right to Information Act, are examples of innovative policies in recent years that have created conducive ground for mass political mobilization. The new government has shown no inclination dismantle these accomplishments.

Few Indian parties, however, have moved rapidly enough with the times. Only one—my own—began to put in place compulsory elections to party posts, starting from the grass-roots level. Instead of leaders being thrust on them from above, young people want to elect their own party leaders. So far, aside from the Youth Congress, they can't.

Young Indians in the Information Age, with social media at their fingertips and a media echo-chamber in hundreds of news channels, are demanding more from political parties in an era of two-way communication. The Google Urban Indian Voters study found that a large percentage of surveyed voters were not satisfied with the available information about political candidates on the internet. Forty-five per cent of urban voters said that they would like to see more information about political parties on the internet to help them make an informed decision. Fifty-seven per cent said they would like to see information on local issues. Forty-eight per cent said they would like to see updates on development activities undertaken in the constituency and 43 per cent said they wanted to see information on party manifestoes.

New voters have given confusing indications of their inclinations in recent years: the protests against corruption, against the maltreatment of women and against restrictive interpretations of Section 377, all suggest an increasing support for cultural liberalism, but there are also signs of enthusiasm for hyper-nationalist rhetoric and a vociferous yearning for a strong and decisive leader.

At the same time, the new voter demands that the benefits of economic growth must reach all Indians—the majority of whom are young, and the majority of whom are poor. As a Member of Parliament, I am struck by the fact that a majority of the voters in every Indian constituency are, by global standards, poor. The basics—food, clothing, shelter, roads, electricity, drinking water, jobs—dominate our politics. This is why my party has focused on inclusive growth—the combination of economic development and social justice—as the lodestar of its work.

If this is important enough when voters are poor, it is deeply significant when they are both poor and young. Young people in India are now asking that their voices be heard, that their issues be addressed and that their roles be recognized. They demand changes from our education system, which will have to cope with hundreds of millions of young people who no longer intend to be farmers and peasants, but will want the education that will equip them to lead viable urban lives. As the fledgling Aam Aadmi Party (AAP) realized, they demand cheaper and more accessible living facilities—a demand which will multiply exponentially as new infrastructure is built and as urban dwellers seek electricity, water, drainage, roads, telephone connections and mass transit. Today, 600 million Indians, overwhelmingly in rural areas, are not even connected to the electricity grid. Tomorrow they will be. And as in Delhi, they will clamour for lower tariffs, free water and better services.

If, say, 300 million Indians were to move from the villages to the towns in the next two decades or less, can we absorb all of them, educate all of them, employ all of them? Our challenge is to connect millions of citizens in a functioning democracy to their own government: not just to announce entitlements that will be showered upon them by a munificent government, but to provide opportunities that they are expected to grasp for themselves, and to create delivery mechanisms that ensure that these opportunities and entitlements are not just theoretical, but real and accessible.

As young India grows into and demands change, our national politics is undergoing a vital shift as well. I believe that a major reason why my party won the 2009 general elections is that our political leadership was able to delink the national polity from the incendiary issues of religious identity and caste denomination that other parties had built their appeal upon. Instead, we put the focus on what the people needed—more development, better governance, wider socio-economic opportunities. AAP has built on our example. It wasn't enough in 2014, but that doesn't invalidate the approach. In some ways it was Congress' success in raising voter expectations and demands that paved the way for the victory of a BJP promising more and better outcomes. The politics of performance prevailed, even if the promise of future achievement by the NDA outshone the reality of past accomplishments by the UPA.

To woo the new voter, we need to devise creative, ambitious responses to connect our young people to the opportunities the 21st century offers. In my visits to the poor and dispossessed when I am in Thiruvananthapuram, I am acutely conscious that the opposite is still the reality for millions of my fellow Indians. They face exclusion and disconnection for a variety of reasons: their place in the traditional social structure, their caste, their poverty, but also because our country has not been able to build the physical means— the roads, the highways, the power-transmission lines, the telephone systems, the schools—to connect them. India's most talked-about young leader, Rahul Gandhi, rightly speaks of two Indias—one connected, one not. Establishing the connection between the two Indias is vital to our country's place in the world, and vital to create an India ready to fulfil its huge potential. Congress lost in 2014, but it can come back in 2019 by embodying the aspirations of young Indians to be connected to the future.

When India succeeds in making that connection, we will be connecting 500 million Indians, over the next two decades, to their own country and to the rest of the world. Half a billion villagers will join the global village. The transformation of India is an exciting prospect in the early 21st century—and young new voters will drive us to it.

INDIA'S DISRUPTED DEMOCRACY

Every year, during India's rainy season, there is, equally predictably, a 'monsoon session' of Parliament. And every year, there seems to be increasing debate about which is stormier—the weather or the legislature.

Take, for instance, the monsoon session of 2011, which began on the first of August. The opening day was adjourned, in keeping with traditional practice, to mourn the death between sessions of a sitting Member of Parliament—but not before a routine courtesy greeting to the visiting Speaker of Sri Lanka's Parliament had been interrupted by a number of Tamil MPs from a regional party rising to their feet to shout demands for his expulsion because of his government's behaviour towards the Tamil minority in that country. Those errant MPs were rapidly silenced, though, and the visitor was allowed to receive a table-thumping welcome from the rest of the House.

Matters were not so swiftly resolved, however, the next day. No sooner had a newly-elected member taken his oath than a number of MPs from the Bahujan Samaj Party, which then ruled India's largest state, Uttar Pradesh, stormed into the well of the House, shouting slogans and waving placards in protest against the Government's land acquisition policies. The Speaker attempted for a few minutes to get them to return to their seats, then gave up the effort and adjourned the house for an hour. When the parliamentarians reassembled, the opposition members—now joined by other MPs from a rival regional party—marched towards the Speaker's desk, their decibel levels even higher. After a few more ineffectual minutes of trying to be heard above the din, the Speaker adjourned Parliament again. One more attempt was made in the afternoon before the House adjourned for the day, with no item of legislative business transacted.

The following monsoon session, in 2012, was hardly an improvement. Demanding the then prime minister's resignation over the allegedly improper allocation of coal-mining blocks to private companies, the Opposition BJP stalled the work of Parliament for three out of the four weeks of the session. The repeated paralysis of Parliament by slogan-shouting members violating (with impunity) every canon of legislative propriety, prompting the hapless Speaker to adjourn the House each day in defeat, ground legislative business to a halt.

Worse was to come in 2014, when India's 15th Lok Sabha passed into history amid ignominy after the least productive five years of any Indian Parliament in six decades of functioning democracy. With entire sessions lost to Opposition disruptions and frequent adjournments depriving legislators of deliberative time, MPs left for home having passed fewer bills and spent fewer hours in debate than any of their predecessors.

If that wasn't bad enough, the final session witnessed new lows in unruly behaviour, with microphones broken, scuffles between members and a legislator releasing a can of pepper spray to prevent discussion of a bill he didn't like. After the Speaker was rushed from her seat choking, with a handkerchief across her nose and mouth, and three asthmatic MPs were taken to hospital, the offender apologized, explaining that he was actually acting in self-defence—against those who sought to prevent him from disrupting the House in less exotic ways.

Indeed, disruption was often par for the course in India's 15th Parliament (my first as a member), many of whose Opposition members appeared to believe that disrupting proceedings is a more effective way of making their point than delivering a convincing argument. In the winter of 2010, an entire session of five weeks was lost without a single day's work, since the Opposition parties united to stall the House, with forced adjournments every single day. While that was extreme, there has not been a single session in recent years in which at least some days were not lost to deliberate disruption.

To those of us who sought election to Parliament in order to participate in thoughtful debate on the ways forward for our country, and to deliberate on the content of the laws by which we would be governed, the experience has been a deeply disillusioning one.

It wasn't always this way. Indian politicians were initially proud of the parliamentary system they had adopted upon Independence, patterned as it was on Britain's Westminster model. India's nationalists had been determined to enjoy the democracy their colonial rulers had long denied them, and had convinced themselves the British system was the best. When a future British Prime Minister, Clement Attlee, travelled to India as part of a constitutional commission and argued the merits of a presidential system over a parliamentary one, his Indian interlocutors reacted with horror. 'It was as if,' Attlee recalled, 'I had offered them margarine instead of butter.'

Many of India's parliamentarians—several of whom had been educated in England and watched British parliamentary traditions with admiration—revelled in the authenticity of their ways. Indian MPs still thump their desks in approbation, rather than applauding by clapping their hands. When bills are put to a vote, an affirmative call is still 'aye', rather than 'yes'. An Anglophile Communist MP, Prof. Hiren Mukherjee, boasted in the 1950s that a visiting British prime minister, Anthony Eden, had commented to him that the Indian Parliament was in every respect like the British one. Even to a Communist, that was a compliment to be proud of.

But six decades of Independence have wrought significant change, as exposure to British practices has faded and India's natural boisterousness has reasserted itself. Some of the state assemblies in India's federal system have already witnessed scenes of furniture overthrown, microphones ripped out and slippers flung by unruly legislators, not to mention fisticuffs and garments torn in scuffles among politicians. While things have not yet come to such a pass in the national legislature, the code of conduct that is imparted to all newly-elected MPs—including injunctions against speaking out of turn, shouting slogans, waving placards and marching into the well of the House—is routinely honoured in the breach. Equally striking is the impunity with which lawmakers flout the rules they are elected to uphold.

There was a time when misbehaviour was firmly dealt with. One of my abiding recollections from childhood was the photograph of a burly socialist parliamentarian, Raj Narain, a former wrestler, being bodily carried out of the House by four sergeants-at-arms for shouting out of turn and disobeying the Speaker's orders to resume his seat. But over the years, standards have been allowed to slide, with adjournments being preferred to expulsions. Last year, 5 MPs in the Upper House were suspended from membership for charging up to the presiding officer's desk, wrenching his microphone and tearing up his papers—but after a few months and some muted apologies, they were quietly reinstated.

Perhaps this makes sense, out of a desire to allow the Opposition its space in a system where party-line voting determines most voting outcomes. Four decades ago, in more gentlemanly times, an Opposition legislator had ended a debate whose outcome (given the size of the ruling party's parliamentary majority) was a foregone conclusion, with the words, 'We have the arguments. You have the votes'. Years later this MP, Atal Bihari Vajpayee, would become prime minister himself, and pride himself in cutting as much slack as possible to the Opposition.

The result is a curiously Indian institution, where standards of behaviour prevail that would not be tolerated in most other parliamentary systems. To those parties who do not get into government and who realize that the outcome of most votes is a foregone conclusion—since the government survives on the basis of its legislative majority—Parliament itself serves not as a solemn deliberative body, but as a theatre for the demonstration of their power to disrupt. The well of the house—supposed to be sacrosanct—becomes a stage for the members of the opposition to crowd and jostle, waving placards and chanting slogans until the Speaker, after several futile attempts to restore order, adjourns in despair. In India's Parliament, many Opposition members feel that the best way to show the strength of their feelings is to disrupt the law-making rather than debate the law.

The result is that the vast majority of the public has lost respect for Parliament and its proceedings. When the daily adjournments take place in the presence of bemused visiting members of other countries' legislatures, it does India's global reputation little good. And when it prevents the adoption of vital legislation, or agreement on important but controversial policies, it leads to the talk of 'policy paralysis' that so bedeviled India's economy in recent years. A paralyzed Parliament contributed directly to the disaffection of investors, which in turn led to economic stagnation, for which every Indian paid a price. It is supremely ironic that the BJP was rewarded by voters in 2014 for the economic failures that its own disruptive behaviour in Parliament had helped cause.

There is an even more fundamental concern here: the frequent disruption showcases both the resilience of India's democracy and the irresponsibility with which its custodians treat it. Pluralist democracy is India's greatest strength, but its current manner of operation is the source of our major weaknesses. India's many challenges require political arrangements that permit decisive action, whereas our parliamentary system increasingly promotes drift and indecision. Indian democracy requires a system of government whose leaders can focus on governance rather than on surviving in power. The disrepute into which the political process has fallen in India, and the widespread cynicism about the motives of our politicians, can be traced directly to the flawed workings of the parliamentary process.

The worry is the cavalier disregard for Parliament revealed in these frequent disruptions risks discrediting the entire process and so delegitimizing parliamentary democracy itself. That is one thing India cannot afford. But its politicians must realize that for themselves.

There is no doubt that Indian democracy has proved an extraordinary instrument for transforming an ancient country of astonishing ethnic diversity, bewildering social divisions and deeply entrenched poverty into a 21st century success story. Only democracy could have engineered such remarkable change with the consent of the governed, and without provoking mass insurrection. Only democracy could have allowed people of such a wide range of ethnic, religious, linguistic and cultural backgrounds to feel they have the same stake in the nation's progress, equal rights under its laws and equal opportunities for advancement in its polity and economy. Only democracy can provide the safety valve for dissent that defuses conflict by giving it a legitimate means of expression. Some observers express astonishment that India has flourished as a democracy; yet the truth is that India could hardly have survived as anything else.

But the 'temple of democracy', as Indians have long hailed their Parliament, has been soiled by its own sacerdotes, and is now in desperate need of a protestant Reformation. The functioning of Parliament has become, to most Indians, an embarrassment, and to many, an abomination. People turn on their televisions and watch in disbelief as their elected representatives shout slogans, wave placards, scream abuse and provoke adjournments—in short, do anything but what they were actually elected to Parliament to do.

The result is that most members of the public see Parliament as a waste of time and money rather than the majestic institution that enshrines India's democracy. The failure to function effectively does more than cheapen the nation's political discourse. It also means that the nation's essential legislative business is delayed; bills lay pending, policies fail to acquire the legal framework for their implementation, governance slows down. The errant MPs are not just letting down the voters who placed their confidence in them: they are betraying their duty to the nation and discrediting democracy itself.

It seems unbelievable that experienced politicians do not understand this, but the complacency with which the political establishment accepts the disruption of Parliament suggests they don't. Since the parliamentary system, unlike the US Congressional one, usually results in predictable outcomes for most votes, with the ruling majority habitually getting its way, Opposition MPs (and any ruling coalition members who disagree with the government position on a specific issue) prefer disruption to debate as a way of preventing an outcome they dislike. This is greeted on both sides of the aisle with a shrug, as if disruption were just as valid a parliamentary technique as a filibuster or an adjournment motion.

In fact, an unwritten but sacrosanct convention ensures that the Speaker almost never uses her authority to suspend or expel errant members except when there is a consensus between the government and the Opposition that she may do so—which of course rarely occurs. (The pepper-spraying MP was, however, suspended for the rest of the session. Even complacency has its limits.)

What the political establishment loses sight of is the broader damage such behaviour does to the standing of Parliament in the eyes of the public, and therefore to democracy itself. It was said that the shambolic performance of elected parliaments in Europe, especially in Germany and Italy between the two World Wars, had a great deal to do with the rise of authoritarianism and fascism in the first half of the 20th century.

When democracy is discredited by its own practitioners, there is much greater public willingness to embrace an efficient-seeming alternative. India's neighbours have proved this often enough, by welcoming the overthrow of elected governments in coups that enjoyed popular support. India has never seemed likely to succumb similarly, but it is a lesson that seems lost on the irresponsible custodians of India's democracy.

If our democracy's founding fathers, like that passionate democrat and scrupulous parliamentarian Jawaharlal Nehru, had not been cremated, they would be turning over in their graves. Yet, in the 2014 general elections, instead of the voters insisting that those who seek to represent them in Parliament actually go there to debate and deliberate—and punishing those who chose to disrupt and destroy at the ballot box—they rewarded the disrupters by voting the BJP into power. In office, the BJP has turned out to be a model of parliamentary rectitude, while the Congress party, now in Opposition, has found itself occasionally unable to resist the temptation to do unto the BJP what the BJP did unto it. (This, sadly, seems to have become the new golden rule of Indian parliamentary politics.)

A former US Ambassador to India, John Kenneth Galbraith, once described the country as a 'functioning anarchy'. A good look at the elected representatives at work in the temple of Indian democracy has often been enough to illustrate what he meant.

TIME TO IMAGINE A PRESIDENTIAL SYSTEM?

The sweeping electoral victory of Narendra Modi's BJP—which enjoys an absolute majority in the Lok Sabha—seems, at first glance, to have ushered in a period of parliamentary stability. Advocates of constitutional change, who feared India's parliamentary system was no longer capable of producing such a result, can now take a breather.

For the three previous decades, the political shenanigans in New Delhi, notably the repeated paralysis of Parliament by slogan-shouting members violating (with impunity) every canon of legislative propriety, seemed to confirm once again what some of us have been arguing for years: that the parliamentary system we borrowed from the British has, in Indian conditions, outlived its utility. Has the time not come to raise anew the case—long consigned to the back burner—for a presidential system in India?

With Mr Modi running the country in a quasi-presidential style already, despite heading a parliamentary system, the question may seem absurd. But since nothing is permanent in politics—least of all the prospects of an indefinite BJP majority—the issue may still be worth examining.

The basic outline of the argument has been clear for some time: our parliamentary system has created a unique breed of legislator, largely unqualified to legislate, who has sought election only in order to wield (or influence) executive power. It has produced governments obliged to focus more on politics than on policy or performance. It has distorted the voting preferences of an electorate that knows which individuals it wants but not necessarily which policies. It has spawned parties that are shifting alliances of individual interests rather the vehicles of coherent sets of ideas. It has forced governments to concentrate less on governing than on staying in office, and obliged them to cater to the lowest common denominator of their coalitions. It is time for a change.

Let me elaborate. Every time Parliament grounds to a screaming halt, the talk is of holding, or avoiding, a new general election. But quite apart from the horrendous costs incurred each time, can we, as a country, afford to keep expecting elections to provide miraculous results when we know that they are all but certain to produce inconclusive outcomes and more coalition governments? Isn't it time we realized the problem is with the system itself?

Pluralist democracy is India's greatest strength, but its current manner of operation is the source of our major weaknesses. India's many challenges require political arrangements that permit decisive action, whereas ours increasingly promote drift and indecision. We must have a system of government whose leaders can focus on governance rather than on staying in power. The parliamentary system has not merely outlived any good it could do; it was from the start unsuited to Indian conditions and is primarily responsible for many of our principal political ills. To suggest this is political sacrilege in New Delhi. Barely any of the many politicians I have discussed this with are even willing to contemplate a change. The main reason for this is that they know how to work the present system and do not wish to alter the ways they are used to.

But our reasons for choosing the British parliamentary system are themselves embedded in history. Like the American revolutionaries of two centuries ago, Indian nationalists had fought for 'the rights of Englishmen', which they thought the replication of the Houses of Parliament would both epitomize and guarantee.

Yet the parliamentary system devised in Britain—a small island nation with electorates initially of a few thousand voters per MP, and even today less than a lakh per constituency—assumes a number of conditions which simply do not exist in India. It requires the existence of clearly-defined political parties, each with a coherent set of policies and preferences that distinguish it from the next, whereas in India a party is all-too-often a label of convenience which a politician adopts and discards as frequently as a Bollywood film star changes costume. The principal parties, whether 'national' or otherwise, are fuzzily vague about their beliefs: every party's 'ideology' is one variant or another of centrist populism, derived to a greater or lesser degree from the Nehruvian socialism of the Congress. We have 44 registered political parties recognized by the Election Commission, and a staggering 903 registered but unrecognized ones, from the Adarsh Lok Dal to the Womanist Party of India. But with the sole exceptions of the BJP and the communists, the existence of the serious political parties, as entities separate from the 'big tent' of the Congress, is a result of electoral arithmetic or regional identities, not political conviction. (And even there, what on earth is the continuing case, after the demise of the Soviet Union and the reinvention of China, for two separate recognized communist parties and a dozen unrecognized ones?)

The lack of ideological coherence in India is in stark contrast to the UK. With few exceptions, India's parties all profess their faith in the same set of rhetorical clichés, notably socialism, secularism, a mixed economy and non-alignment, terms they are all equally loath to define. No wonder the communists, when they served in the United Front governments and when they supported the first UPA, had no difficulty signing on to the Common Minimum Programme articulated by their 'bourgeois' allies. The BJP used to be thought of an as an exception, but in its attempts to broaden its base of support, it sounds—and behaves—more or less like the other parties, except on the emotive issue of national identity.

So our parties are not ideologically coherent, take few distinct positions and do not base themselves on political principles. As organizational entities, therefore, they are dispensable, and are indeed cheerfully dispensed with (or split/reformed/merged/dissolved) at the convenience of politicians. The sight of a leading figure from a major party leaving it to join another or start his own—which would send shock waves through the political system in other parliamentary democracies—is commonplace, even banal, in our country. (One prominent UP politician, if memory serves, has switched parties nine times in the last couple of decades, but his voters have been more consistent than he, by voting for him, not the label he was sporting, at least until he came a cropper in 2014.) In the absence of a real party system, the voter chooses not between parties but between individuals, usually on the basis of their caste, their public image or other personal qualities. But since the individual is elected in order to be part of a majority that will form the government, party affiliations matter. So voters are told that if they want an Indira Gandhi as prime minister, or even an MGR or NTR as their chief minister, they must vote for someone else in order to indirectly accomplish that result. It is a perversity only the British could have devised: to vote for a legislature not to legislate but in order to form the executive.

So much for theory. But the result of the profusion of small parties is that for nearly a quarter-century we had coalition governments of a couple of dozen parties, some with just a handful of members of parliament, and our Parliament has only now seen a single-party majority since Rajiv Gandhi lost his in 1989. As a result, for the longest time India's democracy was condemned to be run by the lowest common denominator—hardly a recipe for decisive action. The disrepute into which the political process has fallen in India, and the widespread cynicism about the motives of our politicians, can be traced directly to the workings of the parliamentary system. Holding the executive hostage to the agendas of a range of motley partners is nothing but a recipe for governmental instability. And instability is precisely what India, with its critical economic and social challenges, cannot afford.

The fact that the principal reason for entering Parliament is to attain governmental office creates four specific problems. First, it limits executive posts to those who are electable rather than to those who are able. The prime minister cannot appoint a Cabinet of his choice; he has to cater to the wishes of the political leaders of several parties. (Yes, he can bring some members in through the Rajya Sabha, but our Upper House too has been largely the preserve of full-time politicians, so the talent pool has not been significantly widened.)

Second, it puts a premium on defections and horse-trading. The Anti-Defection Act of 1985 was necessary because in many states (and, after 1979, at the centre) parliamentary floor-crossing had become a popular pastime, with lakhs of rupees, and many ministerial posts, changing hands. That now cannot happen without attracting disqualification, so the bargaining has shifted to the allegiance of whole parties rather than individuals. Given the present national mood, with the BJP enjoying an absolute majority itself, such anxieties seem remote, but I shudder to think of what will happen after the next elections.

Third, legislation suffers. Most laws are drafted by the executive—in practice by the bureaucracy—and parliamentary input into their formulation and passage is minimal, with very many bills passing after barely five minutes of debate. The ruling coalition inevitably issues a whip to its members in order to ensure unimpeded passage of a bill, and since defiance of a whip itself attracts disqualification, MPs loyally vote as their party directs. The parliamentary system does not permit the existence of a legislature distinct from the executive, applying its collective mind freely to the nation's laws.

Apologists for the present system say in its defence that it has served to keep the country together and given every Indian a stake in the nation's political destiny. But that is what democracy has done, not the parliamentary system. Any form of genuine democracy would do that—and ensuring popular participation and accountability between elections is vitally necessary. But what our present system has not done as well as other democratic systems might, is to ensure effective performance.

The case for a presidential system of either the French or the American style has, in my view, never been clearer. The French version, by combining presidential rule with a parliamentary government headed by a prime minister, is superficially more attractive, since it resembles our own system, except for reversing the balance of power between the president and the Council of Ministers. This is what the Sri Lankans opted for when they jettisoned the British model. But, given India's fragmented party system, the prospects for parliamentary chaos distracting the elected president are considerable. An American or Latin American model, with a president serving both as head of state and head of government, might better evade the problems we have experienced with political factionalism. Either approach would separate the legislative functions from the executive, and most important, free the executive from dependence on the legislature for its survival.

A directly-elected chief executive in New Delhi, instead of being vulnerable to the shifting sands of coalition support politics, would have stability of tenure free from legislative whim, be able to appoint a Cabinet of talents, and above all, be able to devote his or her energies to governance, and not just to government. The Indian voter will be able to vote directly for the individual he or she wants to be ruled by, and the president will truly be able to claim to speak for a majority of Indians rather than a majority of MPs. At the end of a fixed period of time—let us say the same five years we currently accord to our Lok Sabha—the public would be able to judge the individual on performance in improving the lives of Indians, rather than on political skill at keeping a government in office. It is a compelling case.

Why, then, do the arguments for a presidential system get such short shrift from our political class? At the most basic level, our parliamentarians' fondness for the parliamentary system rests on familiarity: this is the system they know. They are comfortable with it, they know how to make it work for themselves, they have polished the skills required to triumph in it. Most non-politicians in India would see this as a disqualification, rather than as a recommendation for a decaying status quo.

The more serious argument advanced by liberal democrats is that the presidential system carries with it the risk of dictatorship. They conjure up the image of an imperious president, immune to parliamentary defeat and impervious to public opinion, ruling the country by fiat. Of course, it does not help that, during the Emergency, some around Mrs Indira Gandhi contemplated abandoning the parliamentary system for a modified form of Gaullism, thereby discrediting the idea of presidential government in many democratic Indian eyes. But the Emergency is itself the best answer to such fears: it demonstrated that even a parliamentary system can be distorted to permit autocratic rule. Dictatorship is not the result of a particular type of governmental system.

The rise of Mr Narendra Modi to near-absolute power paradoxically reaffirms these fears and provides their refutation. It will be argued that the adoption of a presidential system will pave the way for a Modi dictatorship in India. But a President Modi could scarcely be more autocratic than the prime minister we have seen in his first months in office—one who has:

- sidelined all the BJP politicians and statesmen who were senior to him (relegating the most senior to a mentor group, the 'margdarshak mandal', with no functions or authority whatsoever);
- appointed junior figures to key ministerial portfolios to make it clear that he personally will call the shots in their areas of responsibility;
- dismantled the UPA's decision-making 'Empowered Groups of Ministers' and instead disempowered his ministers, deciding his Cabinet's agenda without consultation; and
- dealt directly with the bureaucracy and the Secretaries, bypassing their nominal bosses, the Ministers.

In a parliamentary system, it is the Cabinet that is supposed to be collectively accountable to Parliament, and the ministers who rise to answer questions on the policies they have ostensibly formulated. Under Mr Modi, MPs find themselves in the odd position of interrogating ministers about decisions they may have had nothing to do with—and to explain policies formulated by the bureaucracy directly with the prime minister. How could a President Modi be any different from such a Prime Minister Modi?

In any case, to offset the temptation for a national president to become all-powerful, and to give real substance to the decentralization essential for a country of India's size, an executive chief minister or governor should also be directly elected in each of the states, most of which suffer from precisely the same maladies I have identified in our national system. The case for such a system in the states is even stronger than in the centre. Those who reject a presidential system on the grounds that it might lead to dictatorship may be assured that the powers of the president would thus be balanced by those of the directly-elected chief executives in the states.

I would go farther: we need strong executives not only at the centre and in the states, but also at the local levels. Even a communist autocracy like China empowers its local authorities with genuine decentralized powers: if a businessman agrees on setting up a factory with a town mayor, everything (from the required permissions to land, water, sanitation, security and financial or tax incentives) follows automatically, whereas in India a mayor is little more than a glorified committee chairman, with little power and minimal resources. To give effect to meaningful self-government, we need directly elected mayors, panchayat presidents and zilla presidents, each with real authority and financial resources to deliver results in their own geographical areas.

Intellectual defenders of the present system feel that it does remarkably well in reflecting the heterogeneity of the Indian people and 'bringing them along' on the journey of national development, which a presidential system might not. But even a president would have to work with an elected legislature, which—given the logic of electoral arithmetic and the pluralist reality of India—is bound to be a home for our country's heterogeneity. Any president worth his (democratic) salt would name a cabinet reflecting the diversity of our nation: as Bill Clinton said in his own country, 'my Cabinet must look like America'. The risk that some sort of monolithic uniformity would follow the adoption of a presidential system is not as serious one.

Democracy, as I have argued in my many books, is vital for India's survival: our chronic pluralism is a basic element of what we are. Yes, democracy is an end in itself, and we are right to be proud of it. But few Indians are proud of the kind of politics our democracy has inflicted upon us. With the needs and challenges of one-sixth of humanity before our leaders, we must have a democracy that delivers progress to our people. Changing to a presidential system is the best way of ensuring a democracy that works.

Is that the most important thing for India? Some ask. Dr Ambedkar had argued in the Constituent Assembly that the framers of the Constitution felt the parliamentary system placed 'responsibility' over 'stability' while the presidential did the opposite; he did not refer to 'accountability' and 'performance' as the two choices, but the idea is the same. Are efficiency and performance the most important yardsticks for judging our system, when the inefficiencies of our present system have arguably helped keep India united, 'muddling through' as the 'functioning anarchy' in Galbraith's famous phrase? To me, yes: after more than six and a half decades of freedom we can take our democracy and our unity largely for granted. It is time to focus on delivering results for our people.

It is worth revisiting Dr Ambdedkar's views, since they will be cited against reversing his choice of a parliamentary system over a presidential one. On the question of why a Parliamentary system was chosen, Dr Ambedkar said:

'The Presidential system of America is based upon the separation of the Executive and the Legislature. So that the President and his Secretaries cannot be members of the Congress. The Draft Constitution does not recognize this doctrine. The Ministers under the Indian Union are members of Parliament. Only members of Parliament can become Ministers. Ministers have the same rights as other members of Parliament, namely, that they can sit in Parliament, take part in debates and vote in its proceedings.

Both systems of Government are of course democratic and the choice between the two is not very easy. A democratic executive must satisfy two conditions—

(1) It must be a stable executive and (2) it must be a responsible executive.

Unfortunately it has not been possible so far to devise a system which can ensure both in equal degree. You can have a system which can give you more stability but less responsibility or you can have a system which gives you more responsibility but less stability.

The American and the Swiss systems give more stability but less responsibility. The British system on the other hand gives you more responsibility but less stability. The reason for this is obvious.

The American Executive is a non-Parliamentary Executive which means that it is not dependent for its existence upon a majority in the Congress, while the British system is a Parliamentary Executive which means that it is dependent upon a majority in Parliament.

Being a non-Parliamentary Executive, the Congress of the United States cannot dismiss the Executive. A Parliamentary Government must resign the moment it loses the confidence of a majority of the members of Parliament.

Looking at it from the point of view of responsibility, a non-Parliamentary Executive being independent of parliament tends to be less responsible to the Legislature, while a Parliamentary Executive being more dependent upon a majority in Parliament become more responsible.

The Parliamentary system differs from a non-Parliamentary system in as much as the former is more responsible than the latter but they also differ as to the time and agency for assessment of their responsibility.

Under the non-Parliamentary system, such as the one that exists in US, the assessment of the responsibility of the Executive is periodic. It is done by the Electorate.

In England, where the Parliamentary system prevails, the assessment of responsibility of the Executive is both daily and periodic. The daily assessment is done by members of Parliament, through questions, Resolutions, No-confidence motions, Adjournment motions and Debates on Addresses. Periodic assessment is done by the Electorate at the time of the election which may take place every five years or earlier.

The daily assessment of responsibility which is not available under the American system is it is felt far more effective than the periodic assessment and far more necessary in a country like India. The Draft Constitution in recommending the Parliamentary system of Executive has preferred more responsibility to more stability.'

Has the Indian parliamentary system, in fact, functioned as Dr Ambedkar envisioned? The notion that it provides a 'daily assessment of responsibility' would be laughable—given the performance of the last Parliament with all its disruptions and adjournments—were the need for such responsibility not so acute. Some ask what would happen to issues of performance if a president and a legislature were elected from opposite and antagonistic parties: would that not impede efficiency? Yes, it might, as Barack Obama has discovered. But in the era of coalitions that we have entered, the chances of any party other than the president's receiving an overwhelming majority in the House— and being able to block the president's plans—are minimal indeed. If such a situation does arise, it would test the mettle of the leadership of the day, but what's wrong with that?

In any case, India's fragmented polity, with dozens of political parties in the fray, makes a US-style two-party gridlock in Parliament impossible. Even in the BJP 'wave' of 2014, 37 parties made it to the Lok Sabha. What happens if a future Indian president does not enjoy a majority in Parliament? An Indian Presidency, instead of facing a monolithic opposition, would have the opportunity to build issue-based coalitions on different issues, mobilizing different temporary alliances of different smaller parties from one policy to the next. It would call for the deployment of persuasive skills to get legislation through—the opposite of the dictatorial steamroller some fear a presidential system could produce.

What precisely would the mechanisms be for popularly electing a president, and how would they avoid the distortions that our Westminster-style parliamentary system has bequeathed us? In my view the virtue of a system of directly-elected chief executives at all levels would be the straightforward lines of division between the legislative and executive branches of government. The electoral process to get there may not initially be all that simple. When it comes to choosing a president, however, we have to accept that elections in our country will remain a messy affair: it will be a long while before Indian politics arranges itself into the conveniently tidy two-party system of the US. Given the fragmented nature of our party system, it is the French electoral model I would turn to.

As in France, therefore, we would need two rounds of voting. In the first, every self-proclaimed netaji, with or without strong party backing, would enter the lists. (In order to have a manageable number of candidates, we would have to insist that their nomination papers be signed by at least ten parliamentarians, or twenty members of a state assembly, or better still, both.) If, by some miracle, one candidate manages to win 50 per cent of the vote (plus one), he or she is elected in the first round; but that is a far-fetched possibility, given that even Mrs Indira Gandhi, at the height of her popularity, never won more than 47 per cent of the national vote for the Congress, and Mr Modi enjoys his majority on the basis of a mere 31 per cent. More plausibly, no one would win in the first round; the two highest vote-getters would then face each other in round two, a couple of weeks later. The defeated aspirants will throw their support to one or the other survivor; Indian politicians being what they are, there will be some hard bargaining and the exchange of promises and compromises; but in the end, a president will emerge who truly has received the support of a majority of the country's electorate.

Does such a system not automatically favour candidates from the more populous states? Is there any chance that someone from Manipur or Lakshadweep will ever win the votes of a majority of the country's voters? Could a Muslim or a Dalit be elected president? These are fair questions, but the answer surely is that their chances would be no better, and no worse, than they are under our present system. Seven of India's first eleven prime ministers, after all, came from Uttar Pradesh, which surely has no monopoly on political wisdom; perhaps a similar proportion of our directly-elected presidents will be UPites as well. How does it matter? Most democratic systems tend to favour majorities; it is no accident that every president of the United States from 1789 to 2008 was a white male Christian (and all bar one a Protestant), or that only one Welshman has been prime minister of Great Britain. But then Obama came along, proving that majorities can identify themselves with the right representative even of a visible minority.

I dare say that the need to appeal to the rest of the country will oblige a would-be president from UP to reach across the boundaries of region, language, caste and religion, whereas in our present parliamentary system a politician elected in his constituency on the basis of precisely such parochial appeals can jockey his way to the prime ministership. A directly-elected president will, by definition, have to be far more of a national figure than a prime minister who owes his position to a handful of political king-makers in a coalition card-deal. I would also borrow from the US the idea of an electoral college, to ensure that our less populous states are not ignored by the candidates: the winner would also be required to carry a majority of states, so that crushing numbers in the cow belt alone would not be enough.

And why should the Indian electorate prove less enlightened than others around the world? Jamaica, which is 97 per cent black, has elected a white prime minister (Edward Seaga). In Kenya, President Daniel arap Moi hailed from a tribe that makes up just 11 per cent of the population. In Argentina, a voting population overweeningly proud of its European origins twice elected a son of Syrian immigrants, Carlos Saul Menem; the same phenomenon occurred in Peru, where former President Alberto Fujimori's ethnicity (Japanese) covers less than 1 per cent of the population. The right minority candidate, in other words, can command a majority; to choose the Presidential system is not necessarily to make future Narasimha Raos or Manmohan Singhs impossible. Indeed, the voters of Guyana, a country that is 50 per cent Indian and 47 per cent black, elected as President a white American Jewish woman, who happened to be the widow of the nationalist hero Cheddi Jagan. A story with a certain ring of plausibility in India....

The adoption of a Presidential system will send our politicians scurrying back to the drawing boards. Politicians of all faiths across India have sought to mobilize voters by appealing to narrow identities; by seeking votes in the name of religion, caste and region, they have urged voters to define themselves on these lines. Under our parliamentary system, we are more and more defined by our narrow particulars, and it has become more important to be a Muslim, a Bodo or a Yadav than to be an Indian. Our politics have created a discourse in which the clamour goes up for Assam for the Assamese, Jharkhand for the Jharkhandis, Maharashtra for the Maharashtrians. A Presidential system will oblige candidates to renew the demand for an India for the Indians.

Any politician with aspirations to rule India as President will have to win the support of people beyond his or her home turf; he or she will have to reach out to other groups, other interests, other minorities. And since the directly-elected President will not have coalition partners to blame for his or her inaction, a Presidential term will have to be justified in terms of results, and accountability will be direct and personal. In that may lie the Presidential system's ultimate vindication.

INDIA'S OBAMA MOMENT?

Amongst the many international consequences of the stunning election victory of Barack Obama in the US in 2008 was the widespread introspection around the world on whether such a thing could happen in other countries. Could a person of colour win power in other white-majority polities? Could a member of a beleaguered minority transcend the circumstances of his birth to lead his country?

While many analysts in a wide variety of nations, especially European ones, have concluded that such an event could not occur there in the foreseeable future (in Britain, the very idea is preposterous), India has been an exception. After all, minority politicians have long wielded authority, if not power, in various offices of state in India. And India's 2004 general elections had produced a remarkable sight: they were won by a woman political leader of Italian heritage and Roman Catholic faith (Sonia Gandhi) who made way for a Sikh (Manmohan Singh) to be sworn in as prime minister by a Muslim (President Abdul Kalam) in a country that's 81 per cent Hindu. Not only could it happen here, Indians say, but it already has.

Such complacency is premature. The closest Indian analogy to the position of black Americans is that of the Dalits—formerly called 'Untouchables', the outcastes who for millennia laboured under humiliating discrimination and oppression. Like blacks in the US, Dalits account for about 15 per cent of the population; they are found disproportionately in low-status, lower-income jobs; their levels of educational attainment are lower than the upper castes; and they still face daily incidents of discrimination, being stigmatized for no other reason than their identity at birth. Only when a Dalit rules India can the country truly be said to have attained its own Obama moment.

In theory, a Dalit already has: K. R. Narayanan, born into a poor Dalit family, served as president of India, the highest office in the land, from 1997 to 2002. But the Indian presidency is a largely ceremonial position: real power is vested in the office of prime minister, and no Dalit has come close to holding that office. Indeed, of India's fourteen prime ministers since Independence in 1947, all but five have been Brahmins, members of the highest Hindu caste. The rise of a 'backward class' politician, Narendra Modi, to the prime ministry in 2014 is a significant advance for caste equality in India. But he has endured none of the discrimination that Dalits have historically suffered. Only one recent national election—the general elections of April/May 2009—was seen as likely to produce a plausible Dalit contender for the job of prime minister—the then chief minister of India's most populous state, Uttar Pradesh, Ms Mayawati.

The logic or plausibility behind Mayawati being 'considered' as a prime ministerial candidate was principally electoral. Since 1991, no Indian governing party had enjoyed a secure majority on its own in Parliament, and Indian governments are multi-party coalitions. The then Congress party-led government of Dr Manmohan Singh was made up of 20 parties; it succeeded a 23-party coalition headed by the BJP's Atal Bihari Vajpayee. When the election results are declared, the conventional wisdom each time is that the first challenge for the elected parliamentarians will be to cobble together another coalition. Both the Congress and the BJP, it was assumed in 2009, would seek to make alliances with the dozens of smaller parties likely to be represented in Parliament. But this time they faced a third alternative: Ms Mayawati, whose Bahujan Samaj Party (BSP) was, it was thought, capable of commanding a bloc of at least fifty seats. She had publicly expressed her disdain for both the large national parties; she would much rather lead a coalition than join one. And if the electoral numbers broke down right, she could conceivably assemble a collection of regional and left-wing parties and stake a claim to rule India.

In the event that didn't happen in 2009, and in 2014, she did spectacularly badly, failing even to win a single seat in the Lok Sabha from her strong hold of Uttar Pradesh. In 2009, the Congress party assembled another coalition without her; in 2014, she didn't figure in any governmental discussions. But the seriousness of the prospect was itself a remarkable development: the idea that a Dalit, let alone a Dalit woman, could lead India had essentially been inconceivable for 3,000 years. But India's democracy has opened new pathways to empowerment for its under-classes. The poor and the oppressed may not have much, but they do have the numbers, and that's what matters at the ballot box. Dalits and India's aboriginals (listed in the Constitution as 'Scheduled Castes and Tribes') are entitled to 85 seats in India's 543-member Parliament that are 'reserved' for candidates from their communities. In addition to doing well in these, Mayawati's shrewd alliances, including with some members of the upper castes, which propelled her to power in Uttar Pradesh, give her party a fighting chance in a number of other seats. If, following the experience of one-party rule under the BJP, India returns to a coalition-dependent parliamentary system, that could be all she needs to become prime minister.

The daughter of a government clerk, Mayawati studied law and worked as a teacher before being spotted by the BSP's founder, the late Kanshi Ram, and groomed for political leadership. Her ascent to prominence was marked by a heavy emphasis on symbolism—her rule in Uttar Pradesh featured the construction of numerous statues of Dalit leaders, notably herself—and a taste for lavish celebrations. The unmarried 58-year-old's weakness for 'bling' was demonstrated at her extravagant birthday parties, which she presided over, laden with diamond jewellery, saying (rather like Evita Peron) that her lustre brought glamour and dignity to her people. She takes pride in being the

Indian politician who paid the highest income taxes—some Rs 26 crore, or over $4 million, each year—though the sources of her income are shrouded in controversy. She was accused, but not convicted, of corruption in a number of cases, notably one involving the construction of an elaborate shopping complex near the Taj Mahal, in violation of various zoning laws.

Critics say that Mayawati's promotion of Dalit welfare seemed to start with herself. But there's no denying that the methods that propelled her to power in India's largest state, which sends eighty members to Parliament, helped her build a vital platform to bid for India's most powerful job. Such are the vagaries of democratic politics that in the 2014 elections, she emerged without a single seat in the Lok Sabha, the popularly-elected lower house of Parliament, as the BJP swept to the first single-party parliamentary majority in thirty years. If that pattern continues, the electoral logic of a Mayawati prime ministry becomes impossible.

But she is licking her wounds and biding her time: no sensible political analyst is ready to write her off. With her diamonds and her statues, and a reputation for dealing imperiously with her subordinates, Mayawati is clearly no Obama. But if she succeeds, she will have overcome a far longer legacy of discrimination than the charismatic figure who might one day be known as her American counterpart.

PRESERVING THE PAST

The remarkable aspect of India's cultural heritage is how it continues to suffuse so many aspects of our lives even today. Our geography, our festivals, even the names we give ourselves and our children, often have associations of mythological antiquity and significance. Indian culture is marked by an unparalleled sense of diversity and civilizational continuity. Our heritage is not restricted to hidebound relics; rather, it is a living history in which we partake every day of our lives.

Historically, around the world, it is true that most artistes—sculptors, artisans, painters, musicians, dancers—sought out and often depended upon the patronage of the elite. The sheer scale of some endeavours made this necessary: only the Pharaohs could have marshalled the resources to build the pyramids! Only Shah Jahan could have built the Taj Mahal. In the 21st century, however, this is no longer the case. Especially given its almost omnipresent role in our lives as a nation, it is one of the peculiar tragedies of India that fields such as classical history, art, architecture and the like are still seen as the preserve of the elite. There is an urgent need to remind our people of their own association, role and stake in our cultural heritage—of taking it out of the realm of the courtroom and making it truly a treasure of the people. In short, we need a dedicated effort at democratizing our cultural heritage.

This is particularly the case today, because the greatest assault on our culture does not come (as some of our more blinkered ideologists would suggest) from the West. Rather, the greatest threat to our heritage is the growing ignorance about it amongst our people today, and especially the disconnect from it amongst our youth. It is difficult to treasure something when you do not know its worth; we are, as a vibrant secular democracy, nowhere near the kind of ignorance or intolerance that led to the destruction of the Bamiyan Buddhas in Afghanistan, or the invaluable treasures of Timbuktu in Mali—both priceless and irreplaceable parts of the world's shared cultural heritage—but the neglect of our heritage is a pernicious danger. While it may even appear to be a benign part of our society's modernization, it is a trend we must seek to set right. It is in this context that I particularly appreciate the exemplary role of an institution like the National Museum in offering young people the opportunity not only to study our heritage, but also to learn the skills that will enable them to bring it back into our awareness, and to translate it for the modern world.

It is to India's credit that the National Museum is not just a museum but a university, offering three specialized and interdisciplinary fields of study and research at the masters and doctoral level, in the History of Art, Conservation and Museology. The National Museum Institute provides its students a number of excellent opportunities to gain knowledge and experience about art and cultural heritage. Through these courses, students are empowered with the technical knowledge, skills and abilities to address the pressing need for qualified and competent professionals in these fields; it also inculcates in them the attitudes and holistic values which are crucial in those who will protect, restore and convey our rich heritage to new generations of Indians and to the world.

India has a storied, ancient and vibrant history of over five thousand years as a centre of civilizational enlightenment and a treasure-trove of art and culture. Given our history of religious, cultural and regional diversity, the various peoples of India developed different means of expressing and depicting their ideas, experiences and creative impulses through an exceptionally wide range of material and methods. Art in India traverses the gamut of themes from history to religion, from sculpture to architecture, each medium evolving in unique manners, so as to best express the talents and needs of its creators. Thus, even as India grows in modernity and technological capability, it is important that we continue to nurture our roots, which after all stretch back to mythology, before even the written record of history.

The conservation of our shared cultural heritage is an important challenge today, well acknowledged by government institutions and people worldwide. There is also a growing recognition of the contributions of art and cultural heritage in finding creative solutions for global challenges, and its transversal role in sustainable development is increasingly acknowledged and explored. Art and cultural heritage is a collective patrimony, which tells the history of human existence and development, and is transmitted from one generation to the next. It makes it possible for the present generations to understand their place in history; such a sense of context can bring about a well-grounded mind, in turn enabling us to better cope with the rapid and accelerating pace of change in our society: it is an important element of stability in a rapidly changing world. Art and cultural heritage serve as a unique and dynamic record of human activity; it has been shaped by civilizations responding to the surroundings they inherited and embodies the aspirations, skills and endeavour of countless generations. Stand at Ajanta or Ellora and imagine those monks all those centuries ago chipping away at the rock, without any modern tools or electric drills, chipping away to create such a magnificent legacy to humanity.

In reflecting the knowledge, beliefs and traditions of diverse communities, our heritage gives distinctiveness, meaning and quality to the places and times in which we live, providing both—a sense of continuity and a source of identity. It is a resource for learning and enjoyment, raising our awareness and understanding of the varied ways in which society's values (evidential, historic, aesthetic, communal, etc.) have evolved, and their significance to different generations and communities. This knowledge is a valuable source of community development, cohesiveness, social integration and tolerance among various social groups/communities. There are no restrictions of caste or creed in entering those temples at Ajanta and Ellora, created by Buddhists and Jains for all of us.

In 2013, I was asked to inaugurate a new installation at the Guruvayoor temple in Kerala—not by cutting a ribbon, but by wielding the paintbrush on a mural to fill in the eye of Krishna. What a magnificent evocation of culture and heritage! On another occasion I saw how religious culture can be sustained by secular use—when I was asked, as a visiting minister three years ago, to perform an abhishekam for a Shiva lingam in Mauritius. I mischievously asked if my predecessor, a Muslim, would have been asked to perform the ritual—the answer was yes. These are striking illustrations of the ways in which culture connects our past to our present, and does it in an inclusive manner.

In the contemporary context, contributions from art, archaeological and cultural heritage are now considered our 'cultural capital', and seen as a means for understanding the economic dimension in relation to other forms of capital inputs. Cultural capital may be viewed as a reservoir of tangible and intangible cultural expressions of a society. In particular, the reservoir of tangible cultural capital exists in heritage materials such as monuments, archaeological sites and locations endowed with intangible cultural significance. The main implication of this concept is that cultural activities and heritage materials may be introduced in a broader framework of development, such as assessing investment opportunities and economic impacts. Art and cultural heritage thus provide an important insight into economic development; some measurable economic impacts which result are heritage tourism, job creation and household income, property appreciation and small business incubation.

The link between archaeological and cultural heritage and tourism is the most visible aspect of the contribution to local development—after all, much of the world's tourism is culturally motivated. Heritage tourism must be developed and recognized as an organized industry, that uses cultural heritage as its backbone. Related to this are the opportunities for growth in local communities of small-scale industries. Where cultural tourism is identified as part of an overall development strategy, a comprehensive plan for the identification, protection and enhancement of heritage resources can be put in place, which is also vital for any sustainable effort. Globalization, be it economic or cultural, means change—change at a pace that can be disruptive politically, economically, socially, psychologically. Adaptive application of cultural capital can provide a touchstone, a sense of stability, and a sense of continuity for people and societies to help counteract such disruptions. India's strength in this era is the resilience of its own culture—we have repeatedly shown that we can drink Coca-Cola without becoming Coca-colonized. As Mahatma Gandhi said seventy years ago, India should keep her doors and windows open so that the winds of the world can blow through our house, provided we are grounded solidly enough that we are not blown off our feet.

Art, archaeological and cultural heritage can also contribute to the identity and branding of territory, which is extremely relevant in an age of globalization and fierce competition. This brand identity provides a vibrant base for sustainable and endogenous development. It is, therefore, important that we give more attention to preservation, interpretation and dissemination of cultural resources in order to foster sustainable socio-economic development.

It is, of course, crucial to preserve our irreplaceable tangible and intangible forms of art and culture for future generations. Reading about the Taj Mahal in a textbook can never be compared to seeing the actual façade and drawing first-hand knowledge of our past; museums will lose their charm if they have only replicas of what might have existed in the past; contemporary art practices will have no historical roots from which to draw comparisons or critique. Museums in India have acted as custodians of art and culture so far but their activities should not be limited to only having to collect, preserve and share objects and materials of cultural, religious and historical importance. In the 21st century, museums need to strive to become agents of change and development. As institutions possessing critical resources in society, one of the fundamental objectives of any museum is to impart cultural education effectively.

In educational organizations worldwide, there has been a paradigm shift from instruction-centred learning to student-centred learning where the emphasis is placed on knowledge building and skill acquisition through active participation. The use of information and communication technology needs to be encouraged and promoted in cultural educational organizations in India, so as to prepare students to meet workplace challenges globally. I was very pleased to learn that a dozen National Museum Institute students have won scholarships for further training at the Metropolitan Museum in New York. As a premier institute in the field of art and cultural heritage, the National Museum Institute must also have ready access and connectivity with the world. Global standards must be ours too.

With growing scientific and technological advances, new techniques and methods are being employed to obtain a better understanding of our heritage and devise ways of preserving it. Technological innovations make a welcome impact in areas of research that eventually help us assess the present condition of our (unfortunately, rapidly deteriorating) heritage. Over the last few decades, art historians, museologists and conservators, have embraced technology in various forms. In the image-based field of Art History, the integration of digital technology is no longer a choice—it is a necessity. Museologists have used technology to bring museums to the doorstep of the individual by creating concepts like the 'Virtual Museum' amongst various other things. Conservators are using new age methods like Laser technologies, 3D Imaging technologies etc. for improved and accurate conservation and restoration techniques. It is, therefore, essential to recognize the crucial role of science and technology in keeping our heritage intact, lest our living history be muted and restricted to the written word. I am certain that the National Museum Institute will also adapt to these changes and evolve with the times, employing technology effectively and in doing so lead the way for others to follow.

Through significant efforts in teaching, research and development of technology, while nurturing a spirit of innovation and entrepreneurship along with a strong commitment to our time-tested value system, we have the opportunity to shape the destiny of our nation and the world. At our universities, we aim to create a holistic learning environment, providing fertile ground for nation building today and into the future. We must resolve to make that happen through our respective pursuits of scholarship, research and engagement with society and industry around us. We cannot succeed in the future if we do not preserve our accomplishments of the past.

V

THE PURSUIT OF EXCELLENCE

THE QUEST FOR QUALITY

Quality may be common or uncommon to Indian industry, but for me the first challenge is that it is virtually impossible to define. It is said that quality is something whose presence is never acknowledged but whose absence is always noted. But then quality is rather like India: anything I can tell you about it, the opposite is also true. So it is equally true in our country that quality is often noticed and its absence is generally ignored. Some speak of quality as a feeling rather than a measureable construct: thus an airline can advertise its quality not by indicators like the punctuality of its flights, the taste of its food, or the pitch between its seats, but by a slogan that says, 'We love to fly and it shows.' The ultimate conclusion then, is that quality is not easily amenable to definition but, rather like pornography, you know it when you see it.

And yet the idea of quality relates to something that is quite fundamental to humanity. The idea of quality emerges from a basic human desire to excel. This is indeed pretty fundamental: the minute a baby is born, the mother's expectation changes immediately from praying for a normal child to be born, to developing the child into a super-man or -woman who would excel in everything that the parents could possibly hope the child could do. In other words, the minute the concept of quality touches your life, you are inspired and motivated to raise the bar. You instinctively want to go beyond your current capabilities to target and achieve excellence.

Quality is not merely for a small elite who have the talent and the resources to excel. It inheres in all of us. It is a core aspect of humanity—no matter how rich or poor you are, everyone at some time or the other in their life experiences this aspiration for quality. You can appreciate quality when you are watching a well-played cricket match or eating good food or observing an excellent painting. This is why we have recognized quality today in such a wide variety of fields—honouring quality in zinc, in insulation, in petroleum, banking and education, as well as (of course) in yoga.

As I am sure we have all realized today, quality is inspirational and motivational: it makes you a winner and it makes you appreciate winners. It implies a level of consciousness that comes from working for a higher goal and not just for a petty purpose. This is important for any individual, and also for any country or corporation. Quality, in my view, is not just excellence; it must emerge from the pursuit of excellence for a larger purpose than its own self. To attain true quality, we must set goals that go beyond our immediate needs.

What kind of quality will bring out the best in all of us as a country and aid in the resurgence of India? As the well-known management and quality guru Philip Crosby said, 'quality is the result of a carefully constructed cultural environment. It has to be the fabric of the organization, not part of the fabric.' This applies to our country as well—quality has to be woven into the overall fabric of the Indian nation.

But beyond that statement of the obvious, in what ways can quality be pursued in the context of tomorrow's visible realities? To my mind, in the quest for quality, there are three aspects that are worth thinking about today which can help in the resurgence of India and bring us into the next decade with confidence.

The first is sustainability. We need to emphasize quality in the pursuit of the noble cause of preserving our earth. Every human being will want this, since none of us is exempt from vulnerability to the vagaries of the environment. Every person can identify and relate to both the destructive and the necessary reviving forces around us. We hear of idealistic schoolchildren and concerned adults, government bureaucrats and NGO workers, technologists and economists and of course the media looking at this challenge with mounting vigour and passion. The discussions of global environmental challenges, whether in Copenhagen or Kolkata, Durban or Delhi, have engaged large sections of opinion in our country.

Part of the challenge for India's leadership on this issue is the art of simultaneously raising public consciousness and steering the tenor of the debate beyond the sterile dogmas of received positions. The conventional wisdom may have the merit of being right, but it is, by definition, rarely original and cannot cast light on new ways forward out of old dilemmas. There is therefore great need to think afresh, to come up with innovative approaches and to educate the media, civil society and politicians on what exactly is at stake and why we need to produce new ideas. Quality solutions, in a democracy like ours require a quality debate—and I daresay attitudinal and behavioural changes amongst all of us as well.

The pursuit of quality in this debate, as in many others, will call for enlightened leadership. There's the marvellous story of Alexandre Auguste Ledru-Rollin, the 19th century French politician who became the interior minister in the provisional government that was created in Paris after the Revolution of 1848, who looked out of his window during the tumultuous events of that time and saw a mob rushing past on the street. He promptly headed for the door, saying, 'Je suis leur chef, il fallait bien les suivre' ('I am their leader, I should follow them'). That is one kind of leadership, I suppose, though the fact that this incident is the only thing for which M. Ledru-Rollin is remembered suggests that it is not the most effective or enduring kind of leadership. By and large a leader is expected to lead, even if, from time to time, a good leader knows how to be a good follower. On issues like the environment, our leadership must draw on the best of the ideas and energies of our followership, while giving them guidance and political direction.

Second, I see quality impacting our collective lives when one equates quality with good governance. Developing and preserving good governance is essential for our country and must become the passion of future governments. Good governance transcends all administrative frontiers—whether it relates to infrastructure or economic growth. Good governance means applying quality standards to the process of delivering services to the public. It also requires politicians of all parties recognizing the importance of working together for a common goal.

And for achieving good governance we need good leaders to be groomed young. In the course of my activities as an MP, I have had the occasion of interacting with potential future leaders of India in many forums. I have been impressed by the enthusiasm and enterprise shown by so many young people in dealing with the problems of our country. I am hopeful that such leaders will enter the political mainstream and provide leadership in governance.

The leaders of tomorrow will have to know both how to live with change in a varied world, and how to live with contradictions. As Indians, we like to think of ourselves as an ancient civilization but we are also a young republic; our IT experts stride confidently into the 21st century but much of our population seems to live in each of the other twenty centuries. Quite often the opposites co-exist quite cheerfully.

Third, the most important pursuit has to be to identify quality solutions across the board to our long-standing national problems of clean drinking water, clean air, energy sufficiency, affordable housing, good health and education, whose nature has not changed since independence or even earlier. We still have not solved the questions of providing the aam admi with roti, kapda aur makan and I would add pani, kitab and kaam to this list. We need to find innovative ways to tackle these problems and solve them. The need is imperative. Meeting these goals cannot go on being indefinitely postponed. India must solve these problems, while preserving the earth and practising good governance.

But the fact is that it can be done, and we Indians can do it. When the Indian industrialist Jamsetji Tata was denied admission to Pyke's Hotel in Bombay at the peak of the British Empire, he built a grander, more opulent hotel that was open to Indians—the Taj Mahal Hotel. The Taj is today considered one of the finest hotels in the world, whereas Pyke's has long since closed. When the same Mr Tata set up India's first ever steel mill in the face of implacable British hostility in 1905, a senior imperial official sneered that he would personally eat every ounce of steel an Indian was capable of producing. It's a pity he didn't live to see the descendants of Jamsetji Tata taking over what remains of British Steel, through Tata's acquisition of Corus. It would certainly have given him a bad case of indigestion.

In other words, it's time to set aside the old stereotypes of who can and cannot excel at what in our globalizing world. Quality knows no national boundaries. The smartest executive jets are made by Embraer of Brazil; the tallest building in the world is currently in Dubai, and it overtook the previous tallest building, which was in Taipei; the world's biggest plane is being built in Russia and Ukraine; the world's largest Ferris wheel is in Singapore; the biggest shopping mall is in Beijing; the number One two-wheeler manufacturer in the world is not some Italian company, but India's Bajaj. And the country which is the world's largest consumer of gold, accounting for 20 per cent of the world's consumption, is of course India, where demand for the metal has increased at an average rate of 13 per cent per year over the past decade.

That doesn't surprise anyone, but here's something that once might have. A couple of decades ago no one would have mentioned India and high technology in the same breath. The migration to America of a number of Indian engineers from the 1960s onwards helped create a new perception of India amongst those with whom they worked. The engineers had a solid grounding in their field and excelled in the freedom afforded to them in the US; an Indian invented the Pentium chip, another created Hotmail, a third started Sun Microsystems, and Indians were involved in some 40 per cent of the start-ups in Silicon Valley. Over time, the Indianness of engineers and software developers began to be taken as synonymous with mathematical and scientific excellence. Today, Americans speak of the IITs—the Indian Institutes of Technology, the elite engineering schools from which many of these migrants came—with the same reverence they used to accord to MIT. The image of India has changed from that of a backward developing country to a sophisticated land that produces engineers and computer experts. Sometimes this has unintended consequences. I met an Indian the other day, a history major like me, who told me of transiting through Schiphol airport in Amsterdam and being accosted by an anxious European saying, 'You're Indian! You're Indian! Can you help me fix my laptop?' The old stereotype of Indians was that of snake-charmers and sadhus lying on beds of nails; now Indians are seen as software gurus and computer geeks. So there is no doubt we are capable of developing quality.

However, this cannot happen without engendering a new political ethos. We need people in politics to provide quality leadership just as we are doing in other areas. We have the Quality Council for India, but in addition to that, our country needs a countrywide commitment to quality that can work across these areas and create awareness, promote effective implementation and continuously refine and improve the strategy as we go along.

It is essential that the titans of industry commit themselves to ingrain quality into their business ethos and move ahead in innovation and open and transparent corporate governance. India saw how the sordid drama at Satyam a few years ago proved a wake-up call for every businessman. And as the revival of that company under new management has confirmed, I am very confident that industry can flourish when you adopt good governance, innovation and ethical business practices, which remains the best proven formula to stay ahead of competition. Philip Crosby was not wrong when he said 'Quality is Free'. Savings from quality far outstrips the costs of a quality programme.

It was Mahatma Gandhi who said, 'It is the quality of our work which will please God and not the quantity.' He also memorably said, 'Be the change you wish to see in the world.' Since quality will not come without change, both his exhortations apply to us in tandem. I am sure these two thoughts of Mahatma Gandhi will illuminate our quest for quality in all aspects of our life and work.

EDUCATION IN INDIA

One does not need a stint in the Ministry of Human Resource Development, (as I was privileged to have as Minister of State from October 2012 to May 2014), to realize that education is the most significant instrument of individual self-realization and democratic empowerment in our times. In a fractured, impatient and yet hopeful society like India, it is simply indispensable for social mobility and economic progress. Though for the greater part of human history, martial prowess and mercantile abilities were accorded greater importance, increasingly we have reached a stage of historical evolution where the acquisition and wielding of knowledge trumps all other attainments. In the 21st century, knowledge, and the instrument of its spread, education, will increasingly become the prime determinants of the success and worth of any nation or civilization.

Our society has historically emphasized the importance of education as one of the supreme objects of human existence, while celebrating a strong foundation in imparting education through traditional and non-traditional methods. Traditional methods of guru-shishya parampara thrived in India as did the many monasteries which went on to become important centres of education, receiving students from distant lands, notably as far from our shores as China and Turkey. The Pala Period, in particular, saw a number of monasteries emerge in what is now modern Bengal and Bihar, five of which— Vikramashila, Nalanda, Somapura, Mahavihara, Odantapura, and Jaggadala—were premier educational institutions which created a co-ordinated network amongst themselves under state rule. Nalanda University, which enjoyed global renown when Oxford and Cambridge were not even gleams in their founders' eyes, employed 2,000 teachers and housed 10,000 students in a remarkable campus that featured a library which was nine storeys tall. It is said that monks would hand-copy documents and books which would then become part of private collections of individual scholars. The university opened its doors for students from countries ranging from Korea, Japan, China, Tibet, and Indonesia in the east to Persia and Turkey in the west, studying subjects which included fine arts, medicine, mathematics, astronomy, politics and the art of war.

Amongst them were several famous Chinese scholars who studied and taught at Nalanda University in the 7th century. Hsuan-Tsang (Xuanzang from the Tang Dynasty) studied in the university and then taught there for five years while leaving detailed accounts of his time in Nalanda. Through the years India has paid host to several such scholars who have enriched our educational history. Ibn Battuta, one of the greatest travellers from the old world, found himself being appointed as a judge by Muhammad bin Tughlaq

in Delhi. Similarly, a Portuguese traveller, Fernão Nunes, spent three years in
the Vijayanagara Empire, leaving behind writings which gave us an important
insight into the running of the most prosperous and glittering realm of the era.

In addition to monasteries and formal establishments of learning, informal
institutions and methods of education also flourished in India. Oral education
has always enjoyed an honoured place in Indian culture. Mahatma Gandhi
memorably advocated oral education in place of the prevailing emphasis on
textbooks: 'Of textbooks…' he said, 'I never felt the want. The true textbook
for the pupil is his teacher.' And so, in the little ashram that he created in
South Africa, named Tolstoy Farm, he taught his students through his voice,
imparting his convictions orally, disregarding the need for formal written work.
Gandhiji found inspiration in the ways that knowledge of the Vedas and other
foundational Hindu texts like the Ramayana and the Mahabharata were passed
orally from one generation to another. The oral tradition, sustained through
the generations, had allowed this ancient knowledge to live.

But while such traditions give Indian education its moorings in our culture,
there is no escaping the stark fact that modern India achieved independence
with only 17 per cent literacy. For the next five decades India remained the
poorest, the most illiterate, the most malnourished, and the least gender-sensitive
major country in the world, with over half the world's illiterate adults and 40
per cent of the world's out-of-school children. As late as 2007, South Asia as
a whole had the lowest adult literacy rate (49 per cent) in the world; it had
fallen behind Sub-Saharan Africa (at 57 per cent), even though in 1970 South
Asia was ahead. At that point, the illiterate population of India exceeded the
total combined population of the North American continent and Japan. There
has been a revival in India to 74 per cent literacy (of which more later), but
37 per cent of all Indian primary schoolchildren drop out before reaching the
fifth grade. We have a shortage of schools and a shortage of teachers, and the
problem gets worse every year because of population growth.

Since school education is a state subject in our federal constitution, and
standards vary from state to state, India has made only uneven progress in
educating its population. Whereas most districts in Kerala—given a long tradition
of universal primary schooling and following the introduction of free and
compulsory secondary education by an elected Communist government in
1957, as well as a hugely popular mass campaign for literacy—have attained 100
per cent literacy, Bihar has barely crossed the 50 per cent mark, and it has a
female literacy rate of only 29 per cent. The national literacy level still hovers
around 82 per cent for men and 66 per cent for women. The rise in female
literacy has been dramatic, rising as it has from 9 per cent at Independence.
But one must be wary of these figures. UNESCO defines an illiterate person
as one who cannot, with understanding, both read and write a short, simple

statement on their everyday life. By that definition I suspect that closer to half our population would really qualify as literate.

The traditional explanation for the failure to attain mass education is two-pronged: the lack of resources to cope with the dramatic growth in population (we would need to build a new school every day for the next ten years just to educate the children already born) and the tendency of families to take their children out of school early to serve as breadwinners, sewing footballs or weaving carpets, or at least as help with domestic chores and sibling care at home, or work in the fields. Thus, though universal primary education is available in theory, fewer than three-quarters of India's children between the ages of 6 and 14 attend school at all.

But official national policy is undoubtedly in favour of promoting literacy. As a child at school I remember being exhorted to impart the alphabet to our servants under the Gandhian 'each one teach one' programme; and many of us were brought up on Swami Vivekananda's writings about the importance of education for the poor as the key to their uplift.

Yet it is true that, nearly seven decades after Independence, progress has been inexcusably slow. Obviously, there were policy choices being made here. India spends less than 4 per cent of its GNP on education: 3.6 per cent is the current amount. Successive governments collectively have spent only one-tenth of the amounts on education that they have committed to defence. What is missing is not just financial resources, but a commitment on the part of our society as a whole to tackle the educational tasks that lie ahead. Indian politicians ranging from former Prime Minister Indira Gandhi to former Bihar Chief Minister Laloo Prasad Yadav have proved all too quick to take refuge in sharp rejoinders about people drawing the wrong conclusions from the illiteracy figures. Education, Mrs Gandhi would often say, was not always relevant to the real lives of village Indians, but India's illiterates were still smart, and illiteracy was not a reflection of their intelligence or shrewdness (which they demonstrated, of course, by voting for her). Fair enough, but Kerala's literate villagers are smart too.

We hear more and more from progressive economists about the importance of what they call 'human capital'. Human capital is defined as the stock of useful, valuable, and relevant knowledge built up in the process of education and training. Literacy is the key to building human capital and human capital is the vital ingredient in building a nation. There is no industrial society today with an adult literacy rate of less than 80 per cent. No illiterate society has ever become an industrial tiger of any stripe.

What is striking from the international experience is that whenever and wherever basic education was spread, the social and economic benefits have been quite striking and visible. The development strategies followed in recent decades by Japan, the East Asian industrializing Tigers and China laid a firm basis for equitable growth by massive investment in basic education for all. Literacy was fundamental not only to accelerating the economic growth of these countries, but to distributing resources more equitably and thereby to empowering more people.

It is a truism today that economic success everywhere is based on educational success. And literacy is the basic building block of education. It is not just an end in itself: literacy leads to many social benefits, including improvements in standards of hygiene, reduction in infant and child mortality rates, decline in population growth rates, increase in labour productivity, rise in civic consciousness, greater political empowerment and democratization— and even an improved sense of national unity, as people become more aware than before of the country they belong to and the opportunities beyond their immediate horizons.

Literacy is also a basic component of social cohesion and national identity. The foundations for a conscious and active citizenship are often laid in school. Literacy plays a key role in the building of democracy; my home state of Kerala provides a striking example of how higher levels of literacy lead to a more aware and informed public. As a result of Kerala's high literacy levels, nearly half of the adult population in Kerala reads a daily newspaper, compared to less than 20 per cent elsewhere in India. One out of every four rural labourers reads a newspaper regularly, compared to less than 2 per cent of agricultural workers in the rest of the country. So literacy leads directly to an improvement in the depth and quality of public opinion, as well as to more active participation of the poor in the democratic process.

Absorbing new technologies, raising productivity levels, improving the competitiveness and quality of exports—all hallmarks of development in the 21st century—depend on the skills of a country's workforce. There is an increasing need in India for skilled manpower across all sectors of the economy. With India's increasing economic might, the big and growing gap between the demand for and supply of skilled people is widely felt. A study by the Observer Research Foundation concludes that by 2022 India will need to meet the target of 'skilling and up-skilling' 500 million people. The target cannot be met by the Government of India alone or by conventional educational institutions. It has to be a combined effort by public and private institutions, embracing different government ministries, development partners, NGOs, private and faith-based providers, local community groups, educational institutions and the corporate sector. It will need new vocational training institutions that are yet to be established, as well as recourse to two additional techniques that India has adopted relatively recently, community colleges and distance learning.

Education also plays a vital part in community development, broadly defined as a set of values and practices which permits a community to overcome poverty and disadvantage, knitting the society together at the grassroots and deepening democracy. Higher education is one of the most essential aspects of a developed community. Throughout time, universities have played an important social role through the creation, preservation and the extension of knowledge to and within communities. Universities cannot afford to remain as oases of excellence when the communities sustaining them are silently turning into deserts.

The linkage between universities and communities is vital. There is a need for universities to reach out to communities, and make their policies and structures more flexible and relevant to community development. Community-based learning enriches coursework by encouraging students to apply the knowledge and analytical tools gained in the classroom to the pressing issues that affect local communities. In some African countries, farmers and researchers used community based learning approaches and jointly developed an approach built on farmers' folk ecology and outsiders' knowledge, while going beyond methods that were merely curriculum-driven. India, too, could use distance learning to link farmers to the information that can help them improve their livelihoods.

Community radio can be another beneficial tool for community-based learning. It can play an essential role in giving young people the skills that can lead to better livelihoods and help them seek employment or self-employment. It can also raise awareness on health, which is also a developmental challenge in several developing countries. Community radio can provide non-formal educational opportunities, especially for communities that are not literate. Radio dramas, storytelling and interviews in particular are effective and low cost ways of making community voices an integral part of the learning process. In addressing the challenge of learning for development, open and distance learning can play a particularly important role, building a bridge between knowledge acquisition and skills development and the potential to reduce the inequalities of access that blight conventional education in most countries.

Amartya Sen has reminded us that 'the elimination of ignorance, of illiteracy and of needless inequalities in opportunities [are] objectives that are valued for their own sake. They expand our freedom to lead the lives we have reason to value'. In his most famous poem, the other Nobel Prize-winning Bengali, the immortal poet Rabindranath Tagore, implicitly spoke of education as fundamental to his dream for India. As he wrote in *Gitanjali*, it was in a place 'where the mind is without fear and the head is held high; where knowledge is free' and 'where the mind is led forward…into ever-widening thought and action' that he hoped his India would awake to freedom. Such a mind is, of course, one that can only be developed and shaped by literacy.

But more prosaically, illiteracy must be fought for practical reasons. How are we going to cope with the 21st century, the information age, if a third of our population cannot sign their name or read a newspaper, let alone use a computer keyboard or surf the net? Today's is the Information Age: the world will be able to tell the rich from the poor not by GNP figures, but by their internet connections. Illiteracy is a self-imposed handicap in a race we have no choice but to run.

And we must start early, with India's young children. A key strategy for creating sufficient and appropriate human capital is to focus on basic education for all children. The task of providing elementary education to all children is massive. India is making a major effort now to expand primary education. Our primary school system has become one of the largest in the world, with over 200 million children enrolled. On a typical day, roughly 300 million students are attending classes somewhere in India. But it's not enough.

It is true that while the government recognizes the needs, it has neither the resources nor the ability to deliver quality education to all of India's children. Our state governments have not been able to enrol all children between the ages of 5 and 10 in school, nor are they able to retain the ones they enrol— some drop out because their families can't afford to keep them in school when they could be out to work, some because the teaching is so abysmal that they don't learn anything at school anyway. Ensuring that students achieve decent learning outcomes and acquire values and skills that enable them to play a positive role in their societies is a remote prospect. One ignores at one's peril the role of education in nurturing the creative and emotional growth of learners and helping them to acquire values and attitudes for responsible citizenship.

Despite recent improvements, more Indian kids have never seen the inside of a school than those of any other country in the world. And those who have may not see a teacher, since we hold the world record for teacher absenteeism, or be given the books and learning materials without which the educational experience is incomplete.

Let us spare a thought for the poor teacher—in India, teachers are too often underpaid, under-appreciated and therefore under-motivated. No wonder we have a nationwide shortage of 25 lakh teachers, and several of those who do exist on the rolls, especially in our village pathshalas, don't actually teach: they show up once a month to collect their government salary and are AWOL the rest of the time. Teachers are, or should be, the biggest influence on their impressionable charges, at least after the parents. Their impact on young lives is profound and long-lasting. They shape the character, curiosity level and intellectual potential of their students. In other words, they help shape our society. So far, under-valued and in many cases under-qualified, they are doing an uneven job.

How on earth can we maintain our much-vaunted economic growth rates if we don't produce enough educated Indians to claim the jobs that a 21st century economy offers? We rely on a handful of excellent private and missionary schools to produce the educated elite of our country, and tolerate a large number of uneven (but mostly hopeless) government schools, millions of kids with no schooling at all—and the efforts of a number, not large enough, of charitable organizations.

Our regulatory systems often make matters worse rather than better. When I was MoS at MHRD, I received a visit one day from a kindly, white-haired lady who told me she had been running a school for tribal children on the fringes of Silent Valley in Palakkad, Kerala. Sixty per cent of her students were from tribal families in the valley whose members had never gone to school before; the remaining forty belonged to families classified as below the poverty line. Many of her teachers were volunteers or retirees. But the school had done extremely well for six years, and its impressive examination results had prompted her to apply for recognition from the Central Board of Secondary Education (CBSE), which is run by MHRD in Delhi.

Certainly, CBSE told her; your results justify CBSE affiliation. But under our rules you need a No-Objection Certificate (NOC) from the state government.

So the lady trudged off to the state capital, where after some hours of waiting she was ushered in to see the relevant bureaucrat. No problem for the NOC, he told her; just pay the fee and you will have your certificate.

Relieved, she inquired what the fee was.

The official fee, she was informed, was Rs 17; however, before she could pay that and obtain the certificate, she had to pay the official 35 lakh, or more than 200,000 times the official fee.

Despairing—since that sum exceeded her annual budget for running her school—she took a flight to Delhi instead and came to see me. Upon hearing her story, I immediately called the capable and efficient bureaucrat heading CBSE. Why, I demanded, did we require a certificate whose very existence only served to provide a rent-seeking opportunity to state government officials?

The official saw my point and agreed instantly to recommend to the CBSE governing body that the NOC requirement be dispensed with. It now has, and the lady's tribal school is happily affiliated to the CBSE at no charge.

I tell this story not out of any sense of triumph but because I am acutely aware that there must hundreds of other regulations—all well-intentioned in origin—that set back our efforts across the country to give our most deprived children the opportunity of a decent education.

As the Nobel Prize-winning Chilean poet Gabriela Mistral (a schoolteacher herself) so poignantly said, 'We are guilty of many crimes, but our worst sin is abandoning the child; neglecting the foundation of life. Many of the things we need can wait; the child cannot. We cannot answer Tomorrow. Her name is Today.'

ℒ

Of course, distance learning can be an important tool for ensuring access to quality education. The National Institute for Open Schooling in India reaches out to more than 350,000 learners—many of whom are dropouts, children from the underprivileged castes and learners with disabilities—making it the largest open-schooling system in the world. The programme also has the advantage of being able to provide equivalence with the formal educational system while remaining culturally and linguistically relevant to local needs. And for people with disabilities, especially those in remote rural areas, there is no substitute for distance learning.

India's National Sample Survey shows that the non-availability of schooling facilities in India accounts for about 10 per cent of the 'never enrolled' in rural India and about 8 per cent in urban India. The difference between the sexes is larger in the urban areas. A large number of people, both in rural and in urban India, particularly women, cannot avail of the educational services because of their participation in household economic activities and other socio-economic reasons. In all such cases, the importance of distance learning cannot be overstated.

Distance learning is vital in helping bridge the gender gap as well, since many women prevented by family strictures or religious and social customs from going to high school or college can learn in the privacy of home (and many do). India was wise to set up the Indira Gandhi National University and the National Institute for Open Schooling to help achieve this goal. The saddest aspect of India's literacy statistics is the disproportionate percentage—60 per cent—of women who remain illiterate.

Female literacy was 16 percentage points below male literacy in 2011. At the end of 2011, the male literacy level for children aged 7 years and above exceeded the female literacy level by an overwhelming 16.6 per cent. In terms of female youth literacy (15-24 years age group), India lags behind Bangladesh, Nepal, Sri Lanka, China and Thailand. The proportion of non-literate persons in the 15-19 age group was 15.8 per cent for females as compared to 7.4 per cent for males. In the same age group, the proportion of population who have completed five years of schooling was 83.7 per cent for females as compared to 86.2 per cent for males.

There is no action proven to do more for the human race than the education of the female child. Scholarly studies and research projects have established what common sense might already have told us: that if you educate a boy, you educate a person, but if you educate a girl, you educate a family and benefit an entire community.

A girl who has had more than six years of education is better equipped to seek and use medical and health care advice, to immunize her children, to be aware of sanitary practices from boiling water to the importance of washing hands. The dreaded disease AIDS spreads twice as fast, a Zambian study shows, among uneducated girls than amongst those who have been to school. The World Bank, with the mathematical precision for which they are so famous, has estimated that for every four years of education, fertility is reduced by about one birth per mother.

The more girls go to secondary school, the Bank adds, the higher the country's per capita income growth. And when girls work in the fields, as so many have to do across the developing world, their schooling translates directly to increased agricultural productivity. The marvellous thing about women is that they like to learn from other women, so the success of educated women is usually quickly emulated by their uneducated sisters. And women spend increased income on their families, which men do not necessarily do (rural toddy shops in India, after all, thrive on the self-indulgent spending habits of men). In many studies, the education of girls has been shown to lead to lead to more productive farming and in turn to a decline in malnutrition. Educate a girl, and you benefit a community: QED.

As my former colleague Catherine Bertini, former head of the World Food Programme, once put it: 'If someone told you that, with just 12 years of investment of about $1 billion a year, you could, across the developing world, increase economic growth, decrease infant mortality, increase agricultural yields, improve maternal health, improve children's health and nutrition, increase the numbers of children—girls and boys—in school, slow down population growth, increase the number of men and women who can read and write, decrease the spread of AIDS, add new people to the workforce and be able to improve their wages without pushing others out of the work force—what would you say? Such a deal! What is it? How can I sign up?'

Sadly, the world is not yet rushing to 'sign up' to the challenge of educating girls, who lag consistently behind boys in access to education throughout the developing world, including India. The honourable exception is Kerala. Indeed, as a nation we have a long way to go: we boast one state, Bihar, which even enthroned an illiterate woman as chief minister—as if to showcase its abysmal figure of a 23 per cent female literacy rate, one of the worst on the planet. But her seven daughters did indeed receive an education—so perhaps, after all, there are grounds for hope.

The former UN Secretary-General Kofi Annan put it simply: 'No other policy is as likely to raise economic productivity, lower infant and maternal mortality, improve nutrition, promote health, including the prevention of HIV/

AIDS, and increase the chances of education for the next generation. Let us invest in women and girls.'

Let us indeed do that. And let us educate boys too. We need to achieve 100 per cent literacy across the country, if we are to fulfil the aspirations we have all begun to dare to articulate, and rise to the challenges and opportunities of the 21st century.

⁂

A few years ago I visited a school run by the Bangalore charity Parikrma, which offers a world-class English-language education for slum children. Interacting with the kids, who ranged in age from 5-year-olds who had just started schooling, to 16 and 17-year-olds about to take their board exams, provided no clue to their humble origins. One child spoke boldly of his plans to join the civil services. 'Three years ago,' Parikrma's founder, Shukla Bose, whispered to me, 'I found him selling newspapers at a traffic light.'

The Parikrma model sets out to prove that the poorest and most disadvantaged of India's children can, if given the education, match the best of our elite. But it is not just that Shukla takes in the poorest kids—only those whose families earn less than Rs 750 a month are eligible—it is also that she recognizes that education only succeeds if other factors work in its favour. Of what use is excellent teaching if the child is too hungry to concentrate or too undernourished for her brain to develop? So Parikrma provides all the kids with a full breakfast on arrival in the morning, a solid lunch at mid-day and a snack before they leave for home.

What if they can't afford to get to school from where their parents live? So, bus-passes are provided. But how can you expect poor kids to stay in school if their parents are ill at home and need their children's help? So, Parikrma provides health-care assistance to the entire family during the student's years in school. And what good is a first-rate school education if the child does not have the resources or opportunities to go to college? So, Shukla has been busy fundraising for full scholarships to send her graduating classes to university.

Parikrma's approach is impressive, its experience entirely positive, and the stories of its children heart-warming. Yet, arguably, its experience is not replicable across the country: schools that pay for everything require a level of funding unavailable to most.

Whereas, in Bangalore's government schools, the drop-out rate by the eighth standard is as high as 72 per cent, and the pass rate for the higher secondary exams 8 per cent, Parikrma's children, despite coming from poverty-stricken homes, all stay in school, and fared extremely well when the first group of them took their board exams. What is more, to see the discipline in the smartly-uniformed children (uniforms also provided by Parikrma, of course), the intelligence shining through their scrubbed faces, the confidence in their questions to a visitor, and above all, the hope, is to see lives transformed and futures built where there was only despair.

Parikrma's is not the only example of such educational endeavour. The Shanti Bhavan school in Tamil Nadu, run by the hugely impressive Abraham George—a former army officer who made his fortune in computers and is determined to give it back through his philanthropic George Foundation—also educates slum children to the highest standards, though it does so in a boarding-school format. I am sure there are other charitable organizations trying to do similar work elsewhere in the country. Their methods and operating principles may vary, but the essential thing is this: they all realize that India is never going to be a great 21st-century power if it doesn't educate its young—all of them, not just the ones who can afford an education.

I asked the Parikrma high school kids what they wanted to do in life. Sixteen opted for computer programming—a reflection of our era. One wanted to join the army, half a dozen the IAS, and one girl the CBI, 'because I want to bring justice to our society'. Our society needs justice—and it will only have it when we have enough schools to do justice to the potential of all our children.

❧

The meaning of success in modern India has undergone a paradigm shift, particularly in the past two decades. Before the 1990s, as I have mentioned earlier in this volume, India was often referred to as 'an elephant' owing to its own slow pace of economic and social progress, lethargic policy reforms, and the modest dreams of its population, which were made worse by the weight of its own burgeoning population. As we know, the watershed moment arrived in 1991 when India undertook a slew of economic policy reforms under Dr Manmohan Singh. The economic reforms, featuring conscious liberalization, measured privatization, and increasing globalization, opened a wonderland of opportunities for India. In the following two decades, India changed much faster and more dramatically than either the world or we ourselves expected it to.

As I've pointed out in other essays in this volume, we have 605 million people below the age of 25, while in the age group 10-19, poised for higher education, we have 225 million. This means that for the next forty years we would have a youthful, dynamic and productive workforce when the rest of the world, including China, is ageing. The International Labour Organisation (ILO) has predicted that by 2020, India will have 116 million workers in the work-starting age bracket of 20 to 24 years, as compared to China's 94 million. It is further estimated that the average age in India by the year 2020 will be 29 years as against 40 years in the USA, 46 years in Europe and 47 years in Japan. In fact, in twenty years the labour force in the industrialised world will decline by 4 per cent, in China by 5 per cent, while in India it will increase by 32 per cent.

Since the reforms of 1991, Indians have started to believe that they can really achieve their dreams through hard work and education. Young Indians are driven by the aspiration that if they adequately educate and train themselves they have the potential of achieving anything in the world: financial prosperity, social recognition, global job opportunities, and cosmopolitan lifestyle. With our favourable demographics and the enormous economic opportunities available in a globalizing world, education is the ticket for realizing India's potential.

A sound quality school education is a prerequisite to empower our young population to pursue these opportunities. Realizing the importance of school education, the UPA government launched a series of schemes in the school education sector to ensure that the gaps at every level of school education are filled.

It is sadly true that even today India has been unable to achieve the universalization of elementary education. This prompted the Government of India to launch its flagship scheme of the Sarva Shiksha Abhiyan (SSA) in 2001. However, it did not completely achieve the targets set out on the launch of the scheme. In order to accelerate the achievement of universal education, the UPA government passed the landmark Right of Children to Free and Compulsory Education (RTE) Act, 2009. The SSA then became the main vehicle for achieving the goals of the RTE, with a mandate to provide free and compulsory education to children between the ages of 6 and 14. The scheme addresses the educational needs of about 194 million children in over 1.1 million schools (0.8 million primary and 0.3 million upper primary). With the implementation of the RTE, the constitutional goals of equality and freedom have begun being achieved through education. The Gross Enrolment Ratio (GER) for the 6-10 age group increased from 88.6 per cent in 2000 to reach 116 per cent at the end of 2011 and for the 11-13 age group it increased from 59.3 per cent to 85.5 per cent over the same period.

The RTE is also a great leveller, brushing aside social discrimination, and allowing the different strata of our society to merge into a harmonious whole. In 2013, under the 25 per cent reservation provided under the RTE Act, 66,306 out of 0.2 million students from the economically and socially weaker sections received admission into 8,500 private schools in Pune district. In 2014, 12,500 students were admitted to various schools in Indore district using the RTE provisions. These are small examples of the larger impact that RTE is creating across the country.

It is still a challenge to carry the momentum of primary school enrolments to the secondary school level, where the GER drops to 69 per cent by

Class VIII, 39 per cent by Class XI and XII and 18 per cent by the time of college. Clearly, the dropout rate is disquieting and many students are facing issues in continuing their education beyond the primary level. The prime reasons, as I've noted, include pressure from the family to abandon school for income-generating activities, taking care of younger siblings, assisting the family in household chores, and in some cases even to marry earlier than the law allows. Infrastructural issues like the lack of toilets can also drive children away from school: girls past a certain age need privacy to change, and if there's no toilet at school they'll go home and perhaps not come back. Government funds are allocated to address these challenges, and there has been a significant improvement in the availability of drinking water and of girls' toilets.

In order to provide a boost to the GER at the secondary level, the Indian government launched the Rashtriya Madhyamik Shiksha Abhiyan (RMSA) scheme in March 2009. Among the objectives of this scheme is to provide universal access to secondary level education by 2017 and universal retention by 2020. RMSA aims to universalize secondary school education in the age group of 15-16 by providing a secondary school within 5 km, and a higher secondary school within 7 km, of all habitations, by strengthening 44,000 existing secondary schools, opening 11,188 new secondary schools, mostly by upgrading upper primary schools, appointing 1.79 lakh additional teachers, and constructing 80,500 additional classrooms.

The UPA government tried to overcome the issue of gender disparity by implementing the gender-specific elements of SSA and RMSA. At the primary level, SSA is further aided by the National Programme for Education of Girls for Elementary Level (NPEGEL) in the educationally backward block (EBBs) which helps enrolled female students to regularly attend classes, and by the Kasturba Gandhi Balika Vidyalaya (KGBV) scheme which creates residential upper primary schools for girls from SC, ST, OBC and Muslim communities. At the secondary education level, RMSA is aided by three schemes: Construction and Running of Girls' Hostel for Students of Secondary and Higher Secondary Schools Scheme, Mahila Samakhya Scheme and National Scheme of Incentive to Girls for Secondary Education (which places Rs 3,000 in a bank account for girls below 16 which they can only collect, with interest, when they pass Class X and attain the age of 18).

Apart from infrastructure deficit, many schools are facing perennial problems with regard to the quality of teachers, teacher absenteeism, suitability of curriculum, rural-urban disparity, lack of uniformity and parity in teaching methods, the challenge of schools penetration in conflict-ridden districts, the issue of utilization of physical infrastructure in difficult terrain and harsh weather conditions, to name merely the most obvious. In order to overcome these barriers to education, the UPA government undertook a number of efforts, ranging from curriculum reform to the introduction of Teacher Eligibility Tests. In 2013, it launched the National Repository of Open Educational Resources (NROER) to help us reach the unreached and include the excluded. The NROER aims to offer 'resources for all school subjects and grades in multiple languages. The resources are available in the form of concept maps, videos, audio clips, talking books, multimedia, learning objects, photographs, diagrams, charts, articles, wikipages and textbooks'.

This flagship initiative on open education resources incorporates Information and Communication Technology (ICT) in education. It will help us to realize the goals of both the National Education Policy and the National Curriculum Framework. Over time these initiatives will not only change the way we impart education in India but will greatly impact how children will learn and how they will exchange ideas. It will open doors for new ways of interactive learning for the students and indeed for the teachers. ICT in education can be an answer to the traditional maladies to a significant extent. It will give easier access to the same teaching material to all students in India in languages of their choice. However, we all also know that electricity and connectivity are vital to this form of education. The UPA government also launched a Rs 20,000 crore project to take high-speed broadband cables to 250,000 villages across India, facilitating e-services in diverse fields including education. It will bring millions of Indians to information that can make a difference in their lives, and enable them to benefit from long-distance education, massive open online courses and other methods that could bring them instruction of a higher quality than is locally available in the village.

These measures are important for us to carry forward the momentum in school education that has been built over the past nearly seven decades. After India gained independence, it inherited a fragile education system from the British. In 1950-51, we started with just 200,000 primary schools and 13,600 upper primary schools. By the end of 2011, the number of schools had increased to 1.2 million—around 750,000 primary schools and 450,000 upper primary schools. Literacy rates, as we have seen, have also recorded a tremendous increase since Independence, although we still have a lot to do.

The Manmohan Singh government, for its part, adopted a multi-pronged strategy to achieve the national policy objectives of universal, affordable and quality education. From expanding the scope of the SSA and the Mid-day Meal Scheme, and the passage of the RTE Act in 2009 for improving and deepening enrolment at the primary and elementary level of schooling, the RMSA for increasing retention rates for secondary education, and the creation of new universities, IITs, NITs, IIITs and IIMs and a variety of schemes for increasing the scope and quality of vocational education, the government devised policies and allocated resources to every level of education. But we also know all that we have done is not enough in itself.

As the world approaches the deadline for attaining the Millennium Development Goals (MDGs) in the year 2015, the goals of achieving universal primary education and of promoting gender equality and empower women are directly relevant to our work in school education. India has already achieved the targets for poverty reduction, net enrolment ratio in primary education, and gender parity in primary education, amongst others, but we are going to miss the target, despite significant progress, of improving retention rate from Class I to Class V and of increasing the youth literacy rate. And we are a long way short of the target we hope to attain in gender parity in secondary and higher education. We remain conscious that the possibility of achieving these MDGs in the near future (if not by 2015) and our ability to provide a conducive environment to our young population brimming with aspiration hinges on one critical factor: our ability to provide universal and quality school education.

Education is one of the most potent tools at our disposal to deliver on promises of the visions of Gandhi, Nehru and Ambedkar. As with all our endeavours for development, it too must remain consciously true to these ideals. It is only in dedicating ourselves to these civilizational, constitutional and indeed universal values that we can provide meaningful development, which secures the rights and progress of all citizens towards the goal of ensuring their freedom, equality and empowerment.

There has never been a better time to be an optimistic and patriotic Indian. This is not to dismiss the daunting challenges that face the country today. Crushing poverty, illiteracy, unemployment, malnutrition, disease, discrimination based on caste, community and gender, all continue to be the defining elements of everyday life for an unacceptable number of our fellow citizens. And yet, despite these persistent, age-old handicaps, India today is better placed than it has ever been in its history to meet all these challenges with a realistic chance of overcoming all of them in our lifetimes.

Those of us who wallow in dirges about our gloomy present and get misty-eyed about our glorious past may do well to learn some songs of hope about the future of India. They are going to need them soon. For India in the second decade of the 21st century, the best is yet to come, and the key that will unlock and unleash our long suppressed potential, in one word, is—education.

The creation of the Indian state from the retreating British Empire remains one of the most daring acts of will, suffused with a liberal sprinkling of hope, in recent human history. We were blessed with having, in our Founding Fathers, a group of individuals remarkable in the breadth of their intellect, the scope of their vision and the depth of their integrity. The idea of India finds its moral voice in Gandhi, its political expression in Nehru, its aesthetic sensibility in Tagore, its administrative cohesion in Patel, its nationalist pride in Bose, its composite culture in Azad, and its constitutional ethic in Ambedkar. That we have yet to attain proper fulfilment of the destiny they charted for us is no fault of their vision. Rather it reflects our own collective failings and the dimensions of the task at hand.

Since Independence, education has played a vital role in every aspect of nation-building. The strong bond of citizenship that unites us Indians today, the shared pride in our heritage, the common respect for our national institutions, all these have emerged through the efforts of generations of dedicated teachers, who have ensured that our education amply reflects both our cultural values and national aspirations. They have provided the narrative framework in which the next phase of the story of India is set to unfold and capture the world's attention. Whether this story unfolds at a pace and in a direction consistent with the understandably impatient expectations of our more than 500 million youth or not, will depend largely on the kinds of educational opportunities and vocational skills that we are able to provide them.

The task for our policy makers in the field of education is cut out. The last twenty years of economic reforms have set free the animal spirits of our economy. But the animal can leap farther: this process of growth and prosperity needs to be sustained and even accelerated. Doing it will require a significant investment in improving the quality of our human resources. I address related aspects of this issue in the three essays that follow.

Over the next twenty years, India faces the challenge and opportunity of growing at a rate of 8 per cent and more, with a youthful, productive working-age population that vastly outnumbers those available in the rest of an ageing world. A well-educated, highly-skilled workforce will be an essential prerequisite for driving this momentum. We know that the price of failure is too high: the Naxalite movement shows what might become of frustrated and unemployed young men. We must therefore be all the more determined to succeed. The key elements—ideas, resources, and political will—are in place. And yet there are grounds for concern. Prime Minister Narendra Modi often says all the right things. But indications in his first six months of office of an increasing 'saffronization' of education—the desire to correct a perceived 'secular' imbalance in history textbooks, for instance, and a bewildering emphasis on such atavistic priorities as teaching Sanskrit and 'Vedic mathematics'—give cause for worry. These are prescriptions that do not match the diagnosis I have outlined above. If what our nation needs is to make its population literate, enhance human capital, improve quality across the board and equip our people to rise to the challenges and opportunities of an increasingly competitive globalized world, Sanskrit, Vedic maths and paeans to the greater glory of ancient Hindu science don't help at all. I delve in greater detail into what has been accomplished and what specifically needs to be done in some of the essays that follow. The big question remains: is our new government prepared to do it?

TOWARDS A KNOWLEDGE SOCIETY:
HIGHER EDUCATION IN INDIA

India is entering the global employment marketplace with a self-imposed handicap of which we are just beginning to become conscious—an acute shortage of quality institutions of higher education. For far too long we have been complacent about the fact that we had produced, since the 1960s, the world's second-largest pool of trained scientists and engineers. They were more than our then-protected economy could absorb, and their talents outran the facilities and opportunities available to them in India, so many tens of thousands of them left to make their fortunes elsewhere, founding companies in Silicon Valley, inventing the Pentium chip, and even winning America a couple of Nobel Prizes. Their success meant that 'IIT' soon began to be spoken of in the same breath as 'MIT', and the Indianness of engineers or software gurus is now taken as synonymous with technical excellence. But their success also masked another reality—that there just aren't as many of them as there should be.

Talk to senior Indian executives whose businesses require them to recruit competent staff with scientific or engineering training, and they'll confirm that their demand for such talent vastly exceeds the supply. Once the elite institutions are accounted for—the IITs, BITS, the Indian Institute of Science— what remains is of decidedly uneven quality. For every Narayana Murthy produced by a local or Regional Engineering College, there are hundreds of graduates whom Indian employers, let alone international ones, do not consider ready for prime time. In fact, one of the under-reported stories of today's employment market is that companies like Tata and Infosys are actually hiring people they do not consider to be up to par—and spending six to nine months, and sometimes longer, re-educating them. This is not merely professional training—these companies have set up campuses essentially to make up for the deficiencies in the education of the ostensibly-qualified graduates they have hired. Our university system simply isn't producing enough well-educated graduates to meet the needs of Indian companies today, let alone for their planned growth tomorrow.

Ironically, India has one of the largest higher education systems in the world and ranks second in terms of student enrolment, exhibiting a healthy growth in the number of institutions and enrolment since Independence. India now has 621 universities and 33,500 colleges, but only a few world-class institutions, including notably the globally-renowned IITs whose graduates have flourished in America's Silicon Valley. But these are still islands floating in a sea of mediocrity.

Indeed, the greatest contribution to the world by India in recent years is the export of the educated professional. Soon after Independence we produced a steady stream of such professionals—doctors, engineers, entrepreneurs or teachers in international institutions—who have taken India to the world. We have educated a number of doctors who are leading research teams and patient care in the best hospitals in the world. We have produced engineers who have created multiple successful start-ups around the world, and have seen international banks and multinational corporations being led by Indians who were educated in our elite business schools. These exports have stemmed from the middle class, a growing and dynamic segment of the population, who see education as the only means to social and economic prosperity.

This development points to two paradoxical trends. Despite serious handicaps of means and resources, the country has built up a very large system of education and has created a large pool of men and women equipped with robust scientific and technological capabilities, sensitive humanist and philosophical thought, and profound creativity. In over six decades, we have succeeded in massively expanding the reach of higher education in our country. Today, in terms of enrolment, we have just overtaken USA and now, in absolute terms, we have the second largest number of students in higher education.

In the first decades after Independence, the two 'E's of the Indian education system were understandably, 'Expansion', which I have summarized, and 'Equity'—ensuring the inclusion of the excluded and marginalized groups, those left out for reasons of caste, religion, region and gender. In the process we may have neglected the third E—'Excellence'. We have now begun to focus on the quality of learning outcomes, but much more remains to be done.

The first E—Expansion—is at the heart of our efforts to ensure that the demographic blessing does not become a curse. With the adoption, especially, of the Right to Education Act (RTE), access to education for all was a policy imperative behind which we have put our full weight. The expenditure on education has grown from 3 per cent of GDP to 4.8 per cent of a larger GDP, through, it is still short of the long-announced target of 6 per cent. There have been notable successes. Since adopting RTE, we have achieved GER in primary education of 104 per cent: we have actually found more students in the target age group than we thought were out there, and succeeded in attracting them to schools. The challenge, however, is sustaining these rates of enrolment into higher education. By Class VIII, the GER drops to 69 per cent. In Class XI and XII it is 39 per cent. So clearly we are not retaining those primary school children through high school. And when we come to college, we stand nowhere near the global GER of 29 per cent, with a much lower GER, currently at about 20 per cent. What we call a 'good education', in relative terms, is still easily available only to a privileged few. Private participation in education has succeeded in leveraging our resources and endowments, on the other hand it has also brought in concerns of commercialization, unfair practices and a scramble for purchasing 'merit'.

The painful history of millennia of a stratified and fractured social structure along caste and religious lines has left wounds across the body and soul of our system of education too, which have yet to heal. Coupled with this stratification is a glaring economic divide between haves and haves-not. We have tried finding answers to this baffling adversity in the shape of policies of positive discrimination, differential treatment and subsidy regimes. A fine balance is needed between merit and social justice, and this is a unique challenge to India, unparalleled anywhere else. Nations of comparable size like Brazil and China have a greater uniformity in terms of social and cultural attributes which makes our task a lot more difficult.

This brings me to the second theme—Equity. There can be little disagreement that a broad-based, easy access education system that yet systematically neglects the needs of some part or parts of the population needs urgent reform. The challenge of equity involves including the excluded—those left out of the educational system for reasons of caste, religion, gender, distance or other handicaps. We have made progress towards overcoming all of these disadvantages, but I would like to point specifically to a significant unrealized opportunity— one that potentially holds the answer to our demographic dilemma, and a sustainable, scalable answer at that: educating girls. This is why the Government of India, under the UPA, focused strongly on improving women's education, and why I hope and trust this emphasis will not be lost under its successor.

We have faltered, however, in our quest for the third E—Excellence. We have outstanding educational institutions, but these are still the exception rather than the norm. At the same time, our economy has not been able to employ many of the excellent products of our higher education system, or offer enough of a challenge to many of our best and brightest, which is why so many of them have left the country in search of the proverbial greener pastures abroad.

Market forces will, however, demand that in the process of dissemination of knowledge at every level, we do take into account the fourth 'E'—the newest factor I added to this catechism of Indian education policy thinking— Employability. This is an inevitable policy imperative to balance the forces of markets with the demands of research, the pursuit of knowledge and the imperative of equity.

The quality and employability of the vast majority of our graduates are being seriously questioned. Employers' associations like FICCI, CII and Assocham have conducted studies that have established widespread and high levels of dissatisfaction with the quality of graduates available for employment. I have spoken to CEOs who feel that once you get beyond the top institutions, the graduates they hire from the rest need a year's remedial education—not on the job training, which every major company provides, but a year's actual education to make up for the deficiencies of what they have (not) learned in college. That is why Infosys has built a campus in Mysore and TCS in Thiruvananthapuram. Companies are entering the education space in all but name.

The government, for its part, has launched multi-pronged initiatives to address the gap between educational qualifications and the needs of employers. On this front we have a peculiar situation. At one level, we boast with pride about the half-a-million engineers we produce annually, and the fact that we are home to the world's second largest pool of trained scientists and engineers. But at another level, given the over-supply of persons with higher education, 'over-qualified' persons are hired for jobs that do not require graduate degrees. Some 60 per cent of our engineers, for instance, find themselves in jobs that do not require an engineering degree (and I am not even counting those engineers who get no jobs at all).

New discernible trends point towards a few other systemic issues that must be addressed through policy as well as practice. There is a massive problem of skill mismatch between qualifications and jobs undertaken. A policy that encourages non-graduate technical and non-technical diploma/certificate holders into lower graduate intensity occupations would help to close the skills gap and reduce the pressure on graduate higher education. The skill mismatch situation has seen marked improvement in certain sectors over time. Research has identified the closing of this 'quality' skill gap in high graduate intensity occupations, professionals such as engineers, advocates, medical and legal professionals and other high technology service industries such as telecommunications and information technology. Clearly this has been a positive outcome of targeted policy response to the demand from these sectors over the past decades. The market has, in many ways, led the way and policymakers must be increasingly cognizant of market demands during policy formulation. But the government for its part has also risen to the challenge. We have been encouraging more and more industry and academia interactions so that our universities increasingly meet the needs of the marketplace.

Today, our vision for the 21st century must be to make India a knowledge society, a society capable of both creating theoretical knowledge of global significance and then materially benefitting from it; a society where pursuit of learning and innovation should not be constrained by any lack of access, infrastructure or support; where education is relevant to society, and provides the skills and competencies that society demands. We must understand clearly that we are talking of a knowledge society—one that is committed to excellence as an end in itself—and not just creating a knowledge economy.

In comparison to other developing nations, our country lags behind in technical institutions. More important, there is widespread concern that not a single Indian university features in the top 200 universities of the world. A summary by the Times Higher Education team about the weightage given to various aspects in their rankings explained that 30 per cent weightage each was given to research and citations (which are of course, of published research). Since India's universities are teaching institutions where little research is done, and research is done in small institutions where there is very little teaching, we start off with 60 per cent of the weighting against us—an obvious disadvantage in the global university rankings.

Yet we must also be wary of such rankings. In an editorial opinion in the *Hindu*, two professors, one of whom taught at the Jawaharlal Nehru University (JNU), argued against these rankings, commenting on their lack of insight into intangible features of an institution. They described JNU's unique system of deviation points devised to bring to the campus students from deprived communities and backward regions. The university makes an effort to bring these students at par with others while integrating them with the larger university culture, and making them prominent contributors to making the university a vibrant celebration of intellectual prowess. The article pointedly argued: under what scale or ranking can this unique system be evaluated?

While these rankings remain a matter of debate, the government plans to finance research clusters across the country with the intention of doubling the GDP allocation to research from 1 per cent to 2 per cent. And to help overcome this shortfall, the last UPA government introduced the Universities for Research and Innovation Bill in 2012, seeking to set up fourteen universities for research and innovation which could be established privately, funded publicly or created through a public-private partnership. These institutions would be of national importance, with the objective of achieving excellence in knowledge while building links between academia and the industry and conducting research on issues affecting society at large. But their establishment was thwarted by the Standing Committee of Parliament and the bill now seems to have been withdrawn by the BJP government.

We clearly need to create, across India, an ecosystem of research and teaching around related disciplines. If we can bring several such institutions to life, we could also be in position to attract the best minds from abroad to work in our laboratories and research think tanks and produce solutions which could answer the foremost questions of the world. The UPA's education bills unfortunately have been a victim of the dysfunctionality of our Parliament: those in the Opposition who prefer disruption to debate ensured that they were not even discussed, let alone passed. One can only hope that now they are in power, the former Opposition will here too, as in so many areas, adopt the policies they had obstructed when we tried to pursue them.

It is well known that a strong culture of research and innovation is a very important driver to ensure technical and technological leadership, which ultimately translates to the growth of a strong, robust and self-sufficient economy. A look around the world today very clearly proves that investments in long-term research have a very direct impact on that nation's continued future success. Long-term economic growth depends ultimately on innovation and inventions. There is a strong correlation between innovation and productivity. It is, therefore, of critical importance for academia and industry to participate and focus on research and innovation for growth.

What are the major challenges that we face in this endeavour?

First, a weak PhD research ecosystem. In the global world of hi-tech, India is not perceived to be in the top tier of research. 'IT hub of the world' is good, but ultimately, being the global 'back office' does not lend itself to a perception of an innovator or an inventor. This is ironic, because I recall being invited by the University of Toronto to open an India Innovation Centre there in 2011, and the buzz then was all about 'Indovation'. We have not been able to deliver on that promise.

As I had occasion to note when addressing FICCI in 2013, India's share in global research output is far too low—at 3.5 per cent—for a country with 17 per cent of the world's brains. No Indian college or university ranks among the top 200 of the prestigious Times Higher Education Supplement list, which is based on peer evaluations, and there are only a handful in the top 500, whereas China has 23 institutions in the Top 500.

The number of PhDs produced in computer science engineering in India is about 125, which—even though it represents a quadrupling in the last seven years—is still low compared to other leading economies. The US and China each produce close to 2,000 PhDs a year. The interesting part is that nearly 25 per cent of the PhDs in computer science graduating in the US are of Indian origin. This reiterates the truth that if you provide an environment where the best young minds find a receptive ambience to fulfil their creative energies, you can lay the platform for real and sustained innovation.

Second on my list is the lack of adequate faculty. The handful who devote their lives to research represent the privileged elite at the apex of the higher education system in India. However, as we go down the pyramid, the scenario is very different. The rapid expansion of the Indian higher education system has led to a severe shortage of faculty as also major challenges of quality. The student-to-teacher ratio in the average institution of higher education is 26:1, as against the global norms of 15:1. As of March 2011, only 161 universities and 4,371 colleges had been accredited by the National Assessment and Accreditation Council (NAAC). Even prestigious institutions like IITs have a shortage of 30–35 per cent of faculty and state universities suffer shortages of almost 50 per cent of the faculty they need. Caste-based reservation policies, mandating that certain positions be reserved for certain social groups, have also meant that these vacancies cannot be filled by available candidates of the wrong caste provenance.

Third is the lack of industry investments in a career path for innovation. What career do we offer in industry for innovators? Of course, every graduating engineer cannot become a researcher, let alone an innovator. But let us try and understand why not many of the brightest talents from our best institutes are looking at career opportunities in this space. The answer is simple: because there are not that many career opportunities. While there may be attempts in some pockets, our technology industry has simply not created enough jobs for innovators. We have not glamorized the field enough, we have not provided enough incentives, nor made the necessary investments for research and innovation. Indian industry has to carry the torch of innovation as a mantra, if we have to transition into the area of being a superpower in the hi-tech innovation space. And this is not a philanthropic initiative. Indian industry is realizing that its long term survival and prosperity depend on its ability to innovate and become creators of technology, and not just consumers of it.

Scale is a critical aspect. We are a country of over 1.2 billion people of diverse skills, and more important, with two-thirds of this number under the age of 35—it is a no-brainer to use this demographic dividend to our advantage. We must think scale in whatever we do, and make sure that the steps we take in the area of research of innovation include a broad swathe of stakeholders—and just as important, that the fruits of this innovation make a difference to the lives of significant numbers of our masses.

This brief look at some of the problems with our research and innovation ecosystem prompts a look at some possible approaches to transform this landscape. What are the some of the big changes required to do all of this? The short answer is that we need to become leaders in creating products for which research and innovation is critical. To accomplish this, Indian academia must pursue the task of providing active and sustained mentoring from the top PhD granting institutions to non-PhD granting institutions, coupled with funding from different sources. This can potentially help the research ecosystem in a big way. The top technical institutes need to take the lead here, by driving a culture of world-class research within their own institutes, and laying down benchmarks which the emerging instructions can follow.

We need to reverse the doctoral brain drain by adapting the best practices from across the globe, not only in terms of overall infrastructure development (such as a lab with state of the art equipment), but also advancing the state of the art in research, with milestones defined towards those targeted outcomes.

Our industry has responsibilities too, though theirs are even simpler. The way forward has to be through close partnership with academic institutions. Make research the cornerstone of corporate success in the technology world. Identify strategic opportunities unique to and relevant markets like ours, and make the necessary investments to leapfrog developed nations in specific technologies. Seek out institutions of higher education and fund research there, working out creative arrangements on intellectual property, licenses and royalties on the resultant output.

Academia can make a big impact by fostering an environment where more students look at research as a career option which in turn will help industry. We can build a thriving culture of close collaboration between industry and academia which can lay the foundation for creating a large pool of world-class researchers and innovators. This can enable this country to make the transition to being a significant player in the hi-tech world. Without this, any journey that we undertake on the road to a better future will remain unfulfilled.

The clamour usually arises for immediate tangible goals. A key short-term goal for the new government is to identify strategic pillars for research, engineering and management. In research, the government should take a leaf from the IT services industry and define a milestone-based goal—to define a number of opportunities in the field of research, be it with corporate labs, government set-ups or academic institutions. In engineering, the government should promote a focus on the quality of education but also on the all-round personality development of students. The 'currently employable' percentage of graduating engineers stands at only 17.7 per cent per year; raising this to over 50 per cent is an urgent priority. Conceptually, given the effort put in by students, teachers and institutions, there is no reason why every graduating engineer cannot be employable. But currently, they are not. At the under-graduate level, students must be exposed to various career options and career paths, to ensure that at least the majority of those taking up engineering and related disciplines are those who evince a genuine interest and aptitude in the field.

These efforts must be complemented by long-term goals, which can change the entire context of appreciation in which the education system must operate. The ideal must be to create a sustainable and vibrant education ecosystem where each student in India gets ample opportunities in areas of his or her choice, but that is more easily said than done. To get there, we need to establish India as a leader in the field of research and innovation. We will need to create an environment where research-led innovation plays a significant role in the day-to-day life of an average Indian citizen. We need to change the world's perception so that India is seen as a global leader in providing world-class education, cutting-edge research and a land of ample opportunities. We obviously aren't anywhere near there yet, which is why this is a long-term goal.

When I left India for post-graduate studies in 1975, there were perhaps 600 million people in India, and we had five IITs. When I came back in 2008, we were nearly double that population, and we had seven IITs, one of which has essentially involved the relabelling of an existing Regional Engineering College. To keep up with demand—and the needs of the marketplace—shouldn't we have had twenty IITs by then of the same standard as the original five? Or even thirty? The UPA government created nine more in 2009, but they are still struggling to hire the top-class faculty and attain the quality benchmarks of their illustrious forerunners.

It doesn't need to be this way. Our higher education is over-regulated and under-governed, with the University Grants Commission (UGC), Medical Council of India (MCI) and All-India Council for Technical Education (AICTE) issuing one-size-fits-all directives to prospective universities about the size of their buildings, the number of classrooms and teachers, and what they are allowed to teach. Our regulatory institutions are stifling academic advancement rather than promoting it. And the MCI is a national scandal, stifling the creation of necessary capacity in medical education so that many talented young people are driven away from the profession of medicine while the nation clamours for medical attention.

The challenge of educating and training this vast population under the age of 25 is too vast for the government to meet with its own resources. It is for this reason that the last two decades have also seen the increasing participation of the private sector at all levels of our education system. To their credit, private sector institutions have responded to our national needs with enthusiasm, and (especially in the field of technical and medical education) have made a significant contribution to educating and preparing our youth for the 21st century. Given the size and potential of our population, even foreign universities are now showing a keen interest in creating institutions in India. However as with other sunrise sectors of our economy such as telecom and aviation, the entry of private players in this socially sensitive sector has raised various concerns with regard to equality of access and quality of outcomes. To address these issues, the previous government has prepared legislation which, when in place, will create a more flexible and creative regulatory framework for this absolutely vital segment of our economy and society. It didn't pass the Standing Committee of Parliament.

If our students are ill-served, our teachers are no less so. We do not have enough professors, researchers and scientific scholars in our university system, and we do not make it attractive enough for others to join their ranks. As it is, many qualified teachers are leaving university jobs to join the remedial institutes set up by private companies, where the conditions and the rewards are much better. If private-sector higher education came in, it would once again help make the academic profession the prestigious and well-remunerated career it is in the West.

The major problem remains that our national educational policy remains completely out of step with the times. Whereas countries in the Middle East, and China itself, are going out of their way to woo foreign universities to set up campuses in their countries, India turns away the many academic suitors who have come calling in recent years. Harvard and Yale would both be willing to open branches in India to offer quality education to Indian students, but have been told to stay away. Those Indians who choose to study abroad easily get opportunities to do so—currently nearly 100,000 of them in the United States alone. They would not need to go abroad—nor their parents to spend an estimated $3 billion a year in sending them afar—if we opened up the higher educational space in our country to institutions of international repute, and authorized the setting up of double the number of universities as we currently have.

There is no question that the need exists, the demand is huge, and that our growing and youthful population could easily fill several hundred new campuses. Nor is there a shortage of able and willing institutions ready to come into India. But many of these would not brook the interference of our unimaginative and over-directive UGC. And there's the rub: they would offer stiff competition to the vested interests, well-represented in our Parliament, who have made the higher education sector their chasse gardée, a source of largely illicit revenue flowing from a supposedly non-profit vocation.

. Many foreign institutions willing to invest in India would also necessarily be for-profit ventures in the private sector, and our ideologues recoil in horror at the prospect. Official India, sanctified by court judgments, is convinced that education is a holy sacrament that can only be administered by disinterested souls operating from purely non-commercial motives. Since such souls are few and far between, we have university places available to barely 5 per cent of those who clamour for them. Meanwhile, ordinary Indians would scrape and save to buy their children the best possible education, but it's simply not available. The need for education reform has never been clearer, and was recognized by the previous government of Prime Minister Manmohan Singh. Still, India's spending on higher education is only 1.22 per cent of GDP, which is quite low compared to US spending at 3.1 per cent or, closer to home, South Korea's at 2.4 per cent of GDP. The figure should be higher. So too should India's share in global research output, which is far too low at 3.5 per cent for a country with 17 per cent of the world's brains.

Education is now recognized as a national priority. More resources are being committed, the corporate sector is being encouraged to get involved, and there is a welcome emphasis on innovation. International co-operation, exemplified by the mutual learning implicit in the E-9 exercise, is also being tapped. The next ten years could witness a dramatic transformation of the educational space in India. But it won't happen without a huge national effort. The rest of the E-9, engaged in similar endeavours themselves, will be watching.

The new government would do well to look anew at all the areas where its predecessors had seen that government can make a difference. They could well revive, rather than withdraw, some major legislative initiatives of my former ministry that were pending in Parliament when we left office. Several, like the Foreign Education Providers Bill, Educational Tribunal Bill, National Accreditation Regulatory Authority Bill, Prohibition of Unfair Practices Bill, Higher Education and Research Bill, and Universities for Research and Innovation Bill—there were eleven in all—would, if passed by Parliament, help change the regulatory and governance structure of our higher education system in a way that promotes innovation and creativity rather than simply produce graduates who are largely unemployable. The recommendations of the Kakodkar Committee for reforms in the IIT system and a serious effort to raise spending on research to 2 per cent of the government budget are also important.

I look forward to a future for India where we will reclaim our rich heritage, as a country seen as a hub for educational and innovative excellence. We can become not only a leader in global technologies, but also in adapting these technologies to humanitarian applications and for the promotion of the welfare of our people. Indian students, schooled in the Indian context, will promote innovations that not only better the lot of their compatriots here, but also across the developing world. India must be a thought leader in this field, but also a leader with a heart—one that understands that the purpose of innovation is to improve the quality of life of human beings across the globe. It is a mission we had dedicated ourselves to since the days of yore, when scholars from across the world came to visit Nalanda, Takshashila and Vikramshila, not merely to learn from the wisdom of India but also to serve at the various charitable institutions (hospitals and the like) that these great institutions maintained. Given a conducive environment, I have no doubt we can once again attain such prominence.

I believe that, if we fulfil our plans, we can realize the new 'Indian Dream' of prosperity, peace, equality and welfare—the dream which was most eloquently articulated by Pandit Jawaharlal Nehru in his momentous 'Tryst with Destiny' speech at the midnight moment of our independence, when he spoke of 'the ending of poverty and ignorance and disease and inequality of opportunity'. This Indian Dream is not going to be fulfilled by sleeping on it—we must dream with our eyes open and on our feet, marching firmly on the road to progress. The educational vision of the UPA government, if embraced and carried forward by its NDA successors, will enable us to make the Indian Dream a reality in our time.

These are obvious ideas that require one elementary but elusive thing—a change of policy at the top. There is a crying need to sweep the cobwebs out of education policy and oblige the government to rethink the policies that are manifestly failing the country, creating capacity and promoting excellence. The alternative will be to see Indian companies moving abroad because the talent isn't available to them at home, and the ranks of frustrated unemployed swelling across India, easy prey for the blandishments of terrorists and Maoists. If we are to avoid an apocaplytic fate, we must give them a better chance of employment through more and improved educational possibilities. So let a thousand educational flowers bloom. Now.

STEPHANIA: THE QUEST TO EXCEL

Some years ago I received a gushing fan letter from someone who had chanced upon a copy of the programme brochure of the St. Stephen's College Shakespeare Society production of *Antony and Cleopatra* in 1974. She couldn't believe her eyes at the galaxy of names on the cast list. The title roles were played by me and a young Mira Nair (St. Stephen's, all-male in those days, borrowed its female thespians from Miranda House, and repaid the compliment in kind, so that the previous year I had taken the lead in Miranda's production of Brecht's *Saint Joan of the Stockyards*). Pompey was Amir Raza Husain, who would go on to become a renowned theatre director and impresario; Enobarbus, Ramu Damodaran, later Private Secretary to Prime Minister Narasimha Rao; Roman legionaries included Arun Singh, Asoke Mukerji and Gautam Mukhopadhyaya, now our ambassadors in Paris, New York and Yangon; and amongst the slaves and spear-carriers stood the brilliant novelist-to-be Amitav Ghosh and the future advertising guru Piyush Pandey. 'All of you together on one stage!' gushed the fan. 'What was it like? Did you all have a sense of destiny, knowing what you would become?'

I no longer recall my reply, but I don't believe any of us were unduly concerned about what we would become: at College, we just were. And if the fan had known about the Stephanian 'ShakeSoc types' who for one reason or the other didn't act in that particular production, she would have had even more to be awestruck about. The likes of Kabir Bedi and Roshan Seth, Stephanian stage legends both (as, in a slightly more modest vein, was Kapil Sibal) had passed out a couple of years earlier. But Rajiv Mehrotra, already a TV star on Doordarshan, declined to audition, future novelists Rukun Advani and Anurag Mathur didn't make the cut, and celebrity-quizmaster-to-be Siddhartha Basu, much to everyone's surprise, auditioned but was passed over for a role. (He instead wrote an acerbic review of the production in the campus newspaper, *Kooler Talk*, describing my Antony as a 'flippant, underfed Romeo').

Sense of destiny? Not consciously, except in the sense that by getting into College, you had already arrived; there was an implicit sense that the possibilities were limitless. Yet none of us would have felt that there was anything particularly unusual about our peers: St. Stephen's in those days simply attracted people like that. Hindsight, however, prompts something of the sense of wonderment apparent in the anonymous Wikipedia entry that informs the world, rather breathlessly, that my 'contemporaries included the politician Salman Khurshid, the documentary filmmaker Rajiv Mehrotra, the quizmaster Siddhartha Basu, the novelists Amitav Ghosh, Rukun Advani and Anurag Mathur, the theatre impresario Amir Raza Husain, the editor and politician Chandan Mitra, the columnist Swapan Dasgupta, the economist and media crusader Paranjoy Guha Thakurta, the IAS officer-turned social activist Harsh Mander, the television personality Sunil Sethi, the diplomat Jayant Prasad, the World Trade Organization executive Harsh Vardhan Singh and the advertising guru Piyush Pandey.' It's true, they did—and these, plus the Test cricketer Arun Lal, the composer Param Vir, and a slew of IAS officers (I recently counted seventeen Secretaries to the Government of India whom I had known at St. Stephen's) were guys we hung out at the dhaba with, borrowed tutorial notes from, complained about the mess food to, cut classes and saw movies and competed for female attention with…not A-listers of the future of whom we should have been in awe.

In those days I thought of Amitav Ghosh as a bright and rather persistent campus reporter for All-India Radio's 'Roving Microphone'. Piyush Pandey might, I hoped, play cricket for India one day, but his rustic manner and Hindi colloquialisms seemed to have nothing to do with the country's prevailing advertising culture. After voting for Salman Khurshid and seeing him trounced in the election for the College Presidency, I did not imagine the glittering political future that awaited him on the national stage. (Harsh Mander's passionate engagement in social service work, though, already prefigured the idealist IAS officer and NGO activist he would soon become.) When I borrowed 'tutes' from an intense and soft-spoken Param Vir, I had no idea he would one day be hailed as a genius composer on London's West End. And today's IAS heavyweights include Stephanians who were inveterate punsters, practical jokers and participants in the drag contest to elect a 'Miss Fresher'—hardly material, at first sight, to be finance secretary one day.

And yet, what does the very name 'St. Stephen's' convey to outsiders? Let's face it: to non-Stephanians, the term 'St. Stephen's' conjures up three overlapping concepts, none of which is meant to be flattering—elitism, Anglophilia and deracination. (There is even a rather obscure dictionary definition of a Stephanian as a 'charcoal fossil'—a kind of rock, of course, but 'charcoal fossil's metaphorical possibilities are enough to start a chortle amongst many of the College's self-deprecating alumni.)

When I was given the rare privilege of delivering the 125th Anniversary Golden Jubilee Lecture at the College in 2005 (the 100th anniversary had featured another old boy, Pakistan's then President Zia ul-Haq), I was able to take for granted that few in the audience (which included serving and former cabinet ministers, ambassadors and generals, not to mention the assorted CEO and cricket star) would contest that there is a spirit that can be called Stephanian: most of us had spent three or five years living in and celebrating it. Stephania was both an ethos and a condition to which we aspired. Elitism—an elitism of merit, not birth—was part of it, but by no means the whole.

In any case 'Mission College' elitism was still elitism in an Indian context, albeit one shaped, like so many Indian institutions, by a colonial legacy. There is no denying that the aim of the Cambridge Brotherhood in founding St. Stephen's in 1881 was to produce more obedient subjects to serve Her Britannic Majesty; their idea of constructive missionary activity was to bring the intellectual and social atmosphere of Camside to the dry dustplains of Delhi. Improbably enough, they succeeded, and the resultant hybrid outlasted the Raj.

The St. Stephen's I knew in the early 1970s was an institution whose students sustained a Shakespeare Society and a Criterion Club, and organized Union Debates on such subjects as 'In the opinion of this House the opinion of this House does not matter'. We staged plays and wrote poetry, and the Wodehouse Society I revived ran India's only faculty-sanctioned Practical Joke Competition (in memory of P.G. Wodehouse's irrepressible Lord Ickenham). It was St. Stephen's that invented the 'Winter Festival' of collegiate cultural competition which was imitated at universities across the country. If that sounds deplorably effete, we invariably reached the annual inter-college cricket final, and turned up in large numbers to cheer the Stephanian cricketers on to their accustomed victory. (One of my few worthwhile innovations as President of the Union, aside from improving the mess food on 'vegetarian day', was to supply throat lozenges free of charge to the more raucous of our cheerleaders at the cricket final. I am told this is one more Stephanian tradition that, along with our cricket team, has bitten the dust.) We maintained a careful distinction between the Junior Common Room and the Senior Combination Room, and allowed the world's only non-Cantabridgian 'gyps' to serve our meals and make our beds. And if the punts never came to the Jamuna, the puns flowed on the pages of *Kooler Talk* (known to Stephanians as 'KT', or 'Katie') and the cyclostyled Wodehouse Society rag *Spice* (whose typing mistakes, in Ramu Damodaran's hands, were deliberate, and deliberately hilarious.)

This was the St. Stephen's I knew, and none of us who lived and breathed the Stephanian air saw any alien affectation in it. For one thing, St. Stephen's also embraced the Hindi movies at Kamla Nagar, the trips to Sukhiya's dhaba and the chowchow at TibMon (as the Tibetan Monastery was called by Stephanians); the nocturnal Informal Discussion Group saw articulate discussion of political issues, and the Social Service League actually went out and performed social service; and even for the 'pseuds', the height of career aspiration was the IAS, not some firang multinational. The Stephanian could hardly be deracinated and still manage to bloom. It was against Indian targets that the Stephanian set his goals, and by Indian assumptions that he sought to attain them. (Feminists, please do not object to my pronouns: I only knew St. Stephen's before its co-edification.)

At the same time St. Stephen's was, astonishingly for a college in Delhi, insulated to a remarkable extent from the prejudices of middle-class Indian life.

It mattered little where you were from, which Indian language you spoke at home, what version of religious faith you espoused. When I joined College in 1972 from Calcutta, the son of a Keralite newspaper executive, I did not have to worry about fitting in: we were all minorities at St. Stephen's, and all part of one eclectic polychrome culture. Five of the preceding ten Union Presidents had been non-Delhiite non-Hindus (four Muslims and a Christian), and they had all been fairly elected against candidates from the 'majority' community. But at St. Stephen's religion and region were not the distinctions that mattered: what counted was whether you were 'in residence' or a 'dayski' (day-scholar), a 'science type' or a 'ShakeSoc type', a sportsman or a univ topper (or best of all, both). Caste and creed were no bar, but these other categories determined your share of the Stephanian experience.

This blurring of conventional distinctions was a crucial element of Stephania. 'Sparing' with the more congenial of your comrades in residence—though it could leave you with a near-fatal faith in coffee, conversation and crosswords as ends in themselves—was manifestly more important than attending classes. And in any case, you learned as much from approachable faculty members—like David Baker, Mohammed Amin, Ranjit Bhatia, P.S. Dwivedi, Vinod Choudhury and others too numerous to mention—outside the classroom as inside it. (It was at one of Amin-Sahib's Mediaeval History lectures that he memorably translated the words inscribed above the stage in the College Hall—Jesus said, 'I am the Light of the World'—as 'Jesus ne kaha, main Noor Jehan hoon'.)

Being ragged outside the back gate of Miranda House, having a late coffee in your block tutor's room, hearing outrageous (and largely apocryphal) tales about recent Stephanians who were no longer around to contradict them, seeing your name punned within KT, were all integral parts of the Stephanian culture, and of the ways in which this culture was transmitted to each successive batch of Stephanians.

We did, however, have an ambiguous relationship with the hothouse world of Indian politics outside the campus. Our student's union, of which I won the Presidency with 65 per cent of the vote in a three-cornered contest in 1974, was explicitly apolitical—the party-affiliated bodies that dominated Delhi University campus politics at the time, the Jan Sangh's ABVP (starring a certain Arun Jaitley of Shri Ram College), the Congress-backed NSUI, and the Commmunist SFI and AISF, were not allowed to set up branches at St. Stephen's, and we were not members of Jaitley's Delhi University Students' Union. Our union was even called a 'society' till I persuaded the principal to allow us to call ourselves a 'Students' Union Society'.

Yet some of us were to go on to develop political avatars. My campaign manager in 1974, and Chancellor of the Exchequer in my Cabinet, was Chandan Mitra, in those days a passionate leftist (as was his then Trotskyite pal Swapan

Dasgupta). Both went on to be avatars of the political right that has now come into ascendancy in New Delhi. I myself did not conceal my sympathies for the Swatantra Party, and my bitter disappointment at its dissolution and merger into Charan Singh's BLD in 1974, which I expressed publicly in the College auditorium when Piloo Mody addressed the student body that year. It is to St. Stephen's that I can trace the roots of my current dismay at the dwindling space for liberal ideas in our political discourse and my determination, from within the Congress party, to stand up for the values of democratic freedom, personal liberty, social liberalism, pluralism and individual initiative that Rajaji, Masani and Mody had so brilliantly articulated in my youth. (Indeed, I find it ironic that an illiberal party like the BJP should have cornered the market on 'liberal' thought in our country.)

I had graduated and left for studies in the US when the Emergency came, allowing the college authorities to suspend elections and appoint a student president—none other than my deputy Chandan Mitra! But contemporaries who stayed on at St. Stephen's have told me of Stephanian resistance to the dictates of the Emergency. The Sanjay Gandhi slogan 'More Work Less Talk' quickly became transmuted at St. Stephen's to 'More Workless Talk'. Its Hindi version, 'Baatein Kam, Kaam Ziadah' received a pointed rejoinder in a notice pinned on a board in the College's senior staff room 'Baatein Kam, Chai Ziadah'.

And of course there was the memorable incident of Natwar Singh visiting the college which I have related in the chapter, 'The Fall of an Old Retainer'. I didn't take the Foreign Service exams that all my contemporaries expected me to ace; instead I joined the UN—and years later, when the opportunity arose, joined Natwar's 'dregs of society' myself.

Three years is, of course, a small—and rapidly decreasing—proportion of my life, but my three years at St. Stephen's marked me for all the years to follow. Partly this was because I joined college a few months after my sixteenth birthday and left it a few months after my nineteenth, so that I was at St. Stephen's at an age when any experience would have had a lasting effect. But equally vital was the institution itself, its atmosphere and history, its student body and teaching staff, its sense of itself and how that sense was communicated to each individual character in the Stephanian story. Too many Indian colleges are places for lectures, rote-learning, memorizing, regurgitation; St. Stephen's encouraged random reading, individual note-taking, personal tutorials, extra-curricular development. Elsewhere you learned to answer the questions, at college to question the answers. Some of us went further, and questioned the questions.

Standing at the college on the 125th birthday of St. Stephen's, I remembered the values the college had taught me, in the classroom and outside it. St. Stephen's influenced me fundamentally, gave me my basic faith in all-inclusive, multi-spirited, free-thinking cultures, helped shape my mind and define my sense of myself in relation to the world, and so, inevitably, influenced what I have done later in life—as a man, as a United Nations official, as a writer and now as a politician. Stephania encouraged the development of qualities that would stand me in good stead in each of these activities.

The great humanist and Stephanian Gopalkrishna Gandhi summarized the qualities of Stephania by the Urdu word 'tahzib'. In a speech at the college in 2009, he went on to explain:

> To seek opportunity, but not be an opportunist,
> to make one's money but not rake it in,
> to look for a shaabaash, but not chase after popularity,
> to advance without flattery, to retreat without abandoning,
> to offer loyalty but not cronyism,
> to make a point without wanting to win the argument,
> to make an impression without wanting to leave a mark,
> to make a difference without wanting to be hailed as a Prophet,
> is to have tahzib.
> To work for success rather than for victory,
> and never to want to flash that revolting two-finger sign mimicking the letter 'V',
> is to have tahzib.

So when I look back at college today, I celebrate the secularism, the pan-Indian outlook, the well-rounded education, the eclectic social interests, the questioning spirit and the meritocratic culture that are the vital ingredients of the Stephanian ethos. These are what the idea of Stephania contributes to the idea of India I have described in my books and speeches around the world. The Stephanian peers who were heirs to this ethos are, to my mind, embodiments of a spirit India needs sorely everywhere—the spirit of the quest to excel.

THE INTANGIBLE KERALA HERITAGE

A little over a year ago, I visited a modest village about an hour's drive from Kozhikode, on Kerala's Malabar Coast. There, down a dirt road, stood a recreation of the home of the most celebrated poet and cultural catalyst in the history of the Malayalam language—Thunchath Ezhuthachan. This was Thunchan Perumba, a centre in the same location as the house and school where the bard was born, lived and taught in the 16th century, and where he invented modern Malayalam literature.

There is another reason Ezhuthachan represents the best of Kerala literary and cultural tradition. He was born in an era where the knowledge and transmission of culture was confined to a handful of Brahmins. Despite being born into a socially underprivileged caste, the Chakala Nairs, whose members were forbidden from studying sacred texts, Ezhuthachan defied the ossified traditions of his time and gently but firmly thwarted the attempts by the entrenched interests of the day to keep him away from learning. Ezhuthachan mastered the Vedas and Upanishads without the support, let alone the blessings, of the upper castes. In this, he captured what all Malayalis are proud of—the determination to overcome all obstacles in the pursuit of education and the development of culture. The thriving literary culture of Kerala is a reflection of this proud tradition.

Though I am a Malayali and a writer, I do not consider myself a Malayali writer: despite setting some of my fictional sequences in Kerala and scattering Menons through my stories, I cannot write in my mother tongue. And yet I am not inclined to be defensive about my Kerala heritage, despite the obvious incongruities of a Kerala writer lauding his Malayali heritage in the English language.

As a child growing up in Mumbai, Kolkata and Delhi, my experience of Kerala had been as a reluctant vacationer during my parents' annual trips home. For many non-Keralite Malayali children, there was little joy in the compulsory rediscovery of their roots, and many saw it as an obligation. For city-dwellers, rural Kerala (and Kerala is essentially rural, since the countryside envelops the towns in a seamless web) was a world of rustic simplicities and private inconveniences. When I was 10 years old, I told my father that this annual migration to the south was strictly for the birds. But, as I grew older, I came to appreciate the magic of Kerala—its beauty, which is apparent to even the most casual tourist, and also its ethos, which takes a greater engagement to uncover.

What does it mean, then, for Keralites like me, who have lived most of our lives outside Kerala, to lay claim now to our Malayali heritage? What is it that we learn to cherish, and of which we remain proud, wherever we are?

Non-Malayalis who know of Kerala associate it with its fabled coast, gilded by immaculate beaches and leafy lagoons. But my parents were from the interiors, the rice-bowl district of Palghat, nestled in the last major gap near the end of the Western Ghats. Palghat—or Palakkad—unlike most of Kerala, had been colonized by the British, so my father discovered his nationalism at a place called Victoria College. The town of Palghat is unremarkable, even unattractive; its setting, though, is beautiful. My parents belonged to villages an hour away from the district capital, and to families whose principal source of income was agriculture. Their roots lay deep in the Kerala soil, from which have emerged the values that I cherish in the Indian soul.

As Malayalis, the beauty of Kerala is bred into our souls; it animates our very being. Hailing from a land of forty-four rivers, innumerable lakes and 1,500 km of 'backwaters', the Keralite bathes twice a day and dresses immaculately in white. Kerala's women are usually simple and unadorned. But they float on a riot of colour: the voluptuous green of lush Kerala foliage, the rich red of fecund earth, the brilliant blue of life-giving waters, the shimmering gold of beaches and riverbanks.

Yet there is much more to the Kerala experience than natural beauty. Since my first sojourn as a child in my ancestral village, I have seen remarkable transformations in Kerala society. This success is a reflection of what, in my 1997 book, *India: From Midnight to the Millennium*, I call the 'Malayali miracle': a state that has practised openness and tolerance from time immemorial; which has made religious and ethnic diversity a part of its daily life rather than a source of division; which has overcome caste discrimination and class oppression through education, land reform and political democracy; which has honoured its women and enabled them to lead productive, fulfilling and empowered lives. Indeed, Kerala's social development indicators are comparable to those of the US, though these have been built on one-seventieth the per capita income of America.

And what is striking is that every Kerala woman reads. As a child I grew up listening to my paternal grandmother read aloud from her venerable editions of the Ramayana and the Mahabharata. And I saw, too, my maternal grandmother running a big house and administering the affairs of a large brood of children and grandchildren with firmness and courage. In both cases they had been widowed relatively young, but in neither case was their gender a disqualification in their assumption of authority. Keralites are used to seeing women ruling the roost. My own mother, now closer to 80 than she would like to admit, still drives her own car to our ancestral home in a Palakkad village, scorning male help. She likes to be in charge.

'In the exceptional nature of Kerala's social achievements', Amartya Sen has written, 'the greater voice of women seems to have been an important factor'. The literacy of Kerala women has produced a lower birthrate than China's, without the coercion China needed. A girl born in Kerala can expect to live twenty years longer than one born in Uttar Pradesh, and she can expect to make the important decisions in her life, to attend college, choose a profession, do what others might consider 'men's work', and inherit property (something which, before the law was changed in 1956, Indian women could not expect to do, unless they were Malayalis following the 'Marumakkathayam' matrilineal system).

When M.F. Husain painted a series on Kerala for our co-authored book, *God's Own Country*, everywhere there were the women: striding confidently through the green, holding aloft their elephants, steering their boats through a storm, and simply—how simply!—reading. The mere fact that every Kerala girl above the age of 6 can read and write is little short of a miracle, in a country where more women are illiterate than not. Kerala's women have become doctors and pilots, Supreme Court justices, ambassadors; they have shone in sport, politics, armed forces. 'If Kashmir is all about men and mountains,' Husain said, 'Kerala is all about women and nature.'

Fittingly, it was a woman ruler, Rani Gouri Parvatibai, then queen of Travancore, who in 1817 decreed that 'the State should defray the entire cost of the education of its people in order that there might be no backwardness in the spread of enlightenment among them, that by diffusion of education they might become better subjects and public servants'. Her royal successors followed the policy, and, after Independence, elected communist governments in the state enshrined free, compulsory and universal education as a basic right. Today, Kerala outspends every Indian state in its tax outlays on education, and Keralites support over fifty newspapers. No village is complete without a 'reading room' that serves as a community library, and the sight of villagers reading their newspapers in public, is a ubiquitous one in Kerala, whether on the verandahs of their homes or in the 'chayakadas' (tea shops) where animated arguments around the day's news over steaming sweet cups of tea are a regular feature of daily life.

It is not accidental that Keralites have a deep-rooted love of books and reading, nor that the slightest village boasts a 'reading room' or library, sometimes both. The writer M.T. Vasudevan Nair told me that 'copying texts neatly and artistically was a very common and dignified pastime for middle-class housewives until the first quarter of last century'. Books were borrowed, copied by the women of the household, and then circulated to family and friends—not great for an author's royalties, but wonderful for the transmission of literary culture. The public library movement is strong in Kerala, with some 3,000 libraries in the state, many dating back to the 19th century and created by the governments of Travancore, Cochin and Madras. The long and sustained involvement of the State in library affairs has contributed immensely to the educational, social and economic development of Kerala.

Reading both reflects and shapes Kerala's open mind. Part of the secret of Kerala is its openness to the external influences—Arab, Roman, Chinese, British; Islamist, Christian, Marxist—that have gone into the making of the Malayali people. More than two millennia ago, Keralites had trade relations not just with other parts of India but with the Arab world, the Phoenicians and the Roman Empire, so Malayalis have had an open and welcoming attitude to the rest of humanity. Jews fleeing Roman persecution found refuge here; there is evidence of their settlement in Cranganore in AD 68. And 1,500 years later, the Jews settled in Kochi, where they built a magnificent synagogue that still stands. Kerala's Christians belong to the oldest Christian community in the world outside Palestine. And when St Thomas, one of Jesus's twelve apostles, brought Christianity to Kerala, he made converts among the high-born elite, the Namboodiri Brahmins. Islam came not by the sword, but through traders, travellers and missionaries, who brought its message of equality and brotherhood to the coastal people. The new faith was peacefully embraced and encouraged: for instance, the all-powerful Zamorin of Calicut asked each fisherman's family in his domain to bring up one son as a Muslim, for service in his Muslim-run navy, commanded by sailors of Arab descent, the Kunjali Maraicars.

In turn, Malayalis brought their questing spirit to the world. The great Advaita philosopher, Shankaracharya, was a Malayali who travelled through India in the 8th century AD, laying the foundations for a reformed and revived Hinduism. To this day, there is a temple in the Himalayas whose priests are Namboodiris from Kerala.

Keralites never suffered from inhibitions about travel: an old joke suggests that so many Keralite typists flocked to stenographic work in Mumbai, Kolkata and Delhi that 'Remington' became the name of a new Malayali sub-caste. In the nation's capital, the wags said that you couldn't throw a stone in the Central Secretariat without injuring a Keralite bureaucrat. And there was none of the ritual defilement associated with 'crossing the black water'. It was no accident that Keralites were the first, and the most, to take advantage of the post-oil-shock employment boom in the Gulf; at one point in the eighties, the largest single ethnic group in Bahrain was reported to be not Bahrainis but Keralites. The willingness of Keralites to go anywhere to do anything remains legendary: when Neil Armstrong landed on the moon, my father's friends laughed that he discovered a Malayali already there, offering him tea.

But Keralites are not merely intrepid travellers. They have also behind them a great legacy of achievement. In the 5th century AD the Kerala-born astronomer Aryabhatta deduced, 1,000 years before his European successors, that the earth is round and that it rotates on its own axis; it was also he who calculated the value of π (3.1614) for the first time. I could go on, citing great artists, musicians and poets, enlightened kings, learned sages throughout history. But there would still be so much more: the great Kerala martial arts and the systems of classical dance, notably Kathakali and Krishnanattam, which are admired the world over; Keralite cuisine and traditional medicine.

Yet even more important than any of these are the intangible elements of the Kerala heritage. Thanks to social reformers like Sree Narayana Guru, Chattambi Swami, Mahatma Ayyankali and a host of others, social justice and equality prevail here, and Kerala's working men and women enjoy greater rights and a higher minimum wage than anywhere else in India. It is the first place on earth to democratically elect a communist government, remove it from office, re-elect it, vote the communists out and bring them back again repeatedly. When Italy subordinated the communists to democracy, the world spoke of Euro-communism, but Kerala had already achieved Indo-communism much earlier. Despite their tolerance of discredited ideologies, Malayalis are highly politically aware. When other states were electing film stars to Parliament or as chief ministers, a film star tried to do the same in Kerala and lost his security deposit.

Malayalis rank high in every field of Indian endeavour, from the top national civil servants (in the last government, the prime minister's two principal aides, his seniormost secretary and his national security adviser, were Malayalis) to the most innovative writers and filmmakers. All Kerala mourned the loss of Dr Verghese Kurien, the father of India's 'White Revolution' in milk production, who in the best Keralite tradition, based himself in Gujarat!

All this speaks of a rare and precious heritage which is a legacy for all Malayalis—a heritage of openness and diversity, of pluralism and tolerance, of high aspirations and varied achievement. To be a Malayali is to lay claim to a rich tradition of literature, dance and music, of religious diversity, of political courage and intellectual enlightenment. The Kochi-Muziris Biennale, which was launched in December 2012 (on the euphonious date of 12/12/12) was India's first and only Biennale, and proved an outstanding showcase of contemporary culture.

At the same time I would never promote a parochial Kerala chauvinism. I am proud of being Keralite; I am also proud of being Indian. But that is true of all Keralites. This land imposes no narrow conformities on its citizens: you can be many things and one thing. You can be a good Muslim, a good Keralite and a good Indian all at once. Kerala's 'minorities' suffer no 'minority complex'; they know they enjoy the same rights and opportunities in politics, government, business or society as the so-called 'majority community'. Our founding fathers wrote a constitution for a dream; we have given passports to our ideals. We are all Malayalis first; our religion, our caste, our region come later, if at all.

And so the Indian identity that I want, in my turn, to give my half-Malayali sons imposes no pressure to conform. It celebrates diversity: if America is a melting-pot, then to me India, like Kerala, is a thali, a selection of sumptuous dishes in different bowls. Each tastes different, and does not necessarily mix with the next, but they belong together on the same plate. And the important thing is that Mathai and Mohahammedkutty and Mohanan still sing the same songs and dream the same dreams together—preferably in Malayalam!

This is the expanded vision of socio-cultural heritage that I believe we should preserve, promote and protect. The Malayali ethos is the same as the best of the Indian ethos—inclusionist, flexible, eclectic, absorptive. Whether we grow up in America or in India, whether we can write Malayalam or barely speak it, whether we are Keralites, Calcuttans or Californians—we can all cherish what being Malayali has given us, and celebrate this common heritage together. It is typical that Kerala's premier festival, Onam, is truly non-denominational, celebrated with equal enthusiasm and ownership by Keralites of every faith community. It enshrines an idea of a land where it doesn't matter what the color of your skin is, the kind of food you eat, the sounds you make when you speak, the God you choose to worship (or not), so long as you want to play by the same rules as everybody else, and dream the same dreams.

There is a verse of the poet Vallathol which my father loved to recite, and translates as: 'When we hear the name of India, we must swell with pride/ when we hear the name of Kerala, the blood must throb in our veins.' It is, in some ways, an odd sentiment for a Malayali poet, for Keralites are not a chauvinistic people: the Keralite liberality and adaptativeness—such great assets in facilitating emigration and good citizenship—can serve to slacken, if not cut, the cords that bind diaspora Keralites to their cultural assumptions. And yet Vallathol was not off the mark, for we Keralites take pride in our collective identity as Malayalis; our religion, our caste, our region come later, if at all. There is no paradox in asserting that these are qualities that help make Malayalis good Indians in a plural society. You cannot put better ingredients into the Indian thali.

SOARING TO THE FUTURE:
INDIA'S MARTIAN CHRONICLES

The news that the Mars orbiter spacecraft Mangalyaan, launched by India on 5 November 2013, left the Earth's orbit, traversed the moon, and ten months later reached its ultimate destination, by entering Mars' orbit 400 million kilometres (249 million miles) away, brought great pride to Indians. Space missions have become a matter of national celebration for India, which is already one of the top countries in terms of rocket and satellite technology.

Mangalyaan, India's first inter-planetary satellite, was purpose-built for the Mars mission—and it was made entirely indigenously. Indian-educated scientists designed and fabricated it in barely fifteen months—astonishingly fast for a country of chronic delays, where 'Indian Standard Time' is a common joke. They also did so at a remarkably low cost, with the total bill coming in at under $73 million, or about a fifth of what the few other countries that have sought to explore Mars have spent. Indeed, its budget was exceeded by that of the Hollywood outer-space blockbuster, *Gravity*! While Indians often lament their country's dysfunction, inadequate infrastructure, antiquated industrial processes, and uneven manufacturing record, it rose to the challenge and delivered.

Five years earlier, India's 2008 lunar mission, called Chandrayaan, was the occasion for another national celebration. Though it was intended to explore the moon for two years, the spacecraft was declared lost after 312 days. While scientists at the Indian Space Research Organization (ISRO) believe that they gained valuable lessons from the experience, the partial failure of the Chandrayaan mission still haunts them.

But the challenge was even greater when it comes to Mars, and India succeeded where others had failed. It is a sobering fact that of a total of fifty-one Mars missions sent out by five countries, thirty ended badly. Among India's Asian rivals, neither Japan, which launched a Mars orbiter in 2003, nor China, which followed suit in 2011, was able to complete its mission successfully.

India triumphantly joined the three space programs that have succeeded—those of the Soviet Union, the United States, and the European Union. But unlike them, it became the first country in history to reach Mars's orbit at the very first attempt. Mangalyaan's objective is to look for the presence of methane gas, a sign of possible life. Success would mark a scientific advance for humanity; failure, Indian scientists aver, would still provide a learning experience.

Despite the joy at India's unique accomplishment, the ISRO's chief scientist, K. Radhakrishnan, is not interested in comparisons with other countries:

'We are in competition with ourselves,' he declared, 'in the areas we have charted for ourselves.' India is increasingly regarded around the world as the leading developing country in the field, with the human-resource capacity and technological skills needed to work on the cutting edge of outer-space challenges.

India's adventures in space exploration are not merely about its scientists' ambitions. At United Nations forums, India has consistently been a voice for international cooperation in outer space. It speaks of being able to offer other countries, particularly from the developing world, an opportunity to participate in space exploration. Its moon mission in 2008, which carried a payload for some twenty countries, won the International Lunar Exploration Working Group's International Cooperation Award.

Yet, unavoidably, some triumphalism has crept into the narrative. One of India's more astute young commentators, Sreeram Chaulia, captures this heady exuberance well: 'Every milestone in advanced rocket science', he writes, 'is a shot in the arm for national self-confidence, showing that India is headed for global leadership. When the chips are down, or if there is a national calamity, memories of the Mars orbiter blazing a trail in the sky will sustain the faith that the future belongs to India.'

This is precisely the attitude that raises the hackles of domestic critics, especially on the left, who argue that a country facing India's crippling social and economic problems cannot afford the luxury of indulging in space exploration. Critics have portrayed the Mars mission as an irresponsible ego trip by pampered scientists disconnected from the harsh realities of Indian poverty and suffering. This may not be entirely fair, however. India embarked on its quest for rocket and satellite technology and space exploration when it was far poorer, impelled by its own ancient scientific tradition and the conviction of its first prime minister, Jawaharlal Nehru, that such aspirations could co-exist with a determined effort to end poverty.

Indeed, India's space scientists have produced tangible benefits for ordinary citizens, launching meteorological satellites that have predicted cyclones and helped save thousands of lives, as well as telecommunications satellites that have knit a vast country together through shared networks. Mitigating natural disasters and enabling nationwide broadcasting can hardly be considered to be disconnected from India's real priorities.

With the air still thick from political recriminations in the wake of the general elections, the Mars mission is the one thing that can literally rise above us all.

GO EAST (AND WEST), YOUNG MAN!

To travel is to wilfully leap into the unknown—to give up the assured security of home for the exigencies of the world. This is true whether one journeys from home to a nearby town to see a mela, or to another continent in search of work. Over time, the world and its mores seep, imperceptibly, into our lives and into our minds. We inch closer, howsoever marginally, to becoming—as the Greek philosopher Diogenes first called himself—a 'citizen of the world'.

Predictably, travel arouses a swathe of responses: the world can repel or inspire reflections. For some, like Gandhiji or Darwin, travel provided intellectual and moral reasons to empathize with others; for some others, like Sayyid Qutb or Pol Pot, the world inspired justifications to murder in name of religious purity and class-consciousness. For most of us who fall somewhere between these polarities, travel forces our minds to adapt, to rethink, to reevaluate our prejudices and to recalibrate our passions in ways far removed from conventional education. Travel, in other words, is learning by other means.

Remarkably, in the education curricula of our country, travel rarely figures. An odd picnic during the school year is the most that one might experience. Beyond that, for large sections of India's poor and middle class, the world is reduced to one's city, one's family and nowadays whatever the television channels proffer. The wide world and its wonders mean little.

Predictably, the idea of India—whether as a geographical or cultural space— is increasingly lopsided in the minds of many. The less privileged know little beyond their own areas, or what they see in Bollywood movies. The children of the elite of India's major cities know more about Manhattan or London than they do about, say, Bhubaneswar or Thiruvananthapuram. Many parts of India are virtually foreign countries to their young minds, through no real fault of theirs. Who wants to think about Dantewada when there is a jet plane taking off to Dubai? Our collective consciousness slowly fragments along familiar lines of global capital flows and worldly aesthetics.

Should this matter?

In a heterogeneous democracy like ours, where resources and geographies are different, where peoples and cultures change with every district—it is paramount that we are able to see past our immediate environs. The overbearing tyranny of small disaffections dictates our public discourse. The acrimony in our Parliament and media is emblematic of our inability to listen to, far less agree with, each other. Technology has amplified marginal dissonances. We may know more facts about others, but our discourse suffers from Asperger's syndrome: the terrible inability to empathize.

Our collective challenge is then how we do offer, to the generations of Indians who follow, opportunities to recognize our collective destiny? Lester Pearson, the late Canadian prime minister, said in his Nobel Peace Prize Lecture: 'How can there be peace without people understanding each other, and how can this be if they don't know each other?' To him, and to others, knowledge of the other was critical to demystify, to get past clichés and to learn to treat each individual according to the 'content of their character'. The best way to do this is to travel. Why not explicitly encourage such personal explorations as a matter of public policy? World travel may be limited by the high level of resources required and the difficulty of obtaining visas. But why not promote travel within India?

My friend, Keerthik Sasidharan, who is in his early thirties, suggests that we could create a pan-Indian quasi-governmental agency along the lines of AISEC (Association Internationale des Étudiants en Sciences Économiques et Commerciales) to act as a hub for students who seek to travel. This agency could provide logistical support to students—guidance about possible destinations, a database of student hostels, basic medical assistance and volunteer opportunities in each Indian city. It could also accredit and screen related enterprises like youth hostels, tour providers and social service organizations needing volunteers. In essence, by involving itself in such an enterprise, the State can protect the young travellers, and implicitly make India more accessible.

Another possibility is a centrally facilitated nationwide school children's exchange programme. Let children from Srinagar come and spend two weeks in a year in Thiruvananthapuram and vice versa. Let the Kashmiri children learn about the vast oceans, while Malayali children learn about the snow-clad mountains. Let them interact and play, fight and make friends. This could create friendships that might last a lifetime. But it would need organizational support and subsidies, which the State can provide.

Or take our young writers in Indian languages, who are rarely able to venture beyond the prisms, and the prisons, of their vernaculars. They have just as keen and sensitive perspectives on life as our English language writers, but their horizons are necessarily more limited, and a national perspective often eludes them. They are doubly discriminated against—for being young and being outside the scope of the English language press. Creating a national programme that funds young writers to travel the country and write about it in their local languages is a useful step towards our collective cosmopolitanism.

The resources for all this do not all have to come from the State. But the government could establish a National Endowment for the Discovery of India that is open to private tax-deductible contributions and that can be used to finance the ideas outlined above. If we are to grow into a country that is open minded, we must learn to not just leave the windows of our homes open to the world, as the Mahatma advised us, but also step out and engage with the world.

The best place to start is in India itself—large, multiple, diverse, and in many ways unknown to its own citizens. To encourage young Indians to travel through their own land would reify the idea of India for the next generation. It would be a journey well worth undertaking by all of us.

If we do this, *The Discovery of India* need no longer be a seventy-year-old title in libraries and bookstores, but a core mission of every Indian. Can we, as a state and society, rise to this challenge?

INDIA'S YOUTH: BUILDING A NATION,
SEIZING THE WORLD

Thirty-three years ago, when I was fresh out of college and about to proceed to the United States for post-graduate studies, a leading national newspaper asked me to do an article for their Independence Day supplement. The Emergency had just been declared; politicians had been locked up, the press censored; even one of my short stories had been banned. Around me, newspapermen and journalists were cowed and resentful. The freedoms for which our Independence struggle had been waged seemed in peril, and yet weren't we, the literate minority, disqualified by our privileged status from objecting to measures designed, as the government claimed, to benefit the 'common man'?

I was angry, cynical and confused—a combination of emotions appropriate both to my age, and to the times. This is how I began my article: 'Independent India is 28 years old today. I was 19 a few months ago. In school they told me I was the citizen of tomorrow. Around me I saw the citizens of today, and wondered what purpose I was going to serve. They seemed worn and jaded and cynical. To my fellow citizens of the future, Independence Day merely meant early mornings in starched uniforms on parade grounds, relieved only by the comforting thought of no more classes. In college they were more sensible. They just gave us a holiday, and the chowkidar unfurled the flag.'

But even collegiate cynicism had its limits. 'Independence', it went on in adolescent passion, 'conjures up visions of mammoth patriotic rallies outside Red Fort; a reminder of freedom and self-reliance and the hope of unexploited progress. But when the drums have been beaten and the cavalcade has passed, the cheering invariably seems to subside into a desultory grumble. Our capacity for unproductive complaint is seemingly limitless; but then we appear to have developed the art of destructive criticism to the proportions of a national characteristic. Perhaps it is because, as a former colony, we are used to bemoaning our lot without being able to do anything about it.' Decrying 'the strange spectacle of a nation without nationals, of Indians who are not involved in India', I lamented the absence of a 'sense of belonging' to a larger idea of India. I argued: 'That one is an all-too-dispensable part of the Indian reality is surely all the more reason why one should take one's role all the more seriously, instead of affecting the dislocated detachment that has become the untaxed perquisite of citizenship.' That was my point: we had to belong, we had to care, we had to be involved in what became of our independence. This 'sense of belonging' (the phrase with which I titled the article) would be vital 'to me and those of my generation who now stand on the threshold of that which has, over the last 28 years, been made to mean so little.'

That generation is now in its prime, and it is only fair to ask whether our sense of belonging is any greater now than it seemed to be amongst those who were the age we are now. They suffered by comparison with their parents, who had fought for and won the very independence whose value they seemed to be frittering away. How do we seem now to the generation following ours? If, 28 years after 1947, independence had 'been made to mean so little', does it mean much more today, 68 years on?

At one level, yes. The idea of India has come to mean much more today than it did then. Even if we are nearly seven decades removed from the magic moment of that 'tryst with destiny', we have weathered four wars and an Emergency, conducted sixteen general elections and hundreds of state elections, changed our governments peacefully, defused separatist movements in places as far afield as Punjab and Mizoram, and seen Rashtrapati Bhavan occupied by three Muslims, a Dalit and a woman. Bollywood, yoga and chicken tikka masala have conquered the globe; we have won two cricket World Cups and invented the IPL. And the mass media, especially our countless television channels, have brought us all together in the nationalism of shared experience: We have watched corrupt officials 'stung' on camera, applauded stirring moments on the sports field, screamed a collective 'chak de!' and mourned together for the victims of Kargil. The Information Age gave Indians a greater sense of who we are: a multi-religious people united by the Mahabharat on television, a land of IIT graduates with a third of the world's illiterate children. 'We are like this only', goes the wry line, as we acknowledge the paradoxes of our country. We are large, we contain multitudes.

So young educated Indians had to care, and needed to be involved in what became of our independence. Repeating these words today is not merely indulging in nostalgia; it is to urge that today's young seize opportunities that were not available to their parents at the same age. Amongst these opportunities is the prospect for advancement in a globalized world. But young people cannot do this on their own. Indian society and industry have to make it possible for them.

In the last two decades India has gone from being one of the least globalized economies in the world to one of the most dependent on international commerce. Right up to the late 1980s, foreign travel was a rare and much-coveted luxury for the middle-classes. If one got to go abroad, one had to depend on the largesse of foreigners, since you could carry out of India only a measly foreign exchange allowance of (for much of that time) $8. Foreign goods were largely unavailable; visitors from abroad, bringing what, for them, were routine consumer items, were greeted almost as if they had introduced frankincense and myrrh to Bethlehem.

Today, to mint a cliché, India is not what it used to be. The world has changed, and in order to take advantage of it, India has changed too. Our markets are more open, we enjoy a wider range of consumer items than ever, and those who go abroad (far more than ever before) finance their travel and expenses with foreign exchange. Business process outsourcing has tied large numbers of Indians to foreign work environments and business partners. The world is no longer a strange, intimidatingly inaccessible place for most Indians. And in turn, the world sees India differently too.

Indian companies continue to expand outwards. They continue to set up overseas subsidiaries and partnerships. From the behemoths like Tata Consultancy Services in China and Bharti Airtel across Africa to small diamond trading units in Belgium or agricultural firms like Harrisons Malayalam buying plantation land in South Africa, to turnkey infrastructure project firms like GVK Power & Infrastructure in Indonesia, and many more examples too numerous to mention, Indian firms continue to expand and operate successfully in the rest of the world.

Now the India that is going global is also a remarkably young country. India's youth population remains an under-utilized economic asset. Census figures tell us that nearly one-fifth of India belongs to the 15-24 age group. This provides us with a unique opportunity as a society. We are at a golden moment of being able to create a more globally-aware generation to shore up India's place in a globalized world.

The need is acute. Either we train and prepare our young people for a 21st century global economy, or we face disaster. Each year, we will add around 5 million young adults (between 15-24 years) per year. These are 5 million potentially productive workers. But if they are unemployed or unemployable, they are also potential revolutionaries, Naxalites or stone-pelters. The frustrations of jobless young men lie behind most of the violent protests in the world.

Indian companies that operate outside India should be encouraged, through the diligent application of tax incentives, to use our young people as interns and specialist trainees. There are two benefits from such an arrangement: the firms get the ability to scrutinize and develop talent in-house for the future, while the young person gets the opportunity to work in a professional setting in a foreign country. Over the period of the contractual agreement, it is only natural that this young intern will travel around, interact with the local societies and—over a period of time—we will have Indians who know the world much better than the generation before.

There are many models we can study to fine-tune such a program. The French, for example, have a governmental division that oversees its VIE (internship) program, which is subordinated to the Secrétariat d'etat au Commerce Exterieur (State Secretariat for Foreign Trade). Young French citizens apply to go work abroad for French firms via this agency. Their remuneration is such that one part of it is fixed, while the other is contingent on local wage levels. Often the retention levels at the firms that engage them are high as well. Over the years, the French have created a pool of young people who have served in far-flung areas—and reinforced Paris' own global vision and sensibilities.

In India, our industries and firms are at the cusp of expanding globally in an unprecedented fashion. Our young people are raring to travel, work and experience the world. There is no reason why we cannot bring them together and why a systematic competitive program run by the government can't create a new generation of Indians who—while they enrich their own lives' experiences—will help build and project India's reach into the world.

The young already dominate India demographically. They can dominate India—and the world—economically too. Just let's give them the chance.

THE SUN ALSO RISES: SOLAR ENERGY FOR INDIA

In all the brouhaha about the Indo–US nuclear deal in 2008, not enough attention was paid to then Prime Minister Manmohan Singh's announcement the same year of a credible energy plan for India that goes way beyond the nuclear. By far the most welcome component of his six-point plan to increase the country's reliance on sustainable sources of energy was the prime minister's declaration that the development of India's capacity to tap the power of the sun would be central to the strategy.

'In this strategy, the sun occupies centre stage,' the former PM memorably said, 'as it should, being literally the original source of all energy. We will pool all our scientific, technical and managerial talents, with financial sources, to develop solar energy as a source of abundant energy to power our economy and to transform the lives of our people.' Dr Singh added, and this was no hyperbole: 'Our success in this endeavour will change the face of India.'

As a layman who has no particular competence to weigh in on the scientific aspects of the debate over climate change, I have often wondered why a country like India, with its abundance of natural sunshine, hasn't done more to focus on developing solar energy. The prime minister made it clear that India has no choice, over the next few years, but to move away from economic activity based on fossil fuels to a far greater use of non-fossil fuels. The price of oil alone is proof enough that we have to reduce our dependence on non-renewable (and dwindling) sources of carbon-based energy to renewable and sustainable sources instead.

Of these, solar power is the most obvious one for India. But the existing technology is prohibitively expensive. Solar panels, made from silicon (which itself consumes non-renewable petroleum energy in its manufacture), cost ten times the price of the cheapest fossil fuels. Indian scientists who have worked on reducing these costs are few and far between, and have little success to report. But with the new governmental emphasis on solar energy as a priority, a new research thrust ought to be feasible, given adequate government funding and tax incentives.

It's interesting that all the pressure on India from the international climate change community has focused in the direction of cutting back on our country's carbon emissions. There's no doubt that Indian industry contributes to the global build-up of greenhouse gases, but as New Delhi has repeatedly pointed out, the bulk of that problem was created by two hundred years of Western industrialization, to which India contributed little. Even today, Indian emissions, on a per capita basis, are amongst the lowest in the world. But the debate need not be conducted on that tediously familiar ground. Instead, there's a different point worth making: that of all the possible ways you could combat global warming, the least effective would be the path of simply cutting carbon dioxide emissions.

That conclusion isn't mine: it comes from a panel of eight of the world's top economists, including five Nobel laureates, who were gathered together by the Copenhagen Consensus, a highly innovative mechanism put together by the smart young Danish economist Bjorn Lomborg, author of a remarkable (and admittedly controversial) book, *The Sceptical Environmentalist*. Dr Lomborg convened the panel to examine worldwide research findings on the best ways to tackle ten global challenges: air pollution, conflict, disease, global warming, hunger and malnutrition, lack of education, gender inequity, lack of water and sanitation, terrorism, and trade barriers. The panellists' job, as experts, was to examine, through a cost-benefit approach, a variety of possible solutions to each of these ten challenges. Lomborg set them an interesting challenge of their own: to create a list of priorities enumerating how, in their view, the sum of $800 billion could most effectively be spent over the next hundred years in tackling these problems.

The results were fascinating. Lomborg's panel concluded that the least effective use of resources in slowing down the pace of global warming would be to spend $800 billion over a hundred years solely on cutting back carbon emissions. Such action would, they determined, reduce the planet's unavoidable increases in temperature by less than 0.2 degrees centigrade by the end of this century. Even taking into account the environmental damage that would be caused by the persistence of global warming, the world would in fact be able to prevent only $685 billion worth of damage—while spending $800 billion in the attempt.

The Copenhagen Consensus economists did not draw the conclusion from this that the world should ignore the problem—the effects of climate change are too serious to be neglected. Instead, they concluded that a more effective response than the attempt to reduce emissions would be to significantly increase research on, and the development of, other energy sources than carbon—such as solar energy and (though this would be less welcome in India, where agriculture is meant to feed people, not run their cars) second-generation biofuels.

'Even if every nation spent 0.05 per cent of its gross domestic product on research and development of low-carbon energy', Dr Lomborg argues, 'this would be only about one-tenth as costly as the Kyoto Protocol and would save dramatically more than any of Kyoto's likely successors'.

India can afford to spend that 0.05 per cent—and what's more, we have trained scientists and engineers who, given the proper incentives, can take the challenge on. The scale of India's energy needs, and the abundance of sunshine, should also mean that we should be able to benefit from economies of scale unavailable to smaller countries. There is no question that nuclear efforts are essential as well, which is why the government should be applauded for seeking to end India's nuclear pariah status (currently, our nuclear scientists cannot even get visas to a number of countries as a result of the post-Pokhran sanctions) and to put the country on the road to energy self-sufficiency. But equally, we need to do everything we can to ensure that solar energy should be able to rival nuclear energy in contributing to India's needs by 2020.

The lack of connection of at least 75 million rural households in our country to the electricity grid is a matter of grave concern. With the abundant availability of sunlight in most parts of India, the rapid development and implementation of off-grid solar power technologies would accelerate the electrification of our villages without putting a strain on the environment and at a lesser cost. Research confirms that in remote areas, though initially the cost of off-grid solar is higher than electricity generated by fossil fuels, it is still cheaper than extending the grid. The National Solar Mission needs to do more to provide better access to electricity. Government subsidies can ease the burden on rural households. I rose in Parliament as a member of Mr Modi's new Opposition to urge the government to promote off-grid solar power in rural areas and provide incentives for innovation. Nothing is more vital than providing electricity to rural Indians who are literally disconnected from modern India.

'Our vision is to make India's economic development energy efficient,' the former prime minister had said as he announced his energy plan. 'Our people have a right to economic and social development and to discard the ignominy of widespread poverty.' He's right. May the sun illuminate the way forward.

THE FRUGAL ANSWER TO INDIA'S DOLDRUMS

For the last few years, gloom about the sliding Indian economy was widespread, but misplaced. For macro-economics is not the whole story: to understand why India still offers hope, you have to go micro. To take one example: Google the words 'frugal innovation', as I have done off and on over the last three years, and the first twenty links all relate to India.

At one level, this is not new. Companies have long realized the opportunities that lie in meeting demands at the 'bottom of the pyramid' that had previously been overlooked. India is the country that invented the shampoo sachet more than two decades ago, creating a market for a product that historically the poor had never been able to afford. Indians who don't have either the space or the money to buy a whole bottle of shampoo for Rs 100 could spend Rs 5 for a sachet they'd use once or twice. Repackage the product and you find a whole new market.

But India's path-breaking leadership in 'frugal innovation' goes beyond downsizing: it involves taking the needs of poor consumers (itself a term no one had used before, since who knew the poor could be consumers?) as a starting point and working backwards. Instead of complicating or refining their products, Indian innovators strip the products down to their bare essentials, making them affordable, accessible, durable and effective.

Indians are natural leaders in frugal innovations, imbued as they are with the 'jugaad system' of developing make-shift but workable solutions from limited resources. Jugaad, an untranslatable Hindi word, is a way of life, a philosophy that essentially conveys the quality of somehow making do with what you have, to meet your needs. Some have derided it as enshrining mediocrity: jugaad, they say, is about shoddy work, cutting corners, imitation, making second-rate versions of first-rate products. But in fact, jugaad is not meant to be about pirating products or just making cheap imitations of global brands. It's about innovation—finding inexpensive solutions, often improvised on the fly, within the constraints of a resource-starved developing country full of poor people.

So an Indian villager constructs a makeshift vehicle to transport his livestock and goods, by rigging a wooden cart with an irrigation hand pump that serves as an engine. That's jugaad. Common machines and household objects are reincarnated in ways their original manufacturers had not intended. Everything is reusable or reimaginable. If you have a cell phone but can't afford to pay the bills, you invent the concept of the 'missed call'—a brief ring that is not answered but that sends the signal that you need to speak to the recipient.

Indian ingenuity has produced a startling number of world-beating innovations, none more impressive than the Tata Nano, which, at $2,000, sells for roughly the cost of a high-end DVD player in a Western luxury car. Of course there's no DVD player in the Nano, and no radio either in the basic model, but its innovations (which have garnered thirty-four patents) are not merely the result of doing away with frills (including doing away with power-brakes, air-conditioning and side-view mirrors). Such design choices as reducing the use of steel by inventing an aluminium engine, increasing space by moving the wheels to the edge of the chassis, and inventing a modular design that enables the car to be assembled from kits, all proved conclusively that you could do less with more.

Then there's the GE MAC 400, a hand-held electrocardiogram (ECG) device that costs $800 (the cheapest alternative is over $2,000) and the Tata Swachh, a $24 water purifier (ten times cheaper than its nearest competitor). The ECG uses just four buttons rather than the usual dozen, and a tiny portable ticket machine-style printer, making it small enough to fit into a satchel and even run on batteries. This micro product has reduced the cost of an ECG test to just $1 per patient. The Swachh purifier uses rice husks (which are among India's most common waste products) to purify water. Given that some 5 million Indians die of cardiovascular diseases every year, more than a quarter of them under 65, and about 2 million die from drinking contaminated water, the value of these innovations becomes apparent.

There are many other examples of frugal innovation already in the market, including a low-cost fuel-efficient mini-truck, an inexpensive mini-tractor being sold profitably in the US, a battery powered refrigerator, a $100 electricity inverter and a $12 solar lamp. Medical innovations are widespread: an Indian company has invented a cheaper Hepatitis B vaccine which brought the price down from some $15 an injection to less than 10 cents; insulin's price has come down by 40 per cent thanks to innovation by India's leading biotech firm; and a Bangalore company has invented a diagnostic tool to test for TB and infectious diseases that costs some $200 versus comparable equipment in the Western world retailing for $10,000.

In 2011, the government unveiled a low-cost handheld computer that would cost only Rs 2,250 (about $40). 'Aakash' has a resistive 7-inch touch screen, like Apple's iPad. It comes in a rugged plastic casing, has 2 gigabytes of flash memory, two USB ports, along with headphone and video output jacks and Wi-Fi capability. Aakash uses the Android 2.2 operating system and consumes a meagre 2 watts of power, which is supplied by an internal lithium-ion battery that could be charged using a solar-powered charger. And the government will subsidize 50 per cent of the cost to students, so a young Indian just has to pay $20 to have his own tablet. The initial reviews are good, and even if manufacturing delays led the government to move away from one device to merely announcing procurement standards that any manufacturer was free to match, the idea that India's schoolchildren might soon be learning on and from tablets rather than slates is extraordinary.

Even the financial sector has seen innovation. Just three years ago, there were only 15 million bank accounts in a country of 1.2 billion people. Indians concluded that if people won't come to the banks, you can take the banks to the people. The result has been the creation of travelling tellers with handheld devices, who have converted the living rooms of village homes into makeshift branches taking deposits as low as a dollar. More than 50 million new bank accounts have been established in the last three years, bringing India's rural poor into the modern financial system.

Frugal innovation points to one of the reasons why there is more dynamism in the Indian economy than the conventional Cassandras give the country credit for. It's simply wrong to write India off while 'Indovation' has become the tech world's new buzzword. But, as I have pointed out earlier, we have a lot to do to live up to the buzz and deliver outcomes worthy of our potential.

INDIA'S TWITTER REVOLUTION

On 4 July 2013, Narendra Modi, chief minister of Gujarat and putative prime ministerial candidate of the opposition BJP, became the most-followed Indian politician on the social media site Twitter by crossing 1.82 million followers. (In the interest of full disclosure, if at the risk of immodesty, I should mention that the long-time leader in this race, whom he eclipsed, was myself.) The occasion was enthusiastically celebrated by BJP supporters across the internet, and occasioned a spate of analyses in the mainstream media about the growing impact of social media on Indian politics. (Mr Modi has since gone on to far outstrip his rivals in India in terms of followers, and is currently the third most followed political figure on earth.)

When I began tweeting actively in May 2009—providing a few hundred followers quick updates on the counting of votes in my constituency during the general elections—I could scarcely have imagined where it would lead, the controversies it would envelop me in and (partly as a result!) the way in which India would become one of the world's leading countries in the use of Twitter.

The idea of being able to reach a wide (indeed global) audience in short bites of text not exceeding 140 characters is a deceptively simple one that has captured the imaginations of millions. Twitter is an extraordinary broadcast medium—an interactive Akashvani. Inevitably, movie stars and sportsmen are the biggest tweeters with the largest followings (my brief reign as India's most-followed Tweeter ended just short of the million mark when I was rapidly overtaken, first by Sachin Tendulkar, then Priyanka Chopra, Shah Rukh Khan and Amitabh Bachchan, who have all climbed far ahead in their Twitter fan-base.) But Twitter has a place in our public life too.

Just over five years ago, when I first went on Twitter, it was fashionable for Indian politicians to sneer at the use of social media. Every remark of mine was taken out of context in the press and blown up into a political controversy. The then BJP President, Venkaiah Naidu, even presciently warned me that 'too much tweeting can lead to quitting'. In September 2012, the *Economic Times* carried an article showing that, faced with such resistance, most young Indian politicians were not even active on any social networking site. Few ministers or members of Parliament even maintained any such account, and many of those accounts saw only sporadic—and uninteresting—updates. The journalist and poet Pritish Nandy, interviewed in that article, remarked that even he had more followers than the then prime minister, Manmohan Singh, on Twitter (he had 225,000 to Singh's 195,000 or so) at that time. Others interviewed in that article made it clear that they had no intention of adopting social media in the near future.

Yet the last two years have shown a dramatic acceleration in the pace at which the political world is embracing social media. There is, of course, the BJP's wholesale adoption of Twitter—Modi's allies in the space included Minister of External Affairs Sushma Swaraj, and a cohort of organized supporters, and now that he is prime minister, his entire Cabinet is rushing to emulate him. But other prominent Indian politicians of all parties have leapt in. Just a day after he was sworn in as India's president, Pranab Mukherjee announced that he would be opening a Facebook account to receive and respond to queries from the public. The chief minister of Bengal, Mamata Banerjee, runs a popular and widely read website that the media mines daily for new stories about her views. The youthful chief minister of Jammu and Kashmir, Omar Abdullah, regularly interacts on Twitter, and his much older Rajasthan and Kerala counterparts, Ashok Gehlot and Oommen Chandy, have opened accounts on Facebook as well. More than half the UPA's Council of Ministers went online, and the official number for the current Council is 100 per cent. Even the statistics-dispensing Planning Commission opened an account on social media under UPA, before it was summarily abolished by the NDA. The prime minister's Twitter account has more than quadrupled its following since Mr Modi's election, to nearly 3 million today, five times more than Mr Nandy. (Having followers doesn't mean they are all fans, friends or supporters—many follow you just out of curiosity, some just to attack you. But they are an audience.)

Political issues are being raised and debated regularly, and boisterously, in the social media space. The former finance minister spoke to the public about the Budget, not on TV, but in a Google Hangout. The Planning Commission, the minister for Road Transport and Highways and I have all emulated him. The BBC reported how even 12 per cent of India's population—which is the extent of our internet penetration today—is sufficient to make India the world's third largest internet market, and also the fastest growing for our size, estimated to overtake the USA (in number of persons online) by 2020.

As I discovered during my time in government, I could use Twitter to put out information the mainstream media was not interested in. While I was Minister of State for External Affairs, I used Twitter for India's 'public diplomacy'. My visit to Liberia, for example, was the first ministerial visit in thirty-eight years; my trip to Haiti in the aftermath of the earthquake there was the first Indian ministerial visit ever. Both were ignored here in India by the mainstream media, but through my updates and a couple of links I posted, India's Africa diplomacy and Haiti relief efforts got more widely known because of Twitter. In another example, a girl from my constituency who was amputated in both legs after a railway accident received offers of help from across the world in response to my tweets about her predicament.

I believe that during my ten months in government, I was able to use social media to demystify governance and sensitize people to the daily life of a minister. And after leaving office, I have been able to expand my conversation with politically-engaged people around the globe. Of course, I haven't shared any sensitive information from any political or government meetings on Twitter, but politicians all over the world are tweeting. President Obama has millions of followers on Twitter and Hillary Clinton was tweeting eight to ten times a day when she was on her official visit to India. The UK government encourages frequent use of Twitter and even issues guidelines on effective tweeting. Several current and recent foreign ministers—Bahrain's Khalid Al Khalifa, Norway's Jonas Store, Sweden's Carl Bildt and Australia's Kevin Rudd—tweet frequently, as does former British Foreign Secretary David Miliband and Canada's former Leader of the Opposition Michael Ignatieff. Most of the world's governments run official Twitter accounts.

At the same time it would be wise to be sceptical about the reach and political impact of social media in the Indian context. A 2013 study conducted by the IRIS Knowledge Foundation and the internet and Mobile Association of India (AIMAI) suggests that there are as many as 160 constituencies (out of 543 in India's popularly-elected lower house of Parliament) where the margin of victory is smaller than the number of constituents on social media, or where over 10 per cent of the population is on social media. It estimated that by the 2014 election, as many as 80 million Indians would be using social media, and asserts that this is now a vote-bank that no politician can afford to ignore.

My own view, as the first Indian politician in the social media space, is that this conclusion is somewhat premature. I do not believe, given the numbers, that any Indian election can be won or lost on social media alone. Only a small minority of India's 753 million voters use social media; with constituencies of some 2 million people each, Twitter is of little help in political mobilization. Unlike the US, for example, Twitter would be useless for organizing a mass rally or even convening a large public meeting. Social media cannot be a substitute for conventional campaigning. Yet, it can serve to help set the agenda, because the traditional media—newspapers and television, which do reach most voters—do tap into social media for information about and from politicians. The indirect impact of social media makes it an indispensable communications tool for politicians.

This will certainly become even more important when developments in internet availability on mobile telephones, and the advent of 4G services, make access to social media more universal. Though only 12 per cent of Indians use computers, more than 70 per cent have mobile phones, but very few currently find it easy or affordable to use them to access social media. Telecommunications experts say that revolution is only a few years away—and when it occurs, it will transform the nation's social media space, and politics as well, since a majority of voters will then be on the internet.

That is not yet, and probably not for the next one or two general elections. But in any case, no democratic politician should resist a new communications medium, particularly an interactive one—even if some seem to see it mainly as a public relations tool. Mr Modi's triumph has not noticeably been marred by widespread accusations of the BJP creating 'fake' accounts en masse to boost his follower count. Even doing so shows how Twitter has come to matter in India.

I feel some satisfaction that more and more politicians are online today, issuing messages and actually answering individual questions online. The advantages are clear: one acquires a new, young, literate and global audience for one's views and activities. By being accessible, we earn goodwill. By providing accurate and timely information and opinions, we eliminate the risks of misrepresentation or distortion of our position by others.

The pitfalls of using Twitter are the ever-present risk that something said on a social network could itself be taken out of context or misused by our critics. Responses to questions are particularly vulnerable to being issued in haste and without the usual careful vetting that more formal statements or articles undergo.

That is, of course, how I went wrong at first. When the government's austerity drive of 2009 was announced, a journalist asked me on Twitter, 'Mr Minister, will you travel cattle class?' And I replied, I thought wittily, 'Absolutely! In cattle class, in solidarity with all our holy cows.' The resulting controversy taught me that what you intend to say is less important than what people understand. Since both the questioner (Kanchan Gupta) who used the expression, and I, who repeated it in my response, know that 'cattle class' refers to the airlines' way of herding people in like cattle, rather than to the people themselves, I was bewildered to find myself excoriated as someone who had spoken disparagingly of ordinary people by equating them to cattle! That basic error—of using an expression that is commonplace around the world, but not understood in India—continues to haunt me. As Shakespeare knew, the success of a joke lies not in the tongue of the teller but in the ear of the listener.

It's important to realize that Twitter is only a vehicle—the message is the issue, not the medium. As an MP who through Twitter can reach more people than the largest mass rally can, I believe that what I am trying to do brings into my party's ambit a large number of people who would otherwise be indifferent to politics and the Congress. That's why, after all the criticism, so many leaders have taken to the medium. I just need to take care to ensure that the message is not misunderstood. The idea has always been to inform and engage, rather than to indulge in (misquotable) repartee.

Yes, being responsive on Twitter—though it adds to the sense of public accountability that is invaluable in a democracy—creates its own challenges. Sushma Swaraj has already blamed Twitter's 140-character limit for an imprecisely-worded message about the prime minister that created political ripples within the BJP. Of course, there is the safety net that politicians can always type, delete and retype before pressing enter—but Ms Swaraj reportedly dictates her Twitter messages, so perhaps that is more difficult for her!

There is the ever-present risk that something said on Twitter by a politician could itself be taken out of context or misused by our critics. Recently, well-wishers urged Jammu and Kashmir Chief Minister Omar Abdullah to delete a light-hearted remark that could have been maliciously distorted by his political enemies. He did so, with the curious result that the advice to delete can still be found on Twitter, but the potentially offending remark itself has disappeared!

Some bureaucrats have ventured into Twitter, with the best-known example probably being former Foreign Secretary Nirupama Rao. She in turn may well have been inspired by the success of the Ministry of External Affairs' Public Diplomacy Division, whose officials, with my active encouragement, set up a Twitter page and have been pursuing social media strategies, including a Facebook page and a YouTube channel, to let people know about what Indian diplomacy is up to. This has enabled them to promote India's 'soft power' by creating goodwill among social media users, whether in India or abroad.

But Twitter offers more than the seductive pleasures of gaining attention for your own views. Like other social media, Twitter can help you create knowledge networks, disseminate information and keep track of the world around you well beyond what is available in our daily newspapers. The links posted by people I follow on Twitter give me a wider range of information and insight than any single newspaper can. It also allows strangers to connect on a level playing field: for instance, I have made a number of connections to Pakistani opinion-makers through Twitter, a forum that doesn't belong to either of us but provides us a neutral platform to engage on issues. Yes, there are 'trolls' and other nasties to insult you periodically or badger you on issues that matter to them but not to you. Sometimes I indulge them and even respond mildly; sometimes, when their language becomes too offensive, I 'block' them from reaching me. A few rotten apples can't ruin the entire Twitter basket.

There are dull tweets, over-earnest tweets and repetitive ones. Most of the celebrities on Twitter use their accounts for self-promotion. Once you understand that, you can lightly skim over the less interesting tweets, because the rest might offer you great riches. Twitter has also proved enormously useful in recent humanitarian disasters in Haiti and Japan, helping alert authorities, deliver on-the-spot information and find missing people. And we know of the role it played in keeping Iranian protests alive after their disputed presidential election, and in helping organize the Cairo protestors who led Egypt's Jasmine Revolution.

There's something dangerously addictive, of course, about being able to reach so many people so easily and with such little effort (how long does it take you to type 140 characters?) And when you send your tweet out, you are inevitably curious about others' responses, which keeps you returning to your timeline again and again. So rationing one's Twitter time is essential, or it can take over your day.

The name Twitter initially put me off, and led Indian savants to suggest that it is not a suitable medium for a serious politician—but Google and Yahoo were also silly names that are now household terms. I am convinced that a majority of politicians in 21st century democracies—including India—will be tweeting within ten years from now. Those who are ahead of the curve are rarely appreciated, but we do have the consolation of knowing we got there first.

MY.GOV, YOUR GOV, E-GOV

As I have mentioned elsewhere in the book, e-Governance is a vital part of the answer to corruption, as well as to the challenges of efficiency, accountability and transparency in government. In less than three decades, a blink of an eye when compared to the glacial time spans favoured by Indian history, from when the late Prime Minister Rajiv Gandhi first articulated his vision to take India into the digital age to the present day, the rapid proliferation of information technology, cutting across the rich-poor, the rural-urban, and even the literate-illiterate divide, has had a profound impact on all walks of life. Fortunately, or unfortunately depending on your disposition, this digital revolution has also irrecoverably altered the ways in which the State engages with its citizens and is bound to alter the functioning of government agencies.

To cite three examples—India Post has enabled customers to track speed-posted letters till their destination from its website. The New Delhi police provides contact details for every senior officer, and the means to view an FIR and request a copy online. The Pune Municipal Corporation enables citizens to pay property taxes online. Technology has rendered the actions of the State transparent.

No longer can any agent of state authority—whether a bureaucrat or an elected representative—hide in the labyrinthine maze of secretive rules, records or procedures. The Right to Information Act and the widespread availability of government data, across both new and traditional mediums, have armed citizens with powerful tools to question the way government is conducted. No surprise, then, that today's informed and impatient citizenry demands an efficient service from the State.

Recognizing the potential of technology to promote the ideals of good governance, the Government of India, like many other governments worldwide, is increasingly moving towards digital governance. Though sometimes derided as jargon, terms like digital governance, e-government and e-Governance have passed into the official vocabulary, and have been embraced enthusiastically by both the new Modi regime as well as its predecessors.

The Government of India has in fact been committed longer than most to the use of digital governance to improve the overall quality of government services provided to the citizens as well as to improve its in-house practices and functioning. The push for deployment of IT to further the goals of good governance by the Government of India began as early as the mid-1980s, under the direction of then Prime Minister Rajiv Gandhi, who first decided to increase the pace of ICT use in the day to day business of governance. The National Informatics Centres Network (NICNET) connected district-level and rural-level government offices to government secretariats in the state capitals and was in turn connected to the national network in New Delhi. Enacted in 2000, the Information Technology (IT) Act provided legal recognition for digital signatures in order to catalyse e-commerce. These involve the use of alternatives to paper-based methods of communication and the storage of information in order to facilitate the electronic filing of documents with government agencies, including tax payments.

This policy was amended in the IT Policy (Amendment) Act of 2008 in which digital signatures are referred to as 'electronic signatures'. Since 1995, under the national e-governance plan, the Government of India has been steadily moving towards automating the provision of services across all government departments. One of the many pending draft bills that Opposition disruptions did not allow to pass—the Electronic Delivery of Services Bill, 2011—would have made such provision mandatory. I hope the Modi government will revive it.

It is heartening to see that e-Governance in India has steadily evolved from computerization of government departments to fragmented initiatives aimed at speeding up e-Governance implementation across the various arms of the government at the national, state, and local levels. These fragmented initiatives were unified into a common vision and strategy provided by the National e-Governance Plan (NeGP) in 2006. The NeGP takes a holistic view of e-Governance initiatives across the country, integrating them into a collective vision and a shared cause. This idea has been the organizing principle for the evolution of a massive countrywide infrastructure reaching down to the remotest of villages, and large-scale digitization of government records is taking place to enable easy, reliable access over the internet.

E-governance is now seen as a key element of the country's governance and administrative reform agenda. The NeGP has the potential to enable huge savings in costs through the sharing of core and support infrastructure, enabling interoperability through standards, and of presenting a seamless view of government to citizens. The ultimate objective is to bring public services closer to citizens, as articulated in the NeGP Vision Statement. We may be able to go as far as Finland, which recently made broadband internet access a fundamental right, but we certainly aim to take broadband to all our villages. The unstated side-benefit of such measures is likely to be a significant reduction in the petty corruption that is currently attendant upon the provision of the slightest government service.

As befits a federal system, progress on e-Governance varies widely across states. My own state of Kerala is already in the forefront of implementing various e-Governance government initiatives, some of which have been acknowledged internationally—I'm thinking particularly of Akshaya and Mgov. Coupled with high literacy, this state will have a higher uptake of e-services, which is the key success factor for any progress in e-Governance. It is striking, for instance, that the chief minister of Kerala is the only senior political or governmental leader anywhere in the world whose office and antechamber are visible 24/7 on the internet, via a permanent webcam. Thanks to him, Kerala is a trailblazer there, and it can be in other areas too.

The use of mobile technology is fast catching up everywhere and reaching almost everyone. This has created a truly mobile citizen, especially in a literate and mobile society like that of Kerala. This mobile technology could be leveraged to provide very basic services to citizens like ensuring the availability of rations at the nearby ration shop to providing exam results, facilitating the payment of electricity bills, updating the status of various applications, providing information on vaccinations or the prevalence of diseases, and so on. In agriculture, the government can provide weather information and commodity prices; it can facilitate more effective disaster management through everything from weather updates for fishermen, to delivering coast guard or coastal police alerts. The possibilities are immense.

These applications would be particularly relevant to the rest of India, especially if we can bypass the population's limited access to computers by providing fast, convenient and affordable access to internet services on mobile phones. I have no doubt that the future of electronic services delivery in India will be through mobile devices. With nearly a billion sim cards in operation and over 70 per cent of the population enjoying the use of mobile phones, e-Governance will not just be a reality—it will help bring about the kind of systemic change that can eliminate corruption, empower citizens and give greater profundity to the meaning of democracy than all our efforts in the pre-internet era.

The future is now.

THE NETWORK AGE

The Information Age is essentially an era driven by networks. In the physical realm it began of course with the laying of railway lines on land, and telegraph cables both overland and under the sea, in the 19th century. Then, with the coming of electricity, radio, flight, rocketry and finally computers and mobile telephones, the 20th century saw the complete saturation of our planet and its surrounding space by networks of unimaginable sophistication and complexity.

It never ceases to amaze me that today one is able to stand or sail in the most remote corners of the world and hold in one's hand a device capable of acquiring information from anywhere on the planet and giving access to nearly the entire sum of accumulated human knowledge. If he were around, William Blake would have managed a wry smile to see us hold infinity in our palm in this fashion. Such is the power and all pervasiveness of networks in our times. However, to harness the full potential of physical and electronic networks and convert the information they contain into practical wisdom and wealth requires one more crucial ingredient. That crucial capability is provided by human networks.

Today, the creation of wealth and knowledge, the basis of the enduring strength of nations and civilizations in our time, is essentially a collaborative activity. The solitary genius in the mould of a Newton or an Einstein is more or less extinct; at any rate he is now subject to peer review! The sheer breadth and complexity of our systems across the entire spectrum of human activity require the creation and sustenance of both formal and informal networks of authority and influence. Whether it is government or business, academics or professionals, whether it is the world of sports or the creative arts, networks have become extremely important, to serve as repositories of accumulated wisdom and as crucibles of opportunity.

Given this context, it is more important than ever before that our institutions of higher learning impart not just the core knowledge and skills that provide top-notch competency in a discipline or profession, but that they also provide the paradigm shift of perspective that enables our best and brightest to look beyond their narrow personal goals to appreciate the power and the beauty of human networks and their ability to provide solutions to the enduring and emerging challenges facing the human race. In fact I would go so far as to suggest that the capability to manage networks is the single most important quality of a successful manager. A great deal of what many famous achievers have accomplished has been due to the good fortune that their talents have found a supportive environment in the networks they inhabited. Networks multiplied their reach and influence beyond their own native talents.

But human networks don't create and sustain themselves. They require considerable investment of time, resources, and above all trust. Networks are proof that we are not merely creatures driven by selfish, Darwinian imperatives. The whole is indeed greater than the sum of its individual parts.

In spite of securing admission to the Indian Institutes of Management (IIM) at Ahmedabad and Kolkata, I never studied business management, preferring to go on to the study of international affairs in the US. Therefore, I have never been part of alumni associations of management schools that form the backbone of some of the most successful networks that operate today. However, the two alumni associations that I can lay claim to—St. Stephen's and the Fletcher School of Law and Diplomacy—have been enriching experiences. As a minister, I have been gratified to encounter many Stephanian contemporaries in the upper reaches of our bureaucracy. I remember meeting an alumnus from Fletcher after thirty years in a different country. Though we hadn't met in three decades, there was an instant connect. These alumni networks help connect with a diverse bunch of individuals, who may later be your mentors, friends or even colleagues.

The alumni association of a college also drives interaction between the current students, faculty and the alumni. Besides, the diverse and deep-rooted knowledge of the alumni can be leveraged to build the capabilities of the institution and so benefit the current students. For me it is an absolute pleasure interacting with the newer generation of students of my many alma maters. These interactions remind me that our lives can be lived not just as isolated islands, but as hives of creativity and vitality linked by networks. In the era of the World Wide Web, we are all connected, but some connections are closer than others—none closer than those of our alumni networks.

As a democracy we have moved well beyond the clubbish confines of the old boys' networks of such hallowed elite institutions as the Doon School and St. Stephen's College to broaden and deepen the representation of different segments of society in the bureaucracy, the judiciary and in governance. But they in turn have developed their own networks, the networks of the upwardly mobile. For ultimately, as Forster recognized, the human urge is to 'only connect'—with friends and comrades, but also with strangers and opposites. Thanks to the multiple means available to accomplish this today, ours is truly the Network Age.

VI

ISSUES OF CONTENTION

A HEART DIVIDED: AYODHYA

A 2010 High Court verdict revealed both the strengths and limitations of India as it grapples with its transformation from a land of religious conflict—symbolized by the Partition of 1947 that carved Pakistan out of its stooped shoulders—into a 21st century giant of the era of IT-enabled globalization.

In December 2010 the High Court of India's most populous state, Uttar Pradesh, finally decided a 61-year-old suit over possession of a disputed site in the temple town of Ayodhya. Ayodhya has no software labs; it is devoted to religion and old-fashioned industry. In 1992 a howling mob of Hindu extremists tore down a mosque, the Babri Masjid, which occupied a prominent spot in a town otherwise overflowing with temples. The mosque had been built in the 1520s by India's first Mughal emperor, Babur, on a site traditionally believed to have been the birthplace of the Hindu god-king Ram, the hero of the 3,000-year-old epic, the Ramayana. The Hindu zealots who destroyed the temple vowed to replace it with a temple to Ram. In other words, they wanted to avenge history by undoing the shame of half a millennium ago.

India is a land where history, myth and legend often overlap; sometimes Indians cannot tell the difference. Many Hindus claim the Babri Masjid stood on the exact spot of Ram's birth and had been placed there by Babur to remind a conquered people of their subjugation. Equally, many historians—most of them Hindus—reply that there is no proof that Ram ever existed in human form, let alone that he was born where the believers claim he was. More to the point, they argue, there is no proof that Babur demolished a Ram temple to build his mosque. To destroy the mosque and replace it with a temple, they averred, was not righting an old wrong but perpetrating a new one. The Archaeological Survey of India, however, reported the existence of ruins beneath the demolished mosque that might have belonged to an ancient temple. The dispute remained intractable, and dragged interminably through the judiciary.

To most Indian Muslims, the dispute is not about a specific mosque; the Babri Masjid had lain unused for half a century before its destruction, most of Ayodhya's Muslims having emigrated to Pakistan in 1947. Rather, it was about their place in Indian society. For decades after Independence, Indian governments had guaranteed their security in a secular state, permitting the retention of Muslim 'personal law' separate from the country's civil code and even subsidizing Haj pilgrimages to Mecca. Three of India's presidents have been Muslim, as have been innumerable cabinet ministers, ambassadors, generals and Supreme Court justices, not to mention cricket captains. Until at least the mid-1990s, when Pakistan's soaring birthrate won the race, India's Muslim population was greater than that of Pakistan. For many years, at the cusp of the new century, India's richest man (the IT czar, Azim Premji) was a Muslim. The destruction of the mosque felt like an utter betrayal of the compact that had sustained the Muslim community as a vital part of India's pluralist democracy.

On the other hand, the Hindus who attacked the mosque had little faith in the institutions of Indian democracy. They saw the state as soft, pandering to minorities out of a misplaced and westernized secularism. To them, an independent India, freed after nearly 1,000 years of alien rule (first Muslim, then British) and rid of a sizable portion of its Muslim population by Partition, had an obligation to assert an identity that would be triumphantly and indigenously that of the 82 per cent of the population who considered themselves Hindu.

These zealots are not fundamentalists in any common sense of the term, since Hinduism is a religion without fundamentals: there is no Hindu pope, no Hindu Sunday, no single Hindu holy book and indeed no such thing as a Hindu heresy. Hindu 'fundamentalists' are, instead, chauvinists, who root their Hinduism not in any of its soaring philosophical or spiritual underpinnings— and, unlike their Islamic counterparts, not in the theology of their faith—but in its role as a source of identity. They seek revenge in the name of Hinduism as badge, rather than of Hinduism as doctrine.

In doing so they are profoundly disloyal to the religion they claim to espouse, which stands out not only as an eclectic embodiment of tolerance but as the only major religion that does not claim to be the only true religion. All ways of worship, Hinduism asserts, are valid, and religion is an intensely personal matter related to the individual's self-realization in relation to God. Such a faith understands that belief is a matter of hearts and minds, not of bricks and stone. The true Hindu seeks no revenge upon history, for he understands that history is its own revenge.

The court judgment gave two-thirds of the disputed site to two Hindu organizations, and one-third to the Muslims. This suggested a solution that might permit the construction of both a mosque and a temple on the same site. It is an affirmation of Indian pluralism and at the same time of the rule of law. Interestingly enough, it recalls the arrangements described by European travelers and British administrators in the 18th and 19th centuries, who recorded both Hindus and Muslims worshipping at the disputed site.

But in May 2011, the judgment was stayed on appeal by the Supreme Court, which observed that the High Court had provided a solution that none of the parties to the dispute had sought. Since none had wished for the site to be partitioned, the Supreme Court decided, the status quo should continue.

The road to Paradise for both sets of believers has thus stumbled into the pothole of Purgatory. What the High Court had done was to craft a solution that no political process could have arrived at independently, but which takes the dispute off the streets. Otherwise the violence would go on, spawning new hostages to history, ensuring that future generations will be taught new wrongs to set right.

But the fact that with the Supreme Court's order, the issue is stuck in a judicial standoff, and not a communal riot, reminds the word that democratic India can overcome its most fundamental difficulties without violence or revolution. And in so doing, that it is ready to leave behind the problems of the 16th century as it takes its place in the 21st.

INDIA'S FREE AND IRRESPONSIBLE MEDIA

I am, in a sense, a child of the Indian newspaper. My late father, Chandran Tharoor, started in the newspaper business when barely out of college, representing a pair of Indian papers in post-war London, and spent his working life as a senior advertising executive for some of our country's better-known mastheads. His world fascinated me. My childhood in the 1960s and early 1970s was replete with stories of editorial meetings and battles between the editorial and the advertisement departments, for my father injected newspaper ink into my veins at a young age. I grew up literally with newspapers: from about six or seven years of age, I can remember sitting with my father at 6.30 every morning with chai and multiple newspapers. In addition to the news, he always read the ads, counting the column inches of advertising in his own and the rival newspapers—usually (since he was very good at his job) with a grunt of satisfaction.

My father used to work for the *Statesman*, then a superb newspaper (and again trying to be one). I remember going to the press as a young boy and seeing the linotype machine men at work with their little fonts that had been carved out of very hot metal, putting together words whose idiosyncratic spellings often revealed that they had not had an English language education. (That's why copy editors were indispensable)! I recall handling flongs, the exotic papier-mâché stereotype moulds used in the days before offset printing. Those were the days when you could turn up in some small town and find yesterday's news with today's date on it, in what the newspaper called a 'dak edition'.

Growing up in Bombay and Calcutta, I enjoyed three or four newspapers in the morning; then during the day, the papers from the rest of the country would be flown in, and my father brought them home after work, when I would have a second round of newsprint to digest. So I grew up reading a minimum of seven or eight newspapers a day. (This was not as onerous a task as it might seem, since in those days the big newspapers were just twelve pages long, and some, in bad times of newsprint shortages, carried only eight.) When, at the age of 10, I first published a short story, it was not in a fiction magazine, but in a newspaper, the *Bharat Jyoti*—the Sunday edition of Bombay's venerable *Free Press Journal*. That daily ritual of tea and newspapers gave me an early and abiding passion for the Indian press, one which I have sustained during three decades abroad, when I would have Indian newspapers sent to me in places like Geneva, Singapore and New York.

Those were more innocent times, when no one expected to find sex scandals in the daily news, and editors always knew far more than they shared with their readers. But those were also days when the papers were filled with dull accounts of worthy events, and the front pages regurgitated ministers' speeches with little context, explanation or analysis. There was no real engagement with the substance of what politics means to the Indian people. Investigative journalism was unknown and revelations about errant conduct on the part of our elected officials would only appear if they had first been unearthed by the government.

Obviously newspapers have come a very long way since the days in which I grew up with them. Technology is the most obvious change: today, almost everything is done on computers. No one knows what compositors are any more. Journalists do their own proofreading. Presentation and layout have also dramatically improved. With colour, with newspapers so attractively designed and presented, with lifestyle supplements and multiple sections, anyone who remembers those days knows we are looking at a different product being sold in a different environment.

The economics have also changed: newsprint is more affordable. A twelve-page paper would be considered a joke; multiple sections are now de rigeur. Circulations have shot up along with literacy and disposable incomes, so that the *Times of India* today can call itself the world's most widely-read English-language broadsheet, and Hindi newspapers boast readership numbers that would exceed the wildest fantasies of any editor in the world outside Japan. This is happening when newspapers in the developed West are falling by the wayside, unable to resist the challenge of the internet. Our *Times* is read by some 7.6 million people daily, while the best-selling American paper, *USA Today*, has 2.5 million readers. According to the Indian Readership survey 2014, *Dainik Jagran*, in Hindi, had 16.37 million readers.

But along with this have come other, more substantive, changes, both good and bad. On the positive side, our newspapers are more readable, better edited, better laid out and usually better-written than they were. Investigative stories are frequent and occasionally expose wrongdoing before any official institution does so. The role of newspapers in rousing the social conscience of the Indian public about apparent miscarriages of justice, most notably in the Jessica Lall, Ruchika Girhotra and 'Nirbhaya' cases, has been remarkable.

On the negative side, every newspaper looks at the news less objectively, with a clearly visible slant on the events it is reporting. Newspapers seem more conscious than ever that they have to compete in a tight media environment where it is not they, but TV, that sets the pace. Television news in India, with far too many channels competing 24/7 for the same sets of eyeballs, has long since given up any pretence of providing a public service, with the 'breaking news' story privileging sensation over substance. (Indian TV epitomises the old saw about why television is called a 'medium': 'Because it is neither rare nor well done.')

So newspapers find themselves led by the nose by TV's perennial ratings war. They too feel the need to 'break' news in order to be read, to outdo their TV competitors. They seem to perceive a need to reach readers each day with a banner headline that stimulates outrage rather than increases awareness.

The result has been, to put it mildly, disturbing. Our media, in its rush to air the story, has fallen prey to the inevitable rush to judgement: it has too often become a willing accomplice of the motivated leak and the malicious allegation, which journalists today have neither the time nor the inclination to check or verify. The damage is done in a blaze of lurid headlines—and rectification, if it comes at all, comes too feebly and too late to undo the irreparable damage to innocent people's reputations. The distinctions amongst fact, opinion and speculation that are drummed into journalism students' heads the world over has blurred into irrelevance in today's Indian media.

The cavalier attitude to facts is compounded by a reluctance to issue corrections; my own attempts at correcting blatant falsehoods relating to me in print have been ignored to the point that I have stopped trying. So in 2010 the *Indian Express*, for instance, reported a wholly fictitious 'protocol problem' involving my supposedly having attended the Padma Awards at Rashtrapati Bhavan with a woman who was not (yet) my wife—when the plain, verifiable, fact is that I have never attended a Padma Award ceremony in my life, accompanied or alone! My attempts to point this out, both privately and publicly, got nowhere with the *Express*, which combines excellence in some kinds of investigative journalism (the Dubey murder over national highway funds is a fine example) with a talent for creating blazing stories out of trivia (as with their the banner headlines in 2009 'revealing' that External Affairs Minister S.M. Krishna and I were staying, at our own expense, in five-star hotels, a fact neither of us had hidden and which could have been ascertained from our officially-listed temporary addresses on various government websites).

Part of the problem is a genuine disinclination to take the trouble to research a story, and a disregard for the need to verify it. To take a few examples from 2010, when I was a particularly favoured victim of the practice: *Outlook* ran an appalling piece on my then wife-to-be, Sunanda, in which every second statement was provably false or inaccurate, without consulting either her or her friends about their veracity. (To the magazine's credit, it also ran a flood of letters pillorying it for the piece.) The *Times of India* got taken in by one of the many fake Facebook accounts purporting to be Sunanda's (she was not on any social-networking site at the time) and ran an entire article quoting her supposed views, without ever checking as to whether the accounts was genuine. *Mid-Day* placed words and sentiments in the mouth of one of my sons at my wedding that he would never have thought and did not utter. It also encouraged a doctor to break his Hippocratic oath by revealing not just details but photographs of surgery he had performed on Sunanda after an accident years earlier. Perhaps it is our country's weak libel protections that lead publications to feel they can print anything with complete disregard for character assassination. But it is a sad commentary on how low our print standards have fallen that the very notion of what is 'fit to print' has ceased to have any meaning in India today (and in *India Today* as well, but that's another matter). I have had to endure worse in 2014, after the tragic death of my wife, but will restrain myself from commenting on an ongoing situation.

A friend summarized the problem succinctly for me: 'When I was young, my father wouldn't believe anything unless it was printed in the *Times of India*. Now, he doesn't believe anything *if* it is printed in the *Times of India*.'

As one who has been treated to repeated doses of speculation, gossip, accusation and worse in the course of 2014, I have been made intimately conscious of these limitations of the Indian media. Instead of the restraint and caution one might expect from a responsible press where matters of life and death are involved (and accusations of murder and suicide are flung around with abandon), we have had the spectacle of an unnaturally long-drawn-out media trial, punctuated by frequent eruptions based on motivated leaks, with a meddling politician trying to orchestrate conspiracy theories that are eagerly lapped up by the voyeuristic Indian TV channels, and almost zero probing or even elementary research behind any of the statements aired. Manipulated and malicious leaks were reported uncritically by the media, especially television, without asking even the most basic questions about their plausibility. Sadly, it was not much better in the print media, which—with its ability to provide context, depth and analysis that television cannot—could have compensated for the limitations of television as a medium.

This should be a matter of serious concern to all right-thinking Indians, because free media are the lifeblood of our democracy. They provide the information that enables a free citizenry to make the choices of who governs them and how, and ensures that those who govern will remain accountable to those who put them there. It is the media's job to look critically at elected officials' actions (or inaction), rather than at marginalia that have no impact on the public welfare. Instead, the media's obsession with the superficial and the sensational trivializes public discourse, abdicates the watchdog responsibility that must be exercised by free media in a democracy, and distracts the public from the real questions of accountability with which the governed must confront the government.

The free press is both the mortar that binds together the bricks of our country's freedom, and the open window embedded in those bricks. No Indian leader would go as far as Thomas Jefferson, who said that given a choice between government without newspapers and newspapers without government, he would choose the latter. But government needs newspapers to keep it honest and efficient, to serve as both mirror and scalpel. If instead all we have is a blunt axe, society is not well served.

If India wishes to be taken seriously by the rest of the world as a responsible global player and a model 21st-century democracy, we will have to take ourselves seriously and responsibly as well. Our media would be a good place to start.

THE UNWELCOME MAT

The roots of India's pluralism and warm welcome to foreign cultures run deep. With our inimitable confluence of breathtaking vistas, delectable cuisine, and cultural experiences to whet the heart and soul of the most intrepid and varied traveller, India is often truly 'incredible' in every sense of the word.

India benefits from the future and the past from the international appeal of its traditional practices (from Ayurveda to yoga, both accelerating in popularity across the globe) and the transformed image of the country created by its thriving diaspora. Our rich history, unique blend of cultural diversity, traditional wisdom, and natural beauty is an undeniable draw, not only for non-Indians, but also our thriving diaspora, and many foreign citizens of Indian origin with roots originating in our country.

It is a source of immense pride that, over millennia, our civilization has offered refuge, and more significantly religious and cultural freedom to Jews, Parsis, as well as, different denominations of Christianity and Islam. Chinese scholars, notably Hsuan-Tsang and Fa-Hsien, travelled to study at teach at our ancient universities. The Italian adventurer Marco Polo, the Moroccan-Turkish scribe Ibn Battuta, the Chinese Admiral Zheng He and the French priest Abbe Dubois all visited and wrote vivid accounts of the India they saw—which we might never had enjoyed had the India of their times adopted the kind of visa policies we do today.

Ironically, 21st-century India is one of the world's largest economies, a proud player on the global stage with a long record of responsible conduct on international matters. The country has been attracting tremendous interest from foreign investors with India home to the target consumer not only for multi-national corporate companies, but also foreign governments, and sovereign funds through bilateral cooperation in energy, infrastructure, and even education.

The world is well and truly watching India, and is eager to engage constructively with us. However, our visa system—in both concept and practice, from regulation to application—ensures we continue keep the world at an arm's length. If soft power is about making your country attractive to others, the Indian bureaucracy seems determined to do everything in its power to achieve the opposite effect, in the way in which it treats foreigners wishing to travel to or reside in India.

Visa processes, viewed as time-consuming, unnecessarily demanding, and expensive, became far more cumbersome as a result of the government's reaction to 26/11. For instance, a rule imposed in 2009 restricted travellers on tourist visas to return to India for a period of at least two months after a previous visit. The rationale for this rule was to prevent a future David Coleman

Headley, whose frequent trips to India (interspersed with trips to Pakistan) laid the groundwork for the heinous attack in Mumbai. As usual, the reaction was misplaced and targeted the wrong people. While Headley travelled on a business visa, and not a tourist visa, the terrorists of 26/11 applied for no visas at all. Restricting visas is not an answer to terrorism.

The initial application of the rule also made victims of a wide range of legitimate travellers. Some examples include tourists who wished to make India their base for journeys across the subcontinent; a man who had visited India to visit his gravely ailing mother but was not allowed to re-enter to attend her funeral because two months has not elapsed since his previous visit; a couple that left their luggage in Mumbai while making an overnight visit to Sri Lanka were not allowed to come back to reclaim their belongings; and an NRI who had come to India to get engaged was not permitted to return for his own wedding!

These might have been extreme cases, but our general policy approach is no better. We make it difficult, time-consuming and procedurally irritating to travel to India. We don't allow foreigners to work easily in our country unless they earn a much higher salary than most Indians, and we make it impossible for their spouses to get work permits. When they get here we put them through the nightmarish experience of dealing with the Foreigners' Registration Office (FRRO), which ranks easily amongst our least-known and most-resented government institutions.

A recent example that I have been made aware of is that of a young American development worker with expertise in civil engineering and road reconstruction. Having entered India with the objective of working on development projects, it took her numerous visits and wasted hours to register her arrival. On each occasion she was turned back with instructions to add new supporting documents or replace existing ones. Our system needlessly imposed a long and harrowing process that could have been avoided entirely by the official looking at all her documents in one go and advising necessary changes. Over three successive days spent at the office, she drew solace from the wry observation that she wasn't the only repeat customer. The FRRO has acquired a reputation amongst foreigners in India as a cross between Purgatory and Hades—hardly the right image for a nation that ought to treat others as we would wish our own diaspora to be treated.

The irony becomes stark when ask yourself the question: what does it mean to be a young person in urban India today? It can mean waking up to an alarm clock made in China, downing a cup of tea from leaves first planted by the British, donning jeans designed in America and taking a Japanese scooter or Korean car to get to an Indian college, where textbooks might be printed with German-invented technology on paper first pulped in Sweden.

The young Indian student might call his friend on a Finnish mobile phone to invite them to an Italian pizza while passionately following the fortunes of their favourite English football club! And yet we remain suspicious of foreigners and not gracious in extending a safe welcome to them.

With a frankly tiresome, inconvenient, and unimaginatively-applied system of rules, India's visa bureaucracy succeeds in sending out the message that 'winning friends and influencing people' is not a part of its ethos. As a result the potential of sectors that are impacted by our visa policy remains untapped. One such example is the tourism sector, which has a lot of ground to cover. This is only reaffirmed by the fact that in 2012, around 6.6 million foreign tourists visited India, whereas the top tourist destination in the world, France, with a population and size a fraction of ours, attracted around 83 million!

Though some halting progress was made in the past by extending visa-on-arrival facilities to a handful of foreign nationalities, even these were available at a few selected airports, so tourists had to arrive at the right airport to avoid being turned back! Recognizing this gap, the UPA government has potentially given a massive boost to the country's tourism sector by extending 'visa on arrival' scheme to visitors from 180 countries at a larger list of airports—the first sign that our attitudes might be changing. How it works in practice, however, remains to be seen.

The importance of travel that deepens meaningful cultural exchange, appreciation of other traditions, and humanism should not be underestimated. From time immemorial the accounts of travellers and scholars have been instrumental in bringing civilizations closer together. One might argue that the advent of the Internet Age with digital technology and social media has accelerated the exchange of ideas (or even the clash of civilizations!). However, the virtual cannot replace the experience of living and breathing the vitality of a distant land. In this light, academic exchange that allows scholars and intellectuals access to our country is also imperative.

Despite India's democratic traditions of a free press, scholars and journalists wishing to write about India have to face several unreasonable hurdles to secure a visa. Getting into the country becomes an even bigger challenge, even to those academics and reporters who are deemed to be insufficiently friendly to India. Expressing criticisms of India in the past, irrespective of the merits of the argument, can lead to being placed on a negative list and even to denial of a visa. This is deeply disappointing in a democracy; worse, the intention to avoid negative views about India appearing abroad, results in precisely that.

A manifestation of this inability to accept a different point of view and defend the freedom of expression has also entered civil society in India. The recent withdrawal of a book by an American Indologist under relentless pressure by self-appointed guardians of the Hindu faith, many of whom haven't even read the book, is one such example. Whether or not the criticisms of her work of scholarship are justified is not the point; it is the denial of the right to have an opinion that is detrimental to India's image. While India, always fiercely independent, has no obligation to pay obeisance to academics of any country, this refusal to engage intellectually with an argument, and reluctance to allow physical entry of those with possibly inconvenient views, is detrimental to the goodwill the country engenders as a democracy.

To allow any self-appointed arbiters of Indian culture to impose their hypocrisy and double standards on the rest of us is to permit them to define Indianness down until it ceases to be Indian. To wield soft power, India must defend, assert and promote its culture of openness against the forces of intolerance inside and outside the country. The alienation and antagonism this generates among people, who, for the most part, start off being generously well disposed to India is considerable, and entirely unnecessary.

It is also important to acknowledge this from the perspective of the economy. In recent years, India has suffered, like most developing countries, from declining foreign investment, poor export performance, and a depreciating currency. The government's decision to permit foreign direct investment in multi-brand retail and civil aviation pursued even at the cost of losing a recalcitrant coalition ally, are examples of signals that encourage business engagement that is useful. Yet, business is done with people, and if we are unwelcoming before they step onto our shores, it will only be to our detriment.

At the level of the individual, idealistic young teachers, as well as writers or even business executives looking for early work experience in a prominent emerging market (which they can get in China) are being denied work permits here because their salaries aren't high enough to meet the Home Ministry's arbitrary standards. If they are willing to live on Indian salaries to get to know our country and make a contribution here, why on earth do we deny them?

The impact of our visa policies is not limited to foreigners entering India for business or travel. The reciprocal nature of visa arrangements means the more restrictive we become, the tougher it will be for Indians to travel or work freely abroad. When, on an official visit to Colombia, I was urged by Indian companies to ask for more generous work permits to Indian business executives in that country, it was pointed out to me that Colombia's seemingly unreasonable restrictions on such visas for Indians were still about ten times more generous than the rules India applied for Colombian citizens in identical circumstances.

This critique is not aimed at any specific government. The policies and attitudes I have criticized here have been followed by every government since Independence, of all political hues; they are reflection of the system and not of specific political choices by one party or another. Our bureaucracy, as custodians of our national 'unwelcome mat', has far more to answer than the political ministry of the day. It will take nothing less than a national consensus within our society to make the changes I am advocating here.

India's ability to promote and leverage its soft power in the world will receive a major boost only if and when the country's visa policies are thoroughly re-examined and revised. Only then can Incredible India become a Credible India in the eyes of the world.

PRESERVING ASYLUM IN INDIA

Today the world has over 4 million refugees, and with conflict raging in different parts of the world, the numbers are only increasing. But as the numbers rise, we also run the risk of treating these people as figures in a statistical compilation, and not human beings with needs, fears, hopes and wants. And that is what they are: human beings whose suffering today could mar their tomorrow, unless the world does its share to help them overcome their suffering. World Refugee Day, commemorated every year in India, is an occasion to think of all these families, uprooted and torn; all those homes that have been destroyed; and all those futures jeopardized. But it is also an occasion to think of safe havens granted, asylum ensured, refugees protected, solutions found. It is a day of remembrance, but also of affirmation; a day to recall the pain of loss, but also to nurture the hope of a new life.

India is actually a good country in which to celebrate this special day. After all, history is on our side. India has traditionally welcomed all those who have knocked on its doors seeking refuge and asylum. India's is a civilization that, over millennia, has offered refuge and, more importantly, religious and cultural freedom, to Jews, Parsis, several varieties of Christians, and of course Muslims. Jews came to Kerala centuries before Christ, with the destruction by the Babylonians of their First Temple, and were again given refuge in the 1st century AD when they fled Roman persecution. They settled on the Kerala coast, enjoying a high status in society, and knew no persecution in India until the Portuguese arrived in the 16th century to inflict it. Christianity arrived on Indian soil with St Thomas the Apostle (Doubting Thomas), who came to the Kerala coast some time before AD 52 and was welcomed on shore by a flute-playing Jewish girl. He made many converts, so there are Indians today whose ancestors were Christian well before any Europeans discovered Christianity. Before Cleopatra killed herself, even that great queen thought of sending her son to the safety of India's west coast! Of course, the boy made the mistake of turning back midway to stake his claim to the throne, and met with an untimely and gory end, but that's another story.

The Zoroastrians, fleeing Muslim persecution in Persia in the 10th century, found refuge and a welcome in Gujarat. There is a marvellous story of how asylum was negotiated: the local king, alarmed by the arrival of a shipload of refugees, sent an envoy to tell them there was no room for them. Since they had no language in common, he called for a tumbler full of water and dropped a stone in it; the water overflowed, just as his country would, he argued, if the newcomers were granted asylum. The Zoroastrian captain was not deterred. He called for a glass of milk, and gently stirred a spoonful of sugar into it. Thus, he suggested, would the refugees blend in with their new society, adding sweetness to it without causing any disturbance. So impressed was the king when the envoy told him this story that asylum was promptly granted, and the Parsis, as the Zoroastrians are known in India, have remained successful pillars of Indian society ever since.

But indeed, such traditions of hospitality extend far in our history. In Kerala, where Islam came through traders, travellers and missionaries rather than by the sword, they were embraced rather than rejected: the Zamorin of Calicut was so impressed by the seafaring skills of this community that he issued a decree obliging each fisherman's family in his kingdom to bring up one son as a Muslim to man his all-Muslim navy!

This is India, a land whose heritage of diversity means that in the Calcutta neighbourhood where I lived during my high school years, the wail of the muezzin calling the Islamic faithful to prayer routinely blends with the chant of mantras and the tinkling of bells at the local Shiva temple, accompanied by the Sikh gurdwara's reading of verses from the Guru Granth Sahib, with St Paul's cathedral and the Parsi Anjuman just round the corner.

Similarly, in the city I now represent in Parliament, Thiruvananthapuram, St Jospeh's Cathedral stands diagonally opposite from the Palayam Mosque, both a stone's throw from the famous old Ganapathi temple in the same neighbourhood. It is quite deeply embedded in the Indian psyche that nobody should ever have to face the predicament of being driven out of their home. Our great epics, the Ramayana and the Mahabharata, both, at great length, dwell upon the injustice of the protagonists being forced into exile. And the fact that one of our most popular festivals, Diwali, celebrates a homecoming, demonstrates fully how important the concept of home and the homeland is to an Indian.

Exiles, asylum seekers, and refugees are not, therefore, new to India. Our recent history is a testimony to this, for the birth of our modern nation was accompanied by one of the greatest and bloodiest refugee crises in the world. When Pakistan was hacked off the stooped shoulders of India in the Partition of 1947, between 13 and 15 million people are estimated to have crossed the freshly created borders. Homes were left behind, familiar landmarks, cherished assumptions and friendships; all was lost except their religious identities. Most of these millions who found refuge in India had only the future to look forward to. All they had was hope, and it is from there that the nation picked up. Today's New Delhi, the capital of the republic of India, was itself in many ways a city transformed by these refugees. To this day their memories of loss linger and shape their minds. But with loss came a determination to rebuild, to prevail, to triumph. And so they did.

Indeed, at that point in history, many parts of the world faced the issue of refugees, with the Second World War triggering mass exoduses in Europe, and a number of former colonies finding themselves in circumstances similar to India's. And it was at that time that my old organization, United Nations High Commissioner for Refugees (UNHCR), came into existence. India, for reasons more to do with its colonial past and its non-aligned desire not to take sides in the Cold War, did not sign the 1951 Refugee Convention or the 1967 Protocol, which were seen as catering principally to refugees fleeing communism. But in spirit we stood by the UNHCR, and welcomed its involvement in coping with the largest single refugee movement in human history, when 10 million people fled East Pakistan (today Bangladesh) to seek refuge in India. India remains proud of having done more for the refugees itself, through the use of taxpayer funds and such imaginative measures as an additional postage stamp for refugee relief, than the international community did, but we co-operated closely with the UN then and later, when the bulk of the refugees were repatriated to their homeland. And to this day the relationship survives healthily.

When I use the word 'refugee', of course, I do so in the internationally-accepted definition of the term, which embraces people who have fled their home countries and crossed an international border because of a well-founded fear of persecution in their home countries, on grounds of race, religion, nationality, membership of a particular social group, or political opinion. This means that people who cross borders in quest of economic betterment, or because they are fleeing poverty, anarchy or environmental disaster, do not qualify as refugees. Nor do those who flee from one part of their home country to another because of war, conflict or fear of persecution. When it was announced that I was to deliver the World Refugee Day lecture in 2012, for instance, I received over a hundred messages on Twitter, urging me to speak about the Kashmiri Pandits, the community to which my wife belonged, who were terrorized into fleeing their homes in the Kashmir Valley in 1989 and who sought refuge in Jammu and other parts of India. Though my father-in-law was present at my speech and no doubt would have been able to speak more eloquently of the plight of the Kashmiri Pandits than I could, the fact is that they would be considered internally displaced people (IDP), not refugees, since throughout their travails they continue to enjoy the protection of the Indian State.

The Kashmiri Pandit diaspora, estimated at 2.5 lakh, constitutes India's second largest IDP group. My own wife's family is amongst them; their ancestral home was burned down in 1989-90 by terrorists. (My late wife and I visited the ruins one weekend, under armed protection; nothing remains but memories.) They were amongst those fortunate enough to find new homes and lives in Jammu, but many tens of thousands still languish in camps that were meant to be temporary but within which an entire generation has grown up.

Some 59,000 Kashmiri Pandits are estimated to have moved outside the state—indeed the Home Ministry estimates there are only 808 Kashmiri Pandit families left living in the Kashmir Valley. The homes and temples of many of the rest have been destroyed so that they have nothing to come back to. This is a curious case of a community belonging to what is called the national majority but which finds itself a minority in one part of the country—and suffers the disabilities of vulnerability that can imply.

The violence that periodically erupts in our country has resulted in this tragic phenomenon of internal displacement. Unlike refugees, 'internally displaced people' have not crossed an international border and thus still live in, and are the responsibility of, the country to which they belong. We are, as a result of riots and targeted violence, home to the world's eleventh largest population of IDPs.

There are a variety of factors which cause internal displacement: armed conflict between the State (government) and non-State actors (armed militant groups); natural disasters such as a cyclone, a flood or an earthquake; and violence between ethnic groups and religious minorities, often due to contention over issues such as land rights and mineral resources. Fleeing such problems, IDPs are forced out of their homes fearing for their lives.

While this phenomenon is common in conflict-racked societies and civil war situations, it shames us as a prospering democracy that we have so many IDPs. Of the twelve nations which have suffered the forced migration of a million or more people within their countries, only two are classified as 'stable' countries—India and Turkey.

Though numbers are not entirely reliable, we have some from the IDP database created by the Norwegian Refugee Council (NRC), which tracks IDPs around the world on behalf of the UN. With about 5 lakh IDPs, India's Northeast has witnessed the biggest exodus of people who were forced to leave their homes. In recent years we have witnessed a number of examples. In 2010 along the Assam-Meghalaya frontier, 4,000 Nepali-speaking people were displaced by violent clashes in which their community was targeted by members of the Khasi tribe; in 2011, at least 50,000 people lost their homes after inter-tribal clashes between the Rabha and Garo people in Assam and Meghalaya; and over the years the violence between Bodos and Muslims has driven lakhs into camps and shelters.

There are other cases. The communal carnage in Gujarat in 2002 displaced a lakh and a half within the state. Some of that displacement seems likely to be permanent, as people of a particular community hesitate to return to mixed areas where they were once victimized. Naxalite violence, sometimes linked to clashes over land and tribal rights but quite often simple banditry, and the subsequent government operations against the insurgents, have also caused the forced displacement of about 1.5 lakh people in Andhra Pradesh, West Bengal and Chhattisgarh. Communal riots in Orissa in 2007 and 2008 forced thousands to leave their homes. Many of these IDPs have been obliged to take shelter in camps, particularly in the Northeast where some camps go back as far as the Nellie massacre of Bangladeshi migrants in the 1980s.

But many internally displaced people live outside camps too, and it is all but impossible to estimate exactly how many of them there are. The fact is that at least a million of our countrymen and women are displaced inside our country. Some of the clashes that caused their displacement have pitched two minorities against each other (two different tribes, for instance); sometimes it is two different kinds of minorities—a religious minority against a visible ethnic minority, as happened in Khokrajhar, in Assam.

In the summer of 2012 we saw panic-stricken Northeasterners fleeing a number of Indian cities where they had been living and working because of alleged threats of reprisal attacks on them retaliating for the anti-Muslim violence in Assam. Whether the threats were real or fake—designed merely to intimidate and cause fear—there is no doubt that they had an effect on many thousands of people. Special trains had to be laid on from Bangalore to accommodate the demand. Some of those who fled started coming back as things quietened down, but their temporary displacement raises hard questions about what it means to be a certain kind of Indian in India. Northeasterners have often complained of discrimination and harassment based purely on their visible difference from the people they are living amongst. Such incidents are a betrayal of the acceptance of difference that lies at the heart of Indian civilization.

There is a great deal we can do as a society and a State. Clearly protection for vulnerable minority groups must be a priority for local, state and central governments. This may require a national policy, though the lack of any legislation on IDPs remains a serious shortcoming. The world community has issued Guiding Principles on Internal Displacement which could go into the framing of a suitable law. The Kenyan government introduced an Internally Displaced Persons Bill, 2012, to alleviate the suffering of IDPs in that country, provide legal definitions, and allocate responsibilities to the government and funds for the purpose. India could do something similar.

We also need to evolve a policy on IDPs aiming to get them out of camps and into productive, normal lives either in their new environment or back home if the circumstances that prompted their displacement have changed. Displaced people must be specifically targeted by pro-poor schemes such as the Public Distribution System (PDS), the National Rural Health Mission (NRHM), the Mahatma Gandhi National Rural Employment Guarantee

Scheme (MGNREGS) and the Total Sanitation Campaign (TSC).

To implement these better and to appreciate fully the dimensions of the problem, we need better data on IDPs. The statistics for IDPs living outside of camps are mostly unreliable. This data needs to be updated regularly and the situation of IDPs monitored through frequent field surveys. Let's go farther and create a central government monitoring agency for IDPs. It's time we tackled this human problem head-on.

Still, in addressing the challenges of India's refugee policy, one must focus on those who seek asylum in our country from foreign lands.

I am aware that UNHCR is very satisfied with the Government of India's policy towards refugees. As an Indian and a former UNHCR official, I am conscious that, formally, the Government of India has still not signed up to the international refugee instruments. However, the practice of the government has been exemplary, and many in the international humanitarian community consider India's conduct to be a model. Part of the reason for India's reluctance to sign the Refugee Convention and Protocol is that we take our international obligations very seriously and do not undertake legal commitments that we are not 100 per cent certain about our ability to fulfil. In many countries the opposite is the case: a lot of commitments are made on paper but are not in fact implemented in practice. So India is indeed doing much better in reality than many countries that have actually ratified these conventions. It is rather the obverse of the old laws against homosexuality, which existed on paper but were never applied in practice, so that homosexuals were able to live freely and openly in India, organize associations and publish newsletters and so on, well before the Delhi High Court found the laws themselves to be unconstitutional and struck them down in 2010 (only to be reversed by the Supreme Court in 2013). The gulf between the legal position and the reality has always been a large one in India, and this remains true in relation to refugees as well.

And yet, as an old-fashioned liberal myself, it troubles me that a country with our proud traditions and our noble practices remains legally neither committed nor obliged to do anything for refugees, even if we behave humanely in practice. I think it is high time the government reviewed its long-standing reluctance to sign up legally to what it is already doing morally. The convention and the protocol involve no obligations that we have not already undertaken voluntarily; to refuse to sign them out of an anxiety not to be 'bound' to the wishes of the international community is unworthy of a major country like India that is increasingly moving from being a subject of the international system, a rule-taker as it were, to a rule-maker within it. Our judiciary has already shown the way forward on this: in 1996 the Supreme Court ruled that the State has to protect all human beings living in India, irrespective of nationality.

India is today home to over 200,000 refugees, mainly from Sri Lanka, Myanmar, and Tibet, but also including people from Afghanistan, Iraq, Somalia, Eritrea, Ethiopia, Sudan, Congo, and even Palestine. Most of these refugees are assisted directly by the Government of India, and the UNHCR report for 2011 states that our nation's policy is 'liberal and tolerant'. The organization, for its part, mainly focuses on the urban refugees in New Delhi and the Sri Lankans in Chennai. Altogether about 22,000 of the total number of foreigners seeking refuge or asylum in India fall under its purview.

There are classically three solutions to the plight of refugees: voluntary repatriation home, when the circumstances that prompted them to flee have changed, such as happened to the bulk of the Bangladeshi refugees in 1972; local integration in the country of asylum, of which the best example in India is the Tibetan refugees; and resettlement in a third country, an option that has been used for a modest and (rightly) little-publicized handful of cases, including some Pakistanis and the few Vietnamese boat-people who were rescued by Indian ships and reached our shores in the 1970s and 1980s. Pending one of these three solutions, the host country must provide asylum to the refugees, very often for a lengthy period of time, affording them protection from refoulement, or deportation to their country of origin, legal rights and the opportunity to lead decent lives until a durable solution for their situation can be found.

One of the most lauded efforts of the Government of India has been in the treatment of the Tibetan refugees here. For over fifty years India has supported what is now over 1 lakh people, granting them vast areas of land to build settlements, access to education and livelihood, and much more. As the Tibetan Government in Exile's Secretary for Information says, they enjoy equal rights with Indian nationals, with the exception of the vote. And this is in spite of the diplomatic and political difficulties this causes to the Indian authorities in the conduct of its relations with China. So too are Sri Lankan refugees allowed to make India a second home, so that till they can return, they are not prevented from living their lives fully and with meaning, including engaging in productive employment. In a sense, the treatment of these refugees here has set the bar high and the aim should be to secure such a place and position for all refugees everywhere.

But there are also refugees in India who face some of the most harrowing difficulties. Tibet and Sri Lanka are linked to India by peculiar historical connections and circumstances, which permit its refugees to enjoy a better position. But those who come from other countries such as Myanmar, Afghanistan, Iran or Somalia have had to bear serious disadvantages owing to technical and legal issues.

One of the problems is that while India has not subscribed to international conventions on the topic, it has also not set up a domestic legislative framework to deal with refugees. The result is that issues are dealt with in an ad hoc manner. All foreigners without documents are subject to the Registration of Foreigners Act of 1939, and the Foreigners Order of 1948, which means they always face the possibility of being deported. They are, in principle, given the protections of Indian democracy: under Article 21 of the Constitution they enjoy the right to life and of course they enjoy access to public services. They may even find work in the informal sector, but while these windows are available and open, they do not let in a great deal of sunshine into the asylum-seekers' lives.

Work in the informal sector, for instance, is an extremely competitive affair. For the 22,000 refugees in Delhi alone, access to work is not easy considering that over 500,000 Indians from poorer parts of the country also reach the city each year in search of employment. Language barriers, social prejudices, and unfamiliarity with India further complicate matters, making things difficult for refugees. Indeed, even well-educated refugees in Delhi have no option but to compete in the informal sector. A UNHCR report quotes, for example, a Somalian man asking whether he should abandon his medical qualifications and take up making paper plates, which was the only option available to him.

Access to public services is also difficult. The pressure of India's domestic population on basic amenities such as transport, health, education, etc. means that refugees must also join the queue and hope to get lucky. Special provisions are difficult to provide and in an alien cultural environment, this causes disorientation and makes life as unpleasant as it can get for these people. A typical grievance of refugees is how they often think they have passed the worst by escaping the troubles of their homelands, little realizing that across the border life could turn out to be unexpectedly more distressing. This takes a serious toll on their psychological and physical well-being. Moreover, at this specific moment in history when security concerns are on an all-time high, refugees are placed under perpetual suspicion, which further complicates their life in exile.

What is perhaps even more heartbreaking is the effect all this has on the younger refugees. Children, completely uprooted from familiar environments, have to face the uneasy option of studying in government schools, where cultural and language barriers are even more strongly felt. Confidence is broken and each day is agonizing, making them feel more alien than their parents. And if education is removed, their only other option is to contribute to the family's income by working. It is difficult to speak meaningfully of empowerment of those suffering in the process and the children are left with only the bleakest hopes for their future.

Steps have been taken in this regard, however. At the end of 2011 the government issued a circular to all states and union territories drawing a very clear distinction between the ways in which people with a well-founded fear of persecution should be treated in contrast to economic migrants. Such de facto refugees would be eligible for long-term stay visas, issued for a year at a time but renewable five times. Private sector employment will henceforth be possible, as will access to high quality education, along with the usual advantages of being present in the country with a visa. Technicalities are in fact still being worked out, since most refugees do not have passports to stamp their visas on (and UNHCR documentation is crucial here). This order certainly opens the door and takes an enormous step in making refugees feel at home in India.

So the barrier of securing residence permits and job opportunities has been crossed, but it is clear that implementation of the new order will take time. Not all the states that have received the central government's order have in fact taken the necessary steps to implement it. Each case has to be considered individually and local police officers have to provide the preliminary documentation. The order will take time to be interpreted and understood fully, transmitted across the country, and then put into effect. Nevertheless this is a great leap forward and in spite of all sorts of bureaucratic difficulties, in the end the new order will benefit people.

One challenge faced by refugees in India which has always been a concern is the great poverty in which refugees in India have to live. UNHCR gives a subsistence allowance to all those under its purview, but this is far from a comfortable or dependable source of income. Refugees must be enabled to stand on their feet and the government and UNHCR should facilitate this. Now with the new order this will be possible, at least in theory, but it will require refugees to compete with locals (and economic migrants) for scarce opportunities in a competitive job market.

At least there is arguably nothing that should prevent refugees from entering the job market. They should, therefore, be allowed work permits in as many sectors as possible. Indeed, by allowing them to join the system, the system as a whole could benefit. The aim is to create a model that goes beyond protection to one of self-reliance.

Another challenge we in India need to overcome is that of stereotypes and conservative mindsets. Refugees are often racially, socially, and otherwise discriminated against, especially (and I am sad to acknowledge this) those coming from Africa. To improve their lot, the outlook of our local communities needs to be changed. Indians need to be educated and sensitized to the circumstances of these people so that, in addition to their poverty, they do not need to face issues of hostility and discrimination from their neighbours here. This is a long-term challenge and one that requires the cooperation of the government, society, and ordinary people across the country if it is to be overcome.

I have some understanding for the government's preference to be quiet on these matters and do its work behind the scenes. We live, for instance, in a time when domestic migration is facing violent reactions in a state like Maharashtra, so any seeming encouragement to an influx from outside may not be wise to trumpet out loud. And yet these are also times that call for courage and vision on the part of those in authority. It is time to nail our colours to the mast, to show the nation and the world what we believe in and stand for, rather than saying, 'Don't mind that we haven't signed up to anything, just look at what we are doing.' It is time to move on beyond such a modest position.

It is also crucial to work for the formulation of a national framework to deal with refugees. The creation of a structure, perhaps modelled on the circumstances of the Tibetans, would ease things considerably. While the ultimate aim is that the refugees should be able to return to their homes voluntarily, opportunities towards at least basic self-reliance, should be provided. This is not easy, especially in a country like India with all its internal constraints. But it can be and should be done, keeping in mind India's own traditions and the larger ideals of humanity.

The State need not completely bear the weight of such responsibilities. Civil society partnerships, NGOs, and other private organizations should be encouraged to support refugee activities, and it is certain that such efforts will meet with success. There is no dearth of empathy in the country and this will help the cause of the refugees. Cooperation between all players must be given a boost and we should develop better frameworks to deal with refugees.

As for the creation of a legal framework within the country, there was talk that the Home Ministry was working on a comprehensive refugee law, which now appears to have been shelved, no doubt out of fear that economic migrants from some of our neighbouring states would seek to take advantage of it in large numbers. If a law is ever to be proposed, I can only hope, as a Member of Parliament, that it will turn out to be a liberal and generous law. Ironically the international agencies like UNHCR are in fact so happy with the way things are, at the moment, that they are not pressing for any new law. But I would welcome new legislation because the only risk with our current unofficial but generous policies is that they could easily be changed by different governments without needing to get legislative approval to do so. Of course, since our record has been progressive for the last many years, the possibility of an absolute reversal in practice is slim. We have, as I stated earlier, done a lot for refugees without a law in place, and UNHCR could and should focus on actual work done for helping refugees instead of demanding laws that turn out to be restrictive by the time they are written and end up backfiring.

As a member of UNHCR's Executive Committee and a nation with a long and proud record of asylum and refugee protection, India can and should do more than it has done so far. India, rather perversely, does not grant

UNHCR independent recognition in our country and allows it to work only as a subsidiary of UNDP. This should be changed so that the organization, as it does everywhere else, is able to work freely and to maintain independent links to the government.

Refugees are a global phenomenon of our times. We live in an era which, in Kofi Annan's days at the UN, we used to term as one of 'problems without passports'—problems that cross all frontiers uninvited, problems that no one country or one group of countries, however rich or powerful they might be, can solve on their own. Refugees crossing borders in fear and despair are emblematic of this term—they literally embody problems without passports, and for them we must find solutions that offer blueprints beyond borders. The problems of refugees worldwide are problems that demand global solidarity and international co-operation. India, as a pillar of the world community, as a significant pole in the emerging multipolar world, must play its own part, on its own soil as well as on the global stage, in this noble task. In so doing, we would uphold our own finest traditions and the highest standards of our democracy, as well as demonstrate once again that we are what we have long claimed to be, a good international citizen—an upstanding member of the international community in an ever-closer knit and globalizing world. This is a worthwhile aspiration for all of us who care about what India stands for, at home and in the world.

THE MISFORTUNE AT THE BOTTOM OF
THE PYRAMID

The shocking ouster of the Nobel Prize-winning Bangladeshi economist Mohammed Yunus as managing director of Grameen Bank, the microcredit institution he founded, which blazed a trail for microfinance around the developing world, has thrown a harsh spotlight on the crisis engulfing a business that was till recently seen as a harbinger of hope for millions.

Yunus's tussle with his government, which tried earlier to retire him on grounds of age (he was 70) before firing him from his own board, is entangled in his country's complicated politics. But Bangladeshi Prime Minster Sheikh Hasina's remark that Yunus had 'spent years sucking the blood of the poor'—though palpably unfair in his case—echoes similar charges being made in neighbouring India against companies and banks that had been inspired to emulate Grameen.

Last November, the state of Andhra Pradesh, one of India's most populous, cracked down heavily on private microfinance institutions (PMFIs), told borrowers they did not need to repay their loans and banned many of their activities. State authorities said they were prompted to take decisive action by a spate of suicides committed by borrowers from microfinance institutions who were unable to pay their debts. Some eighty such people were reported to have taken their own lives last year—an alarming figure, even if it is tiny in proportion to the 26.7 million active borrowers from PMFIs in India.

Andhra Pradesh officials charged that PMFIs, which had lent some Rs 80 billion (nearly $2 billion) in the state, levy 'usurious' interest rates (between 24 and 30 per cent, which works out to 2 to 2.5 per cent a month) to sustain their promoters' extravagant salaries and profits. In addition, too many borrowers had taken multiple loans from different sources and were unable to repay them. Aggressive agents were marketing the loans with no heed to the borrowers' capacity to repay. It was alleged, too, that coercion was being used to exact repayment, leaving victims with no way out but to end their own lives.

One of the institutions that received unwelcome attention was SKS Microfinance, once a poster child for the PMFIs, which had done so well and grown so large that its initial public offering last year was oversubscribed thirteen times and raised $350 million. The salaries paid to its top executives—as a reward, essentially, for lending successfully to the poorest of the poor—came in for excoriating criticism across India's political spectrum. SKS' chairman, Vikram Akula, reportedly made $13 million by selling some of his shares last year. Is it moral, critics asked, to profit from providing services that alleviate poverty?

But the counter-argument is that professionally-run private microcredit is better than no credit at all, which is what most of the poor live with. State banks are supposed to lend generously to India's rural poor, but their activities are mired in inefficiency and corruption. Loans often require bribes to be paid first, and the banks' procedures are bewildering to the unlettered. The only alternative—the traditional moneylenders—extort far more than 30 per cent a year, and do so, often, at the point of a knife, or worse.

The problem raises a larger question: should the poor be served by modern financial institutions raising their funds in the capital markets, or must they rely exclusively on non-profit sources of support? The late Indian management guru C.K. Prahalad suggested in his bestselling book *The Fortune at the Bottom of the Pyramid* that businesses could make healthy profits by serving the poor—and so satisfy both their shareholders and the interests of social development. But while selling five-rupee sachets of shampoo to poor consumers is considered clever marketing, lending Rs 5,000 to a starving peasant who might not be able to pay it back is seen as usury. Both activities, after all, are financed by investors looking for returns on their capital and motivated more by profit than compassion. But one is clearly less socially acceptable than the other. A high salary earned by a cosmetics or soft-drink manufacturer attracts no attention; one paid to the CEO of a company that thrives on lending the poor appears unseemly at best, immoral at worst.

Yet PMFIs had succeeded remarkably by meeting a genuine need. Only 50 of India's some 1,000 microfinance institutions are private ones (as opposed to NGOs), but 80 per cent of the market is accounted for by the top four PMFIs. India's PMFIs, many of which doubled their revenues annually, grew at 100 per cent over the 2009-10 fiscal year, reaching over 100 million borrowers, whereas rural co-operatives, which also make small loans, grew at 3 per cent, to some 45 million borrowers. State banks are farther behind.

Yet PMFIs are lending in a market vitiated by a populist political culture. Whereas microcredit institutions rely on a very high repayment rate (often exceeding 98 per cent) for their business model to work, government-run banks and state-supported co-operatives tend eventually to write off their loans when elections come around, with state and national governments waiving poor farmers' debts for understandable political reasons. Private institutions cannot do that; a refusal to repay essentially knocks the bottom out of their business.

There are other complications. The village moneylender, though often a shark, at least belongs to the community and knows his clients. A PMFI, as a faceless institution, relies on good faith and peer pressure to get its money back. The moneylender is happy to lend money for any purpose, including non-productive expenditure like weddings and dowries, whereas for a PMFI to succeed requires lending for economically-sustainable and income-generating activities. PMFIs looking to attract private equity capital emphasized growth over sustainability, lent indiscriminately to people who couldn't pay them back, and attracted opprobrium.

Indian regulators are sorting out the tangle of issues that have arisen in recent months and plunged the microfinance industry into crisis. Ironically, however, none of these problems seems to have befallen Bangladesh's Grameen Bank, which survives largely on donor grants and sustainable repayments. Yunus' ouster, it is suggested, has much more to do with his having once expressed political ambitions. But association with a suddenly tarnished industry cannot have helped either.

Yunus's accomplishments, for which he has won global recognition, cannot be ignored merely because his idea has been transmuted into less reputable businesses. While microfinance is here to stay—and continues to benefit millions in India—it is essential that its practices be reformed to ensure that the dross does not totally dull its sheen.

CONCERNED AUTHORITY,
CONCERNED POPULACE

One of the questions people keep asking me since my entry into politics is what can we do about corruption. What would I do, one citizen recently asked me in an online chat, if I became the 'concerned authority' to deal with corruption? No such prospect—the Lokpal isn't a Member of Parliament!—but in fact corruption is a national malaise and a social ill, not just one that a 'concerned authority' can solve. We are all complicit—those who demand bribes and those who give them.

As one who has long urged an end to public apathy about politics, I was inspired by seeing the passion of Anna Hazare's followers against corruption, which I share, and I have no doubt that during his mass movement, he touched a chord amongst millions of Indians. But we must remember that the supporters of his Jan Lokpal Bill were not the only Indians who are disgusted by corruption. So are many who were never part of his movement. When many of his followers constituted the Aam Aadmi Party against his wishes, they could never quite come to terms with the fact that there are patriotic and principled Indians amongst their critics too, and that we must reach out to each other in good faith.

Anna Hazare's movement persuaded Indians in general, and the political class eventually, that a strong Lokpal is a key part of the answer. Parliament finally legislated the creation of a strong anti-corruption ombudsman, with genuine. autonomy and authority and substantial powers of action. It is too early to judge how well it will work, or indeed whether the unintended consequence many feared—of creating a large, omnipotent and unaccountable supra-institution that could not be challenged, reformed or removed—has been belied. If the current governmental bodies tasked with investigation, vigilance, and audit are deemed to be insufficiently impervious to corruption, it is worth asking what guarantee there is that the new institution of Lokpal could not be infected by the same virus—and if so, what could be done about it, since it would literally be a law unto itself.

A number of related steps need to be taken to tackle corruption at its source. Campaign finance reform, simplification of laws and regulations, administrative transparency, and the reduction of discretionary powers enjoyed by officials and ministers, are all of the highest priority too. The Right to Information Act (RTI) enacted by the first UPA government was in fact the first step in this direction. A credible Lokpal will be another.

But one of the things that was highlighted by the Anna Hazare phenomenon is the extent to which corruption is a middle-class preoccupation, when in fact the biggest victims of corruption in our country are in fact the poor. For the affluent, corruption is at worst a nuisance; for the salaried middle-class, it can be an indignity and a burden; but for the poor, it is often a tragedy.

The saddest corruption stories I have heard are those where corruption literally transforms lives for the worse. There are stories about the pregnant woman turned away from a government hospital because she couldn't bribe her way to a bed; the labourer denied an allotment of land that was his due because someone else bribed the patwari to change the land records; the pensioner denied the rightful fruits of decades of toil because he couldn't or wouldn't bribe the petty clerk to process his paperwork; the wretchedly poor unable to procure the below poverty line (BPL) cards that certify their entitlement to various government schemes and subsidies because they couldn't afford to bribe the issuing officer; the poor widow cheated of an insurance settlement because she couldn't grease the right palms…The examples are endless. Each of these represents not just an injustice but a crime, and yet the officials responsible get away with their exactions all the time. And all their victims are people living at or near a poverty line that's been drawn just this side of the funeral pyre.

One of the reasons that I was an early supporter of economic liberalization in India was that I hoped it would reduce corruption by denying officialdom the opportunity (afforded routinely by our license-permit-quota Raj) to profit from the power to permit. That has happened to some degree, especially at the big-business level. I am, similarly, a strong supporter of computerizing government records and applying e-Governance to transactions that currently require paperwork—and bribes to expedite their processing. But I underestimated the creativity of petty corruption in India that leeches blood from the veins of the poorest and most downtrodden in our society.

The problem of corruption runs far broader and deeper than the headlines suggest. Corruption isn't only high-level governmental malfeasance as typified by the 2G and CWG scandals. Overcoming it requires nothing short of a change in our society's mindset. Everyone claims to be against corruption; the debate is on the means to be used to tackle it. For it would be dangerous to reduce the entire issue to a simplistic solution which won't end corruption by itself. Inspectors and prosecutors can only catch some criminals; we need to change the system so that fewer crimes are committed, and that means changing attitudes too.

For ultimately, corruption flourishes because society enables it. Every time we agree to pay part of the cost of a flat in 'black', negotiate a discount from a store in exchange for not insisting on a bill, or offer 'speed money' to jump a queue, we are complicit in corruption. Every businessman who rationalizes an illicit payment as a 'facilitation fee,' or airily dismisses a lavish gift in cash or kind as part of 'the price of doing business', is complicit in corruption. When I expostulate with such friends they tell me: 'If we don't do it, our work won't get done'. Or even more tellingly: 'If we don't do it, someone else will, and he'll get the business, we won't'. Corruption is spawned by the human desire to get ahead of the competition; self-righteousness alone won't end it.

Once, at the end of yet another argument about corruption, a friend challenged my suggestion that the corrupt only survive because the non-corrupt pay them. If we all stopped offering bribes, I argued, people couldn't demand them, since no one would pay them. That's impossible, my friend replied; there would always be someone looking to get an advantage for himself by paying someone off. 'You can't change India,' he sighed.

But we must. Mahatma Gandhi did. It will take a similar mass movement—abetted by efficient systems of e-Governance and firm executive action—to deliver India its second freedom: freedom from corruption.

THE DARK TRUTH ABOUT BLACK MONEY

One of the more popular campaign promises of the victorious Narendra Modi campaign in 2014—and the most difficult to fulfil—was his commitment to 'bringing back' to India the billions of dollars of 'black money' reputedly stashed abroad by tax evaders, corrupt officials and the like.

No one in our country disagrees that black money is a serious problem or that the black money squirreled away abroad should be identified and brought back, if possible. Black money is particularly pernicious for a developing country like India, because it siphons resources away that could be spent for much needed investments in health, education, roads and general public welfare. There were debates on black money in each one of the first eight Lok Sabhas, but despite learned judges like Santhanam and Wanchoo heading committees that issued voluminous reports, the problem seems only to have got worse over the years.

Black money in India is generated by various practices: real estate transactions, diversion of government resources from welfare programmes, kickbacks on government contracts (especially those involving international procurement) and malpractices in international trade, especially under-invoicing.

What is the scale of the problem? Various numbers, including some fanciful ones, were flung about in the course of the political debate on the issue. One internet and SMS allegation doing the rounds, and cited by the yoga guru and black money crusader, Baba Ramdev, claims that it is Rs 1,456 lakh crore of black money. That would be equivalent to some $30 trillion, whereas our entire GDP is only 1.5 trillion—so something like twenty times our current GDP is supposed to be illegally sitting abroad! We should not get our economics from a yoga teacher. The more realistic number generally cited comes from a widely-circulated report called *The Drivers and Dynamics of Illicit Financial Flows from India 1948 to 2008*, published in November 2010 by the reputable US-based organization, Global Financial Integrity. It concludes that we have lost a total of $213 billion in illicit money since 1948, the present value of which in today's dollars would be about 462 billion, or Rs 20 lakh crore, which is serious money.

Even when it comes to Swiss banks, the burden of the BJP's song for some years now, official Swiss bank figures show that only 0.07 per cent of all the assets in Swiss banks are held by Indians—some 2.5 billion dollars out of 3.5 trillion dollars held in Swiss banks by foreigners, or under Rs 10,000 crore. We are not, therefore, the country with the largest Swiss bank deposits ('more than all the other countries combined', one BJP MP had alleged while in Opposition). Even one illegal rupee in a Swiss bank is unpardonable. But the real dimensions of the problem should be understood accurately.

But the Swiss banks are a red herring in the black money debate. Swiss banks pay 1 per cent interest at the most; it is highly unlikely that Indians with black money are leaving it there, and far more probable that the bulk is being reinvested more profitably elsewhere, including in our own country. Why not? In India, in the last decade, housing prices have risen ten times since 2000, the Sensex has gone up six times, and government bonds offer 8 per cent while the best terms abroad are at 3 per cent. This makes India a very attractive investment destination for Indian money, which can be routed back to the country in a practice called 'round-tripping'—taking illegal money out but bringing it back as a legitimate investment, especially through investment havens like Mauritius.

In our desire to facilitate foreign investment, we have unwittingly made 'round-tripping' easier, through, for example, the anonymity guaranteed by participatory notes: 55 per cent of the foreign institutional investments in India in 2009-10, totalling $85 billion, were made through the participatory notes route. Whereas our domestic investors have to fulfil stringent 'know your customer' norms, these are much more lax for participatory notes. While we need productive investments from abroad, we must not allow them to become a contemporary equivalent of the old 'voluntary disclosure schemes' under which the government used to soak up black money.

At the same time, there are specific concerns. Forty per cent of the total FDI coming into India comes from Mauritius. We have been trying to renegotiate the Tax Treaty we have with Mauritius, but inevitably our strategic interests in that country will affect how far we can push its government to accede to our demands. The fact is, however, that there is no taxation on capital gains in Mauritius, so that if an entity sets up a paper company there, our Double Taxation Avoidance (DTA) Agreement becomes in fact a double non-taxation agreement for us. Our Income Tax Department had the power to examine and verify whether the resident status of a company in Mauritius was genuine or not. The NDA government, whose leading lights are today waxing indignant on the issue, withdrew that power by Circular 789 of April 2000, under which a simple certification from the Mauritius government is now accepted. This has rendered 'round-tripping' from Mauritius much easier, because India no longer has the power to question the residential status of a company there.

It is also mildly amusing that some of the BJP leaders seem to presume that the tax haven countries are just waiting to hand over information and money to us, if only our government is tough enough to ask. The opposite is true. Whatever India can do in relation to the banks of foreign countries is subject to the domestic laws of those countries and of course of international law, including treaties to which India is a party. Under the Indo-Swiss DTA Agreement, information on Swiss bank deposits cannot be revealed by them until we provide the names of the individuals we are investigating, of the banks where they have their money, and evidence of criminality; the Swiss have made it clear will not support 'fishing expeditions' for names in their banks. In addition, we are bound to secrecy clauses; releasing names (except for prosecution) would violate our undertakings and jeopardize future co-operation.

No wonder that Switzerland is ranked number one on the 2014 Financial Secrecy Index compiled by the Tax Justice Network. Since 1934, breaking bank secrecy is a criminal offence in Switzerland, whereas tax evasion is not a crime under their law.

To suggest that the Government of India has not been strong in its efforts is particularly unfair because, since the Pittsburgh G-20 Summit in 2009, India has led the push in the G-20 against banking secrecy and opaque cross-border financial dealings that protect black money. India has joined the Financial Action Task Force, pushed the G-20 to restructure and strengthen the OECD's Global Forum on Transparency and the Exchange of Information for Tax Purposes. The Head of the Global Forum on Tax Transparency rates India 'first in terms of promoting the standards, in terms of fighting tax evasion, and having the international community lining up behind it'. Similar praise has come from the director of the OECD Centre for Tax Policy and Administration. And this was all for the much-maligned UPA government.

The UPA government took a number of related steps. It enacted legislation incorporating counter-measures against non-cooperative countries, whose companies, for instance, must pay a 30 per cent withholding tax. The provisions on transfer pricing were tightened. There is a provision in thirty of our DTAAs requiring assistance for collection of taxes, including taking measures of conservancy, and the UPA government kept trying to put this into the other agreements as well. There are eight more income tax overseas units set up, more manpower has been deployed to the transfer pricing and international taxation units, and a large number of officers have been given specialised training. With all its efforts, the UPA government was able to make specific requests in 333 cases to obtain information from foreign jurisdictions and has already obtained over 9,900 pieces of information regarding suspicious transactions by Indian citizens.

Many speakers in the Lok Sabha debate on black money in 2011 referred to Hasan Ali Khan, the Pune stud farm owner with billions stashed abroad. But though the case is shocking, he did get caught: his prosecution is evidence of the government at work to pursue the holders of black money abroad. The fact is that there is a lot of domestic black money too—notably in politics. Election campaigns are awash in black money; most candidates are reputed to spend far more than the permissible limits, and the difference has to come in unaccounted (black) money. Root and branch reform is necessary.

While it is very easy to shout slogans or·to clamour for political change, the real question the country's political parties need to ask is what can we do together to resolve the problem of black money. I would like to suggest a brief list: We have to tackle the problem of tax evasion, which would require cooperation with the government on tax reform and rationalization and on financial sector reform. We need to incentivise compliance. We have to tackle black money coming from real estate, which again requires cooperation on effective land titling, on reformed land revenue and land record systems, and the elimination of policy distortions, including rationalizing taxation, such as onerous stamp duties which promote evasion. We have to tackle black money in education, which means removing the scarcity of good education supply in our country, which permits some colleges to take black money to provide access to good education. We need effective implementation of government spending programmes, especially their financial management. Action to strengthen law enforcement and criminal justice will help eliminate terrorism-related funding, which also relies on black money. And we do need to tackle electoral reforms to ensure that politics does not remain a major locus of black money. The Lokpal Bill is one of several measures needed to tackle corruption effectively.

In other words, I would respectfully say to the BJP leaders who campaigned to bring the Modi government to power in the name of returning black money that it would be far better to work together to deal with the real problems facing this country. Instead of adjourning the House as the BJP repeatedly did over the issue, we need to use the House to create the policies and reforms that will enable us effectively to deal with black money here and abroad. I am sure the new Opposition—the Congress party—stands ready to co-operate with such an endeavour.

THE UNFORGIVABLE HORROR OF TORTURE

As an Indian official of the United Nations, I was proud of our government's decision in 1997 to sign the UN Convention against Torture and other Cruel, Inhuman and Degrading Treatment or Punishment. But our failure to ratify our own signature has long remained a cause of dismay. Ratification by our government requires enabling legislation from our Parliament to bring our national laws into conformity with international standards. Our existing laws do not define torture as clearly as the UN Convention does, nor have we so far made torture a criminal offence, punishable by the full force of the law. I am proud that in 2010 our government finally proposed a bill that accomplishes both these objectives, and that I was able to speak in Parliament in its support.

When I entered government in 2009, one of the first questions I asked was why we had not yet ratified the UN Convention Against Torture. There was no convincing answer, though some bureaucrats ventured a set of procedural excuses. When I retreated temporarily to the back benches in 2010, my maiden speech in the Lok Sabha was to support the passage of the bill outlawing torture.

At the time when India was seized with well-deserved excitement over the worldwide success of *Slumdog Millionaire*, an issue peripherally raised by the movie was entirely ignored amidst all the hoopla. The film opens with and features horrifying scenes of police brutality, with the cops torturing the principal protagonist, Jamal, including with electric shocks, to get him to confess to cheating in the quiz show. How come there wasn't a huge public uproar in India over this? Not only is there no outrage, we all seem to take such scenes for granted: the general view appears to be that this sort of thing probably happens all the time.

Well, it shouldn't. No civilized democracy conducts or condones torture, whether of its citizens or others. The police may have fallen into the pattern of routinely continuing practices left over from colonial days, when police were instruments of repression, but that's no excuse today. Mistreating any member of the public is in fact against the law in democratic India, and any policeman who behaves as the cops in the movie did are now liable to ten years' rigorous imprisonment and a severe fine. But, as the screenwriters assumed, it seems to happen anyway, and unless society rises up in anger against this kind of police behaviour, it may well continue. As a 21st-century Indian I do not want foreign screenwriters assuming that this sort of thing happens routinely in our country, and the passage of the anti-torture bill will, I hope, ensure that it does not.

The problem of police brutality appears to be widespread in our country and allegations of torture have even been reported in my own constituency of Thiruvananthapuram, the capital of the enlightened state of Kerala. And yet how many of the custodians of the law in our country have ever been prosecuted for torture in India? How many have been punished for mistreating their fellow citizens in this way? The passage of this bill strengthened the hands of those who campaigned against the practice of torture, whenever and wherever it occurs. But it would be disingenuous to suggest that it has ended such misbehaviour altogether.

Not long ago I had the opportunity to read a confidential report from a highly respected international human rights organization about the prevalence of practices of torture in our country. I cannot begin to describe my feelings of shock and grief in reading some of the testimonies of the sufferers. As an MP I am aware that the maintenance of law and order is a state subject, but torture is not a state subject. Torture is a moral affront to the conscience of every Indian.

Law, after all, is a reflection of the values and aspirations of a society. Concepts of justice and law, the legitimacy of government, the dignity of the individual, protection from oppressive or arbitrary rule, and humane treatment by the state are found in every decent society on the face of this earth. Our national movement was based on such principles. As Gandhiji said, 'It has always been a mystery to me how men can feel themselves honoured by the humiliation of their fellow beings.' Let us honour him not just by outlawing, but by ending, the humiliation that torture inflicts on innocent and guilty people alike.

Our nationalist movement fought for the human rights of Indians against British rule. We did not win our freedom in order to torture our own people with impunity. Soon after Independence, India participated, with fervour and conviction, in the drafting of the Universal Declaration of Human Rights. The ideals of our nationalist movement have never in any way lagged behind the highest international standards of democracy and human rights. The setting up of the National Human Rights Commission some two decades ago was a further affirmation of this. We have no reason to fall behind the rest of the world on the issue of torture.

Torture is wrong. It's morally unacceptable, legally unjustifiable, and practically ineffective. It shouldn't be allowed to happen anywhere in India. And if and where it does, it has nothing to do with the kind of India our leaders are trying to build today. It's time for every thinking Indian to stand up and raise their voices against the practice. Torture must stop. And the next time a movie shows an Indian policeman resorting to torture, I hope it also shows him being tried and sentenced for it. That may be the only way to bring about the shift in attitudes we need to ensure that torture has no place in our society—or on our screens.

KERALA'S ECONOMY: EMERGING OR SUBMERGING?

Recently, a friend described something he saw while undertaking a journey by the Kerala Express from New Delhi to Thiruvananthapuram. After traversing more than three-fourths of its 3,000 km journey across eight states, the train chugged past Coimbatore early in the morning of the third day. It was just past 7 a.m. My friend could see neatly dressed people—both men and women—coming out of houses set in rows of colonies, locking the doors behind them. Most of them had small bags and tiffin boxes, indicating that they were going to their workplaces. Every road that came into view was full of people either on cycles, or on foot moving towards bus stops.

About an hour after leaving Coimbatore station, the train crossed over the border through the Palakkad gap of the Western Ghats into Kerala's lush landscape. As is the common sight anywhere in the state, the view was of small and medium-sized houses set amidst clumps of coconut, jackfruit and mango trees. The houses invariably had small verandahs and in many of them my friend spied young and middle-aged men, shirtless and lungi-clad, seated sipping tea and reading newspapers.

The irony of the situation did not escape him. People in Coimbatore had already started off for work an hour ago, while here in Kerala, able-bodied men were only just getting up from their beds and most probably checking out news about far away worlds and events unrelated to their immediate daily lives. Apparently, they were in no hurry to go for work, either because they had no work to attend or no desire to get to their assigned workplace!

I was once invited to address the Trivandrum Management Association on the subject 'Energizing Kerala'. I found that odd, because the only place in the world where Keralites seem to need energizing is in Kerala itself. Look around, and one sees Keralites everywhere, working extremely hard, from clerical jobs in other Indian cities or in the Gulf to nursing slots in the United States, achieving remarkable success. One would think that rarely in the history of human civilization have a people been so wanted by employers abroad, but remain indolent in their own land. India, I have long argued, is more than the sum of its contradictions. For Kerala it may be the other way around!

So what is it that holds them back here? How did this need for 'Energizing Kerala' itself arise? Is it lack of resources (investment), stultifying attitudes, misplaced policies, inefficiencies in governance, suffocating politics? All of the above?

Figures culled from the Kerala State Planning Board's Economic Review

2013 reveal that:

- Kerala has an average unemployment rate of 16.5 per cent, three times the all-India rate of 5.8 per cent. Strikingly, unemployment afflicts primarily the educated and the skilled. There has also been an influx of migrants from other parts of India—an astounding 1.7 million at last count—to fill unskilled jobs that locals, even when otherwise unemployed, just do not want to do;
- Kerala staggers under a debt ratio of 28.5 per cent, down from 35.11 per cent in 2004-05, but still one of the highest in the country and the highest in south India, which is difficult to sustain in the long run (and is getting worse in a climate in which it had to borrow from the Reserve Bank to pay its own employees their Onam bonuses in 2014);
- The economy is heavily tilted towards services, which accounted for more than 60 per cent of the state's total economic activity in 2012–13. Manufacturing accounted for 21 per cent, but more than half of this is attributed to construction, mainly of homes; and
- There is a grave over-dependence on remittances (as much as 26 per cent of the state's revenues, compared to only 3 per cent for the country as a whole) from the approximately 2.28 million Keralites working in the oil-rich Gulf states. The government estimates that there are 43.7 non-resident Keralites per 100 households, outstripping any Indian state.

According to the State Planning Board, the remittance level crossed Rs 65,000 crore in 2012–13. This explains how the high income, rapid growth, and strong social indicators coexist in the state with high unemployment and a slim manufacturing and industrial base. Without its NRK (non-Resident Keralite) remittances, Kerala would only have been another Cuba. Today, one tends to forget that before the Gulf phenomenon happened, Kerala's jobless lakhs had been moving through the gaps in the ghats to every nook and corner of the rest of the country in search of employment and economic freedom.

Economists often speak of the 'curse of oil', which occurs when an economy becomes excessively dependent on a single lucrative natural resource, which in turn squeezes the rest of the economy and distorts its structure. This is the story in many oil-rich Gulf states. Ironically, we see in Kerala a mirror image of this phenomenon, which we can call the 'curse of remittances'. If one day, political developments in the Gulf states were to reverse the migration patterns and slash remittances, what would happen to Kerala?

The irony is that Kerala has long been recognized to have done many things right. For years the darling of development experts, non-governmental organizations and social activists, the 'Kerala Model' seemed to show that impressive levels of human development indicators—in health, education and quality of life comparable even to some rich countries, as I have explained in an earlier essay in this volume—could be achieved without a correspondingly high level of income.

In my book, *India: From Midnight To The Millennium*, I wrote of 'the Malayali miracle'; a state that has practised openness and tolerance from time immemorial, which has made religious and ethnic diversity a healthy part of its daily life, rather than a source of division; which has overcome caste discrimination and class oppression, implemented land reforms and practised true participative political democracy. All this gave Kerala's workforce greater rights and a higher minimum wage than anywhere else in India and enabled its women to lead productive, fulfilling and empowered lives as compared to the majority of their counterparts elsewhere in India.

But in the recent past there has been a new debate on the 'Kerala Model' of development. Can you build high growth and strong human development indicators on such a flimsy basis? Is it sustainable? Sadly, the focus in the new debate on Kerala is now increasingly on its failures: low employment, low levels of food intake and low incomes, accompanied by high levels of alcoholism and the nation's worst suicide rate. India's changes in the era of globalization have accentuated the original shortcomings.

The state's political economists and ideologues are blindly dogmatic when talking about globalization. There have even been panicky calls for re-engaging with peasant agriculture even by delinking from globalization. And all this in a state which has a 1/366 share of the national food grain production!

My own view is that the 'Kerala Model' is still eminently sustainable within the new national and international development paradigms, provided we embrace the opportunity to change. Kerala has to move beyond the basic issues, boldly tackle 'second generation' problems such as creation of infrastructure, move from an agrarian to at least a manufacturing if not heavily industrial economy, develop itself as a knowledge economy, improve the quality of higher education and vocational training to meet the requirements of a modern workforce, and build on its existing successes in tourism and hospitality services. All this will create meaningful employment opportunities and increases in income levels. But, of course, it is more easily said than done.

One essential prerequisite for achieving this would be to bring about a change in perceptions of the state, notably our reputation for having a far keener sense of rights than responsibilities. Even though strikes in individual factories and establishments have become relatively uncommon, our extremely politicized environment has come to haunt us, especially the notorious hartals over marginal political issues, with cars being blocked in the streets, shops closed and life paralyzed. Such behaviour has driven investment away, especially to neighbouring Tamil Nadu. This is why I publicly declared I would never support a hartal or bandh, even if my own party called one; and when it did (to express Congress' outrage over the shocking murder of communist apostate T.P Chandrasekha), I was true to my word, refusing to support it and calling on people to disobey the appeal, on the grounds that we had better ways to convey the strength of our feelings than to disrupt people's lives by political coercion.

It is time for re-balancing. We must open our mental horizons to the world, outgrow our shopworn ideologies and create investment and business-friendly conditions. This does not mean betraying the true interests of the workers, but finding them appropriate and useful work. It does not mean giving up on egalitarian values or of placing profit over people and environment, but rather, using profits to benefit all sections of the populace engaged in productive labour.

I firmly believe that ultimately the Kerala that will succeed is the one open to the contention of ideas and interests within it, unafraid of the prowess or the products of the outside world, wedded to the democratic pluralism that is our civilization's greatest strength. A Kerala determined to liberate and fulfil the creative energies of its people is possible, if its people change their attitudes towards work. When that happens, God's Own Country will no longer deserve the business reputation of being the devil's playground.

CHANGING BENGAL: THE WAY FORWARD

For years it was fashionable to see Kolkata as the epitome of all the ills of our urban culture. Poverty, pollution, pestilence—you name it, Kolkata had it. (Forgive my alliteration: you could stick to that one letter of the alphabet, P, and still find no difficulty cataloguing Kolkata's woes: power-cuts, poverty, potholes, pavement-dwellers, political violence, paralyzed industry.) As business capital and professional talent fled the city from the late 1960s onwards, the city, and the state of which it was the capital, spiralled into increasing irrelevance. 'Kolkata,' I found myself writing in *India: From Midnight to the Millennium*, 'has become a backwater.'

It wasn't always that way. When, as a 12-year-old in late 1968, I first learned of my father's transfer from Bombay to Kolkata, I had embraced the news with great excitement. Kolkata still had the lingering aura of the former First City of the British Empire, a place of importance and of remembered grandeur. It was the bustling commercial metropolis of the jute, tea, coal and iron and steel industries; more important, it was the city of the greatest cricket stadium in India, Eden Gardens, the pavement bookstalls and animated coffee houses of College Street, the elegant cakes of Firpo's Restaurant and—recalling the whispers of wicked uncles—the cabarets of the Golden Slipper, the acme of all Indian nightclubs. It was the city of the visionary Rabindranath Tagore and the brilliant Satyajit Ray; for juveniles of less exalted cultural inclinations, it had India's first disco (the Park Hotel's suggestively-named 'In and Out') and, *JS*, India's only 'with it' youth magazine. Former Kolkatans still spoke of the brilliance of the Bengali stage, the erudition of the waiters at the Coffee House, the magic of Park Street at Christmas.

By the mid-1980s, much of that list had disappeared. What remained, instead, were the dirt and the degradation, the despair and the disrepair, that made Kolkata the poster-child for the Third World city. The global image of what had once been a great metropolis remained a cross between the 'Black Hole' of historical legend and the tragic 'City of Joy' of modern cinema. The best you could hope for was salvation in the slums.

Even culturally, for all its achievements, Kolkata has been reduced to a provincial capital. The city continues to be the custodian of the best of the Bengali tradition, but it no longer produces work that the rest of India looks up to for inspiration. The major innovations in theatre, in art, in music, in writing, even in cinema, are taking place elsewhere in India. Kolkata's intellectual life, including in the pages of its newspapers, does not dominate—let alone anticipate—the national debate. Some of the best Kolkata journalists have left the city; even Bengalis with everything going for them here, like Pritish Nandy and Chandan Mitra, are thriving in Mumbai and Delhi. Non-Bengalis who made their reputations in Kolkata have preferred to preserve them elsewhere: Jug Suraiya has become a famous chronicler of the capital's suburbia, and the likes of M.J. Akbar, Swapan Dasgupta and Suhel Seth have also relocated their talents to New Delhi. Kolkata is left with its bhadralok, who stay not because, but in spite, of what the city offers them.

Of course all this is not purely Kolkata's fault: it cannot help the increasing centralization of everything in the capital, and the corresponding desire of many ambitious and talented people to move to where the action is. But the state of Bengal can still be held responsible for the widespread sense that Kolkata, complacently resting on its past laurels, no longer cares whether it matters to the rest of India or not. When a great city collectively loses the desire for greatness, its lights dim in more ways than one. It used to be said that when Kolkata catches a cold, the rest of India sneezes. For many years till quite recently, if Kolkata had a cold, the rest of India looked away—and hoped that the virus isn't catching.

Well, I am glad to acknowledge that Kolkata seems to have turned the corner. On repeated visits to the city I had felt that nothing had changed, that the only alternative to decline was stagnation. As the 21st century gets under way, I have discovered this is no longer true. Two things have happened: the problems are abating, and the spirit of change is in the air.

I am not suggesting that Kolkata has suddenly become a paragon of civic virtue. But the streets are cleaner, the garbage is being picked up, hawker encroachments cleared, and power-cuts are largely a thing of the past. There are still people sleeping on the pavement, but very much fewer than ever before: reforms in the Bengal countryside mean that destitute villagers no longer flock to Kolkata for survival, and the state has just undergone a political transformation after thirty-four years of increasingly sclerotic Left Front rule. Old city landmarks like the Town Hall have been magnificently restored; the Indian Musuem has had so many decades of dust and grime cleaned off it that it's only now that one can see what a splendid white marble building it is, not the dingy greyish-brown one I recall from my childhood. It may be true that one of the reasons that load-shedding does not regularly plunge the city into darkness is that, instead of the cliché that nothing succeeded like success, Kolkata has demonstrated that nothing succeeds like failure: the exodus of major industry in the last thirty years has reduced demand for power consumption. But there is also something positive in the air.

The signs of progress are everywhere: in the new roads and housing developments that are expanding the metropolis; in the long flyover over Lower Circular Road that has eased traffic congestion from the airport; in the stylish new buildings that have come up where collapsing colonial structures used to stand; in the hi-tech new Science City which both amuses and educates the young; in the gleaming Vidyasagar Setu, which bids fair to rival the great Howrah Bridge as both artery and symbol; in the dazzling prosperity of Salt Lake City, which used to be a mangrove swamp on the way to the airport; in the air-conditioned supermarkets and restaurants that are attracting a new breed of affluent customers. Kolkata feels like a real city once more.

If Kolkata offers encouragement to those who see it moving forward, what lessons can we draw for Bengal itself? Clearly, openness to industry is indispensable to the state's future. This is going to require a serious land policy that takes into account the interests of both farmers and industry: the latter needs land to establish itself, the former needs to be fairly compensated. Without land, there can be no industry, and no one with the interests of Bengal at heart can reasonably take the position that farming lands must never be alienated. The problem often lies with the interference of political goons who prevent farmers from selling land they had already committed to sell. The fact is that Bengal, like my home state of Kerala, suffers from an excess of politicization of everything. The joke is that one Bengali is a poet, two Bengalis is an argument, three Bengalis is a political party, and four Bengalis is two political parties. It's a joke, but it contains an uncomfortable element of truth. Bengal produces more politics than it can consume, and so it often gets consumed by its politics. Progress requires less politics and more action.

Another area requiring priority attention in Bengal is the power sector, which has been languishing despite the improvements in supply rendered possible by reduced demand. Additional production of power, and its effective distribution at viable prices, is essential if industry is to grow. I remember my late father, who was so fond of Bengal that he founded a Bengal-Kerala Cultural Society and ran it single-handedly for many years, joking that Bengalis have Banerjee, Chatterjee and Mukherjee but no energy! Energy in both senses of the word is indispensable for Bengal's growth and development. Fortunately Bengal is now led by a chief minister who, however controversial she may be, is not only a Banerjee but is a bundle of energy.

A final plea for Bengal as it moves forward is to revive its finest educational traditions. Presidency College used to be the finest educational institution in India; it is no longer that, and has not been for three decades. Where are Bengal's great colleges and universities? The state that gave us Shantiniketan and Visva-Bharati, the state of Derozio and Michael Madhusudan Dutt, which produced R.C. Dutt and Sri Aurobindo, where Jagdish Chandra Bose and C.V. Raman worked and taught, the motherland of Rabindranath and Kazi Nazrul Islam, the crucible from which Amartya Sen sprang, no longer boasts the educational pedigree and intellectual distinction that was the envy of the rest of India. Great educational institutions, the nurturers of fine minds, are not born overnight—which makes it all the more urgent that the work of creating them anew must begin yesterday, not tomorrow.

The fact is that Bengal cannot afford to remain dependent on handouts from New Delhi to compensate for gaps in the state's income because of the inhospitable environment for investors in the past. It cannot languish towards the bottom of the list in the World Bank's 'Doing Business in India' report, because it takes 200 days to obtain approvals and permits in Kolkata against 80 days in Hyderabad. It cannot have one of the lowest rankings (lower than Orissa) in per capita information technology exports. It cannot be a state whose best minds and most skilled workers seek to flee because opportunities for remunerative work are stifled by opportunistic politics. These are the things that I believe determined and confident leadership in the state government can change.

Most of you would be familiar with the story of the sinking of the ocean-liner *Titanic* in the early years of the last century, or at least have seen the film. For almost a hundred years till now, it was believed that the sinking of the *Titanic* on her maiden voyage from Southampton in England to New York in America was caused by the ship moving too fast and the crew failing to see the iceberg before it was too late. But now a new book, authored by a descendant of one of the officers of the ship, says that it was not an accident caused by speed, but by a steering blunder. It seems that the ship had plenty of time to miss the iceberg but the helmsman actually panicked and turned the ship the wrong way, and by the time the error was corrected, it was too late and the ship's side was fatally holed by the iceberg. The error occurred because at the time, seafaring was undergoing an enormous upheaval as a result of the conversion from sail to steam ships. The change meant there were two different steering systems and different commands attached to them. When the first officer spotted the iceberg two miles away, his order was misinterpreted by the quartermaster, who turned the ship left instead of right.

In a sense, Bengal's development failure has been like the story of the *Titanic*. As with the confusion caused by the new era where sail ships were being replaced by steamships, those who had ruled the state for more than three decades appeared unsettled by the global changes which have moved the economic system far beyond their old paradigms and theories. By opposing computers and mobile phones, blocking land acquisition for development work, and impeding economic reforms, they steered the ship of state left instead of right. Bengal must steer it back urgently, otherwise it is heading into the iceberg.

The most important challenge is to make the state hospitable to investors. I say to my friends on the Left: this does not mean betraying your workers, but finding them work. It does not mean giving up your values, but adding value to your economy. It does not mean placing profit above people, but rather, using profits to benefit the people.

The fact is that there is nothing wrong with the ship—Bengal, its people, its resources or its potential. But you have to move with the times and not be left behind where other states are moving forward by steering in the right direction. I have great hope in the creativity and resilience of the Bengali people. As I see the atmosphere of purposeful change around us, I am optimistic that Bengal will not be left behind.

VII

A SOCIETY IN FLUX

ASTROLOGY AND THE ASPIRING INDIAN

As always, the general elections in India have, in addition to the usual cast of political aspirants, campaign managers, publicists and vote-brokers, also brought into prominence an array of astrologers, numerologists and pandits. Candidates have been flocking to such soothsayers in large numbers, seeking advice on everything from the precise minute to file their nomination forms to the appropriate alignment of the doors of their campaign offices. Indians, after all, manage to live in that rare combination of modernity and superstition that defines them as a breed apart from the other peoples.

Where else in the world is so much made of an individual's astrological chart, that mysterious database which determines opportunities in life, marital prospects, and willingness to undertake certain risks? I once wrote that an Indian without a horoscope is like an American without a credit card. The truth of that observation shows no signs of fading away in the 21st century.

It seems particularly entrenched in our political world. As a believing Hindu, I make no claims to pure rationalism myself, but I am still bemused to read of the swearing-in of a minister that was delayed because a politician's astrologer told him the time was not auspicious to take the oath, or of a candidate's nomination papers being filed at the last possible minute to avoid the malign influences of the stars at other times of the day. Both are frequent occurrences in Indian political life.

It's not just a question of taking the oath of office on an auspicious day, and at the time determined by an astrologer; the stars even decide the date and time that a minister moves into his office and begins his work. Many a minister does not report to work for days after his swearing-in; files pend while the planets realign themselves more auspiciously. Superstition can also influence the selection of the minister's room in the government building, the allotment of the ministerial bungalow, and the placement of the furniture in the office, all of which are guided (if not actually directed) by gurus and pundits on the basis of time-honoured, if scientifically untested, principles.

My favorite story of this ilk is of the chief minister who refused to move into his official residence because a pundit claimed it was not built according to the correct spiritual principles of vaastu and that he would not fare well in it. The bungalow was accordingly redone, at great public expense, with new doorways being made and windows realigned to satisfy the pundit. At last the chief minister moved in—only to lose his job, and his new home, the next day in an unexpected political crisis.

Why on earth do otherwise intelligent, educated people put themselves in thrall to such superstition? I am all in favour of the innate human desire to propitiate the heavens. I am even prepared to entertain the notion that the cosmos might be sending us signals in every planetary realignment. But what makes us so credulous as to believe that soothsayers understand the code?

Not long ago, the chief minister of Tamil Nadu, the former actress Jayalalitha, decided to add an extra 'a' to the end of her name because a numerologically-minded astrologer told her that the new spelling would be more propitious for her turbulent political career. She promptly went on to win an election in her state—and then lost the next one. She won again, but as these words are written, she is in jail, having been convicted for corruption under her new name, though the transgressions apparently occurred under its old, less auspicious, spelling.

Of course it is entirely possible that Ms Jayalalithaa has attained political successes that a mere Ms Jayalalitha might not have. But on what possible basis can it be argued that the addition of a superfluous vowel made all the difference? One can scarcely believe that the heavens dispense their favours according to the number of vowels in mortals' names. But many Indians are firm believers, as the increasingly eccentric spellings of the names of movie stars and film titles will confirm. One of India's finest actors, Irfan Khan, suddenly rebaptized himself Irrfan, a change that many swear prefigured his career transformation.

New Delhi's political circles are rife with gossip about a former prime minister who was guided daily by a godman, and a former finance minister whose decisions were influenced by astrology (though tempered, it seems, by a former cabinet secretary who passed himself off as an amateur astrologer). The leader of Bihar's Rashtriya Janata Dal, Laloo Prasad Yadav, reportedly filled his swimming pool with mud and garbage because a pandit told him it would stop the 'leak' of members defecting from his party.

Most Indian politicians wear rings with stones tailored to specific planetary conjunctions that are auspicious for them, or designed to ward off malefic influences from planets unfavourably situated on their birth charts. Many swear it works for them; others take the agnostic view that one has nothing to lose by possibly propitiating the planets, except the price of the ring, a sort of Hindu version of Pascal's famous wager.

It turns out, however, that Indian politicians are not the only ones vulnerable to seduction by the Indian 'miracle mafia'. Former Indian Foreign Minister Natwar Singh reveals in his memoir that no less a personage than Margaret Thatcher was impressed by an Indian godman, Chandraswami, whom she received in her office shortly after becoming Conservative party leader. The godman impressed her enough with his mind-reading skills that she visited him again wearing, on his instructions, a red dress and sporting a religious talisman he had given her. At this second encounter, Chandraswami prophesied accurately that she would become prime minister within four years and serve for nine, eleven or thirteen years (she served for eleven).

There was one crucial difference from her Indian counterparts, though. When Natwar Singh, meeting her soon after she had become prime minister, whispered, 'Our man was proved right,' her reaction should not have surprised him.

'For a moment, she seemed flustered,' he recalled. 'Then, she took me aside and said: 'High Commissioner, we don't talk about these matters.' Indians do: our only saving grace is that we are superstitious, but not hypocritical.

OF CLUBS AND COLONIAL DRESS CODES

A controversy erupted in Chennai in 2014 after a Madras High Court Judge, Justice D. Hariparanthaman, was denied entry into the Tamil Nadu Cricket Association Club wearing a dhoti. Arriving at the club premises as he was to participate in a book release function organized by a former chief justice of the High Court, the judge was barred from entering since his choice of attire violated the club's dress code. Apparently the club only allows members or guests dressed in 'full trousers, shirts or T-shirts with collars and leather shoes' to enter the club premises. Ironically, the incident occurred at a time when the state government-owned Co-optex had organized a 'dhoti day' to promote the traditional garb across the state.

Justice Hariparanthaman, with due judicial restraint, termed the incident as 'unfortunate'. Politicians were a little less reticent. 'Dhoti is an integral part of Tamil culture. Denying entry to a person in dhoti is condemnable,' declared 90-year-old former Chief Minister M. Karunanidhi of the DMK, calling on the state government to intervene. Congress leader Gnanadesikan said it was 'regrettable' that a High Court judge was denied entry for wearing dhoti. 'It is not important who went there wearing dhoti,' he clarified, 'but a rule barring the entry into a club for a dhoti-clad person in Tamil Nadu is unacceptable.'

PMK founder Dr S. Ramadoss, an ally of the BJP, urged the government to amend the Act for Registration of Cooperative Societies to end 'the culture of clubs denying entry to those turning up in dhoti'. The PMK leader demanded an end to 'such British-era practices' and expressed regret that even former Supreme Court Justice V.R. Krishna Iyer was denied entry in 1980s in the Gymkhana Club in Chennai. He demanded that the state government move necessary amendments to the laws to ban clubs that do not honour Tamil culture.

Whether the government will go quite so far remains to be seen, though it may be on thin legal ground if it attempts to do that. Strictly speaking, there's nothing in the lawbooks, or the Constitution for that matter, that makes snobbishly objecting to a dhoti and chappals a punishable offence. After all, restaurants and hotels are within their rights to refuse to serve someone in a swimsuit or shorts, and temples often refuse to allow female worshippers to wear pants—and how do you legislate against that?

For the record, the same thing has happened to me, and in the same city. I was denied entry to my own sister's wedding reception at the Madras Gymkhana in 1982 because I was wearing an expensive silk kurta which, of course, didn't have a collar; a sloppier T-shirt, which did, would have been acceptable to the custodians of the club's peculiar standards. On another occasion, I had to tuck my kurta into my pants since the club in question only permitted 'tucked-in shirts'.

All these stipulations are, of course, colonial relics. They go back to the time when the clubs were set up by 'propah' Englishmen and Indians who aspired to be like them—the brown sahibs who fulfilled Macaulay's dream of constituting an intermediate class between the rulers and the ruled, 'a class of persons', as he put it in his famous Minute on Education, 'Indian in blood and colour, but English in taste, in opinions, in morals, and in intellect'. And, he might have added, in attire as well.

The Englishmen and the brown sahibs banded together in clubs that kept out those who weren't, or couldn't be, like them. Membership was selective and perpetuated the culture. As the English gradually left, what remained of the colonial ethos could be found in the club menus (which often featured bland items, designed for the addled colonial palate, that are rarely served in any self-respecting Indian home), their libraries—and their dress codes.

It was hardly surprising that in this particular incident, Tamil Nadu Cricket Association Club officials, under fire for defenestrating the judge, took umbrage not at their overzealous staff, but at the member who had invited Justice Hariparanthaman to the club—because he had failed to brief the guest properly on the dress code. 'The member has apologized to us', a club official was reported as saying. There was no word of any apology to the judge.

In all fairness, though, any private club is entitled to make and impose its own rules on its members, and several politically-incorrect denizens of clubdom have argued that clubs are well within their rights to frame their own codes to 'maintain decorum'. One particularly indiscreet soul confided to a journalist that the ban on the dhoti was only 'to prevent wardrobe malfunction under the influence of alcohol'. A member of the Madras Boat Club was quoted as pointing out, 'If someone wants to come to the club, it is better that they adhere to the rules. No one is forced to come here'.

This is unexceptionable: in a democracy, we all enjoy freedom of association, and that includes the freedom to associate obnoxiously only with people who dress like us.

But the argument can't be allowed to rest there. If clubs seek the right to be discriminatory in their practices, they must be obliged to confine their discrimination to their own members. They should simply not be permitted to hold public functions which include attendance by members of the general public. They cannot be allowed to have it both ways—to claim the privilege of exclusivity as a club, and enjoy the income from leasing out their premises and facilities to the great unshod. If they want to host book releases, they should have no choice but to accept that books are read by people of all sizes, ages, and attires.

The Tamil Nadu Cricket Association Club has promised to review its rules, but don't bet on any change. Once the current flap (which even featured an agitated debate at the Tamil Nadu Legislative Assembly) dies down, the club will undoubtedly go back to its hidebound ways. The entire logic of club culture is that it wants to keep the rest of the world out—to enjoy being an oasis of anglicized privilege that looks askance at the sartorially-challenged. But if someone files a PIL contesting their right to do this, one can only hope the case is heard by Justice Hariparanthaman.

HEALTH MINISTER, OUR KIDS NEED SEX ED

Iactually rather like our new health minister, Dr Harsh Vardhan. He is a pleasant, friendly, rather avuncular individual. I imagine that as a medical practitioner he must have had a gentle and reassuring bedside manner; certainly no one who has spent two minutes with him would ever accuse him of wanting to harm a fly.

And yet his recent remarks, first on discouraging the use of condoms to prevent AIDS and suggesting that fidelity was the preferred route, and then the blunt statement on his website that sex education in schools should be banned, risk doing great harm, not to flies but to human beings.

In his 'vision document' for Delhi, Dr Harsh Vardhan declared unambiguously: 'So-called "sex education" to be banned. Value Education will be integrated with course content. Yoga should be made compulsory.' I am all in favour of values education, and even of yoga, but I am at a loss to understand how the banning of sex education—and the related promotion of ignorance about sex—can do any good for our society.

Perhaps it is a generational problem: the health minister is an old-fashioned moralist with little idea about the recent changes in the sexual habits and practices of today's young Indians. A generation of parents has convinced itself that brushing problems under the carpet will ensure they don't exist. Don't teach kids sex education, and they won't practice sex. Wrong: they'll do it, but they'll do it unaware of the dangers, the means of protection, or the consequences of unprotected sex. The result could be sexually transmitted diseases, unwanted pregnancies resulting in clandestine abortions, and even HIV/AIDS. Ignorance kills.

I remember my former boss, United Nations Secretary-General Kofi Annan, telling me about a disconcerting experience he had had with an African president (whom I shan't name, since he is still in office). The president, an octogenarian Christian, interrupted Mr Annan when he was talking about condom use in the battle against AIDS. 'Mr Annan,' the president said disapprovingly, 'you are the Secretary-General of the United Nations. I don't want to associate you with condoms.' And he changed the subject, leaving Kofi Annan nonplussed.

Many senior Indians share the attitude of this distinguished statesman: sex and condoms are not subjects that important people in positions of political authority talk about. They are necessary evils, no doubt, but not to be discussed in polite company. But if you don't discuss them—don't acknowledge how important they are and how essential it is for your government, and your population, to be aware about them—you shroud yourself, and your society, in darkness. And the public health consequences can be horrendous.

This is why the promotion of ignorance is irresponsible, not virtuous. Fidelity may indeed be a better AIDS prevention measure than condoms, as our health minister believes, but saying so doesn't make every man or woman faithfully monogamous. Public health requires us to take into account the way people actually behave, not the way we wish they would behave. Since AIDS kills 2 million people a year around the world, we shouldn't be taking chances on its spreading in India.

That doesn't mean we should caricature the health minister's views. 'Any experienced NGO activist knows that condoms sometimes break while being used. That is why government campaigns in India, whether through the National Aids Control Organisation or the state governments, should focus on safe sex as a holistic concept which includes highlighting the role of fidelity to single partners,' Dr Harsh Vardhan has said in explaining his initial remarks. If he can ensure that the government continues to promote sexual awareness and not just abstinence, and the easy availability of condoms in addition to lectures on morality, Indians will be safer.

'For the past two decades,' Dr Harsh Vardhan added in his explanatory remarks, 'I have been stressing the need for safe sex using a combination of condoms and discipline which is in line with the Abstinence-Be Faithful-Condom (ABC) line of UNAIDS that has yielded great success in Uganda and forms part of the anti-AIDS campaigns of several countries. As the health minister,' he declared, 'I find it justified to include this simple message in the communication strategy of the government's anti-AIDS programmes. Condoms promise safe sex, but the safest sex is through faithfulness to one's partner. Prevention is always better than cure.'

These are unexceptionable remarks, but morality should not become a mask for promoting ignorance. I count on the health minister to act in full accordance with the letter and spirit of Dr Harsh Vardhan's explanation. Educate our kids about sex; make condoms easily and widely available (and affordable); provide no-questions-asked counselling for those with sex-related problems; and only then rely on the preaching of virtue. Otherwise you would be undermining our chance of preventing the spread of disease—and worse.

Alas, within five months of assuming charge, Dr Harsh Vardhan was defenestrated from the Health Ministry. Mysterious are the ways of politics and, governmental responsibility in the new dispensation.

IS CASTE BACK, OR DID IT EVER DISAPPEAR?

The news that a survey (conducted in over 42,000 households across India by the National Council of Applied Economic Research (NCAER) and the University of Maryland) has established that 27 per cent of Indians still practice caste untouchability, is not, in many ways, news at all. All of us have grown up in an India where we have seen such behaviour, though the kind of people who read English-language op-eds probably think of it as something that happens in rural, backward village Bharat, rather than the urban India they inhabit.

But this survey also packs a few other surprises. It shows almost every third Hindu (30 per cent) admitted to the practice (that is, they refused to allow Dalits, the former 'untouchables', into their kitchen or to use their utensils), but bizarrely enough, data from the survey showed that untouchability was also practised by Sikhs (23 per cent), Muslims (18 per cent) and Christians (5 per cent). These are faiths that pride themselves on their enshrining of equality and the brotherhood of faith. Dr Amit Thorat, the survey's lead researcher at NCAER, was quoted by the *Indian Express* as saying, 'These findings indicate that conversion has not led to a change in mindsets. Caste identity is sticky baggage, difficult to dislodge in social settings.'

These findings—confirming the persistence of the iniquitous practice of caste discrimination across India's religious communities—came on the heels of the outrage that greeted a prominent journalist, Rajdeep Sardesai, on social media when he tweeted his joy that two members of his caste of Goud Saraswat Brahmins ('GSBs') had been elevated to the Cabinet in the latest government reshuffle.

Part of the problem, undoubtedly, was surprise that a sentiment one might associate with, and therefore more easily accept from, someone of a more traditionalist, perhaps rural, background emerged from Sardesai, an English educated urban professional and a certified liberal. People of his ilk (mine too!) tend to disavow caste loyalties as unworthy relics of a more unequal pre-Independence past. As intellectual heirs of a freedom movement that explicitly rejected caste, and outlawed caste discrimination, we aren't supposed to admit to caste feeling even if, in some cases, it lurks somewhere beneath the surface.

Any elitism Sardesai acquired at the elite educational institutions he attended (Campion and Cathedral Schools in Bombay, followed by Oxford University) would normally be assumed to be an elitism of merit, of respect for education and cosmopolitan values. Caste pride sits oddly with such a background.

Or does it? I am conscious of my own bias in the opposite direction. The son of a Keralite newspaper executive who dropped his caste name (Nair) at college in response to Mahatma Gandhi's exhortations to do so, moved to London and brought his children up in westernized Bombay, I am a product of a nationalist generation that was consciously raised to be oblivious of caste.

I still remember my own discovery of caste. I was a 10-year-old representing the VI Standard in an inter-class theatrical event at which the VIII Standard's sketch featured Chintu (Rishi) Kapoor, younger son of the matinee idol and producer Raj Kapoor and later to become a successful screen heartthrob in his own right. I had acted, elocuted a humorous poem and MCed my class's efforts to generous applause, and the younger Kapoor was either intrigued or disconcerted, for he sought me out the next morning at school. 'Tharoor,' he asked me at the head of the steps near the toilet, 'what caste are you?'

I blinked my nervousness at the Great Man.

'I—I don't know,' I stammered.

My father, who never mentioned anyone's religion, let alone caste, had not bothered to enlighten me on such matters.

'You don't know?' the actor's son demanded in astonishment. 'What do you mean, you don't know? Everybody knows their own caste.'

I shamefacedly confessed I didn't.

'You mean you're not a Brahmin or something?'

I couldn't even avow I was a something. Chintu Kapoor never spoke to me again in school. But I went home that evening and extracted an explanation from my parents, whose eclectic liberality had left me in such ignorance. They told me, in simplified terms, about the Nairs; and so it is to Rishi Kapoor, celluloid hero of the future, that I owe my first lesson about my genealogical past.

So I grew up thinking of caste as an irrelevance, married outside my caste, and brought up two children to be utterly indifferent to caste, indeed largely unconscious of it. Even after I entered the hothouse world of Indian politics I did not consciously seek to find out the caste of anyone I met or worked with; I hired a cook without asking his caste (the same with my remaining domestic staff) and have entertained all manner of people in my home without the thought of caste affinity even crossing my mind.

Surely, so has Rajdeep—which is what makes his tweet all the more surprising. But perhaps it's those who reacted to him with such savagery who need to pause and reflect. India is a land of multiple identities, and one of the key identities, inescapably, is caste. To some, it's an instrument of political mobilization; as the Yadav ascendancy in north India has repeatedly demonstrated, when many Indians cast their vote, they vote their caste. English-speaking urban Indians may scorn such behaviour even while accepting it as part of India's political reality. After all, none of us would object if a Dalit leader advertised her pride in being a Dalit, or called for Dalit solidarity. Part of the outrage at Rajdeep Sardesai is, of course, because he's not a member of an oppressed community celebrating its achievements: he is someone at the top of the heap, not merely a Brahmin but a Goud Saraswat Brahmin at that, and he's thrilled about members of this privileged tribe acquiring even more power and prominence.

But could it be that his attitude reflects not so much casteism as an admission of its diminished appeal as a badge of identity? Had Sardesai celebrated the elevation of two Campionites, or even two Oxonians, in the same spirit, no one would have objected (except maybe people who went to rival educational institutions). But isn't it possible that his unreflective celebration of two GSBs suggests that his attitude to caste is so casual that he thinks of it as nothing more than the equivalent of any one of the other labels he can also claim?

Had Sardesai thought consciously that his tweet would be interpreted as casteist, he surely would not have issued it. Instead, perhaps, there's an element of post-modernism about the entire fiasco: he said what he did not because his caste matters so much to him, but precisely because it doesn't. He doesn't base his friendships, his hiring decisions or his political preferences on the basis of caste, and so he unselfconsciously applauded his fellow GSBs the way he might have applauded two members of the same cricket team, the same journalistic fraternity or the same social club as himself. GSB is just another type of identity he shares with others.

At least, that's what I choose to believe: I haven't asked him myself. But I don't need to. Caste won't disappear from the Indian landscape: too many political and administrative benefits (and disadvantages) derive from your caste affiliation for that to happen. For many Indians, it still matters greatly that they inter-marry with, dine with and admit into their homes only people of approved castes. For someone like Sardesai, who married outside his caste, abhors caste prejudice and thrives in an eclectic social environment, caste doesn't matter in quite the same way. To upbraid him for casteism is like calling Jawaharlal Nehru casteist for allowing people to refer to him as 'Pandit' Nehru.

In other words, caste will always be there, but as Sardesai unconsciously reveals, for many of us it doesn't pack the same punch it used to. If it becomes more and more one of many interchangeable, mutable forms of identity—one fraternity of many that an Indian can lay claim to—it can cease to matter so much. The majority of Indians aren't there yet, which is why Sardesai's tweet was greeted with such shock. But if we can't escape being conscious of caste, let's be conscious of it like Sardesai—as the equivalent of an old school tie, nothing more, nothing less. That will remove its sting. And then maybe more people will let Dalits into their kitchens when the next survey rolls around a few years from now.

DELHI UNIVERSITY'S FYUP FIASCO

The problem of over-regulation and political interference in education continues to afflict India's efforts to improve the quality of higher education. The renewed controversy about Delhi University's four-year undergraduate programme (FYUP), the UGC's sudden ultimatum declaring the course not to be in conformity with the National Education Policy, and the undermining of Vice Chancellor Dinesh Singh, have all brought the nation's attention to an issue that has sadly been mishandled by the new government.

Delhi University is the premier university in the country, its pre-eminent position reinforced by its location in the nation's capital and its reputation for attracting students from across the country. Whether it is the quality of its faculty, the diversity and brilliance of its students, or the wide-ranging achievements of its alumni, the university ranks at the forefront of all these parameters and is rightly regarded as the fountainhead of our nation's intellectual capital. Whether you like the FYUP or not, whether you think Vice Chancellor Dinesh Singh is a brilliant and committed educationist or an academic dictator, the university (of which I am an alumnus, 1972-75) should not have been allowed to suffer in the course of this contentious debate.

The FYUP was formally introduced into DU when I served in the Ministry of Human Resource Development, and I am familiar with the passionate views of its critics amongst both faculty and students. The former felt the new concept was insufficiently thought through and ill prepared for; they were also resistant to the new teaching demands the changed system would make on them. Many students, including the principal student unions (both the Congress-backed NSUI and the BJP's ABVP) disliked being asked to put in an extra year to earn the honours degree they used to be able to earn in three years; they were also resentful of being made the guinea pigs in a new experiment while students in most other universities could emerge with a bachelor's degree in three years.

The Left, as usual, denounced the introduction of a four-year degree as reflective of a creeping 'Americanization' of India's education system. Whatever one may think about the US, there's no arguing with the fact that it has the best and most efficient higher education system in the world, much of it run in the private sector and for profit. Of course there are excellent state-funded higher education systems in countries like France and Germany, but they require a level of government resources that we simply do not have available in New Delhi. Though the US was not specifically in the university's mind, as far as I know, when it came up with FYUP, one might as well ask: Why not import useful aspects of the American system if we can't afford to replicate it ourselves?

Still, MHRD officials, led by Minister M.M. Pallam Raju, and I tried to address the issues raised by both groups in a reasonable and responsive manner. But we did not overrule the university as it set about implementing FYUP. My fundamental argument in this debate was one of principle: I did not think it was healthy for politicians and bureaucrats to overrule universities on matters that are clearly within their academic prerogatives. I dare say that those professorial friends of mine who most vociferously demanded my intervention to 'save' the university would have been among the first to object if I had interfered on a matter infringing their own areas of responsibility.

So instead I asked: has the university adopted FYUP in conformity with its own rules, regulations and established procedures? I was assured by the senior officials of the ministry—most of whom are still there, serving the new government—that indeed it had. The FYUP proposal, I was told, had been the subject of numerous consultations with faculty, students and parents; it had been presented to and approved by the University's Academic Council and its Executive Council, that too by lopsidedly overwhelming majorities. In that case, I said, I saw no basis for a minister to intervene. Students and faculty should work out their objections and concerns within established University processes.

Nonetheless, Pallam Raju went the extra mile and set up a committee of experts under the UGC to look into the working of the FYUP and the process of its implementation. This was not to question the policy itself, but the academic rigour with which it was carried out. Course design, syllabi and patterns of instruction are legitimate areas for teachers to be heard by administrators. MHRD and UGC have an overall responsibility in educational policy-making. So the committee was a sensible mechanism to reconcile the two camps and ensure that the University's interests were safeguarded.

It is presumably this committee that has advised the UGC to find the new system in violation of the established education policy, which decrees a 10+2+3 format. I must say I am puzzled that such an obvious objection was not raised earlier, when the FYUP was first being rolled out. The UGC's surprising directive to DU last week to scrap FYUP on these grounds smacks of political expediency—the fulfilment of a BJP campaign promise—rather than of principle.

It may be heresy to say it, but education as a sector remains the last frontier largely untouched by reforms. Higher education in India is still largely over-regulated and under-governed. The economic reforms of the last twenty-odd years have unleashed our economic potential, and the governance reforms of the last ten years have raised our civic awareness. However, we as a nation need to completely overhaul our educational systems and processes if we are to realize the full potential of the demographic dividend that awaits us in the coming decades. Resisting change comes too easily to us, but inertia does not facilitate progress.

While government expenditure on education went up to 4.8 per cent of GDP under the UPA, the truth is that the investments that we make in our educational sector do not yield satisfactory returns. Teaching and research at all levels of the academic spectrum, which are professions that attract the most promising minds in our competitor nations, have largely become another sarkari naukri that offer a job for life replete with perks and benefits but with little incentive for performance or disincentives for non-performance. Relative to the national per capita income, our teachers enjoy a salary structure that is one of the most favourable in the world. And yet by any measure of performance, as repeatedly shown in a number of professional surveys and global rankings of universities, we are languishing at modest to mediocre levels of educational achievement. There are honourable exceptions, but we are not in any position to consider ourselves beyond change, improvement or reform.

The academic community has repeatedly responded to concerns about academic quality by arguing that academic institutions and processes need to be freed from the clutches of government functionaries and their overbearing interference. Paradoxically in the case of DU, when the UPA government tried to go by this policy, all hell broke loose. This unwillingness to abide by due process when the outcome is unfavourable has increasingly become entrenched not just in academia but in our national character. The BJP has now gone to the other extreme by using the UGC to ask all universities to disband four-year undergraduate degrees, which is an absurd infringement of academic freedom. Autonomy is the only answer to this dilemma.

I had urged the vice chancellor (who was a batchmate of mine at St. Stephen's) and his critics to engage with each other in a spirit of academic give-and-take, so as to ensure that both sets of concerns about FYUP were fully taken into account in the implementation of the new policy. Now he is gone, and a serious, well-intentioned effort to introduce change has been scuppered, with even less consultation than when it was introduced.

The four-year undergraduate degree (which is, incidentally, the international standard) may or may not be inherently superior to the three-year degree. However, the vice chancellor of Delhi University must, in principle, be accorded the respect and autonomy to follow the statutes that govern the University and, with the approval of the Academic Council and Executive Council, carry out the changes that they believe will strengthen DU's position as a centre of excellence. The freedom to experiment, to innovate and perhaps even to fail, is a freedom that must be recognized and cherished. That freedom, along with the vice chancellor, was demolished by the events of this year.

The victims of the mishandling of this entire episode are many: the principle of academic autonomy, the quest for educational reform, the ministry's reputation for consistency and integrity in policy-making, the vice chancellor's credibility, the university's reputation, and above all the students themselves. Both those students who joined the FYUP last year and those who were about to seek admission to DU when the government asked the UGC to perform its flip-flop have been plunged into confusion and uncertainty. They—and Delhi University—deserved better from our new rulers.

FILLING STOMACHS AND MINDS:
THE MID-DAY MEAL SCHEME

Of the many sad news stories that find their way from India into the international press, the saddest in a long while concerned the deaths of twenty-two children in July 2013 in a government school in the poor rural district of Chapra in Bihar. The children were poisoned by their mid-day meals—a vital part of a programme of government-provided nutrition in the schools—which it appears were cooked in oil carelessly stored in used pesticide containers. The sheer horror of parents seeing their kids safely off to school, only to hear they had been killed by something intended to benefit them, is unbearable to contemplate.

Reaction was swift—predictable breast-beating about the inefficiency of India's government services, particularly in rural areas, the country's woeful standards of hygiene, and the inattentive implementation of even flagship national schemes by the country's twenty-eight state governments. 'Free school meals kill children', one headline screamed. The mid-day meal scheme itself has been trashed by critics in India and abroad as wasteful and counter-productive, with one critic in a British newspaper even going so far as to say that there is 'little evidence to suggest that schoolchildren are actually getting any nutritional value from it at all'.

The truth, however, is quite the opposite. The scheme, which costs the Government of India an estimated Rs 10,000 crore a year (to feed 120 million schoolchildren in over a million government primary schools across the country), little more than three cents a child, has been an extraordinary success. By providing free and balanced nutrition to schoolchildren, it has provided a powerful incentive to poor families to send their kids to school and, equally important, to keep them there throughout the day. Attendance rates have improved, sometimes by as high as 10 per cent, and dropout rates have declined thanks to the scheme. Social barriers in a stratified society have been broken by a scheme that obliges children of different castes to sit together and eat the same meal at the same time and the same place.

Children whose families could not afford to feed them properly have gained measurably. In drought-affected areas, the mid-day meal scheme has allowed children who would otherwise have starved to overcome the risks of malnourishment. One scholar, Farzana Afridi, has written in the *Journal of Development Economics* that the scheme 'improved nutritional intakes by reducing the daily protein deficiency of a primary school student by 100%, the calorie deficiency by almost 30% and the daily iron deficiency by nearly 10%'.

Critics of the scheme, who see it as symptomatic of big-government run amok and ask why it is necessary for any government to feed schoolchildren, forget that if governments didn't pay for it, no one else could. The idea originated three decades ago in the southern state of Tamil Nadu, whose then chief minister, the film star M.G. Ramachandran, expanded a pilot scheme of his predecessor K. Kamaraj by introducing free meals in all schools, in a measure widely critiqued as populist and fiscally irresponsible. Children, his detractors argued, go to school to learn, not to eat. (They overlooked the fact that if the children cannot eat, they cannot learn: empty stomachs make it difficult to fill minds.) The critics were silenced by the voters, who expressed their support for the scheme at the elections, and by its results—improved literacy rates and nutrition levels in Tamil Nadu. Soon other states were imitating the scheme, and in 1995, the central government followed suit, supplementing state government budgets so that children throughout the country could enjoy the same benefit. Today, 87 per cent of the government schools in the country implement the scheme.

Its benefits have ensured the mid-day meal scheme's popularity, but the quality of its implementation has varied across states, with some more capable than others of maintaining the standards required to provide a reliable service. Many of the northern states, like Bihar, have been laggards in creating kitchens and storage facilities, providing utensils and administering the scheme. The Government of India provides funds for cooks and helpers and has devised guidelines for the scheme's implementation, but schools come under state governments, who have not always been models of reliability. The rule requiring cooked meals to be tasted by at least two adults before being served to the children has often been ignored, as it was in the case of the Chapra tragedy.

Attempts to enforce the rule have met with unexpected resistance from teachers, who are obliged to rotate tasting duty: they object that they are at school to teach students, not to taste their food, and some teachers' unions have refused to perform this task. Sadder still has been the reaction of some parents in Bihar who have pulled their children out of school rather than risk them being poisoned. Such concerns are understandable, but they are manifestly an over-reaction. The Chapra tragedy has at least focused attention on a scheme that public opinion has largely taken for granted. It would be a great pity if, in examining what went wrong, deficiencies in the scheme's implementation were to obscure its very real accomplishments.

The mid-day meal scheme has transformed lives and helped educate a generation of poor schoolchildren. It should be emulated by other developing countries, not shunned because of a preventable tragedy.

INDIA'S MISSING AND ABUSED WOMEN

In the 1920s, a young Tamil girl sang and starred in her school musical. It was, ostensibly, a private event with few outsiders. Yet so exceptional was her singing that the newspaper *Swadesamitran* ran her photograph and wrote about the event. Seeing that photo in the newspaper, her household 'was appalled' for, as the music historian V. Sriram writes, 'good, chaste women never had their photographs published in papers'.

Today, this seems like an archaic, if minor, prejudice based on gender: one fostered by a conservative, ill-educated, economically stagnant and culturally insular society of the 1920s. There are more vicious examples of gender discrimination now, from dowry deaths to multiple rapes in Delhi. Yet the census of 2011 reveals the worst discrimination of all: there are even more 'missing women' in India than Amartya Sen first realized, a quarter of a century ago.

In fact, like a virus out on the loose, these prejudices of the mind feast and fester on in our souls to create an unequal and unjust society. Gender-based prejudices take on many forms: from the psychologically terrifying to the subtly demoralizing. Yet, nowhere is this gender based inequity seen more vividly than when we look at the declining sex-ratios.

The 2011 census revealed that for the under-6 age group, there were only 914 girls for every 1,000 boys. This child-sex ratio, or CSR, was 927 girls per 1,000 boys in the 2001 Census; in fact the CSR has declined in twenty-eight of the thirty-five states. The CSR in India suggests things are getting worse for girls and women in India, even while the economy is getting better.

More alarming is the inverse correlation between declining child-sex ratio and increased economic growth. In Gujarat, where economic growth is much heralded, this shortfall of girls is seen starkly between backward and non-backward districts, with the former at 923 and the latter at 873. Ironically, regions with large tribal communities, in general, have better CSRs than the high-growth areas of the country. Alarmingly, states like Tamil Nadu, which were historically gender agnostic, have begun to show a marked decline in CSRs as well. All in all, during the decade of unprecedented wealth creation, India became a terrible place to be conceived female.

Notwithstanding the fact that some states like Haryana and Punjab have had historically low ratios since 1880s, and they have shown dramatic improvement in the past decade, the fact that in 2011 they continue to have CSRs less than 850 girls for 1,000 boys demonstrates that much more needs to be done. Their natural rate is estimated to be around 952: that's a hundred girls missing for every 1,000 boys.

This said, it is also important to remember that there could be other reasons that affect the natural birth rate of boys. Professor Emily Oster at the University of Chicago has argued that since women who carry Hepatitis B virus are likely to have a higher number of boys, there is a biological aspect to this gender divide. She estimates 20-30 per cent of 'missing women' in India can be ascribed to the Hepatitis B. This Hepatitis B and in-vitro gender phenomenon is seen in far-flung populations of Taiwan and natives in Alaska. If further validated, this gender divide has a epidemiological and public health aspect that deserves closer attention.

But that explanation for 20-30 per cent of our missing women still doesn't explain the rest of the 70-80 per cent. We need not belabour the question of why this is so: two socio-economic pressures, dowry and the greater economic value of being male, explain our disgraceful prejudices against girls. But what can we learn from these depressing census figures?

First, rising education in itself is not enough. We're becoming more literate and less gender-friendly.

Second and sadly, increased female education is neither a sufficient nor necessary condition to ensure stable gender ratios. Numerous studies had led us to believe that educating girls could transform society. Not true in this respect, alas.

Third, income growth can simply increase access to technological tools that perform selective abortions. Richer people aren't necessarily wiser nor more decent. Punjab and Haryana continue to prove that it is possible for a mediaeval mindset to flourish amidst post-modern shopping malls.

Fourth, legal restrictions haven't been effective. We already have the Pre-conception and Pre-Natal Diagnostic Techniques Act, 1994, but it hasn't improved CSR. Worse, as Home Secretary G.K. Pillai acknowledged: 'Whatever measures that have been put in over the last 40 years have not had any impact on the child sex ratio.'

Fifth, India's modernization has worsened the practice of dowry rather than reduced it. Professor Siwan Anderson at the University of British Columbia has argued that caste continues to perpetuate dowry because India's endogamous marriage practices restrict the supply of marriage partners—and as a result efficient matching of individuals doesn't occur. Caste, in a sense, acts as a barrier in the free market of marriage. Then dowry becomes a method to bid for mates, signal social status and perpetuate an arms race to reach the top of the pecking order. Free enterprise has unshackled the economy, but the beneficiaries are operating in a restricted marriage market, limited by caste. They just demand higher dowries now.

What does the shortage of girls mean for us as a society? In economics, when the supply of a good is limited, the 'price' of that good rises if and only if there exists an orderly and legal market to transact. In its absence, you get blackmarketing, violence, theft and trafficking to possess that good. It doesn't take much imagination to connect the dots and recognize what this means when one gender is in short supply. Cases of polyandry are being reported from Haryana. In China, where the one-child policy has created a similar imbalance, there are horrifying stories of predatory bands of young males on the prowl for scarce women.

Can policy-makers do something about it? Governments can't usually alter cultures, but laws can be creatively used to help. There are two approaches—a 'negative' and a 'positive' approach. A 'negative' approach seeks to use the power of the State to restrict the ability of citizens to technologically discriminate the foetus on the basis of its gender. It denies the freedom of the present generation in order to protect the right to exist of future generations. This would involve stricter implementation of existing laws and making punishments more stringent. But this approach in general has yielded suboptimal results. In any case, in a democracy like India's, it's hard to tell people what they can't do, or to enforce legislation that tries to do that.

The positive approach focuses on incentives. How about tax breaks for mixed-caste marriages? Grants for having female children? If girls are undervalued because they don't earn as much as men, countervailing policies can be made. Since our growing economy unduly favours men, there is a role for government to help create employment opportunities for women. Mandating benefits for gender-neutral employers, or ensuring legal protections for female staff, can increase women's employment opportunities and in turn contribute to increasing the economic 'value' of a girl child.

All however is not dismal. Much of India has to learn to from Punjab's achievement over the past decade. In 2001, the CSR in Punjab was 798. In 2011, that has risen to 846—a 48-point increase! It shows that we can stem, prevent and reverse the slide. That would not just be beneficial for our collective future but also in accordance with the injunctions of our most orthodox texts. Changing CSR numbers might seem like a 21st-century fad, but in fact it's consonant with our ancient wisdom. The *Manusmriti*, no less, proclaims: 'where women are not revered, all rites are useless'.

But they are not revered. Linked to the phenomenon of the missing woman is the shameful abuse of the ones who are here. The horrifying rape and murder of a student physiotherapist in Delhi in December 2012 focused national attention on the widespread phenomenon of violence against women. The attention was overwhelmingly focused on rape, but in the process, the fact of generalized violence against women was overlooked. Men are, of course, physically stronger than women, so the one thing they can usually do is to impose themselves violently on the weaker sex. Wife-beating may not be as common as it used to be, but it persists nonetheless: many a bruise that a woman, out of pride, tries to pass off as the result of a household accident has in fact been caused by a man. Honour killings, assumed to a problem of Islamic societies, have occurred in India, as some fathers and brothers have killed their own daughters and sisters for having too readily adopted the sexual mores of the 21st century, and done so with men of the 'wrong' caste or religion. In parts of India we still worship women who have, often under intolerable pressure, cast themselves on the funeral pyres of their dead husbands. We have the uniquely Indian practice of burning brides whose parents have not paid as much dowry as expected.

Of all places, Kerala, sadly, has begun to prove that even education does not necessarily breed decency toward women. I write this with deep regret, having often, in my books and columns, celebrated the empowerment of Kerala's women (and been put right on the subject by Keralite women who know better.) But it is now widely reported that violence against women is rising in Kerala—some figures show a 300 per cent increase. Kerala's women are educated, and so are their men, but women still do not escape the iron law of social conformism, and many have driven up the state's suicide rates to record levels. The large number of Keralite men working in the Middle East, separated from their families and imbibing from their new surroundings a traditionalist attitude towards women, does not help; they often return home unprepared to deal with the expectations of the educated women they have left behind, and when clashes occur, the resort to violence is all too common. If violence against women is on the rise in educated Kerala, then we have a national problem that policy-makers cannot afford to ignore. Every time a woman is the victim of violence anywhere in our country, each Indian is diminished.

What can we do about it? Talking about it in the English-language media is hardly enough. Awareness of the problem must be increased, especially amongst those who don't read liberal and enlightened newspapers or books and may not even be conscious that they have the right to reject and resist violence. What is needed is social change, and that comes painfully slowly in our country. A national campaign to shame every man who assaults a woman might be one way—of using the mass media to change the masses. There's a challenge to the more public-spirited of our PR and advertising gurus. Are they man enough to take it on?

As for that young girl who was once chided for getting her photograph published in the newspaper—in 1998 she went on to be awarded the Padma Vibhushan, India's second highest civilian award. She was D.K. Pattammal, the grand matriarch of Carnatic music. As her life exemplifies, in every seed, there is nestled a mighty banyan—awaiting its opportunity to bloom.

EMPOWERING INDIAN WOMEN

The horrific gang-rape and death of a young woman in Delhi in December 2012 shocked and outraged India like never before. But this tragedy did not just bring forth feelings of fear and anger, it also, quite ironically, created an atmosphere of greater sensitivity and receptivity to the entire spectrum of issues relating to gender equality. The suffering of Nirbhaya, as she was called by the media and as she is known to most Indians today (though I would have preferred to use her real name, Jyoti Singh, which her father proudly revealed to the world) was a mirror placed before Indian society, and the reflection we see was ugly and grotesque beyond belief.

And yet I do dare to suggest that we must not give up on hope for a better and more just future for India's women. It is not enough for one who, being both a male and a politician, is a twice-damned target of popular anger in the wake of Nirbhaya, to express my own sense of outrage and horror at not just what this braveheart had to go through on that bus that gloomy December night, but at what millions of unknown and unrecognized Indian women, born and unborn, have to go through on a daily basis. It is essential to recognize that their struggle is a struggle not merely confined to their gender but it is the struggle of every right minded and patriotic Indian citizen who wants a more just and more equal India.

The question of how women are treated in Indian society was not a question ever lacking in salience. It has been a recurrent theme in our discourse on social reform; indeed, no other area has been the subject of as much sustained attention or effort from every quarter—the government, NGOs, the media, society—with such consistency. It is a concern that reveals itself in every conversation of national importance, whether it pertains to economic development, empowerment and poverty eradication, education and employment, crime, law and order, governance—or even national security.

The broad theme that I want to address is thus one of women's rights in society, and how they can be promoted and secured. Measurable and sustainable gains in this endeavour will require that we address not only the manifestations of misogyny in various fields, but also the root of the problem—which is, simply, that we still struggle with entrenched social attitudes, transmitted norms and imbibed values that militate against equality for women, in some cases elevating and yet diminishing them as idealized mothers and wives, and in the worst cases seeing them as no more than property or objects for use. Such beliefs are akin to a cancer on the soul of our society: providing symptomatic relief is crucial if we are to function at all, but our condition will improve only when we treat the underlying malaise.

A government, and more broadly a society, has two primary tools at its disposal to effect a change in prevalent societal perceptions and norms: legislation, and education. The former is a top-down approach, imposed for the greater good, or simply to prevent acts the legislators—though not all society—see as morally repugnant. It is based on instrumental logic, seeking most commonly to punish the acts that it would deter, and to a lesser extent to reward the acts it would encourage. It can play a leading role, establishing a right with all the force of the law, sometimes long before society as a whole is willing to accept such a right in such a form. Laws are believed to evolve, over time, from customs and norms; legislation-driven reform may be seen as an attempt to reverse-engineer that process.

Education is a more organic approach to social change. Particularly in the modern world, it is the arena through which children are socialized into the world. It is the vehicle for a host of values, principles and beliefs, and we have ample evidence that ideas imbibed in childhood (or during the schooling experience) are remarkably resilient, persisting to define both conduct and judgement of the individuals who imbibe them long after they reach adulthood. By ensuring that our children imbibe the values we wish them to embody in later life, we can achieve a manner of social change that is not only sustainable but in fact self-sustaining. These are, in the long run, the same values that they will inculcate in their children—and those children in theirs in turn, and so on.

Though I have pointed out, in a previous essay in this volume, that education alone does not guarantee respect for women, as the rising statistics for gender violence in highly-educated Kerala confirm, one could still argue that taken together, especially over an extended period of time, education and legislation together are fairly powerful tools. They can establish rights, protect them, and over time establish them as the standards for societally-valued conduct, thereby ensuring that they are passed on to succeeding generations. Over time, one would believe, they can erode even the most formidable resistance, until the practices we believe are best consigned to history will indeed be found only in the archives. Against such efforts is arrayed the not-insignificant inertia of years of tradition and social custom, generations upon generations raised believing that a certain idea was practiced because it was correct, and correct because it has always been practiced. That this resistant strain continues to dominate so much of our social milieu would lead to one of two conclusions: that we have vastly underestimated its staying power, or that the reach of either of our tools—legislation or education—has not been as great as we need and desire.

This understanding of the power of education and legislation does not, after all, come as a revelation. India has a rich history of social reform movements which sought to bring about precisely such a change in values and mindsets, using a judicious mix of both top-down and grassroots-origin methods. When

Raja Rammohun Roy initiated the pioneering work of the Brahmo Samaj, for instance, practices like sati were rampant. The Brahmo Samaj advocated the abolishment of sati, on the (wholly reasonable!) grounds that burning innocent young married women on their husband's funeral pyre was an atrocity, and that such a practice was too abhorrent to be justified on any moral grounds. The Brahmo Samaj actively advocated widow remarriage, not only as the humane and practical alternative to sati, but also as an answer to the traditional view that a widow was somehow impure or a source of misfortune. The noted social reformer Ishwarchandra Vidyasagar led by example when he arranged for the marriage of his son to a widow, something that was unheard of in his day. It was in no small part due to the efforts of these early reformers that the colonial administration was persuaded to outlaw sati altogether, although it was many years before punishment could be known to descend with certainty on any who violated that law. In turn, even as the declaration that sati was illegal crystallized disparate strands of resistance amongst the more traditional elements, it empowered the reformers to act with both legal and moral force on their side.

In that sense, legislation often marks a watershed moment in the struggle. Consider the Hindu Marriage Act of 1955: it was a response to the inbuilt inequalities in the traditional systems of marriage, and a guarantee that both spouses could enjoy equal rights under any marriage. As policymakers and legislators of this country, it is imperative for us to keep in mind the interests of all those who are affected. It is no mean feat in a country where the division of marital property is left to the discretion of the judges that the law is finally at par with international standards where a woman gets a 50 per cent share in marital property; and where children are living with their mother, she is entitled to more than that share of the property. The very concept of visitation rights—that the parent who does not have custody is still entitled to play a part in the lives of their children—embodies an evolution in the human rights discourse, whereby rights are not only equally awarded but equally unbundled between genders. Going by precedent, it was found that courts grant only 5-35 per cent of the man's income to the woman, even if the woman has children to support. The Hindu Marriage Act (Section 27) always provided that property jointly acquired by a married couple could be divided by the courts and allocated equally to the married couple. The 2010 amendment was undertaken to ensure that men and women do actually get equal shares in such property.

Similarly, the year 2013 was an important one for Indian legislation, since it marked the passing of the Criminal Law (Amendment) Bill. This amendment was passed by the Lok Sabha on 19 March, and by the Rajya Sabha only two days later. Again, while it was catalyzed by the Delhi gang-rape, a case for more stringent penal provisions against sexual violence could have been made far earlier.

The National Crime Records Bureau (NCRB) states that there were 309,546 crimes against women reported in the country in 2013. This is as compared to 244,270 in 2012—an increase of almost 27 per cent. Andhra Pradesh, accounting for nearly 7.1 per cent of the country's population, accounted for the highest number of crimes against women. These numbers remain alarmingly high even when viewed in light of our overall population figures as well: while no society has succeeded in eradicating rape or gender-based violence, over 300,000 instances in a country of 1.2 billion people means one in every four thousand people has been the victim of such a crime. It also amounts to over 800 instances of gender violence every day, or over 30 incidents every hour. Every other minute, somewhere in India, a woman is facing some ill-treatment—perhaps a catcall, perhaps an inappropriate touch, perhaps a nightmarish violation she will not survive. To make matters worse, the NCRB figures also indicate that rape is the single fastest growing crime reported in India, and even then we know that a large number of offences go unreported.

What these statistics point to is the dichotomy—the blatant hypocrisy, really—between how women are treated in our mythology and in real life. As a goddess, the woman is worshipped as the embodiment of the feminine power, a source of energy and knowledge, a harbinger of fortune and good luck. Real women are raped, molested and suppressed on a daily basis: one in every 6,000, one every other minute, and counting. Years after we abolished dowry, we continue to register hundreds of cases of dowry-related violence and harassment. We know that some of these are fabricated, or efforts to harass the groom's family. Herein lies a lesson: legislation cannot prevent such conduct, it merely drives it underground, and creates its own problems vis-à-vis enforcement.

The challenge remains what it has always been: to change societal perceptions so that individual worth is not calculated based on gender, and human rights are not unequally shared based on an accident of birth. Ironically, rape is looked upon with disdain even in the most fervent patriarchy—because it brings dishonour to the family, by 'defiling' a woman who is seen as the rightful property of her husband and the embodiment, quite literally, of the family's honour. And before we pass judgment on societies whose laws and customs still reflect these norms, let us remember the number of instances in India where young women and men have been exiled, tortured or killed precisely because their actions (usually, asserting a degree of sexual or marital autonomy) were seen as bringing dishonour to the family; let us remember also that the family itself has often been the enforcer of such edicts.

And, before we dismiss even these instances as the preserve of remote corners of our nation, views not shared by 'people like us', let us recall also the significant opposition faced by the provision regarding marital rape that was proposed as part of the recent amendment. Even today, I receive on a daily basis long and eloquently argued emails warning that recognizing as a crime 'marital rape' will lead to the breakdown of the system of marriage, and the devastation of Indian society as we know it, and that it is my duty as a minister to prevent such an outrage. There are those who, in the 21st century, can demand—daily, and repeatedly—that their government be a democracy, but can only think of the bedroom as a dictatorship. Feminists (or all those who may not self-identify as feminists but believe in the equality of the genders) think of rape as a crime because it impinges on the autonomy of a woman and violates that autonomy.

We have often heard it said that the mark of a healthy society is the treatment that is meted out to its women. This is not merely an assertion, but a truth that is borne out by substantial research, and it leads me to my next point: the education of women and girls.

One of the more difficult questions I found myself being asked through my years as a public official, both abroad and in India, especially when I addressing a generalist audience, is: 'what is the single most important thing that can be done to improve the world?' It's the kind of question that tends to bring out the bureaucrat in the most direct of communicators, as one feels obliged to explain how complex are the challenges confronting humanity; how no one task alone can be singled out over other goals; how the struggle for peace, the fight against poverty, the battle to eradicate disease, must all be waged side-by-side—and so mind-numbingly on. I finally realized, though, that there is a simple answer. To ensure that attitudes towards women's rights are inculcated, in a sustainable and self-sustaining manner, as I have explained in my essay on education in this volume, we can adopt a two-word mantra—'educate girls'.

It really is that simple. And not only is it of immense value for the girl in question, but also an exceptional benefit to the nation. Scholarly studies and research projects have established what common sense might already have told us (and what Gandhi often did): that if you educate a boy, you educate a person, but if you educate a girl, you educate a family and benefit an entire community. The evidence is striking. Increased schooling of mothers has a measureable impact on the health of their children, on the future schooling of the child, and on the child's adult productivity. The children of educated mothers consistently out-perform children with educated fathers and illiterate mothers. Given that they spend most of their time with their mothers, this is hardly surprising.

A World Bank project in Africa established that the children of women with just five years of school had a 40 per cent better survival rate than the children of women who had less than five years in class. A Yale University study showed that the heights and weights for newborn children of women with a basic education were consistently higher than those of babies born to uneducated women. A UNESCO project demonstrated that giving women just a primary school education decreases child mortality by five to ten per cent.

The health advantages of education extend beyond childbirth: educated girls marry later, and are less susceptible to abuse by older men. They tend to have fewer children, space them more wisely and so look after them better; women with seven years' education, according to one study, had two or three fewer children than women with no schooling. The reason Kerala's fertility rate is 1.7 per couple while Bihar's is over four is that Kerala's women are educated and, unfortunately, half of Bihar's are not.

As the veteran Indian feminist Kamala Bhasin so memorably put it:

Main padhna seekh rahi hoon, ki zindagi ko padh sakoon,
Main likhna seekh rahi hoon, ki apni kismat khud likh sakoon,
Main hisaab seekh rahi hoon, ki apne adhikaron ka bhi hisaab rakhoon.

(I am learning to read, so I can read life;
I am learning to write, so I can write my destiny;
I am learning mathematics, so I can keep an account of my rights.)

It is a cause that ought to be the abiding passion of every right thinking citizen of our country. It is certainly an unambiguous policy objective of the Government of India. Our National Education Policy document, adopted in 1986 and amended in 1992, states: 'Education will be used as an agent of basic change in the status of women. In order to neutralize the accumulated distortions of the past, there will be a well-conceived edge in favour of women. The National Education System will play a positive, interventionist role in the empowerment of women. This will be an act of faith and social engineering.'

Despite our clear priorities, it is clear that in our own country, we have a long way to go to fulfil this particular tryst with destiny. Although since Independence, the country has made significant strides in improving the overall literacy rates for women and, across the board, enrolment rates for women right from the primary level to college have been going up, yet much more needs to be done. According to the figures available with the HRD Ministry, at Independent India's first census in 1951, the country had a literacy rate of 18.3 per cent, a mere 27.2 per cent for men and an abysmal 8.9 per cent for women. Since then, in 2011 this rate has moved up to a healthy 82.1 per cent for men and stands at a more acceptable 65.5 per cent for women. Without going into the quality and reliability of our literacy-related statistics, it remains a matter of deep national concern that even today nearly one out of every three women in our country is illiterate. It is evidence for one of the two assertions I mentioned, that our efforts at reform do not yet have the reach or coverage that we require.

To elaborate further, as per the MHRD's provisional statistics for the year 2009-10, while 17.1 per cent of all eligible males had enrolled for higher education, merely 12.7 per cent of all eligible young women were able to avail of the same opportunity. This figure hides, within itself, a shocking and unacceptable rural-urban divide. While around 30 per cent of all urban women enrol for some form of higher education, a little over 8 per cent of all rural young women are able to enrol for a higher degree. Similarly at the higher secondary level, while 38.3 per cent of eligible boys are enrolled at this level, only 33.3 per cent of girls are able to avail of educational opportunities at this level. Our experience suggests that while at the primary level the enrolment rates for girls and boys are roughly identical, sustaining the girl child through the education system remains a challenge.

For its part, the Government of India has launched many ambitious programmes for improving the overall enrolment ratio and to address the gender bias. The Right to Education Act, the Sarva Shiksha Abhiyan, the Kasturba Gandhi Balika Vidyalaya scheme, the Mid-Day Meal Scheme, the Mahila Samakhya Scheme, provision of free textbooks, provision of separate toilets for girls are some of the schemes and measures that address the challenges of educating the girl child at the primary level. At the secondary level, under the flagship Rashtriya Madhyamik Shiksha Abhiyan, specially targeted schemes such as the Girls' Hostel Scheme, and the National Incentive to Girls for Secondary Education Scheme (where a sum of Rs 3,000 is placed in a fixed deposit of eligible school going girls under the age of 16, who are entitled to withdraw it along with interest upon passing their Class X exam and reaching 18 years of age)—all these schemes aim to ensure that those girls who enrol at the primary level are given some support to continue their education to the secondary level and beyond.

At the university level too, the Government of India has adopted a multi-pronged strategy to ensure greater participation of women at all levels of higher education. Due to widespread concerns about the safety and dignity of unaccompanied young women living away from home, the Government of India has devised a special scheme administered by the UGC for construction of women-only hostels for colleges in order to provide dedicated and secure residential spaces for the women students/ researchers/ teachers and other staff. This is absolutely vital if we are to encourage our young women to take up academic pursuits at the highest levels without any fear whatsoever of facing harassment and inconvenience.

The government realizes that merely increasing participation and providing infrastructure to women in education is not enough. These efforts must be complemented by the development of Women's Studies departments in our universities and colleges. Ultimately, with the right kind of content, we should be able to stimulate knowledge and awareness about women's education and other gender equality related issues through a well-integrated process of teaching, research and documentation.

Gender equality in education is not merely a practical necessity or a vital precondition for prosperity. It is all that and much more. It is a fulfilment of our moral and constitutional obligation to treat our citizens equally. All our claims to be the world's largest democracy will ring hollow in the face of persistent gender discrimination with regard to access to education and in particular to top quality education. The continuing difference between our enrolment ratio for boys and girls at most levels of our education system is no less a national shame than the appalling sex ratio caused by the reprehensible practice of sex selection and female foeticide. As another one of my distinguished former colleagues at the UN, the UNICEF's then head, the energetic Carol Bellamy, while releasing her flagship report called 'State of the World's Children in 2004', said bluntly: 'the failure to invest in girls' education puts in jeopardy more development goals than any other single action.'

India's educated women represent the paradox of a country which, for all its maltreatment of women, gave the world its first women doctors and amongst its first women pilots, CEOs and one of the first female heads of government. But they are not exempt from being patronized by the patriarchy: it was not so long ago, after all, that a male chief minister addressed an audience of professional women in the city by talking about the sanctity of motherhood and of dutiful wives singeing their fingers to make the perfect chappati, and he is now prime minster! Men need to be educated too—especially men who wield power in our still make-dominated society.

The duty and the right to Stand Up and Speak Out is not the burden of only women. All right-thinking men share it too. Let me end by quoting a poem first made famous by that great modern icon of feminism, Hilary Clinton, 'Silence' by Delhi's own Anusuya Sengupta, who wrote it while a student at Lady Shri Ram College:

Too many women in too many countries
speak the same language of silence.
My grandmother was always silent, always aggrieved
Only her husband had the cosmic right (or so it was said)
to speak and be heard.
They say it is different now.
(After all, I am always vocal and my grandmother
thinks I talk too much)

But sometimes I wonder.

When a woman shares her thoughts, as some women do,
graciously, it is allowed.

When a woman fights for power, as all women would like
to, quietly or loudly, it is questioned.

And yet, there must be freedom—if we are to speak

And yes, there must be power—if we are to be heard.

And when we have both (freedom and power) let us now be
understood.

We seek only to give words to those who cannot speak
(too many women in too many countries)

I seek to forget the sorrows of my grandmother's silence.

The suffering of Indian women may not be over anytime soon, but the
silence that masked it for millennia is gone. Together we will all stand up, we
will all speak out and we will make sure that the reality of Indian women
is more faithful to our civilizational self-image and popular rhetoric. There is
one form of energy that is greater than all the energy that can come out of
thermal, hydel, solar or nuclear power: it is woman power, and it can electrify
the future.

PROHIBITION IN KERALA

'Why on earth has Kerala gone for Prohibition?' friends kept asking me for much of the second half of 2014.

Their surprise is, at one level, understandable: Kerala has long been regarded as a haven for tipplers. Despite the closure of the ubiquitous arrack shops by the A.K. Antony government in 1996, alcohol of various (and varying) other qualities has been widely available throughout the state. Its reputation as a tourist paradise has also floated on a sea of easily available libations: the local palm toddy, the increasingly popular 'Indian Made Foreign Liquor' (whose popularity grew after the ban on arrack and the resultant coarsening of the less-intoxicating toddy to appeal to hardened arrack-drinkers), and the more expensive fare distilled in Scotland, albeit at five-star prices. Kerala had even acquired the dubious reputation of being the state with the highest per capita consumption of spirits in India (in vain did some of us try to explain that it was not because we were particularly prone to drunkenness, but because we were honest enough to declare, and pay excise, on everything we drank, unlike, say, Punjab.)

So no one had ever thought that Kerala would ever consider going the Gujarat way and ban booze. Until, to universal exclamations of astonishment, we did.

Some 712 bars were to be closed after a final binge at the festival of Onam, Kerala's equivalent of Christmas and Diwali rolled into one. Sundays have been declared dry days; even five-star hotels cannot serve liquor on the Sabbath. The hundreds of outlets of the government-owned Kerala Beverages Corporation, or Bevco, which daily feature long queues of faithful swillers, will also be closed, at the rate of 10 per cent a year: community organizations are already clamouring for the outlets in their neighbourhoods to be amongst the first to be shut down. Soon, the only places that you will be able to get a drink in Kerala, aside from friends' homes, will be five-star hotels, of which the state boasts just eighteen—and there too, not on Sundays.

It should be pointed out, though, that however counter-intuitive this might seem, the decision has been widely hailed across the state. The influential Christian churches (all seven denominations of the Biblical faith) have applauded loudly, as have the political parties identified with the Christian community. The almost equally vocal Muslim leadership, including the ruling coalition's ally, the Muslim League, has done so as well. Working-class women, despairing of their feckless and bibulous husbands, have hailed the decision, as have traditionalists, Gandhians and assorted moralists, of which our country has no shortage. No public figure of any consequence in Kerala has stood up to oppose the decision.

And yet, there are objective reasons for surprise. Excise duties on liquor are a vital source of income for the state government, accounting for 22 per cent of Kerala's revenues. Another 26 per cent depends on tourism, both domestic and foreign. In addition, much of Kerala's economic viability depended upon attracting foreign investors, especially into the knowledge and services sectors, where the quality of life available in the state had to be a major draw (IT professionals in Bangalore tend to flock to that city's bars and pubs after their long hours on the job). In a state which boasts little other industry and no other significant sources of income (except remittances from its working population abroad), it had been widely assumed that, morality aside, Kerala simply could not afford to do without widely, conveniently-available, and heavily-taxed liquor.

The assumption is right. But to make such a rational case overlooks the simple truth that politics is profoundly irrational. The ruling Congress party in Kerala is led by a moralistic Gandhian who led a campaign for the state's bars to be closed. The issue was sparked off by the pending renewal of the licences of 438 bars which had been stalled by the election code of conduct, which the Congress chief did not want renewed once the code's restrictions were lifted. The pragmatists in government resisted his call to scrap the licenses altogether, until they found themselves being portrayed, in intra-party arguments, as agents of the 'liquor mafia' and worse. That was more than they could bear: if responsible stewardship of the state's finances meant being tarred with the 'liquor mafia' brush, the chief minister decided, he would rather let the state go into debt than see his personal reputation sullied. Prohibition was the only choice available to salvage his image. He would not only not renew the 438 pending licenses; he would withdraw the licences of every single bar in the state, except those catering to the affluent in five-star hotels.

The somewhat bizarre one up-manship of senior politicians competing with each other to prove they were holier-than-thou would have been amusing had the consequences not been so drastic. Once the decision was taken, there was no going back; no one wanted to be branded as a votary of the demon drink. But in the days since it was announced, and even while the applause is yet to die down across the state, grim reality has begin to beckon. Bar workers and distillery employees, some 20,000 across the state, will be thrown out of work; they and their families will soon be clamouring for relief, in a state with levels of unemployment so high that lakhs of Keralites go outside the state each year looking for work. Tourism operators are already being stung by cancellations; one source claimed to me that 50 per cent of the convention bookings in Kerala this winter—a majority of those scheduled for non-five-star hotels—have already been cancelled. IT companies contemplating moving to the clean, green, tech-friendly environment available in Kerala say the fact that their employees might not easily be able to enjoy a drink after work has given them pause.

Worse, few expect the decision will actually reduce drinking in Kerala. The Tamil Nadu government's alcoholic beverages corporation, TASMAC, has announced that it will open a string of new outlets along the length of the Kerala border, to cater to the demands of Keralite consumers, whose excise duties will now fill Tamil Nadu's coffers rather than Kerala's. Smugglers are reported to be readying plans and selecting routes to bring in quantities of liquor from Tamil Nadu and Karnataka to cater to the demands of parched Keralites. Worries are mounting that poor customers and those too far inland to shop in Tamil Nadu will be vulnerable to illicit and spurious or adulterated hooch, which might even kill them. The failure of Prohibition in states like Andhra Pradesh and Haryana—both of which ended their liquor bans because their revenues suffered while their neighbours, prospered—and the even more famous example of the United States, offers a salutary warning.

The ban targets drunkenness, social disorder and male irresponsibility (many labourers blow up a large proportion of their salaries at Bevco instead of spending them on household essentials), and so is widely popular. But it will also hurt the backpacking foreign tourist who wants a chilled beer on a hot day, the three-star hotel resident who seeks a glass of wine with her meal, and the hard-working professional who wants to let his hair down on a Sunday. If all these people desert 'God's own Country', Paradise will not easily recover.

Keralites have sustained a welfare state with the best social development indicators in the country, buttressed by an array of government schemes that provide everything from well-stocked community health centres in the villages to subsidized medicines, unemployment insurance and one-rupee-a-kilo rice to BPL (Below the Poverty Line) cardholders. The government pays the salaries of tens of thousands of teachers, doctors, nurses, social workers and extension workers of all kinds. It does so through revenues made up overwhelmingly of excise on alcohol, tourism and remittances from Keralite workers abroad. When two of these three sources are drastically reduced, social services and the government payroll will have to be cut. Will the Keralite, accustomed to such benefits, accept that this is the unavoidable price to pay for the virtues of temperance? (No prizes for guessing the answer: Keralites are second to none in wanting to have their cake and eat it too.)

Some rumblings of discontent are already being heard amongst the very political leaders who have ostensibly endorsed the government's decision, though they are muttered in undertones rather than openly expressed. For any politician who opposes the ban will be instantly tarred as an advocate of alcohol, an agent of the 'liquor mafia', and a bar-loving enemy of good, wholesome Gandhian values. So political leaders remain unanimous in acquiescing in the decision, even while privately whispering their concern about its implications.

Half a century ago, my late father, talking about Bombay's Prohibition policy under which liquor could be obtained by anyone with a doctor's certificate certifying him to be an alcoholic, explained to me that 'India is not only the world's largest democracy; we are also the world's largest hypocrisy'. As his home state stumbles into a policy that none of its makers truly believes in but none can afford to disavow, I'd like to raise a toast to him: fifty years on, Dad, you're still right.

MINORITIES AND POLICING

In the aftermath of the horrors of Mumbai, 26/11, the hard work of reconstruction, of rebuilding—of reimagining our country—never quite occurred. One genuine cause of satisfaction must be that there was no demonization of our Muslim minority, which the terrorists must have hoped to provoke. The victims of the killers were from every faith, and Indians of every religion have stood united in their anger and determination.

And yet it was just the weekend before the attacks that the then prime minister had urged senior police officers not to widen 'the fault lines in our society' and to act to 'restore the faith of the people—especially those belonging to religious and ethnic minorities and the weaker sections—in the impartiality and effectiveness of the police'. His words reflected a real conundrum: the general public feels it is not adequately protected against the random violence of terrorists, but every pro-active policing effort seriously alienates India's largest minority community. Young Muslim men have been picked up and brutalized for no reason other than their demographic profile, and yet the sneering triumphalism of the terrorists' Islamist propaganda seems to leave the authorities little choice. But if the efforts to stamp out the sources of terror merely incite the sullen resentment within which terrorism breeds, every crackdown will prove counter-productive. There has to be a better way.

And there is. Indian dealt effectively with Sikh extremism by the skilful use of the talents of a pluralist state. The Khalistanis never succeeded in making their cause one of the Sikh community versus the Indian state. Instead, we saw the majority of Sikhs stay loyal to their country, as a largely Sikh police force, led by a charismatic Sikh officer, K.P.S. Gill, ably combated the minority of Sikh terrorists, while the Indian state orchestrated a democratic political process which brought elected Sikh leaders to power in Punjab. There is absolutely no reason why a similar approach cannot work with the Muslim community, the overwhelming majority of whom are proud and loyal Indians. To do so we must start by getting more Muslims into the security forces.

There are well-known historical and sociological reasons that explain why Muslims are under-represented in the country's police forces, the Central Reserve Police and crucial gendarmeries like UP's Provincial Armed Constabulary. Obviously, we cannot infuse a significant number of Muslims into these forces overnight. But it's obvious that we need to enhance the recruitment and retention of minorities in the police forces and to conduct police outreach to minority communities. Such an approach would simultaneously reduce a major source of grievance in the Muslim community, increase the trust between the police and the people they are policing, and dramatically improve our own intelligence about currents within a community whose vulnerability to the blandishments of terror is high.

We can learn some lessons from how other democracies have dealt with similar concerns. Despite the Sachar Commission Report, few in India want to see an additional layer of reservations for minorities in state institutions. But Britain, which abjures quotas altogether, follows a policy of 'positive action' to help under-represented groups compete more effectively in the selection process for police jobs, and conducts extensive outreach work through mosques, black churches and community groups.

We in India also need to recognize that if we want under-represented Muslims to compete effectively for police jobs, they need to feel the police is part of them, rather than an external entity. It's clear we need to:

- actively solicit applications from minorities for the police at all levels (including the Provincial Armed Constabulary and the Central Reserve Police);
- offer special catch-up courses open only to members of the minority communities that will prepare them for the entrance examinations; at the moment few feel qualified to take the exams, and fewer still pass; and
- require police officers to work with community organizations, mosques and madrasas to encourage minorities to apply.

In other words, instead of more 'reservations', with the resentment that it breeds, let us make it easier for minorities to join the police. But let's not stop with recruitment: we also need to focus on the retention and progression of minority officers. Unless young people from minorities see that the police service offers real career opportunities and a good quality of life in the workplace, they will not overcome their negative perceptions. The fact that, in many Western countries, there are several officers from the visible minorities now at senior officer rank, sends a powerful message to these communities. In India, the promotion of minority police personnel at senior and middle levels and using them as visible symbols of the police force would constitute a powerful model to the minority community.

We could also take a leaf out of Britain's book in what they do to combat racism within the police, as well as enhance cross-cultural knowledge, offering training courses to white officers that include a 'long weekend' spent living with a minority family. Britain is far from perfect—as the recent discrimination case filed by Deputy Commissioner Tariq Ghafoor suggests—but many Hindu policemen, especially in Gujarat and the suburbs of Mumbai, would benefit immeasurably by spending a few days in a Muslim mohalla. Let's face it: if our police are not properly and continuously trained in minority relations, the current problems will continue.

Of course India is not Britain, and no foreign idea can simply be imported wholesale into our country. But we must acknowledge the grave risk to the national fabric of any community being alienated from the police. Our police forces must reflect the diversity of India. Such a policy would be the 'other side of the coin' to a tough security policy which is indispensable to reassure the common urban resident, terrorized by the bomb blasts, that the government can keep them safe.

TERRORISM AND INDIA

Every year since the 26 November 2008 attacks, I have undertaken a personal pilgrimage to the city of Mumbai. '26/11', as we call it now, was the day when this city, representing the best and the brightest of our civilizational values, was attacked in an act of terror unmatched in its ruthlessness and savagery. Since then, for me this day has been a day of resolve and remembrance. Every year on this day I have returned to Mumbai to pay homage to the brave martyrs of our security forces and to the innocent victims of this cowardly attack. Too many people think that you can do anything to India, and Indians will in time forgive and forget. My visits to Mumbai every year on this day—attending memorials, participating in ceremonies and rallies, quietly visiting the sites that were attacked, speaking to some of the survivors—are a personal affirmation of my belief that we must never forget.

The sacrifices and senseless slaughter that Mumbai witnessed on those fateful three days must never be forgotten. The lone surviving perpetrator, Ajmal Kasab, was hanged in 2012, but the masterminds of this bloodletting still find sponsorship, sanctuary and support across the border. As long as they roam free, no proud Indian can forgive or forget. The spirit of India, the idea of India, are not vanquished by this act: if anything it has brought us together to an unprecedented level of solidarity.

And yet it is necessary, even at the risk of sounding academic, to try to understand the origins of terrorism as a historical force before we begin to appreciate its implications for modern India and its democracy. In his book, *Inside Terrorism*, Bruce Hoffman tells us that the word 'terrorism' was first popularized during the French Revolution. 'In contrast to its contemporary usage, at that time terrorism had a decidedly positive connotation...Hence, unlike terrorism as it is commonly understood today, to mean a revolutionary or anti-government activity undertaken by non-state or subnational entities, the *regime de la terreur* was an instrument of governance wielded by the recently established revolutionary state.'

Hoffman further adds that ironically, perhaps, terrorism in its original context was also closely associated with the ideals of virtue and democracy. The revolutionary leader Maximilien Robespierre firmly believed that virtue was the mainspring of a popular government at peace, but that during the time of revolution must be allied with terror in order for democracy to triumph. He appealed famously to 'virtue, without which terror is evil; terror, without which virtue is helpless', and proclaimed: 'Terror is nothing but justice, prompt, severe and inflexible; it is therefore an emanation of virtue.'

Hoffman states that despite this divergence from its subsequent meaning, the French Revolution's 'terrorism' still shared at least two key characteristics in common with its modern-day variant. First, the regime de la terreur was neither random nor indiscriminate, as terrorism is often portrayed today, but was organized, deliberate and systematic. Second, its goal and its very justification—like that of contemporary terrorism—was the creation of a 'new and better society' in place of what it proclaimed as a fundamentally corrupt and undemocratic political system, an ideology not dissimilar to the rabid utopias proclaimed by Hafiz Saeed and his ilk. Indeed, Robespierre's vague and utopian pronouncements about the revolution's central goals are remarkably similar in tone and content to the equally turgid, millenarian manifestos issued by many contemporary terrorist organizations. Whether it is the jehadis of the LeT and Al Qaeda, the Maoists, or the LTTE, while the specific grievances of different movements may vary a great deal, they share common strands of self-righteous rage, violent tactics and utopian delusion. Democratic societies, including India, must understand this pathology before they begin to formulate a response against this menace that is firmly grounded in their own civilizational ethos and constitutional values.

International terrorism is a method, rather than a political ideology. It has, at various times in the last 150 years, been used by the right and the left, by sub-national groups and internationalists, by secessionists and nation-builders, both successfully and unsuccessfully.

⁂

But putting all academic understanding aside, for most Indians, terrorism was defined in blood on the night of 26/11. While most of the nation was glued to an India-England ODI in Cuttack, news came of some gunfire in South Mumbai. Initial reports suggested a gun battle between rival gangs. But the unfolding events showed our darkest fears coming true. Be it the Oberoi or the Taj, the Leopold Cafe or the Chhatrapati Shivaji terminus, the beloved VT, terror had come to Mumbai in the most savage and brutal manner possible. The city that never sleeps did not blink an eyelid as it watched with shock and horror, its most beloved and iconic landmarks being devastated by an orgy of death and destruction. It was a night lasting sixty-eight hours, whose nightmares continue to haunt and horrify our collective consciousness.

The terrorists, who heaved their bags laden with weapons up the steps of the wharf to begin their assault on the Taj, knew exactly what they were doing. Theirs was an attack on India's financial nerve-centre and commercial capital, a city emblematic of the country's energetic thrust into the 21st century. They struck at symbols of the prosperity that was making the Indian model so attractive to the globalizing world—luxury hotels, a swish café, an apartment house favoured by foreigners. The terrorists also sought to polarize Indian society by claiming to be acting to redress the grievances, real and imagined, of India's Muslims. And by singling out Britons, Americans and Israelis for special attention, they demonstrated that their brand of Islamist fanaticism is anchored less in the absolutism of pure faith than in the geopolitics of hatred.

The attack on the Chabad House and the killing of its residents was particularly sad, since India is justifiably proud of the fact that it is the only country in the world with a Jewish diaspora going back 2,500 years where there has never been a single instance of anti-Semitism. This was the first time that it became unsafe to be Jewish in India—one more proof that this terror was not homegrown.

That year on 26/11, the platitudes flowed like blood. Terrorism is unacceptable; terrorists are cowards; the world stands united in unreserved condemnation of this atrocity. Commentators in America tripped over themselves to pronounce this night and day of carnage India's 9/11. But India has endured many attempted 9/11s, notably a ferocious assault on our national Parliament in December 2001 that nearly led to all-out war against the assailants' presumed sponsors, Pakistan. In 2008 alone, terrorist bombs took lives in Jaipur, in Ahmedabad, in Delhi and (in an eerie dress-rehearsal for the effectiveness of synchronicity) several different places on one searing day in the state of Assam. Jaipur is the lodestar of Indian tourism; Ahmedabad is the primary city of Gujarat, the state that is a poster child for India's development, with a local GDP growth rate of 14 per cent; Delhi is the nation's political capital and India's window to the world; Assam was logistically convenient for terrorists from across a porous border. Mumbai combined all the four elements of its precursors: by attacking it, the terrorists hit India's economy, its tourism, and its internationalism, and they took advantage of the city's openness to the world. A diabolical grand slam.

So the terrorists hit multiple targets in Mumbai, both literally and figuratively. They caused death and destruction to our country, searing India's psyche, showing up the limitations of its security apparatus and humiliating its government. They dented the worldwide image of India as an emerging economic giant, a success story of the era of globalization and an increasing magnet for investors and tourists. Instead the world was made to see an insecure and vulnerable India, a 'soft state' bedevilled by enemies who could strike it at will.

But terrorism and India have had a long history. We Indians have learned to endure the unspeakable horrors of terrorist violence ever since malignant and delusional men in Pakistan, wearing the khaki of military honour and the clerical robes of piety, concluded, after four unsuccessful wars, that it was cheaper and more effective to bleed India to death than to attempt to defeat it in conventional war. Attack after attack has been proven to have been financed, equipped and guided from across the border.

Yet, periodically, Pakistani civilian leaders speak of their commitment to peace, and India wearily resumes its pursuit of dialogue with Islamabad, all the while conscious that the elected leaders it is speaking to are not the ones who are really calling the shots in that country. The Pakistani Army, whose very raison d'etre (and disproportionate share of national resources) depends on sustained hostility to India, are the real rulers of Pakistan. If the nominal government crosses the military's red lines in its approach to India, they will be quickly hauled back, if not actually overthrown.

This lends a somewhat surreal quality to India's relations with Pakistan. Agreements are concluded with authorities who do not themselves possess the power to implement what they have undertaken. The classic example of this was the agreement to set up a Joint Working Group on Terrorism. It did not produce a single shred of useful information, simply because Pakistani intelligence refused to provide any of it to Pakistani officials to share with their Indian counterparts.

India sees progress in the investigations and trial of seven Pakistanis accused of involvement in the Mumbai terror attack case in Islamabad's Anti Terrorism Court as an important marker of Pakistan's commitment to combat terrorism emanating from its soil. But the case has moved at a glacial pace. The trial has been subject to repeated adjournments, non-appearances of lawyers, vacation of judges and frequent changes of prosecution lawyers. The principal accused, Zakiur Rahman Lakhvi, enjoys a comfortable life in prison, equipped with numerous cell phones from which he commands his followers; he has even fathered a child during his incarceration (there are officially no conjugal rights for prisoners in Pakistan). The principal conspirator, Hafeez Sayeed, roams freely around the country, making incendiary, hate-filled speeches against India, while the government bleats that he has no case to answer. India keeps insisting that Pakistan must show tangible movement in bringing all those responsible for the Mumbai terrorist attacks, including those under trial, to justice quickly, but it has no answer to Islamabad's wilful disregard of this requirement,.

Continued terrorism from Pakistan and areas under its control remains a core concern for India. It is critical for India and also for the security of the region that Pakistan shows determined action to dismantle all terrorist networks, organizations and infrastructure within its own territory. Pakistan must also uphold the sanctity of the Line of Control, which is the most important Confidence Building Measure between the two countries. This includes ending unprovoked firing on our posts, and ending repeated transgressions of the LOC by the Pakistan Army, which have adverse consequences for our bilateral ties. We do not accept the argument that the transgressions across the LOC or incidents of unprovoked firing are the handiwork of non-state actors. Everything along the LOC is firmly under the control of the armies on both sides.

Yet, despite these continuous provocations, India's government remains committed to peace. We do so not because of any external compulsion or internal weakness, but because it is in our history, our culture and in our embrace of a constitutional, pluralist, democratic system of governance to do so. The unscrupulous and unrestricted use of violence is not an instrument of state policy in India, as it seems to be in Pakistan. A tit for tat policy, as advocated by the more short sighted and hot headed elements in our society, neither serves our long term national interests nor attains the more immediate and urgent objective of stopping terror attacks. Resilience, vigilance and patience—these are the vital ingredients in any successful democratic response to cross border and home grown terror. Those who dream of bleeding India dry through a thousand cuts will drown in their own hatred before our great nation runs out of either blood or spirit.

In any case, given India's preponderant size and presence in South Asia, and as a country that seeks to focus on its own enormous development challenges, we should do everything we can to defuse hostility on our borders. Not talking to Pakistan is not much of a policy; it has been tried for years, yielding no significant benefit. If India's pursuit of peace strengthens like-minded Pakistani politicians who are struggling against their own hawks, it is worth attempting. The benefits of peace, for both sides, would be enormous.

But India has always been a status quo power that wishes to live in peace, while Pakistan, craving Kashmir, uses every means at its disposal to alter the status quo. We in India are committed to resolving all outstanding issues with Pakistan, including the issue of Jammu and Kashmir, through bilateral dialogue on the basis of the Simla Agreement, for which there needs to be an environment free from terror and violence. India has long been in favour of placing the Kashmir dispute on the back burner and promoting trade, travel and the rest; it is Pakistan that has taken the view that there cannot be normal relations with India until Kashmir is settled, on terms acceptable to Islamabad. Unless Pakistani peacemakers are willing to advocate a policy of across-the-board engagement with India despite the lack of a solution to the Kashmir dispute, our progress will remain halting and limited.

Friendship has to be built on a shared perception of the danger of terrorism to both states—of a sincere acceptance by the Pakistani military establishment that those who attacked the Taj in Mumbai are just as much their enemies as those bombing the Marriott in Islamabad. This would require more than fuzzy words from civilian politicians—it needs genuine cooperation from all Pakistani authorities, including useful information-sharing and real action to arrest, prosecute and punish the perpetrators. This has not been forthcoming, and there is some doubt whether it will ever be.

It is widely accepted that terrorism emerges from blind hatred of an 'Other',

and that in turn is the product of three factors: fear, rage and incomprehension—
fear of what the Other might do to you, rage at what you believe the Other
has done to you, and incomprehension about who or what the Other really
is. These three elements fuse together in igniting the deadly combustion that
kills and destroys people whose only 'sin' is that they feel none of these things
themselves.

It is not particularly chauvinist to point out that India, fundamentally, has been
a peace-loving nation and society. As the third largest contributor of peacekeepers
to the United Nations, India has been instrumental in promoting the peaceful
resolution of conflicts. India has consistently and peacefully helped various other
developing nations to facilitating democracy in their respective nations. India
helped conceive the idea of the United Nations Democracy Fund (UNDEF)
and, along with the United States, it remains the principal funder of UNDEF.

A democracy is made of its people, for its people and by its people. Over
the years the various Indian governments have placed the welfare of the Indian
people over any destructive external agendas. Even in 1948, when the Kashmir
issue arose, our first prime minister, Pandit Jawaharlal Nehru, took the issue to
the UN so that a peaceful solution could have been sought. It was Nehru's
proposal that a plebiscite be held immediately to ascertain the wishes of the
people. Though Nehru's decision to appeal to the UN has been seen within
the country as a blunder that snatched diplomatic stalemate from the jaws of
imminent military victory, I think that it is unreasonable. After all, Pakistan could
just as easily have raised the issue at the UN, and it would have found some
support. India has been consistently committed to find a sustainable solution for
Kashmir through peace talks, albeit unsuccessful.

Unlike various developed nations that have invaded other countries without
the approval of its people, India has refrained from resorting to violent terrorist
measures unless the safety of its people is at threat. It understands that terror
cannot be dealt with through terror. Unlike our neighbours, the army in India
does not make foreign policy. That is the prerogative of an elected civilian
government that is determined to engage in dialogue with its eyes open. Apart
from being trained for combat, army officials are taught to serve the nation
and work for the greater good of its people. We saw a striking example of
this in 2014 in the extraordinary rescue and relief efforts conducted by the
Indian Army during the floods in Jammu and Kashmir.

Apart from external organizations trying to create terror internally, Indian
democracy has also been a hotbed for internal terrorism. The previous government
identified sixty-five terror groups active in the country, out of which thirty-
four are in the state of Manipur. This is not something new for India. Since
Independence various internal groups have threatened Indian democracy. From
Naxalites to various independent groups in Northeast India, from groups spreading

communal violence to those fighting for new states, Indian democracy has had to tackle the issue of internal terror on an ongoing basis. Many of these groups have been predominantly leftist by nature. In April 2006, then Prime Minister Manmohan Singh called the Maoist insurgency 'the single biggest internal security challenge ever faced by our country'.

Various other insurgency movements have been mushrooming in our nation. But one needs to understand is that no terrorist organization, however well motivated, well trained and well financed, can hold a democracy to ransom. The whole emanation of the idea of India, to borrow Rabindranath Tagore's famous phrase, is the idea of a plural civilization, a civilization that has been created by generations of people of various backgrounds coming together to contribute to our history, and a civilization capable of infinite resilience and fortitude. Nehruji spoke about India as a palimpsest written over by new, succeeding waves of people coming to this country, making the India we know today and yet not erasing what has gone before. The high turnout at the recent assembly elections in Chhattisgarh has sent out an unambiguous message to the Naxalites that the people of Chhattisgarh have immense unshakeable faith in the country's democratic polity.

The Naxalite movement gained steam in some of the poorest regions of our country. While India tackles poverty, one of the more interesting debates that has arisen since the spectre of terrorism invaded the global consciousness is the one about poverty and terror. Some have argued, perhaps a bit too simplistically, that terrorism is caused by poverty and that the eradication of poverty will lead to the elimination of terror. Certain development advocates have been particularly assiduous in purveying this line, no doubt in reaction to the even more simplistic discourse of those who argue that terrorism is a form of evil, divorced from any understandable 'root cause', that must be ruthlessly stamped out in a 'global war'.

There is no doubt that terrorist groups require a steady flow of new member-martyrs, they need the support of non-terrorists to survive. Support in terms of money or sanctuary from those sympathetic with their avowed political ambitions is essential. So is support from those who feel alienated from non-violent means of political change. And support from those who live in fear of its perpetrators but are unable to successfully face them down. Terrorism is bred from alienation and nurtured by hopelessness, deprivation and the frustrations of those who feel powerless. So the argument that terrorism has understandable causes has gained ground in some circles. But repudiation was bound to come sooner or later from the growing band of scholars who study such things.

The American economist Alan B. Krueger of Princeton and Czech Professor Jitka Malecková of Charles University in Prague have examined this question in the context of Palestinian support for terrorism and established, from a diligent perusal of public opinion polls, that the support for terror attacks on Israel is lower amongst the poor and unemployed people than amongst the relatively better off Palestinians (students, professionals, merchants). The same is true, they showed, for supporters of the Hezbollah in Lebanon and of the extremist, even racist Gush Emunim in Israel. So when doctors and engineers participated in the 2007 bomb assaults in London and Glasgow, Krueger was not surprised. He told the *Wall Street Journal*: 'Each time we have one of these attacks and the backgrounds of the attackers are revealed, this should put to rest the myth that terrorists are attacking us because they are desperately poor. But this misconception doesn't die.'

My London-based Indian friend Salil Tripathi, a thoughtful analyst of such issues, concurs. He wrote in the *New Statesman*: 'Some 15 of the 19 hijackers on 11 September, 2001 came from wealthy families in a prosperous country—Saudi Arabia. Osama Bin Laden's background was famously opulent; his deputy Ayman al-Zawahiri is an affluent paediatrician. There are many good reasons to eliminate poverty. But we should not expect terrorism to decline as a result.'

And yet—I am tempted to say, 'Not so fast, my friends.'

Of course eliminating dire poverty will not, in itself, solve our problems in this age of terror. The pilots of 9/11 were not poor; not only were they educated and reasonably well off, their pilots' licenses could have guaranteed them comfortable middle-class lives. But those, like me, who focus on the factors that make terrorism possible are not drawing so simple a causal connection as to suggest that poverty causes terrorism. My own argument is a little more complicated. It is, first, that poverty helps create the conditions that provide succour and sustenance to terrorists, who can scarcely work in isolation: they need support, bases, safe havens, supplies, allies, and they find these amongst a general population that is broadly alienated from the world order the terrorists are attacking, an order that denies them hope. Yes, it is not just poverty at work here. Those who support, applaud and orchestrate terrorism are not driven solely by a sense of economic injustice. A sense of oppression, of exclusion, of marginalization, also gives rise to extremism, and this comes particularly to people who see no other hope of overturning the political dispensation that alienates them.

Second, terrorists need a rationale for their actions—a narrative of injustice to inspire their pawns, the suicide bombers and their ilk, and to win broad sympathy for their cause. That rationale is most easily found in tales of poverty and suffering seemingly created by an unjust world order. If we can eliminate poverty, we would significantly dent that rationale, and dilute the support base for terrorism.

It is sadly true that other factors will continue to spawn terrorists. My friend Nasra Hassan, a Pakistani former colleague of mine at the UN, wrote a remarkable article for the *New Yorker* in 2001 in which she suggested that indignity, political humiliation and a sense of desperation about the possibility of bringing about political change were the main motivations for would-be Palestinian suicide bombers. (She came to this conclusion by interviewing several terror-recruits in Israeli prisons.) Terrorism is a weapon of asymmetrical warfare; it is the instrument of the weak against the implacable power of a state system that enrages them. It has been used by anarchists in 19th-century Russia, Irish nationalists in 20th-century Britain, Basque separatists in 21st-century Spain and by the advocates of Tamil Eelam in Sri Lanka.

So ending poverty alone will not end terror. But it will make terrorism that much more difficult to promote. If we can create a world in which all people have access to—at a minimum—the opportunity to live beyond starvation, to receive an education, and to have realistic hopes for a better future, including the possibility of some say in their own political arrangements, we might be able to stop the lugubrious litany of reflections on terror. That would be a positive goal to work for, in India and around the world.

Terrorism is, after all, an assault on the common bonds of humanity and civility that tie us all together. Our commitment to democracy should make us stronger in the face of terror and we should not relent till this scourge is extinguished effectively. I believe strongly that we must work to create a world in which Indians can prosper in safety and security, a world in which a transformed India can play a worthy part. At the international level, the advocacy of a Comprehensive Convention on Terrorism is a worthy pursuit in this direction. Domestically, this is a time in our national evolution when we must rethink the assumptions of our political philosophy and rise to the need to refurbish our institutions with new ideas.

An India led by rational, humane and open-minded ideas of itself must develop a view of the world that is also broad-minded, accommodative and responsible. That would be in keeping with the aspirations that Nehru launched us on when he spoke of our tryst with destiny. As we embark on the second decade of the 21st century, the time has indeed come for us to redeem his pledge.

This means firmly rejecting any word or deed that could fan the flames from whose cinders have emerged extremist groups like the Students' Islamic Movement of India and the 'Indian Mujahideen', made up largely of young Muslim men disaffected from the Indian state. There is no doubt that the tragic Gujarat pogrom of 2002 served as the perfect recruiting poster for such terrorist groups, since it enabled them to argue that the only answer to a state that allowed such things to happen to Muslims was to fight fire with fire and state power with terror. A state in which communal disturbances are prevented by enlightened action, and where inflammatory rhetoric and worse, rioting, is put down with a firm hand, will be a state in which terrorism has little chance to flourish.

India must protect its minority populations, empower them politically, and enable them to partake fully of the opportunities the state offers. This would require education, training and resources to take advantage of such opportunities, from recruitment to the police forces to seed capital for entrepreneurship. The government also needs to send regular signals of reassurance to minorities— and to Muslims in particular, since their vulnerability is accentuated by the circumstances of India's Partition, and because so many terrorist groups derive support and funding from Islamist groups across the border. It is not yet clear that the BJP regime of Prime Minister Narendra Modi fully appreciates the importance of this. In professing to be religion-neutral, but giving free rein to Hindu chauvinists to spew bigotry and division for petty political purposes, the government is missing an opportunity to embrace the Muslim minority in its narrative of aspiration. Promoting development and integration of minorities into the national mainstream is essential for India if it wishes to minimize the numbers of those who might be seduced by the siren call of terrorism.

Whether India has the second or third largest Muslim population in the world (depending on the exact numbers in Pakistan), there is no doubt that India's is by far the largest Muslim minority in the world, both in numbers and as a proportion of the population. At the same time Islam is deeply rooted in Indian soil, with few Indian Muslims—even those of relatively recent Persian, Afghan or Arab origin—having links, or owing allegiance, to the lands of their forebears. Though conservative Islamist doctrine has sprung from Indian minds (the Deoband School, whose doctrines inspired the Taliban, is situated in India), none of the dozens of prominent Islamic seminaries or theologians has ever advocated armed insurrection against the Indian state.

The migration to Pakistan, upon Partition, of a significant proportion of the Muslim elite and its educated middle-class, meant that India's Muslims were always disproportionately poorer and less educated than their counterparts in other communities. Successive governments have tried to address this problem with only a modest degree of success, and many Muslims objectively suffer from unfavourable socio-economic conditions—which some ascribe to discrimination against them. If a narrative of injustice and discrimination gains ground across the community, it can provide propitious conditions for terrorists to exploit. It is all the more in the interests of the Indian state to ensure that the economic development of India fully embraces its Muslim minority.

India's democratic politics undoubtedly complicate both the perception of the problem and the response to it. Bomb blasts in Indian cities have often led to crackdowns and arrests of suspected terrorist sympathisers, which have inevitably swept up large numbers of young Muslim men, many completely innocent but whose lives and livelihoods are ruined by their detention. Politicians have been quick to seize on such arrests as proof of malice, if not downright discrimination, on the part of government and security agencies, and in the process have often declaimed support for many whose innocence is somewhat more questionable. Combating terrorism in a pluralist democracy is never easy, and it is particularly complicated in India, given that our hothouse politics rarely observes the restraints that are common in democracies elsewhere. Still, preventing and combating terror are both essential, and it is the duty of the government to be both adept and sensitive to all aspects of the challenge.

Of course India can recover from the physical assaults against it. It is a land of great resilience that has learned, over arduous millennia, to cope with tragedy. When the terrorists have tried to create panic in any corner of the nation, this spirit of the people has consistently defied their purpose. Bombs and bullets alone cannot destroy India, because Indians will pick their way through the rubble and carry on as they have done throughout history.

But what can destroy India is a change in the spirit of its people, away from the pluralism and co-existence that has been our greatest strength. That these tragic events never led to the demonization of the Muslims of India was vital, for if it had done so the terrorists would have won.

So I go to Mumbai every 26/11 to reaffirm the human spirit, the Indian spirit—the spirit of Mumbai. The phrase 'never again' has been used elsewhere across the world. Every November 26, it resonates in every Indian heart. Let us mourn what happened in Mumbai 2008. Let us pay homage to all the victims of this senseless outrage and tribute to those who overcame the terror. But at the same time let us strive together to ensure that it never happens again.

I have no doubt that whoever governs India, this spirit will not die. We will create a safe, prosperous and just India. In doing so we will ensure that the politics of hope will always prevail over the purveyors of hatred. India will be a beacon of strength and stability for the rest of the subcontinent. I want 26/11 to be marked not merely by reflection and mourning, but by also celebrating and reaffirming our faith in the idea of India.

On 26/11/2008, we lowered our heads in mourning. Every 26/11 to come, let us raise them again in hope.

VIII

INDIA BEYOND INDIA

LOOKING BACK AT 29 YEARS AS A UN OFFICIAL

There are two stories I like to tell about my time at the UN. The first relates to numbers. When I joined the Office of the UNHCR on 1 May 1978, we were a small organization of a few hundred people headquartered in Geneva, all of whom seemed to know each other on first-name terms, with relatively tranquil field offices that prided themselves on not being 'operational', but 'representative'. I joined on the first day of a Conference of Representatives convened by the new high commissioner, Poul Hartling, to meet his top staff, and was startled to hear my senior colleagues celebrating the fact that, following the headline-making drama of the 1971 Bangladesh refugee crisis, UNHCR had lapsed into its old familiar obscurity. 'We are not a household name,' several said emphatically, 'and we don't wish to be. We are more effective working quietly with governments behind the scenes.'

It didn't last. Within months of my joining, UNHCR found itself coping with a veritable explosion of earth-shaking refugee crises. The Vietnamese boat people fled communist rule in small boats and flooded neighbouring countries; Afghans sought refuge in Pakistan and Iran in the millions after the Soviet invasion of their homeland; starvation and oppression convulsed populations in the Horn of Africa, sending millions of Ethiopian and Somali refugees across fragile borders; and Nicaraguans started escaping a brutal civil war in their country against the dictatorship of Somoza. Before long, a household word was precisely what UNHCR became: one week I calculated that we were mentioned in five of the top six news stories of the flagship news bulletin of the BBC World Service.

I had joined an organization of some 400 staff worldwide, with a total budget of some $200; within a year-and-a-half, UNHCR's staff had tripled and its budget had quadrupled to cope with these new challenges.

A decade later, after a richly satisfying career at UNHCR (of which more later), I was invited to join the small peacekeeping staff in the UN Secretary-General's office in New York in late 1989, towards the end of the Cold War. There were precisely six civilian professional officers on the staff and three military advisers; that was the total size of the Office of Special Political Affairs, which ran UN peacekeeping. In the field there were five relatively stable operations that had not changed significantly in years. But soon after I joined, the same thing happened. The end of the Cold War meant that a large number of operations became both possible and necessary that could not have occurred during the tense days of the superpower standoff, when the UN kept the peace only where all major powers agreed it should. Namibia was brought to independence, the civil war in Angola came to an end, and so did the one in Mozambique; war brought Pol Pot's oppression in Cambodia to a close, warlords dragged Somalia into crisis, Saddam Hussein's invasion of Kuwait led to Desert Storm and the imposition of peace by the international community—and the biggest of them all, the chaotic and tragic civil war in Yugoslavia dragged in the UN. During my seven years in peacekeeping the small office became a Department of Peacekeeping Operations; we went from six civilians and three military to over 400 Headquarters personnel, from five operations to eighteen, and from 5,000 troops in the field to over 80,000. I had the rare privilege of being closely involved, as Special Assistant to the Under-Secretary-General, in this incredible expansion.

The moral of the story, I joked to my UN colleagues: if you are a small organization that wants to expand, increase your budgets and staff and make headlines, hire me!

The second story I like to tell is about what my own career illustrates about the UN—and I'm not talking about numbers alone. Since the best crystal ball is often the rear view mirror, my personal reminiscence tells us a lot about the question of change at the UN. For, the UN has not just changed enormously since its establishment, it has been transformed in the three-decade career span of this one former UN official. If I had even suggested to my seniors when I joined the organization in 1978 that the UN would one day observe and even run elections in sovereign states, conduct intrusive inspections for weapons of mass destruction, impose comprehensive sanctions on the entire import-export trade of a member state, create a counter-terrorism committee to monitor national actions against terrorists, or set up international criminal tribunals and coerce governments into handing over their citizens (even sometimes their former presidents) to be tried by foreigners under international law, I am sure they would have told me that I simply did not understand what the UN was all about. (And indeed, since that was in the late 1970s, they might well have asked me—'Young man, what have you been smoking?')

And yet the UN has done every one of those things during the last two decades, and more. The United Nations, in short, has been a highly adaptable institution that has evolved in response to changing times. Expansion, mutation, growth and evolution—these have been the hallmarks of an institution that has become indispensable to a world full of global issues that are relevant to all mankind. My career is a testimony to the extraordinary need for, and benefits of, international co-operation to address global crises.

These stories are about organizational expansion, but my most precious memories of my twenty-nine years at the United Nations relate to the fact that it has given me the opportunity to help my fellow human beings in the most basic way. For example, when I was heading the UNHCR office in Singapore, early in my career with the UN, it was immensely rewarding that

I could put my head to the pillow at night knowing that things I had done during the day had made a real difference to other people's lives.

I could recount a number of stories from those days, but one episode stands out in my memory because it crystallized my inner satisfaction. A Vietnamese family tried to escape their troubled country on a vessel powered by a dodgy tractor engine. It gave way in the middle of the South China Sea. They ran out of food. They ran out of drinking water. They began subsisting on rainwater and hope. But that was not enough to feed the couple's two small children, an infant and a baby, at sea. So the parents slit their fingers for the children to suck their blood in order to obtain some nourishment to survive.

When the family was rescued by an American ship, they were too weak to even stand; they had to be lifted bodily from their boat and taken on board the larger vessel. They were brought to Singapore port, where I was engaged in a running tug-of-war with the Singapore authorities over the refugees' right to disembark on humanitarian grounds (the government insisted on verifiable guarantees of resettlement before the refugees could be allowed off the ships). My staff and I had to rush this family to a Singapore hospital, which meant begging and pleading with the authorities to bend all sorts of rules to allow this to happen instantly because their lives were in danger. We succeeded, and rushed them to intensive care, not knowing if they would survive. To see that same family, three or four months later, well-dressed, well-fed and ready to embark on their new lives in the United States, offered the kind of satisfaction that few jobs do.

As to lessons from that great tragedy (and the impressive international response), I learned for myself how useful the UN could be, as a young man running the UNHCR office (and the refugee camp that went with it) in Singapore at the peak of the Vietnamese 'boat people' crisis. It was obvious that some of the things I did could be done just as well by non-governmental organizations, church groups, compassionate individuals—all of whom I indeed enlisted in the cause as partners, donors and volunteers at the camp. But the UN could also do things that these good people could not —because, as an inter-governmental body, the UN has clout with its member states. Only the UN could negotiate with the government the terms under which refugees rescued at sea could be brought in to the port; only the UN could arrange their disembarkation; only the UN was allowed to be responsible for the camp; only the UN could work out the guarantees of resettlement in foreign countries without which the refugees could not disembark; only the UN, in the end, could persuade immigration officials of a dozen foreign countries to admit refugees and resolve problem cases. The UN, I realized through my own work, isn't just a way of bureaucratizing our consciences; it makes a real difference to real human beings, a difference that only the UN can make. And that's why I'm proud to have served it.

This doesn't mean, of course, that every one of my twenty-nine years of service was filled with such satisfaction. I learned and grew immensely by leading the team in the Department of Peacekeeping Operations handling the former Yugoslavia, and that was undoubtedly the most intense experience of my years at Headquarters. There were years of seventeen-hour days and seven-day weeks, and throughout it, the frustration of knowing that for all your efforts, the blood was continuing to flow in the Balkans. And yet, even there one could point to the intangible satisfaction of being directly involved in one of the great events of our time, and so leaving one's smudgy thumbprints on the footnotes of the pages of world history.

(Francis Fukuyama's idea of 'The End of History'—that the central debate in human history had been resolved with the triumph of the West in the Cold War, and that liberal democratic capitalism had essentially no challengers as the organizing principle of all human politics—seemed almost comically overstated in my own UN experience. In the years immediately after its publication, conflicts arose in so many states—the former Yugoslavia, Georgia, Moldova, Rwanda, Somalia, the list goes on—over fundamental issues of history, ethnicity and identity that had nothing to do with Fukuyama's thesis. It was as if history was reminding the world that reports of its demise had been exaggerated!)

When I later headed the UN's public information efforts, I enjoyed a different kind of challenge. It was my job to help shape the UN's message to the world and to deliver it every day. We did this through press relations, live radio broadcasts, TV programmes, publications, advocacy campaigns and an internet website that received over 2 billion hits a year in my time. In addition, my department handled relations with non-governmental organizations, outreach to civil society and educational institutions, and we ran the library at Headquarters, as well as guided tours of the building. So there was a wide variety of tasks for my colleagues in New York and at seventy-seven UN Information Centres around the world (which I had to cut to sixty-three as part of a budget-trimming exercise, a reversal of my old experience of expansion). Of course the UN never had just one message—each day we were juggling breaking news stories as well as long-term issue campaigns, and trying to respond to media interest in everything from peacekeeping operations to personnel problems. This kept us intensely involved with our colleagues in the various substantive departments of the UN, and it gave me, as the Under-Secretary-General, a fascinating overview of the range of challenges the UN dealt with every day.

My own role tended to combine a number of different elements. Many UN agencies had their own communications establishments, so there my role was one of co-ordination on system-wide issues. But the personal element came in because it was a job that allowed me to exercise my own creativity.

I could initiate new ideas to expand the UN's communications frontiers a little, such as my idea in 2004 to develop and announce a 'top ten list' of stories the world needed to hear more about, but which the media were neglecting. That was an innovation that has bought us good results in terms of global attention for forgotten issues. I was also privileged to launch a series of seminars on 'Unlearning Intolerance', where religious figures and scholars of diverse persuasions addressed questions including Islamophobia and anti-Semitism. The discussion was free, critical, reasoned, receptive, and uninhibited. It is in restoring those elements to otherwise impassioned discourse that the true strength and uniqueness of the United Nations lies. Where else but the UN could all countries of the world have joined in a resolution to remember the Holocaust and resolve to work together to dispel hatred, bigotry, racism, and prejudice and to refrain from religious incitement?

And then there was the management challenge that dominated my last seven years at the UN. Heading the Department of Public Information also gave me the rich satisfaction of stimulating the creative energies of the talented men and women from around the world who had brought their talents to the organization—as a manager of more than 750 colleagues in sixty-three countries, it was my job to lead them, guide them, provoke them and of course to learn from them too. What individuals contribute in institutions like the United Nations, is their intelligence, their drive, their integrity, their willingness to put in all the long hours it takes. When you work for an institution like the United Nations, the institution itself is at the centre of some of the great human events of our time. And so to be able to work with the United Nations means making your contribution to forces far larger than any individual is normally privileged to do.

Yet I can't conclude my recollections of the UN without a special word for one individual—Kofi Annan, the man I worked with most closely for the longest time (the entire second half of my career), and for whom I have the highest respect. When the UN and he won the Nobel Peace Prize in 2001, there was no doubt in my mind that the prize recognized the work of the thousands of unsung United Nations staff striving anonymously behind the headlines—bearing the brunt of the outflow of Afghan refugees, waging the long and thankless battle to overcome poverty in Africa, fighting the scourge of HIV/AIDS and other killer diseases, patrolling the frontlines in sixteen peacekeeping operations around the world. But it was also a tribute to the way that the United Nations, under this remarkable Secretary-General, had become the one indispensable global organization, something the Nobel Committee itself recognized in its citation, proclaiming 'that the only negotiable route to global peace and co-operation goes by way of the United Nations.'

I believe profoundly that, at its best and its worst, the UN is a mirror of the world—it reflects our hopes and aspirations but also our divisions and disagreements. The challenge for the UN is to mirror the pluralism and diversity of its membership, while at the same time acting effectively to address the great challenges the world faces. Above all it is the small countries, the poorest people, the weakest states, that need the UN most, and we must be able to fulfil their expectations. But we should also recognize our limitations. To work for the UN you have to be both an idealist and a realist: an idealist, because without ideals you may as well go and work somewhere else, but also a realist, because the UN pursues its ideals within the limits of the politically possible. As Dag Hammarskjold, our great second Secretary-General, put it, the UN was not created to take humanity to heaven but to save it from hell. That is sometimes the best we could do.

As for myself, my motivations in my UN service were no different from my motivations in life in general, including today in Indian politics: to do my best at whatever I undertake. To strive to leave the world a better place for my having been in it. To defend democracy and diversity. And to be motivated always by a faith in pluralism, and in the infinite possibilities of the human spirit. The UN, in its ideals and at its best in practice, incarnates those values that make the world worth living in for the vast majority of humanity. I remain immensely proud of having served it.

EMERGING POWERS AND GLOBAL
GOVERNANCE: INDIA

Take a random set of headlines from the summer of 2014 and what do we see? Our media is dominated by coverage of the Israel–Palestine conflict, the rise of ISIS and the horrors they are perpetrating, the events between Russia and Ukraine and the shooting down of a civilian airliner, and, to move away from conflict, the spread of the deadly Ebola virus, and the creation of a BRICS bank just as the G-8 goes back to being a G-7 again. All these events transcend national boundaries with implications for the globe as a whole, but with no common agreed global mechanism to deal with them, other than the UN and its agencies, with all their limitations.

Global governance is not exactly the most precise concept dreamed up by political scientists today. It is used to describe the processes and institutions by which the world is governed, and it was always intended to be an amorphous idea, since there is no such thing as a global government to provide such governance. 'Global governance' is a term that tries to impose a sense of order, real or imagined, on a world without an organized system of government. To describe it I would focus on four essential aspects.

The first is history. The institutions of global governance today are those that emerged after the disasters of the first half of the 20th century, and I think we must never forget the past if we are to understand the present and focus on the future. In the first half of the 20th century, the world saw two World Wars, countless civil wars, mass expulsions of populations, and the horrors of the Holocaust and Hiroshima. It was a period in which I think the world really must have wondered whether we as a collective humanity were likely to survive. Tolstoy had already written that memorable line that if you were not interested in war, it didn't matter; war was interested in you. And that's what essentially happened in the first half of the 20th century.

Then things changed. In and after 1945, a group of far-sighted leaders were determined to make the second half of the 20th century different from the first. So they drew up rules to govern international behaviour, and they founded institutions in which different nations could cooperate for the common good. That was the idea of 'global governance'—to foster international cooperation, to elaborate consensual global norms and to establish predictable, universally applicable rules, to the benefit of all.

The keystone of the arch, so to speak, was the United Nations itself. The UN was seen by world leaders as the only possible alternative to the disastrous experiences of the first half of the century. It stood for a world in which people of different nations and cultures could look on each other, not as subjects of fear and suspicion but as potential partners, able to exchange goods and ideas to their mutual benefit. The UN was seen by visionaries like former US President Franklin Delano Roosevelt as the only possible alternative to the disastrous experiences of the first half of the century. As Roosevelt stated in his historic speech to the two US Houses of Congress after the Yalta Conference, the UN would be the alternative to the military alliances, balance-of-power politics and all the arrangements that had led to war so often in the past.

His successor, the US president who presided at the birth of the UN, Harry Truman, argued passionately in San Francisco, when the Charter was signed, that the sacrifices that soldiers had made in the Second World War would only be justified if you had an arrangement in which all countries felt they had an equal stake. Truman put it clearly: 'You have created a great instrument for peace and security and human progress in the world,' he declared to the assembled signatories of the United Nations Charter in San Francisco on 26 June 1945. '…If we fail to use it, we shall betray all those who have died in order that we might meet here in freedom and safety to create it. If we seek to use it selfishly—for the advantage of any one nation or any small group of nations—we shall be equally guilty of that betrayal.'

'We all have to recognize,' Truman said, 'no matter how great our strength, that we must deny ourselves the license to do always as we please. No one nation…can or should expect any special privilege which harms any other nation… Unless we are all willing to pay that price, no organization for world peace can accomplish its purpose. And what a reasonable price that is!' That was a very clear and strong vision, and there's no question that the setting up of the global institutions in 1945 is something that we can all look back on with a sense of admiration, and dare I say it, gratitude.

Not that Paradise descended on earth in 1945. We all know that tyranny and warfare continued, and that billions of people still live in extreme and degrading poverty. But the overall record of the second half of the twentieth century is one of amazing advances. A third world war didn't occur. The world economy expanded as never before. There was astonishing technological progress. Many in the industrialized world now enjoy a level of prosperity, and have access to a range of experiences, that their grandparents could scarcely have dreamed of; and even in the developing world, there has been spectacular economic growth. Child mortality has been reduced. Literacy has spread. The peoples of the developing world threw off the yoke of colonialism, and those of the Soviet bloc won political freedom. Democracy and human rights are not yet universal, but they are now much more the norm than the exception. And yet we all know there's still a long way to go.

The second important feature is the global nature of the determining forces of today's world. There are broadly two contending and even contradictory forces in the world in which we live today; on the one hand are the forces of convergence, the increasing knitting-together of the world through globalization, modern communications and trade, and on the other are the opposite forces of disruption, of religious polarization, of the talk of the clash of civilizations, and of terrorism. The two forces, one pulling us together, the other pulling us apart, are both concurrent phenomena of our times, and these are taking place in a world in which—to take an Indian example—the terrorist attacks in Mumbai on 26/11 were in many ways emblematic of this paradoxical phenomenon. Why do I say this? Because the terrorists of 26/11 used the instruments of globalization and convergence—the ease of communications, GPS systems and mobile telephone technology, five-star hotels frequented by the transnational business elite, and so on—as instruments for their fanatical agenda. Similarly, on 9/11 in New York, rather than as forces to bring the world closer together, the terrorists also used similar tools—the jet aircraft being crashed into those towers emblematic of global capitalism, while the doomed victims of the planes tried to make frantic calls to their loved ones.

Both 9/11 and 26/11 were grotesque moments in that way. At the same time 9/11 had already reminded us of the cliché of the global village, because it proved that we are living in a village in which a fire that started in a dusty cave somewhere in Afghanistan, in one corner of the global village, could be strong enough to melt the steel girders holding up the tall skyscrapers at the opposite end of the global village. We have to recognize both the positive and negative forces of the world today, and from it, a consciousness of the increasing mutual interdependence that characterizes our age.

Global governance, as I've mentioned, rests on the realization that security is not indeed just about threats from enemy states or hostile powers, but that there are common phenomena that really cut across borders and affect us all. This idea has gained strong ground through the nineties and through the first part of this century. There is an obvious list of such problems: terrorism itself, the proliferation of weapons of mass destruction, of the degradation of our common environment, of climate change (quite obviously because we cannot put up a fence in the sky to sequester our own climate, it affects everyone), of persistent poverty and haunting hunger, of human rights and human wrongs, of mass illiteracy and massive displacement. There are financial and economic crises (because the financial contagion becomes a virus that spreads from one country to others), the risk of trade protectionism, refugee movements, drug trafficking. And we must not overlook epidemic disease. As we worry about Ebola let us remember the SARS epidemic in China a few years ago; initially there was an attempt to keep it quiet, but it was very easy for the virus to hop on a plane and show up in Toronto, and suddenly it became a global phenomenon, no longer something that could be contained in any one country. The same is true of AIDS, the same was true of swine flu (H1N1) and is true of Ebola today.

Today, whether one is from India or from Indiana, whether you live in Narita or Noida, it is simply not realistic to think only in terms of one's own country. Global forces press in from every conceivable direction; people, goods and ideas cross borders and cover vast distances with ever greater frequency, speed and ease. The internet is emblematic of an era in which what happens in New York or New Caledonia—from democratic advances to deforestation to the fight against AIDS—can affect lives in New Delhi. As has been observed about water pollution, we all live downstream.

Indians therefore realize they have a growing stake in international developments. To put it another way, the food we grow and we eat, the air we breathe, and our health, security, prosperity and quality of life are increasingly affected by what happens beyond our borders. And that means we can simply no longer afford to be indifferent about the rest of the world, however distant other countries may appear.

The third aspect is the emergence of institutions and processes that reflect this reality of increasing global convergence. Global institutions benefit from the legitimacy that comes from their universality. Since all countries belong to it, the UN enjoys a standing in the eyes of the world that gives its collective actions and decisions a legitimacy that no individual government enjoys beyond its own borders. But the institutions of global governance have been expanding beyond the UN itself. There are selective inter-governmental mechanisms like the G-8, military alliances like NATO, sub-regional groupings like the Economic Community of West African States, one-issue alliances like the Nuclear Suppliers Group. Writers connect under International PEN, soccer players in FIFA, athletes under the International Olympic Committee, mayors in the World Organization of United Cities and Local Governments. Bankers listen to the Bank of International Settlements and businessmen to the International Accounting Standards Board. The process of regulating human activity above and beyond national boundaries has never been more widespread.

Individual countries may prefer not to deal with such problems that transcend borders directly or alone, but they are impossible to ignore. So handling them together internationally is the obvious way of ensuring they are tackled; it is also the only way. Perhaps we can call for 'blueprints without borders': some scholars of international affairs have begun to speak of an idea they call 'responsible sovereignty', the notion that nations must cooperate across borders to safeguard common resources and to tackle common threats. I think that's a very sensible and succinct way of looking at the world which we have now come to, over six decades after the institutions of global governance were created, in a very different world, and in itself in a reaction to a very different world that preceded it. As far back as 1992, former UN Secretary General Boutros Boutros-Ghali in his report, 'An Agenda For Peace', stated that 'the time of absolute and exclusive sovereignty has passed'.

In parallel is emerging the fourth idea, that there are universally applicable norms that underpin our notion of world order. Sovereignty itself, however understood, is one, and linked to that idea is the principle of non-interference in other countries' internal affairs, equality and mutual benefit, non-aggression and co-existence across different political systems, the very principles originally articulated by India's first Prime Minister Pandit Nehru in his Panchsheel Doctrine with the People's Republic of China in 1954. (Today's China does not speak very much of the Panchsheel, the Five Principles of Peaceful Co-Existence, but its principles are embedded in the Chinese concept of a 'harmonious world'.) At the same time, there has evolved a new set of global norms of governance that complement these principles, including respect for human rights, transparency and accountability, rule of law, equitable development based on economic freedom, and at least to most nations, political democracy. These are seen as broadly desirable for all countries to aspire to, and while no one suggests that they can or should be imposed on any nation, fulfilling them is seen as admirable by most of the world and broadly accepted as evidence of successful governance.

Now these four broad aspects are descriptive of global governance, rather than prescriptive. But I would suggest that we should examine them in the context of a significant change in the way the world has evolved since the end of the Second World War. While we have all benefited from the global governance structures that evolved since 1945, we still have to recognize that these reflect the realities of 1945 and not of today, when a large number of emerging powers have begun asserting themselves on the world stage. That's why the time has come to think seriously about the challenges and the opportunities in global governance in the future, at a time when we are witnessing the weakening of traditional power centres in the world.

As we look around the world of today, we cannot fail to note the increase in the number of major powers across the world since the structures of the international system were put in place in 1945. It is an undeniable fact that the emerging powers have moved very much from the periphery to the centre of global discourse and global responsibility, and they have now a legitimate and an increasingly voluble desire to share power and responsibility in the global system. The dominance of a handful of small, industrialized Western countries, especially in the international financial institutions (the so-called Bretton Woods organizations), looks increasingly anomalous in a world where economic dynamism has shifted irresistibly from the west to the east. (In arguing the case for more democratization of the international system, I would like to add here, parenthetically, the increasing role of what are called social forces—NGOs, civil society movements—which we don't perhaps give enough account of in our discussion on global governance, but which we cannot be indifferent to, or unconscious of.) With all of this, and the emergence of new powers and forces which, unlike China, were omitted from the high table in 1945, we have clearly reached a point where there is need for a system redesign of global governance to ensure that all countries benefit. Clearly, what we in India are looking for is a more inclusive multilateralism, and not, as some American and Chinese observers once suggested, a G2 condominium.

As an Indian, I have no doubt that we must be globally active if we are to create and maintain the society we want at home. And our success at home is the best guarantee that we will be respected and effective abroad.

Because the distinction between domestic and international is less and less meaningful in today's world, when India thinks of global governance it must also think of its domestic implications. The ultimate purpose of any country's foreign policy is to promote the security and well-being of its own citizens. India wants a world that gives us the conditions of peace and security that will permit us to grow and flourish, safe from foreign depredations but open to external opportunities. This is the perspective from which India approaches global governance.

At the same time there is a consensus in our country that India should seek to continue to contribute to international security and prosperity, to a well-ordered and equitable world, and to democratic, sustainable development for all. These objectives now need to be pursued while taking into account 21st century realities: the end of the Cold War, the dawning of the Information Era, the ease of worldwide travel and widespread migration (5 per cent of the world's population currently lives in countries other than those in which they were born), the blurring of national boundaries by movements, networks and forces transcending state frontiers, the advent of Islamist terrorism as a pan-global force, the irresistible rise of China as an incipient superpower while retaining its political authoritarianism, the global consciousness of 'soft power', and the end to the prospect of military conflict between any two of the major nation-states.

Emerging powers like India are crucial players in the world's efforts to address a matrix of challenges—several interconnected socio-economic and environmental issues that pose a threat not just to the concept of nation states, but to humanity itself. We live in a world, after all, of poverty and inequality, malnutrition and epidemic disease, in which, as of June 2014, the number of people displaced from their homes exceeded 50 million—higher than the numbers of people affected by the Second World War. So we all need to pursue, across the globe, a variety of common objectives, including, but not limited to:

Ensuring peace, racial harmony, security
Resolution of conflicts, rehabilitation and rebuilding
Mitigating climate change
Protecting information highways and the internet
Stimulating and regulating the development of space technology
Governance of oceans, and of the 'global commons'

Today, emerging powers like India and China are indispensable to any global agreement on issues like trade (where the fate of the Doha Round hinged on India's acceptance of a deal that it feels could undermine its food security), and climate change. They are demanding accountability and responsibility from the traditional economic powerhouses.

India can legitimately argue that it has already earned its right to play a crucial role through its contributions to the existing structure of global governance. Take peace and security, for instance: India has been the largest troop contributor to UN missions since their inception. With participation in over forty-three peacekeeping missions seeing a contribution of more than 160,000 troops and a large number of police personnel, India has expended its blood and treasure to achieve some of the most arduous goals of global governance, the maintenance of international peace and security. In 2014 alone, India has contributed over 7,000 troops and civilian police personnel to UN peacekeeping missions across the globe.

The world, as the cliché goes, has changed. I grew up at a time when borders seemed unalterable, the USSR a permanent reality, and the Cold War a fixture of life. So much has changed so startlingly for the previous generation, that no one is prepared to write off the prospects of further change in the next one. The challenge for the newly emergent powers is to help shape the world order that is transforming itself even as they seek to find a newly prominent place in it.

∽

Multilateralism is a key issue. India's multilateral diplomacy has evolved significantly over time; as the world has changed, so have India's priorities in the international system. It used to be said about Indian diplomacy that it's like the love-making of an elephant: conducted at a very high level, accompanied by much bellowing, and the results are not known for two years. Fortunately this is less true of Indian diplomacy today: it has become more sprightly and adaptable to changing global realities.

Today, India's imperative is a domestic one: of ensuring growth, prosperity and security to its people. This requires peace and stability in its neighbourhood, since investors will not be attracted to war-zones, and successful relationships with countries that can be sources of India's security—including its energy security and its food security. To this end, India has had to bolster its bi-lateral and multi-lateral engagements with a wide variety of forums.

Traditionally, Indian multilateralism has largely been defined by its role in the UN, and specifically by its membership in two developing country bodies— the G-77 (of 120 developing countries) and the Non-Aligned Movement (NAM)—of both of which it was a founding member. Born half a century ago in the middle of a world riven by antagonism between the USA and the USSR and the alliances they led, NAM had been the vehicle for developing countries to assert their independence from the competing claims of the two superpowers. But with the end of the Cold War, there are no longer two competing blocs to be non-aligned between, and many have questioned the relevance of a movement whose very name signifies the negation of a choice that is no longer on the world's geopolitical table. The G-77, similarly, serves as a global 'trade union' of developing countries at a time when India sets far greater practical store by its membership of the G-20, the 'management' of the world economy.

Its membership of both the G-77 and the G-20, both the trade union body and the management, points to the new Indian approach to global governance. In the second decade of the 21st century, India has been moving increasingly beyond non-alignment to what I have described, in my 2012 book, *Pax Indica: India and the World of the 21st Century*, as 'multi-alignment'—maintaining a series of relationships, in different configurations, some overlapping, some not, with a variety of countries for different purposes. Prominence in the non-aligned movement remains a necessary reflection of India's anti-colonial heritage. But it is no longer the only, or even the principal, forum for India's international ambitions. Thus India is simultaneously a member of NAM and of the Community of Democracies, where it serves alongside the imperial powers that NAM decries. Similarly it seeks greater authority for itself in the form of a seat on the Security Council of the UN while, at the same time, focussing intensively on its seven immediate neighbours in the South Asian Association for Regional Co-operation, or SAARC.

An acronym-laden illustration of what multi-alignment means lies in India's membership of RIC (the trilateral forum with Russia and China, which meets annually), IBSA (the South-South co-operation mechanism that unites it with Brazil and South Africa), of BRICS (which brings all five of these partners together) and of BASIC (the environmental-negotiation group which adds China to IBSA but not Russia). India is the only country that belongs to all of these groupings, and not merely because its name begins with that indispensable asset to any multilateral acronym, a vowel! All these groups serve

India's interests in different ways, and it makes a valuable contribution to each. That is the way in which India pursues its place in the world, and the traditional forums like the non-aligned movement and the G-77 are largely incidental to it.

For India is coming of international prominence at a time when the world is moving, slowly but inexorably, into a post-superpower age. The days of the Cold War, when two hegemonic behemoths developed the capacity to destroy the word several times over, and flexed their muscles against each other by changing regimes in client states and fighting wars half a world away from their own borders, are now truly behind us. Instead, we are witnessing a world of many rising (and some risen) powers, of various sizes and strengths but each with some significant capacity in its own region, each strong enough not to be pushed around by a hegemon, but not strong enough to become a hegemon itself. They co-exist and co-operate with each other in a series of networked relationships, including bilateral and plurilateral strategic partnerships that often overlap with each other, rather than in fixed alliances or binary either/or antagonisms. The same is true of the great economic divide between developed and developing countries, a divide which is gradually dissolving; on many issues, India has more in common with countries of the North than of the global South for which it has so long been a spokesman. Neither in geopolitics nor in economics is the world locked into the kinds of permanent and immutable coalitions of interest that characterized the Cold War.

My metaphor of choice is the World Wide Web: an interlinked and networked world, not one of binary opposites. The new networked world welcomes every nation; it has little room for the domination of any superpower. Relationships are contingent and overlap with others; friends and allies in one cause might be irrelevant to another (or even on opposite sides). The networked world is a more fluid place. Countries use such networks to promote common interests, to manage common issues rather than impose outcomes, and provide a common response to the challenges and opportunities they face. Some networks would be principally economic in their orientation, some geopolitical, some issue-specific.

Take BRICS, for instance. BRICS now represents over 26 per cent of the global landmass, 43 per cent of its population, 20 per cent of the Global GDP (but closer to 50 per cent of current annual growth in global GDP) and 18 per cent of the market capitalization of the world's stock exchanges. When they talk about economic co-operation, when they set up their own development bank, the rest of the world has to sit up and pay attention. Or IBSA: it's not just a vehicle for South-South co-operation in trade, investment and development, which we've all heard before, but it represents an emerging partnership amongst three countries which share, in the words of former

Indian Prime Minister Manmohan Singh, 'the principles of pluralism, democracy, tolerance and multiculturalism'. The political content of these new groups may only be incipient, but they suggest changing realities the rest of the world would be unwise to ignore.

In such a world, India's 'multi-alignment' serves a variety of purposes. It helps India recast some assumptions and norms on global governance as it makes the transition from being among the rule-takers in the global arena to a rule-maker, a state capable of playing a global agenda–setting role. Multi-alignment also constitutes an effective response to the new trans-national challenges of the 21st century, to which neither autonomy nor alliance offer adequate answers in themselves. An obvious example is dealing with terrorism, which requires diplomatic and intelligence co-operation from a variety of countries facing comparable threats; but also shoring up failing states, combating piracy, controlling nuclear proliferation and battling organised crime. In addition to such issues there are the unconventional threats to the peace that also cross all borders (pandemics, for instance), and the need to preserve the global commons—keeping open the sea lanes of communication across international waters so that trade routes and energy supplies are safeguarded, ensuring maritime security from the Horn of Africa to the Straits of Malacca, protecting cyberspace from the depredations of hostile forces including non-governmental ones, and the management of outer space, which could increasingly become a new theatre for global competition.

Here the old forums can play a useful role in pushing the new agenda: India's then prime minister, Dr Manmohan Singh, used the sixteenth summit of NAM to call for 'global governance structures that are representative, credible and effective'.

This leads me, almost inevitably, to UN reform, because that is perhaps the first consequence that follows from the analysis that I have given you. UN reform is sort of like a malady where all the doctors gather around the patient, and they all agree on the diagnosis, but they can't agree on the prescription. That is the problem we've been facing for the last twenty-two years of debate on UN reform, since the General Assembly took it on the agenda in 1992, with the creation of the Open-Ended Working Group on Security Council reform.

The challenge is immense, not least because of the competing ambitions, all mutually incompatible, of an assortment of Member States that see themselves as potential winners or losers in any new arrangement. (I remember when the initial talk was all about Germany and Japan, the then Italian Foreign Minister Susanna Agnelli saying, 'What's all this talk about Germany and Japan? After all, we lost the war, too.')

So that is not something that is going to happen overnight, but India continues to push for an expansion of the Security Council in both categories—permanent and non-permanent. But it's not just the Security Council; we'd like to see the General Assembly strengthened as the primary intergovernmental legislative body, which it is not yet; it has become too often a rhetorical forum, or a declaratory forum rather than one which acts as a legislative body which drive the action of the UN organization. We'd like to see the Economic and Social Council becoming a more meaningful development-oriented body, and a serious instrument of development governance. And we would like to see a greater sharpening in focus on the working of the UN funds, agencies and programmes, whose effectiveness is so important for so many of the world's vulnerable and developing people.

I say all this not just as an academic exercise, because as somebody—not just as an Indian MP and former minister, but as somebody who has devoted three decades of his life to multilateral cooperation at the United Nations—I will say very strongly that my big fear remains that if reform does not come, that countries will inevitably look to alternative solutions. If reform of the United Nations does not take place, countries will simply be tired of being excluded, and they will say: 'Why should we waste time and energy and support and political focus on a place where they will not have us at the high table when there are others who are willing to acknowledge us and admit us?' The G20, to take the obvious example, is a body that has no charter, that does not require two-thirds vote for amendment, that does not need to be hamstrung by over two decades of debate, in deciding on its composition. And suddenly a new high table can be created which would be in effect the risk of an unelected directoire in world affairs of countries deciding that they have positioned themselves to be able to dictate to the rest of the world. And it could really undermine the one really effective universal organization we have built up on the underpinnings of national and international organization. So not reforming, and being petty in throwing obstacles to reform is terribly short-sighted, not only because it does not address the fundamental problem of representation and balance in global governance, but because it could undermine the very institution that many of these countries—particularly the medium-sized countries that are in the forefront of opposition to reform—have seen as a bulwark for their own security and safety.

I do want to turn to the international financial institutions, the Bretton Woods institutions as well, because of course we tend to focus excessively perhaps on political institutions; geopolitics is always more interesting to laymen than financial institutions. But the fact is that it is rather bizarre, once again, that they reflect the realities of over seven decades ago (those institutions were designed in 1944), rather than of today. Frankly it does seem slightly absurd that till recently, Belgium disposed of the same weighted vote as China in these institutions. And we really will need to see reform; the G20 Summit in Pittsburgh in September 2009 agreed in principle to a systemic redesign of the international financial structure, and in some ways that was what legitimized it in the eyes of many of us as the premier forum for international economic cooperation. It is a meaningful platform for north-south dialogue, because the south is not completely outweighed by the north in the composition of the G20.

The 2009 summit in Pittsburgh took a concrete decision to reform the Bretton Woods institutions. The intention is clear: to pursue regulatory reform but also to dilute the disproportionate power wielded by the old 'developed' economies of the Western world at a time when the 'emerging' economies had not yet emerged. Voting share targets were in fact agreed in Pittsburgh—to shift 5 per cent of the IMF quota share and 3 per cent of the World Bank's voting power from the developed world to the developing and transition economies. However, this actually falls short of what India, along with Brazil, Russia and China, have called for; the BRIC countries have demanded 7 per cent of the IMF quota share, and 6 per cent of the World Bank's. Nonetheless, they accepted the Pittsburgh outcome as an acceptable. First step towards the longer-term objective of broad parity between the developed countries and the developing/transition economies. But since the Pittsburgh decision in 2008, there has been no further movement on the issue. It is a measure of the BRICS countries' frustration at this that they have decided to create a New Development Bank headquartered in Shanghai: the message appears to be, if you can't give us a worthy place in your structure, we are quite capable of creating our own.

Let me stress: without reform, which will ensure buy-in from the emerging powers, these institutions will lose their relevance and their effectiveness. Already the setting up of a BRICS Bank is a clear signal that emerging powers are not content to be bit players on a world stage constructed by the main actors of 1944.

If that seems contestable to some in the West, I think we can only point to the recent global financial crisis, which showed how important it is that the surveillance of risk by international institutions, early warning mechanisms and so on are needed for all. In other words, they are needed so that the developing countries can also have some oversight over the mistakes the developed countries are making, as well. It's important that in this context, the developing countries should have a voice in overseeing the global financial performance of all countries rather than it simply being a case of the rich supervising the economic delinquency of the poor, which has been the pattern of much of the nearly seven decades of international global governance. So the inclusion of developing countries in the oversight mechanisms, and the inclusion of developed countries in the mechanisms that need to be overseen is going to be essential, as well. And to that I might add, en passant, the need for multilateral and regional development banks to have additional and adequate resources to fulfil their mandates.

The need for increased, more democratic and more equitable global governance cannot be denied. Jobs anywhere in the world today depend not only on local firms and factories, but on faraway markets for the goods they buy and produce, on licenses and access from foreign governments, on international financial trade rules that ensure the free movement of goods and persons, and on international financial institutions that ensure stability—in short, on the international system constructed in 1945. We just have to bring them into the world of the 21st century.

Our globalizing world clearly needs institutions and standards. Not 'global government', for which there is little political support anywhere but 'global governance', built on laws and norms that countries negotiate together, and agree to uphold as the common 'rules of the road'. India is committed to a world in which sovereign states can come together to share burdens, address common problems and seize common opportunities. If we are determined to live in a world governed by common rules and shared values, and to strengthen and reform the multilateral institutions that the enlightened leaders of the last century have bequeathed to us, then only can we fulfil the continuing adventure of making this century better than the last.

At the same time, much of what we are in the process of accomplishing at home—to pull our people out of poverty and to develop our nation—enables us to contribute to a better world. This is of value in itself, and it is also in our fundamental national interest. A world that is peaceful and prosperous, where trade is free and universally-agreed principles are observed, and in which democracy and respect for human rights flourish, is a world of opportunity for India and for Indians to thrive.

As Indian diplomats are fond of saying, we come from a very long tradition of internationalism or universalism. The old Sanskrit saying, 'Vasudevaya Kutumbakam' (The whole world is one family) has animated India's approach, since time immemorial, on the global stage; we have never been an insular, internally-focused country, we have always been externally focused. Even at the moment of Independence in 1947, when the flames of partition with Pakistan were burning, our great first prime minister, Jawaharlal Nehru, at that tragic moment, was still able to speak not only of his dreams for India, but for the world. In his historic speech about India's 'tryst with destiny', Nehru, speaking of our country's hopes, said: 'Those dreams are for India, but they are also for the world, for all the nations and peoples are too closely knit together today for any one of them to imagine that it can live apart. Peace has been said to be indivisible; so is freedom, so is prosperity now, and so also is disaster in this

One World that can no longer be split into isolated fragments.'

So we see ourselves very consciously as a responsible international citizen seeking to help fulfil those dreams for the world. And on that basis we wish to see a world that is more equitable, that allows more voices to be heard, that allows more players to have a part in that classic spirit of 'Vasudevaya Kutumbakam', that we are all one family, and we have to sort out that family's business together.

As a major power, India can and must play a role in helping shape the global order. The international system of the 21st century, with its networked partnerships, will need to renegotiate its rules of the road; India is well qualified, along with others, to help write those rules and define the norms that will guide tomorrow's world. Rather than confining itself to being a subject of others' rule-making, or even a resister of others' attempts, it is in India's interests (and within India's current and future capacity) to take the initiative to shape the evolution of these norms as well as to have a voice in the situations within which they are applied.

DILEMMAS OF GLOBAL GOVERNANCE

Every year since 2011, some fifty young leaders around the world under 35 years of age from about thirty different countries have been meeting in Delhi at the Asian Forum on Global Governance. The Forum, which I helped put together with the Observer Research Foundation and the German ZEIT-Stiftung, seeks to provoke thinking on a wide range of issues, as well as expand networks and form friendships that will last a lifetime. It builds on a similar 'summer school' on global governance run every year in Hamburg, whose alumni include some of India's brightest young leaders.

I take pride in the fact that I have had the opportunity to play the midwife in this fruitful partnership between the two institutions from India and Germany. India is in the throes of dynamic change and serves as the perfect destination for young international-minded leaders who want to understand the nature of transformation and transition in Asia and the world. Germany, with its tradition of European solidarity and experience of thought leadership, is the perfect foreign partner.

Each year's theme relates in one way or another to the challenges of negotiating governance in our multipolar world, and reflects the understanding that conversations and dialogues on crucial global challenges are perhaps the only way forward for the planet. These conversations must start now, if they haven't already, and these conversations should start with young people across the world who are destined to become change-makers.

There are several reasons why such initiatives are important today. These include the economy, ecology, technology, demography and geography—each of which surprises us by how much and how fast they change. The world today has no similarity to that of the 1950s or even the 1990s. In fact the surprise that greeted the award of the Nobel Peace Prize to the European Union in 2012 confirms how much we have forgotten of history and how much we have taken today's peace for granted. That Europe was the continent which for a thousand years served as a battleground for brutal and bloody wars, civil conflicts and massacres right up to 1945, and is now a place where war even between traditional antagonists is inconceivable, is no mean accomplishment. We know the EU is currently suffering the Eurozone crisis. That too is a reminder that economics and geopolitics do not necessarily march in step—that we must consider them both separately and together.

Amongst the key pertinent questions facing the world are: How do traditional governance frameworks adapt to the paradigm of constant change? Why are post-World War II frameworks still in place to run the world's premier institutions? How are political, economic or social disruptions likely to reshape them? What is the role of the emerging and developing world in negotiating new frameworks? What is the role of new technologies, new media, non-state actors? Which nations will assume leadership? And can we have a more equitable and representative world order which does not have to compromise on the speed and efficiency of decision making?

Clearly there is no single answer to many of these questions. Yet it is important to pose them.

Each step forward on the route to a new governance paradigm is going to be negotiated. Negotiations are unlikely to yield results if a zero-sum game is pursued. The idea for a forum like this is to create a space for debates, a fertile breeding ground for discussions, and most of all to promote greater understanding of the multiplicity of perspectives.

What the Forum has been doing is to present and provoke conversations around five key governance issues: rebalancing of governance centres and consequently of global power itself; traditional security and who will catch the ball in the period of change and transition; climate change, energy and poverty, each of which is an enduring narrative of our times; the role of trans-national corporations and other non-state actors; and perhaps most important, new rules and modes for financial and economic cooperation.

My previous book, *Pax Indica: India and the World of the 21st Century*, looked at these issues from an Indian prism. As India seeks to shape governance frameworks, and define its forward trajectory, it will need the key virtues of flexibility, adaptability, resilience and persistence. Simultaneously, it is likely that India's multiple external engagements will sometimes complement and at other times challenge the norms, rules and frameworks that govern our nation.

Aside from governments and nations, the emergence and proliferation of non-state actors including multinationals and civil society will continue to exert unique pushes and pulls. Some of the questions worth asking are whether we confront these new voices, or co-opt them, thereby reducing their novelty, or partner with them? What are the various interests at play? Can market efficiency alone help to respond more effectively to the systemic, societal, political or ecological challenges that confront our civilizations?

All of us are operating within a technological paradigm that is constantly evolving. Five years ago nobody had heard of Twitter, let alone predicted that it would be used as an agent of massive socio-political change across West Asia and North Africa. It is a sobering fact that the pace of technological change is perhaps the most unpredictable of all externalities, and paradigm shifts cannot ever be fully accounted for in our predictions and projections of the future. We do not know today what technology will alter the world even in three years' time, so we must remain modest when we seek to predict the future or even to anticipate our own roles.

In any case negotiations will be the fulcrum around which the world will evolve. Some would like the framework for negotiations to be value based, failing to recognize that values that seem to them to be universal to some, are alien to others. Some suggest that the framework should be based on interests that are defined through conversations. The Delhi Forum provides a venue for many of these conversations. It is fitting that India will be the stage on which many new roles will be rehearsed and enacted.

WHEN DEMOCRACY IS A BAD IDEA: THE 'LEAGUE OF DEMOCRACIES'

Amidst the continuing brouhaha about issues of race and gender that emerged in the 2008 US presidential campaign, the world quickly lost sight of the most important question that arose in the candidates' more desultory skirmishing over international affairs. That relates to John McCain's advocacy of the establishment of a 'League of Democracies,' and the mounting clamour for Barack Obama to espouse the same idea as his own.

McCain broached the idea more than once in major foreign policy speeches. The League is something he said he'd establish in his first year in office, a close-knit grouping of like-minded nations that could respond to humanitarian crises and even compensate for the United Nations Security Council's distressing tendency to be hamstrung by the likes of Russia and China when it needed to take decisive action against the world's evildoers. The idea was embraced enthusiastically not just by neocon Republicans spoiling for an alternative to the UN, but even by Obama supporters, who were quick to point out that the notion of such a body had been championed by Democrat-minded academics like John Ikenberry, Anne-Marie Slaughter and especially Ivo Daalder, who is also a foreign-policy adviser to the Illinois Senator.

Anthony Lake, Obama's most senior international affairs counsellor, signed on as well. 'Crises in Iran, North Korea, Iraq and Darfur', he wrote, 'not to mention the pressing need for more efficient peacekeeping operations, the rising temperatures of our seas and multiple other transnational threats, demonstrate not only the limits of American unilateral power but also the inability of international institutions designed in the middle of the 20th century to cope with the problems of the 21st.' In other words, the institutions so painstakingly built up out of the ashes of the Second World War have passed their use-by date, and it's time to move on to UN 2.0, or perhaps, in the argot of the day, UN Vista.

Neocon guru Robert Kagan rejected the notion that a League of Democracies would supplant the UN: '[not] any more than the Group of Eight leading industrialized nations or any number of other international organizations [could] supplant it. But the world's democracies could make common cause to act in humanitarian crises when the UN Security Council cannot reach unanimity'. The League's strength would be that it 'would not be limited to Europeans and Americans but would include the world's other great democracies, such as India, Brazil, Japan and Australia, and would [therefore] have even greater legitimacy'.

The idea found unlikely adherents on the other side of the pond.

Labour progressive Alan Johnson is almost giddy with enthusiasm: 'A concert of democracies could promote liberal ideals in international relations and give teeth to the 'responsibility to protect'. It could exercise the power of attraction, a soft power that might act as a goad to democratic reform in many countries seeking the benefits of membership. It could re-anchor the US in an internationalist framework and enhance the influence that America's democratic allies wield in Washington. The concert, perhaps 100 strong, would seek to protect interests, defend principles, reconcile differences, reach consensus, gauge and grant international legitimacy to actions, signal a commitment to the democratic ideal and show solidarity with those movements 'trying to pry open a democratic space'. In other words, it would do everything the UN has been trying valiantly to do, with mixed results so far.

One doesn't have to be a starry-eyed devotee of the UN to ask everyone to take a deep breath before the runaway popularity of this idea becomes consensual in Washington. The world has less than three decades ago, come out of a crippling Cold War. We are moving fitfully, and despite undeniable problems, to a post-bloc world, one in which America's biggest potential geopolitical rival, China, is also its biggest trading partner. If we were to create a new League of Democracies, who exactly are we leaving out? China and Russia, for starters—a former superpower and a future one, two countries without whom a world of peace and prosperity is unimaginable. Instead of encouraging their gradual democratization, wouldn't we be reinforcing their sense of rejection by the rest? Would the result not be the self-fulfilling prophecy of the emergence of a League of Autocracies with these two at the helm?

That's if the idea worked; but would all democracies join such a League? Democracies like India and France have proved prickly in the past about countries like the US or Britain assuming that their internal political arrangements might govern their foreign policy choices. Many democracies have other affinities that are as important to them; India, for instance, may count solidarity with other former colonies, or with other developing countries, or even with fellow members of the Commonwealth, as more important than its affiliation with a League of Democracies. South Africa may judge that its shared experience of racist oppression with Zimbabwe outweighs its shared democratic tradition with Britain. The American notion that a collection of democracies would inevitably be an echo-chamber for an American diagnosis of global problems is a fantasy.

The claim that a League of Democracies would be less likely to be paralyzed into inaction over, say, sanctions on Iran, than a Security Council with the likes of Russia or China on it, overlooks the basic fact that it is in the nature of democracies to differ, to argue amongst themselves, and to be responsive to the very different preoccupations of their own internal constituencies. America itself is least likely to be swayed by sentimental appeals to democratic virtue: had a League of Democracies existed during the apartheid years, would Washington have been persuaded by a democratic majority to intervene against Pretoria? The very question points to the risibility of its premise.

The advocates of a League of Democracies argue that it would intervene more effectively in cases like Sudanese atrocities in Darfur or the cruel indifference of the military regime in Myanmar to the sufferings of its cyclone victims. In fact the reasons why such interventions have not occurred is because they are impracticable. Humanitarian aid could not have been delivered effectively in the Irrawaddy Delta in the teeth of active resistance by the Myanmarese Junta, or in Darfur by going to war with the Sudanese army, unless the countries wishing to do this were to be prepared to expend a level of blood and treasure that democracies rarely risk for strangers. It is one thing to march into a chaotic, government-less Somalia to protect the delivery of aid, quite another to confront the military force of a sovereign state defending its own territory. (And even then, at its peak, the Somalia operation cost the international community seven times the value of the humanitarian aid it was delivering.)

It is also specious to argue that collective action by a group of democracies (when the UN is unable to act) would enjoy international legitimacy. That, too, is a delusion. The legitimacy of democracies comes from the consent of the governed; when they act outside their own countries, no such consent exists or applies. The reason that decisions of the United Nations enjoy legitimacy across the world lies not in the democratic virtue of its members, but in its universality. The fact that every country in the world belongs to the UN and participates in its decisions gives the actions of the UN—even that of a Security Council that reflects the geopolitical realities of 1945 rather than today—a global standing in international law that no more selective body can hope to achieve.

This is the time to renovate and strengthen the UN, not to bypass it. As the post-Cold War 'unipolar moment' slowly but surely makes way for a world of multiple power centres and a rising new superpower, there has never been a greater need for a system of universally-applicable rules and laws that will hold all countries together in a shared international community. We all hope that, in an era of instant communications and worldwide information flows, this community will be an increasingly democratic one. Subtracting today's democracies from it will have the opposite effect.

The hothouse of American presidential politics too often provides fertile ground for bad ideas to flower. The League of Democracies is one that needs to be nipped in the bud before it can take root.

WARRING FOR PEACE

Years ago, while I was toiling at the United Nations, the international community—gathered together at the level of heads of state and government at a Millennium Summit in New York—endorsed the idea that they had a collective responsibility to protect civilians whose own governments were unable or unwilling to do so. Sovereignty was all very well, the world leaders agreed, but it came with certain duties to the people in whose name it was exercised, and if sovereign governments couldn't prevent massive human rights abuses (or worse, inflicted them on their own people), then the world had the duty to do something about it. The new doctrine was immediately dubbed 'R2P', short for 'responsibility to protect'.

This was a twist to the earlier arguments for 'the right to humanitarian intervention', turning the issue on its head: the principle was no longer about the right of foreigners to intervene in third countries for humanitarian purposes, but rather their responsibility to protect people, if necessarily through intervention. The evocative image behind R2P was that of the 1994 genocide in Rwanda, when perhaps a million people died in a mass slaughter conducted by machete-wielding Tutsi militia—a horror that could have been prevented had the international community taken on such a responsibility, and intervened with a few thousand troops, instead of withdrawing the UN Blue Helmets who already happened to be there.

It all sounded very noble and altruistic. The UK's telegenic and hyper-articulate then prime minister, Tony Blair, memorably declared that in the future, the West would go to war in the name of its values, not just of its interests. The wars of the future, Blair and his acolytes argued, would be fought for peace and human rights, not over something as crass as national interests, oil (perish the thought!) or imperial lust for territorial aggrandizement. The only catch in all this was in applying the principle to an actual case. As Rwanda had revealed, governments were all-too-unwilling to risk blood and treasure for the sake of foreign lives. Would armies actually intervene out of disinterested humanitarianism, or only do so when such declared intent in fact masked more cynical motives?

Indeed, the first major military intervention after the Millennium Summit—the Iraq war in 2003—was initially sought to be couched in the language of humanitarianism by its proponents. But this was hotly rejected by the votaries of R2P, who argued that the war was squarely anchored in Washington's geopolitical interests rather than in any real concern for suffering Iraqi civilians. Blairite altruism never quite recovered its credibility in the aftermath of Iraq.

R2P came to life again, though, with the aerial military intervention by NATO forces in Libya. Since the UN Security Council resolution that authorized the action permitted countries to use 'all necessary means' to stop the assaults by Gaddafi's forces on Libyans rising up against his oppressive regime, the bombardments were described as humanitarian in intent, aimed at saving Libyan lives. The idea was supposed to be to level the playing field so that a peaceful settlement could be negotiated by the contending parties, as had happened in Egypt and Tunisia. This was meant to be a war for peace.

It didn't work out that way. The Western air forces did not simply stop their action once they had neutralized Gaddafi's attacks on rebel-held Benghazi. They went on pounding ground targets, causing considerable civilian casualties. An attack on Gaddafi's compound, which killed one of his children, suggested that the objective had moved well beyond the imposition of a 'no-flight zone' to protect civilians on the ground to getting rid of Gaddafi himself—in effect, regime change. Exactly as it eventually transpired.

My American writer friend David Rieff, who was once an enthusiastic interventionist in the civil war in Yugoslavia (but has since recanted—see his book, *At the Point of a Gun*) now criticizes 'the messianic dream of remaking the world in either the image of American democracy or of the legal utopias of international human rights law'. This is not just because it isn't easy to do, nor that it involves taking more lives than it saves. It's also, simply, because Rieff, and gradually other Americans, are coming around to the view that intervention isn't right in any circumstances. He even told the *New York Times*'s Maureen Dowd that 'Gaddafi is a terrible man, but I don't think it's the business of the United States to overthrow him. Those who want America to support democratic movements and insurrections by force if necessary... are committing the United States to endless wars of altruism. And that's folly.'

This sounds rather like the traditional non-aligned objection to any interference in the internal affairs of sovereign states. Countries like India, China and Brazil, which abstained on the Libyan resolution, have long been profoundly allergic to any attempt by countries to impose their will on Third World nations by the force of arms. The experience of colonialism underlies many of these attitudes—nations that have won their freedom after centuries of subjugation by foreigners supposedly acting out of a 'civilizing mission' are understandably none too keen on seeing the same conduct re-emerge under the garb of humanitarianism, or even R2P. And yet those in the developing world who would resist such intervention have no answer to the question— if the world had been prepared to protect the Rwandans from genocide in 1994, would you have considered that an inadmissible interference in Rwanda's sovereignty?

The squeamishness is not only on the part of the developing country ideologues. The potential intervenors have their own hesitations. In the 1820s,

US President John Quincy Adams declared about America: 'Wherever the standard of freedom and independence has been or shall be unfurled, there will her heart, her benedictions and her prayers be. But she goes not abroad, in search of monsters to destroy...she is the champion and vindicator only of her own.' Adams' statement recognized that the principal duty of a democracy is to its own voters and legislators. The imposition of its values on others is, indeed, not its business.

It doesn't help, of course, that such attempts at imposition have often gone awry, as the years of chaos in Iraq after the American military triumph in 2003 demonstrated. War creates casualties. Often these exceed the beneficiaries; it has only been a few decades since an American general so fatuously declared in Vietnam that 'it was necessary to destroy the village in order to save it'. If you want peace, you must prepare for war—only in order not to have to go to war. Once you do, peace is no longer possible; the logic of war renders the very idea absurd, as we are seeing every day in Libya. The French philosopher Blaise Pascal remarked, centuries ago, that 'he who would act the angel, acts the beast'. To pretend that angels must do beastly things for angelic purposes is either naïve, or cynical, or both.

This is why the only true warriors for peace are United Nations peacekeepers, whose job is to prevent the recurrence of conflict, rather than to engage in conflict in the name of ending it. When the war ended in Libya, amidst all the smoke and the rubble lay one more discredited notion, that of going to war in the name of peace.

HOW RELEVANT IS NON-ALIGNMENT?

As the world settles into the permanent fluidity of the post-Cold War era, questions are understandably being raised about the relevance and direction of the Non-Aligned Movement (NAM) that emerged from it. Born half a century ago in the middle of a world riven by antagonism between the USA and the USSR and the alliances they led, NAM had been the vehicle for developing countries to assert their independence from the competing claims of the two superpowers. But with the end of the Cold War, there are no longer two rival blocs to be non-aligned between, and many have questioned the relevance of a movement whose very name signifies the negation of a choice that is no longer on the world's geopolitical table.

With the passing of the binary superpower-led world, NAM has redefined itself as a movement for countries that are not aligned with any major power. Since this is a state of affairs that is true of most countries in the world outside NATO, the globe's only surviving military alliance, it is hardly sufficient to justify the maintenance of the movement. So NAM has been shaping a persona that is increasingly vocal about resisting the hegemony of the sole superpower, the US, and in asserting the independence of its members—overwhelmingly former colonies in the developing world—from the dominance of 'Western imperialism'. The somewhat old-fashioned sound of the term revives charges that the movement is out of date. More seriously, this perception is compounded by the increasing visibility within NAM of countries like Iran and Venezuela, both nations whose strident hostility to the USA underscores NAM's anti-Western image. The very location of the Summit serves to undercut the West's attempts to isolate Iran internationally and so proclaims NAM's defiance of the currents of the times.

Does such an orientation sit well with the rest of the membership, which includes such partners of Washington as India, Pakistan, Saudi Arabia, Kenya, Qatar and the Philippines? Some of these countries would probably feel less comfortable with the political rhetoric of NAM than with its economic arguments, at a time when predatory global capitalism is increasingly under challenge around the world—but others have been noticeably receptive to US economic policies. In any case economics is the domain of the G-77, the 'trade union' of the developing world, not NAM, whose raison d'etre is political.

NAM does, however, embody the desire of many developing countries to stake out their own positions distinct from the Western-led consensus on a host of global issues—energy, climate change, technology transfer, the protection of intellectual property especially in pharmaceuticals, and trade, to name a few. In its determination to articulate a different standpoint on such issues, NAM embodies many developing countries' desire to uphold their own strategic autonomy in world affairs and the post-colonial desire to assert their independence from the West.

The Arab Spring that convulsed the Middle East affected several NAM members directly. The countries that have undergone the most significant changes—Egypt, Libya, Tunisia and Syria—are all members of NAM. The movement should therefore be a logical vehicle to pursue a resolution of the issues swirling around the turbulence of the region. But its members are too hopelessly divided to forge a common position—and the anti-Assad views of many of them on Syria, for instance, or their rejection of the fanatical ambitions of ISIS, are not very different from those of the West. Nonetheless the NAM summits discuss the developments in the Arab world in the hope of evolving a shared understanding of the region's future evolution. Whether this will amount to much more than words remains to be seen.

For a country like India, whose two decades of economic growth have made it an important player on the global stage, the non-aligned movement remains a necessary reflection of its anti-colonial heritage. But it is no longer the only, or even the principal, forum for its international ambitions. As we have seen before, in the second decade of the 21st century, India is moving increasingly beyond non-alignment to 'multi-alignment'—maintaining a series of relationships, in different configurations, some overlapping, some not, with a variety of countries for different purposes. Thus India is simultaneously a member of the NAM and of the Community of Democracies, where it serves alongside the same imperial powers that NAM decries. It has a key role in both the G-77 (the 'trade union' of developing countries) and the G-20 (the 'management' of the globe's macro-economic issues).

An acronym-laden illustration of what multi-alignment means lies in India's membership of IBSA (the South-South co-operation mechanism that unites it with Brazil and South Africa), of RIC (the trilateral forum with Russia and China), of BRICS (which brings all four of these partners together) and of BASIC (the environmental-negotiation group which adds China to IBSA but not Russia). India belongs to all of these groupings; all serve its interests in different ways. That is the manner in which India pursues its place in the world, and the NAM is largely incidental to it.

THE ARAB SPRING, INDIA AND CHINA

The tumultuous events in Egypt and the 'Arab Spring' have been commented upon extensively by experts far more knowledgeable than I am about the Arab world. And yet there is one aspect of what has happened that none of the experts seems to have focused on—something with wider global implications.

Let me explain. Perhaps one of the more interesting sidelights of the dramatic events in Cairo, as millions poured into Tahrir ('Liberation') Square and the Egyptian police melted away in the face of demonstrators, looters, democrats and vandals alike, was the reaction of the People's Republic of China. Beijing's official spokesperson on Sunday called for a 'return to order' in Egypt, expressing concern at the troubles besieging this 'friendly country'. Praying for calm, the Chinese government made it clear that the restoration of law and order was its principal priority.

What made China—once a reliable supporter of the cause of 'liberation' for 'oppressed peoples' seen as groaning under the yoke of pro-Western authoritarian regimes—take such a tack this time? It is easy enough to say that China is no longer the communist country it used to be, and that Mao's old enthusiasm for spreading the faith of the Little Red Book has long been supplanted by a preference for the Big Green Chequebook instead. That is, of course, true, and few are the 'liberation movements' these days that can count on cash, ideological support or practical assistance from Beijing. Nor is it wrong to point out that despite a consciousness of a US threat to its own global superpower ambitions, China does not fundamentally see itself in political competition with the USA and is making little effort to wrest pro-Washington governments away from the American embrace.

All that is commonplace enough. But there is something more behind the Chinese position. What China's statement about Egypt reveals is that the mandarins in Beijing are thinking about themselves—and their own stake in the success across the world of authoritarian systems which, whatever their foreign policy orientations, are more akin to their style of rule than to Washington's. When the Soviet Union collapsed in 1990-91, no one was more worried than the Beijing establishment. They too had embarked on reforms, after all, driven by the same realization as Moscow that the communist system was not only morally and ideologically bankrupt, but worse still, did not work in practice. Communism's biggest weakness was not that it was undemocratic, but that it could not deliver the goods. The fact that the USSR's embrace of reform had led so rapidly to the collapse of the ruling Communist party, and even to unravelling of the entire country, gave pause to the enthusiasts of change in China—those who had been tempted by the Gorbachev-like impulses of one-time party leader Zhao Ziyang. They anxiously studied the Soviet reform experience for lessons they could draw upon to avoid a similar fate themselves.

And from this emerged a simple insight: what an authoritarian system in the throes of reform needs to do is to pursue perestroika but not glasnost. Political change, for such regimes, is a bad idea, but economic success is essential.

Gorbachev's big mistake, the bosses in Beijing concluded, was that he mixed up the genuine need for perestroika (the restructuring of the failed and inefficient Communist economic and bureaucratic system) with the unnecessary turn towards glasnost (openness, liberalism and democratic pluralism in the political system). The former, as the Chinese communists saw it, was an imperative they had already realized by then; the latter, which Gorbachev saw as a necessary accompaniment—rather like the chhole without which a bhatura isn't worth having—would simply guarantee their own extinction. Whereas the Russian communists had wrongly believed the package came as a whole and couldn't be disaggregated, the Chinese decided it could be. They proceeded to demonstrate that you could operate a capitalist economic model within an authoritarian, repressive one-party state.

In this they found considerable sympathy from regimes around the world which, while pro-Western in their foreign policy, remained the antithesis of Western Enlightenment values at home. The survival of such regimes—from Putin's Russia, still more messy than Beijing would like, to a variety of Arab and African dictatorships—vindicated China's view that its way of doing business (and running government) had far more resonance and viability than the free-for-all democracy practised in untidy places like India and nominally advocated by America and the European Union.

The fact is that they are not wholly wrong. The 'Jasmine Revolution' in Tunisia and its knock-on effect in Egypt (with the prospect of the contagion spreading to Libya, Sudan, Yemen and/or Jordan in the uncertain future) is instructive for all sorts of reasons, but perhaps the most striking of them is that it is not authoritarianism per se that the crowds in the streets are demonstrating against. Dictatorial rule has been accepted in each of these countries for decades. What the protestors were shouting for was not just freedom but dignity—the dignity that comes from having jobs worth doing, food to eat, hopes of a better life for their kids. As long as authoritarianism can deliver economic benefits, most people in most developing countries will put aside their natural desire for democratic self-expression and concentrate on making a good life for themselves and their families instead. It is when an authoritarian state fails to deliver on these basic necessities that the people finally pour into the streets.

This is the central Chinese insight. A rock song of the 1970s memorably told us that 'freedom's just another word for nothing left to lose'. When the heavy hand of the state takes care of your material aspirations, its heaviness seems less important. Opposing it would jeopardize a lot of material benefits: this is why Chinese dissidents have so little support in their materialistic society. When the state doesn't deliver the goods, then opposing it makes sense: you have nothing left to lose. The biggest failures of Hosni Mubarak in Egypt and Zine Al Abidin Ben Ali in Tunisia may not have been their repressive politics but their failed economics. If young men hadn't been unemployed and struggling to make ends meet, feed themselves and have the self-respect to offer a home to the young women they desired, they would not be calling for the overthrow of their government. That is worth bearing in mind as the so-called experts allow the scent of jasmine to envelop us all.

And yet one is tempted to ask the question: would a different political approach have avoided regime collapse? In other words, could democracy have provided an outlet for the grievances of jobless and frustrated youth that would have fallen short of bringing governments down? The Indian experience offers an instructive model.

Unlike most developing countries—including every single one in the Arab world—India did not choose, upon attaining its independence from colonial rule, to adopt an authoritarian system in the name of nation-building and economic development. Instead, it voted for democracy. British rule left India impoverished, diseased and undeveloped, with an appalling 18 per cent literacy rate; the British-determined partition with Pakistan added communal violence, the trauma of destruction and displacement, and 13 million refugees to this list. India's nationalist leaders would have been forgiven if they had argued that they needed dictatorial authority to cope with these immense problems, especially in the most diverse society on earth, riddled with religious, linguistic and caste divisions. But they did not.

They decided, instead, that democracy, for all its imperfections, was the best way to overcome these problems, because it gave everyone a stake in solving them. Democracy reflected India's diversity, since Indians are accustomed to the idea of difference. From a source of division in the polity, democracy has turned out to be the best—indeed the only—mechanism for managing India's differences within the framework of an agreed system for accommodating the contention of divergent interests. It helps that Indian nationalism has always been the nationalism of an idea. It is the idea of one land embracing many—a land emerging from an ancient civilization, united by a shared history, sustained by a pluralist political system. India's democracy imposes no narrow conformities on its citizens. The whole point of Indian pluralism is you can be many things and one thing: you can be a good Muslim, a good Keralite and a good Indian all at once. As I have long argued (perhaps once too often!) that if America is famously a 'melting-pot', then to me India is a thali, a selection of sumptuous dishes in different bowls. Each tastes different, and does not necessarily mix with the next, but they belong together on the same plate, and they complement each other in making the meal a satisfying repast.

Amid India's myriad problems, it is democracy that has given Indians of every imaginable caste, creed, culture, and cause the chance to break free of their lot. There is social oppression and caste tyranny, particularly in rural India, but Indian democracy offers the victims a means of escape, and often—thanks to the determination with which the poor and oppressed exercise their franchise—of triumph. The significant changes in the social composition of India's ruling class since Independence, both in politics and in the bureaucracy—with leaders from the formerly 'untouchable' and backward castes elected to high office—have vindicated democracy in practice.

The result is that though economic difficulties persist—rising food and fuel prices, corruption scandals, unemployment—they have not led to demonstrations calling for regime change. Indians know they can use other means—debates in Parliament, political alliance-making, and eventually the ballot-box—to bring about the changes they desire. This also guarantees a responsive government. Democratic accountability is a perpetual process—Indian governments act today for fear of electoral retribution tomorrow. That is an incentive that Mubarak and Ben Ali never had.

India has always been reluctant to preach democracy to others—its own history of colonial rule makes it wary of preaching its ways to foreign civilizations, and underscores its conviction that each country must determine its own political destiny. Democracy, in any case, is rather like love—it must come from within, and cannot be taught. But for Arab rulers looking uneasily at the lessons of events in Tunisia and Egypt, the example of India might well be worth paying attention to.

GLOBALIZATION, POVERTY AND INDIA

One of the features of this globalized world of particular benefit to India, we are told by the American writer Thomas Friedman, is that the world is flat. Friedman, who has also acquired something of a reputation as the pre-eminent cheerleader for globalization, argues that there has been a 'levelling of the playing field' as a result of the over-capacity built up during the 'dot-com boom', particularly in technological infrastructure and international fiber-optic cabling. This has 'flattened the world', producing a convergence of opportunities that allows any company in any country the chance to join a new global supply chain in both services and manufacturing. We are now in the era of 'Globalization 3.0', as he calls it, and India is perhaps the one country other than China that exemplifies the benefits of this process.

I do not fundamentally disagree with the argument that, thanks to its technological proficiency, India is much better placed to take advantage of this new world than most, and that its abundance of highly-skilled engineers and software technicians plugged into the global networks explains why it is doing so well today. But I am less willing to embrace the sweeping conclusions of a Friedman; I fear that in celebrating the flatness of his world he loses sight of more than one inconvenient hillock.

Friedman wrote some years ago that we have moved from a world dominated by superpowers to one dominated by supermarkets—including, of course, super stock-markets, about whose power he has written with such admiration. In other words, analysts like him suggest that geopolitics has ceded place to the primacy of globalized economics. Western analysts of this persuasion build on that perception to argue that the era of state domination has given way to a world flattened by networked global trade. But this analysis overlooks at least three fundamental realities that most of the world's people still wake up to.

The first is the nature of the state itself, whose withering away the globalizers foresee with (paradoxically) an almost Marxian glee. Yet the state is still indispensable to most people. It provides, or should provide, physical security, law and order, economic infrastructure and basic services. For most people in the world, however, the problem is that their state is not strong enough to deliver on those vital requirements. One can rejoice at the rising living standards of Indians working at call centres, making airplane reservations, tracing lost luggage, fixing credit-card payments, transcribing medical notes and reading CAT scans and MRIs for Americans, but what is the condition of the country they return to? Foreign observers like Friedman wax lyrical about the Infosys campus outside Bangalore, an oasis I too have visited, which would not be out of place in any Western country—but the managers of Infosys have to organize their own electricity, their own 'mass' transportation, their own health club, and so on, because these facilities are absent, unreliable or dilapidated in the city itself.

Today, 'you can innovate without having to emigrate', Friedman writes. But at least in the old days, if America wanted to tap into the best brains trained in India, it had to offer them American salaries and American lifestyles; you had to let them into your neighbourhoods and your schools. Today, you can export jobs to India which command relatively low wages and prestige in the US, and leave the Indians to their potholed roads and their power breakdowns and their water shortages. We cannot celebrate the creation of little enclaves of globalized prosperity, the 21st-century equivalents of the gated communities of Manila or Johannesburg, which house the privileged while outside them the poor fester in their slums.

Indeed, while these may be middle-class concerns, more serious is the seeming obliviousness of the globalizers to the levelling of poverty, disease, and malnutrition stalking his flat new world. One can sing of 3 billion people entering the global market, while forgetting that most of them (and indeed 3 billion people overall around the world) are living under $2 a day. The threat of the combination of poverty, conflict, famine and AIDS in sub-Saharan Africa is arguably the most elemental challenge facing humanity at the start of the 21st century. The American writer Robert Kagan made it fashionable to observe, rather fatuously, that 'Americans are from Mars and Europeans are from Venus'. If so, where are Africans from—Pluto? They, and for that matter the rest of the world's poor, could be on the farthest planet for all the attention the votaries of globalized flatness are prepared to pay them.

The third great omission of the globalization brigade is that of the digital divide. The eagerness to hail 'levelling' and 'flattening' makes sense in the West, since the internet has certainly made information far more widely accessible there. But that is not yet true in the developing world, except for a tiny minority of the empowered. The stark global reality of the internet today is the digital divide: you can tell the rich from the poor by their internet connections. The gap between the technological haves and have-nots is widening, both between countries and within them. The information revolution, unlike the French Revolution, is a revolution with a lot of liberté, some fraternité, and no egalité. So the poverty line is not the only line about which we have to think; there is also the high-speed digital line, the fiber optic line—all the lines that connect our globalized world, but which exclude those who are literally not plugged in to its possibilities.

Advocates of globalization as a force for good, like Thomas Friedman, are convinced that trade and IT are the most important driving forces in the world. Walls are falling and networks are being knit: in Friedman's words, 11/9 (the day the Berlin wall fell) counts for more than 9/11. 'The most important force shaping global economics and politics in the early 21st century [is]... a triple convergence of new players, on a new playing field, developing new processes and habits for horizontal collaboration', he writes. But the forces behind 9/11 can easily disrupt the world made possible by 11/9. Not long ago, for instance, the Indian police reported the arrest of a terrorist cell in Delhi affiliated to the jihadist Lashkar-e-Toiba which allegedly had plans to bomb India's leading IT companies. One might think that in a flat world geography is history, but history has a habit of haunting some parts of the world—and if you live in them, geography can still imprison you in the consequences of your history.

This is true in India as it is in Africa. Thomas Friedman has advanced what he calls his 'Dell Theory of Conflict Prevention', under which no two countries will go to war if they are both part of the same globalized supply chain, for instance making Dell computers. This reminds me of nothing so much as his earlier 'Golden Arches Theory of Conflict Prevention', under which he asserted that globalization had ensured that no two countries with a McDonald's would go to war—which was published just before NATO bombs came crashing down on Belgrade's city centre, not far from the biggest McDonald's in the Balkans. Being part of a global supply chain is not enough either, I am afraid, to prevent war, since most human conflict is fuelled by emotions rather than calculations. After all, China has made it clear that it is quite serious about going to war if Taiwan declares independence, even if every economist would argue that—given the extensive (and increasing) interdependence of Taiwan and the Chinese mainland, and the horrific economic consequences of any disruption—war would make no sense.

I mention this only to suggest that, even in this flat new world, economics cannot explain everything. As Francis Fukuyama discovered before him, it is not yet time for 'the end of history'. Culture, religion, and national pride all continue to play their part in world affairs.

Does this mean that I am a pessimist on the future of India in this flat new world of the 21st century? Not at all; I consider myself an optimist. But then I define optimism as looking at the future with uncertainty. The globalizer says everything will go right; the pessimist is convinced that everything will go wrong; and the optimist argues that the future is uncertain, but there is a possibility that things could go well.

Today, the world is on the threshold of an era of global opportunity and hope. Whatever one might think about globalization it is clear that today we are in a position to build an open and inclusive world economy in which all countries can participate and from which all countries can benefit. For some years now, the UN's Human Development Reports have argued compellingly that poverty is no longer inevitable. For the first time, long-cherished hopes of eradicating poverty seem attainable, because the world has the material, natural and technological resources to do so within a generation—provided that concerted political will and sufficient resources are brought to the task. That is what the Millenium Development Goals are about.

The eight Millennium Development Goals (MDGs) were adopted in the Millennium declaration by the United Nations Millennium Summit in September 2000—the largest single gathering of heads of state and government in human history, at any one time on the planet. The MDGs range from halving extreme poverty to halting the spread of HIV/AIDS and providing universal primary education, empowering women and girls, reducing maternal and infant mortality, and promoting environmental sustainability, all by the target date of 2015. Taken together, they form a blueprint agreed to by all the world's countries and all the world's leading development institutions. They have galvanized unprecedented efforts to meet the needs of the world's poorest—but we cannot truly say that they are on course to being achieved in full anywhere.

The past twenty-five years have seen the most dramatic reduction in extreme poverty that the world has ever experienced. Spearheaded by progress in China and India, literally hundreds of millions of men, women and children all over the world have been able to escape the burdens of extreme impoverishment and begin to enjoy improved access to food, health care, education and housing. Yet at the same time, dozens of countries have become poorer, devastating economic crises have thrown millions of families into poverty, and increasing inequality in large parts of the world means that the benefits of economic growth have not been evenly shared. Today, more than a billion people—one in every six human beings—still live on less than a dollar a day, lacking the means to stay alive in the face of chronic hunger, disease and environmental hazards. In other words, this is a poverty that kills. A single bite from a malaria-bearing mosquito is enough to end a child's life for want of a bed net or $1 treatment. A drought or pest that destroys a harvest turns subsistence into starvation. A world in which every year eleven million children die before their fifth birthday and three million people die of AIDS is not a world that we can be proud to live in.

For centuries, this kind of poverty has been regarded as a sad but inescapable aspect of the human condition. Today, that view is intellectually and morally indefensible. The scale and scope of progress made by countries in every region of the world has shown that, over a very short time, poverty and maternal and infant mortality can be dramatically reduced, while education, gender equality and other aspects of development can be dramatically advanced. The unprecedented combination of resources and technology at our disposal today means that we are truly the first generation with the tools, the knowledge and the resources to meet the commitment, given by all States in the Millennium Declaration, 'to making the right to development a reality for everyone and to freeing the entire human race from want'.

But we must admit that to accomplish this, capitalism alone is not enough. Governments and civil society have to play a part; solidarity cannot be a hollow term. Success will require sustained action. It takes time to train the teachers, nurses and engineers needed; to build the roads, schools and hospitals that are essential; and to grow the small and large businesses which would be able to create the jobs and income that the poor must have to get out of poverty. Capitalism is vital in the third area, and an indispensable partner in the first two, but taxpayers must play a crucial part. We must, for instance, more than double global development assistance over the next five years. And of course we must ensure it is widely and honestly spent.

Poverty cannot be allowed to spread without catastrophic consequences for rich and poor countries alike. I am one of those who stubbornly clings to the belief that poverty can be conquered. And you are conscious, I trust, that over the last three decades, more than twenty industrial states, and more encouragingly, more than a dozen developing countries, have eliminated absolute poverty. Others can do it too.

Overcoming poverty is well within humanity's reach. The wealth of nations has increased sevenfold since 1945. Some individuals today are enjoying riches on a scale previously unimagined. Yet victims of poverty still endure intolerable forms of deprivation; they continue to be marginalized and excluded. Acknowledging the persistence of poverty reminds us of the road we have yet to travel and the battles we have yet to win.

As I've noted, about 3 billion people, half of the world's population, live on less than $2 a day. But it would be wrong of me to imply that the developed world is exempt from the problem of poverty. In industrial countries, many of which suffer high unemployment and eroding social protection, more than 100 million people live below the poverty line today and tens of millions are jobless. Pensions and social security now protect many people in the North from poverty in their last years; but poverty in old age remains the most common experience around the world, and it is an increasing worry as developed-country populations age.

There is no shortage of strategies and plans, analyses and statistics, approaches and measures, to tackle extreme poverty around the world. What we need is a renewed determination and willingness to bring all actors—capitalists and governmental decision-makers—together in one unstinting effort. We should not worry too much about the doctrinal underpinnings for our efforts. Whenever I hear theoretical arguments about eradicating poverty I am reminded of the story of the two French development economists who were having a quarrel about a specific problem. One says, 'You know what we can do about this problem? We can do this and this and this and we can solve it.' And the other one replies, 'Yes, yes, yes, that will work in practice. But will it work in theory?' Let us not worry too much about theory, but focus on ending poverty in practice.

So long as every fifth inhabitant of our planet lives in absolute poverty, there can be no real stability in the world. Poverty is not only a human and moral issue: the enormous and still growing disparities between rich and poor pose a threat to the very fabric of every society. On a universal scale, extreme poverty threatens world peace and the global environment.

It is necessary, too, to tackle poverty on a broad front. If our efforts are to prove effective, we have to move forward in several areas simultaneously. After all, what is the use of providing a farmer with high-yielding varieties if his crop cannot fetch a fair price to earn a living? What could be more cruel than immunizing a child only to see it die of starvation? What is the use of education if unemployment is the only reward awaiting the educated?

Indeed, there are broader questions, too, that the United Nations needs to ask whenever poverty is discussed—questions of sustainable development and of good governance. What is the merit of economic growth if it benefits only the rich? How can one defend growth if it despoils the environment and in turn increases the costs to society? Who can sustain creative energy under conditions of instability or corrupt institutions? What is the point of international development cooperation in the face of increasing barriers to trade and declining commodity prices?

There are no simple answers to these complex questions, but they should be in our minds as we discuss the issues before us today. It is the shared responsibility of all countries to help eradicate poverty through carefully chosen, country-specific programmes. There is no single solution; but what will surely make a difference is to stay the course until success is achieved. The United Nations, which has made the eradication of poverty a prime concern, must continue to press for a more supportive international environment for the efforts to end poverty.

If I may turn away from the policy issues and look at the problem of poverty briefly as an author—my first novel, *The Great Indian Novel*, begins with the proposition that India is not, as people keep calling it, an underdeveloped country, but rather, in the context of its history and cultural heritage, a highly developed one in an advanced state of decay. Such sentiments are, of course, the privilege of the satirist; but, the notion of decay apart, I relish reminding readers that there is more than one way to look at the question of poverty. When my cantankerous old narrator declares, at the beginning of the novel, that 'everything in India is overdeveloped', he is deliberately provoking his readers to forget their usual view of an underdeveloped country as one devoid of everything the world today values. In telling the story of India I try to evoke an idea of development that transcends—but does not deny—the conventional socio-economic indices.

I do this because, poverty has many faces. It is much more than low income. It also reflects poor health and education, cultural deprivation, lack of knowledge and limited communication opportunities, the inability to exercise human and political rights and the soul-destroying denial of dignity, confidence and self-respect.

The notion that 'man does not live by bread alone' is one that is widely accepted. Of course we must end poverty, and give men and women enough bread to live on. But music, dance, art and the telling of stories are indispensable to humanity's ability to cope with the human condition. After all, why does man need bread? To survive. But why survive, if it is only to eat more bread? To live is more than just to sustain life—it is to find meaning in life. And the poorest men and women in the developing world feel the throb of culture on their pulse, for they tell stories to their children as their fires are lit at dusk and the shadows fall—stories of their land and its heroes, stories of the earth and its mysteries, stories that have gone into making them what they are.

For whom, after all, is development? It is not an abstract endeavour of states, a set of figures on GNP tables. Development is about people—human beings with needs and rights. Without culture, development becomes mere materialism, a subject for economists and planners rather than a matter of people. And if people are to develop, it is unthinkable that they would develop without culture, without song, and dance, and music, and myth, without stories about themselves, and in turn, without expressing their views on their present lot and their future hopes. Development implies dynamism; dynamism requires freedom, the freedom to create; creativity is both a condition and a guarantee of culture.

Let us not forget that there exist, around us, many societies whose richness lies in their soul and not in their soil, whose past may offer more wealth than their present, whose culture is more valuable than their technology. We must strive to eradicate poverty, but we must also ensure that we end that poverty of the spirit that ultimately is as harmful to humanity as lack of food or medicine. Let us work for a world in which we can fill both stomachs and souls at the same time.

THE MILLENNIUM DEVELOPMENT GOALS: MISSING THE MARK?

The target date for fulfilling the Millennium Development Goals is 2015, and as these words emerge at the dawn of 2015, the world knows it will not meet those goals this year. So as that deadline looms, attention is already shifting to replacing them beyond 2015 with a new set of Sustainable Development Goals (SDGs). Meanwhile, looking back on the MDGs, the jury is still divided on whether we should regard the effort to fulfil them as a failure or a partial success.

I was at the UN in September 2000, when world leaders met at the Millennium Summit and pledged to work together to free humanity from the 'abject and dehumanizing conditions of extreme poverty', and to 'make the right to development a reality for everyone'. These pledges include commitments to improve access to education, health care, and clean water for the world's poorest people; abolish slums; reverse environmental degradation; conquer gender inequality; and cure HIV/AIDS.

It's an ambitious list, but its capstone is Goal 8, which calls for a 'global partnership for development'. This includes four specific targets: 'an open, rule-based, predictable, non-discriminatory trading and financial system'; special attention to the needs of least-developed countries; help for landlocked developing countries and small island states; and national and international measures to deal with developing countries' debt problems.

Basically, it all boiled down to a grand bargain: while developing countries would obviously have primary responsibility for achieving the MDGs, developed countries would be obliged to finance and support their efforts for development.

This hasn't really happened. At the G-8 summit at Gleneagles and the UN World Summit in 2005, donors committed to increasing their aid by $50 billion at 2004 prices, and to double their aid to Africa from 2004 levels by 2010. But official development assistance (ODA) last year amounted to $119.6 billion, or just 0.31 per cent of the developed countries' GDP—not even half of the UN's target of 0.7 per cent of GDP. In current US dollars, ODA actually fell by more than 2 per cent during each year of the 2008-11 recession.

The UN admits that progress has been uneven, and that many of the MDGs are likely to be missed in most regions. An estimated 1.4 billion people were still living in extreme poverty in 2010, and the number is likely to be higher today, owing to the lingering effects of the global economic crisis. The number of undernourished people has continued to grow, while progress in reducing the prevalence of hunger stalled—or even reversed—in some regions.

About one in four children under the age of five is underweight, mainly due to lack of quality food, inadequate water, sanitation, and health services, and poor care and feeding practices. Gender equality and women's empowerment, which are essential to overcoming poverty and disease, have made at best fitful progress, with insufficient improvement in girls' schooling opportunities or in women's access to political authority.

Progress on trade has been similarly disappointing. Developed country tariffs on imports of agricultural products, textiles, and clothing—the principal exports of most developing countries—remained between 5 per cent and 8 per cent in 2008, just 2-3 percentage points lower than in 1998.

The time has come to reinforce Goal 8 in two fundamental ways. Developed countries must make commitments to increase both the quantity and effectiveness of aid to developing countries. Aid must help developing countries improve the welfare of their poorest populations according to their own development priorities. But donors all too often feel obliged to make their contributions 'visible' to their constituencies and stakeholders, rather than prioritizing local perspectives and participation.

There are other problems with development aid. Reporting requirements are onerous and often impose huge administrative burdens on developing countries, which must devote the scarce skills of educated, English-speaking personnel to writing reports for donors rather than running programs. And donor agencies often recruit the best local talent themselves, usually at salaries that distort the labour market. In some countries, doctors find it more remunerative to work as translators for foreign-aid agencies than to treat poor patients.

Meanwhile, donors' sheer clout dilutes the accountability of developing countries' officials and elected representatives to their own people.

We must change the way the world goes about the business of providing development aid. We need a genuine partnership, in which developing countries take the lead, determining what they most acutely need and how best to use it. Weak capacity to absorb aid on the part of recipient countries is no excuse for donor-driven and donor-directed assistance. The aim should be to help create that capacity. Indeed, building human-resource capacity is itself a useful way of fulfilling Goal 8.

Doing so would serve donors' interest as well. Aligning their assistance with national development strategies and structures, or helping countries devise such strategies and structures, ensures that their aid is usefully spent and guarantees the sustainability of their efforts. Donors should support an education policy rather than build a photogenic school; aid a health campaign rather than construct a glittering clinic; or do both—but as part of a policy or a campaign, not as stand-alone projects.

Trade is the other key area. In contrast to aid, greater access to the developed world's markets creates incentives and fosters institutions in the developing world that are self-sustaining, collectively policed, and more consequential for human welfare. Many countries are prevented from trading their way out of poverty by the high tariff barriers, domestic subsidies, and other protections enjoyed by their rich-country competitors.

The European Union's agricultural subsidies, for example, are high enough to permit every cow in Europe to fly business class around the world. What African farmer, despite his lower initial costs, can compete? The onus is not on developed countries alone. Developing countries, too, have made serious commitments to their own people, and the primary responsibility for fulfilling those commitments is theirs. But Goal 8 assured them that they would not be alone in this effort. Unless that changes, the next five years will be a path to failure.

IMF: INSOLVENTS MAY FLOURISH;
INDIA MUST FIX!

The appointment of France's finance minister, Christine Lagarde, as managing director of the International Monetary Fund (IMF) in July 2011, brought an end to a race which, for all its illusions of drama and contest, was in fact entirely predictable.

The so-called Bretton Woods institutions—the World Bank and the IMF, set up in the New Hampshire town of that name by the Allied Powers of World War II in 1944—have long rested on a cosy deal within the Western world, under which the former would always be headed by an American and the latter by a West European. The ten managing directors of the IMF since then have all been Europeans (four from France, two from Sweden, and one each from Belgium, Germany, Netherlands and Spain). All eleven presidents of the World Bank, needless to say, were American.

America's continued dominance may well reflect its status as a genuine economic superpower, but Europe's is a reflection of arrangements that have long been questionable. The fact is that Europeans have dominated the IMF's Executive Board, the body responsible for the organization's day-to-day management. Despite accounting for barely 20 per cent of global GDP in purchasing power parity terms, the member states of the European Union collectively account for 31 per cent of the votes on the IMF Board, and in practice cast up to 36 per cent of the votes (since there are only twenty-four directors, smaller countries entrust their voting rights to the bigger ones—thus Italy casts the votes of Greece, Albania, East Timor and Malta, and the Netherlands votes on behalf of a group that includes Israel, Armenia and the Ukraine). This 36 per cent vote share gives the EU countries an undue advantage in the race to get the 50.1 per cent needed to elect an IMF head.

The irony is that Europe is a borrower from the IMF. Instead of the insolvency of European countries like Greece, Spain or Ireland leading to a reduction in the EU's voting weight on the board, the problems of Europe have cynically been used to justify Lagarde's appointment. It is precisely because of Europe's financial problems, Europeans argue, that a European is needed to head the IMF to deal effectively with them. (Wolfgang Munchau in the *Financial Times* explained that an IMF boss 'will have to bang heads together in meetings of European finance ministers, and will have to converse effectively with some notoriously difficult heads of government and state'.) Oddly, the same argument was never used when the Asian flu was being dealt with by a European IMF director, Michel Camdessus, who was clearly unfamiliar with the mores of the continent. Had Asia's economic troubles in the late 1990s led

New Delhi to call for an Asian IMF head, we would have been laughed out of court. The acronym IMF, it used to be said by shame-faced Third Worlders, stands for 'Insolvents Must Fawn'. With a European in charge, this may have to be amended to 'Insolvents May Flourish'.

So once again a European has become the chief of an institution supposedly controlled by 187 member nations, in a process which effectively discriminates against 93 per cent of the world's population. As the Venezuelan commentator Moises Naim trenchantly wrote, before the decision was taken: 'In its daily work, the IMF demands that the governments that seek its financial assistance adopt market principles of efficiency, transparency and meritocracy in exchange for its help. Yet that same institution selects its leader through a process completely at odds with those values.'

This is a system ripe for reform. Europe and the world could have benefitted from having an IMF chief from a developing country with experience of successfully managing a serious economic crisis. Mexico's Augustin Carstens, for instance, had impressive substantive credentials, and was arguably the most qualified candidate for the job amongst those in the fray. An Indian might have been a worthwhile contender, reflecting our country's increasing influence in the global economy. The Indian economist Arvind Subramanian, a former IMF staffer, argued that 'the lack of a strong voice from India is unfortunate because the strength and legitimacy of multilateral institutions, which are in India's long-term interests, are at stake. The danger here is that if India, along with others, sits on the sidelines and the international debate is not strongly engaged, there will be decision making by default. This will only serve to perpetuate the status quo, of an important multilateral institution that remains basically non-universal in its legitimacy, deficient in wisdom and objectivity, and unduly politicised.'

That is exactly what has now happened. The dominance of a handful of small industrialized Western countries in the international financial institutions looks increasingly anomalous in a world where economic dynamism has shifted irresistibly from the West to the East. We have clearly reached a point where there is need for a system redesign of global governance in the macro-economic arena, to ensure that all countries can participate in a manner commensurate with their capacity.

The G20 Summit in Pittsburgh in September 2009 set in motion a process for global redesign of the international financial and economic architecture, and has become a meaningful platform for north-south dialogue precisely because the south is not completely outweighed by the north in the composition of the G20. The Pittsburgh summit decided to reform the Bretton Woods institutions by shifting decision-making power (5 per cent of the IMF quota share and 3 per cent of the World Bank's voting power) from the developed world to the developing and transition economies. Nations like India, Brazil, Russia and China, have called for higher figures—7 per cent of the IMF quota share and 6 per cent of the World Bank's voting powers—to be transferred, and their long-term objective is broad parity between the developed countries and the developing/transition economies in the international financial institutions.

It certainly seems uncontestable that the recent global financial crisis showed that the surveillance of risk by international institutions and early warning mechanisms are needed for all countries. In other words, it is important that, in the context of global governance, the developing countries should have a voice in overseeing the global financial performance of all nations, rather than it simply being a case of the rich supervising the economic delinquency of the poor. The Lagarde appointment, instead of being accepted as a defeat, should serve as a spur for India to take the lead to bring about this much-needed change. India's revived economy and its management of the impact of the global recession entitles it to take a more assertive position in the international financial institutions. IMF should now stand for India Must Fix. The time to do that is when Lagarde's term ends in 2016.

FREEDOM OF EXPRESSION AND COMMUNICATION CHALLENGES IN THE AGE OF THE INTERNET

It shouldn't be necessary in this day and age for a politician to affirm his own deeply-rooted belief in freedom of expression and press freedom, but in India this is not something one can take for granted. I think of freedom of expression as a fundamental human right—one that helps to guarantee all my other rights. I have been conscious since my UN days that Article 19 of the Universal Declaration of Human Rights states that people have the right to 'seek, receive and impart information and ideas through any media and regardless of frontiers'.

As a writer and a politician I am conscious how fortunate we are to live in a country that guarantees us that right. Writers in some developing countries have to contend with the argument that development and freedom of expression are incompatible—that the media, for instance, must serve the ends of development as defined by the government, or operate only within the boundaries of what the social and religious authorities define as permissible. The developing world is full of writers, artists and journalists who have to function in societies which do not grant them this freedom. For them freedom of expression is the oxygen of their own survival, and that of their society, but they are stifled. In countries where truth is what the government or the religious establishment says is true, freedom of expression is essential to depict alternative truths which the society needs to accommodate in order to survive.

And yet it is all too often absent, because in many countries, there are those who question the value of freedom of speech in their societies; those who argue that it threatens stability and endangers progress; those who still consider freedom of speech a Western import, an imposition from abroad and not the indigenous expression of every people's demand for freedom. What has always struck me about this argument is that it is never made by the people, but by governments; never by the powerless but by the powerful; never by the voiceless, but by those whose voices are all that can be heard. Let us put this argument once and for all to the only test that matters: the choice of every people, to know more or know less, to be heard or be silenced, to stand up or kneel down. Only freedom of expression will allow the world's oppressed and underprivileged a way out of the darkness that shrouds their voices, and their hopes. The internet has been giving them this choice as never before.

The internet has augmented, but in India not entirely supplanted, traditional media. Media freedom is a vital aspect of the freedom of expression. A free press often marks the difference between a society that is able to protect itself from abuses of human rights and one that falls victim to oppression and injustice. The media must always use its freedom to raise the awkward question, to probe beyond the evident reality, to awaken the dormant consciousness, and therefore, yes, sometimes to subvert the established order. Freedom of the press is ultimately the best guarantee of liberty, of change and of progress. It is the mortar that binds together the bricks of freedom—and it is also the open window embedded in those bricks, which would, in Mahatma Gandhi's famous metaphor, allow the winds of the world to blow freely through the house. As Indians, we know that there is no development without democracy, and no democracy without freedom of speech.

There is widespread recognition today that restraints on the flow of information directly undermine development and progress. In this era of globalization, global interdependence means that those who receive and disseminate information have an edge over those who curtail it.

In the age of the internet, there can be little argument that information and freedom go together. The information revolution is inconceivable without political democracy and vice versa. Already, the spread of information has had a direct impact on the degree of accountability and transparency of governments around the world.

The internet has been made possible by advances in technology that have also transformed the traditional media. Technology that is lighter to carry, simpler to use, and comes at a fraction of the cost, has already changed television reporting. Not so long ago, a ton of equipment was flown into a trouble-spot; a satellite dish the size of a house was set up; a story was born. And where that satellite dish was, the journalists stayed. So that's where the story stayed, until the dish moved on. But now, digital technology is producing cameras a tenth the cost of yesterday's, simple enough to be operated by a non-technician, the reporter himself, with pictures that can be sent down the telephone line.

The simpler to use, more affordable technology has truly democratized television news. Smaller, less well-financed news-gathering organizations and independent operations in developing countries, have all benefited from this revolution. But so has the story in itself; because no story will be too remote to reach, too hard to get to, too expensive to cover, or too difficult to transmit. One reporter and a telephone line will often be enough. And this kind of technological innovation has also made the internet a vital source of news and analysis without any of the limitations of reach that television has.

The new hallmarks of freedom of expression today are the ability to receive, download and send information through electronic networks, and the capacity to share information—whether in a newspaper, on a TV screen, or an online website—without censorship or restrictions. The information society of today can thrive only if citizens are provided with full information to allow democratic participation at all levels in determining their destiny. New digital technology offers great possibilities for enhancing traditional media and combining them with new media. Moreover, traditional media, and especially radio and television, remain the sole form of access to the information society for much of the world's population, including the very poor and the illiterate. Technology has become the biggest asset for those who seek to promote and protect freedom of expression around the world.

This brings me to the era we are living in today, the era of the information revolution, the internet, the World Wide Web, and the extraordinary transformation in the reach and range of our freedom of expression made possible by social media. Just the day after he was sworn in as our thirteenth president, Pranab Mukherjee announced that he would be opening a Facebook account to receive and respond to comments and queries from the public. In fact his fellow Bengali, Chief Minister Mamata Banerjee, has beaten him to it, with a popular and widely-read website that the media mines daily for news stories about her views. When I first went on social media in 2009, it was fashionable for Indian politicians to sneer at the use of Twitter and Facebook. Today, our new prime minister has made it clear that these are essential tools for credible and accountable political leaders by obliging all members of his new Council of Ministers to open social media accounts and run them actively.

The reach of social media has been facilitated by rapid technological developments as well. When we speak of social media we do not mean only media running on a desktop computer or a mainframe server. In a famous study, my good friend Nik Gowing of the BBC highlights how in a moment of major, unexpected crisis, the institutions of power—whether political, governmental, military or corporate—face a new, acute vulnerability of both their influence and effectiveness, thanks to new media technologies. It is no longer possible to ignore the issue of the uncontrolled impact of instant news on the workings of society and more generally on the impact of new media technologies on political affairs.

As Gowing points out, 'It was a chance video taken by a New York investment banker that dramatically swung public perceptions of police handling of the G20 protests [in the UK]. Those 41 seconds swiftly exposed apparently incomplete police explanations of how and why a particular protestor, Ian Tomlinson, died. They alone forced a level of instant accountability from the police about their orders, behaviour and operation.'

When US-led NATO warplanes bombed villages in Afghanistan's Azizabad village a couple of years ago, US forces initially claimed only seven people died. NGOs said the bombing killed up to ninety. Only after mobile phone video emerged two weeks later did US commanders accept they had to re-

examine evidence. In a re-investigation, the US had to revise the death toll
to fifty-five. As Gowing argues, 'Such examples confirm how new information
technologies and dynamics are together driving a wave of democratization and
accountability. It shifts and redefines the nature of power in such moments.
It also creates a new policy vulnerability and brittleness for institutions, who
then struggle even harder to maintain public confidence.'

Globally, it is true that most major institutions of power still do not appreciate
the full scale and implications of the dramatic new real-time media trend and
its profound impact on their credibility. Increasingly, a cheap camera or mobile
phone that is easily portable in a pocket can undermine the credibility of a
government despite the latter's massive human and financial resources. The
new lightweight technologies available to almost anyone mean that they enjoy
a new capacity for instant scrutiny and accountability that is way beyond the
narrower, assumed power and influence of the traditional media.

The world is full of examples of what Gowing calls 'non-professional
information doers': hundreds of millions of amateurs with an electronic eye
who can now be found anywhere. As many as 5 billion people worldwide—
including 84 per cent of Americans, more than 70 per cent of Chinese and
perhaps 60 per cent of all Indians today—now use mobile phones. They all
get messages out. And they do so more rapidly than the official mechanisms
can. Their strength is that they enable people to issue and disseminate material,
including raw footage and compellingly authentic images, before the mainstream
media, or for that matter governments, can do so. Inevitably, this means they
shed light where officialdom would prefer darkness, as China learned when
video footage of a shootout involving Uighur separatists in 2008 made it to
the world media despite Beijing's denials.

The core implications are striking. We have all heard about the so-called
24/7 news and information cycle, but with social media the pressure of the
news cycle can build up not just over a few hours but often in no more than
a few minutes. As images, facts and allegations emanating from cell phones
and digital cameras go viral, they undermine and discredit official versions,
present an alternative reality in the face of government denials and, fuelled
by dissenters and expatriates, rebound onto the evolution of the situation
itself. Twitter and digital cameras had a huge impact on the Iranian protests
after the disputed re-election of President Mohammed Ahmedinejad. Despite
Tehran's attempts to manage the crisis, social media kept the protests alive for
far longer, and with more prolonged intensity, than they could have survived
without that digital fuel.

With such instant scrutiny, governmental power is rendered more vulnerable.
The Wikileaks saga demonstrated this too, since the publication of classified
material on the internet circumvented both government control and the

restraints that are normally observed by traditional media. In the old days, governments assumed they could command the information high ground in a crisis. That is simply no longer true.

This brings me, inevitably, to the Arab Spring. The role of social media websites—such as Facebook, Twitter, Google, YouTube and Skype—in the political revolutions in Tunisia, Egypt, and Libya, with ripples elsewhere in the Middle East, notably Syria, has given new impetus to the discussion of social media on world politics. The eminent American journal *Foreign Affairs* debated the issue last year. One analyst, Clay Shirky, argued eloquently that 'these tools alter the dynamics of the public sphere. Where the state prevails, it is only reacting to citizens' ability to be more publicly vocal and to coordinate more rapidly and on a larger scale than before these tools existed'. On the other hand, author Malcolm Gladwell responded that, for Shirky's 'argument to be anything close to persuasive, (he) has to convince readers that in the absence of social media, those uprisings would not have been possible'.

My own position is somewhere between them. Of course uprisings can occur (and have occurred) without Twitter or even Google, but media always has an impact on the reach and spread of word about an uprising, and therefore has an impact on its intensity and sustainability. In this case, I would argue that satellite television—notably Al Jazeera and its imitators—as well as mobile phones and SMSes, had probably more of an impact on the unrest across these North African Arab countries than Facebook or Twitter. But impact is undeniable. As the American commentator Peter Osnos puts it, 'It is pointless to dispute that digital advances have played an enormous role in recent years in the speed of communications, and, in some situations, Egypt and Tunisia certainly among them, these technologies have played a meaningful part in the rallying of crowds and in garnering international recognition. A global generation of mainly young people will continue to refine and use the capacity to reach out to each other. Turmoil reflects the conditions of the era in which it occurs, and social media are very much a factor of our age.'

This is why China has paid particular attention to censoring the internet, employing 40,000 cyber-police to monitor blogging sites, shutting down any sites that get out of line and banning Twitter. When a US-based Chinese-language site called for a Jasmine Revolution in China, the Great Firewall of China blocked all searches for the word 'jasmine', even if you were merely looking for jasmine tea! Clearly the authoritarians in Beijing are quite aware of the enormous potential of social media to disrupt even their politics.

Of course, there can be a more positive and non-confrontational use of social media in a crisis, as we saw with the catastrophe of the tsunami, earthquake and nuclear accident in Japan. Within days of the Japanese earthquake and tsunami in 2011, 64 per cent of blog links, 32 per cent of Twitter news links and the top twenty YouTube videos carried news and information about the crisis in Japan. Nine days after Japan's catastrophic earthquake, two urgent pleas for help appeared on the Twitter stream of US Ambassador John Roos: 'Kameda hospital in Chiba needs to transfer 80 patients from Kyoritsu hospital in Iwaki city, just outside of 30km (sic) range', said the first. 'Some of them are seriously ill and they need air transport. If US military can help, pls contact [so-and-so] at Kameda.'

The back-to-back tweets, marked to @AmbassadorRoos, his Twitter address, popped up on Roos's mobile phone, so that a digital SOS reached him instantly. A year earlier, before Roos opened his Twitter account, getting the US Ambassador's attention in such a direct and immediate way would not have been possible. Roos activated the US military in response to the tweets, they in turn contacted the Japanese Self-Defense Forces, and the patients were transported to safety. In other words, this time, troops were mobilized by Twitter.

Japan's disaster has spotlighted the critical role that social media websites such as Twitter are increasingly playing in responses to crises around the world. They may have been designed largely for online socializing and just for having fun, but such sites and others have empowered people caught up in crises. Their strength is that they enable people to share vivid, real-time unfiltered images and text reports before any other source, including governments or traditional media, can do so. There is no doubting the potential of social media to create information, whether video or text, and communicate it immediately, without the delays necessarily wrought by editorial controls, cross-checking or even the synthesizing that occurs in a humanitarian operation's situation room. In Japan, the International Atomic Energy Agency (IAEA) took to YouTube to get its messages out. In the week following the earthquake and tsunami, people viewed more than 40 million disaster-related items.

The US Federal Emergency Management Administration, or FEMA, has even become a leading proponent of social media. 'Nobody invented Twitter to be an emergency messaging or disaster tool,' FEMA director, William Craig Fugate, has acknowledged. 'It was developed for an entirely different purpose.' But volunteers using social media sites have played pivotal roles in responses to various types of global crises, from the BP Horizon oil spill to the unrest in the Middle East to the earthquakes in Haiti, Chile, New Zealand and Japan. There were 70 million tweets on the Haiti earthquake alone, and social media proved indispensable in providing information to draw crisis response maps and dispense assistance.

Google engineers also developed a software program that enables people to take snapshots of the lists of names posted on the walls of refugee or displaced-person shelters and scan them into a program called Person Finder, thus entering thousands of survivors' names into a searchable database. Person

Finder also incorporates names that were once scattered through many other missing-persons databases. YouTube, which is owned by Google, created its own video person finder. Within an hour of the Japanese earthquake, Google's crisis response team—launched after the disaster in Haiti—had posted a 'Person Finder' website that quickly grew to include 450,000 records, says Jamie Yood, of Google. 'If you're looking for someone, you can post, 'Hey, my cousin is a teacher in Sendai, we're looking for him'. Someone else will post, 'I've seen him in a shelter; he's fine'. As Fugate says, 'We've got to stop looking at the public as a liability and start looking at them as a resource.' What makes social media so different from other emergency response tools, he says, is that it 'allows a two-way conversation in the impact zone, so that we can link people with information, resources and ideas'. Similar efforts were used in the Kashmir floods in 2014.

More people than ever access the videos on mobile phones, says a Google spokeswoman. Now about 700 million people a day watch videos on their mobile phones, ten times the number just two years ago. So social media is going to be inescapable in all future international crises and disasters. On any given day, people are sending 200 million Twitter messages, nearly a billion and a half tweets every week. There are two ways to look at this: that it's symptomatic of information overload, or that it represents a huge audience of information-generators and consumers that people in positions of public responsibility ignore at their peril. My own sympathies are very much towards the latter view.

The media shapes our awareness of events and, by so doing, sometimes shapes events themselves. Events that the media ignores find it difficult to obtain traction in the modern world; events that the media focuses on, on the other hand, become impossible even for powerful governments to ignore.

We know that in India's neighbourhood, in the fight against terrorism, some countries have enacted or are considering measures that restrict press freedom. But the fight against terrorism cannot be won unless the media are allowed to play their crucial role of informing citizens and acting as a watchdog.

I understand that some South Asians feel strongly that in our cultures, freedom comes with responsibilities, and that untrammeled freedom of the press carries risks of social and political disruption that cannot be allowed. The example of the Danish cartoons of the Prophet Mohammed is often cited; few Asian governments would be happy to permit the publication of material so derogatory as to offend and provoke a large segment of the population. Similarly, your freedom to move your fist stops just short of my face. Such restraints are obvious, and no reasonable advocate of freedom of the press would seek absolute freedom for the media, unconstrained by the well-being of the society in which it flourishes.

But there is a world of difference between accepting this principle and implementing it reasonably. Societies are self-correcting mechanisms; when the press goes too far it rapidly discovers the limits for itself. The press everywhere adopts the restraints appropriate for its social environment; no American newspaper, for instance, would print the so-called 'n' word when referring to black Americans—not because the government disallows it but because the editors are conscious of what is the decent and socially acceptable thing to do. Asian editors are capable of the same judgements, as they demonstrated during the episode of the Danish cartoons. Leaving governments to decide what is reasonable and responsible substitutes the judgement of the authorities for the judgement of the media, and so risks that press freedom itself might be jeopardized.

We have seen a couple of troubling developments in past years that have thrown some of these questions into sharp focus. The arrest in 2007 of a cartoonist in Bangladesh and the suspension of publication of the leading Bengali weekly, *Prathom Alo*—over a cartoon that sought to satirize not the Prophet but the social custom of naming everybody after the Prophet—is a disturbing example of this. If restraints are expected, fine; but if that means giving free license to the most intolerant elements of a society to censor ideas that are not in themselves blasphemous, then we are all in trouble. As a South Asian myself, I understand and respect the view that Asian societies are not European ones, and that not every standard applicable in Europe can be transplanted wholesale to South Asia. But most South Asians are capable of understanding a joke in the spirit in which it was intended. Let us not empower the humourless, because their agenda has little to do with society as it exists but everything to do with the society they wish to create, one in which people of their political persuasion will prevail.

Few would argue today against the statement that information and freedom go together. Despite the Chinese exception, the information revolution of today is largely inconceivable without increasing political democracy—and vice versa. Already, the spread of information has had a direct impact on the degree of accountability and transparency of governments around the world—including, as we have seen in the recent earthquake, China's.

At the same time I should admit that governments are not the only danger to press freedom. In many countries, media concentration and media ownership by large conglomerates presents another subtle challenge to a vigorous, independent press and endanger its role as a 'check and balance' to political and economic power. Democratizing access to information can serve as a check, not only on governments, but also on press barons and media magnates, and that is why the issue of democratizing information is so vital today.

And if we look at the larger question of freedom of expression, going beyond the media to individual works of art and literature, South Asian societies themselves can be part of the problem. Consider the evidence from the first half of 2008: Salman Rushdie, whose books are already banned in Pakistan and Bangladesh, is driven out of Mumbai by protests at his presence organized by Samajwadi Party hooligans and extremist Muslim groups. Taslima Nasreen is not merely banned in her native Bangaldesh but actively hounded, fearing for her life; when she seeks refuge in democratic India, she is not only obliged to live in hiding, but the erstwhile communist government of West Bengal claimed it was unable to protect her, and a Congress union minister from that state, once a byword for liberal culture and intellectual freedom, demanded that she apologize 'with folded hands' to her tormentors. India's Picasso, M.F. Husain, a national treasure, spent his last years in exile in Dubai and London because he could not stand the harassment of multiple lawsuits that were been filed against him and did not set foot in his native land again for fear of being hauled off to a police lock-up. The film *Jodhaa Akbar* couldn't be screened in Rajasthan because Rajput groups objected to the very name of its heroine. And 2 MLAs in UP persuaded the Mayawati government, through a device absurdly called a 'notice of propriety', to ban a historical novel, *Rani* by Jaishree Mishra, for allegedly depicting the legendary freedom fighter Rani Lakshmibai of Jhansi in a 'bad light'. This had, they claimed, 'badly hurt' the people of the state, particularly in Bundelkhand (whose reading habits must indeed be unusual for a historical romance to have 'badly hurt' them).

It almost seems as if each group in South Asia's diverse polities is vying with the next for the right to be more offended by a work of art than anyone else. I am perfectly happy to allow any sensitive souls to sulk or to dash off outraged letters to the editors of our national newspapers, but when their sense of wounded self-esteem manifests itself in acts of violence and vandalism, in the burning of effigies of authors and artists, and in hounding creative people into exile, then it is Indian civilization itself that is under attack. And I am outraged when the institutions of the Indian state, instead of rising to protect the freedoms guaranteed by the Indian Constitution and fundamental to the preservation of our democracy, submit cravenly to the agents of intolerance. Part of the problem is that we Indians lack the political courage to stand up for the principles our democracy has been erected on. We rush to appease the loudest bigot frothing at the mouth because we fear that his outrage has an authenticity, rooted in the Indian soil, that our educated liberal convictions lack. That does a disservice to the real roots of tolerance in the Indian tradition—and it allows the least tolerant elements of our society to define what is acceptable to the rest of us. If we do not raise our voices against this growing intolerance, we will be left with an India that is no longer the India that Mahatma Gandhi fought to free.

If I sound a little worked up about all this, it's because the dangers across South Asia are all too real. Intolerance has caused enough victims on the subcontinent, and even more elsewhere. When information is controlled and manipulated, you can have tyranny and worse—it wasn't so long ago that 'hate media' incited war and genocide in the Balkans and in Rwanda. When information is freely available, South Asia's new information society has a better chance of being people-centred, inclusive and progressive. After all, the human mind is like a parachute; it functions best when it is open.

Freedom of the press goes hand-in-hand with freedom of information. It is gratifying that more than fifty countries have passed freedom of information laws, thus guaranteeing their citizens the right to know what their government is up to. According to the independent media watchdog freedominfo.org, more than half of these freedom of information laws were passed in the last decade. In South Asia, only India has done so, but the example is instructive. New access-to-information laws have spawned a host of investigative articles on issues such as radiation contamination in Australia, lavish spending by some Canadian officials, corruption in India by elected officials and civil servants, and mercury poisoning in Japan. Freedom of information laws help the press in their work, and they help the public by promoting the accountability of government authorities.

Press freedom is also a precondition for the economic and social progress that is another of the primary objectives of all governments. Recall Amartya Sen's famous argument that there has never been a famine in a democracy with a free press. Famines are the result of a lack of access to food, and Sen has proved, with extensive research, that they occur only when the media is not free to draw attention to the problem. Freedom of expression is also essential to generating awareness about development, about the environment, about education and about critical health issues like HIV/AIDS. And it continues to be a major building block in the UN's post-conflict reconstruction efforts. All these good causes need the media to do its daily work, and do it well. And the media can only be effective if it has extensive access to information.

There is widespread recognition that restraints on the flow of information directly undermine development. Global interdependence means that those who receive and disseminate information have an edge over those who curtail it. The consequences are apparent in all fields of human endeavour.

The new hallmarks of development are the ability to receive, download and send information through electronic networks, and the capacity to share information—including not only newspapers and journals, but also online websites—without restrictions. This is why censorship is so unwise; indeed, it is anti-development. For developing countries need to open up to the outside world, liberalize the mass media, and resist government control and censorship of information, if they are to be able to take advantage of the opportunities that the information revolution has made available to the world.

In India, the case for social media has been gaining ground. We are already one of the world's leading countries in the use of Twitter, and social media is bound to gain as the prospects for e-government improve by the day. Though the Department of Information Technology's new rules on internet intermediaries have created a firestorm in cyberspace, in parallel, the first draft of the Electronic Delivery of Services Bill, 2011, has proposed that all ministries and government departments will have to deliver services electronically, whether through the internet or mobile phones. Though that bill is not yet law, India is not just on the right track, but bids fair to become a model of e-governance in the developing world.

And yet the controversy over the government's alleged desire to censor Facebook, Twitter and other leading lights of the social media obscured our progress in this area and also raised some genuine and urgent questions we need to address about free speech in our society.

The problem arose when the *New York Times* reported that our then telecom minister, Kapil Sibal, had called in senior social media executives from Facebook, Microsoft, Google and Yahoo and allegedly asked them to 'to pre-screen user content from India and to remove before it goes online'. Such a request inevitably sparked off a firestorm of internet protest against the minister, without waiting to hear his side of the story. Facebook pages sprang up to denounce him; web-boards overflowed with nasty comments against the minister, the ruling party and the government, suggesting they were trying to protect a political leader; and the hashtag '#IdiotKapilSibal' started 'trending' on Twitter. All a bit over the top.

As a frequent recipient of disparaging, inflammatory or defamatory content myself, I'm no great fan of unpleasantness on any media, social or otherwise, but I'm strongly opposed to censorship. Freedom of speech is fundamental to any democracy, and many of the most valuable developments in India would not have been possible without it. Freedom of speech is the mortar that binds the bricks of our democracy together, and it's also the open window embedded in those bricks. Free speech keeps our government accountable, and helps political leaders know what people are thinking. Censorship is a disservice to both rulers and the ruled. But—and free-speech advocates hate that 'but'!—every society recognizes some sensible restraints on how free speech is exercised. Those restraints almost always relate to the collectivity; they arise when the freedom of the individual to say what he wants causes more harm to more people in society than restricting his freedom would. Justice Oliver Wendell Holmes, in the US, put it memorably when he said that freedom of speech does not extend to the right to shout 'fire!' in a crowded theatre. (After all, that could cause a stampede, in which people could get trampled upon, injured and even killed, and the theatre's property destroyed—all consequences that outweigh the individual's right to say what he likes.)

Since societies vary in their cultural and political traditions, the boundaries vary from place to place. Free speech absolutists tend to say that freedom is a universal right that must not be abridged in the name of culture. But in practice such abridgement often takes place, if not by law then by convention. I have already mentioned why no American editor would allow the 'n' word to be used to describe Black Americans, and Indian editors frequently write of 'a particular community' rather than risking inflaming passions by naming the community involved. Just as the commonplace practice of women taking off their bikini tops at St Tropez, Copacabana or Bondi Beach could not be replicated on the beaches of Goa, Dubai or Karachi without risking assault or arrest, so also things might be said in the former set of places that would not pass muster in the latter. It's no use pretending such differences (of culture, politics and sensitivity) don't exist. They do, and they're the reason why free speech in, say, Sweden isn't the same as free speech in Singapore.

The problem is particularly acute on social media, because it's a public forum for the expression of private thoughts. The fact is that social media's biggest asset is also its biggest problem. Its strength is that social media enables ordinary people (not just trained journalists) to share vivid, real-time unfiltered images and text reports before any other source, including governments or traditional media, can do so. Even more, any individual with the basic literacy needed to operate a keyboard can express his or her opinion, create information, whether video or text, and communicate it immediately, without the delays necessarily wrought by editorial controls, cross-checking or even the synthesizing that occurs in a 'mainstream' media newsroom.

That gives social media an advantage over regular media as a disseminator of public opinion. If you wanted to express your views in, say, a newspaper, you would have write something well enough to pass editorial muster; your facts and opinions would be checked, vetted and challenged; your prose might be cut for space reasons (or mere editorial whim); and you might have to wait days, if not weeks, to see your words in print. None of that applies to social media. You can write all you want, as you want, in the words you want, on a blog or a Facebook page, put it up with a Twitter link, click a mouse and instantly watch it all go viral. It's a 21st century freedom that no democratic political leader would wish to confront.

And yet this very freedom is its own biggest threat. It means anyone can say literally anything, and inevitably, many do. Lies, distortions and calumny go into cyberspace unchallenged; hatred, pornography and slander are routinely aired. There is no fact-checking, no institutional reputation for reliability to defend. The anonymity permitted by social media encourages even more irresponsibility: people hidden behind pseudonyms feel free to hurl abuses they would never dare to utter to the recipients' faces. The borderline between legitimate creative expression and 'disparaging, inflammatory or defamatory content' becomes more difficult to draw.

Kapil Sibal's main concern was not with politics, but with scurrilous material about certain religions that could have incited retaliatory violence by their adherents. People say or depict things on social media that might be bad enough in their living rooms, but are positively dangerous in a public space. The challenge of regulating social media is that the person writing or drawing such things does so in the privacy of his home but releases them into the global commons. My own yardstick is very clear: I reject censorship. Art, literature and political opinion are to me sacrosanct. But publishing or circulating inflammatory material to incite communal feelings is akin to dropping a lighted match at a petrol pump. No society can afford to tolerate it, and no responsible government of India would allow it.

Personally, I'd rather snuff out that match than close down the petrol pump. But I'm far from sure that prosecuting Facebook or Google is the right way to go about it. After all, could you sue the phone companies for someone sending a defamatory or obscene SMS? The analogy to a newspaper is wrong—these social network sites are more like the postman carrying the newspaper to your door. You would prosecute the newspaper for publishing legally actionable material, but you would not prosecute the postal service.

That said, let me affirm how useful social media is in our society. Social media can be employed to create knowledge networks, disseminate information and keep track of the world around you well beyond what is available in our daily newspapers. The young Indian blogger Mahima Kaul writes: 'Personally, Twitter is a better source of news than any newspaper homepage can hope to be, and Facebook keeps me abreast of my friends in a way email or simple phone calls could not do. But that's not the point right now: in the context of social media, it allows strangers to connect over a decidedly neutral platform and talk about issues. Sure, people get nasty, but there is a distance of a computer screen (mobile) to save you from any unnecessary facetime.'

I have discussed India's experience with Twitter in a separate chapter in this volume, but will digress briefly on the success of the Ministry of External Affairs' Public Diplomacy Division, whose officials, with my active encouragement, set up a Twitter page and have been pursuing social media strategies, including a Facebook account and a YouTube channel, to let people know about what the ministry and diplomatic missions do. This has enabled them to promote India's soft power (even within the country) by creating goodwill among social media users in general, whether in India or abroad. To me, the MEA's initiative was excellent: It put India on a par with the Western democracies which have already adopted social media sites as an instrument of outreach. The MEA's spokesmen are now must-follow tweeters, using the medium to get out the message.

Of course we must examine the advantages—and possible pitfalls—of using social media as a tool for diplomacy. The advantages are clear. India acquires a new, young, literate and global audience for our foreign policy initiatives and positions. By being accessible to internet searchers, we earn goodwill. By providing accurate and timely information, we eliminate the risks of misrepresentation or distortion of our position.

So social media has become a vital instrument of our public diplomacy, the framework of activities by which a government seeks to influence public attitudes with a view to ensuring that they become supportive of foreign policy and national interests. Public diplomacy differs from traditional diplomacy in that public diplomacy goes beyond governments and engages primarily with the general public. In India, at least the way the MEA uses the term, 'public diplomacy' embraces both external and domestic publics, since it is clear that in today's world you cannot meaningfully confine your public diplomacy to foreign publics alone; in the current media environment, whatever message any government puts out is also instantly available to its domestic audience on the internet.

Public diplomacy is not just about communicating your point of view or putting out propaganda. It is also about listening. It rests on the recognition that the public is entitled to be informed about what a government is doing in international affairs, and is also entitled to responsiveness from those in authority to their concerns on foreign policy. Successful public diplomacy involves an active engagement with the public in a manner that builds, over a period of time, a relationship of trust and credibility. Effective public diplomacy is sometimes overtly conducted by governments but sometimes seemingly without direct government involvement, presenting, for instance, many differing views of private individuals and organizations in addition to official government positions.

Public diplomacy should also recognize that in our information-saturated world of today, the public also has access to information and insights from a wide and rapidly growing array of sources. This means that government information must be packaged and presented attractively and issued in a timely fashion if it is to stand up against competing streams of information, including from critics and rivals of the government. Your public diplomacy is no longer conducted in a vacuum; you are also up against the public diplomacy of other countries, sometimes on the very same issues.

This is all the more so in the era of the internet. How does information reach people, particularly young people, today? The emergence of Web 2.0

tools and social media sites like Facebook, Twitter, YouTube and Instagram—to name just a few of the more popular ones—offer governments a new possibility not only to disseminate information efficiently through these channels but also to receive feedback and respond to concerns. Countries like the US, UK and Canada consider Web 2.0 a boon for their public diplomacy and have been quick to embrace and deploy a wide array of internet tools. They also pro-actively encourage their diplomats to blog, so that they can populate the discussion forums with sympathetic points of view. In doing so, they are acutely aware of the effectiveness with which terrorist groups like Al Qaeda and many other militant organizations have harnessed the full power of Web 2.0 tools to propagate their message.

The pitfalls of using social media are the ever-present risk that something said on a social network could itself be taken out of context or misused by our critics. I am a poster child for this experience myself, with innocent remarks and jokes being willfully distorted and misrepresented, usually by political enemies but sometimes by the malicious and often enough by the humourless. Light-hearted remarks, jokes and puns are especially vulnerable; the kind of banter that would be acceptable, even admired, in a mono-lingual culture like the UK's or the USA's is fraught with political peril in multi-cultural India with its varying levels of education and linguistic sophistication.

Responses to questions are particularly vulnerable to being issued in haste and without the usual careful vetting that more formal statements undergo. The nature of the medium calls for speedy issuance of information and instant reaction, neither of which Government processes are designed for!

The principal lesson of the MEA's experience so far is that it works, provided you are willing to make the effort required. And that means having a team in place to deal with all the questions/comments/complaints that come your way, because a non-responsive social media site could be seriously counter-productive. As Mahima Kaul wrote, 'if you are not in it, you are out of it'. This young lady puts it well when she says that the Indian government 'will have to trust its people, and it will have to trust its own ability to respond to the people'.

There is no good reason why an IT powerhouse like India should not be in the forefront of public diplomacy efforts using 21st century technologies and communications practices. Not to deploy social media tools effectively is to abdicate a channel of contact not only with the millions of young Indians who use Facebook and Twitter but also to the huge Indian diaspora that tends to have such an active presence on the net on Indian issues and in turn wields a disproportionate influence on international perceptions of India. To place matters in perspective, Facebook alone currently has over 500 million subscribers, 50 per cent of whom access the site on any given day, and a unique ability to disseminate information virally among its system and beyond through its networks of friends, fans and those who share their information. The average Facebook user has 130 friends, and each of those has 130 more, and so on. When President Obama delivered his famous Africa address in Ghana, the State Department deployed a full range of digital tools and some 250,000 Africans posed questions or made comments on the address—and most received responses from dedicated staff assigned to respond!

As I have argued elsewhere in this volume, my brief stint in government saw me using social media to demystify governance, enhance transparency and openly keep the general public informed about both my routine work and interesting preoccupations while in office. I continued the practice both between my two stints in office and after becoming a member of the Opposition. Though I am seen as something of a pioneer in India, the practice is quite widespread in other democracies. President Obama has been a trailblazer but the practice has been embraced by some 505 government leaders and ministers, according to a recent study by the website Twiplomacy, which established in 2013 that 153 out of the UN's 193 member countries ran official government Twitter accounts. The number has almost certainly gone up since then. Fears of Twitter indiscretions are not entirely misplaced, but very few snafus have occurred; far from leaking secrets on social media, most government leaders have, if anything, erred on the side of caution, using Twitter and Facebook only to promote their own PR, rather than to engage meaningfully with the interested public.

When we speak today about freedom of the press and access to information, we do so standing on a platform of technology. It is clear that technology is the bridge between the right to information, and its realization. That technology is a bridge is nothing new. But we need not envisage it as an expensive multi-spanned high-tech bridge of the type that links two distant points—the type of bridge that, in the twentieth century, came to symbolize modern engineering. Indeed, in keeping with the impetus of today's technological advances, we can think smaller than that, because the liberating power of technology is rather simpler than that. The liberation process can start, for people in remote villages in poor parts of the world, with an internet kiosk, or a satellite link to a one-room school.

Information is liberating in many ways. It is liberating in the traditional political sense of the term—a sense that would probably have been understood by the nationalist leaders of many Asian countries, who used freedom of information, and specifically press freedom, effectively against their colonial masters. Information and freedom go together. The information revolution is inconceivable without political democracy, and vice-versa.

It is also liberating economically. Information technologies are an extremely cost-effective form of capital. Modest but focused investments in basic education and access can achieve remarkable results. Estonia and Costa Rica are well-known examples on other continents of how information access strategies can help accelerate countries' growth and raise income levels. South Asia can do just as well.

Indeed, some of the least-developed South Asian countries—notably, to pick one example, of Bangladesh—have also shown how determined leadership and innovative approaches can connect remote and rural areas to the internet and mobile telephony, and thereby improve the economies of small villages and farmers who were previously condemned to subsistence, because they were tied to local knowledge and local markets. And no-one who comes, as I do, from India could doubt that radical transformation is possible when information infrastructures are taken seriously.

What does this have to do with freedom of expression? Simple: these are two sides of the same information coin. Those of us who believe in liberty and who seek to build a better world should argue for greater access to information for all. We need to find ways to ensure that the information freely available in the West is also freely available to the rest.

Because if the information revolution is to deliver more than proximity— if it is to deliver greater understanding for the greater good and thereby contribute to a better world for all—we need to do two things in South Asia (and for that matter everywhere). First, we need to find ways to provide access to information to *all* people. And second, we need to ensure that this information is truly global—diverse, pluralistic and tolerant.

The substance is every bit as important as the means. The mass media that now rings our globalized world still principally reflects the interests of its producers. Even in the 21st century, what passes for international culture is usually the culture of the economically developed world.

Ask yourselves: who makes the cut to enter the global imagination in our brave new world? Yes, there is the occasional Third World voice, but it speaks a first world language. As far back as the first Congo Civil War of 1962, the journalist Edward Behr saw a TV newsman in a camp of violated Belgian nuns calling out: 'Anyone here been raped and speak English?' In other words, it was not enough to have suffered: one must be able to express one's suffering in the language acceptable to the media.

It is still the unfortunate truth that those speaking for their cultures in our globalized media are often not the most authentic representatives of them. Some believe that the bias inherent in the mass media will be overcome by the internet, and there is no doubt that the internet can be a democratizing tool. In some parts of the world, it has already become one, since large amounts of information are now accessible to almost anyone. But a person's means of access to information has long served as a way by which you could determine his or her wealth—perhaps merely by glancing at the watch on their wrist. And the stark reality of the world today is that you can tell the rich from the poor by their internet connections.

Today, the poverty line is linked to the high-speed digital line, the fibre optic cable—all the lines that exclude those who are literally not plugged in to the possibilities of our new world. There is a marked gap between the technological haves and have-nots, between those who know, and those who don't—both between countries and within them. This gap has come to be called the digital divide.

The digital divide is not just about access to technology. It remains a fact that 69 per cent of the world's websites are in English. That this poses problems may seem blindingly obvious to anyone for whom Chinese or French are first languages. But imagine how much less new media has to offer if your first— and only—language is Manipuri, or Pashto? These aspects are changing with the dizzying evolution of the internet, which will soon have more Chinese-language users than English. But it is difficult to argue that a young Indian researcher, for instance, will find as much information even in Hindi on a key subject as she can in English. And the history the internet discusses, and the markets it describes, and even the entertainment it provides still apply mainly to two continents—Europe and America—half a world away.

So the 'digital divide' is not only a technological one, but also a content divide that marginalizes developing countries. This content divide means that even where people find ways to access new media, there is often a lack of locally meaningful material. Of course we must all help promote the creation of domestic content, in line with the local culture and in the local language. Cultural diversity and pluralism are essential to an inclusive information society. The two concepts—diversity of content and press freedom—can and need to go together.

The world I would like to see develop is one in which there is what I call 'communications pluralism'. I would like everyone to be free to get themselves into the information age. Only this will bridge the content divide. New digital technology offers great possibilities for enhancing traditional media and combining them with new media. Moreover, traditional media, and especially radio and television, remain the sole form of access to the information society for much of the world's population, including the very poor and the illiterate.

Perhaps this is the newest challenge for the governments of South Asia— to work to bring access to information, and the empowerment it offers, to all the world's people. Only then will equity and equality be truly brought to the information revolution. Only then will the subcontinent's poor and underprivileged have a real way out of the darkness that shrouds their voices, and their hopes. Censorship militates against this freedom of access that is the new hallmark of freedom of expression.

The cases filed against the artist M.F. Husain on charges of obscenity had the unintended effect of striking a blow for freedom of expression in India, because Justice Sanjay Kishan Kaul of the Delhi High Court issued a landmark judgement in May 2008, upholding a number of petitions submitted by and on behalf of Husain. This not only ensured that justice was done to an authentic South Asian icon, but it contained observations that are both refreshing and true about the role of art in our society—observations which I hope will guide India's national discourse on this vexed subject in the future.

The great 92-year-old Indian artist had been harassed by malicious lawsuits seeking his prosecution for allegedly having offended the petitioners' notions of morality by the use of nudity in his art, particularly in paintings of Hindu goddesses and in the depiction of the contours of India in the shape of a nude female figure. The piling up of a number of cases—motivated essentially by anti-Muslim bigotry—had driven Husain into self-imposed exile in Dubai and London. Justice Kaul's judgement disposed of several of these cases in a learned, closely-argued and meticulously-footnoted ruling that bears detailed reading and extensive citation.

Justice Kaul begins by quoting Pablo Picasso: 'Art is never chaste. It ought to be forbidden to ignorant innocents, never allowed into contact with those not sufficiently prepared. Yes, art is dangerous. Where it is chaste, it is not art.' Recalling the richness of India's 5,000-year-old culture, the judge adds, 'Ancient Indian art has been never devoid of eroticism where sex worship and graphical representation of the union between man and woman has been a recurring feature.' Describing the nude as a 'perennial art subject', the judge observed that some paintings have been called 'obscene', 'vulgar', 'depraving', 'prurient' and 'immoral'—but it was important to look at art from the artist's perspective. As a judge he had to balance 'the individual's right to speech and expression and the frontiers of exercising that right', to prevent a 'closed mind' becoming 'a principal feature of [our] open society' or 'an unwilling recipient of information' from enjoying a veto over others' rights to the same information.

But despite his appreciation of India's artistic traditions, the learned judge could only, of course, base himself on the legal aspects of the case. He reviews precedents and judgements from the US, UK, Australia and Canada before examining Indian case law (it is striking, by the way, that the law of obscenity in India dates back to Section 292 of the Indian Penal Code of 1860, which also applies in Pakistan and Bangladesh). Under Article 19(2) of the Indian Constitution, the judge observes, 'obscenity which is offensive to public decency and morality is outside the purview of the protection of free speech and expression... but the former must never come in the way of the latter and should not substantially transgress the latter.' How does one determine standards of public decency? Justice Kaul is clear: 'The test for judging a work should be that of an ordinary man of common sense and prudence and not an out of the ordinary or hypersensitive man'. Obscenity, he opines, 'is treating with sex in a manner appealing to the carnal side of human nature or having that tendency.' In legal terms, as opposed to dictionary definitions, of obscenity, something which merely offends, repels or disgusts someone but does not tend to deprave or corrupt him or her cannot therefore be said to be obscene.

That is the standard which Justice Kaul applied to the petitions before him. Husain's paintings are hardly intended to provoke lustful thoughts; in fact, the judge notes, as an artist he 'actually celebrates nudity and considers it as the purest form of expression'. In the case of his painting of *Bharat Mata*, which had offended several petitioners, the judge ruled that 'the aesthetic touch to the painting dwarfs the so called obscenity in the form of nudity and renders it so picayune and insignificant that the nudity in the painting can easily be overlooked'. The complainants who had objected to the painting being available on a website could always choose not to look at it, the judge said, adding tartly that 'it seems that the complainants are not the types who would go to art galleries or have an interest in contemporary art, because if they did, they would know that there are many other artists who embrace nudity as part of their contemporary art.'

'Art and authority have never had a difficult relationship until recently,' the judge observes in his ruling. His judgement goes a long way towards reconciling the two. It is unlikely that his reasoning would be welcomed in any of India's Islamic neighbours, but his larger observations on the case deserve the attention of every thinking Indian.

The most important of these, I believe, is his rejection of the tendency of thin-skinned (or maliciously-motivated) people across the country to claim to be offended by artistic and literary works. If you're easily offended, he argues, don't read the book, look at the painting or open the website that offends you, but don't prevent the artist or writer from enjoying his constitutionally-protected freedom of expression. What is vital, according to Justice Kaul, is to look at the work of art from the artist's point of view—his or her intent rather than the hyper-sensitive viewer's reaction. Lest he be promptly denounced by the Hindutva brigade as a deracinated pseudo-secularist, the judge wisely cites Swami Vivekananda's words in defence of his approach: 'we tend to reduce everyone else to the limits of our own mental universe and begin privileging our own ethics, morality, sense of duty and even our sense of utility. All religious conflicts arose from this propensity to judge others. If we indeed must judge at all, then it must be 'according to his own ideal, and not by that of anyone else'. It is important, therefore, to learn to look at the duty of others through their own eyes and never judge the customs and observances of others through the prism of our own standards.' (Swami Vivekandanda said this in the 1890s.)

But Justice Kaul goes even further in extending the boundaries of the permissible in India. Nudity and sex, he argues, have an honoured place in art and literature: 'in the land of the *Kama Sutra*, we shy away from its very name?' he asks in surprise. 'Beauty lies in the eyes of the beholder and so does obscenity.... [In Indian tradition] sex was embraced as an integral part of a full and complete life. It is most unfortunate that India's new 'puritanism' is being carried out in the name of cultural purity and a host of ignorant people are vandalizing art and pushing us towards a pre-renaissance era.'

This is wonderful language in a High Court judgement. Readers should remember that India, unlike the US, has no absolute right to freedom of expression; in our country, Article 19(2) says that freedom of speech can be curbed by 'reasonable restrictions...in the interests of [the sovereignty and integrity of India], the security of the State, friendly relations with foreign States, public order, decency or morality or in relation to contempt of court, defamation or incitement to an offence.' In other words, a differently-minded judge could have easily interpreted the language about public order, decency and morality more narrowly. We Indians are fortunate that a series of judgements over the years, culminating in this one, have tilted the balance decisively in favour of our freedoms.

Justice Kaul is sensitive to the charge that liberal attitudes to art and obscenity reflect the inclinations of a privileged minority and that most Indians might indeed be offended by the kind of art his judgement protects. He writes: 'Democracy has wider moral implications than mere majoritarianism. A crude view of democracy gives a distorted picture. A real democracy is one in which the exercise of the power of the many is conditional on respect for the rights of the few... In real democracy the dissenter must feel at home and ought not to be nervously looking over his shoulder fearing captivity or bodily harm or economic and social sanctions for his unconventional or critical views. There should be freedom for the thought we hate. Freedom of speech has no meaning if there is no freedom after speech. The reality of democracy is to be measured by the extent of freedom and accommodation it extends.'

These words should give heart not just to admirers of M.F. Husain, but to artists and writers across the country, who in recent years have found themselves the victims of other people's hyper-sensitivities. 'Intolerance', Justice Kaul writes, 'is utterly incompatible with democratic values. This attitude is totally antithetical to our Indian psyche and tradition'. He goes on to warn that the criminal justice system 'ought not to be invoked as a convenient recourse to ventilate any and all objections to an artistic work' and be used as a 'tool' in unscrupulous hands to violate the rights of artists. The judge declares that 'a magistrate must scrutinise each case in order to prevent vexatious and frivolous cases from being filed and make sure that it is not used a tool to harass the accused, which will amount to gross abuse of the process of the court.... [A]part from the harassment element there would be growing fear and curtailment of the right of the free expression in such creative persons.' He decries 'the large number of incidents of such complaints. ...resulting in artists and other creative persons being made to run across the length and breadth of the country to defend themselves against criminal proceedings initiated by oversensitive or motivated persons, including for publicity'.

Justice Kaul's ruling is a remarkable charter for artistic freedom in India. 'I have penned this judgment', he concludes, 'with the fervent hope that it is a prologue to a broader thinking and greater tolerance for the creative field'. Every thinking Indian concerned about freedom of expression should join in the applause. And every South Asian who is not Indian ought to prod his or her country's judiciary to study the Indian judgement very carefully.

Now all of the above begs a simple question. Why is this important?

I suspect that no one would argue that the trifecta I've spoken about—freedom of expression, access to media and availability of information—is a magic formula. It is not a panacea; it will not solve all of India's problems. But we all know that it makes up a very powerful force that can—and must—be harnessed if we are to deliver a tolerable standard of living to all Indians.

And in the 21st century, a new global society is undoubtedly evolving. It will happen irrespective of how we in India respond, but at present, we have some power over how it evolves. Will globalization be a divisive force—one that merely adds to the gap between the haves and the have-nots in this new global society? Or will it be a process that actually delivers on the promise made at the founding of the UN in 1945—of 'better standards of life in larger freedom'? The answers depend, to a very real extent, on how well we can deliver information to those most in need.

And if we get it right, there will also be direct benefits for those of us who already enjoy a high degree of personal and economic liberty. Why? Because media is education, and education is critical to global security. People who are well informed are less likely to be led astray by the purveyors of hatred and intolerance.

If we were to look at other positive uses of social media internationally, it has also proved critical for connecting the world's younger generation on a single platform, thus strengthening bonds between them across borders and cultures. Young people from different geographic and economic backgrounds can be brought together in a positive direction. Students who attended the India-Pakistan Youth Peace Conferences have started using digital media to stay connected and have even invited others from their campuses to join the conversations. Many Indians and Pakistanis, including several in official positions, exchange informal messages on social media. Pakistan's former interior minister Rehman Malik and its former ambassador in Washington, Husain Haqqani, are regular tweeters, as was the late Salman Taseer, governor of Pakistani Punjab, who was assassinated for expressing views with the kind of candour that made him so popular on Twitter.

Today's information society can thrive only if citizens are provided with full information to allow democratic participation at all levels. The media need to be engaged as indispensable key participants of the information society, and governments must welcome the role of press freedom as vital to democracy and good governance.

Bridging the information divide is not going to be easy. The barriers are many. But it is clear that access to information and communication must be made more universal and affordable; that the right to receive and impart information contained in Article 19 of the International Convention on Civil and Political Rights must be protected as a fundamental right; and that in every country, a policy framework should be put in place that is transparent and predictable.

The prospective benefits of the information age are clear; in a nutshell, we now have a powerful tool to address the disadvantages of under-development, of isolation, of poverty and of the lack of political accountability and political freedom. But these benefits will only be made manifest when the entrances and exits to the information superhighway are open to everyone, when they are mapped and signposted in such a way as to allow everyone to know where they need to go, and when the road itself is suitable for all manner of vehicles, from SUVs to trams, and from rickshaws to bicycles.

The ultimate clinching argument might well come from the marketplace, in the dizzying valuations of social media sites which go way beyond their earnings or dividends. Every week, one of the social media firms seems to attract a sky-high valuation. Profitless Twitter is worth close to $40 billion. When Facebook, the poster child of social media, went public in early 2012 its value was at $106 billion. Even though it has lost more than $30 billion since its debut, at its current stock market price, Facebook's value is still higher than that of real-world businesses like Ford ($38 billion). But that's still peanuts compared to Google's value, which is more than $525 billion. The mind boggles at where both will be in the years to come.

In other words, in the era of the internet, freedom of expression through social media is here to stay, and we need to live with it. Quite simply, we will not be able to live without it. The Information Revolution has already occurred; we now live in the age of the information society. Our task in India now is to shape it to our own needs and in our own image.

FLYING WHILE BROWN, AND OTHER JOYS OF AIRPORT SECURITY

I've been a frequent air traveller since I was a few months shy of my sixth birthday, when my parents first packed me off to boarding school two plane rides away from home. Those days of being willingly handed from air-hostess to air-hostess as an 'unaccompanied minor' made me blasé about the rigours of air travel (and very respectful of air-hostesses). Going abroad to study as a teenager, and joining the United Nations at 22, confirmed my ease with the world of the frequent flyer. I saw the average airport terminal as a familiar haven, like a friend's sitting-room. I felt as cozy in a check-in line as a tapeworm in an Indian intestine.

But 9/11 changed all that. Of course we had lived with airport security checks before the World Trade Center was hit. But 9/11, and every suspected airplane security threat thereafter, have made security checks so much more stringent. The assorted divestments, the enthusiastic frisking, the suspicious prying open of your bag, that bleeping wand pushed into awkward spots, have all combined to make flying much less fun than ever. Passengers at airports now look so chronically morose that a passing vulture flying overhead would sense a business opportunity.

The episode of the 'shoe bomber', Richard Reid, has suddenly meant more feet being bared at airports than at the average Hindu temple. A friend of mine refuses to travel by air anymore because he can't bear to have to take his shoes off every time, put them through the screening device and lace them up again. (He's not just finicky—he suffers from lumbago, and finds it quite literally a major pain.) My own solution has simply been to change my style, replacing my customary lace-up Oxfords with a pair of slip-on loafers whenever I fly. I'm only relieved the security people haven't decided I might try to strangle the pilot with my tie.

Generals are always fighting the last war, and security screeners are the same. I'm just grateful it was a shoe bomber they were reacting to. What on earth would they do if the next Richard Reid tried to ignite his underwear?

Then came the fellows who tried to explode liquid chemicals on board. So now ladies have to pack their potions and unguents in three-millilitre bottles and fit them all into a quart-size plastic bag. Since the plot didn't work the first time and no one has tried it since, the only beneficiaries of this are the recyclers, who receive a dumpster-load of discarded water and shampoo bottles from the US government's Transportation Security Administration (TSA) every day, and the concessionaires on the other side of security, facing parched passengers suddenly deprived of their drinks, whose thirst they cheerfully quench at an exorbitant price.

But that's not all that's changed. As security procedures intensified I had thought it wise to travel light and check-in everything I needed for my journey. I had always packed a sturdy suitcase with a combination lock, to ensure I arrived with what I had packed. But the best-laid plans of mice and men are vetoed by the TSA. First the security people wanted you to leave the suitcase open when you checked it in, so they could screen it and examine the contents. Could that explain the stories of pilferage proliferating on the frequent-flyer circuit? The TSA now lets you keep your suitcase locked, provided it's of an approved brand whose combo locks they can open. I promptly purchased a TSA-compliant Samsonite. I take several dozen flights a year in or from the US, and on every single one of them, without exception, I've arrived to find a TSA inspection notice nestling amongst my crumpled shirts. One would think that after the fortieth attempt they might conclude that I was simply one of those people who didn't like to carry explosives in his suitcase. But no, flight number forty-one, and there's that notice again...

It doesn't help, of course, that I bear a name and a countenance of sufficient swarthiness to increase the odds of my suitcase being 'randomly' picked for a TSA inspection. Indians like myself whose features might pass for Middle Eastern have learned to appreciate the special risks of 'flying while brown'. 'There was a time during the 1970s oil boom,' a fellow Indian told me, 'that I rather enjoyed being mistaken for Arab. People assumed I was richer than I was and treated me with respect. Now, after 9/11, I'm anxious to demonstrate I'm Indian. If I were a woman I'd wear a sari all the time, just to show I'm not that kind of brown'.

South-South solidarity quails in the face of the joys of being repeatedly singled out for 'random' secondary security screening. If you're the wrong shade, your hand-luggage is subject to the most thorough check of all. This can involve both indignity and inconvenience. It's bad enough to have strangers' hands, even ones wearing those latex gloves, sift through your most intimate possessions. It's worse when individual items are held up to dubious inspection, amidst loud calls for supervisors to rule on them. (And the security guys all seem to approach the task with the look of a dog who has just been reminded where its bone is buried.) My tongue-cleaner, an Indian hygienic device since Vedic times that involves a U-shaped loop which these days is made of stainless steel, attracts particular attention. I can't imagine how it could be repurposed for use in a hijacking, but I'm braced for the day I'm asked to demonstrate it. Just say aah...

But you don't need exotica to interest the guardians of our collective safety, who all look at you with expressions that might have been filmed by Ingmar Bergman in one of his less frivolous moments. The challenge of finding a pair of nail-clippers that security won't confiscate is one that has defeated most travellers, as the heaps in front of each security officer testify. (And yet you can usually go through security and buy yourself, from an airport store, a nail-clipper just like the one they confiscated, which you will then, of course, have taken away by the security people on your way back home.) Exactly the same thing has happened to me twice with deodorants purchased at airports.

If that's all you have to go through at security, consider yourself lucky. In all fairness, you don't have to be brown to be selected for extra-special attention, though it helps. In their desire to prove the randomness of their biases, I've also seen security people pick passengers in inverse relation to the likelihood of their being a terrorist—elderly grandmothers making their way through security on a walker, say, or a certain white-haired senator from Massachusetts. (It is normally not difficult to tell the difference between Ted Kennedy and a terrorist fanatic bent on mass murder, but I guess the TSA wanted to prove their even-handedness, or their bloody-mindedness.) And I know of people whose experiences were considerably more embarrassing than mine. (Heard about the American businesswoman who was interrogated about her vibrator at a foreign airport, as her colleagues watched and sniggered? Or the mother carrying breast-milk in a bottle for her baby who was ordered to drink it to prove it wasn't a lethal toxin? A friend tells me about his handicapped young son who flies with an oxygen tank. How do we know it's not a deadly poison gas, the TSA wanted to know—failing to note that the kid breathing the stuff hadn't dropped dead.) I have watched in mounting incredulity as one of my own books, which I was carrying as a gift, was taken away to be inserted into a special device after it had already passed security, to make sure, no doubt, that my words wouldn't explode mid-flight.

Every time you think you've got the formula down pat—slip-off shoes, no nail-clippers or other sharp objects, no bottles of water, nothing you can't explain or bear to see displayed to the attentive public in line behind you— some new complication comes up. The full-body scanners that can be found in American airports have not yet invaded the rest of the world, but privacy is clearly secondary to the imperative of rendering every passenger totally incapable of harming an aircraft. It's bad enough that you have to take out your laptop, empty your pockets, slip off your shoes, loosen your belt and shed your jacket to facilitate the inspections—they'll still ask you to spread your arms and legs and prepare to be violated. Worse, you have to smile through the whole ordeal. Because if you dare to complain, they really come down on you. A witticism in an airport security line is like a Swiss tap—turn it on, and you instantly find yourself in hot water. 'Jokes or inappropriate remarks regarding security could lead to your arrest,' signs humorlessly warn you at strategic points. And until they close Guantanamo, I'm taking no chances...

So what's next? I don't know. But it's a measure of how much we have come to accept in today's world that we take those long lines at security in stride and don't even complain too loudly about the intrusiveness of those inspections. I feel sorry for the next 6-year-old who needs to fly alone. The innocence with which I first embraced air travel is simply inconceivable today.

CYBER SECURITY IN INVASIVE TIMES

The revelations that Pakistan-based websites have been unleashing doctored pictures of alleged atrocities against Muslims in order to inflame passions in India once again brought attention to the enormous potential of the Information Age to challenge our security assumptions.

The computer is the instrument of our age; cyberspace is the oxygen of the internet. So much in our interconnected, globalized, and technologically advancing world depends on cyberspace. From our mundane emails to social networking to high priority banking services, government systems, communications, transport, and perhaps most important, our military organizations, all increasingly place reliance on the World Wide Web and everything connected to it.

To a layman, cyber security means simple things: a password that is not stolen, a message that remains confidential, a child that is not exposed to a stalker or paedophile online. When they type in a web address, that is where they should go and not to a spam site. When they click a link that looks genuine, they should not be cheated by a plausible fraud. Their work online should not be tampered with, and so on.

But cyber security ranges across wider terrain. The international relations theorist Joseph Nye has discerned four different types of threats to cyberspace. The most dramatic is cyber war—the unauthorized invasion by a government into the systems or networks of another, aiming to disrupt those systems, to damage them partially, or to destroy them entirely. A specific target is to slow down if not curtail the military systems of the target state: there is no point having excellent missiles and weapons if the delivery systems can be paralyzed. And as our military establishments become more and more dependent on sophisticated technologies, the risk of equally sophisticated attacks on them grows.

Nye's second threat is cyber espionage. Governments can invade the systems of their rivals to steal sensitive information that would be useful for their own purposes. These attacks are usually hard to discover and the case of Operation Shady Rat, the world's biggest hacking ever, is rather phenomenal. For five whole years hackers had access to seventy government and private agencies around the world as they secreted away gigabytes of confidential information, unbeknownst to those at the receiving end. By the time Shady Rat was spotted, forty-nine networks had been infected in the United States alone along with several others in India, South Korea, Taiwan and elsewhere.

Cyber crime is the third kind of threat, and the most familiar. While this also has military and political implications, it affects the lives of ordinary internet users more closely. Just the other day, for instance, a domestic aide of mine, recently introduced to the world of email, came up to me looking rather dazed. He had, he said, just received an email that some lady in Kenya had left him a substantial amount of money. In order to access that money he needed to deposit a relatively small but still significant sum (Rs 40,000 to be exact) at a local bank account here, so that the transfer could be facilitated. Such messages come in daily and there are many who fall prey to them. Cyber crime also includes pornography, internet stalking, and personality imitation.

Finally there is cyber terrorism. This includes websites spreading extremist propaganda, recruiting terrorists, planning attacks, and otherwise promoting terrorists' political and social objectives. It also involves the use of hackers by terrorists to debilitate states and governments, much like in cyber war, with the only difference that this involves a non-State actor. Cyberspace offers a great advantage for the shrouded business of terrorists, making their work murkier than ever to those outside.

Cyber attacks are already happening daily, and as we grow more and more 'connected', the threats also become more complex. Symantec, a leading international cyber security company, recorded that in 2010 alone there were three billion malware attacks. (The figure has undoubtedly gone up since then.) Of these one stands out especially, pointing to the possible use by legitimate governments of cyber weapons. This was the case of Stuxnet, which attacked five Iranian organizations, all reportedly connected with their uranium enrichment and nuclear programmes. By early 2011 the *New York Times* revealed, very plausibly, that Stuxnet was the single biggest weapon used in an attempt to thwart Iran's nuclear ambitions, and the most sophisticated instrument ever used in cyberspace. There is, in a sense, a war constantly on in cyberspace, one that is invisible and to which we are all, in the end, inevitably connected.

In 2012, a similar highly complicated attack called Flame was discovered in Russia, Hungary, and Iran. Flame had been copying documents, recording audio (including keystrokes!), network traffic, Skype calls, as well as taking screenshots from infected computers. And it was passing all this information collected to the computers controlling it. No security alarm went off on any of the infected computers, which raises the question: are any of our systems really safe? Conventional security measures are all outdated and by the look of it, even the 'latest' protections are rendered obsolete sooner than we would collectively desire.

In those cases, the US is the likely suspect, but though nothing can be conclusively established, China has consistently topped the list of official suspects in the world of cyber attacks. The attacks coming from there do not usually aim to destroy or even debilitate as much as to steal information. The Titan Rain attack, for instance, targeted the US military, NASA, and the World Bank. Sensitive information stolen was not only related to military matters but also to markets, trade, and business activities. Similarly Ghostnet infiltrated Indian government systems and accessed classified information of our security agencies, embassies, and the office of the Dalai Lama, doing the same with hundreds of government establishments elsewhere in the world.

Social networking websites are also increasingly becoming targets, not only because of the massive databases they provide, but also in order to spread malware that infect computers. On Facebook there are over 50 million Indian users and even if a small fraction of them click unsuspectingly on a malevolent but seemingly ordinary link, you have that many computers opened up to risk and infection. Cyber attacks, to state the obvious, can be very personal.

Another use of social networks, seen recently in India, is to spread inflammatory material with a motivated agenda, such as the doctored pictures of alleged atrocities against Muslims in Assam and Myanmar that incited violence in Mumbai and threats of retaliation elsewhere. Though this does not constitute cyber terrorism in itself, it constitutes a new security threat that cannot be ignored.

There are no easy responses to all these phenomena. The US created Cybercom in 2009 as a military command dedicated to cyber warfare. In the civilian arena few countries have a credible equivalent. India's own style of dealing with cyber threats leaves much to be desired. It is relatively chaotic and there is a constant insecurity that our cyber-defences are insufficient. This perception has been underscored by frequent reports of successful invasions of Indian cyberspace. Our approach appears so far to have been ad hoc and piecemeal. There are some twelve stakeholders in protecting the cyber defences of India, including the Home Affairs Ministry, the National Disaster Management Authority, National Information Board and a motley crew of others. They are together responsible for the Indian Computer Emergency Response Team, which is the principal national agency. Such a large number of bosses, I would argue, is not conducive to efficiency.

We must be vigilant, but we must also ensure our security measures do not compound the threat. As someone once asked, if Tim Berners-Lee had to ask for permission, would the World Wide Web have been invented? Would Google have been perceived as a security threat right at the start and been prohibited? Would Wikipedia have come into existence? The chances are they would not have been allowed.

The freedom of cyberspace is just as crucial to the debate as its protection is. This is why policy on cyber security is too important to be left to the cyber security experts and too valuable socially to be left to the police. It is not for the gunsmiths to decide who should use the gun and how. The key to cyberspace should never be given to those who would place a lock on it. It should be held by the larger moral force of society.

LOSING OUR HEADS TO KIPLING

Faithful readers—and I know I have a few—are aware that I have had a few unkind things to say about Rudyard Kipling over the years. But there was one work of his I was very fond of when young—and no, I'm not referring to his precious *Jungle Book*, with little (white) Mowgli surrounded by all the menacing (sub-human) animals of the Indian jungle. The words of Kipling's that I most admired, and often recited, were those of his poem 'If':

> If you can keep your head when all about you
> Are losing theirs and blaming it on you,
> If you can trust yourself when all men doubt you
> But make allowance for their doubting too,
> If you can wait and not be tired by waiting,
> Or being lied about, don't deal in lies,
> Or being hated, don't give way to hating,
> And yet don't look too good, nor talk too wise:
> If you can dream—and not make dreams your master,
> If you can think—and not make thoughts your aim;
> If you can meet with Triumph and Disaster
> And treat those two impostors just the same;
> If you can bear to hear the truth you've spoken
> Twisted by knaves to make a trap for fools,
> Or watch the things you gave your life to, broken,
> And stoop and build 'em up with worn-out tools:

And so on it went, but these were the lines that rang resonant in my impressionable mind, especially the bit about Triumph and Disaster. The poem seemed to me to speak immortal truths that all individuals of conviction had to live by: the need to stand up for what you believe in even if your ideas are scorned, your motives suspected, your performance distorted; the need to persist doggedly on the right path despite the hecklers and naysayers around you; the need, above all, to have faith in yourself and not be swayed by either pressure or pleasure. Of course the poem weakened somewhat in its second half, with the lines 'If you can make one heap of all your winnings/ And risk it all on one turn of pitch-and-toss', an exhortation to gamble that I thought irresponsible even in my teenage years, and the nakedly sexist imperialism of the closing lines, 'Yours is the Earth and everything that's in it, /And—which is more—you'll be a Man, my son!' But on the whole, I said to myself, Kipling may have been a racist thug who suffered from bipolar disorder and opium addiction, but he certainly had a way with words, and the words in this poem were not only inspirational, they were rhythmically recitable—and they rhymed pretty well too.

Well, all of us grow up, and in time I too outgrew my lingering respect for Kipling as anything but a wordsmith—a craftsman of high talent without a soul. So it might have passed—with all due contumely for the inventor of the notorious phrase 'the white man's burden' and the equally racist assertion that East and West could never meet. But when I recently discovered that Indian schoolchildren of my acquaintance were still reciting 'If' in elocution contests and learning it by heart for literature courses, I felt I had to raise my voice in protest. Because in celebrating Kipling's poem, we are not merely celebrating a benighted imperialist—we are unconsciously paying homage to a specific incident in the nasty annals of imperialism.

For 'If' was written for a purpose, and the purpose was to honour Kipling's friend Leander Jameson, one of Africa's nastier colonists in the service of Cecil Rhodes' British South Africa Company. Jameson had won fame for a military misadventure baptized by the British media as 'Jameson's Raid'—an assault in 1895 on the elected Boer government of South Africa, which he hoped to overthrow and replace with a more congenial alternative—congenial, that is, to British imperialism. Jameson and his raiders were soundly thrashed and widely pilloried even by many Englishmen; many historians consider that his attack began the unfortunate cycle of events that was to lead to the outbreak of the Second Boer War, the invention of concentration camps and (eventually) to the institution of apartheid. The government in London, which historians believe to have been behind the raid, cynically disowned Jameson and his men and even put him in jail for his pains, much to the outrage of Kipling and his fellow jingoists. The poet wrote 'If' in response, to urge Jameson to ignore his detractors and persecutors.

So what many see as an inspirational poem full of stirring aphorisms for young people to live by is in fact little more than an apologia for an imperialist misdeed. In that, 'If' is little different from the Kiplingesque effort by Britons in India two decades later to raise funds in support of Brigadier Dyer, the butcher of Jallianwallah Bagh. Fine words strung together in praise of the morally indefensible: that was Kipling every time, and the sonorous cadences of 'If', alas, are no exception. It is time to retire this poem from our curriculums—or at least to footnote it thoroughly. It is time to relegate Kipling to the darkest recesses of our history, where he and his ilk belong. For the 'truth [he's] spoken' is indeed the twisted view of an imperialist 'knave', and if we're taken in, it's we who are the fools.

OUR FONDNESS FOR FAKES

We've all received those ubiquitous emails in our inbox, though mercifully most of them these days are caught by our spam filters. Emails offering expensive drugs at hard-to-beat prices—drugs against cholesterol, blood pressure, arthritis and baldness, always bearing familiar brand names like Lipitor, Celebrex and inevitably Viagra. The wiser amongst us delete them instantly. Some are, however, taken in. Those who are uninsured, or who can't afford to pay full price, or who in their cupidity simply imagine that they can save a few bucks, even order these medicines from the internet hawkers. The results are often calamitous. Sometimes the paid-for drugs never arrive. Sometimes they do, and that's worse. They're fakes, in some cases made of little more than powdered cement, artfully disguised to look like the real thing. At best, they will be of no medical benefit whatsoever. At worst, they could kill you.

Counterfeit drugs are a multi-million dollar industry. The fake medicines market is said to be worth over $75 billion a year worldwide. Like counterfeit watches, fake perfumes, imitation designer clothing and pirated films, they thrive in a world where people are all too ready to bend the rules. But what isn't as well known is how these merchants of the meretricious misuse the international trade system to pursue their goals. Places like Hong Kong and Dubai, because of their open and liberal trade policy, their efficient systems devoid of bureaucratic entanglements, and the absence of import and export fees or income tax in their free ports, have become particular targets.

Dubai is particularly attractive to counterfeiters for the same reason that it is attractive to regular traders—because of its strategic location on the Arabian Gulf, which makes Dubai ideal for the movement of goods between Asia, Europe and Africa. The fake-drug merchants have not been slow to catch on. Records show that nearly one third of all counterfeit drugs confiscated in Europe in 2013 came from—which really means through—the United Arab Emirates. The Intellectual Property Unit of the Dubai Customs Authority destroyed 293 tonnes of counterfeit products just in the first five months of 2014.

But there's also a more sinister reason why free-trade zones appeal to the counterfeiters. They use such zones to conceal the real origin of a drug, especially by moving the products from one zone to another, or by relabelling fake or adulterated goods to make them look as of they came from more legitimate sources. The *New York Times* wrote of 'a complex supply chain of fake drugs that ran from [counterfeit drugs manufacturers in] China through Hong Kong, the United Arab Emirates, Britain and the Bahamas, ultimately leading to an Internet pharmacy whose American customers believed they were buying medicine from Canada'.

Fake drugs stir rage in all of us, because any of us could be vulnerable to the dangers of being laid low by a medicine we thought was going to help us. Fake booze is another problem. We all know of the bad old days when smugglers sold you bottles of Johnnie Walker Black Label which contained some spurious spirit they had injected into an empty bottle with a syringe (India was the world's largest market for empty Johnnie Walker bottles.) But if that isn't bad enough, almost half of all alcoholic spirits sold in Russia are counterfeit, killing 43,000 Russians every year.

Not all fakes kill, of course, and counterfeiting of other goods often escapes the same level of censure because people tend to think it doesn't matter as much. What's the harm, people ask themselves, if we can 'beat the system' and enjoy something without really paying for it? If we get something that others think is genuine and only we know the difference, how does it matter?

The short answer is that it does—not just because theft is theft, whether it is of intellectual property or of somebody's wallet. It matters because fakery stifles innovation, depriving the world of the creativity that is our only source of progress. It matters because those of us who buy fake goods are really stealing from creative risk-takers and giving our support to the more indolent counterfeiters, who profit from the ingenuity and hard work of others. In the process, we shoot ourselves in the foot, because we deprive creators of the incentive to create—thereby reducing the number of new products we can one day enjoy. Wearing a fake watch may not harm you directly in the way that consuming a fake drug would, but it diminishes you nonetheless, and dilutes the possibilities of the world in which you live.

It's up to ordinary citizens to ensure that the fakes don't prevail. If each of us refused to buy, wear or consume stolen goods, the counterfeiters would have to look elsewhere for custom. Everything known to human beings can be faked. Thanks to advances in digital technology, 3D laser scanners and counterfeiting software, there is now little that cannot be quickly and cheaply reproduced—and sold around the world as the genuine article. The result is that one in ten of all products sold across the globe is now believed to be counterfeit.

So what kind of a world do we want to live in? One in which nothing is real, nothing is what it seems, or one in which there is a premium on genuineness, on high quality—and on the authentic? A non-profit group called the Authentics Foundation has been running a Fakes Cost More Campaign in Europe recently. Maybe they should bring it to Mumbai too.

Authenticity is an underrated virtue. It's always better to wear a genuine Tata Titan than a fake Cartier, because the latter puts you in the position of pretending to have something you don't, which is as bad as pretending to be someone you're not. Where imagination is usurped by imitation, no one wins.

HOW PROUD SHOULD WE BE OF BOBBY JINDAL?

The election of Bobby Jindal as governor of the US state of Louisiana was greeted exultantly by Indians and Indian-Americans around the world, and now his possible candidacy for the White House has us all agog. There's no question that this is an extraordinary accomplishment: a young Indian-American, just 36 years old, not merely winning an election but doing so on the first ballot by receiving more votes than his eleven rivals combined, and that too in a state not noticeably friendly to minorities. Bobby Jindal became the first Indian-American governor in US history (paving the way for Nikki Haley, born Namrata Randhawa, in South Carolina a few years later), and the youngest currently serving chief executive of an American state. A credible run for the presidency will set the seal on his stunning political career. These are distinctions of which he can legitimately be proud, and it is not surprising that Indians too feel a vicarious sense of shared pride in his remarkable ascent.

But is our pride misplaced? Who is Bobby Jindal and what does he really stand for?

There are, broadly speaking, two kinds of Indian migrants in America: though no sociologist, I'll call them the atavists and the assimilationists. The atavists hold on to their original identities as much as possible, especially outside the workplace; in speech, dress, food habits, cultural preferences, they are still much more Indian than American. The assimilationists, on the other hand, seek assiduously to merge into the American mainstream; they acquire a new accent along with their visa, and adopt the ways, clothes, diet and recreational preferences of the Americans they see around them. (Of course there are the in-betweens, but we'll leave them aside for now.) Class has something to do with which of the two major categories an Indian immigrant falls into; so does age, since the newer generation of Indians, especially those born in America, inevitably tend to gravitate to the latter category.

Bobby Jindal is an assimilationist's dream. Born to relatively affluent professionals in Louisiana, he rejected his Indian name (Piyush) as a very young child, insisting that he be called Bobby, after a (white) character on the popular TV show *The Brady Bunch*. His desire to fit into the majority-white society he saw around him soon manifested itself in another act of rejection: Bobby spurned the Hindusim into which he was born and, as a teenager, converted to Roman Catholicism, the faith of most white Louisianans. There is, of course, nothing wrong with any of this, and it is a measure of his precocity that his parents did not balk at his wishes despite his extreme youth. The boy was clearly gifted, and he soon had a Rhodes Scholarship to prove it. But he was also ambivalent about his identity: he wanted to be seen as a Louisianan, but his mirror told him he was also an Indian. The two of us jointly won something called an Excelsior Award once from the Network of Indian Professionals in the US, and his acceptance speech on the occasion was striking—obligatory references to the Indian values of his parents, but a speech so American in tone and intonation that he mangled the Indian name of his own brother. There was no doubt which half of the hyphen this Indian-American leaned towards.

But there are many ways to be American, and it's interesting which one Bobby chose. Many Indians born in America have tended to sympathize with other people of colour, identifying their lot with other immigrants, the poor, the underclass. Vanita Gupta, in Tulia, Texas, another largely white state, won her reputation as a crusading lawyer by taking up the case of undocumented workers exploited by a factory owner (her story was depicted by Hollywood, with Halle Berry playing the Indian heroine). Bhairavi Desai leads a taxi drivers' union; Preeta Bansal, who grew up as the only non-white child in her school in Nebraska, became New York's solicitor general and has served on the Commission for Religious Freedom, as well as in the Obama Justice Department. None of this for Bobby. Louisiana's most famous city, New Orleans, was a majority black town, at least until Hurricane Katrina destroyed so many black lives and homes, but there is no record of Bobby identifying himself with the needs or issues of his state's black people. Instead, he sought, in a state with fewer than 10,000 Indians, not to draw attention to his race by supporting racial causes.

Indeed he went well beyond trying to be non-racial (in a state that harboured notorious racists like the Ku Klux Klansman David Duke); he cultivated the most conservative elements of white Louisiana society. With his widely-advertised piety (he asked his Indian wife, Supriya, to convert as well, and the two are regular churchgoers), Bobby Jindal adopted positions on hot-button issues that place him on the most conservative fringe of the Republican party. Most Indian-Americans are in favour of gun control, support a woman's right to choose abortion, advocate immigrants' rights, and oppose school prayer (for fear that it will marginalize non-Christians). On every one of these issues, Bobby Jindal is on the opposite side. He's not just conservative; on these questions, he is well to the right of his own party.

That hasn't stopped him, however, from seeking the support of Indian-Americans. Bobby Jindal has raised a small fortune from them, and both when he ran unsuccessfully for governor in 2003, and successfully in 2007 and 2011, an army of Indian-American volunteers from outside the state turned up to campaign for him. Many seemed unaware of his political views; it was enough for them that he was Indian. At his Indian-American fundraising events, Bobby is careful to downplay his extreme positions and play up his heritage, a heritage that plays little part in his appeal to the Louisiana electorate. Indian–Americans, by and large, accept this as the price of political success in white America: it's just good to have 'someone like us' in such high office, whatever views he professes to get himself there. But Bobby has never supported a single Indian issue; he refused to join the India Caucus when he was a Congressman at Capitol Hill, and is conspicuously absent from any event with a visiting Indian leader. It is as if he wants to forget he is Indian, and would like voters to forget it too.

So the *Times of India* emblazons his triumph on the front page, and Indians beam proudly at another Indian–American success story to go along with Kalpana Chawla and Sunita Williams, Hargobind Khorana and Subramaniam Chandrasekhar, Kal Penn and Jhumpa Lahiri. But none of these Indian–Americans expressed attitudes and beliefs so much at variance with the prevailing values of their community. Let us be proud that a brown-skinned man with an Indian name has achieved what Bobby Jindal has. But let us not make the mistake of thinking that we should be proud of how he behaves, or what he stands for.

THE POLITICS OF ENERGY

We live in a post–war world. Today shooting wars are the exception, and they look increasingly unlikely almost everywhere. But are we entering an era of 'resource wars' instead—intense competition over the control of energy, water, even food? Many observers think so. And energy is the principal resource over which global competition is expected.

Consider the evidence. Emerging markets like China, India, Brazil, and Turkey have voracious appetites for energy, and they are all in the race to acquire it. China is expected to account for one-third of the increase in oil demand in the next two decades. It is scrambling for oil and gas concessions in Africa, on land and offshore. It is intensifying its development of a blue-water navy to assert dominance in the South China Sea and beyond, not least to ensure that sea lanes of communication are kept open for its energy supplies. India is comparably active in the Western half of the Indian Ocean. The geopolitics of energy are no longer merely about the US pursuing its security interests in the Gulf.

Everyone needs affordable, reliable energy, which is indispensable for economic growth. In a world where the notion of 'energy independence' is a fantasy, the quest for energy security is unavoidable. I addressed this issue in 2012 at the KazEnergy Conference in Kazakhstan's astonishing new capital of Astana. I recall from my days in the UN, the Kazakh president, Nursultan Nazarbayev, telling the General Assembly that his country was ranked seventh in oil reserves in the world, sixth in gas reserves and second in coal reserves. And it also has uranium! Astana is less than four hours' flying time from New Delhi but we have not been giving it the importance it deserves.

The dominant source of energy in the world is fossil fuels: the combination of oil, gas and coal easily represents over 80 per cent of the world total primary energy supply. Of course, alternative energy must and will be explored: wind power, solar energy, hydropower, geothermal heat, and biofuels are amongst the other sources of energy that are currently being developed around the world, but the vast global infrastructure of oil and gas will continue to supply the majority of world energy needs in the predictable future. Experts say that even by 2030, hydrocarbons will still account for over 70 per cent of the world's energy.

There is insufficient global supply to meet demand. Global energy demand is expected to grow by 32 to 40 per cent in the next two decades, as it did over the previous two. Increasing supply is therefore not the sole answer. Energy efficiencies, conservation, alternative energy and new oil and natural gas fields must be explored, but they will not be enough to meet the rising demands of our growing global economy. The development of renewable energies should go forward while recognizing that oil and natural gas are going to be around for decades.

The global politics of energy can no longer be ignored. In late 2011 the State Department created a Bureau of Energy Resources to focus exclusively on energy, a sign of the growing importance of energy issues to US foreign policy and national security. India's External Affairs Ministry has appointed a Joint Secretary for Energy Security. Other countries are no doubt doing the same. And yet we have not made progress in developing an international system to manage the global competition for energy resources, to match the system for global geopolitics that we have built around the UN.

The global situation, despite the appearance of stability, offers uncertain prospects. The notion of 'peak oil' is broadly discredited; new supplies continue to be found, and both Iraq and Iran have competitively raised their estimates of national oil reserves by some 25 per cent from previous estimates. How much of this is real remains to be proven, and with sanctions on Iranian oil beginning to bite, less of it is entering the global supply chain. Further supply disruptions are not impossible as the pressure for decisive action against the Iranian nuclear programme mounts in some quarters.

Meeting increasing global demand, according to the expert Daniel Yergin, means an increasing share of oil will be from challenging environments such as ultra-deep offshore wells, the Arctic and the Canadian oil sands. North America has flourished: Yergin pointed out that in 2011, the US registered the largest increase in oil production of any country outside of OPEC, and the output of Canadian oil sands had tripled since 2000 (it is now greater than Libya's output before its civil war began in 2011).

Meanwhile, the natural gas market has been transformed by the rapid expansion of shale gas production, especially in the United States. A dozen years ago, shale gas amounted to only about 2 per cent of US production. Today, it is 39 per cent and rising. Future US power plants could be run on gas, which has the merit of being cleaner and more environmentally-friendly than the alternatives. As recently as 2006, the US was expected to become a net natural gas importer, but now it has enough supply for more than 100 years of consumption.

So much for the supply side. On the demand side, curbs are working. The improving gasoline efficiency of cars will help reduce oil demand. Strikingly, the oil and natural gas industry in the US itself invested $71 billion in greenhouse gas-reducing technologies from 2000-2010—nearly twice as much as the federal government. President Obama's stimulus bill allocated another $100 billion towards energy efficiency and alternative energy. The United Nations declared 2012 the Year of Sustainable Energy, proclaiming the goals of universal access to energy, doubling the rate of improvement in energy efficiency and doubling the share of renewable energy in the global energy mix. Fulfilling these targets will not be easy.

In our post-war world, conflict over such issues is unnecessary and avoidable. There is enough for all, provided we pursue these common goals co-operatively. Then we can embrace the future with confidence.

KISSING THE FROG

An IIT graduate—so the story goes—is walking near a pond one day when a frog speaks to him. 'Kiss me,' it says, 'and I will turn into a beautiful princess.' The IITian does a double-take, turns back to check if he has heard right, and sure enough, the frog repeats itself: 'Kiss me and I will turn into a beautiful princess.' He looks thoughtfully at the frog, picks it up and puts it into his pocket. A plaintive wail soon emerges: 'Kiss me and I will turn into a beautiful princess.' He ignores it and walks on. Soon the frog asks, 'Aren't you going to kiss me?' The IIT guy stops, pulls the frog out of his pocket, and replies matter-of-factly: 'I'm an engineer. I don't have time for a girlfriend. But a talking frog is cool.'

No prizes for guessing what a literature graduate would have done in the same situation! Such is the self-image of the engineer in India: rational, hard-working, self-disciplined, steady, focused on the results of his work. Parents pray for the smartest of their kids to become engineers. Any child with better than average marks in science at school is pushed towards the profession, sustained by peer pressure that convinces him there could be no higher aspiration.

And no doubt for some there isn't. But that clearly isn't the whole story. Disturbing research at Oxford University by sociologists Diego Gambetta and Steffen Hertog points to an intriguing—one might say worrying—correlation between engineering and terrorism. If that doesn't raise eyebrows at the IITs, nothing will. But consider the evidence: Osama bin Laden was a student of engineering. So were the star 9/11 kamikaze pilot Mohammed Atta, the alleged mastermind of that plot, Khalid Sheikh Mohammed, and their all-but-forgotten predecessor, the chief plotter of the 1993 World Trade Center bombing, Ramzi Yousef.

The Oxford scholars, after putting together educational biographies for some three hundred known members of violent Islamist groups from thirty countries, concluded that a majority of these Islamist terrorists were not just highly educated, but a startling number of them are engineers. Indeed, according to Gambetta and Hertog, nearly half had studied engineering. A summary of their research in *Foreign Policy* magazine remarked that 'across the Middle East and Southeast Asia, the share of engineers in violent Islamist groups was found to be at least nine times greater than what one might expect, given their proportion of the working male population.'

Is there something about engineering that makes its most proficient graduates vulnerable to the temptations of violent extremism? Gambetta and Hertog seem to think so. They have no patience for the more conventional possible explanation—that engineers might be sought after by terrorist groups for their technical expertise in making and blowing up things. Instead, they argue that the reason there are so many terrorist engineers is that the subject helps produce a mindset that makes one prone to radicalization.

Engineers consider themselves problem solvers, and when the world seems to present a problem, they look to engineering-type solutions to solve it. Engineering, Gambetta and Hertog suggest, predisposes its votaries to absolute and non-negotiable principles, and therefore to fundamentalism; it is a short step from appreciating the predictable laws of engineering to following an ideology or a creed that is infused with its own immutable laws. It is easy for engineers to become radicalized, the researchers argue, because they are attracted by the 'intellectually clean, unambiguous, and all-encompassing' solutions that both the laws of engineering and radical Islam provide. According to Gambetta and Hertog, surveys in Canada, Egypt, and the United States have proved over the years that engineers tend to be more devout, and more politically conservative, than the rest of the population.

I'm not suggesting one should buy wholesale the conclusions of the Oxford researchers; I know a few engineers who wouldn't harm a fly, so I'd be wary of making any sweeping generalizations about an entire profession. But the study does seem to me to open the door to make a nowadays-unfashionable case: the argument in favour of studying the humanities. I have always believed that the well-formed mind is preferable to the well-filled one, and it takes a knowledge of history and an appreciation of literature to form a mind that is capable of grappling with the diversity of human experience in a world devoid of certitudes.

If terrorism is to be tackled and ended, we will have to deal with fear, rage and incomprehension that animates it. We will have to know each other better, learn to see ourselves as others see us, learn to recognize hatred and deal with its causes, learn to dispel fear, and above all just learn about each other. It is not the engineering mindset that facilitates such learning, but the vision of the humanities student. The mind is like a parachute—it functions best when it is open. It takes reading and learning about other peoples and cultures to open (and broaden) minds.

Ignorance and lack of imagination remain the handmaidens of violence. Without extending our imagination, we cannot understand how peoples of other races, religions or languages share the same dreams, the same hopes. Without reading widely and broadening our minds, we cannot understand the myriad manifestations of the human condition, nor fully appreciate the universality of human aims and aspirations. Without the humanities, we cannot recognize that there is more than one side to a story, and more than one answer to a question.

That, of course, is never true in engineering. Perhaps the solution lies in making it compulsory for every engineering student to take at least 20 per cent of his courses in the humanities. Maybe then he might even kiss the frog.

PANDORA'S INBOX

Half a century before the invention of e-mail, T. S. Eliot asked, 'where is the wisdom that has been lost in knowledge? Where is the knowledge that has been lost in information?' If he were alive today, contemplating an electronic inbox on his flickering computer, he might well have added, 'where is the information that has been lost in trivia?'

It is one of the paradoxes of our times that inventions meant to speed matters up inevitably end up slowing us down. When e-mail first came into my life, I was thrilled; instead of correspondence piling up for months as I struggled to find the time to pen a reply, instead of faxes not going through and cables that cost an arm and a leg per word, I now had a means of getting messages through instantaneously, efficiently and free. I became an avid and diligent e-mailer.

And how I regret it.

I get over three hundred e-mails a day, sometimes twice that. Some of them are urgent (but not necessarily important) work-related questions. Some of them are personal letters, friends reaching across time and space to say hello. As I am an Indian MP, many are from job-seekers, favour-demanders and petitioners. Some are one-line queries, others lengthy documents requiring perusal and comment. Many are unsolicited junk mail, offering products and services I did not ask for and do not need, and though an efficient filter catches many of them, it also catches 'real' mail and marks it as spam. (I do not have time to review my overflowing spam-box either, to retrieve them.)

Some are mass mailings of information, both interesting (like an international affairs mailing list I subscribed to years ago when I innocently believed I would have time to read its contents) and diverting (like my daily update of the Doonesbury comic strip). Some—an astonishingly large number—are jokes, of varying quality, both verbal and visual. Many are campaigns—I received several thousand emails recently from Muslim students wanting exams not to take place on Fridays. And increasingly, some are viruses that have attached themselves to the address-books of friends, with attachments which, if opened, could destroy my computer.

Because they are on the screen, I feel obliged to go through them all, if only to make sure that I do not need to read them. And this is a chore that has taking more and more of my time. Whereas, when e-mail first came into vogue, one could spend fifteen to twenty minutes a day on it, now receiving and sending e-mails adds two to three hours to an average day. (Not counting the time lost in attending to false virus warnings, the plague of our times). And since one's other work does not stop, those are hours added to one's day, and therefore subtracted from one's life. A convenience has become a burden.

When I am at my computer, I find myself neglecting more important matters that have come to me by 'snail mail' (or what is nowadays referred to as 'hard copy') in order to dispose of e-mail. E-mails automatically become urgent, because you know that if you do not reply to one immediately, it will soon be swamped by two hundred others and you will forget that you have failed to reply to it. You find yourself scrambling to attend to e-mails of utter triviality for no other reason than to get past them to the possibly important ones that lie behind. The result is 'information fatigue'—a palpable sense of exhaustion from dealing with too much information, coupled with anxiety about coping with the sheer volume of material to be digested, and an ever-shortening attention span in the face of what seems an unstoppable flood of facts. I felt, to recall Eliot, that I understood more when I knew less, and knew more when I had less information to process.

This is a global problem—an estimated fifteen billion e-mails are sent out daily around the world, and the figure continues to increase by the day. As technology advances, it has become more and more difficult to escape the ubiquity of e-mail. No longer is one obliged to open up a desktop computer at the office; now people are plugging in laptops on planes and trains to read their mail, and the latest cell phones have allowed people to check their e-mail wherever they are, even on the Tokyo underground.

It is almost enough to have one longing again for the day when information was a scarce resource and you had to go out to find it. Now there is so much information around that the challenge is to sift the really necessary information for the trivial chaff that surrounds it. And here, to paraphrase Kipling, it is clear that the e-mail of the species is deadlier than the mail.

Addiction to e-mail is increasingly being recognized as a malady. The British national lottery operators, Camelot, once passed an edict banning e-mails on Fridays. They wanted staff to talk to each other instead, at least one day a week. But the experiment was abandoned within a month. People are simply too used to the convenience of copying messages to multiple recipients and hitting the send button: walking to their desks is now an unfamiliar idea.

Part of the problem is that we keep allowing the avatars of progress to persuade us that their new inventions would replace the old ones, when in fact they simply add to both our conveniences and our burdens. The telephone did not supplant the postal system, it merely complemented it; the fax did not replace the telegraph; and the e-mail sits alongside all these prior methods of communication. Now we have more and more means of reaching each other, with less and less worth saying.

There is an inverse relationship between the difficulty and expense of communication, on the one hand, and the quality of what is communicated, on the other. When you paid cable operators by the word, and there was always the risk of garbled transmissions, your messages were crisp, succinct and to the point. When neither length nor complexity affects the cost of a message, however, the field is open for irrelevant and unnecessary communication.

Without even the price of a stamp to deter the prolix, the unmanageable tsunami of e-mail threatens to drown the world in information, unless the servers, switches and wires that sustain the system burn out first. Ease of replication permits matters to get very easily out of hand.

I've finally given up trying to cope. I've decommissioned my email account and set up an auto response that gives emailers ten other options to reach people who can help them (including bringing messages to my attention). So far, it hasn't made much of a difference: e-mails keep flooding the decommissioned mailbox. But it has helped me: I no longer feel obliged to reply.

BIRTHDAYS: A BEASTLY BEATITUDE

Why do we celebrate birthdays? This is a perfectly serious question, prompted by the fact that eight years ago I turned 50, and if the heavens allow me two more, the exalted Shashtiabdapoorthi looms. Our ancient sages valued this landmark so highly that in many tradition-minded families the sixtieth birthday is celebrated with all the pomp of a marriage. (Any readers who missed out on the fun are entitled to an even grander commemoration when they turn 84 and have therefore seen a thousand moons.)

I will receive cards, phone calls and messages of congratulations from family and friends, all for having accomplished—what exactly? Nothing more than merely emerging onto the stage sixty years ago. Whereas the person who did all the hard work that day, the one whose effort and sacrifice and pain resulted in the fortuitous event—my mother—will be ignored by all and sundry. She will go to the temple, as usual, and feed the poor, as she has done on each of her children's birthdays for decades. But no one will congratulate her for what she accomplished on that March Shivratri day six decades ago. Instead, the tributes will come to the least deserving beneficiary: the person whose only real challenge on that occasion was to be able to manage to breathe.

Yes, life is unfair, especially for mothers. And yet, it's true that each passing birthday marks a milestone on the road of life, something by which to measure the way you have lived. Sixty is a particular landmark, prompting some to see that year's birthday party as a 'graduageing' ceremony. Not that most of us use birthdays for any serious purpose: usually it is the occasion for a party, and for the more spiritually-minded, for prayer; some spend it with close family, others with raucous friends; but few use it to take stock of what they have done and where they are going.

Indeed, it takes landmark birthdays to prompt that sort of self-assessment. In my case, 30 did it: it was, after all, the age when my cricketing heroes began to think of retirement, and up till that point I had thought of age entirely in relation to the careers of cricketers, most of whom, in those days, were past their peak by 30. So at 30, I took a long hard look at my life and concluded that there was a great deal more I needed to do to justify my presence on the planet. Thirty was far more significant a threshold than 40, which passed by scarcely noticed. When I was a child that would have surprised me, for 40 had used to seem forbiddingly middle-aged, the point at which all potential had been exhausted, the beginning of an inexorable descent into decrepitude. But by the time I got there, 40 seemed to me to be an insignificant age, populated by striplings and rising stars and the leaders of tomorrow, rather than a turning point. Perhaps it is a reflection of the enhanced longevity of our times that the mid-point has been raised: 40 is still young today, and 50 is the new 40.

But what does that mean? No one I know who has reached 50 seems ready to be put to pasture. The days when office-goers contemplated retirement at 55 are gone almost everywhere, even in the hidebound confines of Indian government service, which now expects its bureaucrats to toil until 60 (and many of us feel that, as for Supreme Court Justices, it should be raised to 62). During my years as a manager at the UN, I used to find it deeply frustrating to lose some of my best staff at 60, an age when many of them seemed to be in the prime of their professional lives and had never been more assured or more productive. (Some, particularly from developing countries, would attempt to claim that their original birth certificates were wrongly filled in or subsequently doctored, a claim whose plausibility was undermined by the fact that they chose to reveal this only when they turned 59.)

Then came 50: an alarming age which seemed to suggest the imminence of irrelevance. At 50, no one can plausibly be described any more as 'young' (an adjective that had dogged me all my life), or as 'up-and-coming' or as an exciting new talent. By 50, you should have pretty much made your mark; for 99.99 per cent of the human population, you know that in the race of life you are closer to the finish line than the starting gate.

And so 50 tends to be a landmark you notice. Intrepid gerontologists may come up with long lists of people whose major accomplishments occurred after they turned 50, but in most cases, 50 represents the narrowing of possibilities, the closing of avenues, both personal and professional. Choices you haven't made till 50 are no longer available for you to make. Of course, there are professions where this isn't true: Indian or Japanese politics, for instance, where you have to be at least 50 to be taken seriously at all. But even your body reminds you daily of the things you can no longer do without feeling the consequences. Comedians tell you that if you wake up after 50 and don't feel a nagging pain anywhere, you're probably dead.

But I'm still here, though my recent career in Indian public life has given me enough stress to shave several years off my life. Fifty-eight, my number as I write this, isn't a landmark of any sort; it is an age of no particular distinction. It's the sort of age which, if it were a cricketing score, would carry an asterisk, meaning 'not out': innings still going on, much more to do, plenty of batting still to come. The new ball has been weathered, some of the uneven bounce in the wicket mastered (or at least understood), an intelligent estimate of the field taken, and the bowling sized up. Of course, the bat is now a bit worn, smudged both from the fours that went off the meat of the bat and the nicks and edges that accompanied your scoring, but you're still there and the great cosmic umpire doesn't seem to be readying to raise his finger. Fifty-eight not out! You squint into the sun. Would somebody please move that sightscreen?